hawkeye
TEAM SPIRIT

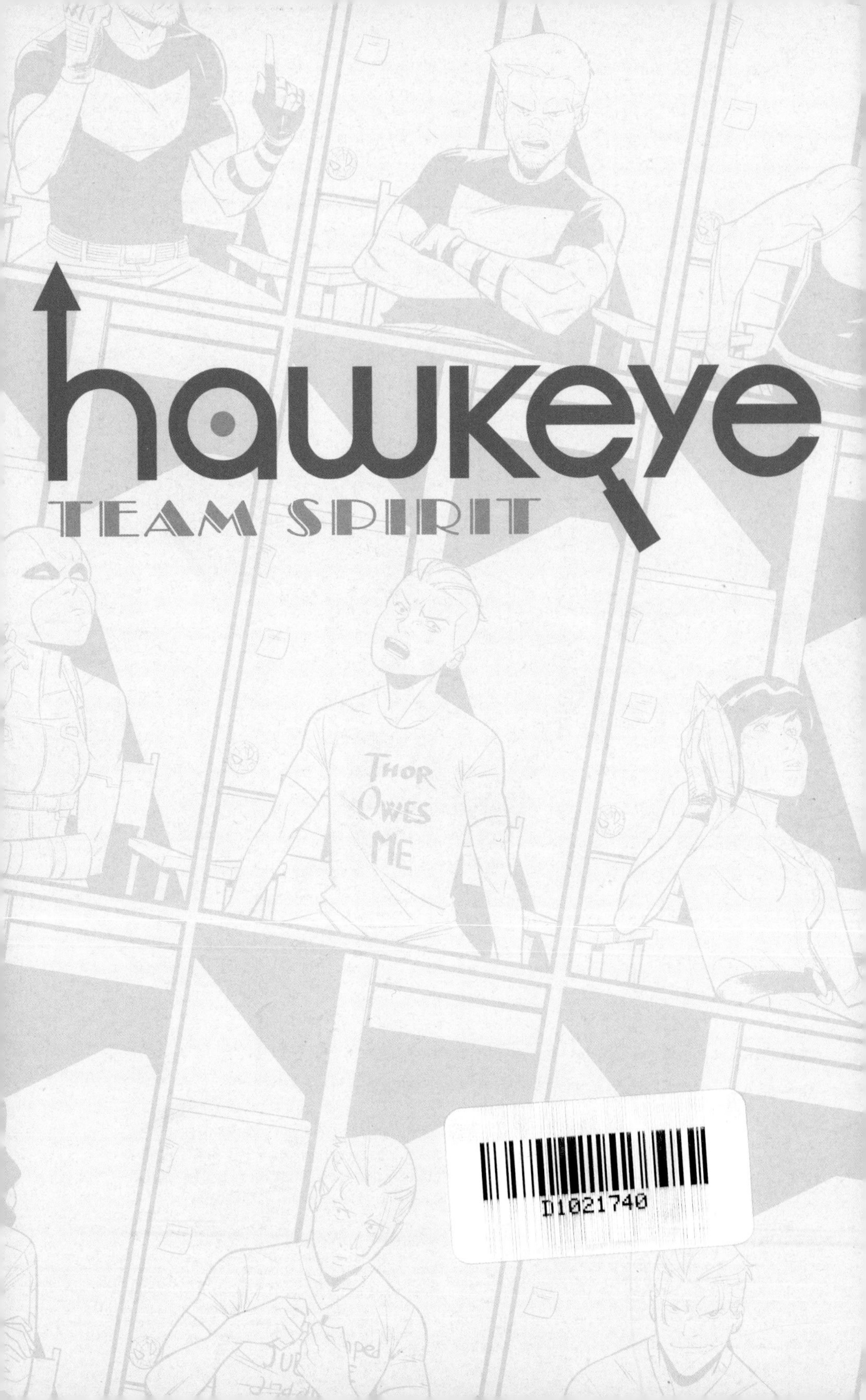
THOR OWES ME

collection editor JENNIFER GRÜNWALD • assistant editor DANIEL KIRCHHOFFER
assistant managing editor MAIA LOY • associate manager, talent relations LISA MONTALBANO
vp production & special projects JEFF YOUNGQUIST • director, licensed publishing SVEN LARSEN
svp print, sales & marketing DAVID GABRIEL • editor in chief C.B. CEBULSKI

HAWKEYE: KATE BISHOP — TEAM SPIRIT. Contains material originally published in magazine form as WEST COAST AVENGERS (2018) #5-10 and WAR OF THE REALMS: JOURNEY INTO MYSTERY (2019) #1-5. First printing 2021. ISBN 978-1-302-93478-1. Published by MARVEL WORLDWIDE, INC., a subsidiary of MARVEL ENTERTAINMENT, LLC. OFFICE OF PUBLICATION: 1290 Avenue of the Americas, New York, NY 10104. © 2021 MARVEL No similarity between any of the names, characters, persons, and/or institutions in this book with those of any living or dead person or institution is intended, and any such similarity which may exist is purely coincidental. **Printed in Canada.** KEVIN FEIGE, Chief Creative Officer; DAN BUCKLEY, President, Marvel Entertainment; JOE QUESADA, EVP & Creative Director; DAVID BOGART, Associate Publisher & SVP of Talent Affairs; TOM BREVOORT, VP, Executive Editor; NICK LOWE, Executive Editor, VP of Content, Digital Publishing; DAVID GABRIEL, VP of Print & Digital Publishing; JEFF YOUNGQUIST, VP of Production & Special Projects; ALEX MORALES, Director of Publishing Operations; DAN EDINGTON, Managing Editor; RICKEY PURDIN, Director of Talent Relations; JENNIFER GRÜNWALD, Senior Editor, Special Projects; SUSAN CRESPI, Production Manager; STAN LEE, Chairman Emeritus. For information regarding advertising in Marvel Comics or on Marvel.com, please contact Vit DeBellis, Custom Solutions & Integrated Advertising Manager, at vdebellis@marvel.com. For Marvel subscription inquiries, please call 888-511-5480. **Manufactured between 12/31/2021 and 2/1/2022 by SOLISCO PRINTERS, SCOTT, QC, CANADA.**

hawkeye
TEAM SPIRIT

WEST COAST AVENGERS #5-10

WRITER **KELLY THOMPSON**
ARTISTS **DANIELE DI NICUOLO** (#5-7),
GANG HYUK LIM (#8-9) & **MOY R.** (#10)
COLOR ARTISTS **TRÍONA FARRELL** (#5-7, #9-10)
& **GANG HYUK LIM** (#8)
LETTERER **VC's JOE CARAMAGNA**
COVER ART **STEFANO CASELLI** & **NOLAN WOODARD** (#5-6),
EDUARD PETROVITCH (#7-8) AND **GANG HYUK LIM** (#9-10)
ASSISTANT EDITOR **SHANNON ANDREWS BALLESTEROS**
EDITOR **ALANNA SMITH**
EXECUTIVE EDITOR **TOM BREVOORT**

WAR OF THE REALMS: JOURNEY INTO MYSTERY #1-5

WRITERS **THE McELROYS**
ARTIST **ANDRÉ LIMA ARAÚJO**
COLOR ARTIST **CHRIS O'HALLORAN**
LETTERER **VC's CLAYTON COWLES**
COVER ART **VALERIO SCHITI** & **DAVID CURIEL**
ASSOCIATE EDITOR **SARAH BRUNSTAD**
EDITOR **WIL MOSS**

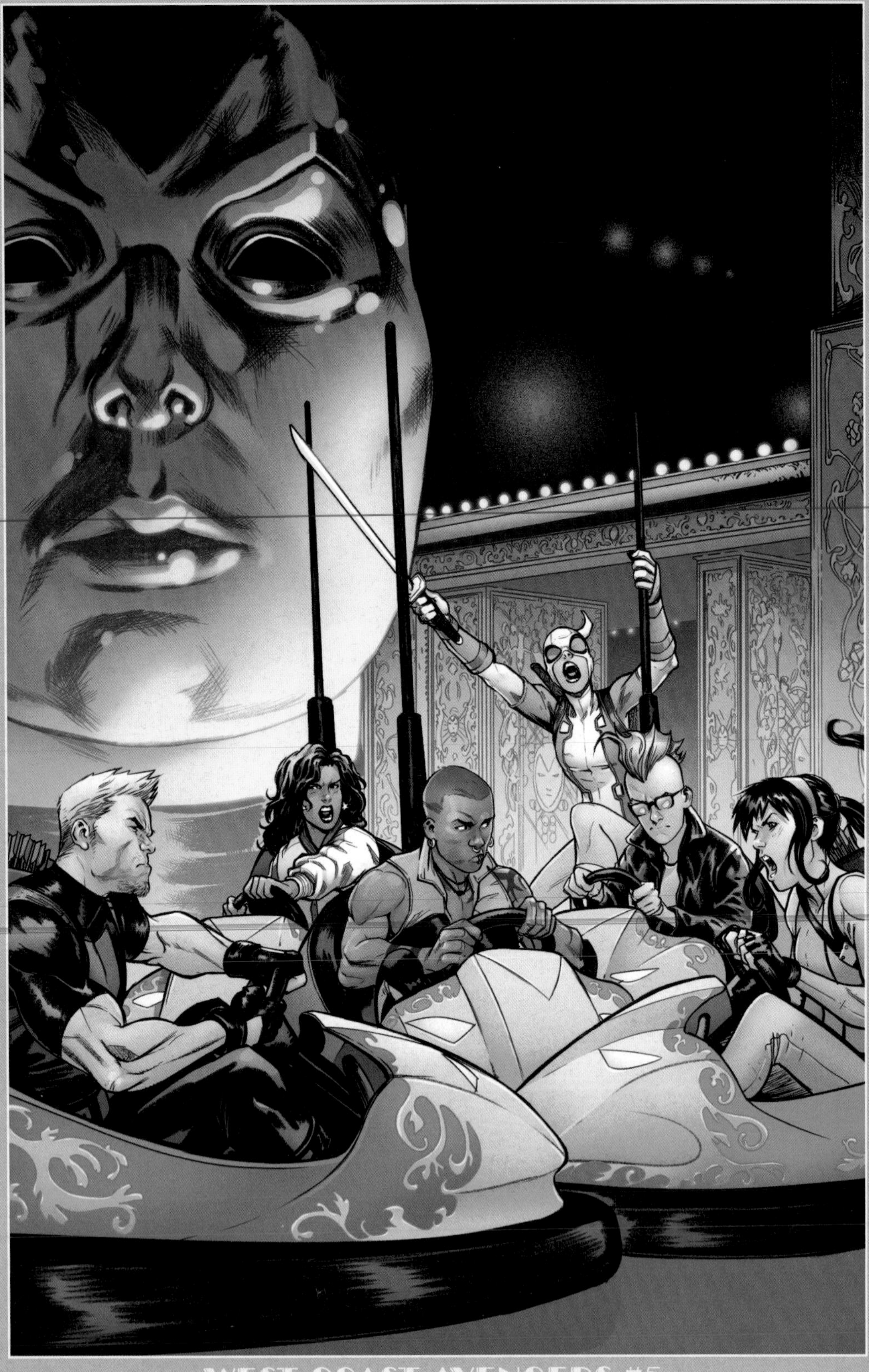

WEST COAST AVENGERS #5

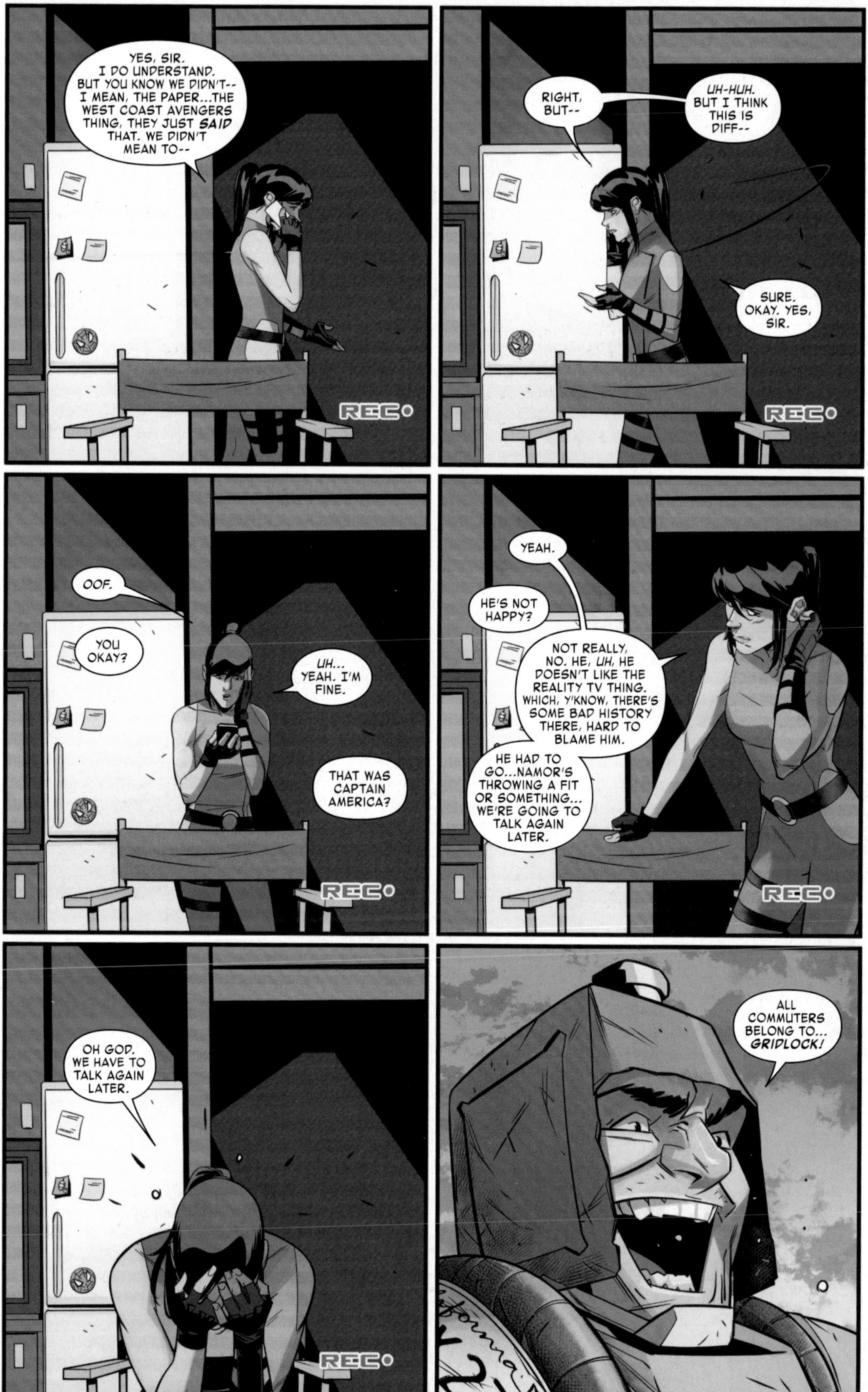
YES, SIR. I DO UNDERSTAND. BUT YOU KNOW WE DIDN'T-- I MEAN, THE PAPER...THE WEST COAST AVENGERS THING, THEY JUST *SAID* THAT. WE DIDN'T MEAN TO--
REC
RIGHT, BUT--
UH-HUH. BUT I THINK THIS IS DIFF--
SURE. OKAY. YES, SIR.
REC
OOF.
YOU OKAY?
UH... YEAH. I'M FINE.
THAT WAS CAPTAIN AMERICA?
REC
YEAH.
HE'S NOT HAPPY?
NOT REALLY, NO. HE, *UH,* HE DOESN'T LIKE THE REALITY TV THING. WHICH, Y'KNOW, THERE'S SOME BAD HISTORY THERE, HARD TO BLAME HIM.
HE HAD TO GO...NAMOR'S THROWING A FIT OR SOMETHING... WE'RE GOING TO TALK AGAIN LATER.
REC
OH GOD. WE HAVE TO TALK AGAIN LATER.
REC
ALL COMMUTERS BELONG TO... *GRIDLOCK!*

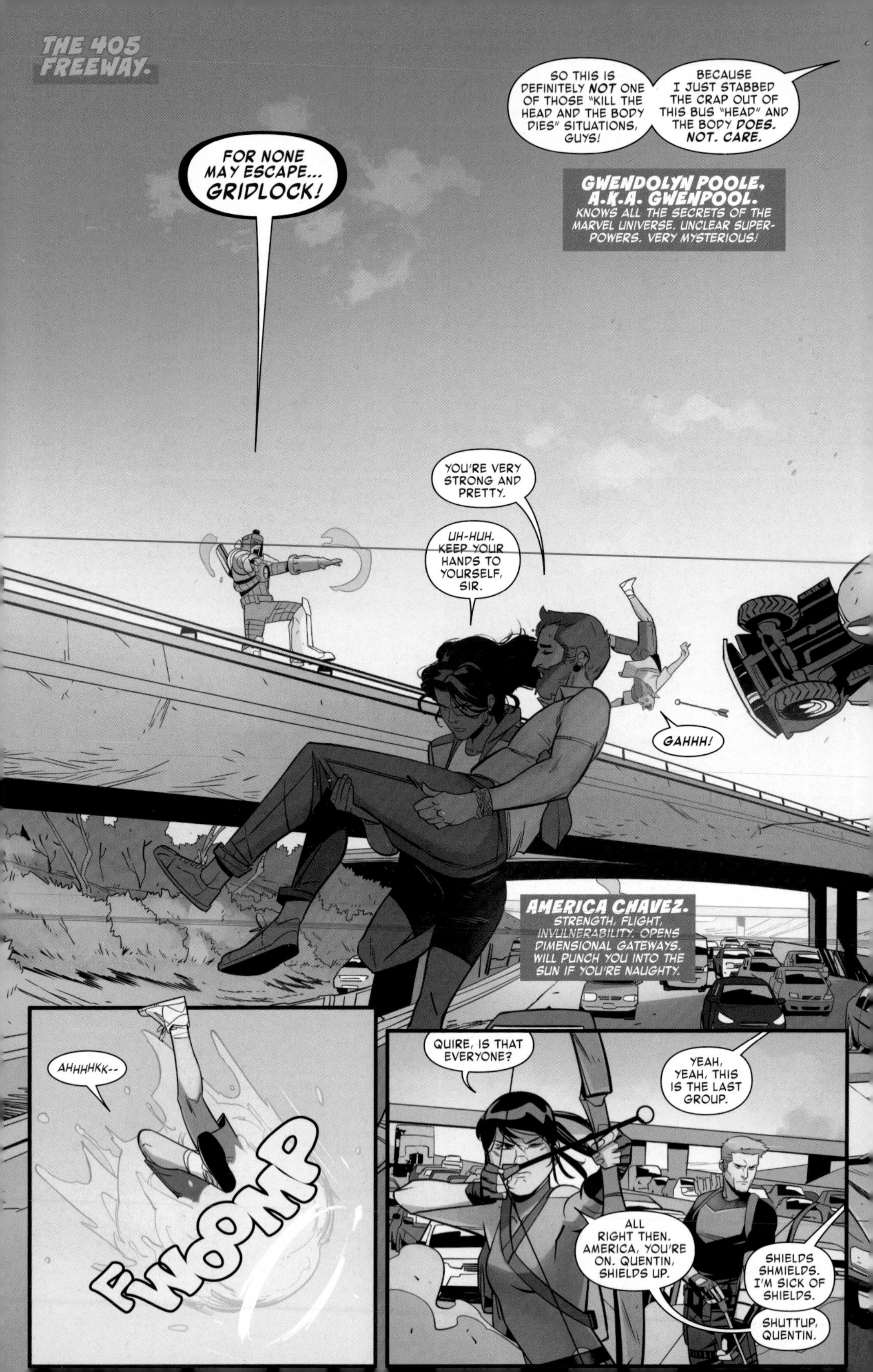
THE 405 FREEWAY.
SO THIS IS DEFINITELY NOT ONE OF THOSE "KILL THE HEAD AND THE BODY DIES" SITUATIONS, GUYS!
BECAUSE I JUST STABBED THE CRAP OUT OF THIS BUS "HEAD" AND THE BODY DOES. NOT. CARE.
GWENDOLYN POOLE, A.K.A. GWENPOOL. KNOWS ALL THE SECRETS OF THE MARVEL UNIVERSE. UNCLEAR SUPER-POWERS. VERY MYSTERIOUS!
FOR NONE MAY ESCAPE... GRIDLOCK!
YOU'RE VERY STRONG AND PRETTY.
UH-HUH. KEEP YOUR HANDS TO YOURSELF, SIR.
GAHHH!
AMERICA CHAVEZ. STRENGTH, FLIGHT, INVULNERABILITY. OPENS DIMENSIONAL GATEWAYS. WILL PUNCH YOU INTO THE SUN IF YOU'RE NAUGHTY.
AHHHHKK--
FWOOMP
QUIRE, IS THAT EVERYONE?
YEAH, YEAH, THIS IS THE LAST GROUP.
ALL RIGHT THEN. AMERICA, YOU'RE ON. QUENTIN, SHIELDS UP.
SHIELDS SHMIELDS. I'M SICK OF SHIELDS.
SHUTTUP, QUENTIN.

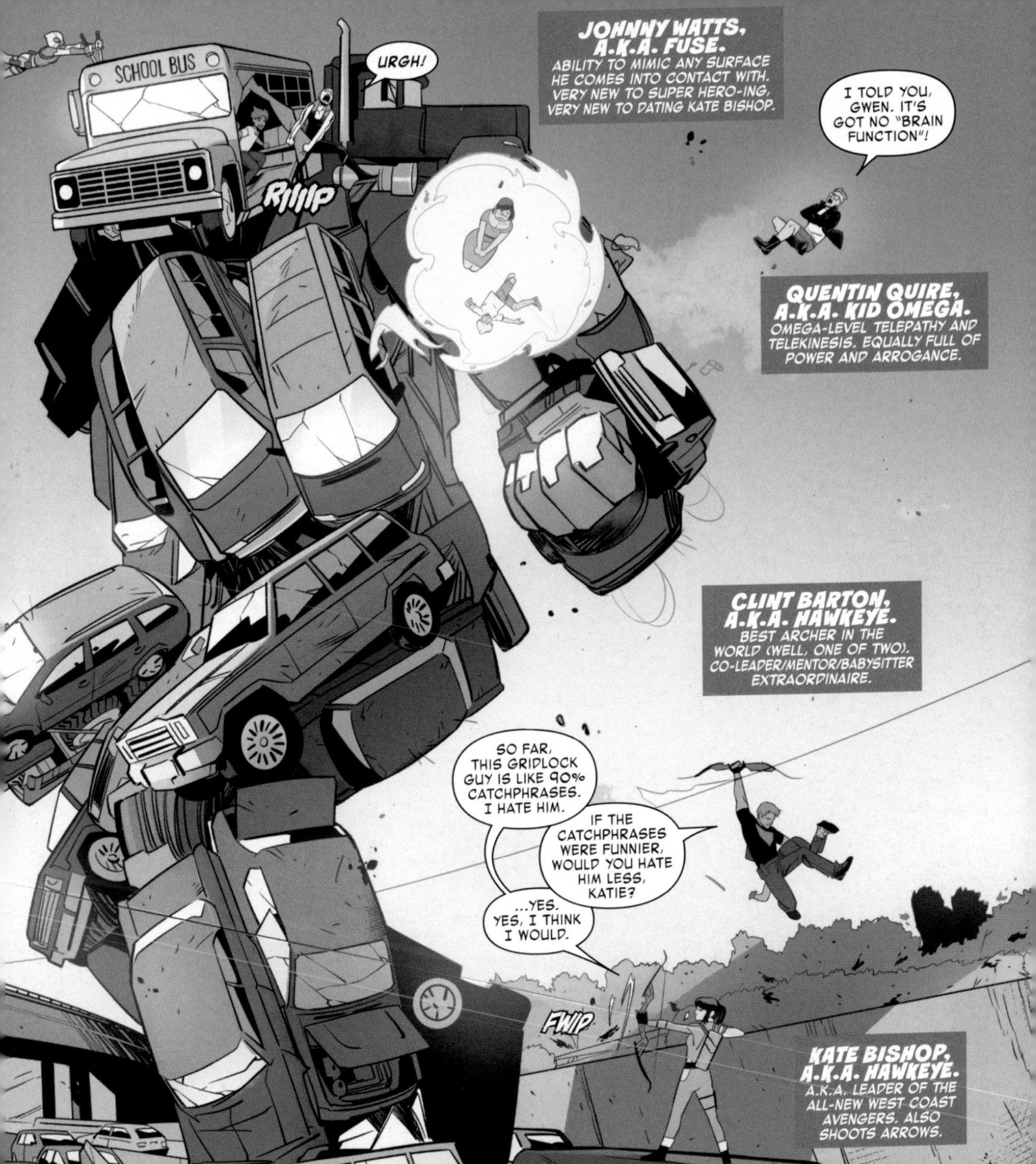
SCHOOL BUS
URGH!
RIIIIP
JOHNNY WATTS, A.K.A. FUSE.
ABILITY TO MIMIC ANY SURFACE HE COMES INTO CONTACT WITH. VERY NEW TO SUPER HERO-ING, VERY NEW TO DATING KATE BISHOP.
I TOLD YOU, GWEN. IT'S GOT NO "BRAIN FUNCTION"!
QUENTIN QUIRE, A.K.A. KID OMEGA.
OMEGA-LEVEL TELEPATHY AND TELEKINESIS. EQUALLY FULL OF POWER AND ARROGANCE.
CLINT BARTON, A.K.A. HAWKEYE.
BEST ARCHER IN THE WORLD (WELL, ONE OF TWO). CO-LEADER/MENTOR/BABYSITTER EXTRAORDINAIRE.
SO FAR, THIS GRIDLOCK GUY IS LIKE 90% CATCHPHRASES. I HATE HIM.
IF THE CATCHPHRASES WERE FUNNIER, WOULD YOU HATE HIM LESS, KATIE?
...YES. YES, I THINK I WOULD.
FWIP
KATE BISHOP, A.K.A. HAWKEYE.
A.K.A. LEADER OF THE ALL-NEW WEST COAST AVENGERS. ALSO SHOOTS ARROWS.
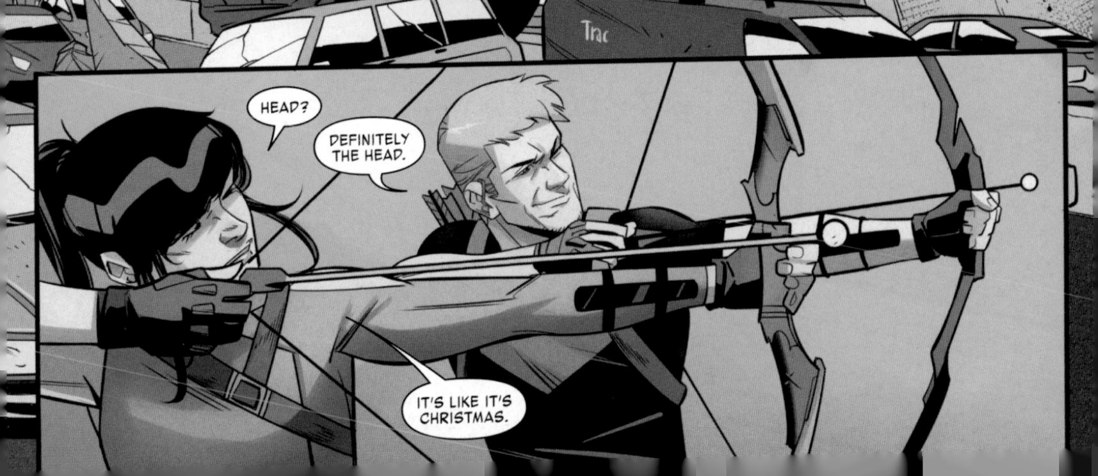
HEAD?
DEFINITELY THE HEAD.
IT'S LIKE IT'S CHRISTMAS.

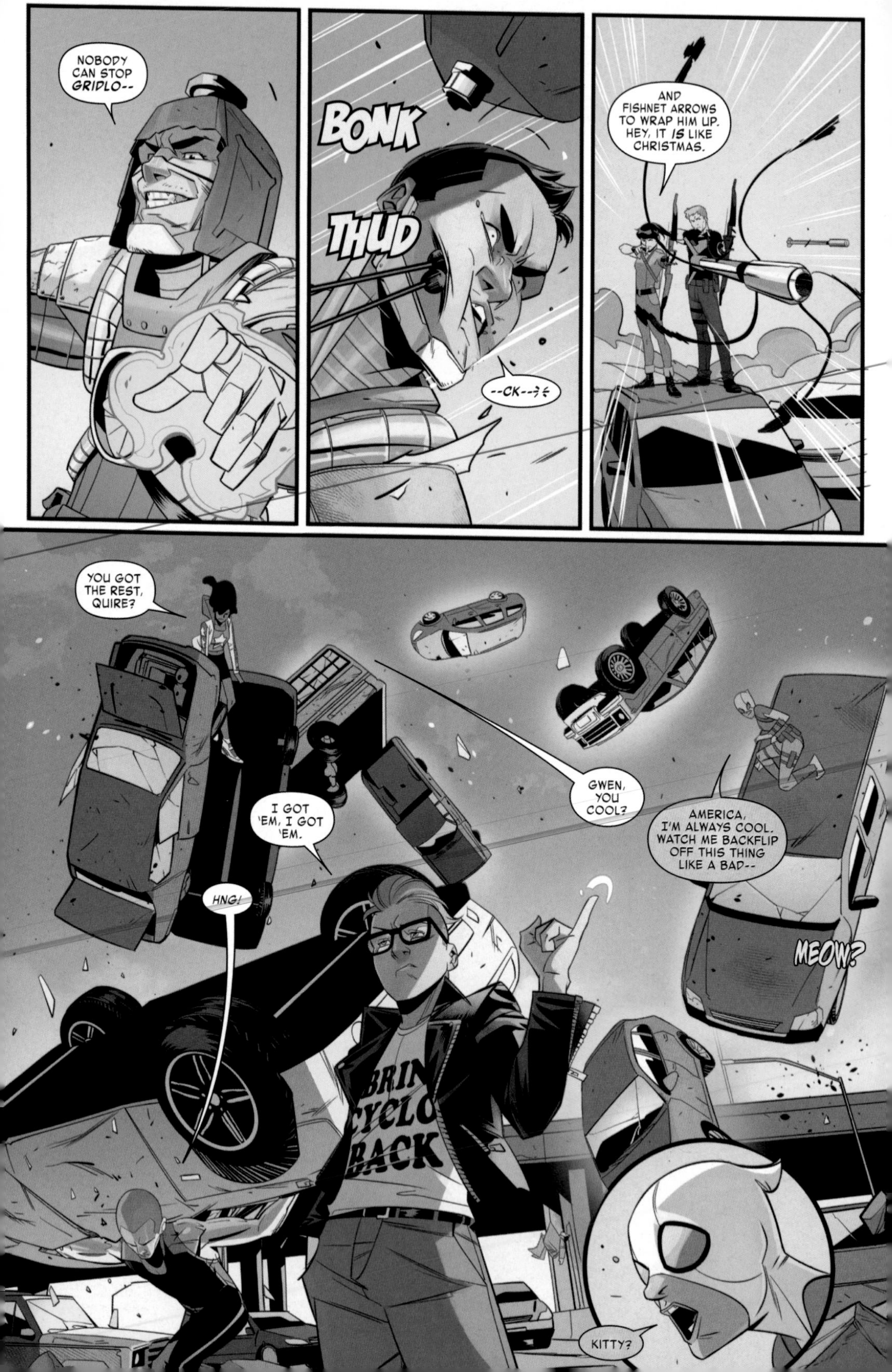
NOBODY CAN STOP GRIDLO--
BONK
THUD
--CK--
AND FISHNET ARROWS TO WRAP HIM UP. HEY, IT IS LIKE CHRISTMAS.
YOU GOT THE REST, QUIRE?
GWEN, YOU COOL?
I GOT 'EM, I GOT 'EM.
AMERICA, I'M ALWAYS COOL. WATCH ME BACKFLIP OFF THIS THING LIKE A BAD--
HNG!
MEOW?
BRIN CYCLO BACK
KITTY?

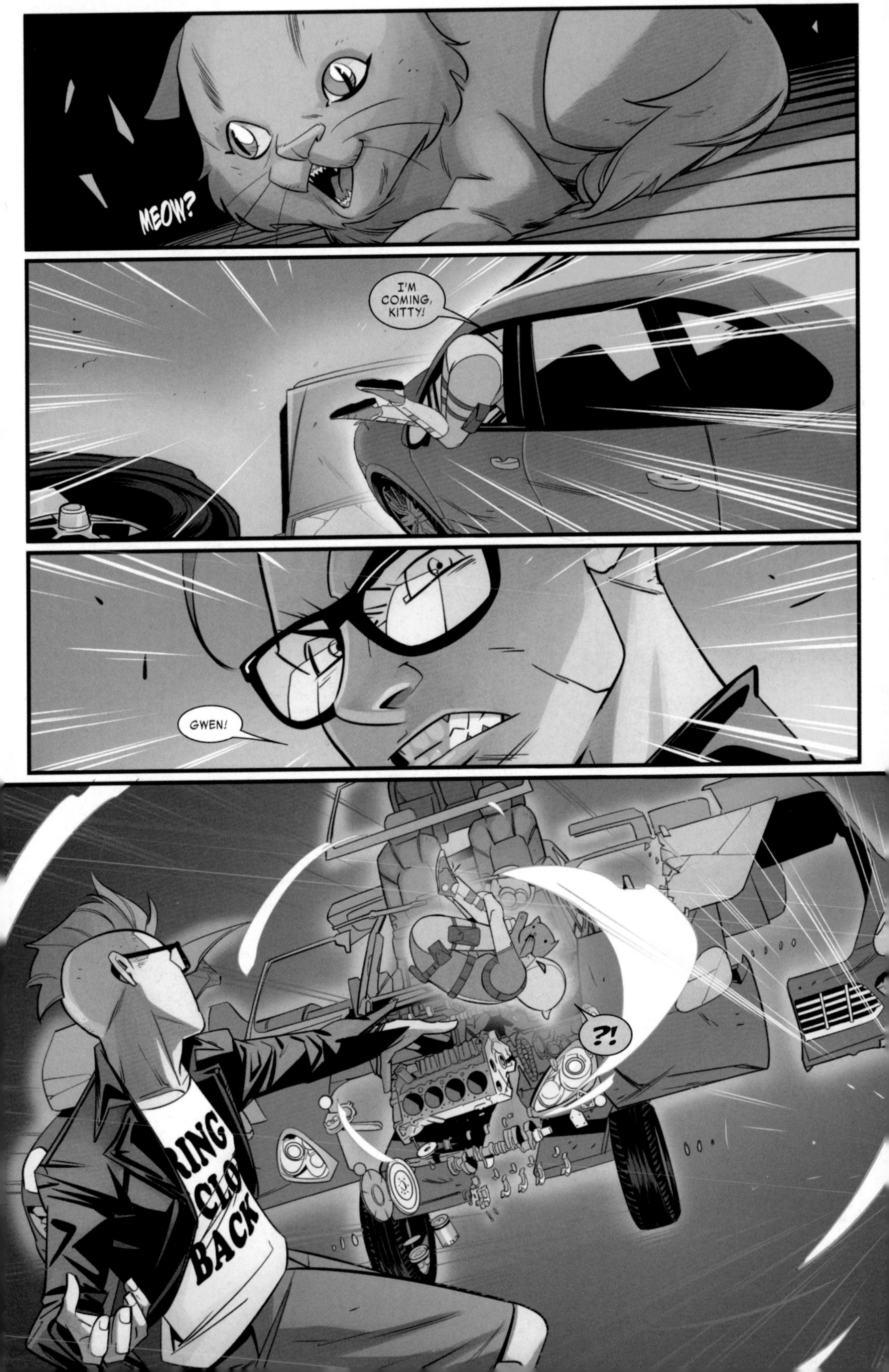
MEOW?
I'M COMING, KITTY!
GWEN!
?!
RING
CLO
BACK

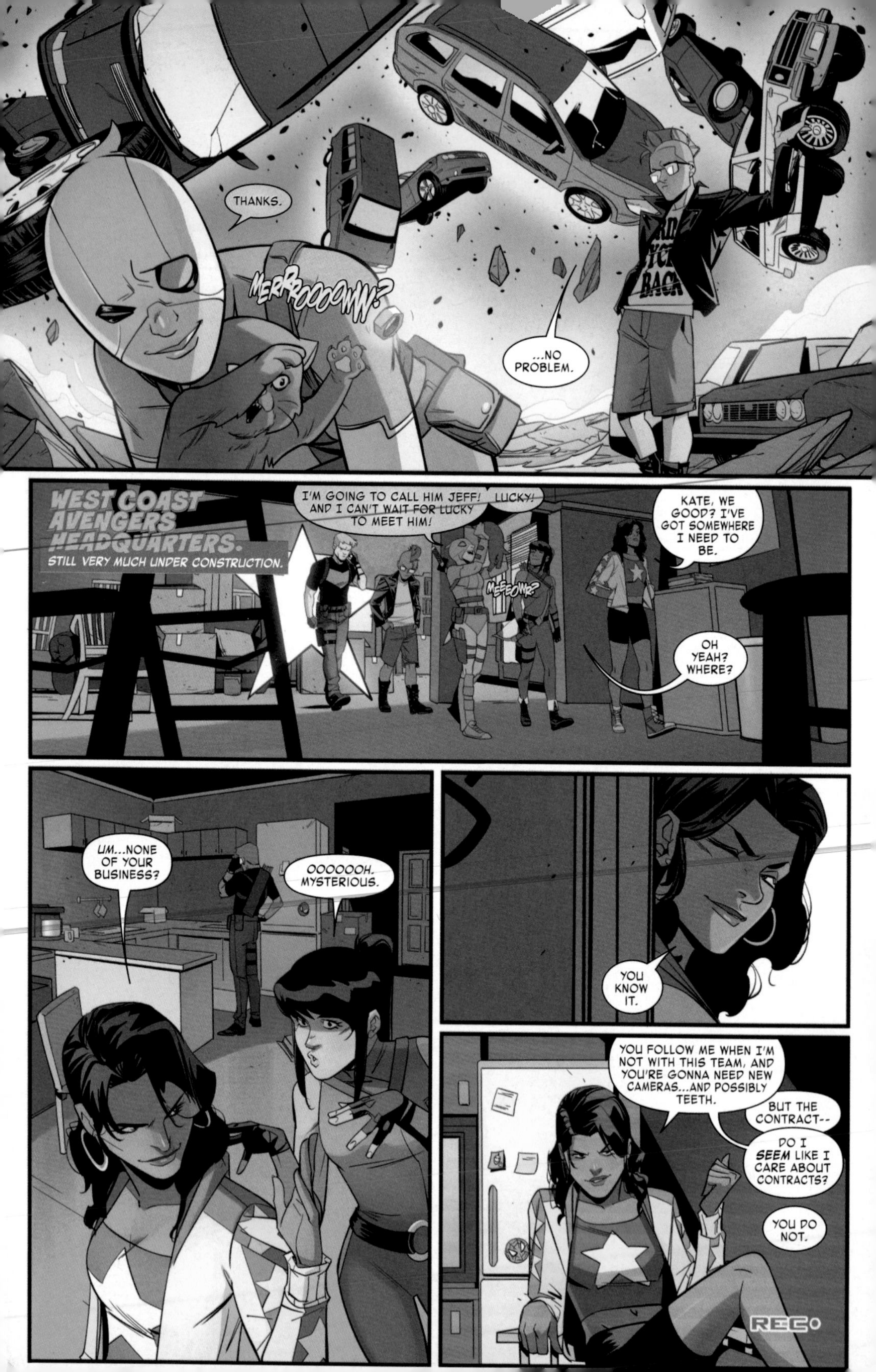

THANKS.
MERRROOOOWWN?
...NO PROBLEM.
WEST COAST AVENGERS HEADQUARTERS.
STILL VERY MUCH UNDER CONSTRUCTION.
I'M GOING TO CALL HIM JEFF! AND I CAN'T WAIT FOR LUCKY TO MEET HIM!
LUCKY!
MEEOWR?
KATE, WE GOOD? I'VE GOT SOMEWHERE I NEED TO BE.
OH YEAH? WHERE?
UM...NONE OF YOUR BUSINESS?
OOOOOOH. MYSTERIOUS.
YOU KNOW IT.
YOU FOLLOW ME WHEN I'M NOT WITH THIS TEAM, AND YOU'RE GONNA NEED NEW CAMERAS...AND POSSIBLY TEETH.
BUT THE CONTRACT--
DO I SEEM LIKE I CARE ABOUT CONTRACTS?
YOU DO NOT.
REC

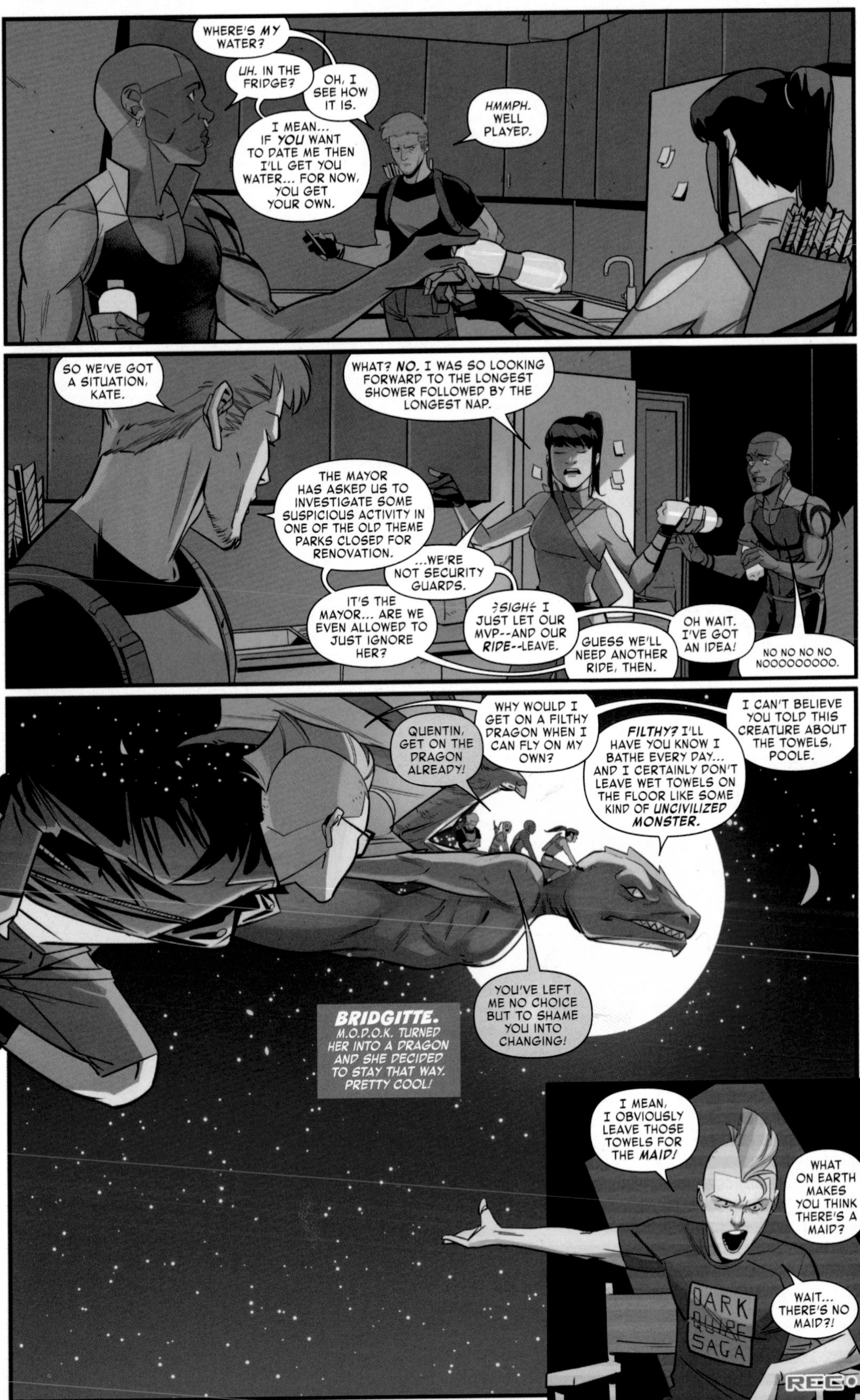
WHERE'S MY WATER?
UH. IN THE FRIDGE?
OH, I SEE HOW IT IS.
I MEAN... IF YOU WANT TO DATE ME THEN I'LL GET YOU WATER... FOR NOW, YOU GET YOUR OWN.
HMMPH. WELL PLAYED.
SO WE'VE GOT A SITUATION, KATE.
WHAT? NO. I WAS SO LOOKING FORWARD TO THE LONGEST SHOWER FOLLOWED BY THE LONGEST NAP.
THE MAYOR HAS ASKED US TO INVESTIGATE SOME SUSPICIOUS ACTIVITY IN ONE OF THE OLD THEME PARKS CLOSED FOR RENOVATION.
...WE'RE NOT SECURITY GUARDS.
IT'S THE MAYOR... ARE WE EVEN ALLOWED TO JUST IGNORE HER?
SIGH I JUST LET OUR MVP--AND OUR RIDE--LEAVE.
GUESS WE'LL NEED ANOTHER RIDE, THEN.
OH WAIT. I'VE GOT AN IDEA!
NO NO NO NO NOOOOOOOOO.
QUENTIN, GET ON THE DRAGON ALREADY!
WHY WOULD I GET ON A FILTHY DRAGON WHEN I CAN FLY ON MY OWN?
FILTHY? I'LL HAVE YOU KNOW I BATHE EVERY DAY... AND I CERTAINLY DON'T LEAVE WET TOWELS ON THE FLOOR LIKE SOME KIND OF UNCIVILIZED MONSTER.
I CAN'T BELIEVE YOU TOLD THIS CREATURE ABOUT THE TOWELS, POOLE.
BRIDGITTE. M.O.D.O.K. TURNED HER INTO A DRAGON AND SHE DECIDED TO STAY THAT WAY. PRETTY COOL!
YOU'VE LEFT ME NO CHOICE BUT TO SHAME YOU INTO CHANGING!
I MEAN, I OBVIOUSLY LEAVE THOSE TOWELS FOR THE MAID!
WHAT ON EARTH MAKES YOU THINK THERE'S A MAID?
DARK QUIRE SAGA
WAIT... THERE'S NO MAID?!

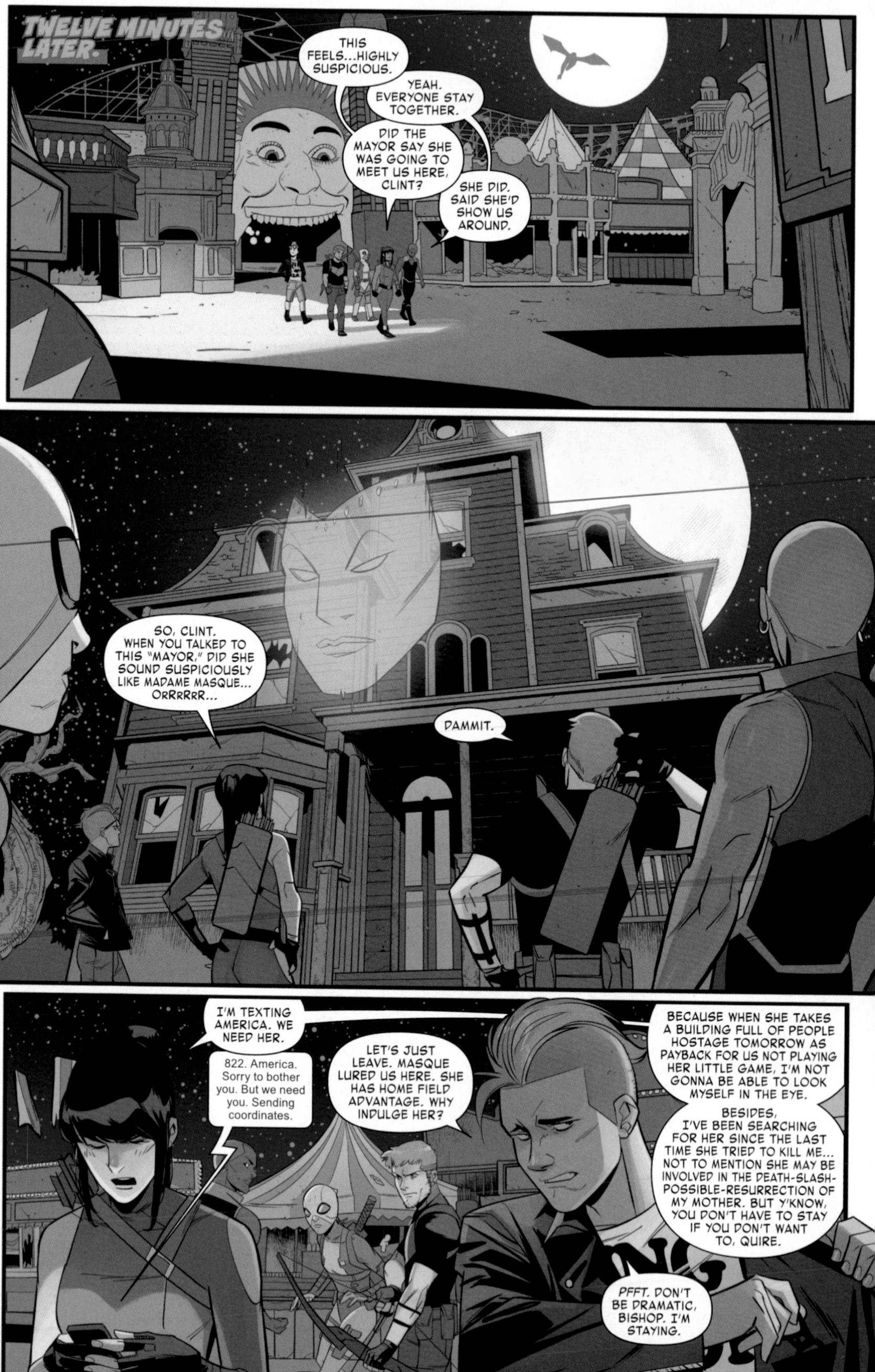
TWELVE MINUTES LATER.
THIS FEELS...HIGHLY SUSPICIOUS.
YEAH. EVERYONE STAY TOGETHER.
DID THE MAYOR SAY SHE WAS GOING TO MEET US HERE, CLINT?
SHE DID. SAID SHE'D SHOW US AROUND.
SO, CLINT. WHEN YOU TALKED TO THIS "MAYOR," DID SHE SOUND SUSPICIOUSLY LIKE MADAME MASQUE... ORRRRRR...
DAMMIT.
I'M TEXTING AMERICA. WE NEED HER.
822. America. Sorry to bother you. But we need you. Sending coordinates.
LET'S JUST LEAVE. MASQUE LURED US HERE. SHE HAS HOME FIELD ADVANTAGE. WHY INDULGE HER?
BECAUSE WHEN SHE TAKES A BUILDING FULL OF PEOPLE HOSTAGE TOMORROW AS PAYBACK FOR US NOT PLAYING HER LITTLE GAME, I'M NOT GONNA BE ABLE TO LOOK MYSELF IN THE EYE.
BESIDES, I'VE BEEN SEARCHING FOR HER SINCE THE LAST TIME SHE TRIED TO KILL ME... NOT TO MENTION SHE MAY BE INVOLVED IN THE DEATH-SLASH-POSSIBLE-RESURRECTION OF MY MOTHER. BUT Y'KNOW, YOU DON'T HAVE TO STAY IF YOU DON'T WANT TO, QUIRE.
PFFT. DON'T BE DRAMATIC, BISHOP. I'M STAYING.

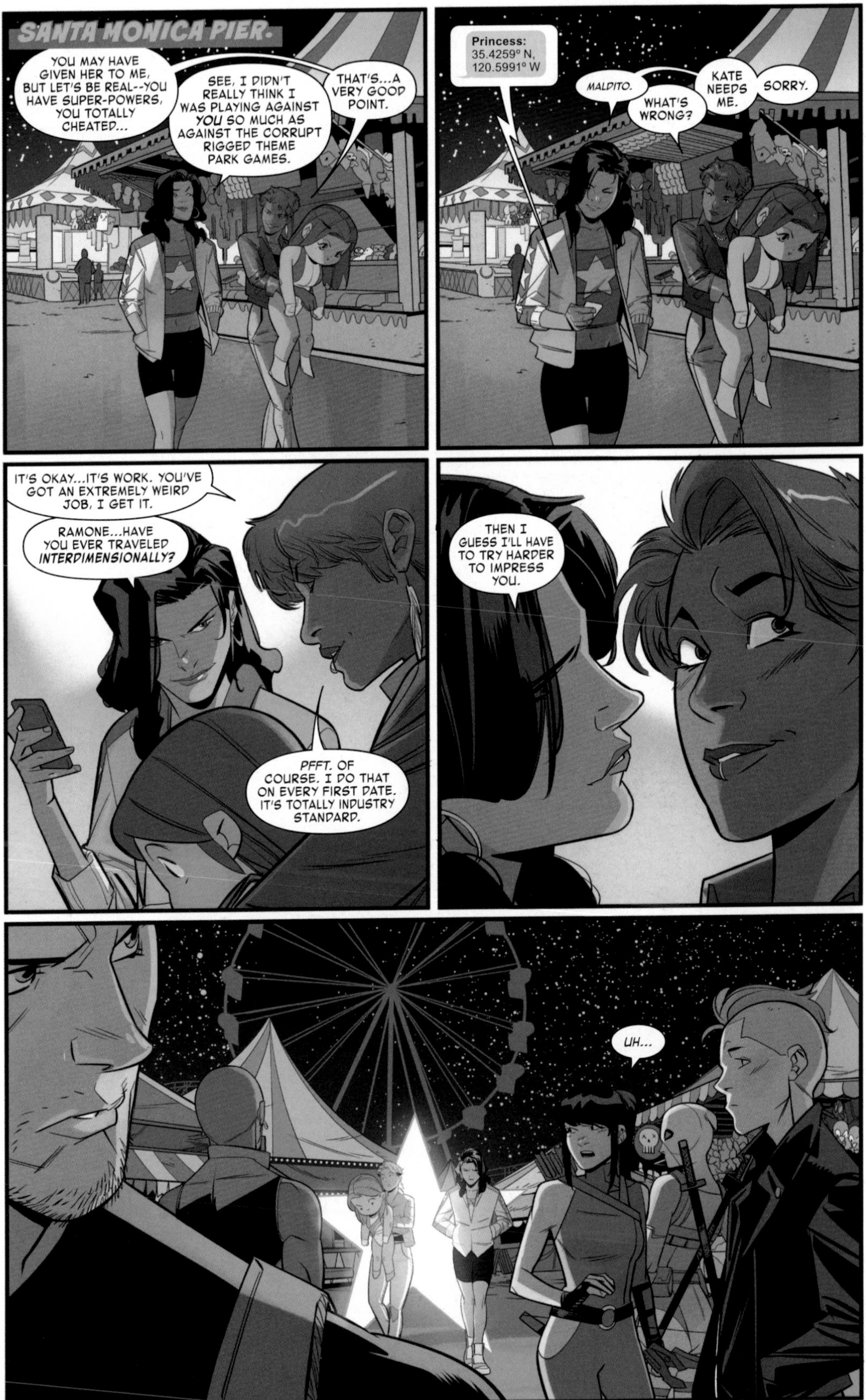
SANTA MONICA PIER.
YOU MAY HAVE GIVEN HER TO ME, BUT LET'S BE REAL--YOU HAVE SUPER-POWERS, YOU TOTALLY CHEATED...
SEE, I DIDN'T REALLY THINK I WAS PLAYING AGAINST YOU SO MUCH AS AGAINST THE CORRUPT RIGGED THEME PARK GAMES.
THAT'S...A VERY GOOD POINT.
Princess:
35.4259º N,
120.5991º W
MALDITO.
WHAT'S WRONG?
KATE NEEDS ME.
SORRY.
IT'S OKAY...IT'S WORK. YOU'VE GOT AN EXTREMELY WEIRD JOB, I GET IT.
RAMONE...HAVE YOU EVER TRAVELED INTERDIMENSIONALLY?
PFFT. OF COURSE. I DO THAT ON EVERY FIRST DATE. IT'S TOTALLY INDUSTRY STANDARD.
THEN I GUESS I'LL HAVE TO TRY HARDER TO IMPRESS YOU.
UH...

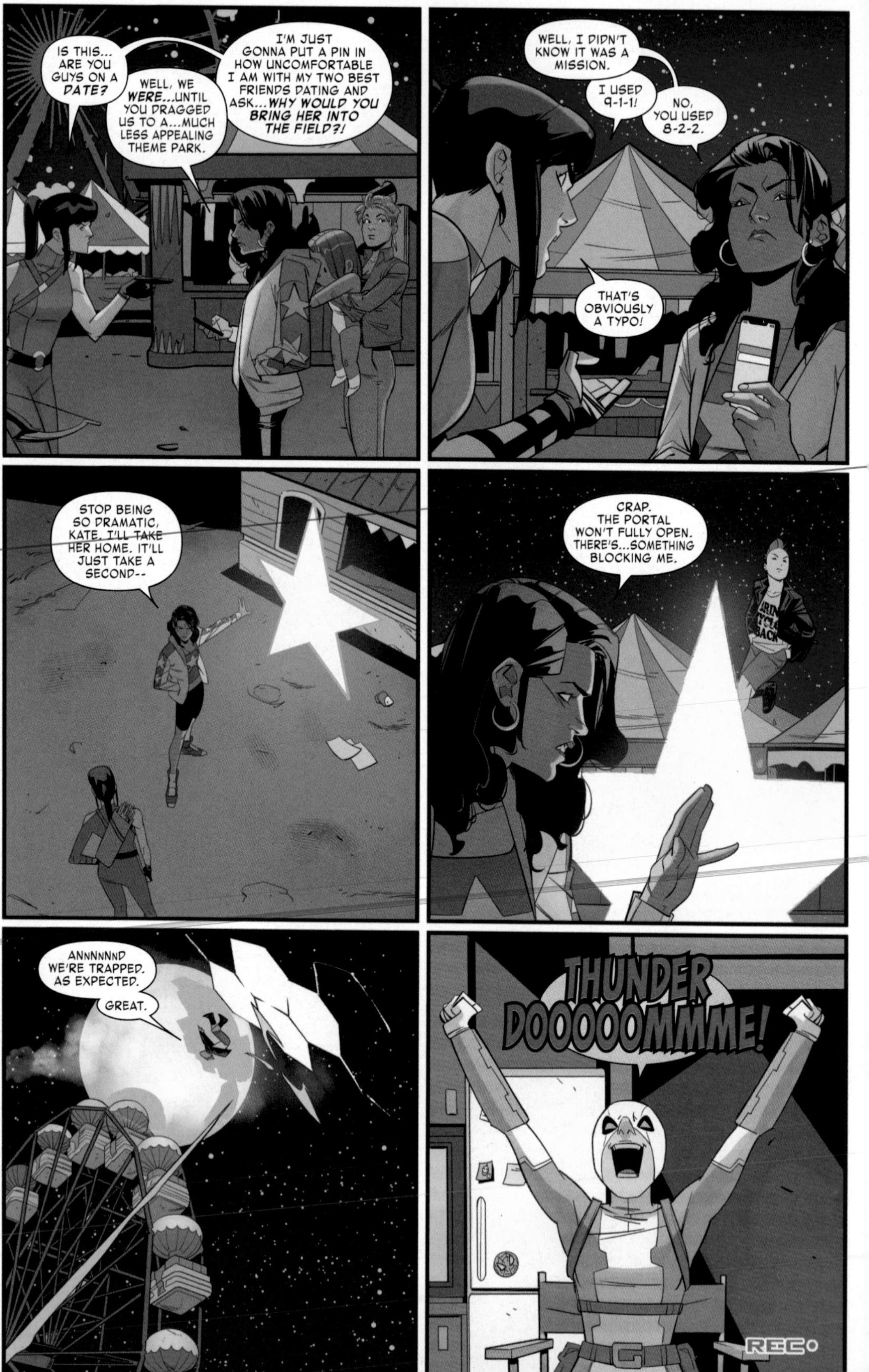
IS THIS... ARE YOU GUYS ON A DATE?
WELL, WE WERE...UNTIL YOU DRAGGED US TO A...MUCH LESS APPEALING THEME PARK.
I'M JUST GONNA PUT A PIN IN HOW UNCOMFORTABLE I AM WITH MY TWO BEST FRIENDS DATING AND ASK...WHY WOULD YOU BRING HER INTO THE FIELD?!
WELL, I DIDN'T KNOW IT WAS A MISSION.
I USED 9-1-1!
NO, YOU USED 8-2-2.
THAT'S OBVIOUSLY A TYPO!
STOP BEING SO DRAMATIC, KATE. I'LL TAKE HER HOME. IT'LL JUST TAKE A SECOND--
CRAP. THE PORTAL WON'T FULLY OPEN. THERE'S...SOMETHING BLOCKING ME.
ANNNNNND WE'RE TRAPPED. AS EXPECTED.
GREAT.
THUNDER DOOOOOMMME!
REC

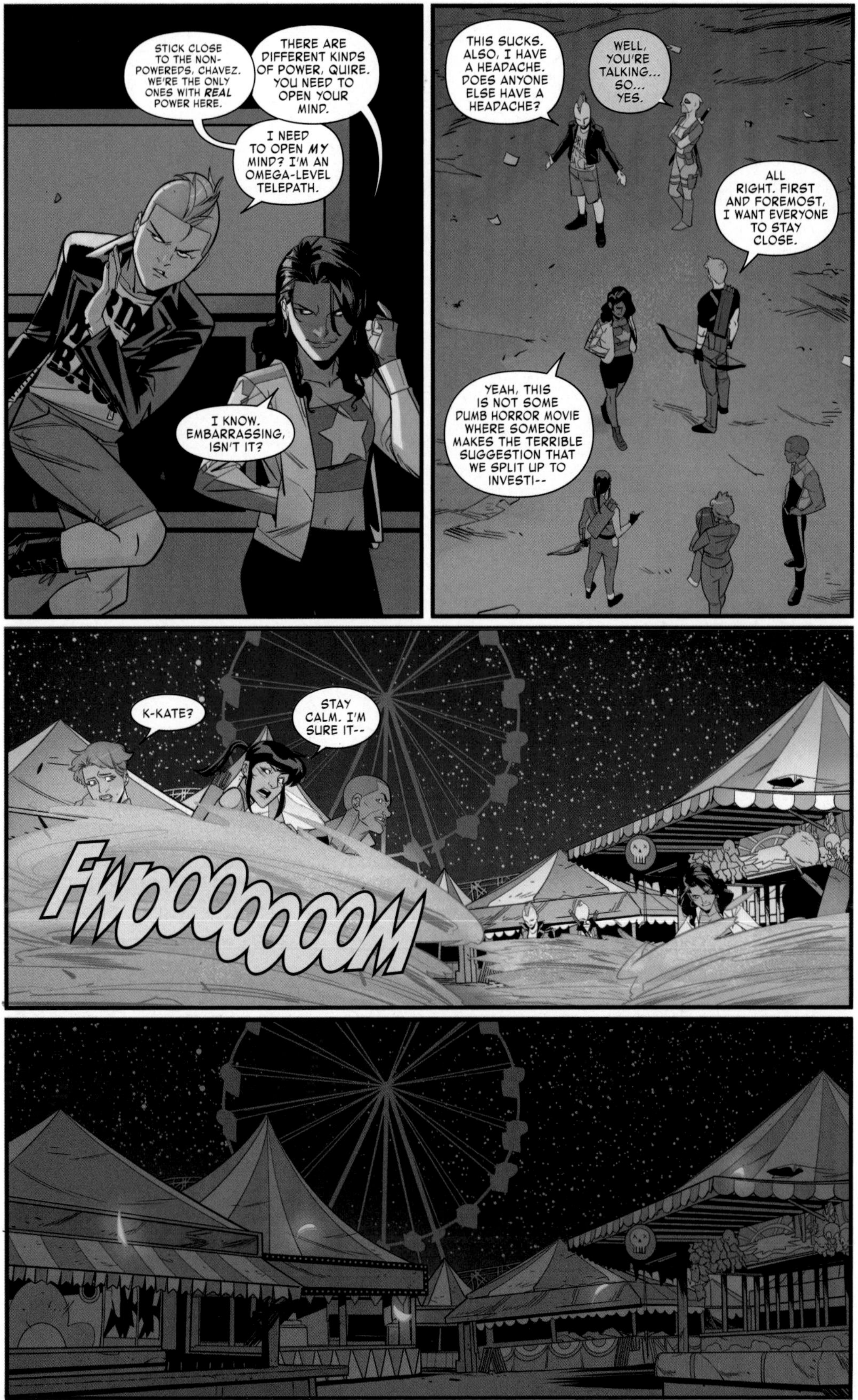
STICK CLOSE TO THE NON-POWEREDS, CHAVEZ. WE'RE THE ONLY ONES WITH REAL POWER HERE.
THERE ARE DIFFERENT KINDS OF POWER, QUIRE. YOU NEED TO OPEN YOUR MIND.
I NEED TO OPEN MY MIND? I'M AN OMEGA-LEVEL TELEPATH.
I KNOW. EMBARRASSING, ISN'T IT?
THIS SUCKS. ALSO, I HAVE A HEADACHE. DOES ANYONE ELSE HAVE A HEADACHE?
WELL, YOU'RE TALKING... SO... YES.
ALL RIGHT. FIRST AND FOREMOST, I WANT EVERYONE TO STAY CLOSE.
YEAH, THIS IS NOT SOME DUMB HORROR MOVIE WHERE SOMEONE MAKES THE TERRIBLE SUGGESTION THAT WE SPLIT UP TO INVESTI--
K-KATE?
STAY CALM. I'M SURE IT--
FWOOOOOOOM

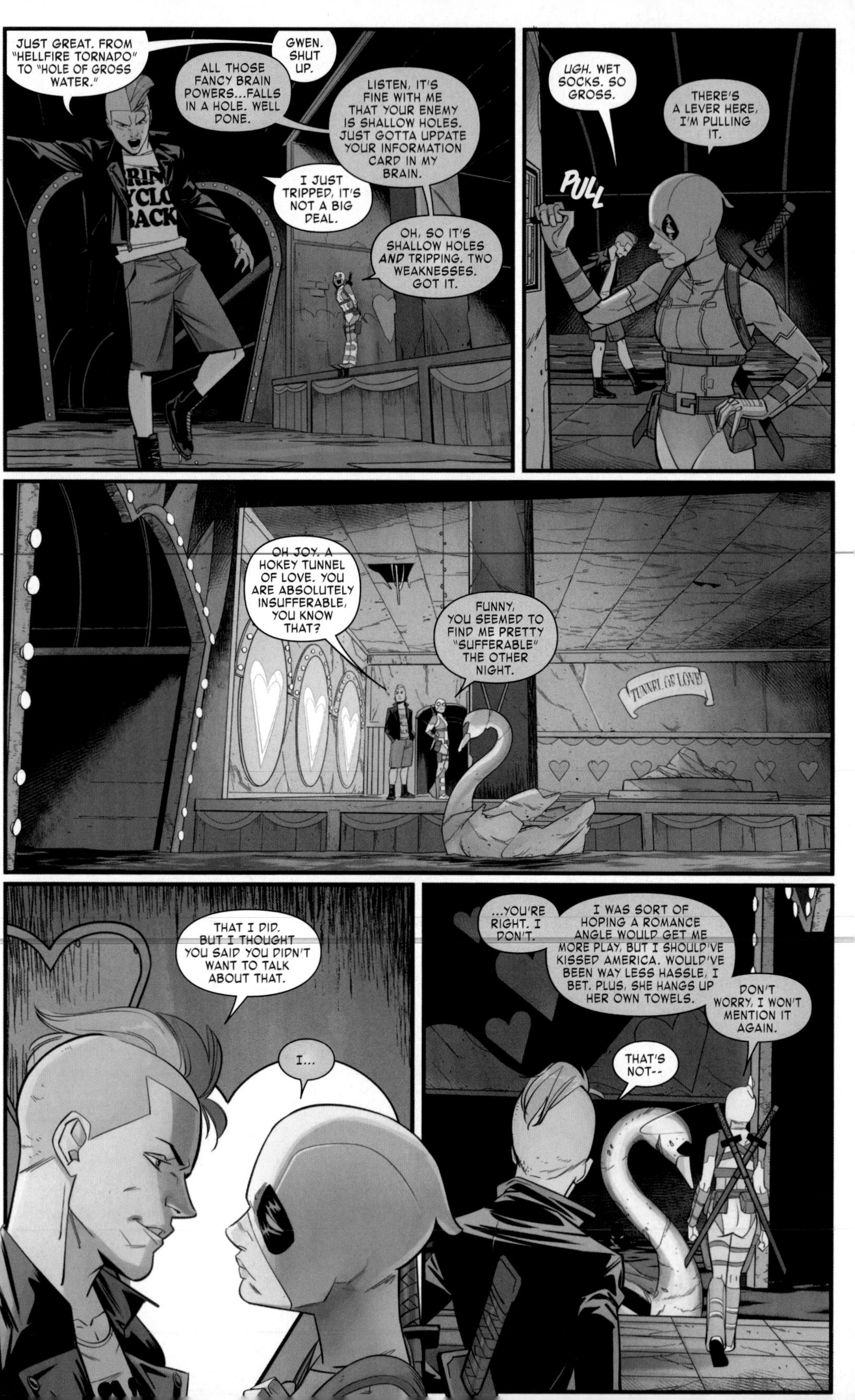
JUST GREAT. FROM "HELLFIRE TORNADO" TO "HOLE OF GROSS WATER."
GWEN. SHUT UP.
ALL THOSE FANCY BRAIN POWERS...FALLS IN A HOLE. WELL DONE.
LISTEN, IT'S FINE WITH ME THAT YOUR ENEMY IS SHALLOW HOLES. JUST GOTTA UPDATE YOUR INFORMATION CARD IN MY BRAIN.
I JUST TRIPPED, IT'S NOT A BIG DEAL.
OH, SO IT'S SHALLOW HOLES AND TRIPPING. TWO WEAKNESSES. GOT IT.
UGH. WET SOCKS. SO GROSS.
THERE'S A LEVER HERE, I'M PULLING IT.
PULL
OH JOY. A HOKEY TUNNEL OF LOVE. YOU ARE ABSOLUTELY INSUFFERABLE, YOU KNOW THAT?
FUNNY, YOU SEEMED TO FIND ME PRETTY "SUFFERABLE" THE OTHER NIGHT.
TUNNEL OF LOVE
THAT I DID. BUT I THOUGHT YOU SAID YOU DIDN'T WANT TO TALK ABOUT THAT.
I...
...YOU'RE RIGHT. I DON'T.
I WAS SORT OF HOPING A ROMANCE ANGLE WOULD GET ME MORE PLAY, BUT I SHOULD'VE KISSED AMERICA. WOULD'VE BEEN WAY LESS HASSLE, I BET. PLUS, SHE HANGS UP HER OWN TOWELS.
THAT'S NOT--
DON'T WORRY, I WON'T MENTION IT AGAIN.

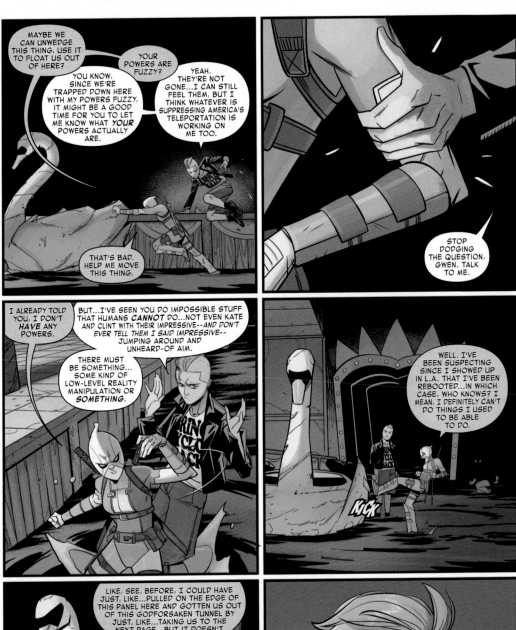

MAYBE WE CAN UNWEDGE THIS THING, USE IT TO FLOAT US OUT OF HERE?

YOUR POWERS ARE FUZZY?

YOU KNOW, SINCE WE'RE TRAPPED DOWN HERE WITH MY POWERS FUZZY, IT MIGHT BE A GOOD TIME FOR YOU TO LET ME KNOW WHAT *YOUR* POWERS ACTUALLY ARE.

YEAH. THEY'RE NOT GONE...I CAN STILL FEEL THEM, BUT I THINK WHATEVER IS SUPPRESSING AMERICA'S TELEPORTATION IS WORKING ON ME TOO.

THAT'S BAD. HELP ME MOVE THIS THING.

STOP DODGING THE QUESTION, GWEN. TALK TO ME.

I ALREADY TOLD YOU, I DON'T *HAVE* ANY POWERS.

BUT...I'VE SEEN YOU DO IMPOSSIBLE STUFF THAT HUMANS *CANNOT* DO...NOT EVEN KATE AND CLINT WITH THEIR IMPRESSIVE--*AND DON'T EVER TELL THEM I SAID IMPRESSIVE*--JUMPING AROUND AND UNHEARD-OF AIM.

THERE MUST BE SOMETHING... SOME KIND OF LOW-LEVEL REALITY MANIPULATION OR *SOMETHING*.

WELL, I'VE BEEN SUSPECTING SINCE I SHOWED UP IN L.A. THAT I'VE BEEN REBOOTED...IN WHICH CASE, WHO KNOWS? I MEAN, I DEFINITELY CAN'T DO THINGS I USED TO BE ABLE TO DO.

KICK

LIKE, SEE, BEFORE, I COULD HAVE JUST, LIKE...PULLED ON THE EDGE OF THIS PANEL HERE AND GOTTEN US OUT OF THIS GODFORSAKEN TUNNEL BY JUST, LIKE...TAKING US TO THE NEXT PAGE...BUT IT DOESN'T WORK ANYMORE.

I CAN DO SOME STUFF...BUT NOT OTHER STUFF.

I'M NOT REALLY SURE WHAT'S GOING ON, BUT IT'S BEEN HAPPENING SINCE WAY BEFORE WE LANDED IN THIS HORROR MOVIE MASQUERADING AS A THEME PARK.

...

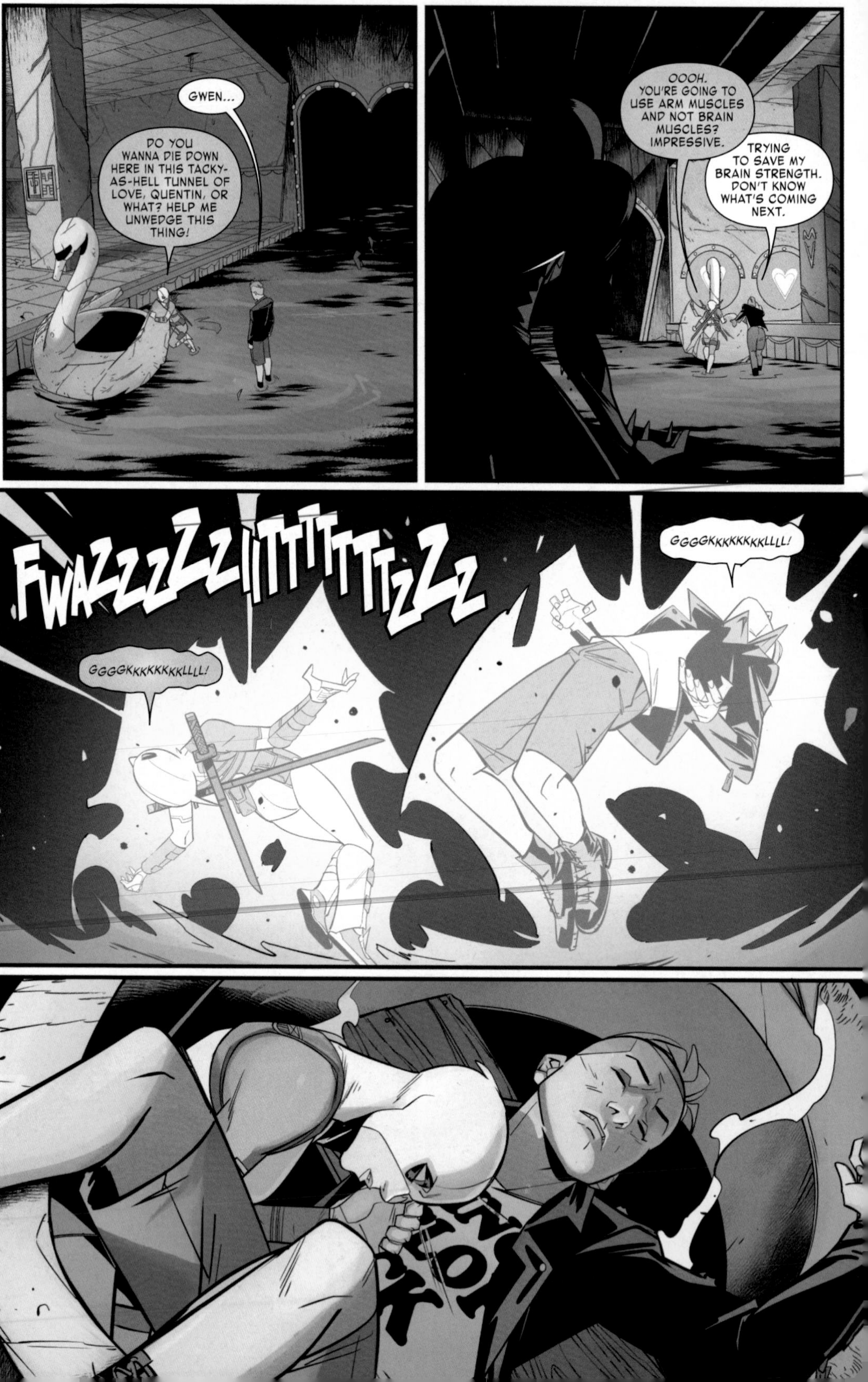
GWEN...
DO YOU WANNA DIE DOWN HERE IN THIS TACKY-AS-HELL TUNNEL OF LOVE, QUENTIN, OR WHAT? HELP ME UNWEDGE THIS THING!
OOOH. YOU'RE GOING TO USE ARM MUSCLES AND NOT BRAIN MUSCLES? IMPRESSIVE.
TRYING TO SAVE MY BRAIN STRENGTH. DON'T KNOW WHAT'S COMING NEXT.
FWAZZZZZZIIITTTTTTTZZZ
GGGGKKKKKKKKLLLL!
GGGGKKKKKKKKLLLL!

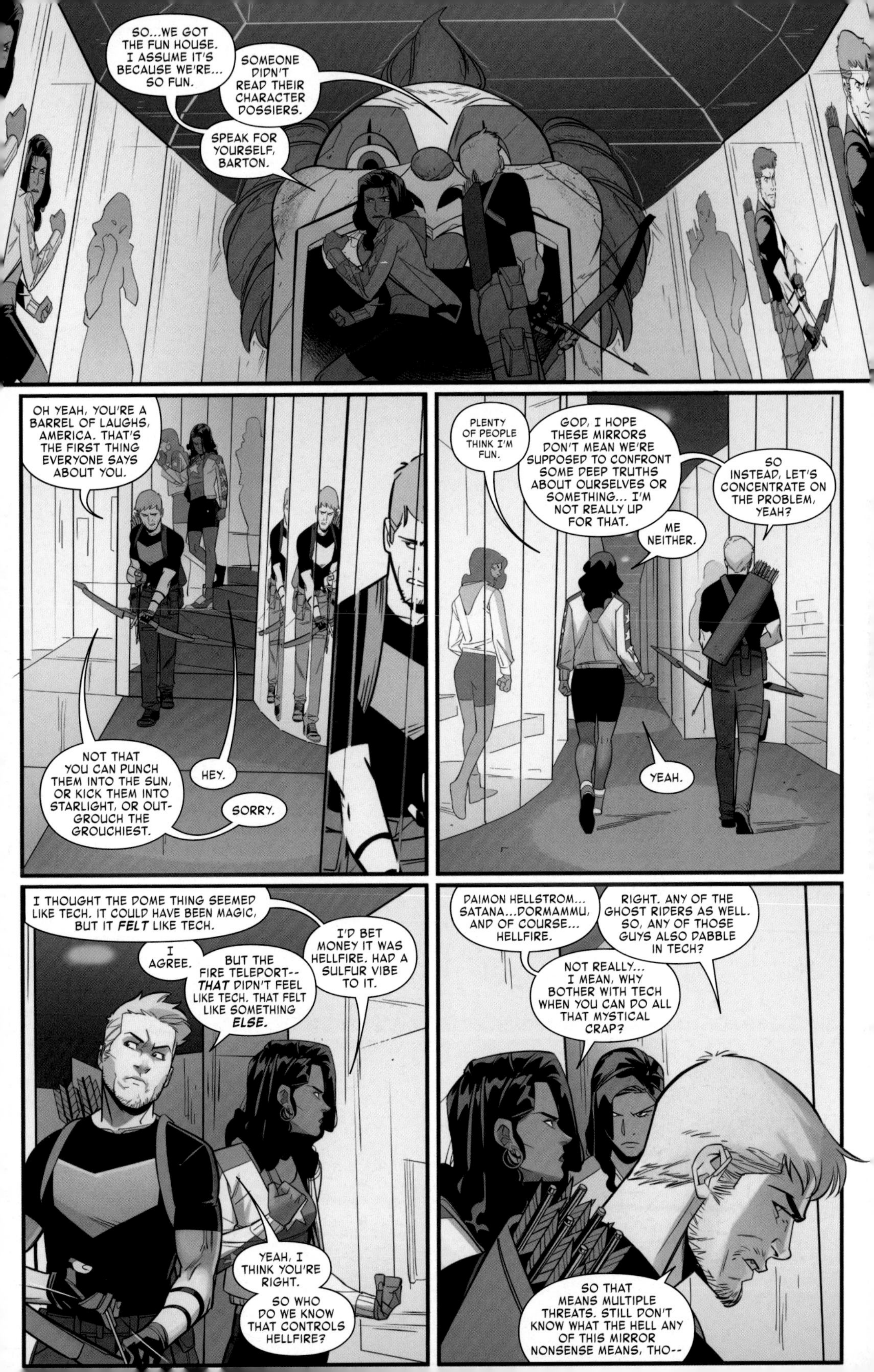
SO...WE GOT THE FUN HOUSE. I ASSUME IT'S BECAUSE WE'RE... SO FUN.
SOMEONE DIDN'T READ THEIR CHARACTER DOSSIERS.
SPEAK FOR YOURSELF, BARTON.
OH YEAH, YOU'RE A BARREL OF LAUGHS, AMERICA. THAT'S THE FIRST THING EVERYONE SAYS ABOUT YOU.
NOT THAT YOU CAN PUNCH THEM INTO THE SUN, OR KICK THEM INTO STARLIGHT, OR OUT-GROUCH THE GROUCHIEST.
HEY.
SORRY.
PLENTY OF PEOPLE THINK I'M FUN.
GOD, I HOPE THESE MIRRORS DON'T MEAN WE'RE SUPPOSED TO CONFRONT SOME DEEP TRUTHS ABOUT OURSELVES OR SOMETHING... I'M NOT REALLY UP FOR THAT.
ME NEITHER.
SO INSTEAD, LET'S CONCENTRATE ON THE PROBLEM, YEAH?
YEAH.
I THOUGHT THE DOME THING SEEMED LIKE TECH. IT COULD HAVE BEEN MAGIC, BUT IT *FELT* LIKE TECH.
I AGREE.
BUT THE FIRE TELEPORT-- ***THAT*** DIDN'T FEEL LIKE TECH. THAT FELT LIKE SOMETHING ***ELSE.***
I'D BET MONEY IT WAS HELLFIRE. HAD A SULFUR VIBE TO IT.
YEAH, I THINK YOU'RE RIGHT.
SO WHO DO WE KNOW THAT CONTROLS HELLFIRE?
DAIMON HELLSTROM... SATANA...DORMAMMU, AND OF COURSE... HELLFIRE.
RIGHT. ANY OF THE GHOST RIDERS AS WELL. SO, ANY OF THOSE GUYS ALSO DABBLE IN TECH?
NOT REALLY... I MEAN, WHY BOTHER WITH TECH WHEN YOU CAN DO ALL THAT MYSTICAL CRAP?
SO THAT MEANS MULTIPLE THREATS. STILL DON'T KNOW WHAT THE HELL ANY OF THIS MIRROR NONSENSE MEANS, THO--

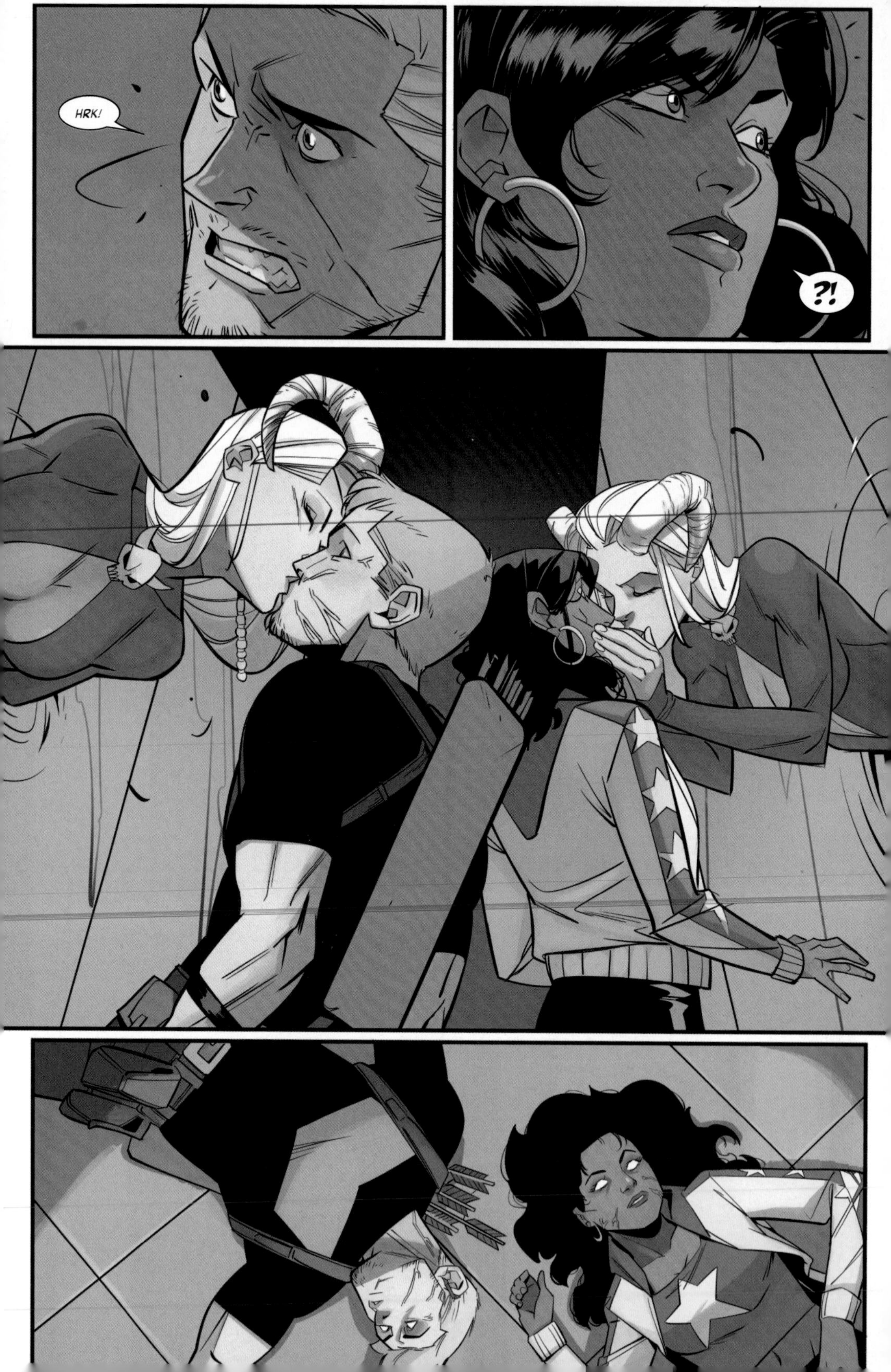
HRK!
?!

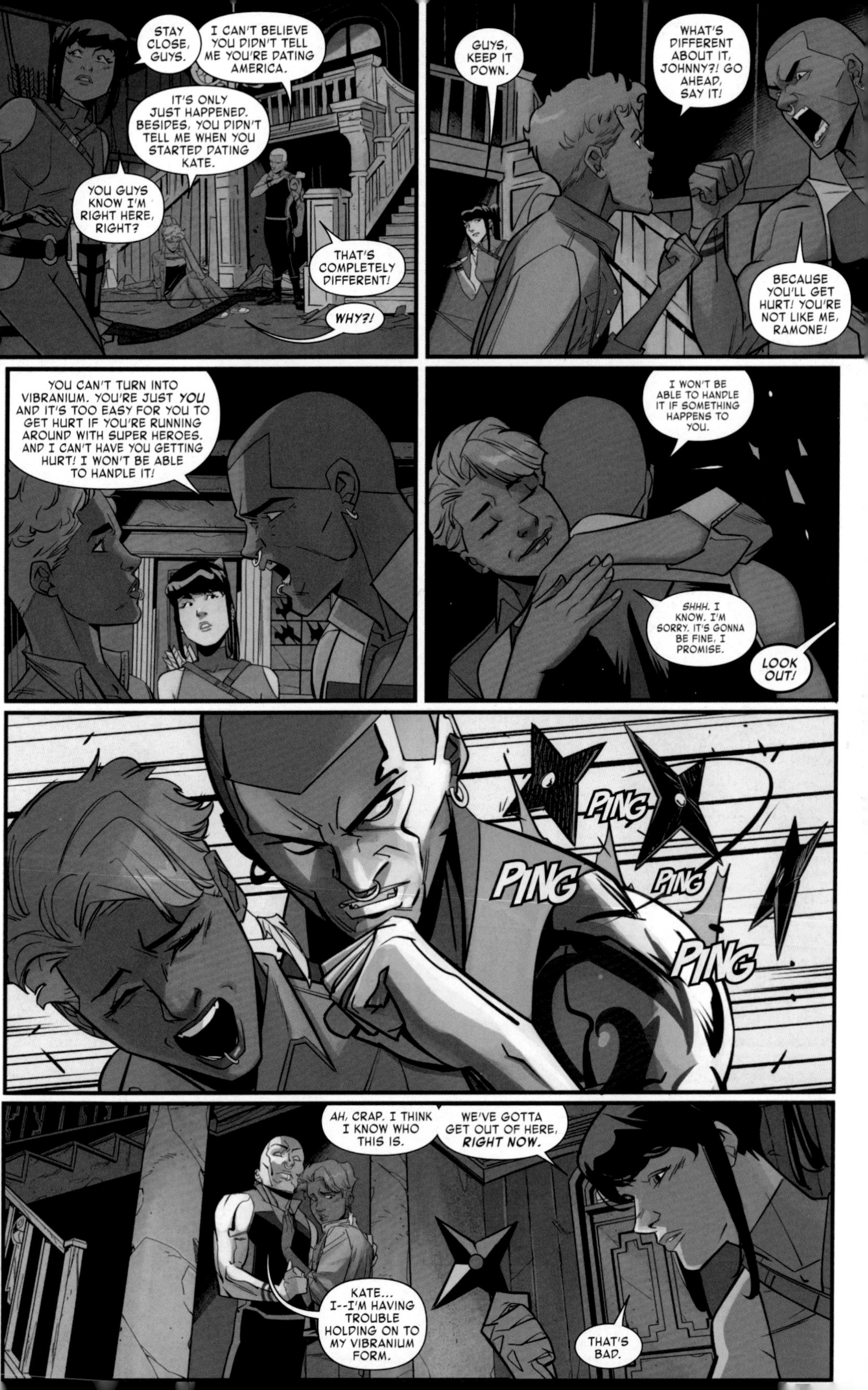
STAY CLOSE, GUYS.
I CAN'T BELIEVE YOU DIDN'T TELL ME YOU'RE DATING AMERICA.
IT'S ONLY JUST HAPPENED. BESIDES, YOU DIDN'T TELL ME WHEN YOU STARTED DATING KATE.
YOU GUYS KNOW I'M RIGHT HERE, RIGHT?
THAT'S COMPLETELY DIFFERENT!
WHY?!
GUYS, KEEP IT DOWN.
WHAT'S DIFFERENT ABOUT IT, JOHNNY?! GO AHEAD, SAY IT!
BECAUSE YOU'LL GET HURT! YOU'RE NOT LIKE ME, RAMONE!
YOU CAN'T TURN INTO VIBRANIUM. YOU'RE JUST YOU AND IT'S TOO EASY FOR YOU TO GET HURT IF YOU'RE RUNNING AROUND WITH SUPER HEROES. AND I CAN'T HAVE YOU GETTING HURT! I WON'T BE ABLE TO HANDLE IT!
I WON'T BE ABLE TO HANDLE IT IF SOMETHING HAPPENS TO YOU.
SHHH. I KNOW. I'M SORRY. IT'S GONNA BE FINE, I PROMISE.
LOOK OUT!
PING
PING
PING
PING
AH, CRAP. I THINK I KNOW WHO THIS IS.
WE'VE GOTTA GET OUT OF HERE, RIGHT NOW.
KATE... I--I'M HAVING TROUBLE HOLDING ON TO MY VIBRANIUM FORM.
THAT'S BAD.

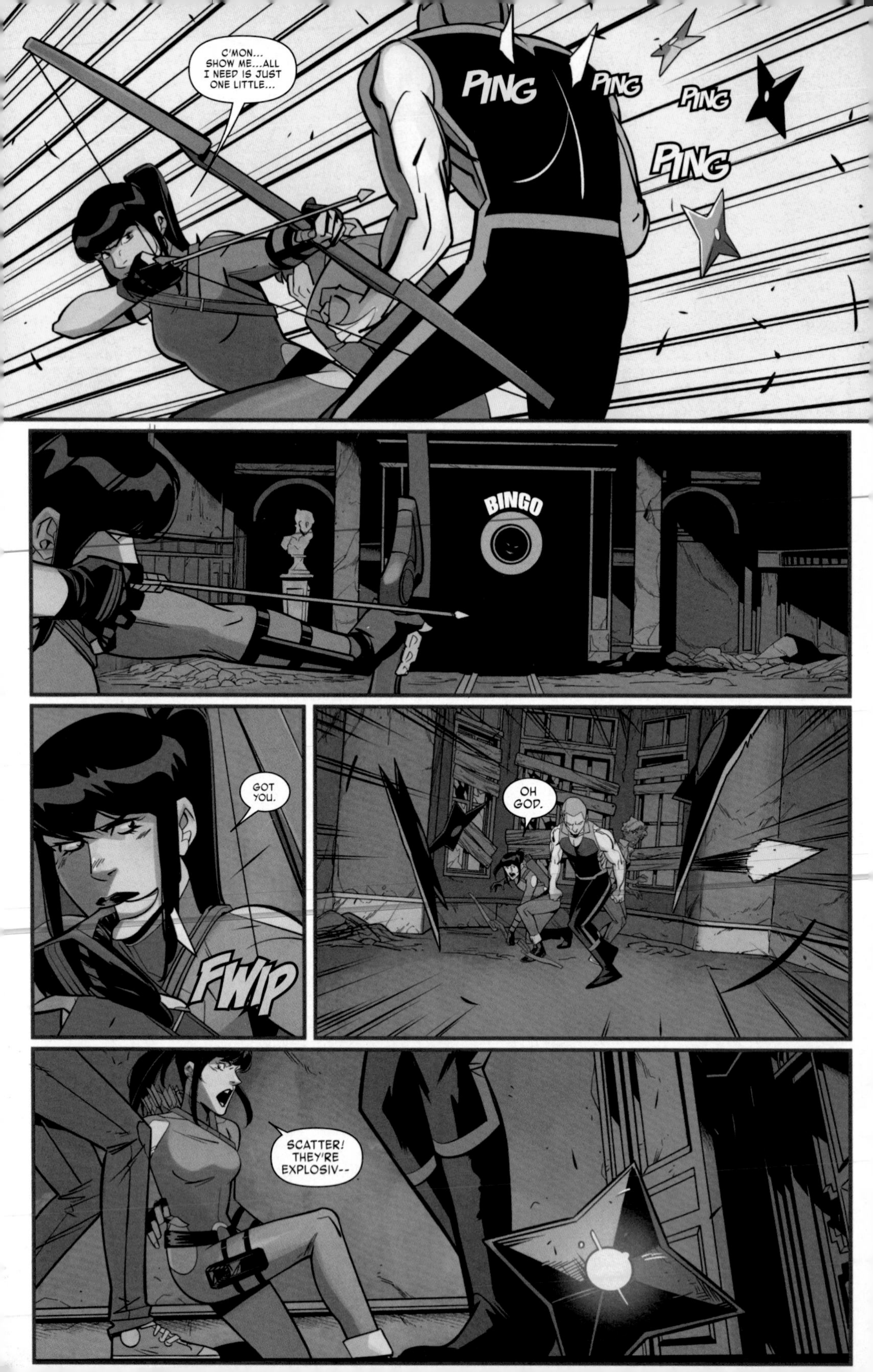
C'MON... SHOW ME...ALL I NEED IS JUST ONE LITTLE...
PING
PING
PING
PING
BINGO
GOT YOU.
FWIP
OH GOD.
SCATTER! THEY'RE EXPLOSIV--

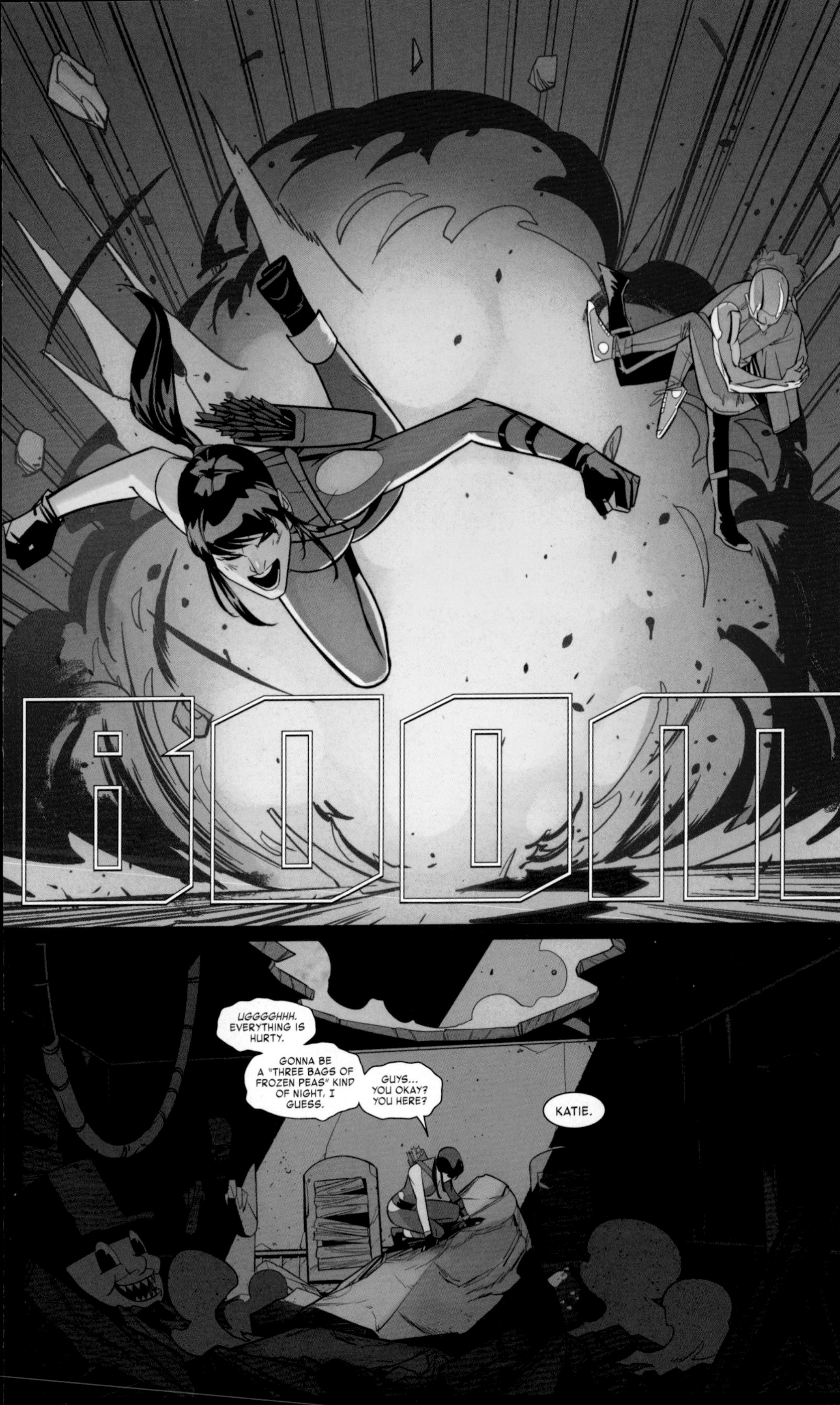
BOOM
UGGGGHHH. EVERYTHING IS HURTY.
GONNA BE A "THREE BAGS OF FROZEN PEAS" KIND OF NIGHT, I GUESS.
GUYS... YOU OKAY? YOU HERE?
KATIE.

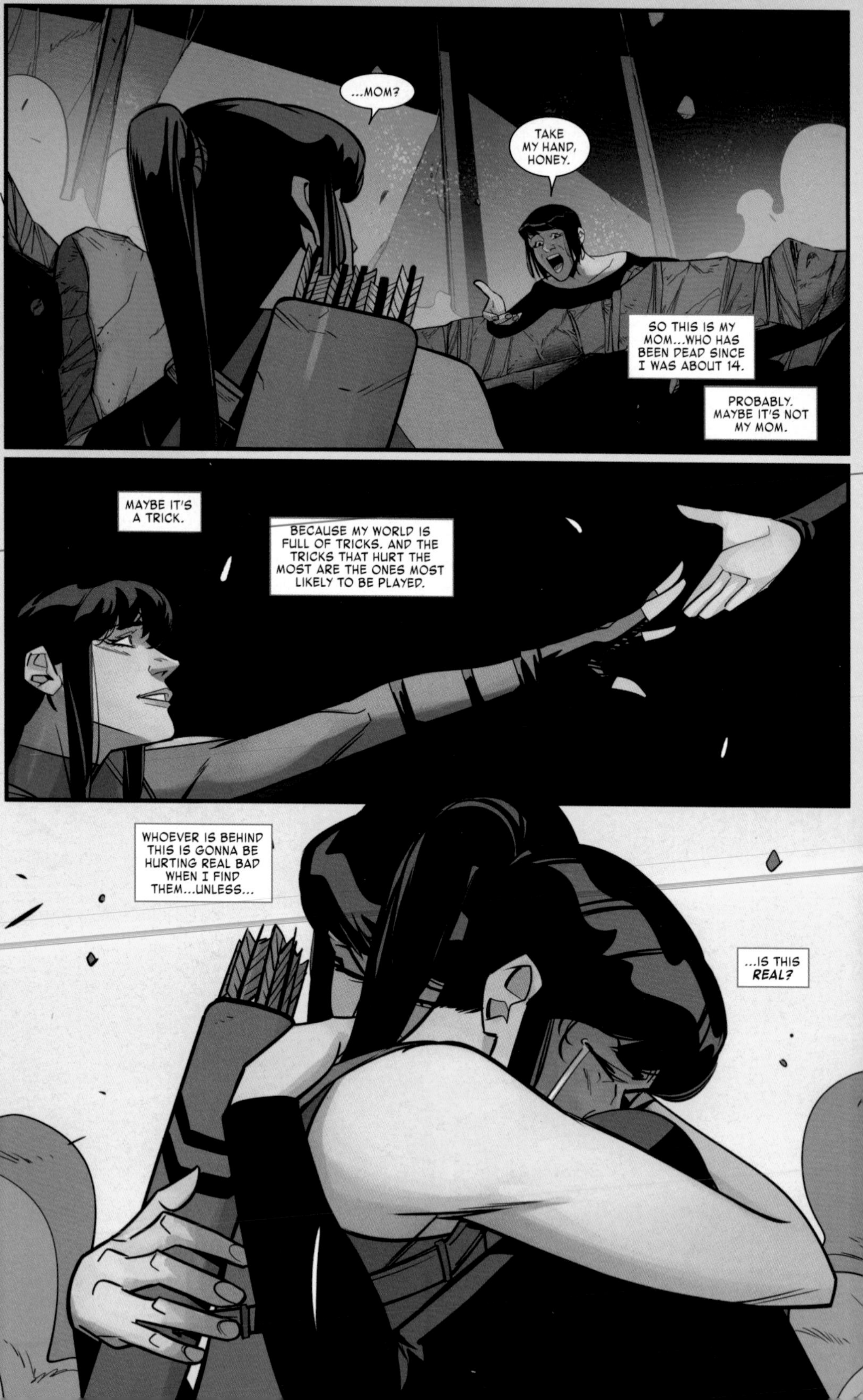
...MOM?
TAKE MY HAND, HONEY.
SO THIS IS MY MOM...WHO HAS BEEN DEAD SINCE I WAS ABOUT 14.
PROBABLY. MAYBE IT'S NOT MY MOM.
MAYBE IT'S A TRICK.
BECAUSE MY WORLD IS FULL OF TRICKS. AND THE TRICKS THAT HURT THE MOST ARE THE ONES MOST LIKELY TO BE PLAYED.
WHOEVER IS BEHIND THIS IS GONNA BE HURTING REAL BAD WHEN I FIND THEM...UNLESS...
...IS THIS *REAL?*

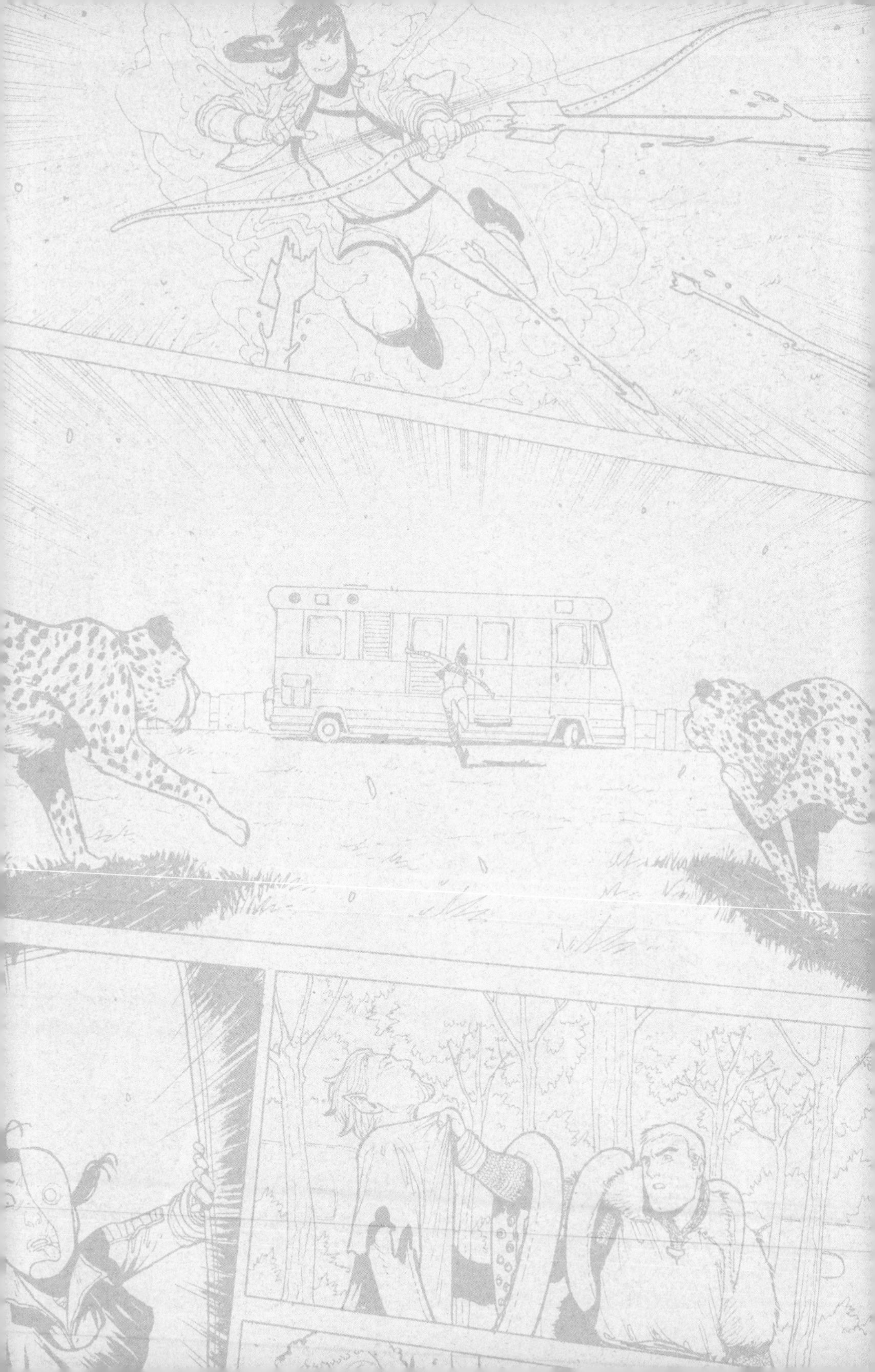

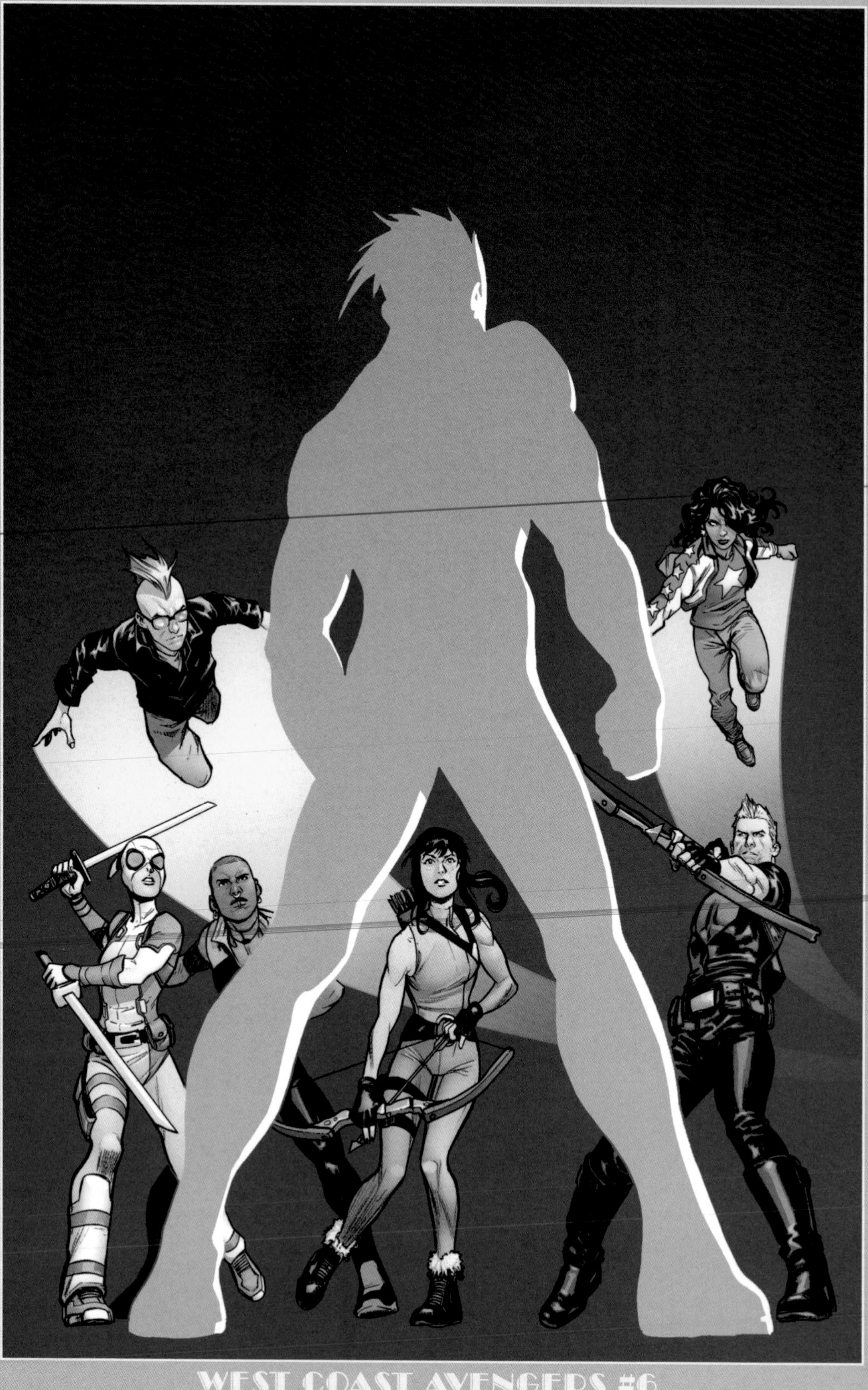

WEST COAST AVENGERS #6

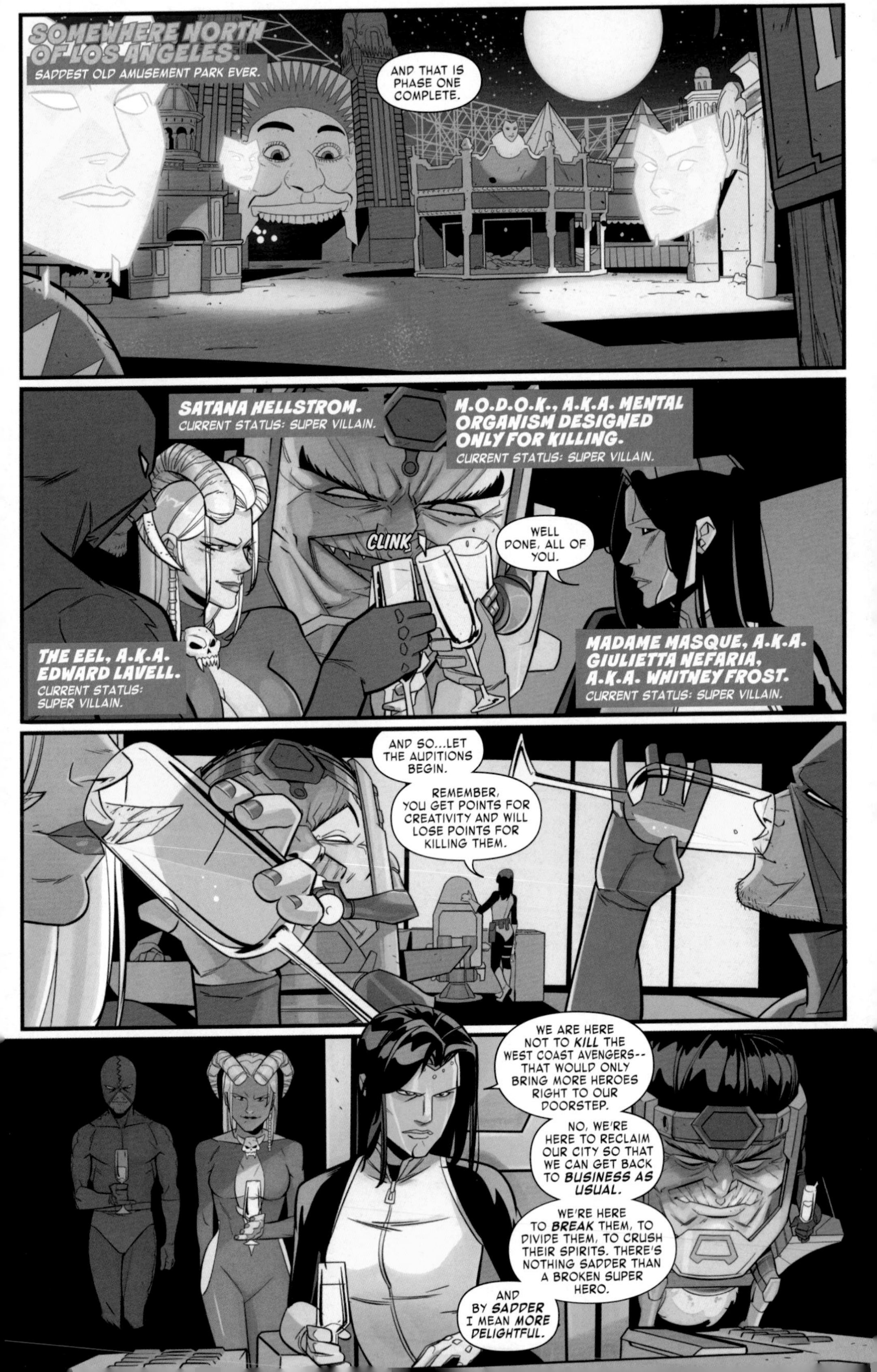
SOMEWHERE NORTH OF LOS ANGELES:
SADDEST OLD AMUSEMENT PARK EVER.
AND THAT IS PHASE ONE COMPLETE.
SATANA HELLSTROM.
CURRENT STATUS: SUPER VILLAIN.
M.O.D.O.K., A.K.A. MENTAL ORGANISM DESIGNED ONLY FOR KILLING.
CURRENT STATUS: SUPER VILLAIN.
CLINK
WELL DONE, ALL OF YOU.
THE EEL, A.K.A. EDWARD LAVELL.
CURRENT STATUS: SUPER VILLAIN.
MADAME MASQUE, A.K.A. GIULIETTA NEFARIA, A.K.A. WHITNEY FROST.
CURRENT STATUS: SUPER VILLAIN.
AND SO...LET THE AUDITIONS BEGIN.
REMEMBER, YOU GET POINTS FOR CREATIVITY AND WILL LOSE POINTS FOR KILLING THEM.
WE ARE HERE NOT TO KILL THE WEST COAST AVENGERS-- THAT WOULD ONLY BRING MORE HEROES RIGHT TO OUR DOORSTEP.
NO, WE'RE HERE TO RECLAIM OUR CITY SO THAT WE CAN GET BACK TO BUSINESS AS USUAL.
WE'RE HERE TO BREAK THEM, TO DIVIDE THEM, TO CRUSH THEIR SPIRITS. THERE'S NOTHING SADDER THAN A BROKEN SUPER HERO.
AND BY SADDER I MEAN MORE DELIGHTFUL.

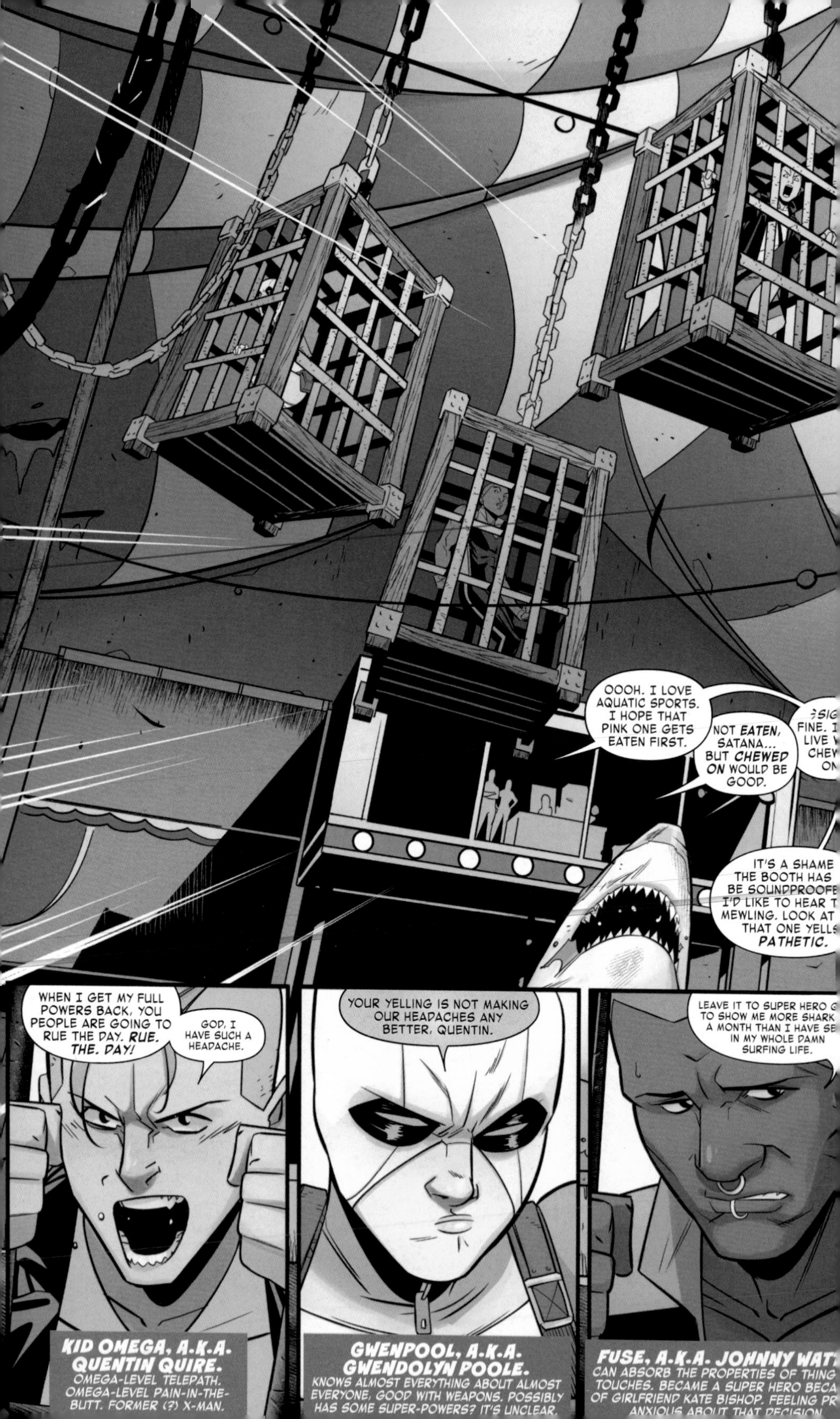
OOOH. I LOVE AQUATIC SPORTS. I HOPE THAT PINK ONE GETS EATEN FIRST.
NOT EATEN, SATANA... BUT CHEWED ON WOULD BE GOOD.
SIG FINE. I LIVE CHEW ON
IT'S A SHAME THE BOOTH HAS BE SOUNDPROOFE I'D LIKE TO HEAR T MEWLING. LOOK AT THAT ONE YELL PATHETIC.
WHEN I GET MY FULL POWERS BACK, YOU PEOPLE ARE GOING TO RUE THE DAY. RUE. THE. DAY!
GOD, I HAVE SUCH A HEADACHE.
KID OMEGA, A.K.A. QUENTIN QUIRE.
OMEGA-LEVEL TELEPATH. OMEGA-LEVEL PAIN-IN-THE-BUTT. FORMER (?) X-MAN.
YOUR YELLING IS NOT MAKING OUR HEADACHES ANY BETTER, QUENTIN.
GWENPOOL, A.K.A. GWENDOLYN POOLE.
KNOWS ALMOST EVERYTHING ABOUT ALMOST EVERYONE, GOOD WITH WEAPONS. POSSIBLY HAS SOME SUPER-POWERS? IT'S UNCLEAR.
LEAVE IT TO SUPER HERO TO SHOW ME MORE SHARK A MONTH THAN I HAVE SE IN MY WHOLE DAMN SURFING LIFE.
FUSE, A.K.A. JOHNNY WAT
CAN ABSORB THE PROPERTIES OF THING TOUCHES. BECAME A SUPER HERO BECA OF GIRLFRIEND KATE BISHOP. FEELING PR

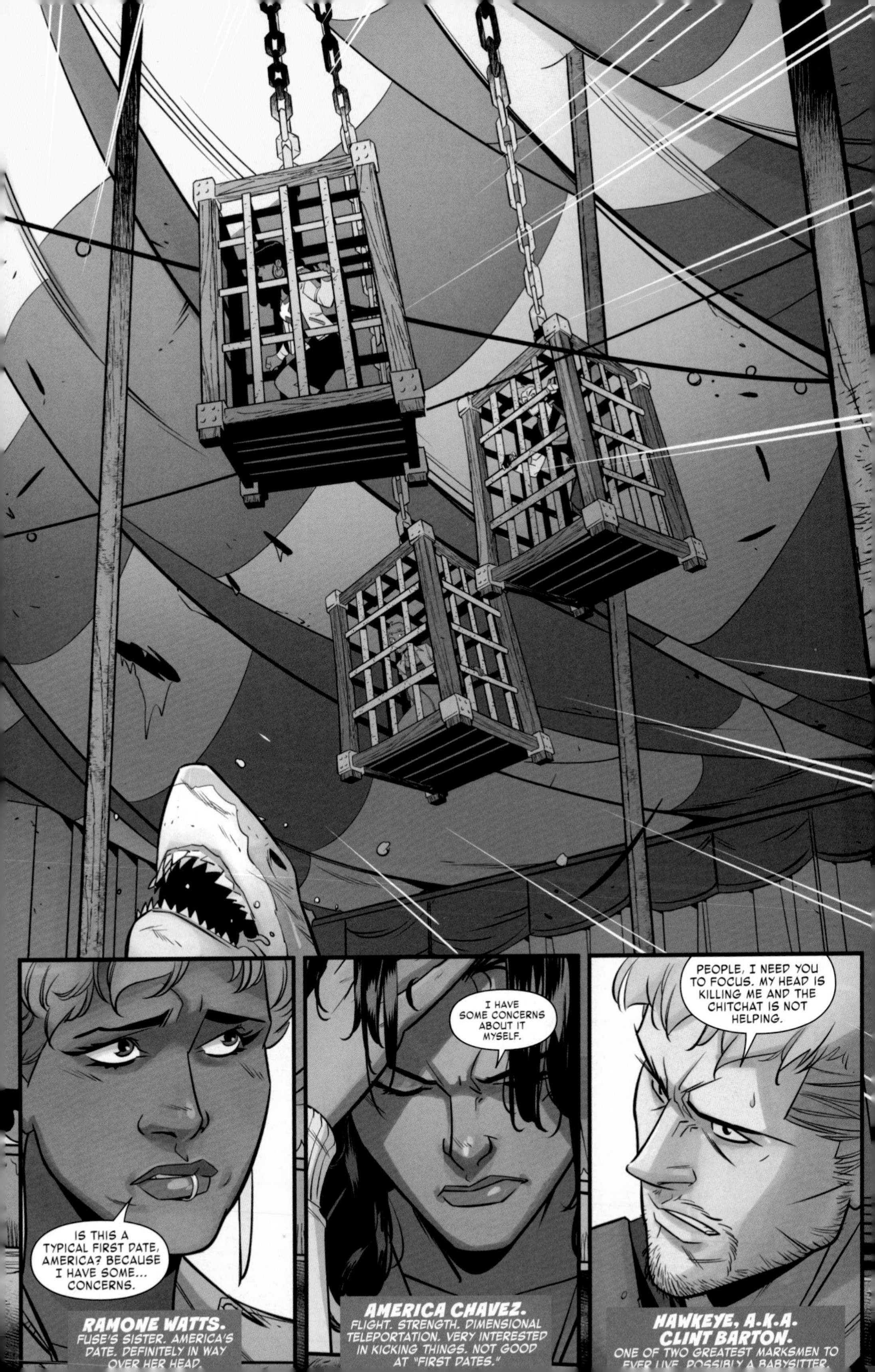

IS THIS A TYPICAL FIRST DATE, AMERICA? BECAUSE I HAVE SOME... CONCERNS.
RAMONE WATTS.
FUSE'S SISTER. AMERICA'S DATE. DEFINITELY IN WAY OVER HER HEAD.
I HAVE SOME CONCERNS ABOUT IT MYSELF.
AMERICA CHAVEZ.
FLIGHT. STRENGTH. DIMENSIONAL TELEPORTATION. VERY INTERESTED IN KICKING THINGS. NOT GOOD AT "FIRST DATES."
PEOPLE, I NEED YOU TO FOCUS. MY HEAD IS KILLING ME AND THE CHITCHAT IS NOT HELPING.
HAWKEYE, A.K.A. CLINT BARTON.
ONE OF TWO GREATEST MARKSMEN TO EVER LIVE. POSSIBLY A BABYSITTER.

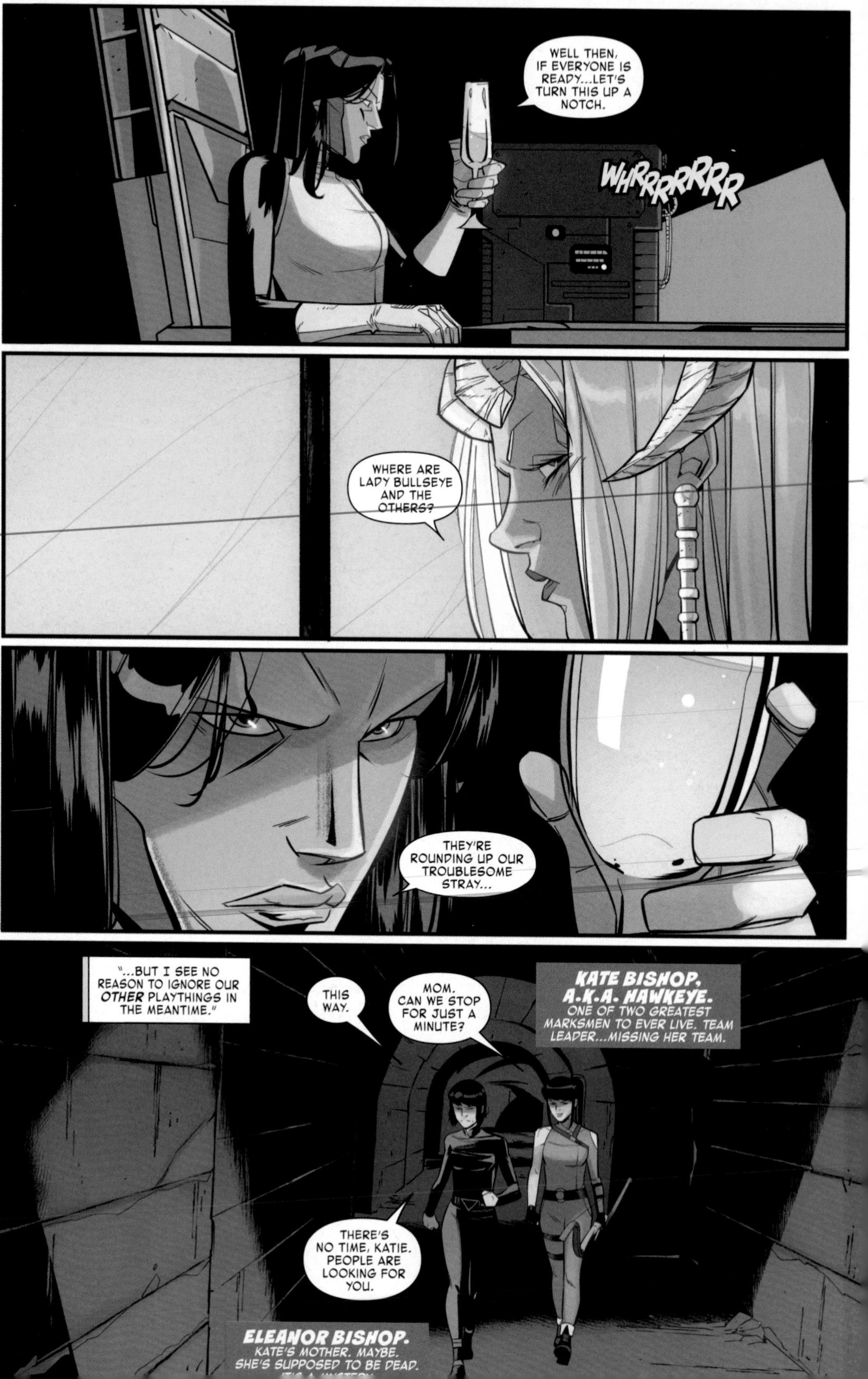

WELL THEN, IF EVERYONE IS READY...LET'S TURN THIS UP A NOTCH.
WHRRRRRRR
WHERE ARE LADY BULLSEYE AND THE OTHERS?
THEY'RE ROUNDING UP OUR TROUBLESOME STRAY...
"...BUT I SEE NO REASON TO IGNORE OUR *OTHER* PLAYTHINGS IN THE MEANTIME."
THIS WAY.
MOM. CAN WE STOP FOR JUST A MINUTE?
KATE BISHOP, A.K.A. HAWKEYE.
ONE OF TWO GREATEST MARKSMEN TO EVER LIVE. TEAM LEADER...MISSING HER TEAM.
THERE'S NO TIME, KATIE. PEOPLE ARE LOOKING FOR YOU.
ELEANOR BISHOP.
KATE'S MOTHER. MAYBE. SHE'S SUPPOSED TO BE DEAD.

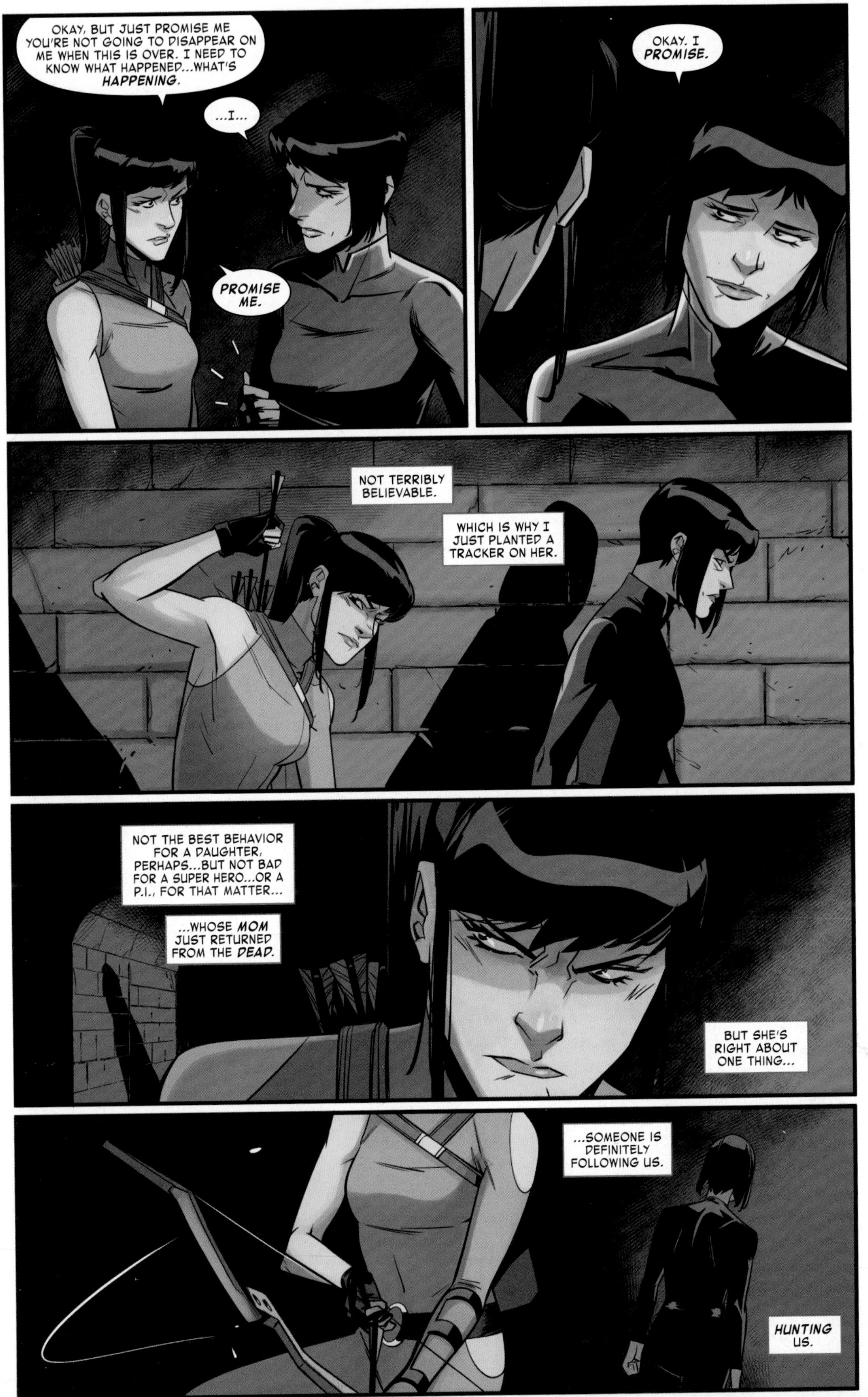
OKAY, BUT JUST PROMISE ME YOU'RE NOT GOING TO DISAPPEAR ON ME WHEN THIS IS OVER. I NEED TO KNOW WHAT HAPPENED...WHAT'S *HAPPENING.*
...I...
PROMISE ME.
OKAY. I *PROMISE.*
NOT TERRIBLY BELIEVABLE.
WHICH IS WHY I JUST PLANTED A TRACKER ON HER.
NOT THE BEST BEHAVIOR FOR A DAUGHTER, PERHAPS...BUT NOT BAD FOR A SUPER HERO...OR A P.I., FOR THAT MATTER...
...WHOSE *MOM* JUST RETURNED FROM THE *DEAD.*
BUT SHE'S RIGHT ABOUT ONE THING...
...SOMEONE IS DEFINITELY FOLLOWING US.
HUNTING US.

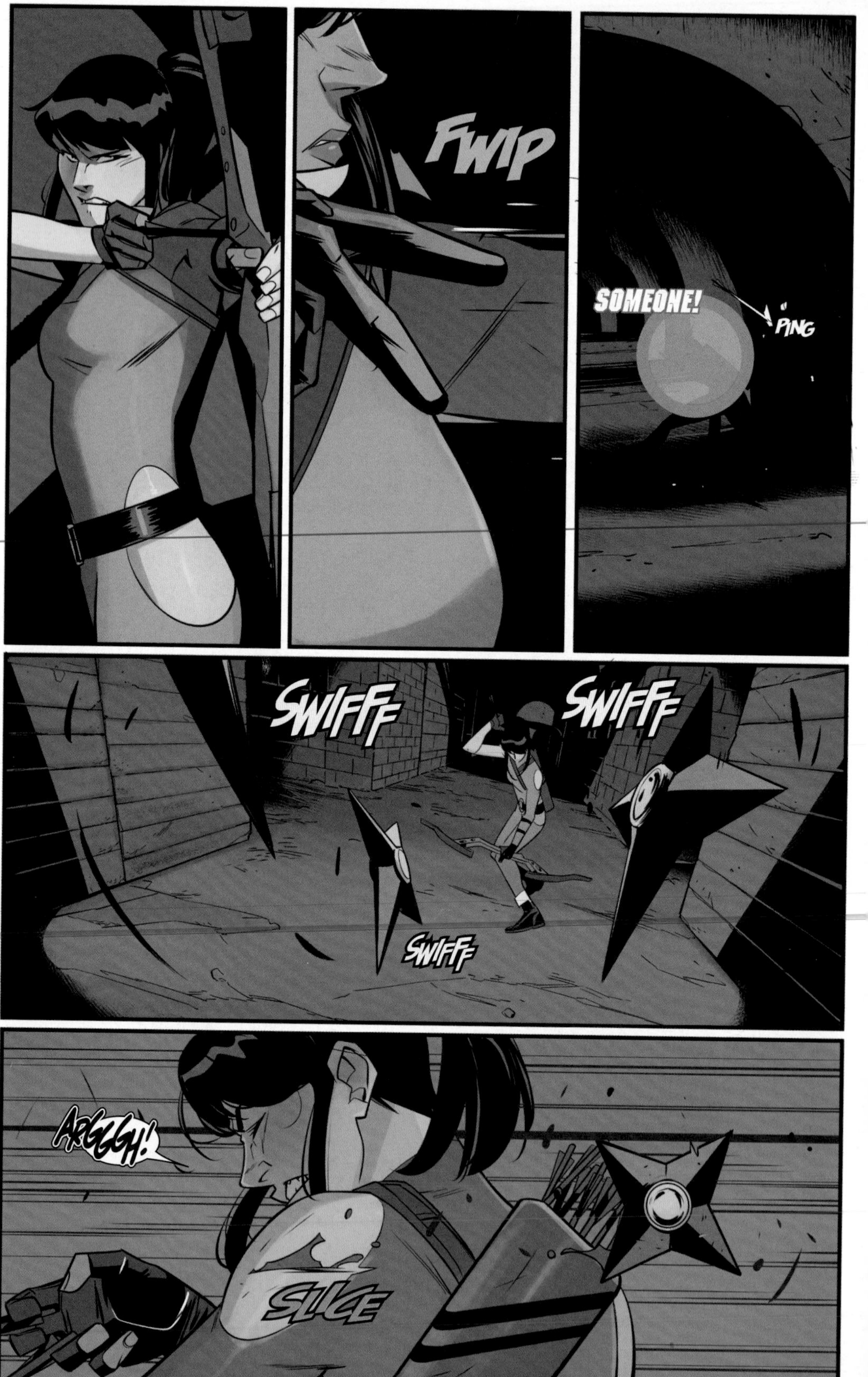
FWIP
SOMEONE!
PING
SWIFFF
SWIFFF
SWIFFF
ARGGGH!
SLICE

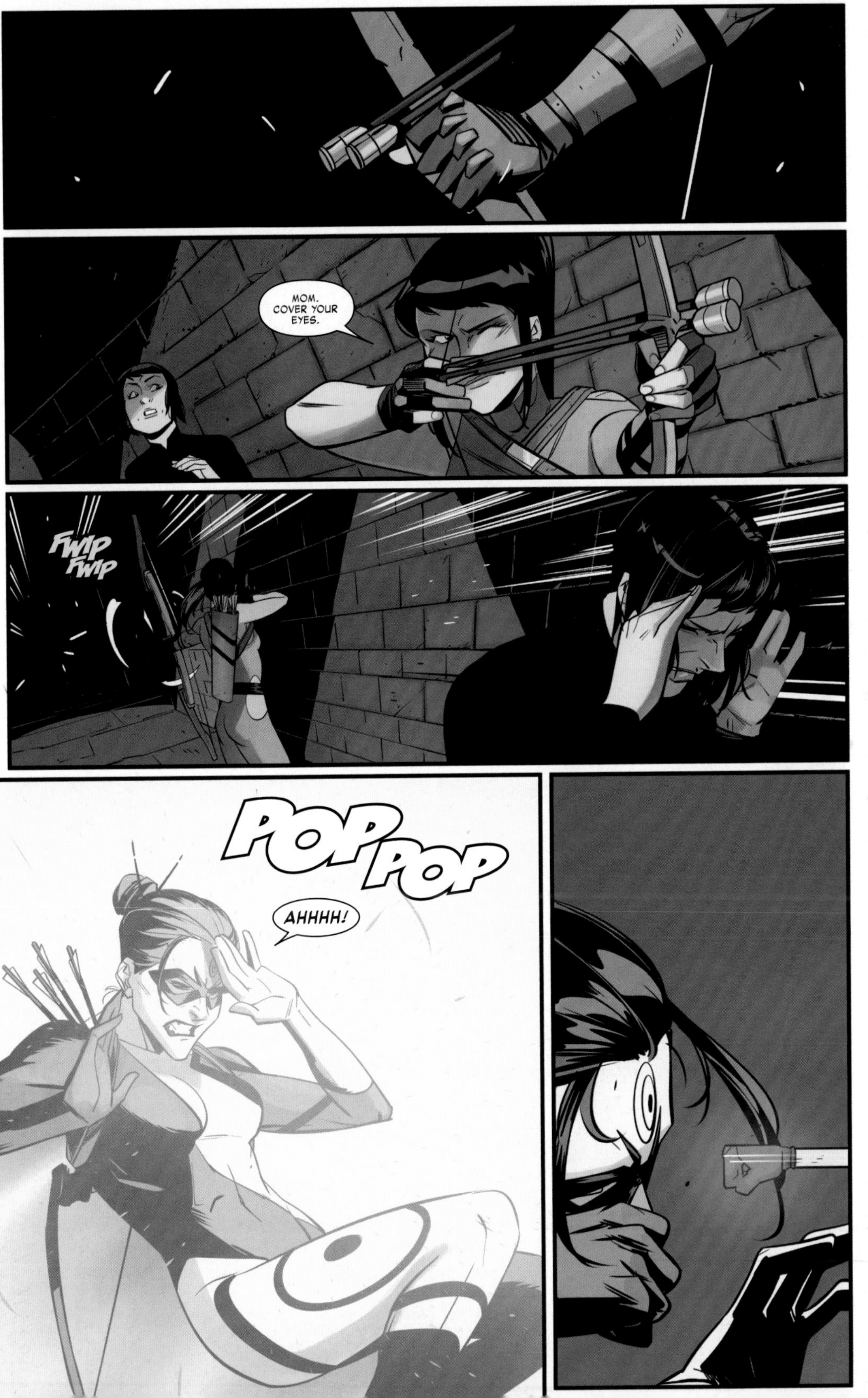

MOM. COVER YOUR EYES.
FWIP FWIP
POP POP
AHHHH!

BOOM

UNGGG!

SMACK

KATE, WE HAVE TO HURRY. SHE WON'T BE ALONE.

OKAY, JUST GIVE ME A MINUTE.

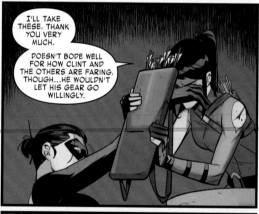

I'LL TAKE THESE, THANK YOU VERY MUCH.

DOESN'T BODE WELL FOR HOW CLINT AND THE OTHERS ARE FARING, THOUGH...HE WOULDN'T LET HIS GEAR GO WILLINGLY.

WHAT'S THIS? EARPLUGS?

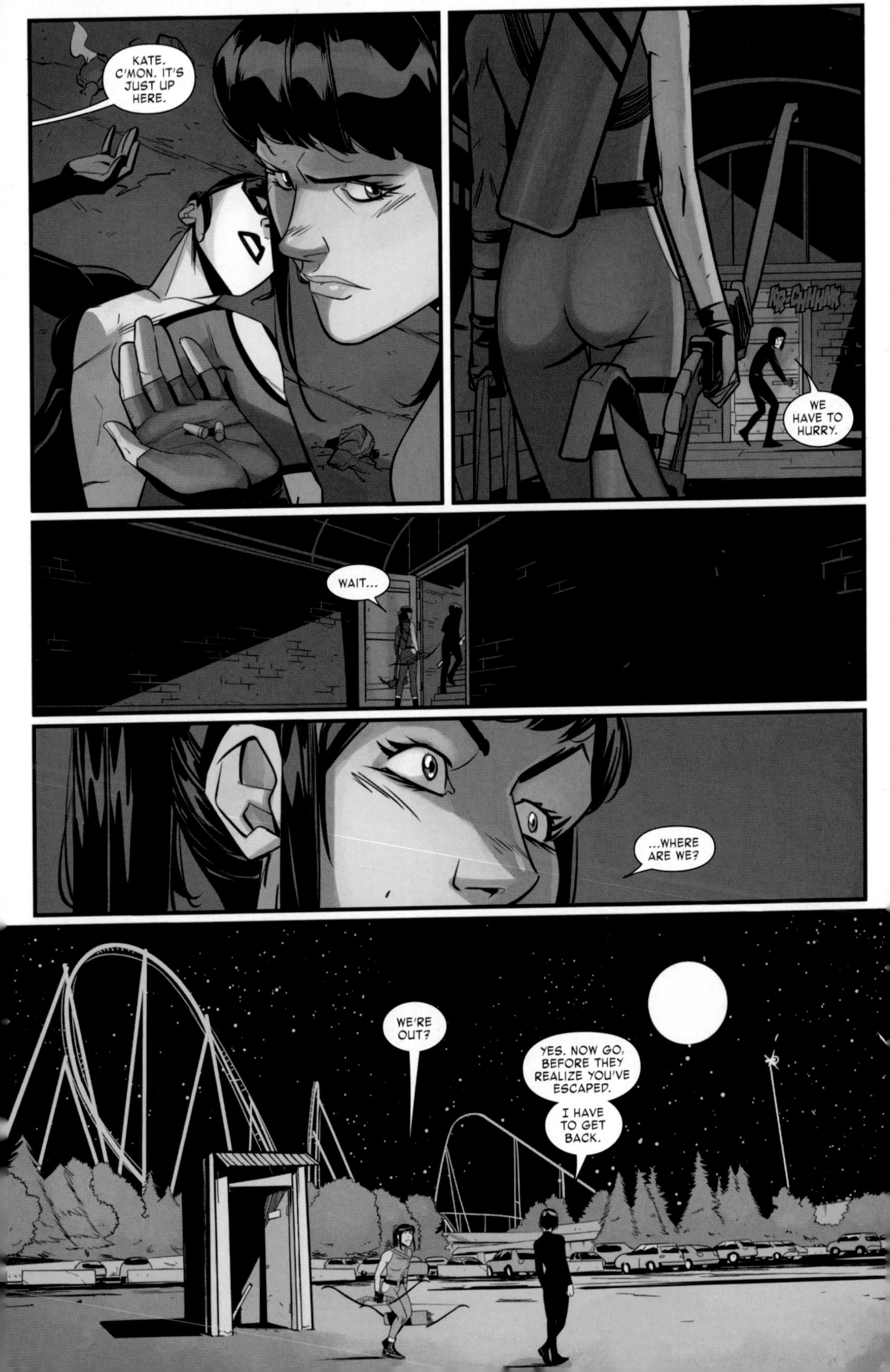
KATE. C'MON. IT'S JUST UP HERE.
KR-CHHHNK
WE HAVE TO HURRY.
WAIT...
...WHERE ARE WE?
WE'RE OUT?
YES. NOW GO, BEFORE THEY REALIZE YOU'VE ESCAPED.
I HAVE TO GET BACK.

BUT I CAN'T LEAVE. MY FRIENDS--WELL, MY FRIENDS AND *QUIRE*--ARE STILL IN THERE.

KATE, I CAN'T GET THEM OUT. YOU HAVE TO GO, NOW. BEFORE THIS GETS WORSE.

I'M NOT LEAVING MY TEAM BEHIND, MOM.

I DON'T KNOW WHAT KIND OF DAUGHTER YOU THINK YOU RAISED...BUT THAT'S NOT AN OPTION THAT WAS EVER ON THE TABLE.

KATE, PLEASE. THERE ARE THINGS HERE YOU CAN'T UNDERSTAND. THINGS BEING SET IN MOTION...IF YOU DON'T GO NOW, I DON'T KNOW THAT I CAN PROTECT YOU.

WELL, YOU NEVER HAVE BEFORE, SO I GUESS IT'LL JUST BE BUSINESS AS USUAL, THEN.

THAT WAS TOO FAR. I'M MAD. I'M SCARED. I'M NOT THINKING.

WOW...I MUST HAVE GOTTEN USED TO THAT HEADACHE...BUT IT LET UP THE SECOND I STEPPED OUTSIDE. NOW IT'S COMING BACK WITH A VENGEANCE.

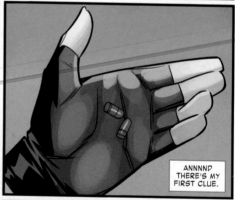

ANNNND THERE'S MY FIRST CLUE.

HANG ON, GUYS. I'M COMING FOR YOU.

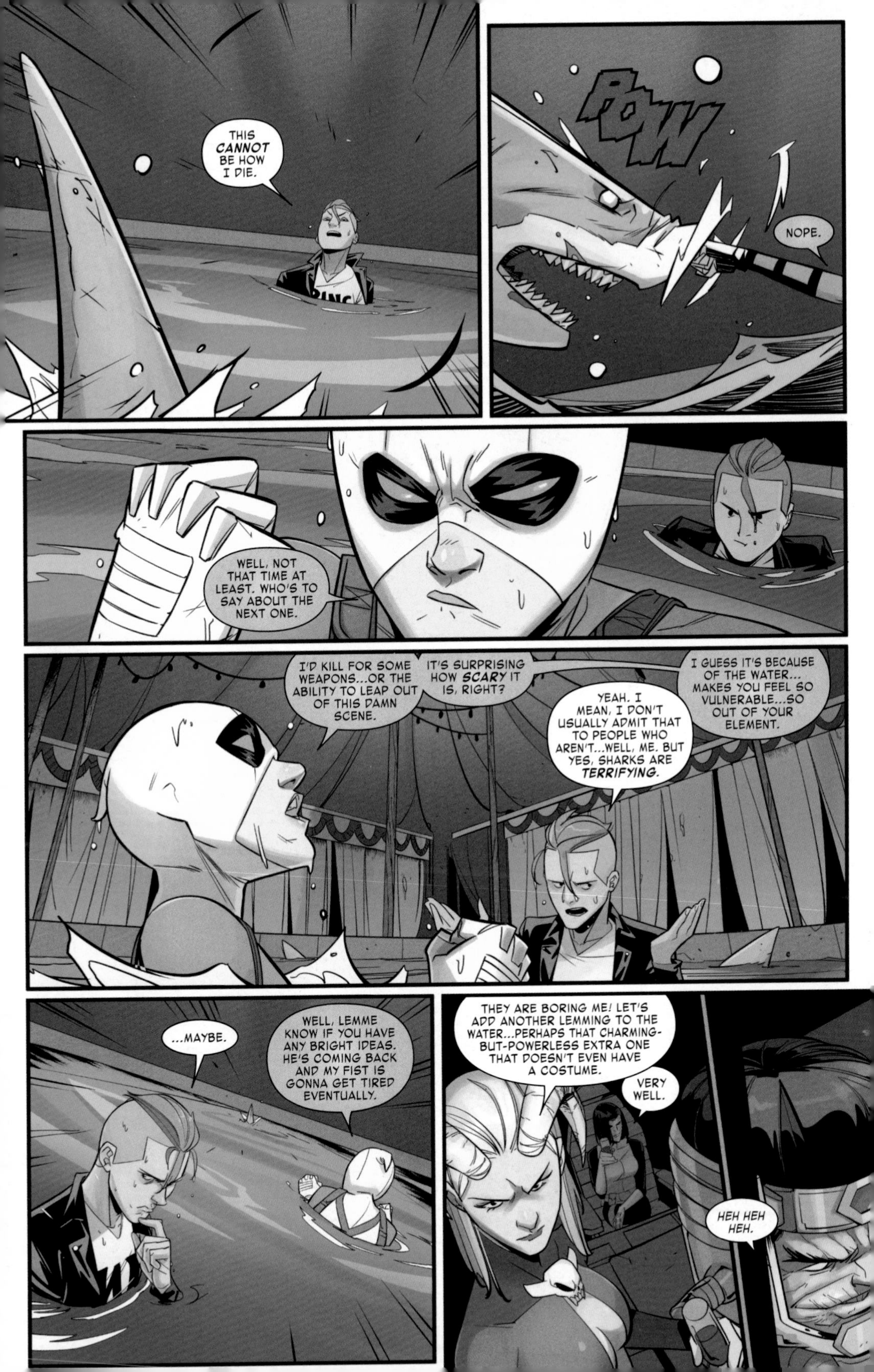
THIS CANNOT BE HOW I DIE.
POW
NOPE.
WELL, NOT THAT TIME AT LEAST. WHO'S TO SAY ABOUT THE NEXT ONE.
I'D KILL FOR SOME WEAPONS...OR THE ABILITY TO LEAP OUT OF THIS DAMN SCENE.
IT'S SURPRISING HOW SCARY IT IS, RIGHT?
I GUESS IT'S BECAUSE OF THE WATER... MAKES YOU FEEL SO VULNERABLE...SO OUT OF YOUR ELEMENT.
YEAH. I MEAN, I DON'T USUALLY ADMIT THAT TO PEOPLE WHO AREN'T...WELL, ME. BUT YES, SHARKS ARE TERRIFYING.
...MAYBE.
WELL, LEMME KNOW IF YOU HAVE ANY BRIGHT IDEAS. HE'S COMING BACK AND MY FIST IS GONNA GET TIRED EVENTUALLY.
THEY ARE BORING ME! LET'S ADD ANOTHER LEMMING TO THE WATER...PERHAPS THAT CHARMING-BUT-POWERLESS EXTRA ONE THAT DOESN'T EVEN HAVE A COSTUME.
VERY WELL.
HEH HEH HEH.

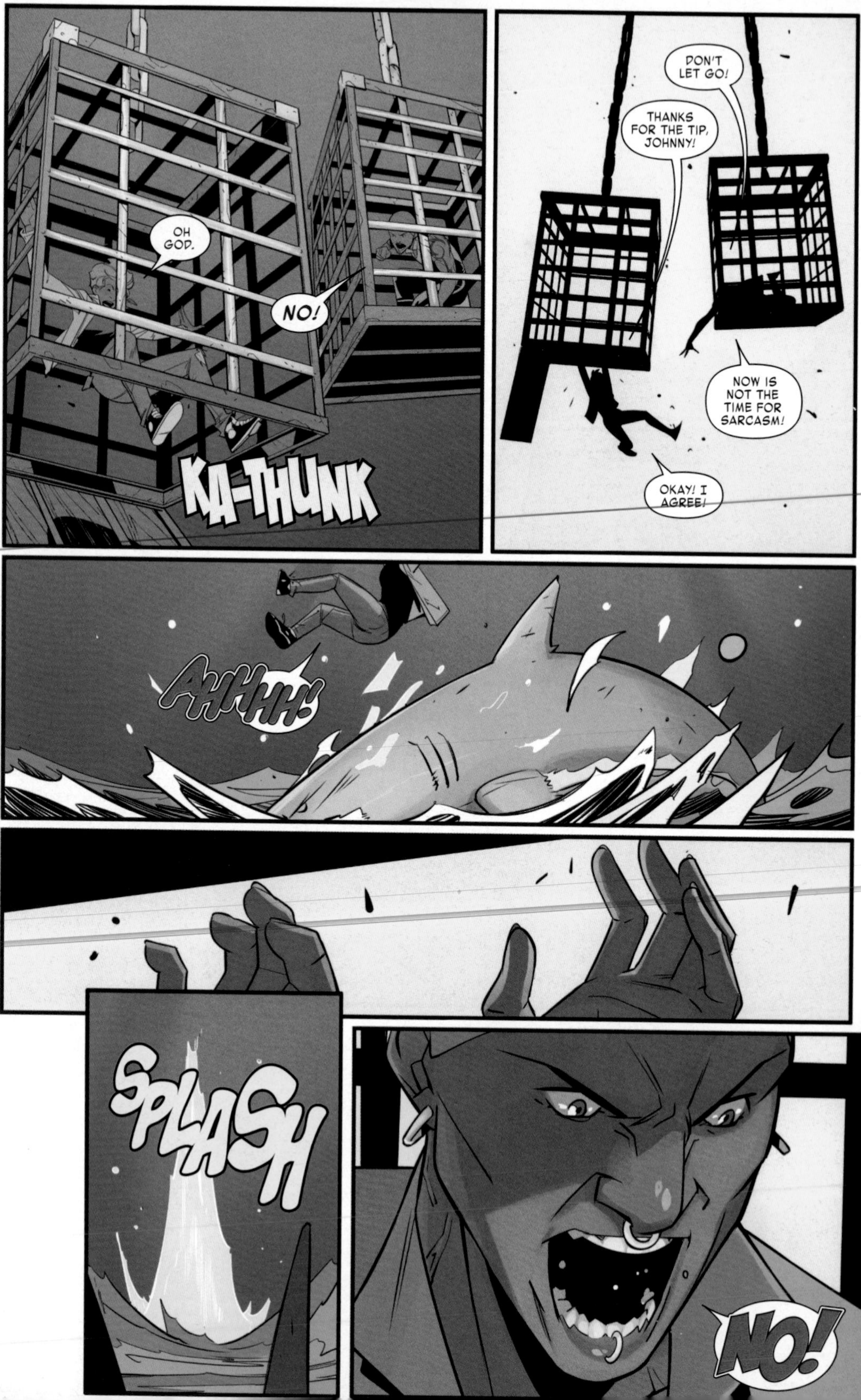
OH GOD.
NO!
KA-THUNK
DON'T LET GO!
THANKS FOR THE TIP, JOHNNY!
NOW IS NOT THE TIME FOR SARCASM!
OKAY! I AGREE!
AHHHH!
SPLASH
NO!

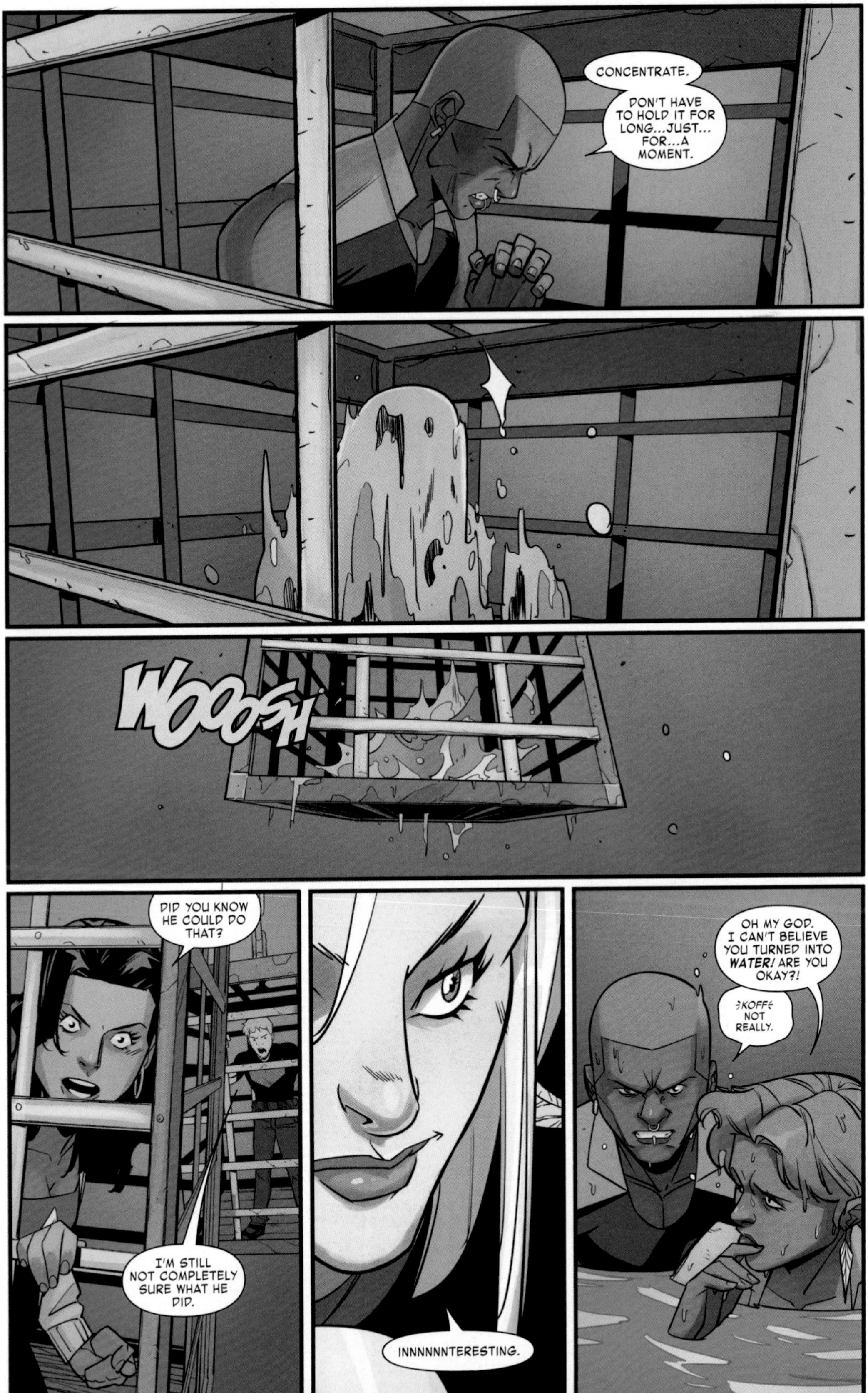
CONCENTRATE.
DON'T HAVE TO HOLD IT FOR LONG...JUST... FOR...A MOMENT.
WOOOSH
DID YOU KNOW HE COULD DO THAT?
I'M STILL NOT COMPLETELY SURE WHAT HE DID.
INNNNNNTERESTING.
OH MY GOD. I CAN'T BELIEVE YOU TURNED INTO WATER! ARE YOU OKAY?!
KOFF NOT REALLY.

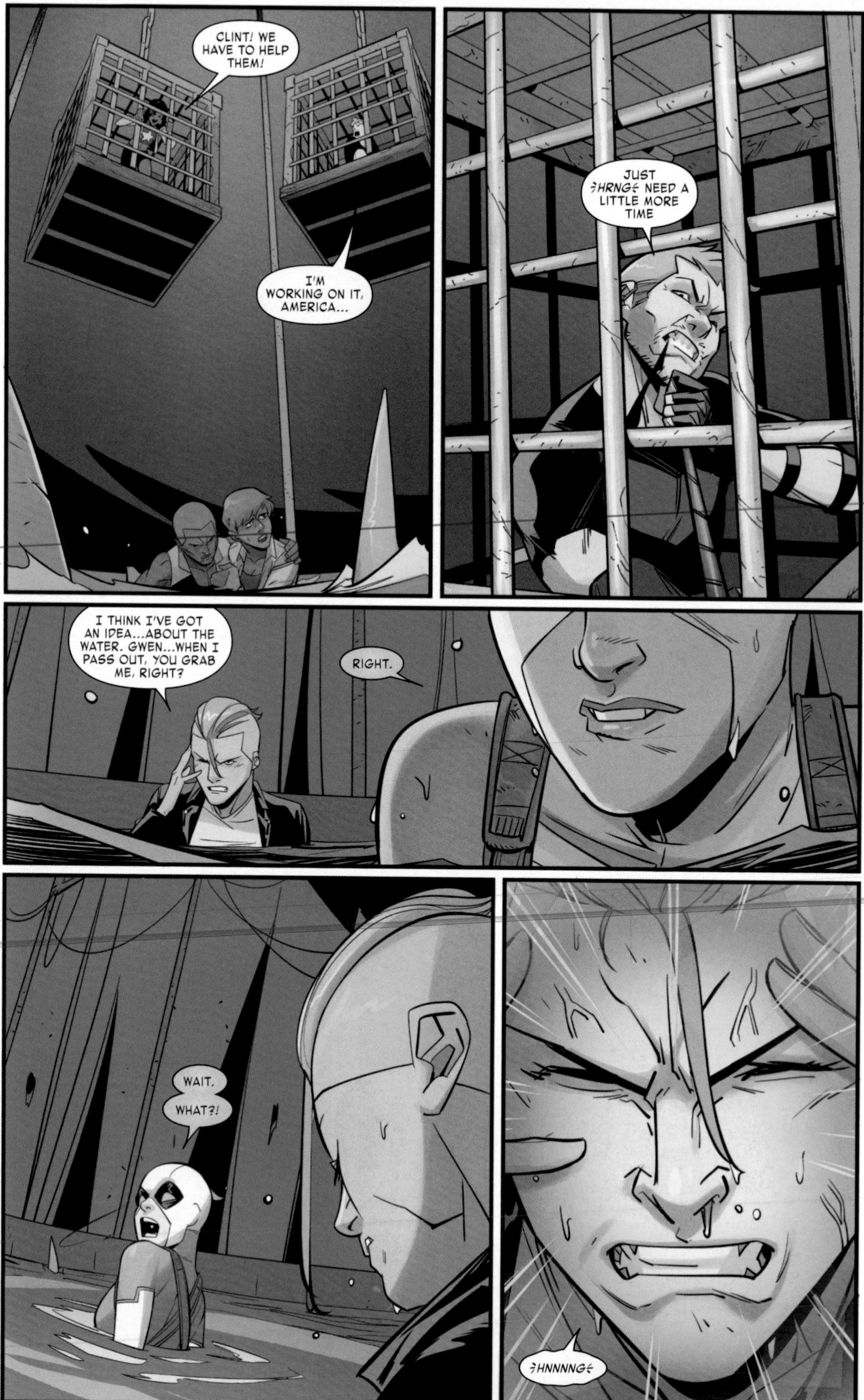
CLINT! WE HAVE TO HELP THEM!
I'M WORKING ON IT, AMERICA...
JUST ≠HRNG≠ NEED A LITTLE MORE TIME
I THINK I'VE GOT AN IDEA...ABOUT THE WATER. GWEN...WHEN I PASS OUT, YOU GRAB ME, RIGHT?
RIGHT.
WAIT.
WHAT?!
≠HNNNNG≠

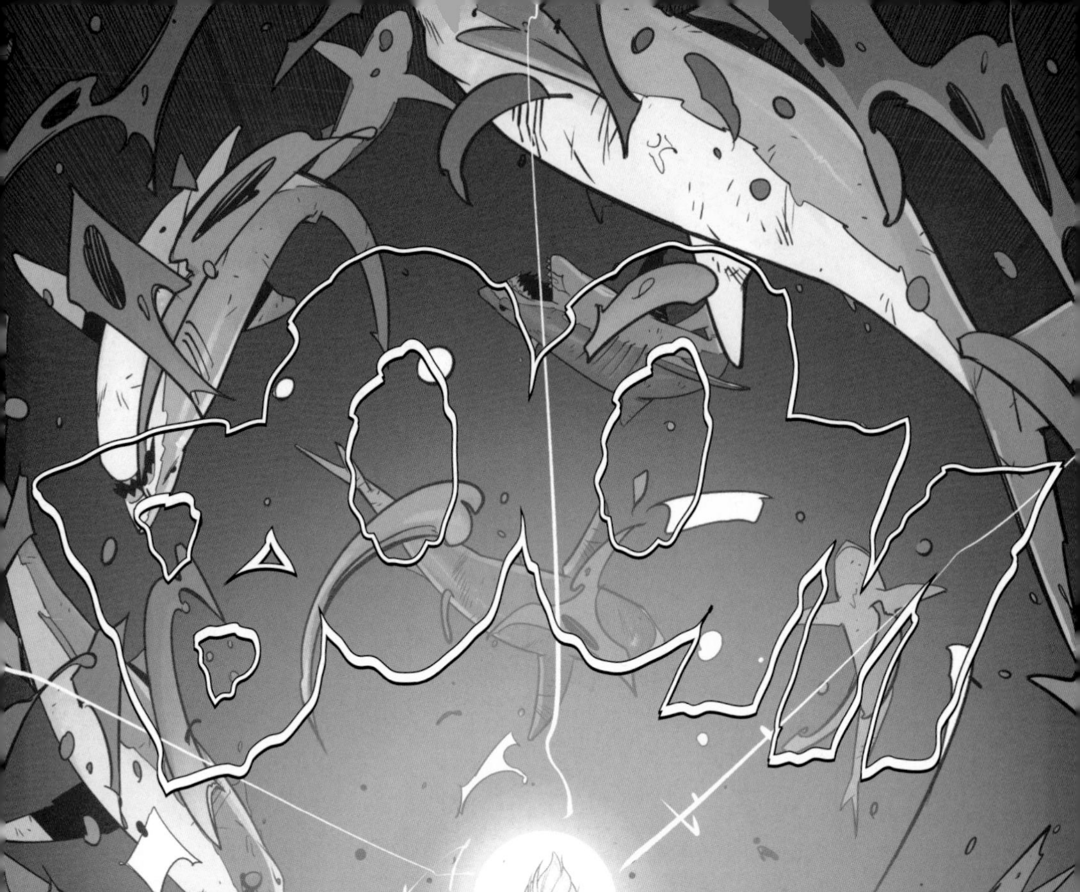
BOOOM
BRING CYCLOP BACK
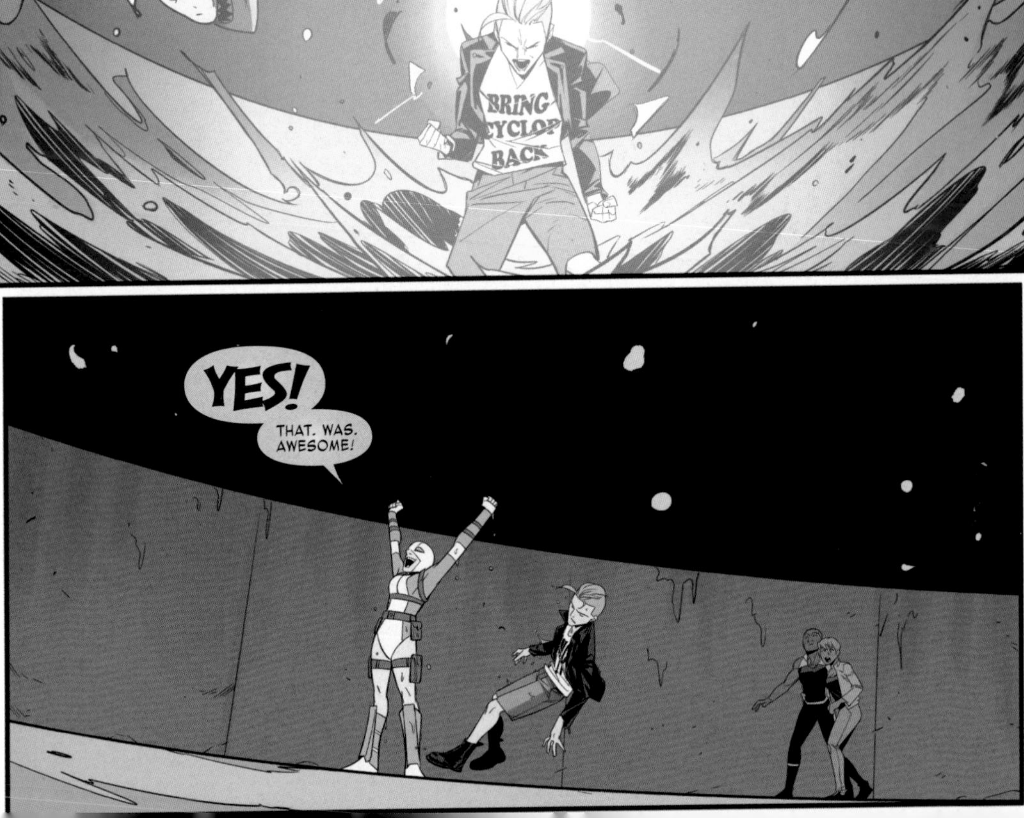
YES!
THAT. WAS. AWESOME!

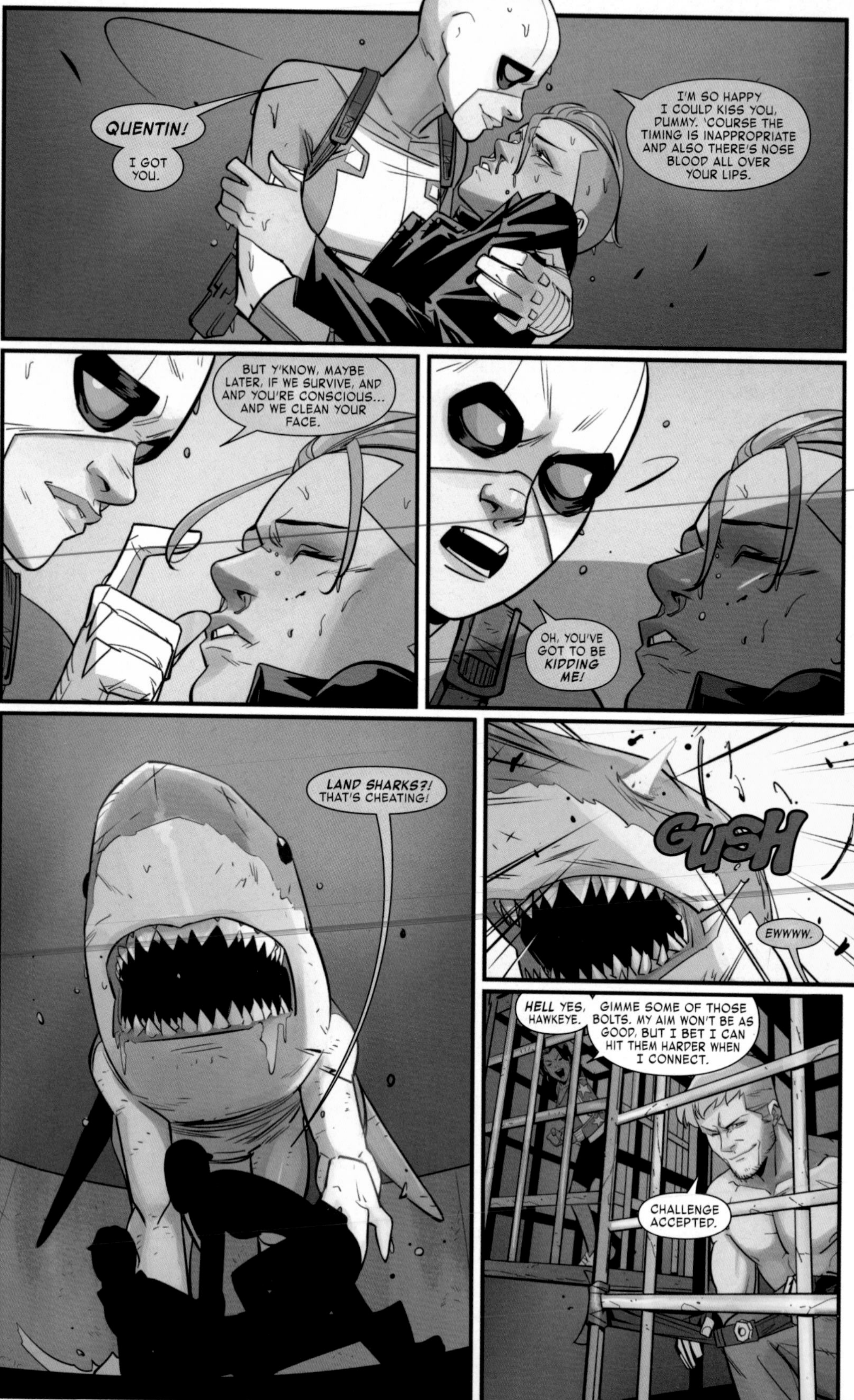
QUENTIN!
I GOT YOU.
I'M SO HAPPY I COULD KISS YOU, DUMMY. 'COURSE THE TIMING IS INAPPROPRIATE AND ALSO THERE'S NOSE BLOOD ALL OVER YOUR LIPS.
BUT Y'KNOW, MAYBE LATER, IF WE SURVIVE, AND AND YOU'RE CONSCIOUS... AND WE CLEAN YOUR FACE.
OH, YOU'VE GOT TO BE KIDDING ME!
LAND SHARKS?! THAT'S CHEATING!
GUSH
EWWWW.
HELL YES, HAWKEYE.
GIMME SOME OF THOSE BOLTS. MY AIM WON'T BE AS GOOD, BUT I BET I CAN HIT THEM HARDER WHEN I CONNECT.
CHALLENGE ACCEPTED.

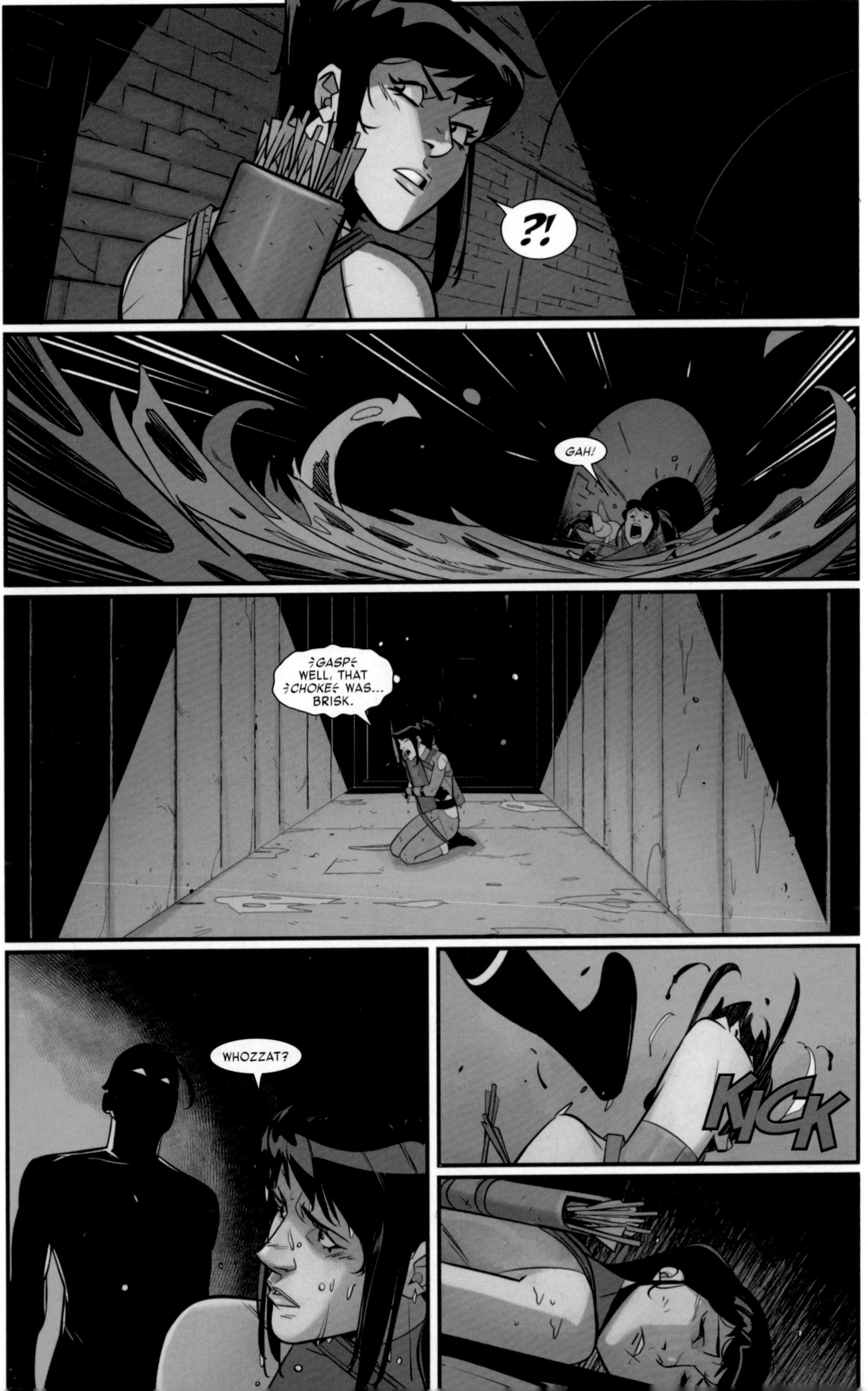
?!
GAH!
⸗GASP⸗ WELL, THAT ⸗CHOKE⸗ WAS... BRISK.
WHOZZAT?
KICK

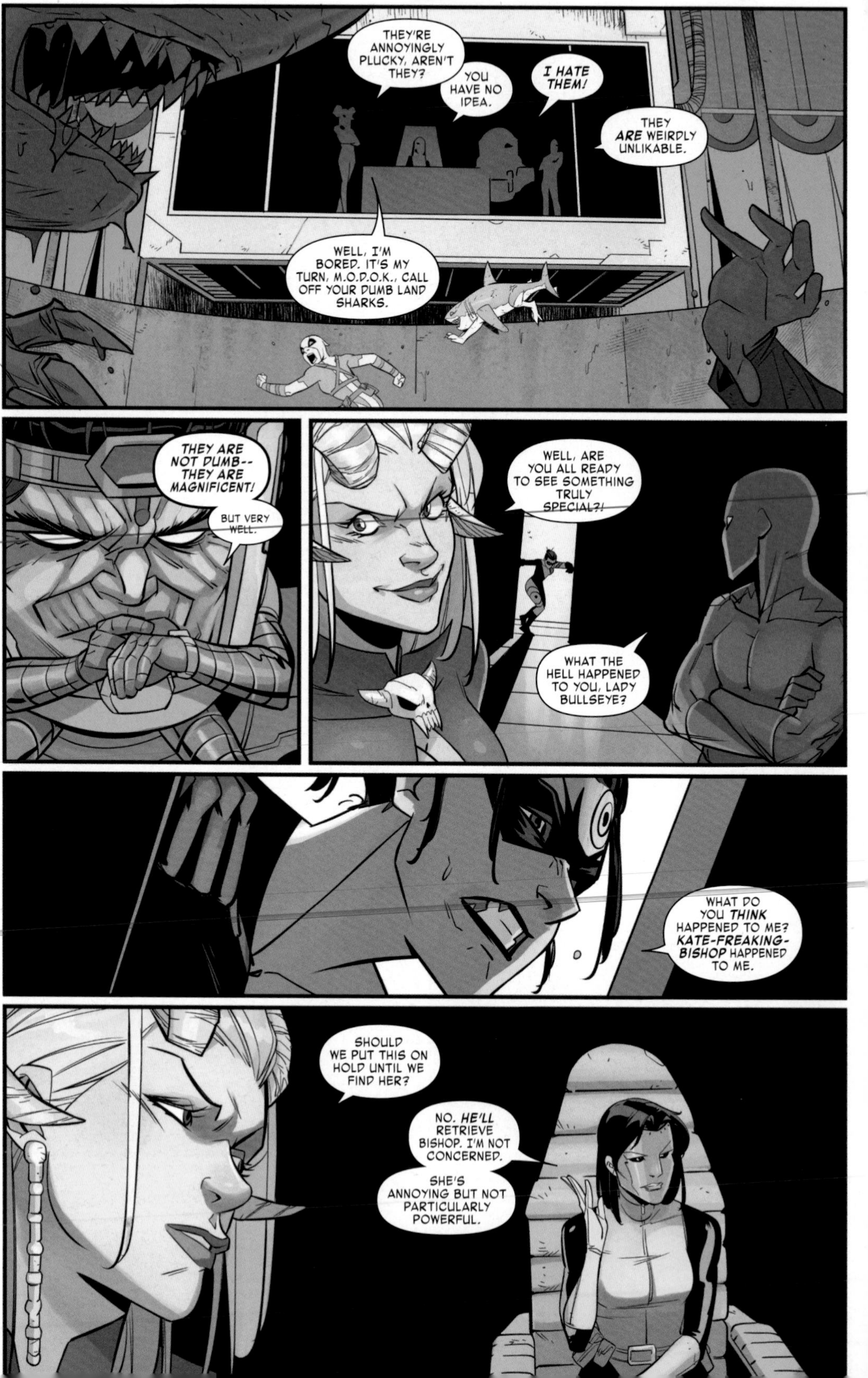
THEY'RE ANNOYINGLY PLUCKY, AREN'T THEY?
YOU HAVE NO IDEA.
I HATE THEM!
THEY ARE WEIRDLY UNLIKABLE.
WELL, I'M BORED. IT'S MY TURN, M.O.D.O.K., CALL OFF YOUR DUMB LAND SHARKS.
THEY ARE NOT DUMB-- THEY ARE MAGNIFICENT!
BUT VERY WELL.
WELL, ARE YOU ALL READY TO SEE SOMETHING TRULY SPECIAL?!
WHAT THE HELL HAPPENED TO YOU, LADY BULLSEYE?
WHAT DO YOU THINK HAPPENED TO ME? KATE-FREAKING-BISHOP HAPPENED TO ME.
SHOULD WE PUT THIS ON HOLD UNTIL WE FIND HER?
NO. HE'LL RETRIEVE BISHOP. I'M NOT CONCERNED.
SHE'S ANNOYING BUT NOT PARTICULARLY POWERFUL.

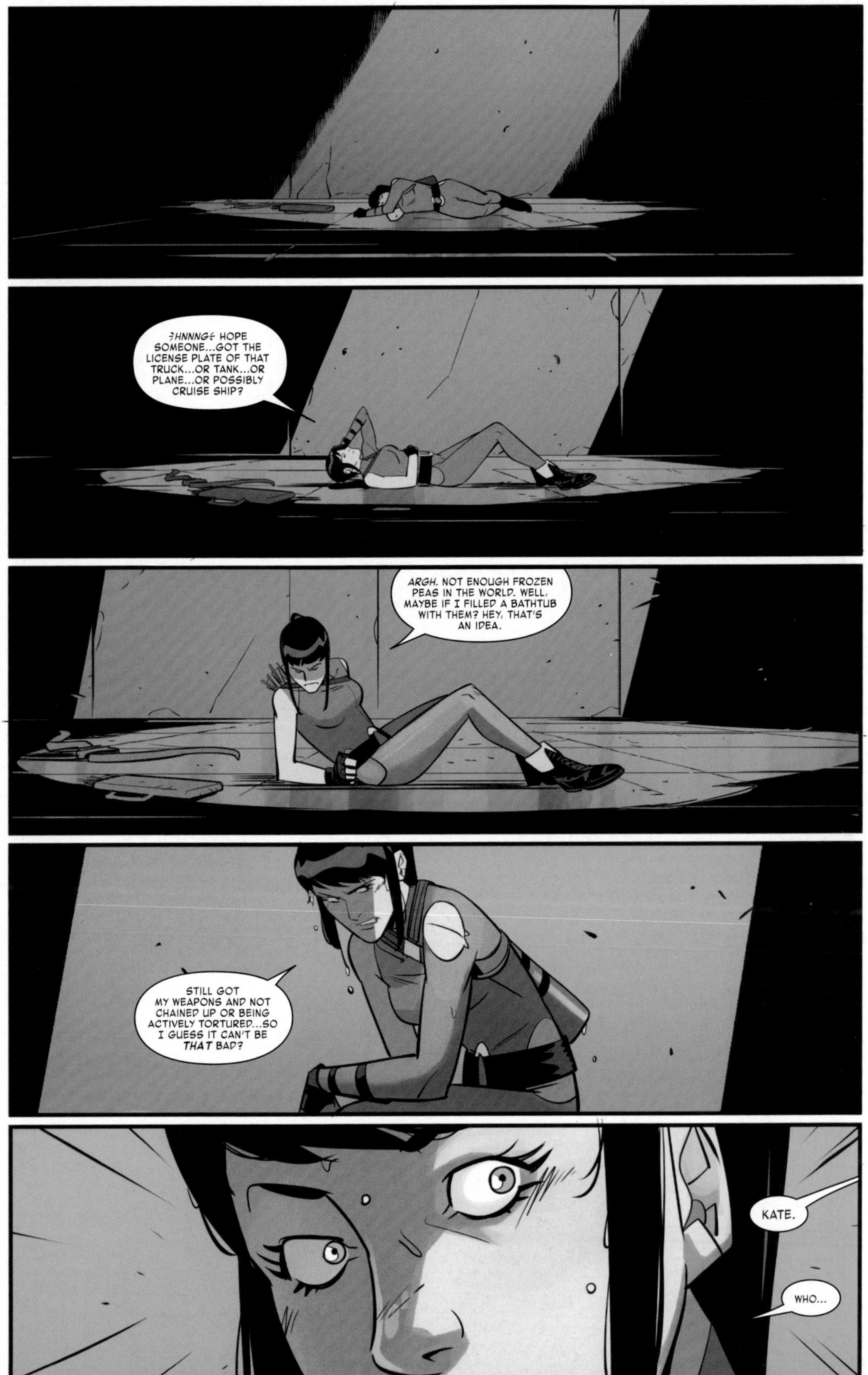

ƎHNNGƐ HOPE SOMEONE...GOT THE LICENSE PLATE OF THAT TRUCK...OR TANK...OR PLANE...OR POSSIBLY CRUISE SHIP?
ARGH. NOT ENOUGH FROZEN PEAS IN THE WORLD. WELL, MAYBE IF I FILLED A BATHTUB WITH THEM? HEY, THAT'S AN IDEA.
STILL GOT MY WEAPONS AND NOT CHAINED UP OR BEING ACTIVELY TORTURED...SO I GUESS IT CAN'T BE THAT BAD?
KATE.
WHO...

SPOKE TOO SOON. IT IS THAT BAD.
...NOH-VARR?
HI. SORRY ABOUT BEFORE, BUT I CAN EXPLAIN EVERYTHING.
NOH-VARR, A.K.A. MARVEL BOY, A.K.A....
...KATE'S EX-BOYFRIEND.

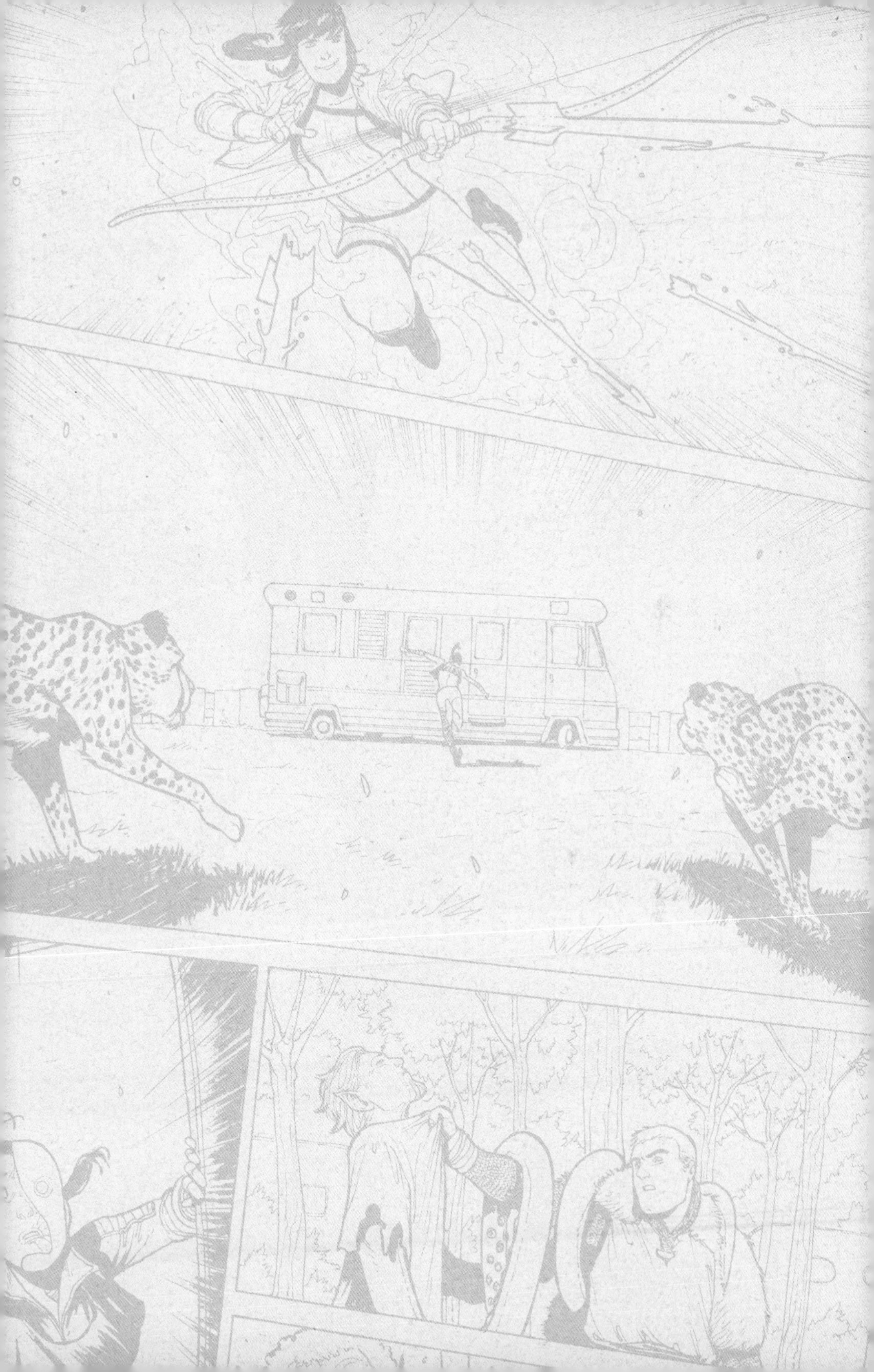

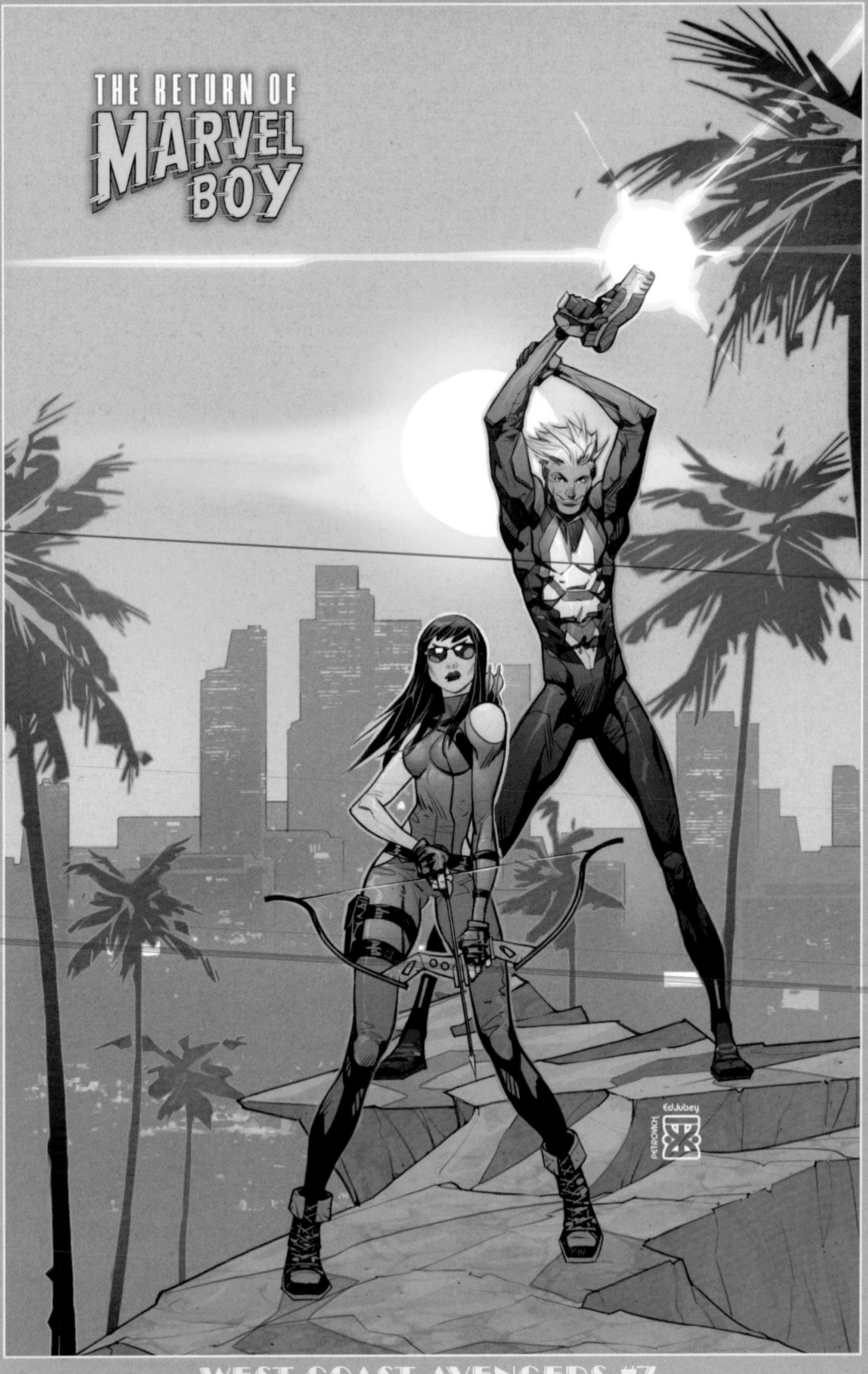
THE RETURN OF
MARVEL
BOY

WEST COAST AVENGERS #7

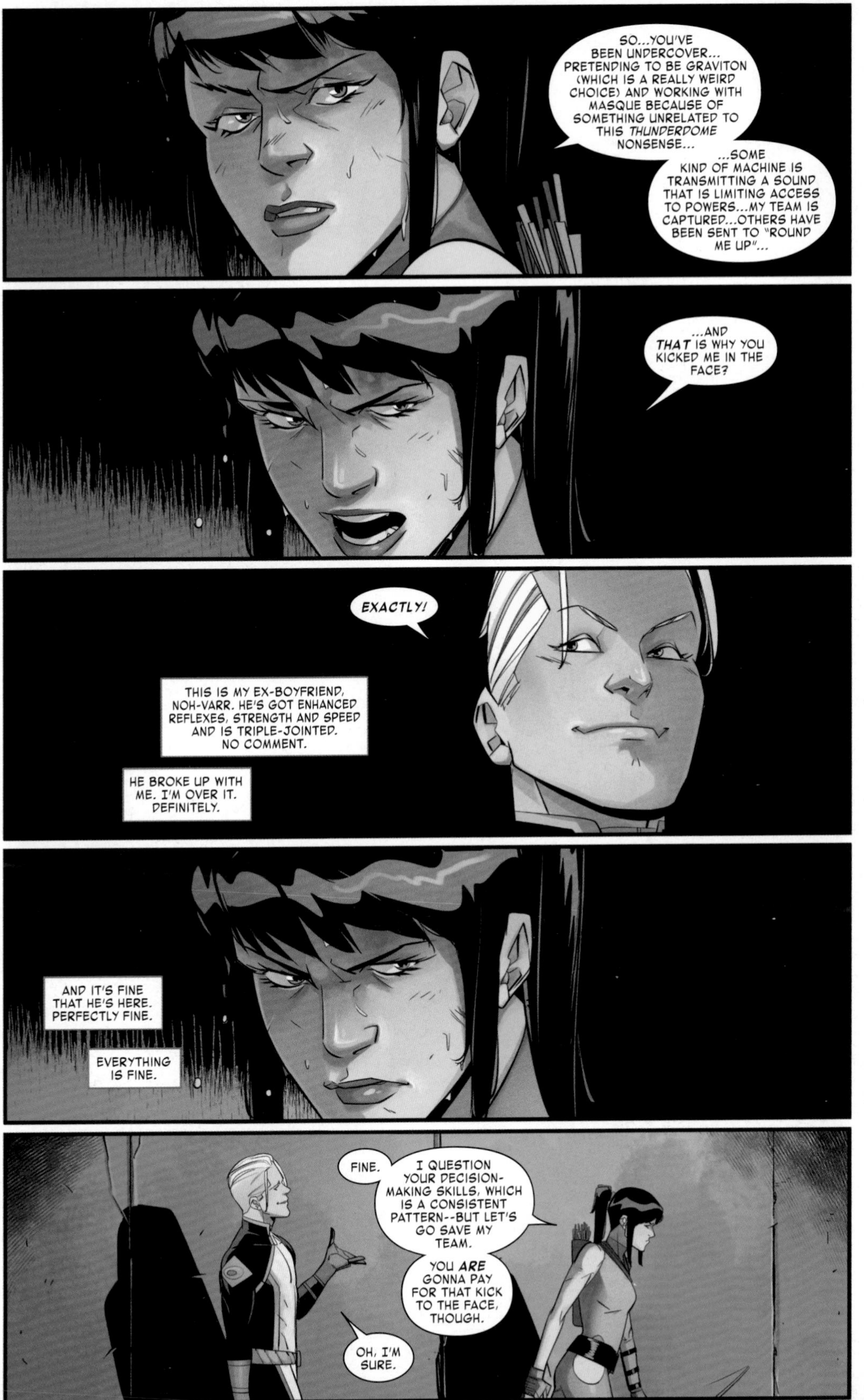
SO...YOU'VE BEEN UNDERCOVER... PRETENDING TO BE GRAVITON (WHICH IS A REALLY WEIRD CHOICE) AND WORKING WITH MASQUE BECAUSE OF SOMETHING UNRELATED TO THIS THUNDERDOME NONSENSE...
...SOME KIND OF MACHINE IS TRANSMITTING A SOUND THAT IS LIMITING ACCESS TO POWERS...MY TEAM IS CAPTURED...OTHERS HAVE BEEN SENT TO "ROUND ME UP"...
...AND THAT IS WHY YOU KICKED ME IN THE FACE?
EXACTLY!
THIS IS MY EX-BOYFRIEND, NOH-VARR. HE'S GOT ENHANCED REFLEXES, STRENGTH AND SPEED AND IS TRIPLE-JOINTED. NO COMMENT.
HE BROKE UP WITH ME. I'M OVER IT. DEFINITELY.
AND IT'S FINE THAT HE'S HERE. PERFECTLY FINE.
EVERYTHING IS FINE.
FINE.
I QUESTION YOUR DECISION-MAKING SKILLS, WHICH IS A CONSISTENT PATTERN--BUT LET'S GO SAVE MY TEAM.
YOU ARE GONNA PAY FOR THAT KICK TO THE FACE, THOUGH.
OH, I'M SURE.

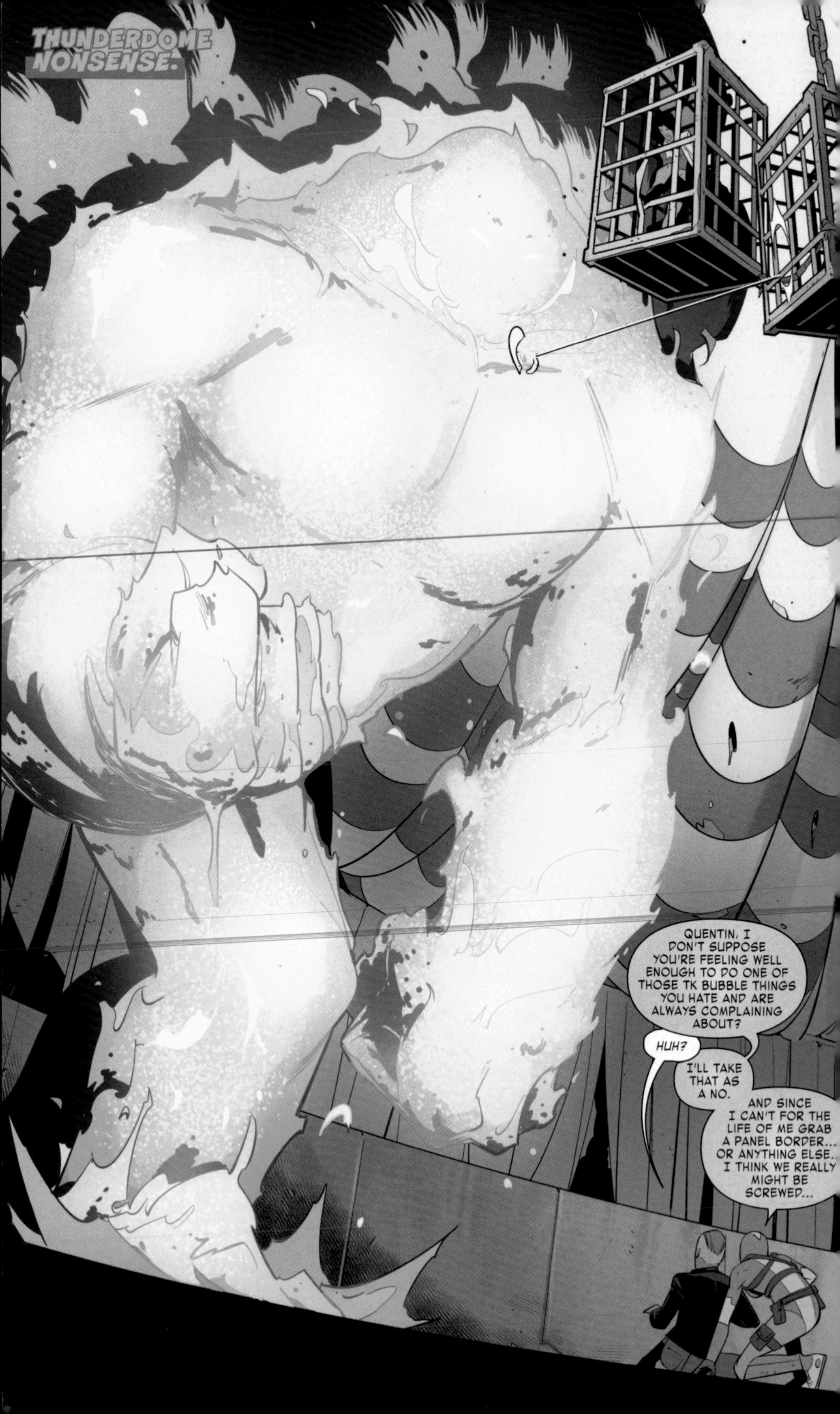
THUNDERDOME NONSENSE.
QUENTIN, I DON'T SUPPOSE YOU'RE FEELING WELL ENOUGH TO DO ONE OF THOSE TK BUBBLE THINGS YOU HATE AND ARE ALWAYS COMPLAINING ABOUT?
HUH?
I'LL TAKE THAT AS A NO.
AND SINCE I CAN'T FOR THE LIFE OF ME GRAB A PANEL BORDER... OR ANYTHING ELSE... I THINK WE REALLY MIGHT BE SCREWED...

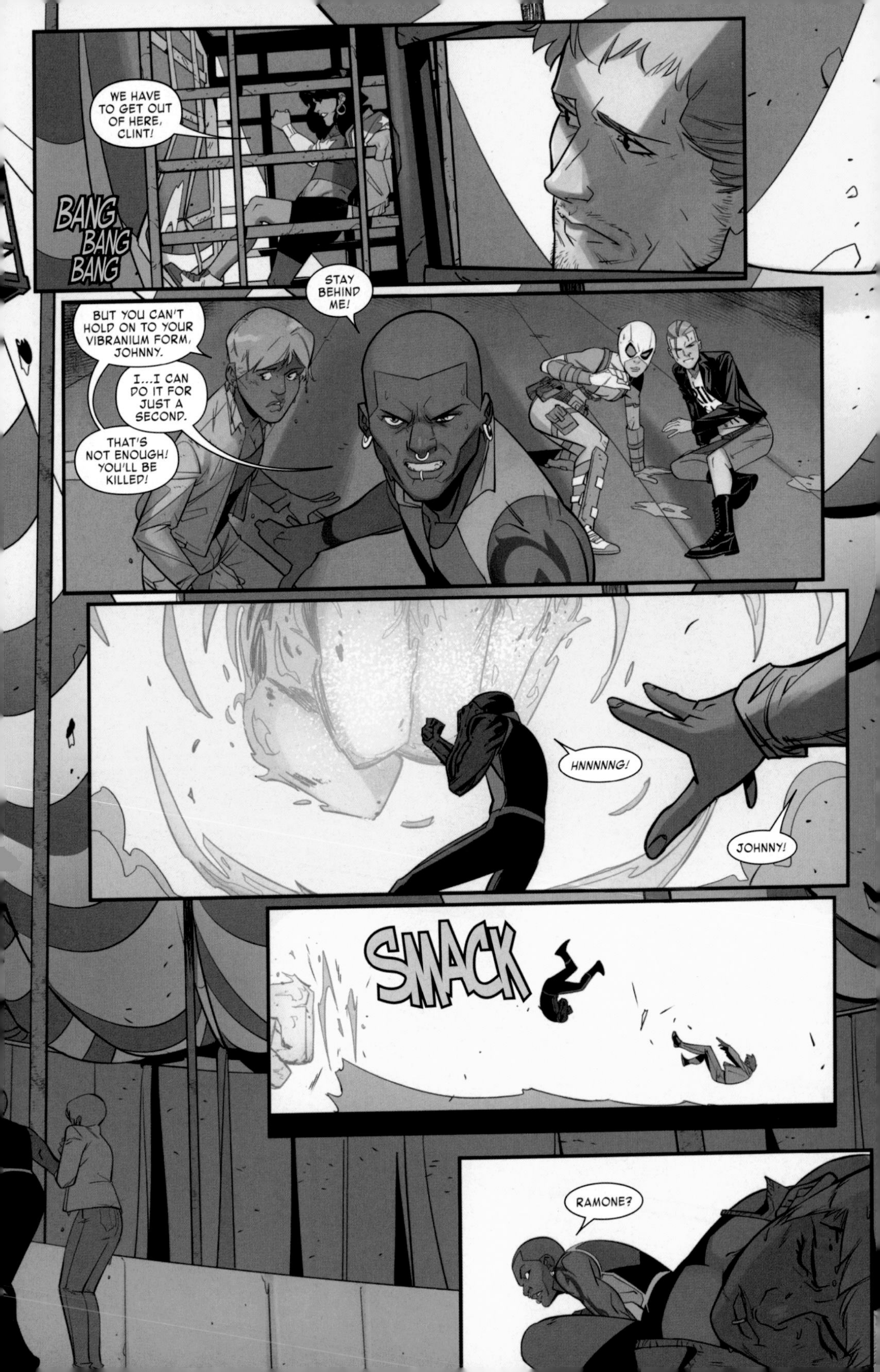
WE HAVE TO GET OUT OF HERE, CLINT!
BANG BANG BANG
STAY BEHIND ME!
BUT YOU CAN'T HOLD ON TO YOUR VIBRANIUM FORM, JOHNNY.
I...I CAN DO IT FOR JUST A SECOND.
THAT'S NOT ENOUGH! YOU'LL BE KILLED!
HNNNNNG!
JOHNNY!
SMACK
RAMONE?

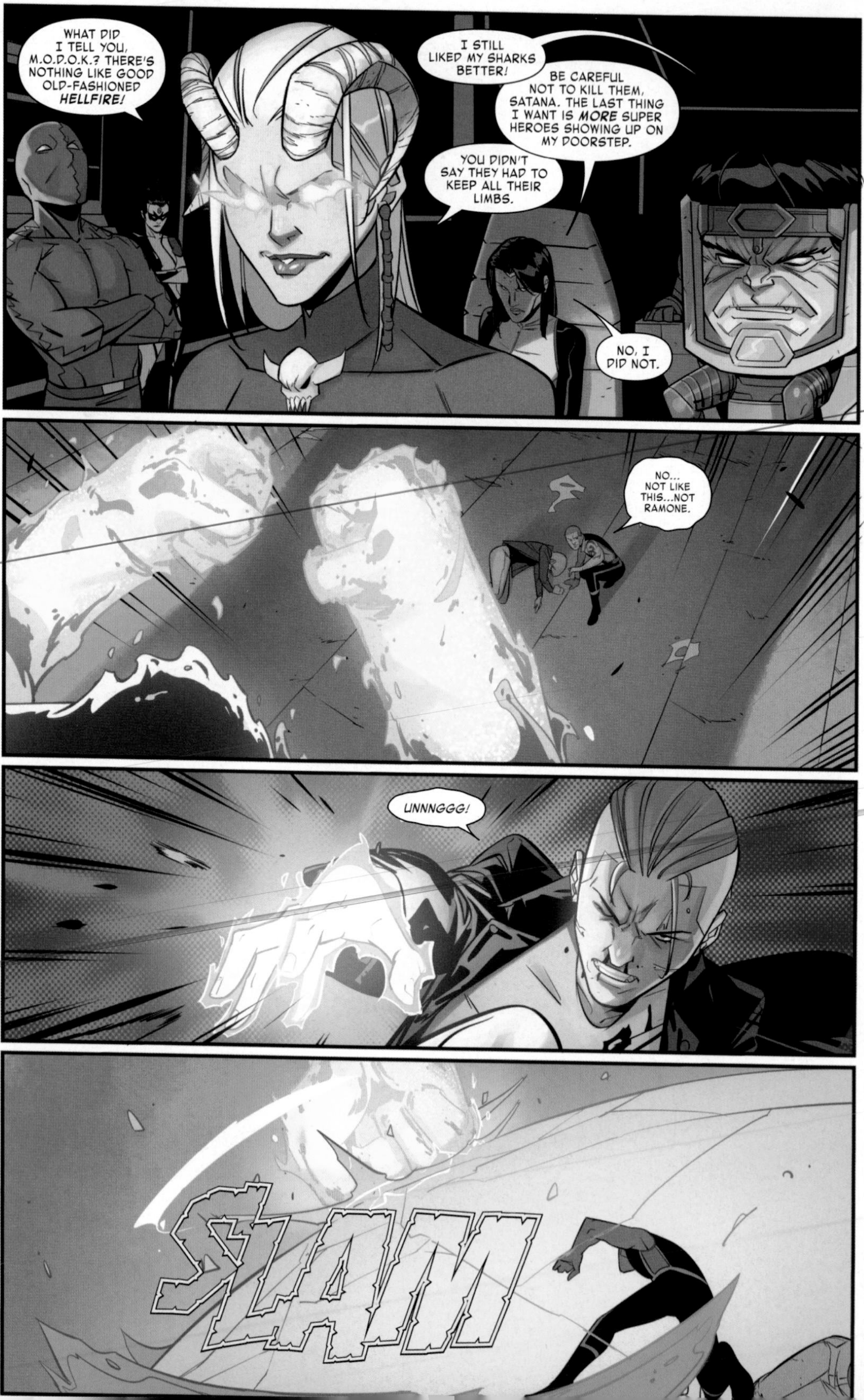
WHAT DID I TELL YOU, M.O.D.O.K.? THERE'S NOTHING LIKE GOOD OLD-FASHIONED HELLFIRE!
I STILL LIKED MY SHARKS BETTER!
BE CAREFUL NOT TO KILL THEM, SATANA. THE LAST THING I WANT IS MORE SUPER HEROES SHOWING UP ON MY DOORSTEP.
YOU DIDN'T SAY THEY HAD TO KEEP ALL THEIR LIMBS.
NO, I DID NOT.
NO... NOT LIKE THIS...NOT RAMONE.
UNNNGGG!
SLAM

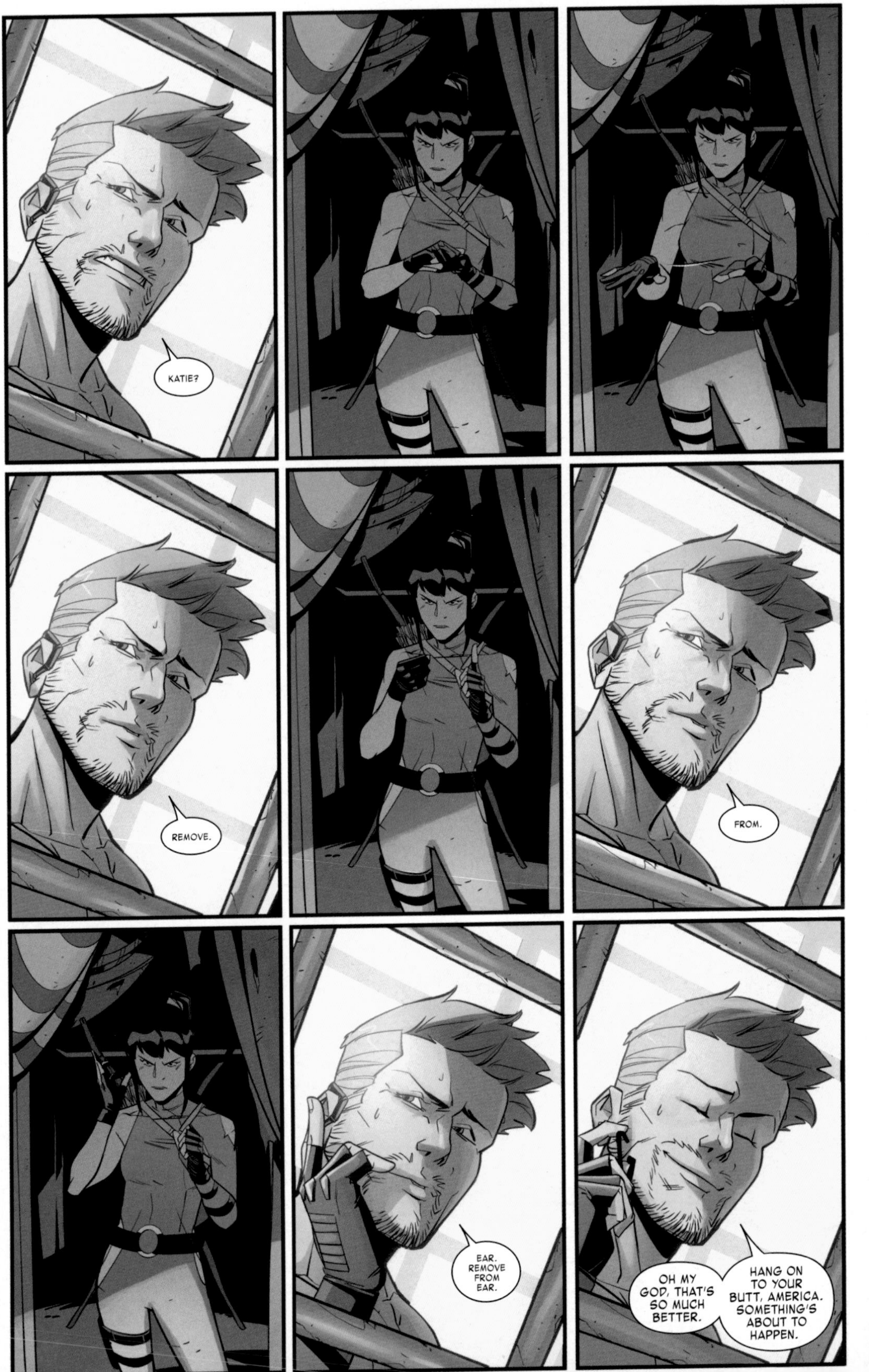
KATIE?
REMOVE.
FROM.
EAR. REMOVE FROM EAR.
OH MY GOD, THAT'S SO MUCH BETTER.
HANG ON TO YOUR BUTT, AMERICA. SOMETHING'S ABOUT TO HAPPEN.

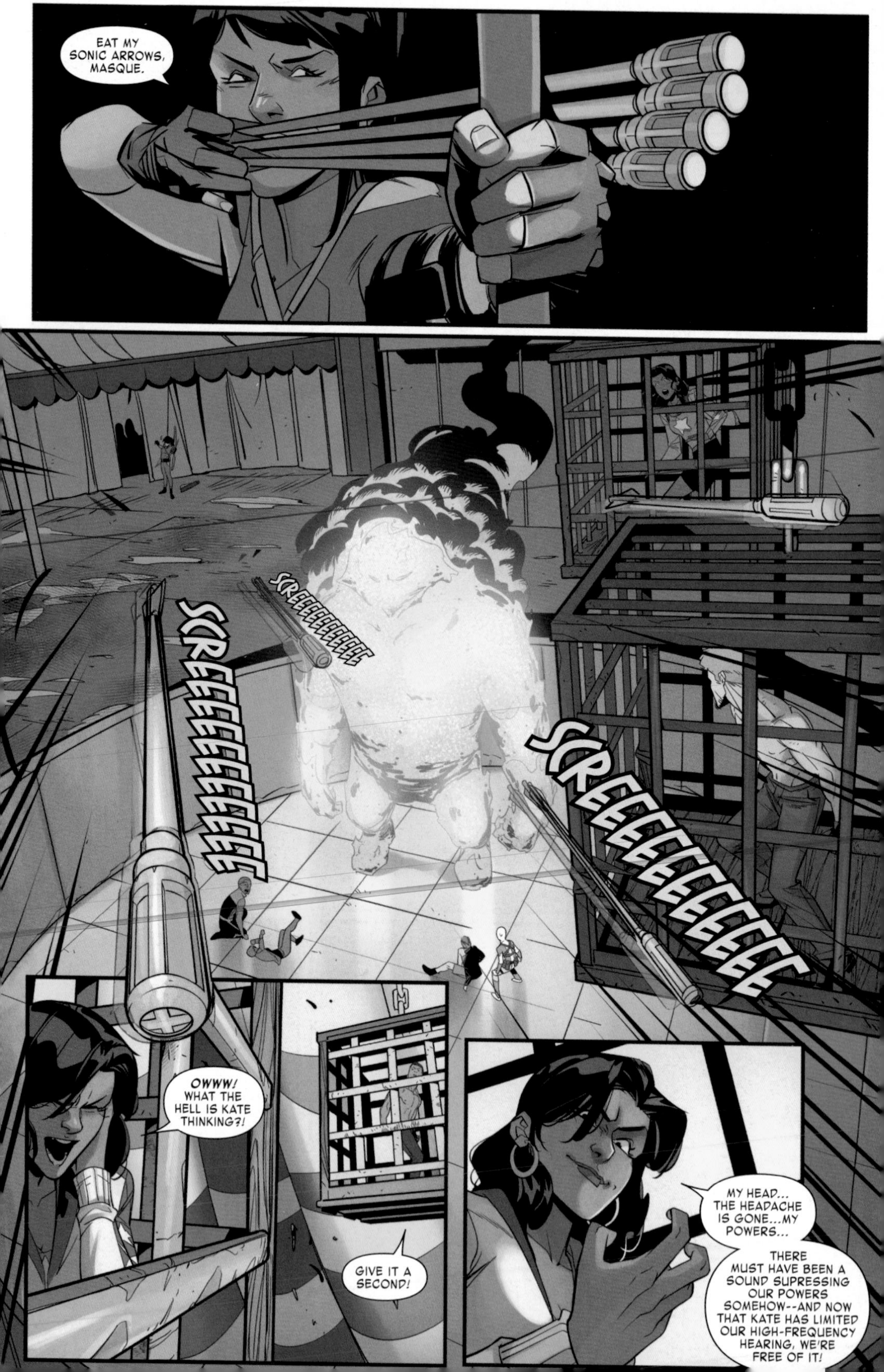
EAT MY SONIC ARROWS, MASQUE.
SCREEEEEEEEEEEE
SCREEEEEEEEEEE
SCREEEEEEEEEEEE
OWWW! WHAT THE HELL IS KATE THINKING?!
GIVE IT A SECOND!
MY HEAD... THE HEADACHE IS GONE...MY POWERS...
THERE MUST HAVE BEEN A SOUND SUPRESSING OUR POWERS SOMEHOW--AND NOW THAT KATE HAS LIMITED OUR HIGH-FREQUENCY HEARING, WE'RE FREE OF IT!

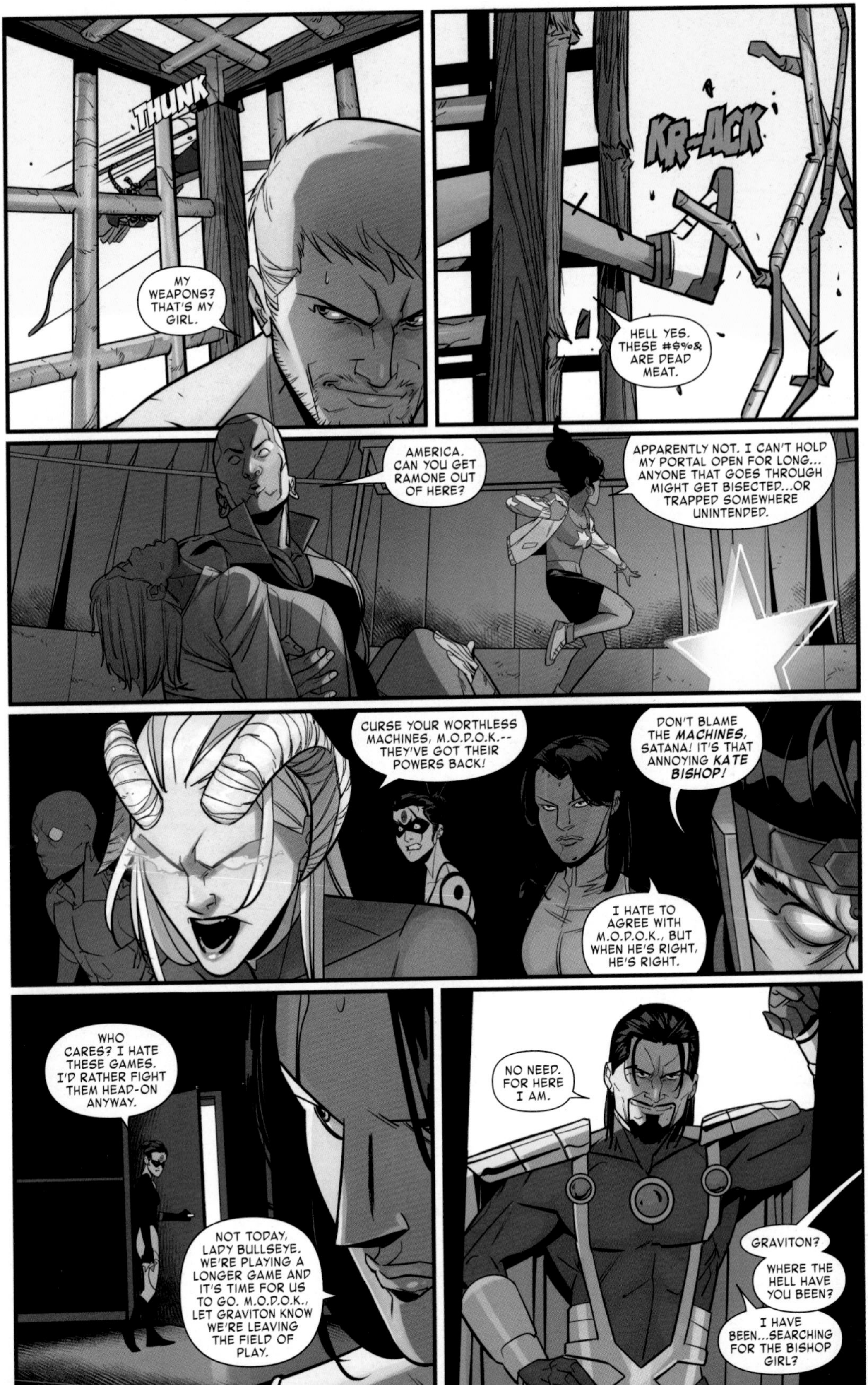
THUNK
MY WEAPONS? THAT'S MY GIRL.
KR-ACK
HELL YES. THESE #$%& ARE DEAD MEAT.
AMERICA. CAN YOU GET RAMONE OUT OF HERE?
APPARENTLY NOT. I CAN'T HOLD MY PORTAL OPEN FOR LONG... ANYONE THAT GOES THROUGH MIGHT GET BISECTED...OR TRAPPED SOMEWHERE UNINTENDED.
CURSE YOUR WORTHLESS MACHINES, M.O.D.O.K.--THEY'VE GOT THEIR POWERS BACK!
DON'T BLAME THE MACHINES, SATANA! IT'S THAT ANNOYING KATE BISHOP!
I HATE TO AGREE WITH M.O.D.O.K., BUT WHEN HE'S RIGHT, HE'S RIGHT.
WHO CARES? I HATE THESE GAMES. I'D RATHER FIGHT THEM HEAD-ON ANYWAY.
NOT TODAY, LADY BULLSEYE. WE'RE PLAYING A LONGER GAME AND IT'S TIME FOR US TO GO. M.O.D.O.K., LET GRAVITON KNOW WE'RE LEAVING THE FIELD OF PLAY.
NO NEED. FOR HERE I AM.
GRAVITON?
WHERE THE HELL HAVE YOU BEEN?
I HAVE BEEN...SEARCHING FOR THE BISHOP GIRL?

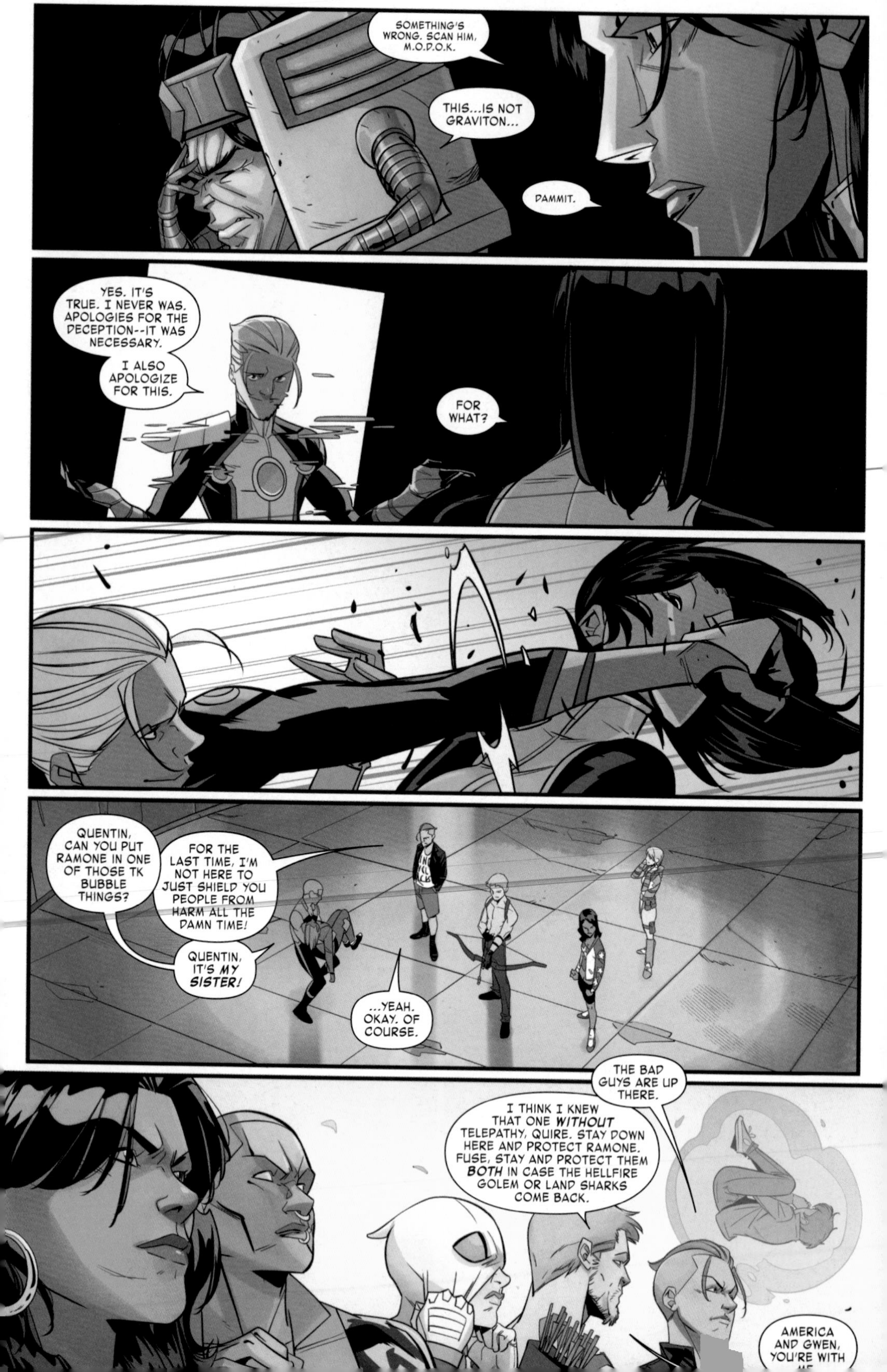
SOMETHING'S WRONG. SCAN HIM, M.O.D.O.K.
THIS...IS NOT GRAVITON...
DAMMIT.
YES. IT'S TRUE. I NEVER WAS. APOLOGIES FOR THE DECEPTION--IT WAS NECESSARY.
I ALSO APOLOGIZE FOR THIS.
FOR WHAT?
QUENTIN, CAN YOU PUT RAMONE IN ONE OF THOSE TK BUBBLE THINGS?
FOR THE LAST TIME, I'M NOT HERE TO JUST SHIELD YOU PEOPLE FROM HARM ALL THE DAMN TIME!
QUENTIN, IT'S *MY SISTER!*
...YEAH. OKAY. OF COURSE.
THE BAD GUYS ARE UP THERE.
I THINK I KNEW THAT ONE *WITHOUT* TELEPATHY, QUIRE. STAY DOWN HERE AND PROTECT RAMONE. FUSE, STAY AND PROTECT THEM *BOTH* IN CASE THE HELLFIRE GOLEM OR LAND SHARKS COME BACK.
AMERICA AND GWEN, YOU'RE WITH

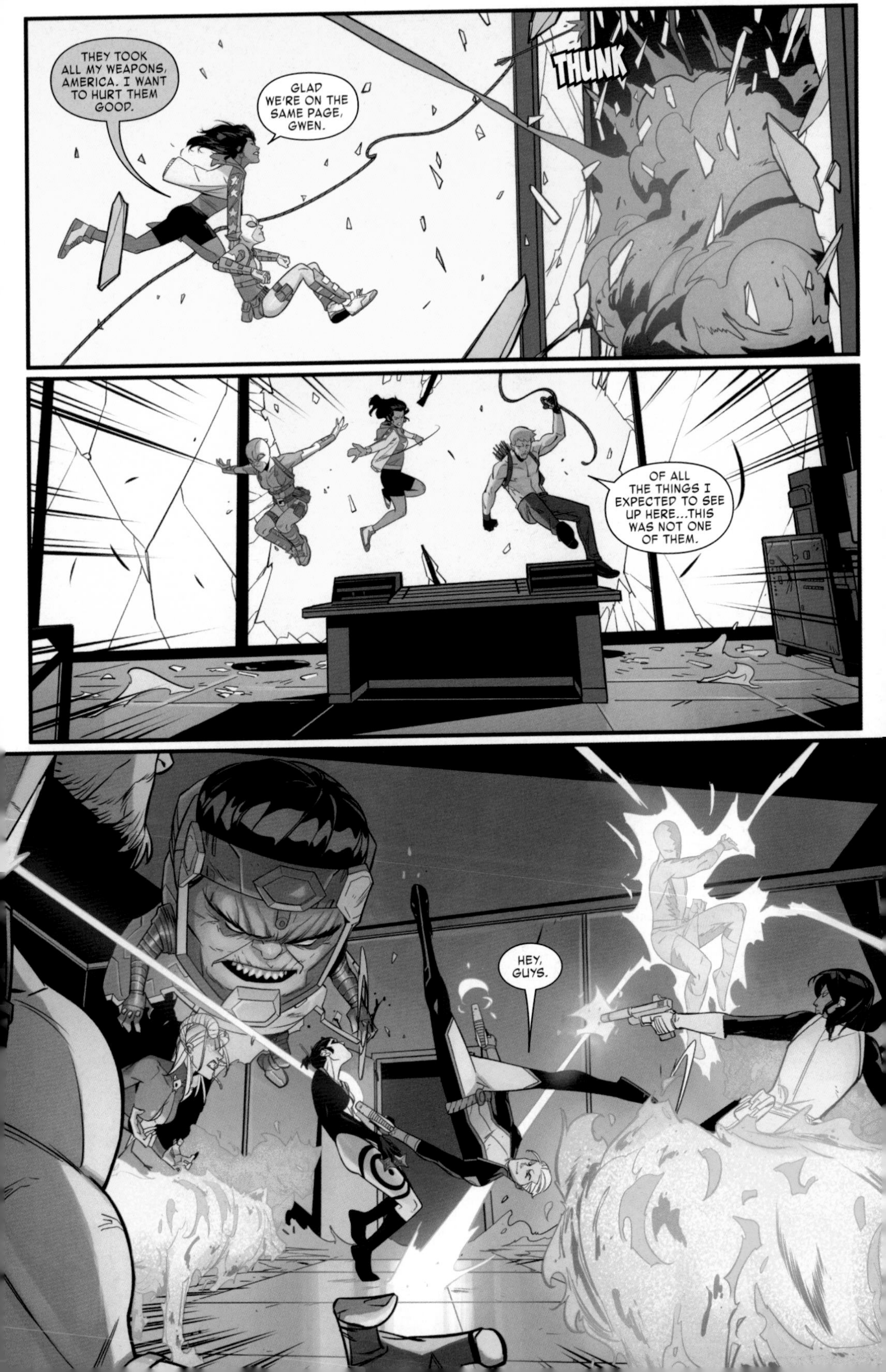
THEY TOOK ALL MY WEAPONS, AMERICA. I WANT TO HURT THEM GOOD.
GLAD WE'RE ON THE SAME PAGE, GWEN.
THUNK
OF ALL THE THINGS I EXPECTED TO SEE UP HERE...THIS WAS NOT ONE OF THEM.
HEY, GUYS.

ALL RIGHT, NOH-VARR MAY BE A JERK, BUT HE'S ON OUR SIDE. BACK HIM UP!

M.O.D.O.K., GET US OUT OF HERE, NOW!

YOU THINK I'M NOT TRYING?!

PROPERTY OF AIM

TRY FASTER!

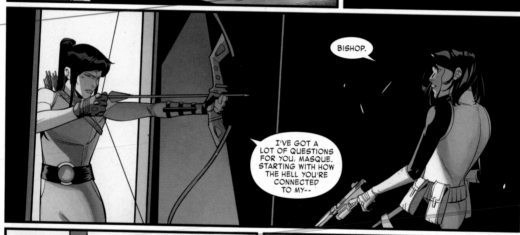

BISHOP.

I'VE GOT A LOT OF QUESTIONS FOR YOU, MASQUE. STARTING WITH HOW THE HELL YOU'RE CONNECTED TO MY--

BAM

HNNNG--?!

AND JUST WHERE IN THE HELL HAVE YOU BEEN?!

NO MATTER. I'M HERE NOW.

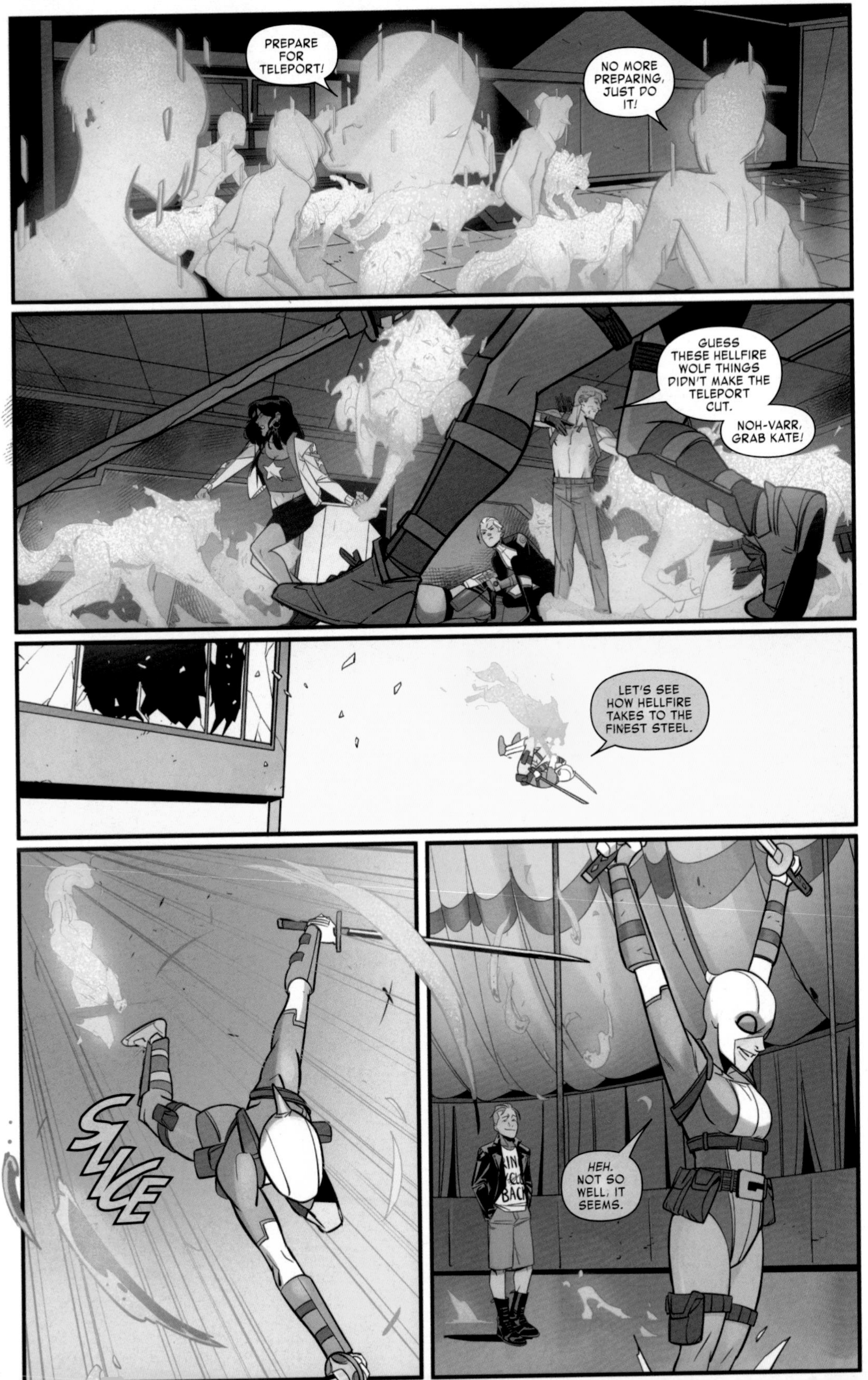
PREPARE FOR TELEPORT!
NO MORE PREPARING, JUST DO IT!
GUESS THESE HELLFIRE WOLF THINGS DIDN'T MAKE THE TELEPORT CUT.
NOH-VARR, GRAB KATE!
LET'S SEE HOW HELLFIRE TAKES TO THE FINEST STEEL.
SLICE
HEH. NOT SO WELL, IT SEEMS.

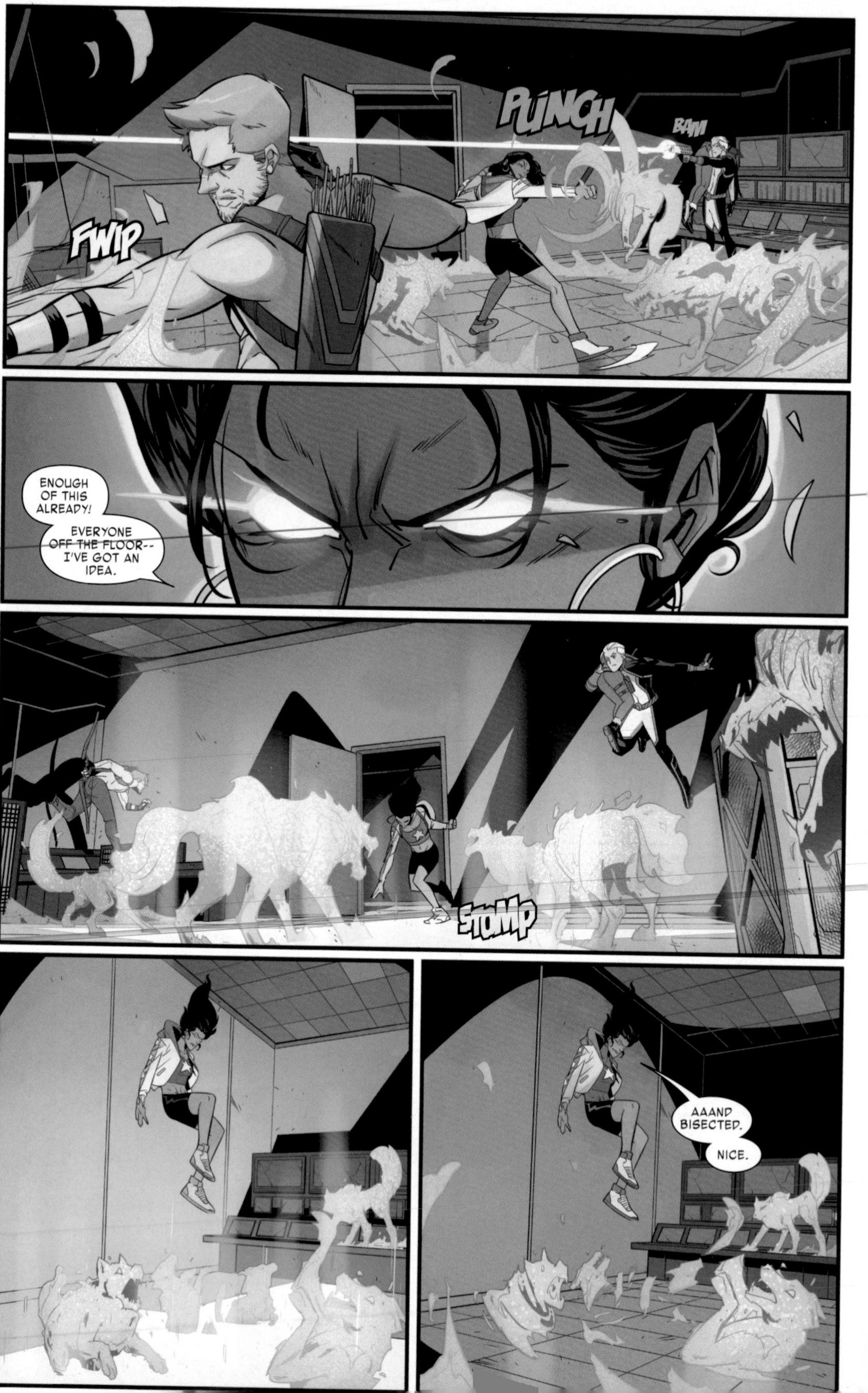
PUNCH
BAM
FWIP
ENOUGH OF THIS ALREADY!
EVERYONE OFF THE FLOOR-- I'VE GOT AN IDEA.
STOMP
AAAND BISECTED.
NICE.

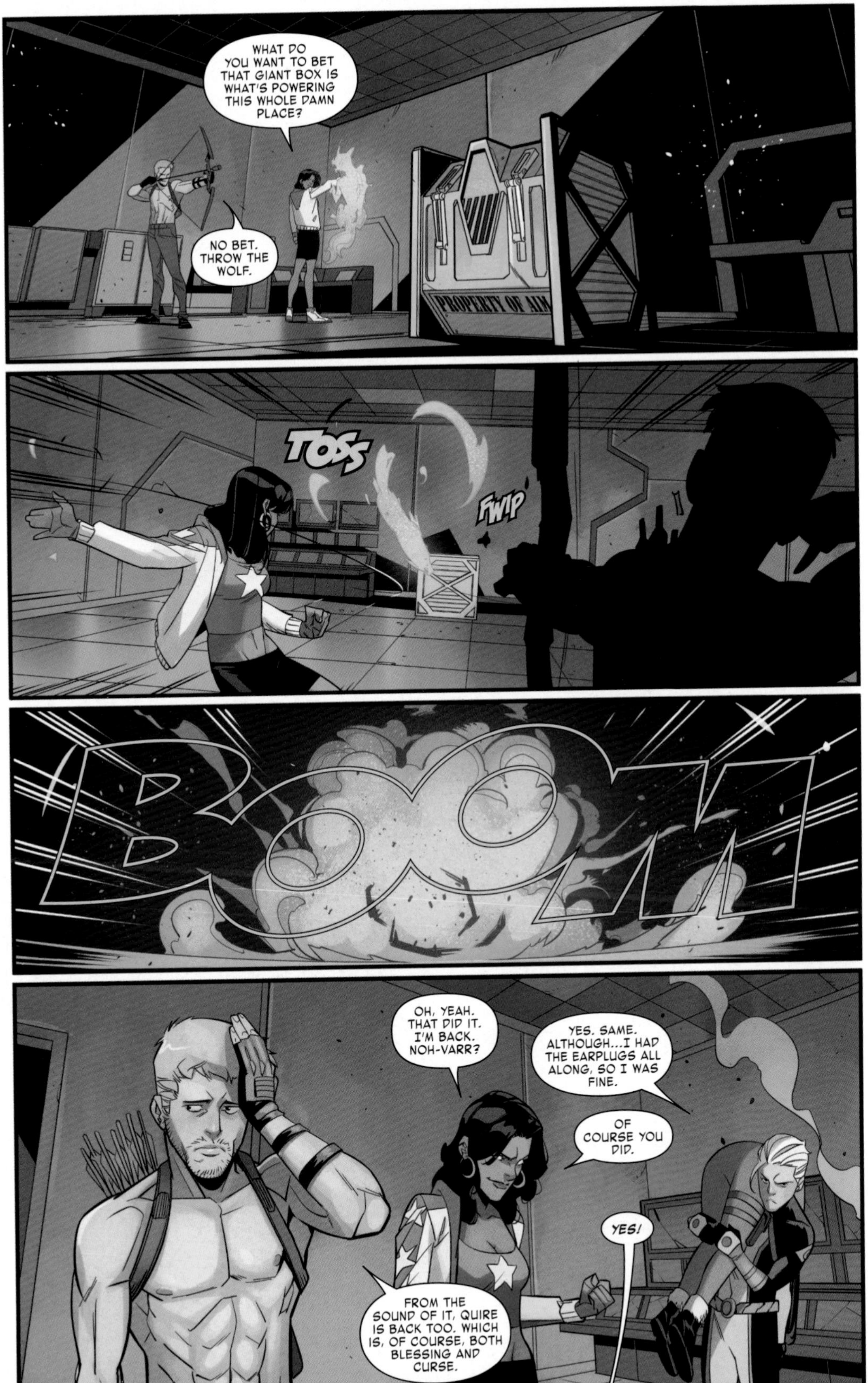
WHAT DO YOU WANT TO BET THAT GIANT BOX IS WHAT'S POWERING THIS WHOLE DAMN PLACE?
NO BET. THROW THE WOLF.
PROPERTY OF AIM
TOSS
FWIP
BOOM
OH, YEAH. THAT DID IT. I'M BACK. NOH-VARR?
YES. SAME. ALTHOUGH...I HAD THE EARPLUGS ALL ALONG, SO I WAS FINE.
OF COURSE YOU DID.
YES!
FROM THE SOUND OF IT, QUIRE IS BACK TOO. WHICH IS, OF COURSE, BOTH BLESSING AND CURSE.

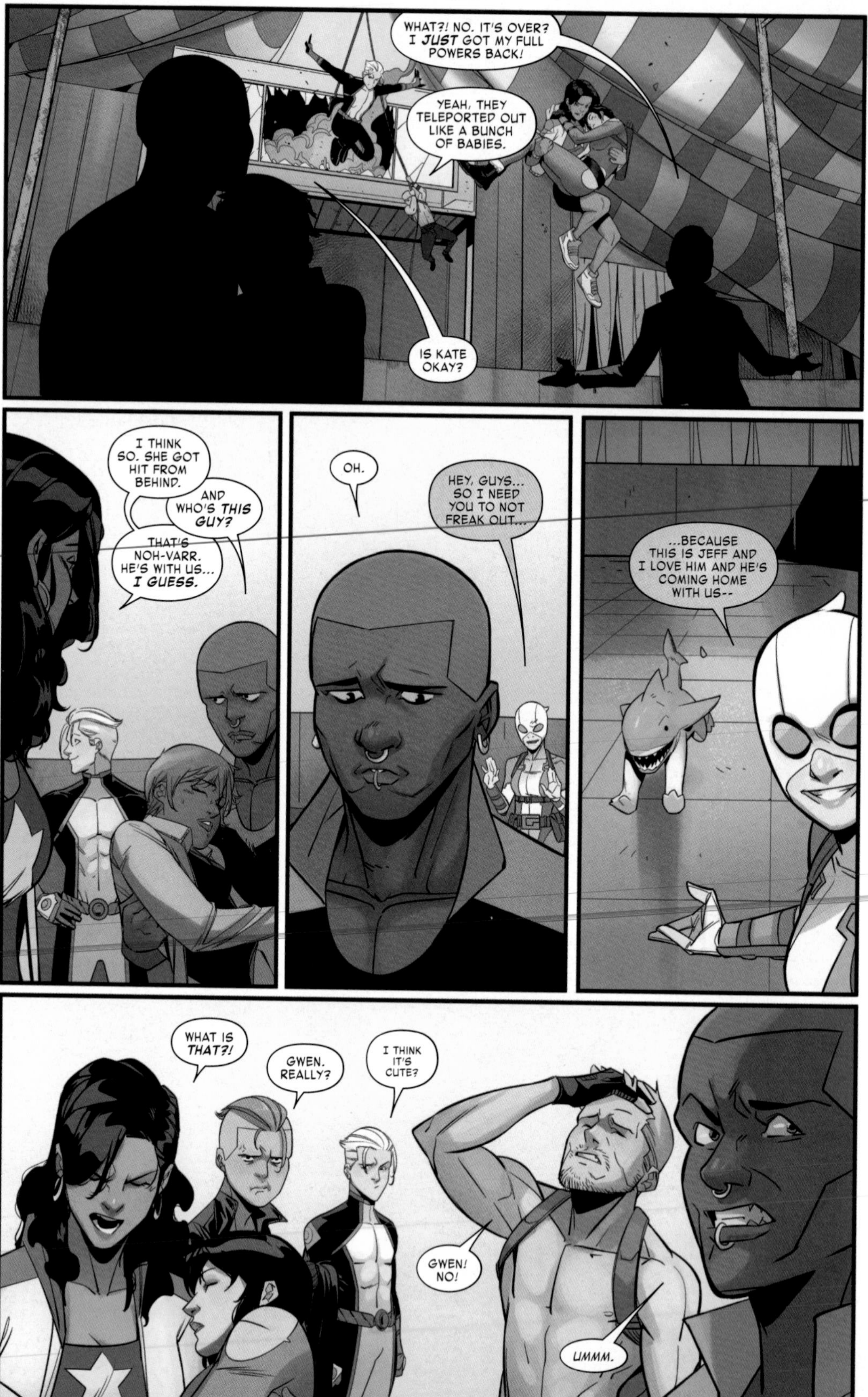

WHAT?! NO. IT'S OVER? I JUST GOT MY FULL POWERS BACK!
YEAH, THEY TELEPORTED OUT LIKE A BUNCH OF BABIES.
IS KATE OKAY?
I THINK SO. SHE GOT HIT FROM BEHIND.
AND WHO'S THIS GUY?
THAT'S NOH-VARR. HE'S WITH US... I GUESS.
OH.
HEY, GUYS... SO I NEED YOU TO NOT FREAK OUT...
...BECAUSE THIS IS JEFF AND I LOVE HIM AND HE'S COMING HOME WITH US--
WHAT IS THAT?!
GWEN. REALLY?
I THINK IT'S CUTE?
GWEN! NO!
UMMM.

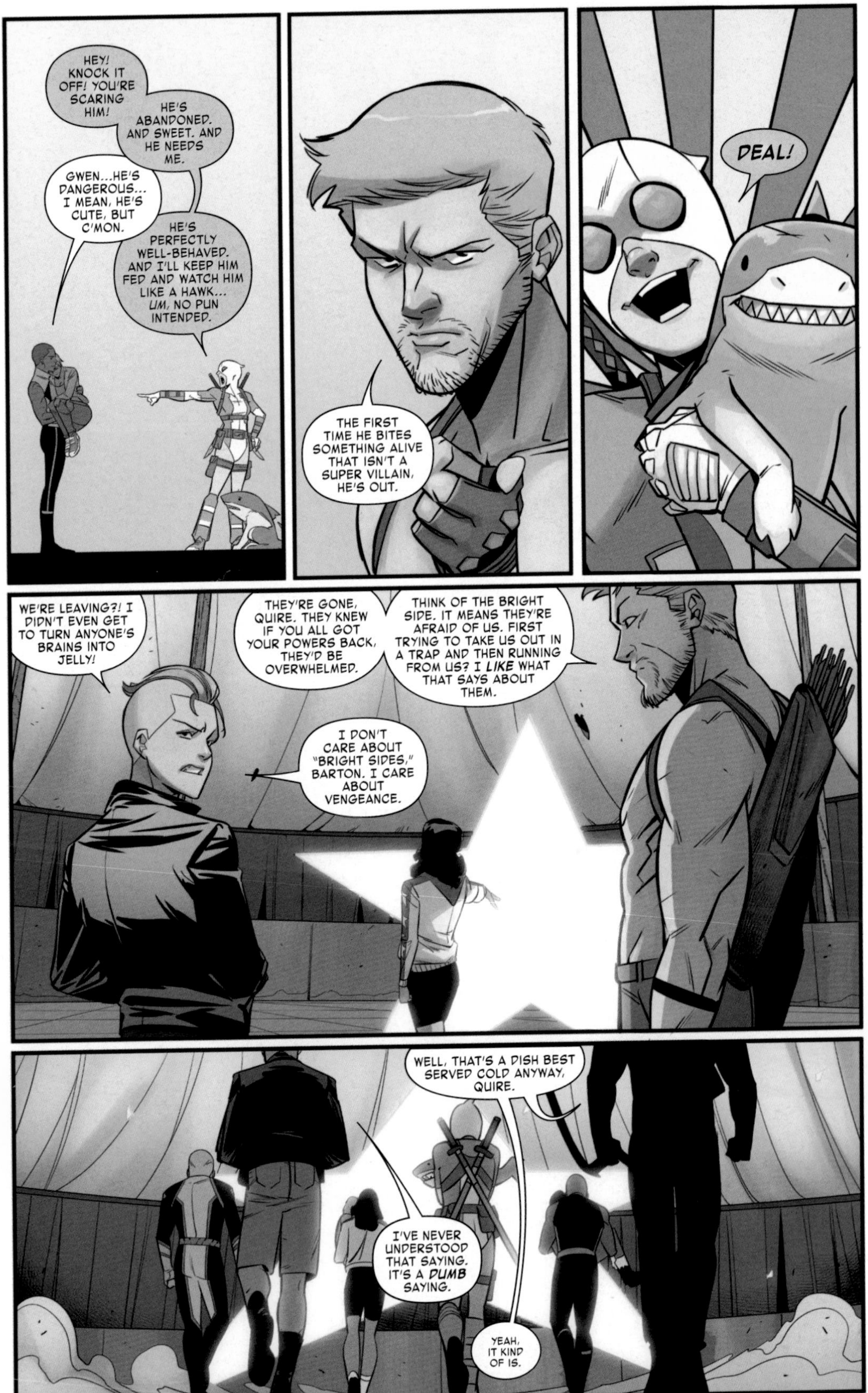
HEY! KNOCK IT OFF! YOU'RE SCARING HIM!
HE'S ABANDONED. AND SWEET. AND HE NEEDS ME.
GWEN...HE'S DANGEROUS... I MEAN, HE'S CUTE, BUT C'MON.
HE'S PERFECTLY WELL-BEHAVED. AND I'LL KEEP HIM FED AND WATCH HIM LIKE A HAWK... UM, NO PUN INTENDED.
THE FIRST TIME HE BITES SOMETHING ALIVE THAT ISN'T A SUPER VILLAIN, HE'S OUT.
DEAL!
WE'RE LEAVING?! I DIDN'T EVEN GET TO TURN ANYONE'S BRAINS INTO JELLY!
THEY'RE GONE, QUIRE. THEY KNEW IF YOU ALL GOT YOUR POWERS BACK, THEY'D BE OVERWHELMED.
THINK OF THE BRIGHT SIDE. IT MEANS THEY'RE AFRAID OF US. FIRST TRYING TO TAKE US OUT IN A TRAP AND THEN RUNNING FROM US? I LIKE WHAT THAT SAYS ABOUT THEM.
I DON'T CARE ABOUT "BRIGHT SIDES," BARTON. I CARE ABOUT VENGEANCE.
WELL, THAT'S A DISH BEST SERVED COLD ANYWAY, QUIRE.
I'VE NEVER UNDERSTOOD THAT SAYING. IT'S A DUMB SAYING.
YEAH, IT KIND OF IS.

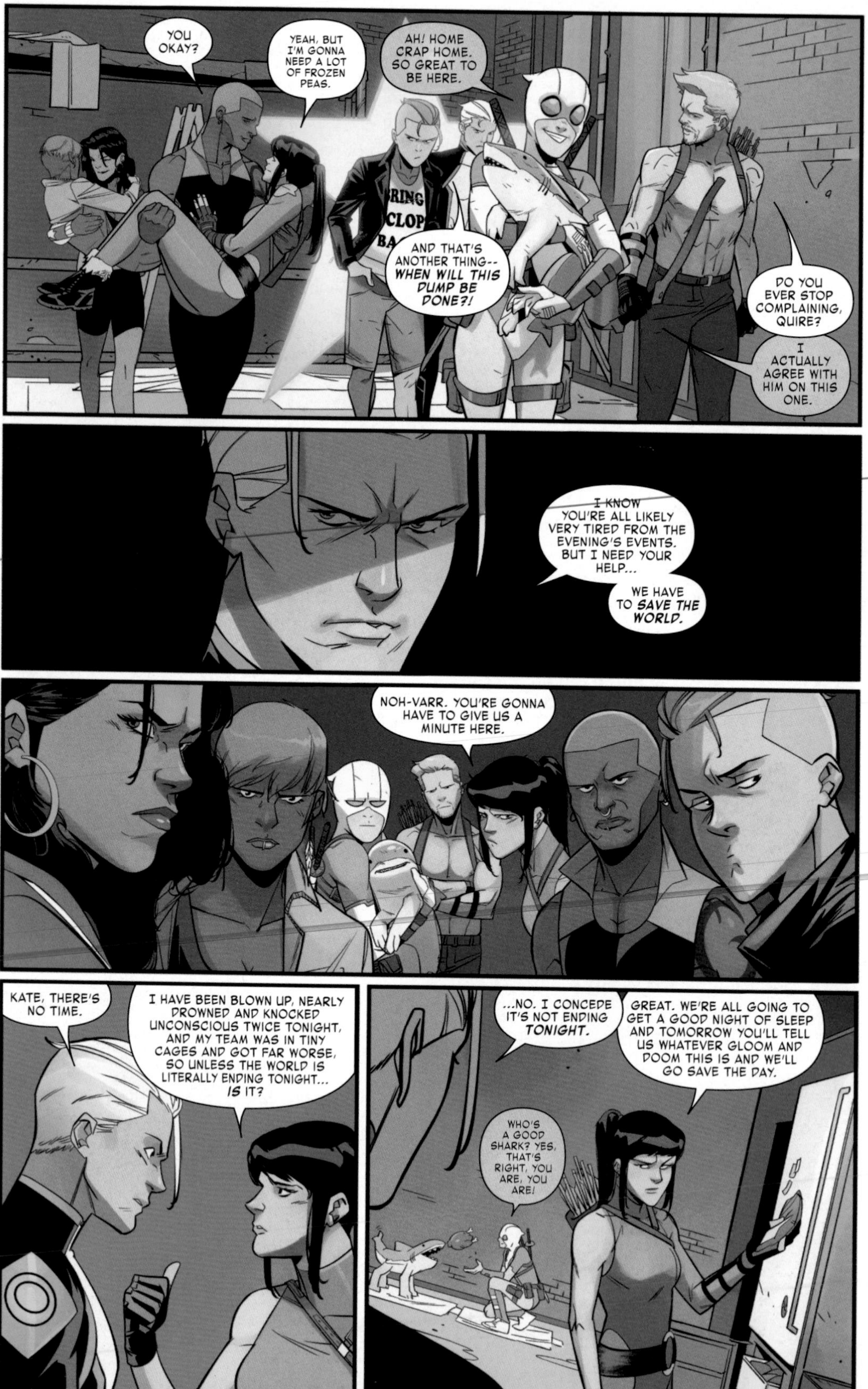
YOU OKAY?
YEAH, BUT I'M GONNA NEED A LOT OF FROZEN PEAS.
AH! HOME CRAP HOME. SO GREAT TO BE HERE.
AND THAT'S ANOTHER THING-- WHEN WILL THIS DUMP BE DONE?!
DO YOU EVER STOP COMPLAINING, QUIRE?
I ACTUALLY AGREE WITH HIM ON THIS ONE.
I KNOW YOU'RE ALL LIKELY VERY TIRED FROM THE EVENING'S EVENTS. BUT I NEED YOUR HELP...
WE HAVE TO SAVE THE WORLD.
NOH-VARR. YOU'RE GONNA HAVE TO GIVE US A MINUTE HERE.
KATE, THERE'S NO TIME.
I HAVE BEEN BLOWN UP, NEARLY DROWNED AND KNOCKED UNCONSCIOUS TWICE TONIGHT, AND MY TEAM WAS IN TINY CAGES AND GOT FAR WORSE, SO UNLESS THE WORLD IS LITERALLY ENDING TONIGHT... IS IT?
...NO. I CONCEDE IT'S NOT ENDING TONIGHT.
GREAT. WE'RE ALL GOING TO GET A GOOD NIGHT OF SLEEP AND TOMORROW YOU'LL TELL US WHATEVER GLOOM AND DOOM THIS IS AND WE'LL GO SAVE THE DAY.
WHO'S A GOOD SHARK? YES, THAT'S RIGHT, YOU ARE, YOU ARE!

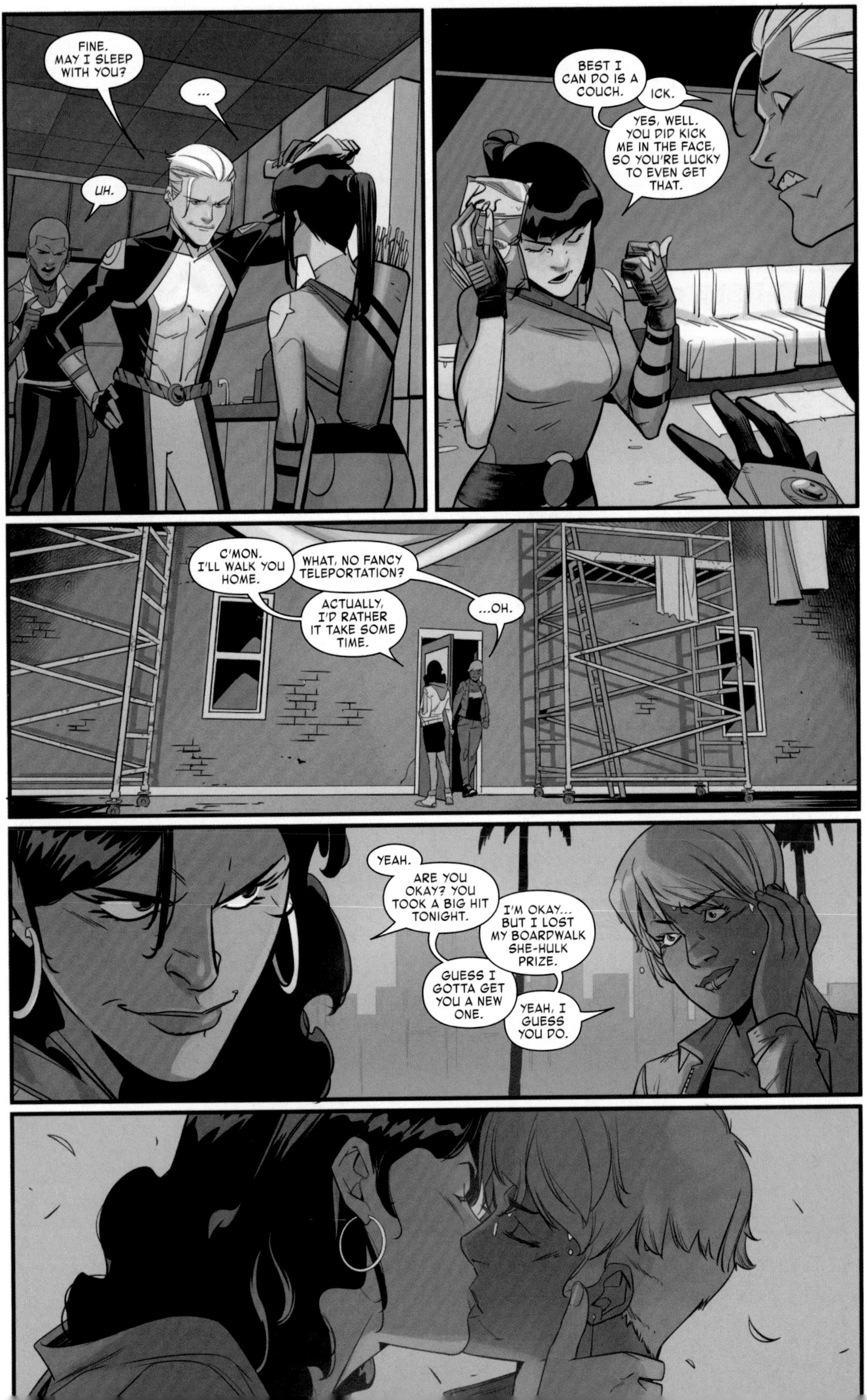
FINE. MAY I SLEEP WITH YOU?
...
UH.
BEST I CAN DO IS A COUCH.
ICK.
YES, WELL. YOU DID KICK ME IN THE FACE, SO YOU'RE LUCKY TO EVEN GET THAT.
C'MON. I'LL WALK YOU HOME.
WHAT, NO FANCY TELEPORTATION?
ACTUALLY, I'D RATHER IT TAKE SOME TIME.
...OH.
YEAH.
ARE YOU OKAY? YOU TOOK A BIG HIT TONIGHT.
I'M OKAY... BUT I LOST MY BOARDWALK SHE-HULK PRIZE.
GUESS I GOTTA GET YOU A NEW ONE.
YEAH, I GUESS YOU DO.

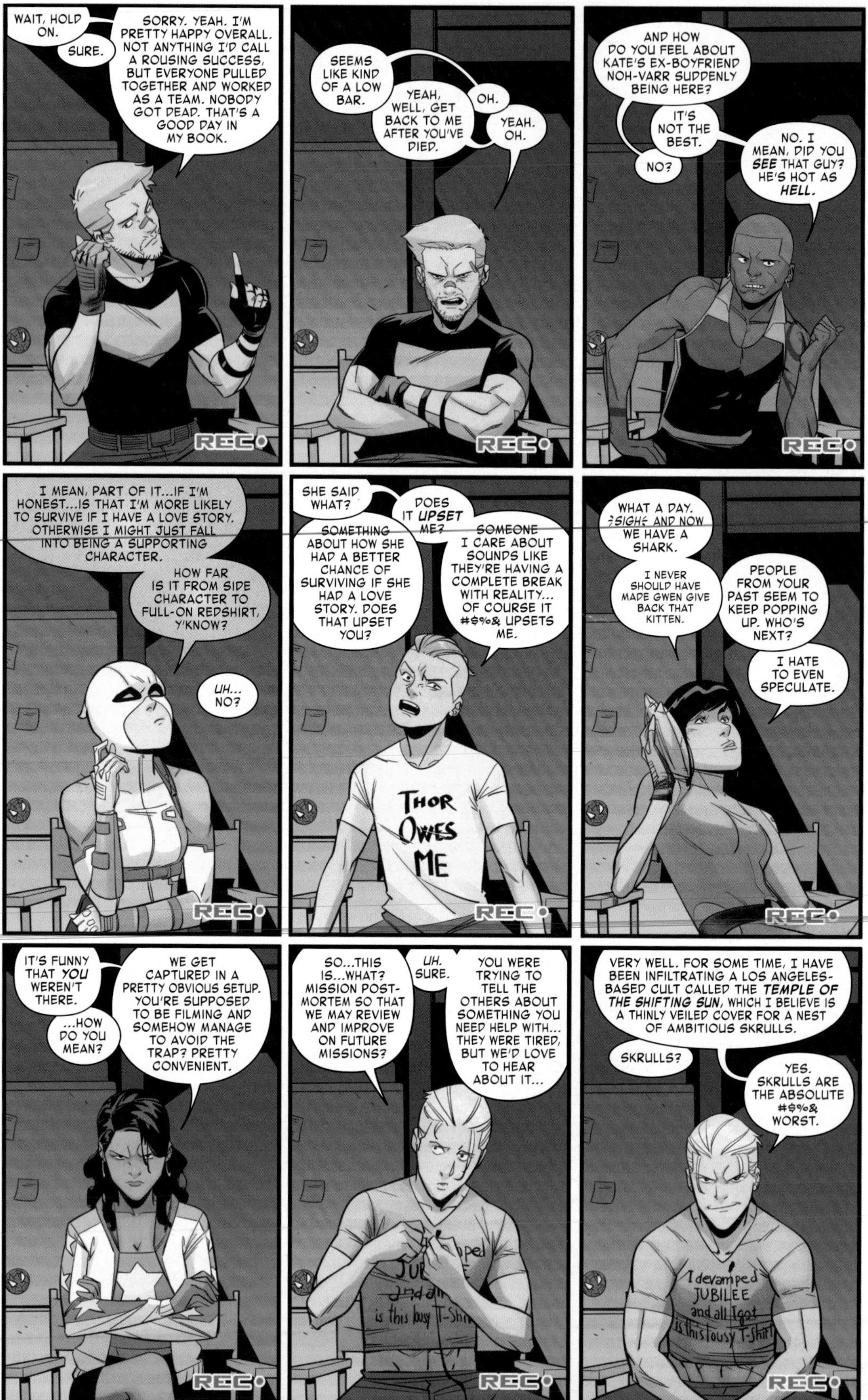
WAIT, HOLD ON.
SURE.
SORRY. YEAH. I'M PRETTY HAPPY OVERALL. NOT ANYTHING I'D CALL A ROUSING SUCCESS, BUT EVERYONE PULLED TOGETHER AND WORKED AS A TEAM. NOBODY GOT DEAD. THAT'S A GOOD DAY IN MY BOOK.
REC
SEEMS LIKE KIND OF A LOW BAR.
YEAH, WELL, GET BACK TO ME AFTER YOU'VE DIED.
OH.
YEAH. OH.
REC
AND HOW DO YOU FEEL ABOUT KATE'S EX-BOYFRIEND NOH-VARR SUDDENLY BEING HERE?
IT'S NOT THE BEST.
NO?
NO. I MEAN, DID YOU SEE THAT GUY? HE'S HOT AS HELL.
REC
I MEAN, PART OF IT...IF I'M HONEST...IS THAT I'M MORE LIKELY TO SURVIVE IF I HAVE A LOVE STORY. OTHERWISE I MIGHT JUST FALL INTO BEING A SUPPORTING CHARACTER.
HOW FAR IS IT FROM SIDE CHARACTER TO FULL-ON REDSHIRT, Y'KNOW?
UH... NO?
REC
SHE SAID WHAT?
SOMETHING ABOUT HOW SHE HAD A BETTER CHANCE OF SURVIVING IF SHE HAD A LOVE STORY. DOES THAT UPSET YOU?
DOES IT UPSET ME?
SOMEONE I CARE ABOUT SOUNDS LIKE THEY'RE HAVING A COMPLETE BREAK WITH REALITY... OF COURSE IT #$%& UPSETS ME.
THOR OWES ME
REC
WHAT A DAY. ⸗SIGH⸗ AND NOW WE HAVE A SHARK.
I NEVER SHOULD HAVE MADE GWEN GIVE BACK THAT KITTEN.
PEOPLE FROM YOUR PAST SEEM TO KEEP POPPING UP. WHO'S NEXT?
I HATE TO EVEN SPECULATE.
REC
IT'S FUNNY THAT YOU WEREN'T THERE.
...HOW DO YOU MEAN?
WE GET CAPTURED IN A PRETTY OBVIOUS SETUP. YOU'RE SUPPOSED TO BE FILMING AND SOMEHOW MANAGE TO AVOID THE TRAP? PRETTY CONVENIENT.
REC
SO...THIS IS...WHAT? MISSION POST-MORTEM SO THAT WE MAY REVIEW AND IMPROVE ON FUTURE MISSIONS?
UH. SURE.
YOU WERE TRYING TO TELL THE OTHERS ABOUT SOMETHING YOU NEED HELP WITH... THEY WERE TIRED, BUT WE'D LOVE TO HEAR ABOUT IT...
REC
VERY WELL. FOR SOME TIME, I HAVE BEEN INFILTRATING A LOS ANGELES-BASED CULT CALLED THE TEMPLE OF THE SHIFTING SUN, WHICH I BELIEVE IS A THINLY VEILED COVER FOR A NEST OF AMBITIOUS SKRULLS.
SKRULLS?
YES. SKRULLS ARE THE ABSOLUTE #$%& WORST.
I devamped JUBILEE and all I got is this lousy T-Shirt
REC

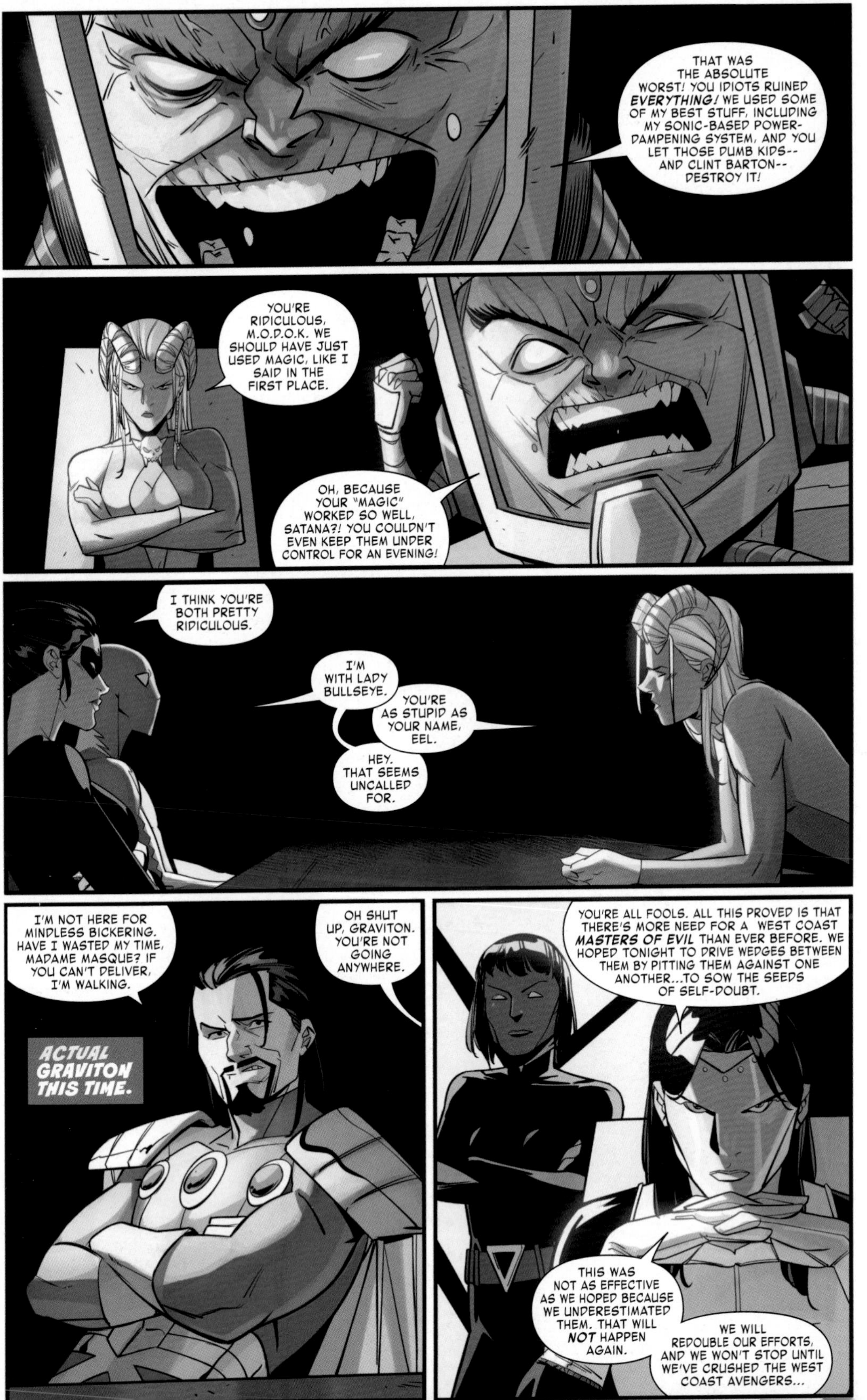
THAT WAS THE ABSOLUTE WORST! YOU IDIOTS RUINED EVERYTHING! WE USED SOME OF MY BEST STUFF, INCLUDING MY SONIC-BASED POWER-DAMPENING SYSTEM, AND YOU LET THOSE DUMB KIDS--AND CLINT BARTON--DESTROY IT!
YOU'RE RIDICULOUS, M.O.D.O.K. WE SHOULD HAVE JUST USED MAGIC, LIKE I SAID IN THE FIRST PLACE.
OH, BECAUSE YOUR "MAGIC" WORKED SO WELL, SATANA?! YOU COULDN'T EVEN KEEP THEM UNDER CONTROL FOR AN EVENING!
I THINK YOU'RE BOTH PRETTY RIDICULOUS.
I'M WITH LADY BULLSEYE.
YOU'RE AS STUPID AS YOUR NAME, EEL.
HEY. THAT SEEMS UNCALLED FOR.
I'M NOT HERE FOR MINDLESS BICKERING. HAVE I WASTED MY TIME, MADAME MASQUE? IF YOU CAN'T DELIVER, I'M WALKING.
OH SHUT UP, GRAVITON. YOU'RE NOT GOING ANYWHERE.
ACTUAL GRAVITON THIS TIME.
YOU'RE ALL FOOLS. ALL THIS PROVED IS THAT THERE'S MORE NEED FOR A WEST COAST MASTERS OF EVIL THAN EVER BEFORE. WE HOPED TONIGHT TO DRIVE WEDGES BETWEEN THEM BY PITTING THEM AGAINST ONE ANOTHER...TO SOW THE SEEDS OF SELF-DOUBT.
THIS WAS NOT AS EFFECTIVE AS WE HOPED BECAUSE WE UNDERESTIMATED THEM. THAT WILL NOT HAPPEN AGAIN.
WE WILL REDOUBLE OUR EFFORTS, AND WE WON'T STOP UNTIL WE'VE CRUSHED THE WEST COAST AVENGERS...

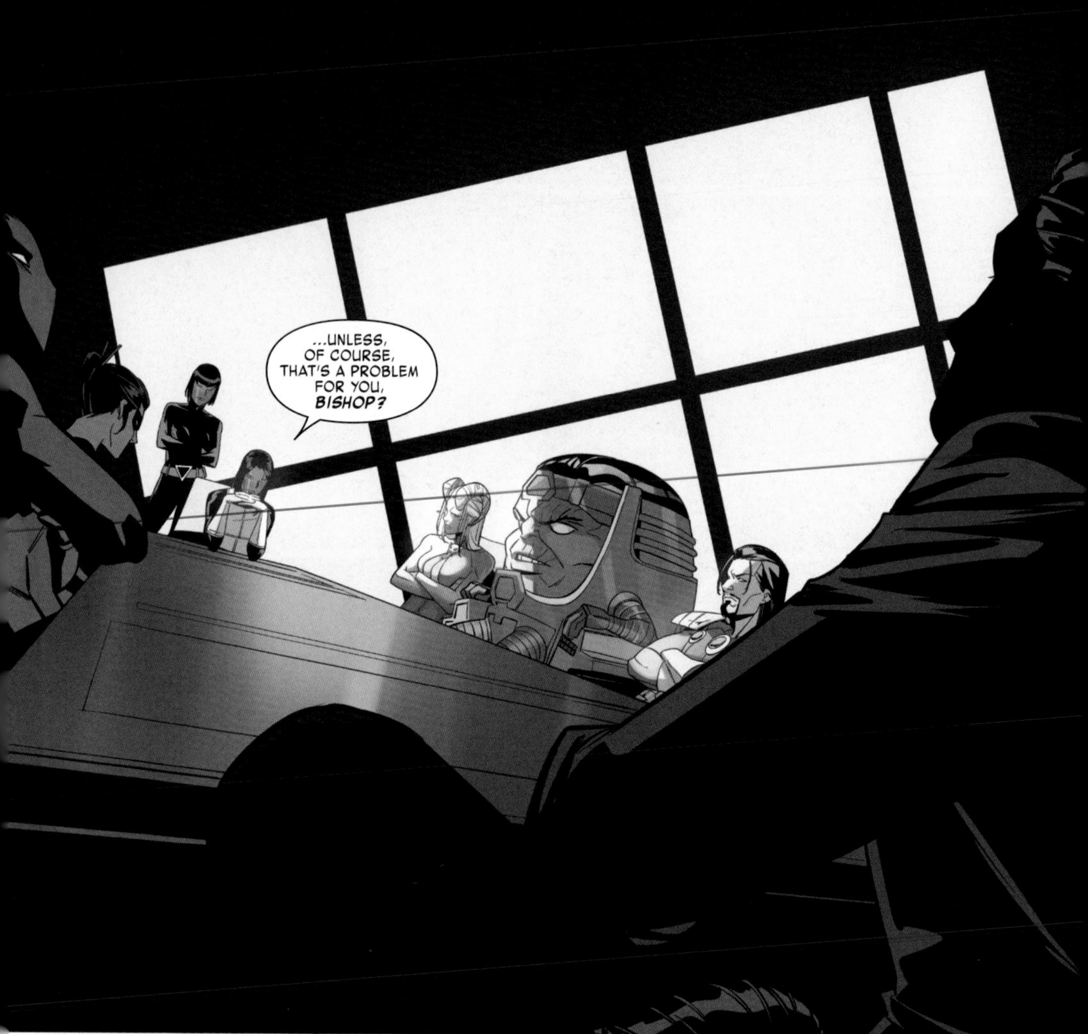
...UNLESS, OF COURSE, THAT'S A PROBLEM FOR YOU, BISHOP?

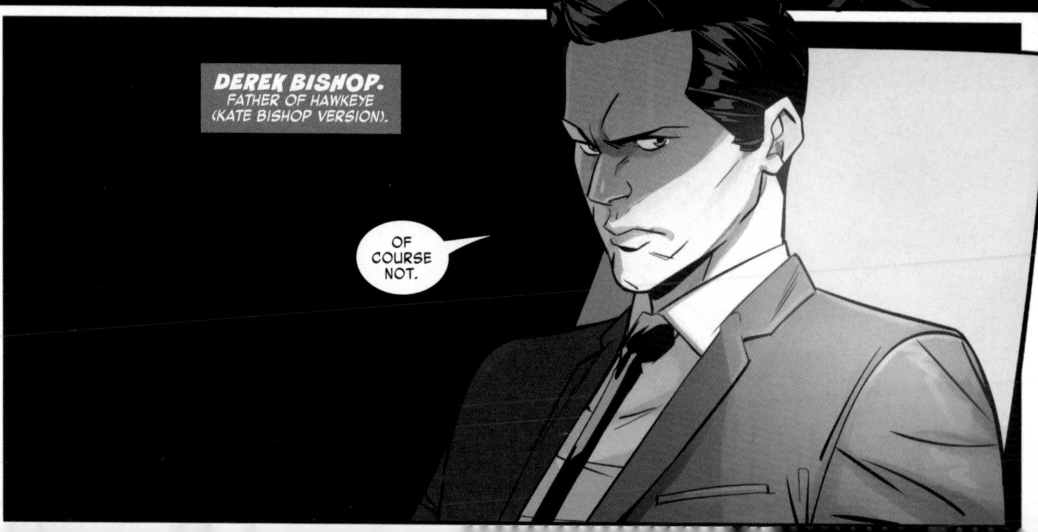
DEREK BISHOP. FATHER OF HAWKEYE (KATE BISHOP VERSION).
OF COURSE NOT.

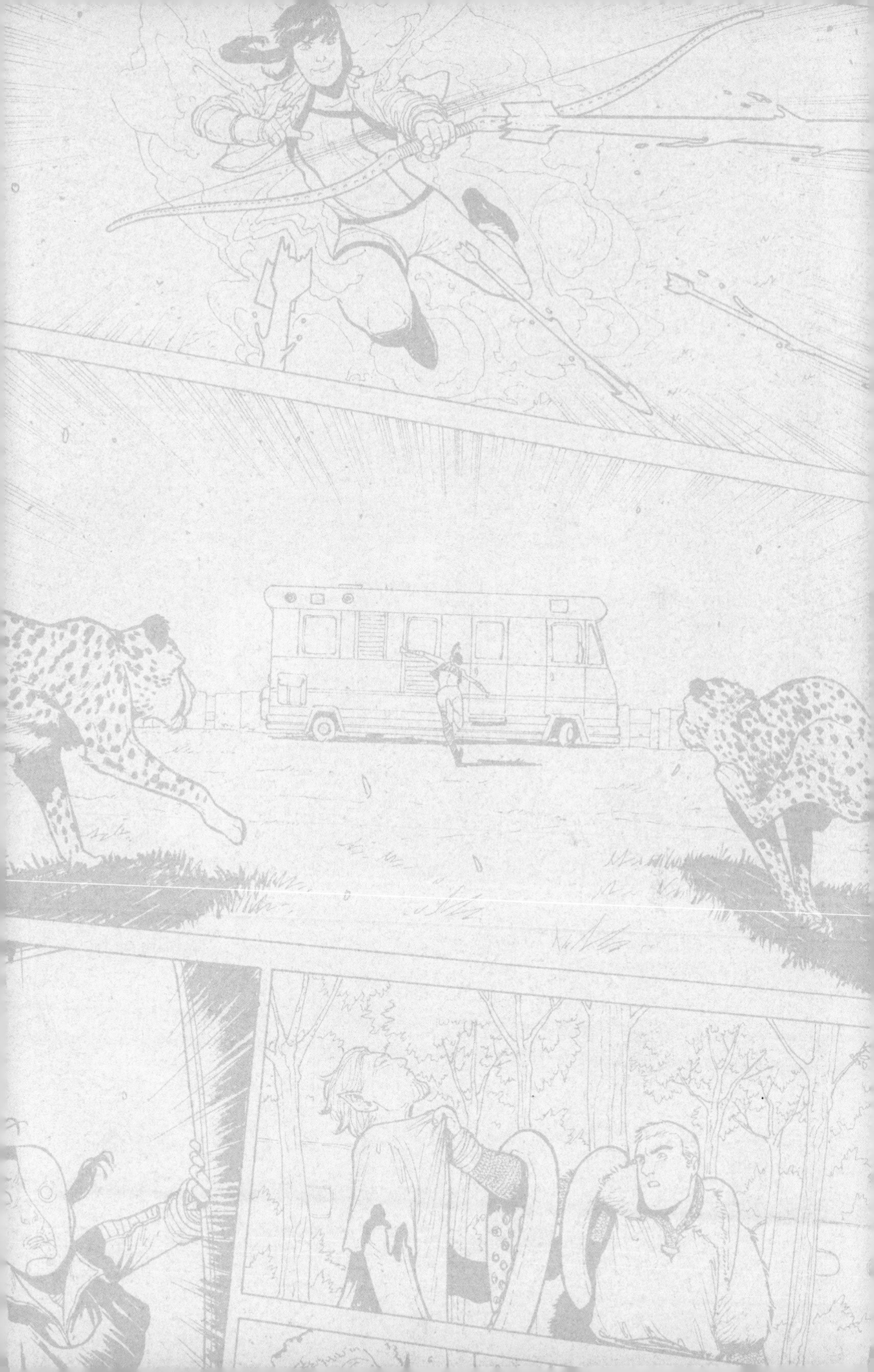

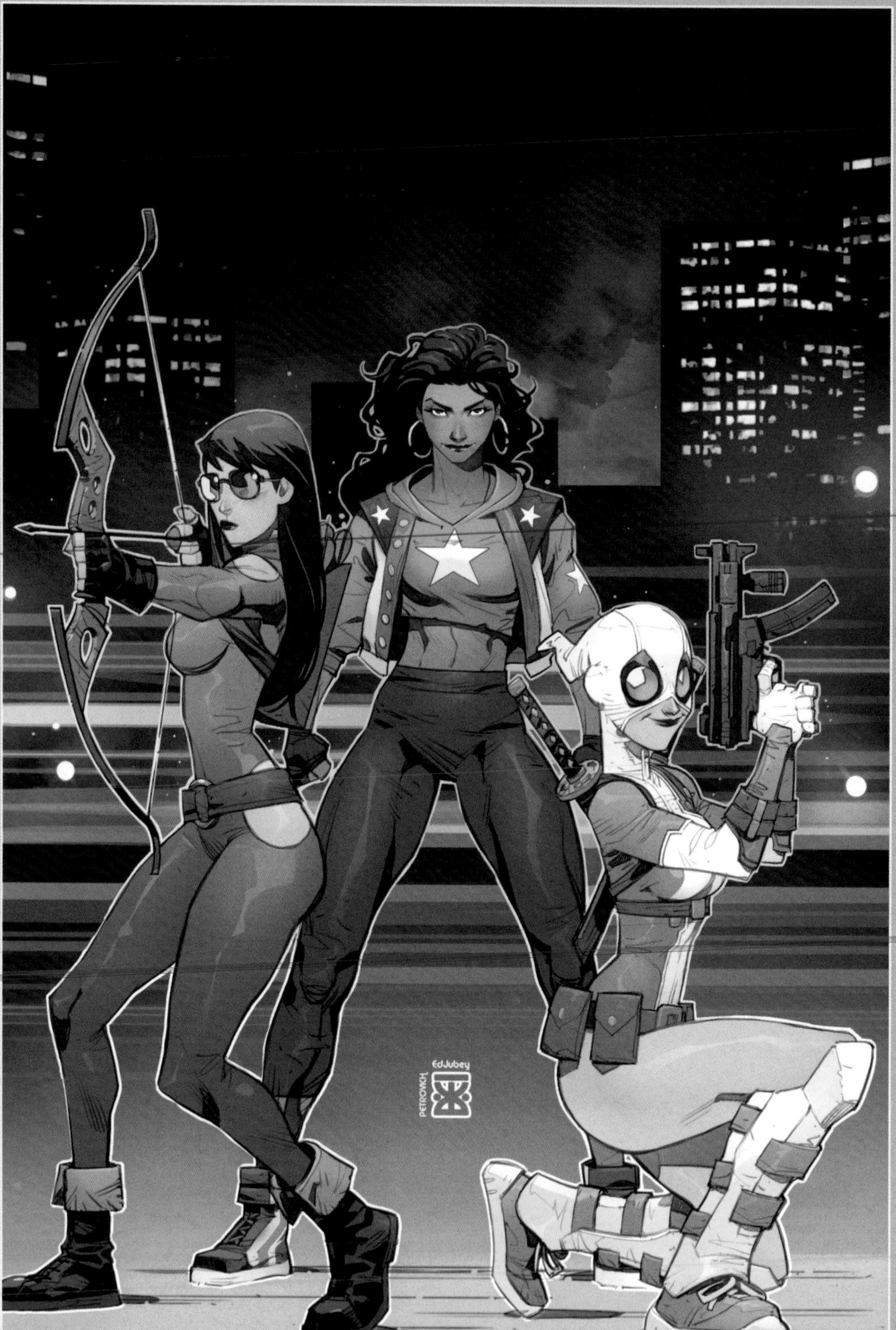
EdJubey
PETROVICH

WEST COAST AVENGERS #8

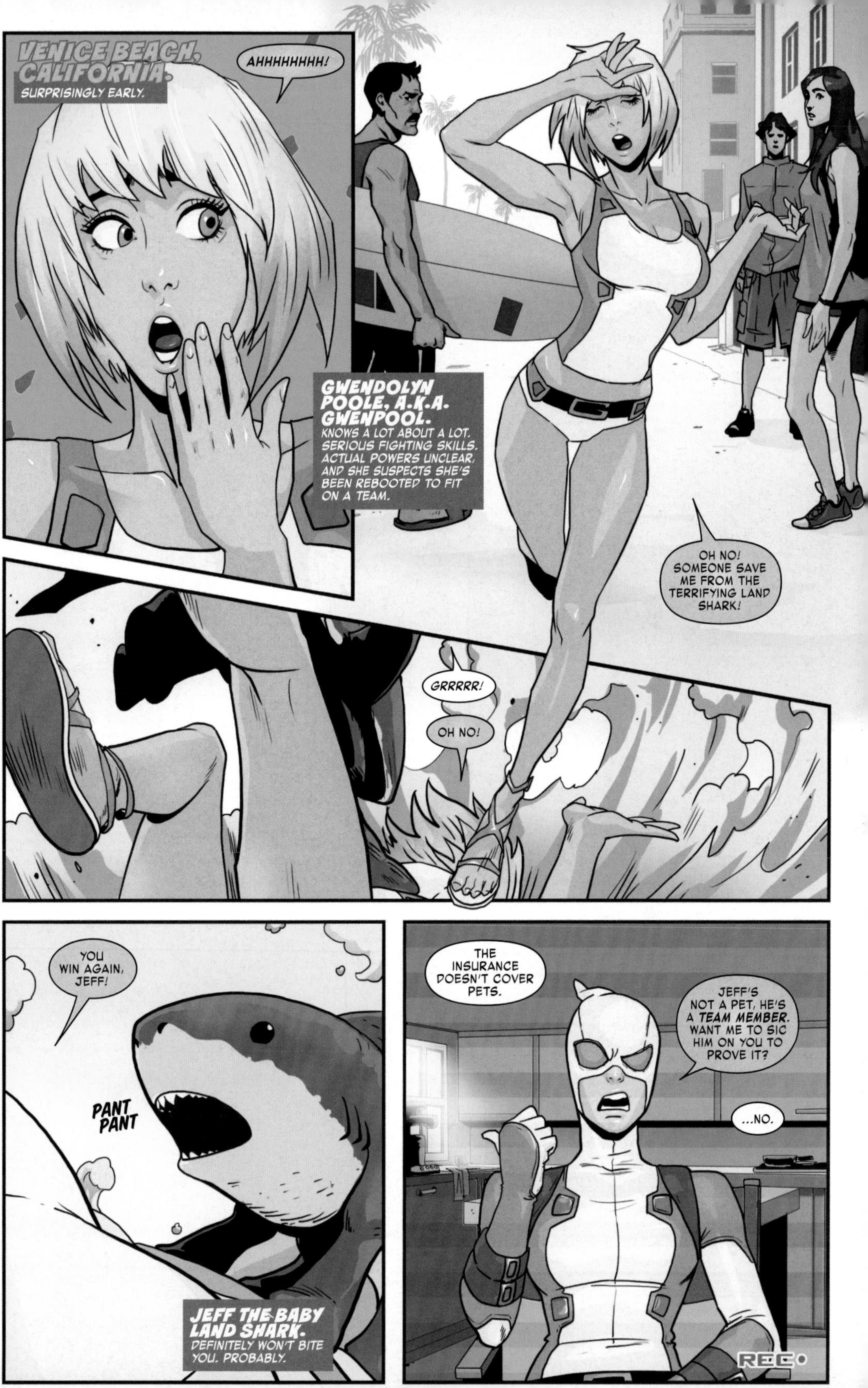
VENICE BEACH, CALIFORNIA.
SURPRISINGLY EARLY.
AHHHHHHHH!
GWENDOLYN POOLE, A.K.A. GWENPOOL.
KNOWS A LOT ABOUT A LOT. SERIOUS FIGHTING SKILLS. ACTUAL POWERS UNCLEAR, AND SHE SUSPECTS SHE'S BEEN REBOOTED TO FIT ON A TEAM.
OH NO! SOMEONE SAVE ME FROM THE TERRIFYING LAND SHARK!
GRRRRR!
OH NO!
YOU WIN AGAIN, JEFF!
PANT PANT
JEFF THE BABY LAND SHARK.
DEFINITELY WON'T BITE YOU. PROBABLY.
THE INSURANCE DOESN'T COVER PETS.
JEFF'S NOT A PET, HE'S A *TEAM MEMBER.* WANT ME TO SIC HIM ON YOU TO PROVE IT?
...NO.
REC

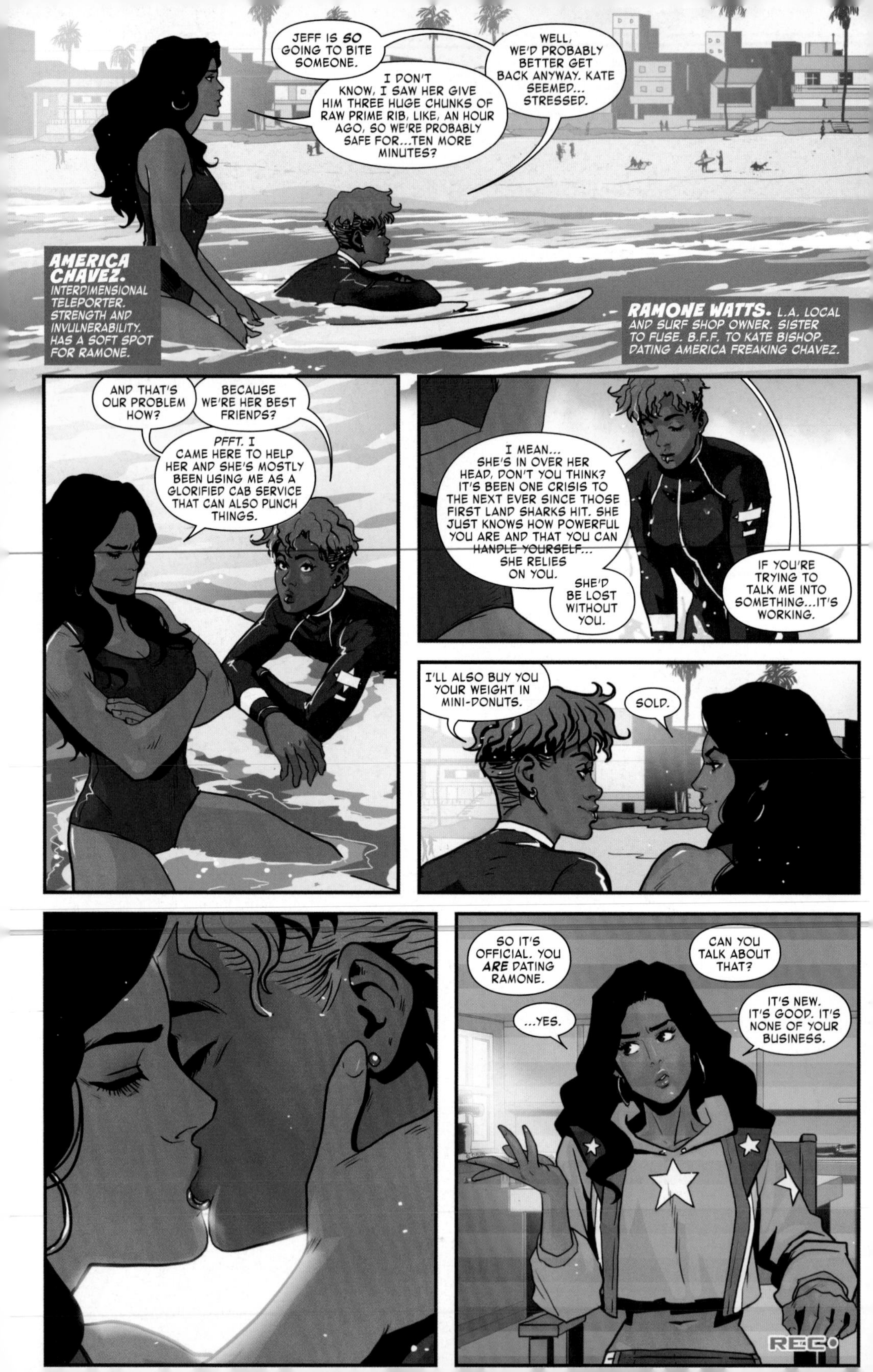
JEFF IS SO GOING TO BITE SOMEONE.
WELL, WE'D PROBABLY BETTER GET BACK ANYWAY. KATE SEEMED... STRESSED.
I DON'T KNOW, I SAW HER GIVE HIM THREE HUGE CHUNKS OF RAW PRIME RIB, LIKE, AN HOUR AGO, SO WE'RE PROBABLY SAFE FOR...TEN MORE MINUTES?
AMERICA CHAVEZ. INTERDIMENSIONAL TELEPORTER. STRENGTH AND INVULNERABILITY. HAS A SOFT SPOT FOR RAMONE.
RAMONE WATTS. L.A. LOCAL AND SURF SHOP OWNER. SISTER TO FUSE. B.F.F. TO KATE BISHOP. DATING AMERICA FREAKING CHAVEZ.
AND THAT'S OUR PROBLEM HOW?
BECAUSE WE'RE HER BEST FRIENDS?
PFFT. I CAME HERE TO HELP HER AND SHE'S MOSTLY BEEN USING ME AS A GLORIFIED CAB SERVICE THAT CAN ALSO PUNCH THINGS.
I MEAN... SHE'S IN OVER HER HEAD, DON'T YOU THINK? IT'S BEEN ONE CRISIS TO THE NEXT EVER SINCE THOSE FIRST LAND SHARKS HIT. SHE JUST KNOWS HOW POWERFUL YOU ARE AND THAT YOU CAN HANDLE YOURSELF... SHE RELIES ON YOU.
SHE'D BE LOST WITHOUT YOU.
IF YOU'RE TRYING TO TALK ME INTO SOMETHING...IT'S WORKING.
I'LL ALSO BUY YOU YOUR WEIGHT IN MINI-DONUTS.
SOLD.
SO IT'S OFFICIAL. YOU ARE DATING RAMONE.
...YES.
CAN YOU TALK ABOUT THAT?
IT'S NEW. IT'S GOOD. IT'S NONE OF YOUR BUSINESS.
REC

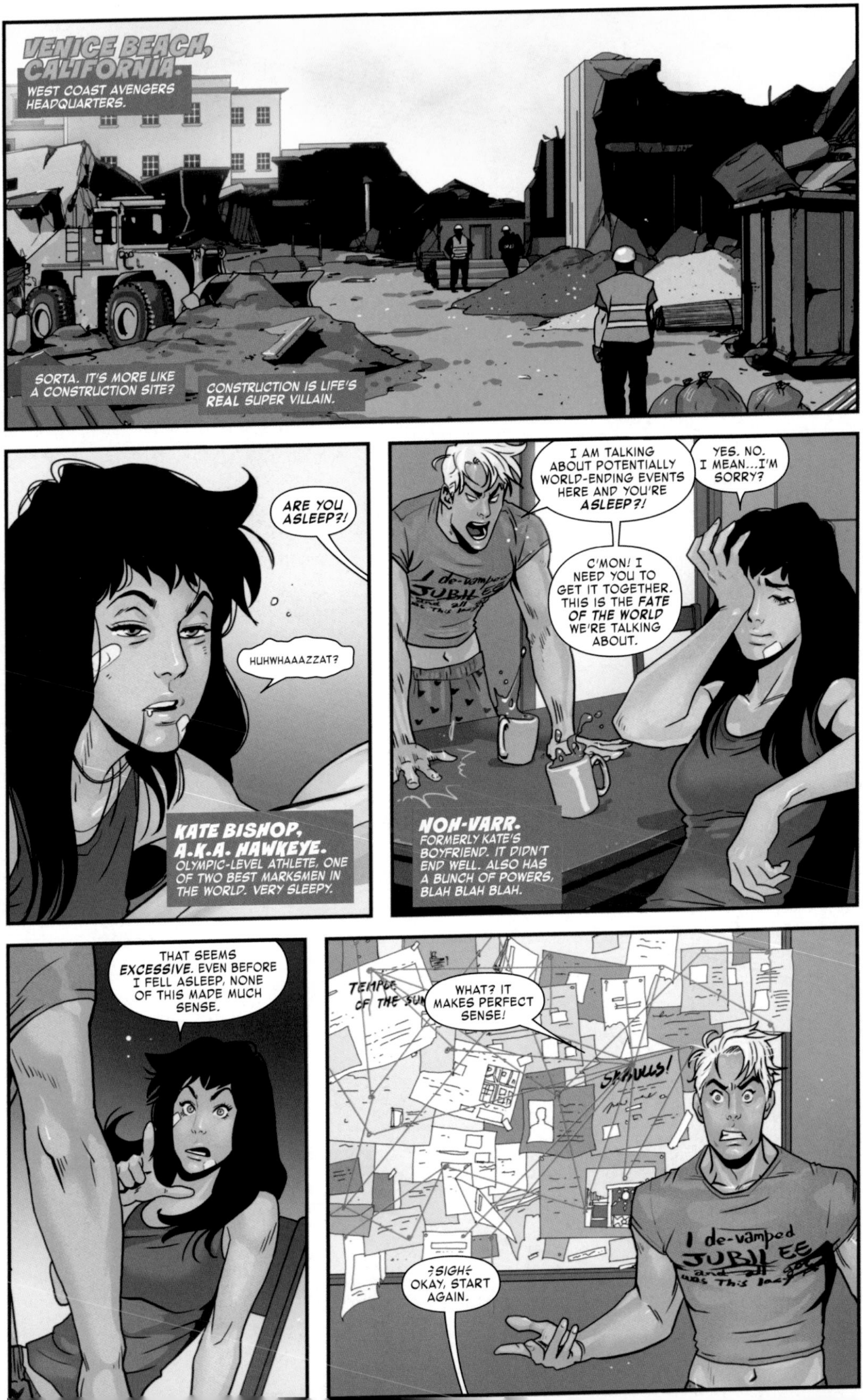
VENICE BEACH, CALIFORNIA.
WEST COAST AVENGERS HEADQUARTERS.
SORTA. IT'S MORE LIKE A CONSTRUCTION SITE?
CONSTRUCTION IS LIFE'S REAL SUPER VILLAIN.
ARE YOU ASLEEP?!
HUHWHAAAZZAT?
KATE BISHOP, A.K.A. HAWKEYE.
OLYMPIC-LEVEL ATHLETE, ONE OF TWO BEST MARKSMEN IN THE WORLD. VERY SLEEPY.
I AM TALKING ABOUT POTENTIALLY WORLD-ENDING EVENTS HERE AND YOU'RE ASLEEP?!
C'MON! I NEED YOU TO GET IT TOGETHER. THIS IS THE FATE OF THE WORLD WE'RE TALKING ABOUT.
YES. NO. I MEAN...I'M SORRY?
NOH-VARR.
FORMERLY KATE'S BOYFRIEND. IT DIDN'T END WELL. ALSO HAS A BUNCH OF POWERS, BLAH BLAH BLAH.
THAT SEEMS EXCESSIVE. EVEN BEFORE I FELL ASLEEP, NONE OF THIS MADE MUCH SENSE.
WHAT? IT MAKES PERFECT SENSE!
SKULLS!
I de-vamped JUBILEE
SIGH
OKAY, START AGAIN.

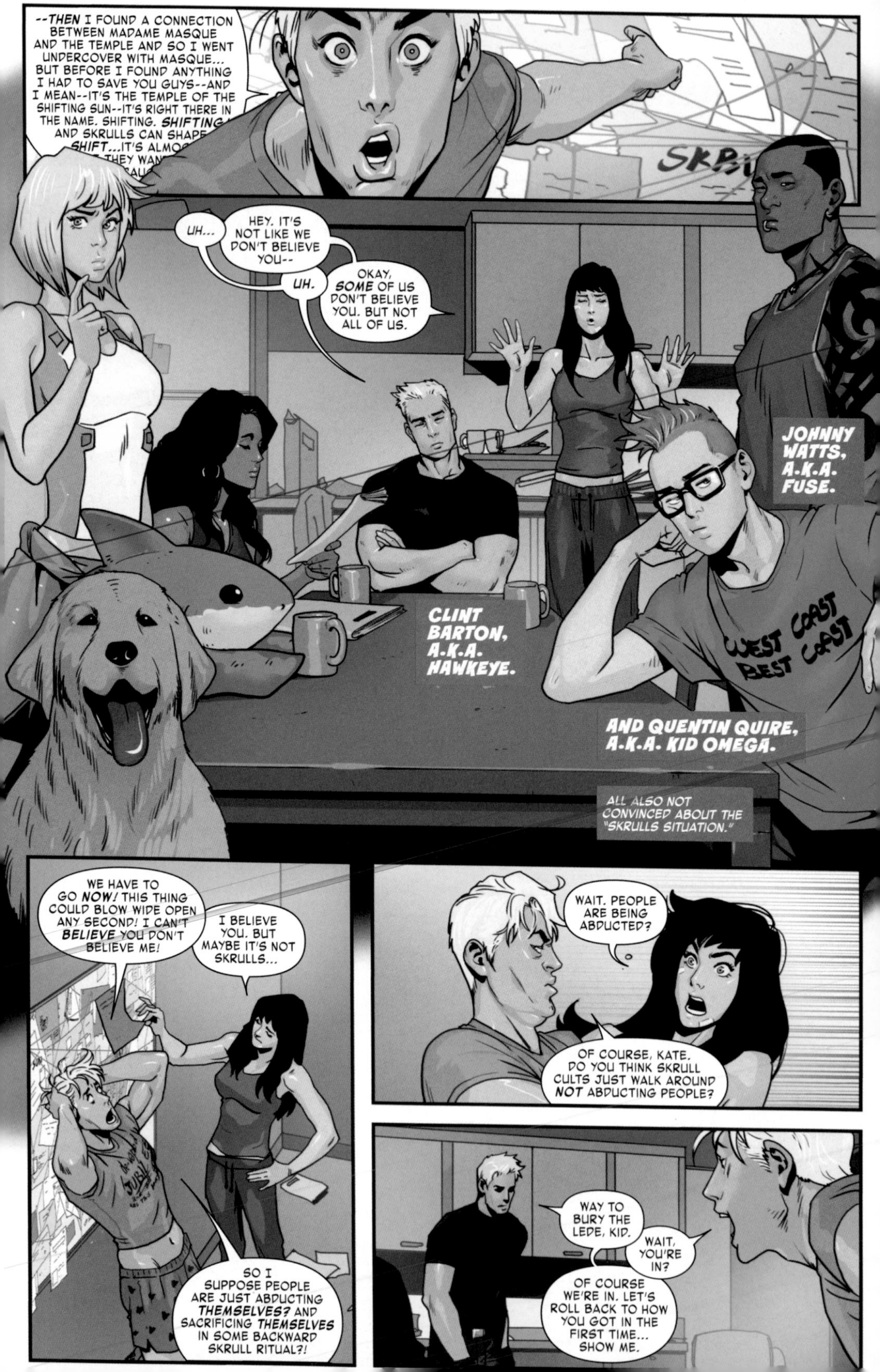
--THEN I FOUND A CONNECTION BETWEEN MADAME MASQUE AND THE TEMPLE AND SO I WENT UNDERCOVER WITH MASQUE... BUT BEFORE I FOUND ANYTHING I HAD TO SAVE YOU GUYS--AND I MEAN--IT'S THE TEMPLE OF THE SHIFTING SUN--IT'S RIGHT THERE IN THE NAME. SHIFTING. SHIFTING! AND SKRULLS CAN SHAPE SHIFT...IT'S ALMO
UH...
HEY. IT'S NOT LIKE WE DON'T BELIEVE YOU--
UH.
OKAY, SOME OF US DON'T BELIEVE YOU. BUT NOT ALL OF US.
JOHNNY WATTS, A.K.A. FUSE.
CLINT BARTON, A.K.A. HAWKEYE.
WEST COAST BEST COAST
AND QUENTIN QUIRE, A.K.A. KID OMEGA.
ALL ALSO NOT CONVINCED ABOUT THE "SKRULLS SITUATION."
WE HAVE TO GO NOW! THIS THING COULD BLOW WIDE OPEN ANY SECOND! I CAN'T BELIEVE YOU DON'T BELIEVE ME!
I BELIEVE YOU. BUT MAYBE IT'S NOT SKRULLS...
SO I SUPPOSE PEOPLE ARE JUST ABDUCTING THEMSELVES? AND SACRIFICING THEMSELVES IN SOME BACKWARD SKRULL RITUAL?!
WAIT. PEOPLE ARE BEING ABDUCTED?
OF COURSE, KATE. DO YOU THINK SKRULL CULTS JUST WALK AROUND NOT ABDUCTING PEOPLE?
WAY TO BURY THE LEDE, KID.
WAIT, YOU'RE IN?
OF COURSE WE'RE IN. LET'S ROLL BACK TO HOW YOU GOT IN THE FIRST TIME... SHOW ME.

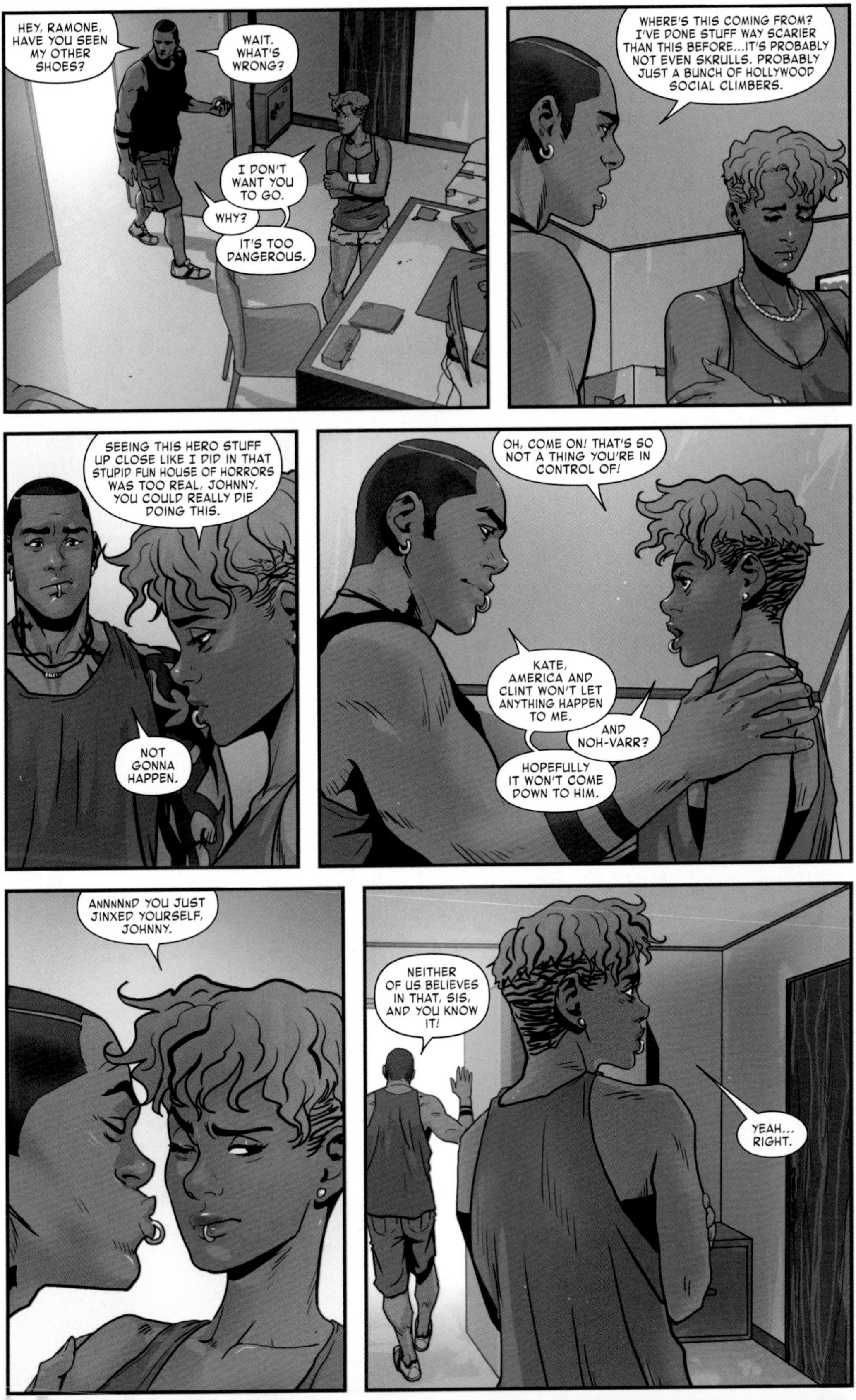
HEY, RAMONE, HAVE YOU SEEN MY OTHER SHOES?
WAIT. WHAT'S WRONG?
I DON'T WANT YOU TO GO.
WHY?
IT'S TOO DANGEROUS.
WHERE'S THIS COMING FROM? I'VE DONE STUFF WAY SCARIER THAN THIS BEFORE...IT'S PROBABLY NOT EVEN SKRULLS. PROBABLY JUST A BUNCH OF HOLLYWOOD SOCIAL CLIMBERS.
SEEING THIS HERO STUFF UP CLOSE LIKE I DID IN THAT STUPID FUN HOUSE OF HORRORS WAS TOO REAL, JOHNNY. YOU COULD REALLY DIE DOING THIS.
NOT GONNA HAPPEN.
OH, COME ON! THAT'S SO NOT A THING YOU'RE IN CONTROL OF!
KATE, AMERICA AND CLINT WON'T LET ANYTHING HAPPEN TO ME.
AND NOH-VARR?
HOPEFULLY IT WON'T COME DOWN TO HIM.
ANNNNND YOU JUST JINXED YOURSELF, JOHNNY.
NEITHER OF US BELIEVES IN THAT, SIS, AND YOU KNOW IT!
YEAH... RIGHT.

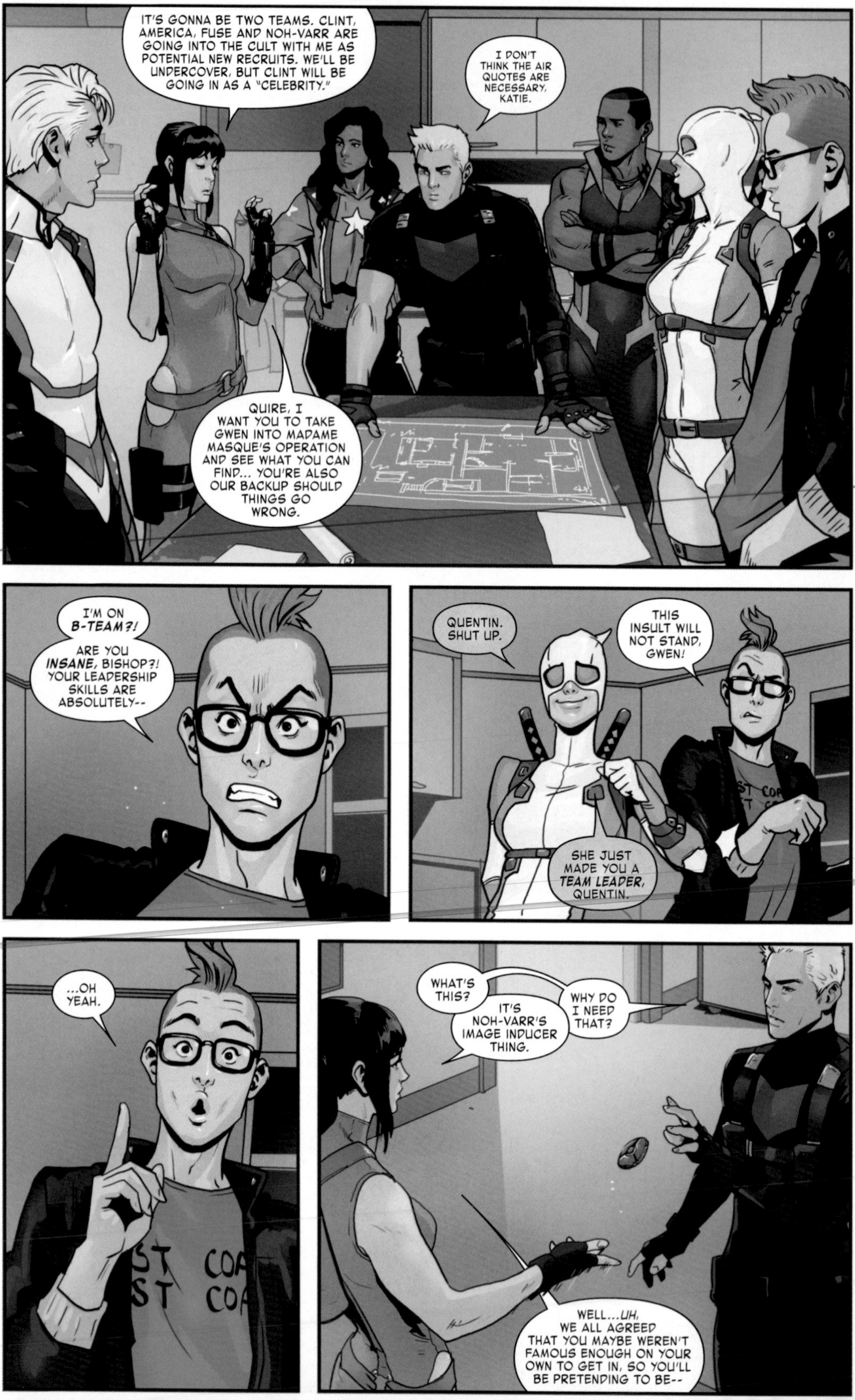
IT'S GONNA BE TWO TEAMS. CLINT, AMERICA, FUSE AND NOH-VARR ARE GOING INTO THE CULT WITH ME AS POTENTIAL NEW RECRUITS. WE'LL BE UNDERCOVER, BUT CLINT WILL BE GOING IN AS A "CELEBRITY."
I DON'T THINK THE AIR QUOTES ARE NECESSARY, KATIE.
QUIRE, I WANT YOU TO TAKE GWEN INTO MADAME MASQUE'S OPERATION AND SEE WHAT YOU CAN FIND... YOU'RE ALSO OUR BACKUP SHOULD THINGS GO WRONG.
I'M ON *B-TEAM?!*
ARE YOU *INSANE,* BISHOP?! YOUR LEADERSHIP SKILLS ARE ABSOLUTELY--
QUENTIN. SHUT UP.
THIS INSULT WILL NOT STAND, GWEN!
SHE JUST MADE YOU A *TEAM LEADER,* QUENTIN.
...OH YEAH.
WHAT'S THIS?
IT'S NOH-VARR'S IMAGE INDUCER THING.
WHY DO I NEED THAT?
WELL...*UH,* WE ALL AGREED THAT YOU MAYBE WEREN'T FAMOUS ENOUGH ON YOUR OWN TO GET IN, SO YOU'LL BE PRETENDING TO BE--

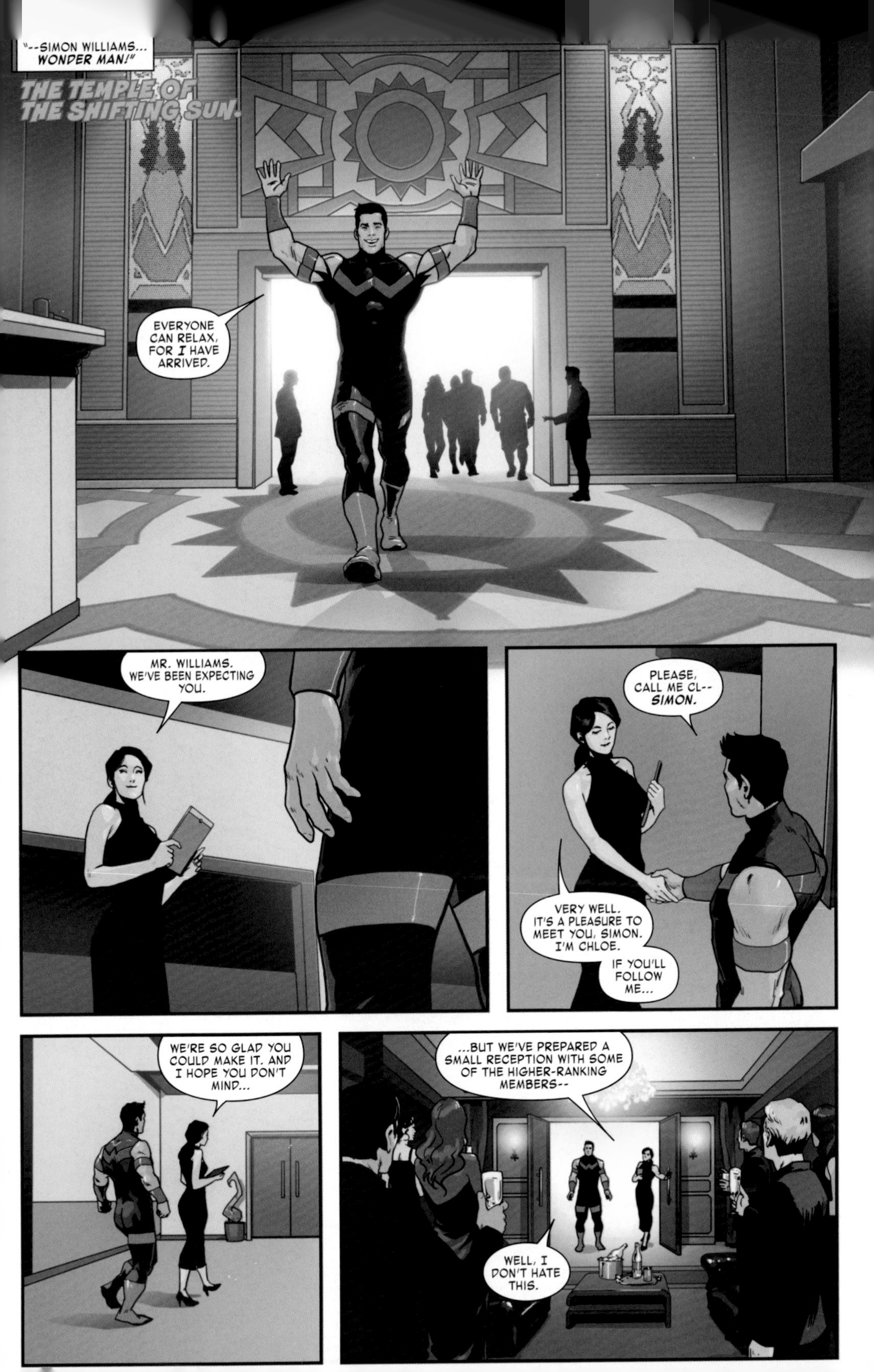
"--SIMON WILLIAMS... WONDER MAN!"
THE TEMPLE OF THE SHIFTING SUN.
EVERYONE CAN RELAX, FOR I HAVE ARRIVED.
MR. WILLIAMS. WE'VE BEEN EXPECTING YOU.
PLEASE, CALL ME CL-- SIMON.
VERY WELL. IT'S A PLEASURE TO MEET YOU, SIMON. I'M CHLOE.
IF YOU'LL FOLLOW ME...
WE'RE SO GLAD YOU COULD MAKE IT. AND I HOPE YOU DON'T MIND...
...BUT WE'VE PREPARED A SMALL RECEPTION WITH SOME OF THE HIGHER-RANKING MEMBERS--
WELL, I DON'T HATE THIS.

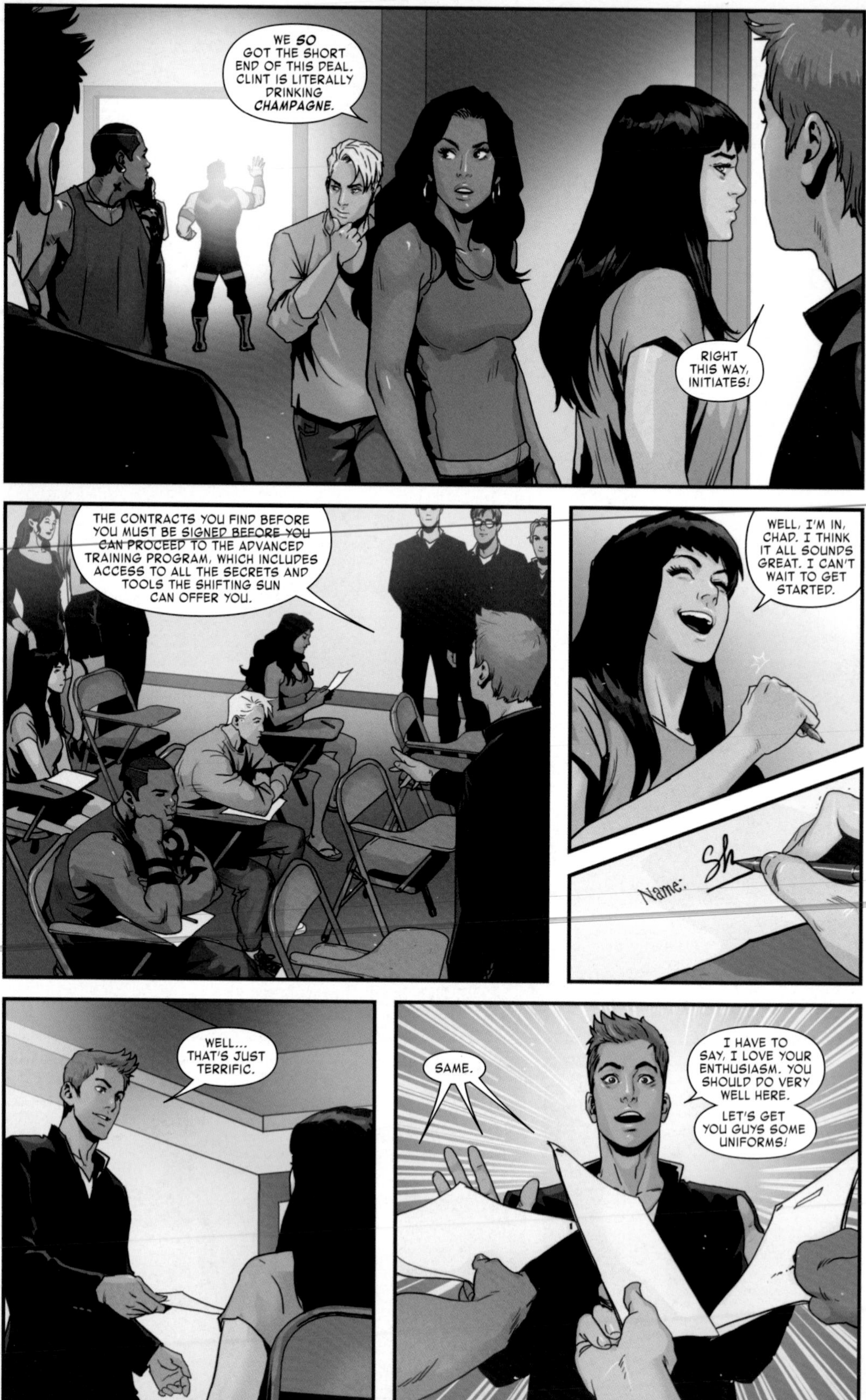
WE SO GOT THE SHORT END OF THIS DEAL. CLINT IS LITERALLY DRINKING CHAMPAGNE.
RIGHT THIS WAY, INITIATES!
THE CONTRACTS YOU FIND BEFORE YOU MUST BE SIGNED BEFORE YOU CAN PROCEED TO THE ADVANCED TRAINING PROGRAM, WHICH INCLUDES ACCESS TO ALL THE SECRETS AND TOOLS THE SHIFTING SUN CAN OFFER YOU.
WELL, I'M IN, CHAD. I THINK IT ALL SOUNDS GREAT. I CAN'T WAIT TO GET STARTED.
Name: Sh
WELL... THAT'S JUST TERRIFIC.
SAME.
I HAVE TO SAY, I LOVE YOUR ENTHUSIASM. YOU SHOULD DO VERY WELL HERE.
LET'S GET YOU GUYS SOME UNIFORMS!

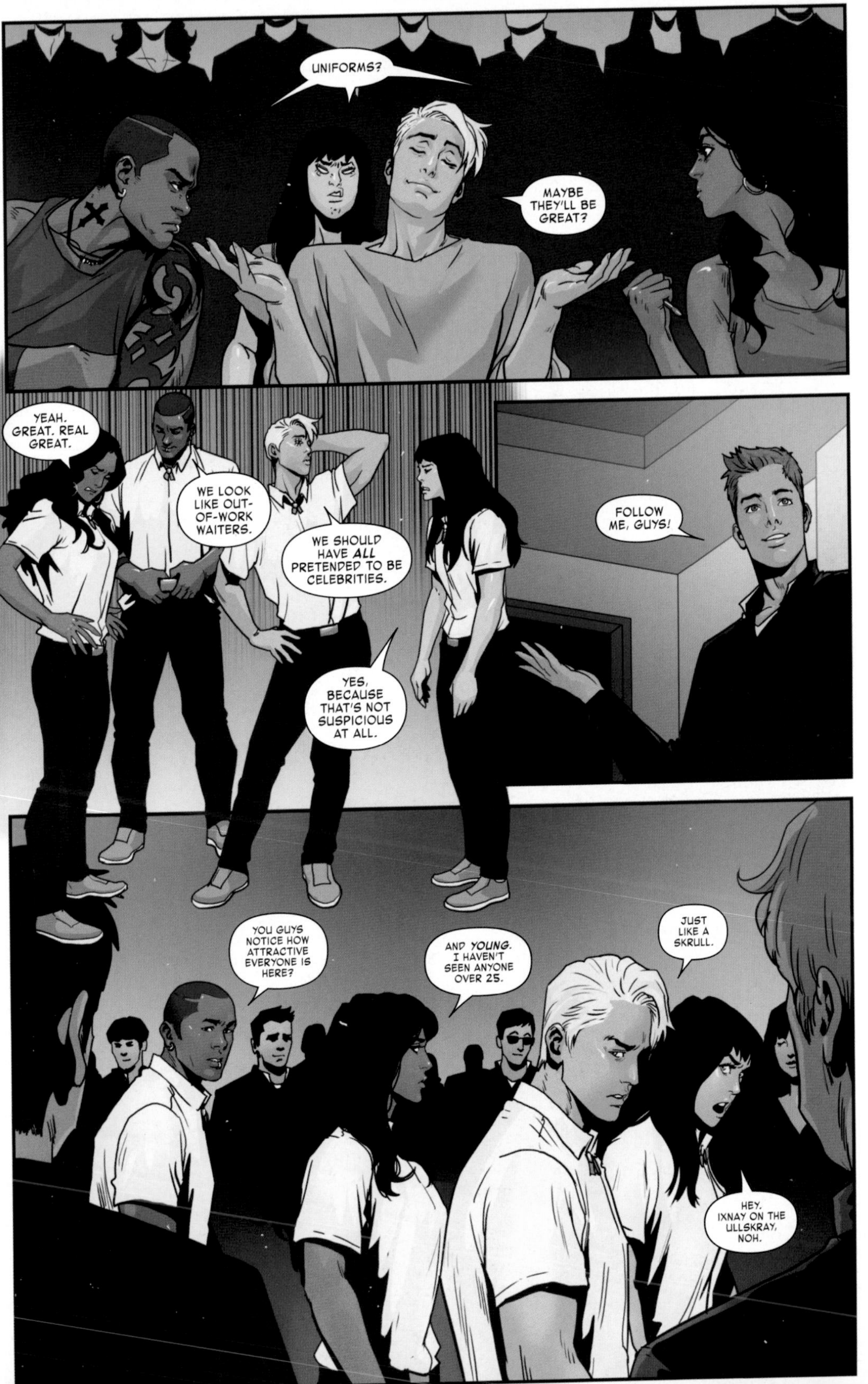
UNIFORMS?
MAYBE THEY'LL BE GREAT?
YEAH. GREAT. REAL GREAT.
WE LOOK LIKE OUT-OF-WORK WAITERS.
WE SHOULD HAVE *ALL* PRETENDED TO BE CELEBRITIES.
YES, BECAUSE THAT'S NOT SUSPICIOUS AT ALL.
FOLLOW ME, GUYS!
YOU GUYS NOTICE HOW ATTRACTIVE EVERYONE IS HERE?
AND *YOUNG.* I HAVEN'T SEEN ANYONE OVER 25.
JUST LIKE A SKRULL.
HEY. IXNAY ON THE ULLSKRAY, NOH.

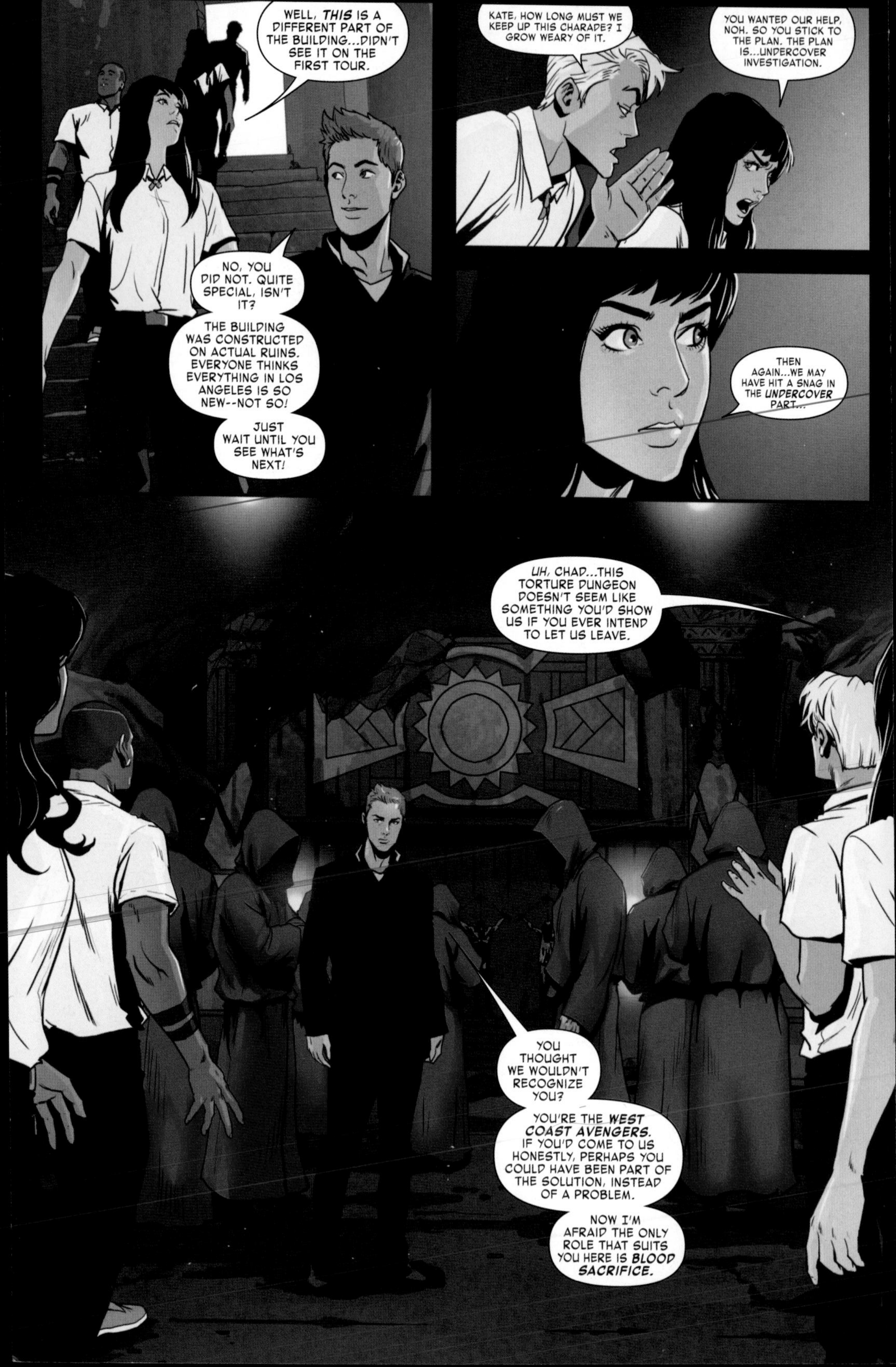
WELL, THIS IS A DIFFERENT PART OF THE BUILDING...DIDN'T SEE IT ON THE FIRST TOUR.
NO, YOU DID NOT. QUITE SPECIAL, ISN'T IT?
THE BUILDING WAS CONSTRUCTED ON ACTUAL RUINS. EVERYONE THINKS EVERYTHING IN LOS ANGELES IS SO NEW--NOT SO!
JUST WAIT UNTIL YOU SEE WHAT'S NEXT!
KATE, HOW LONG MUST WE KEEP UP THIS CHARADE? I GROW WEARY OF IT.
YOU WANTED OUR HELP, NOH. SO YOU STICK TO THE PLAN. THE PLAN IS...UNDERCOVER INVESTIGATION.
THEN AGAIN...WE MAY HAVE HIT A SNAG IN THE UNDERCOVER PART...
UH, CHAD...THIS TORTURE DUNGEON DOESN'T SEEM LIKE SOMETHING YOU'D SHOW US IF YOU EVER INTEND TO LET US LEAVE.
YOU THOUGHT WE WOULDN'T RECOGNIZE YOU?
YOU'RE THE WEST COAST AVENGERS. IF YOU'D COME TO US HONESTLY, PERHAPS YOU COULD HAVE BEEN PART OF THE SOLUTION, INSTEAD OF A PROBLEM.
NOW I'M AFRAID THE ONLY ROLE THAT SUITS YOU HERE IS BLOOD SACRIFICE.

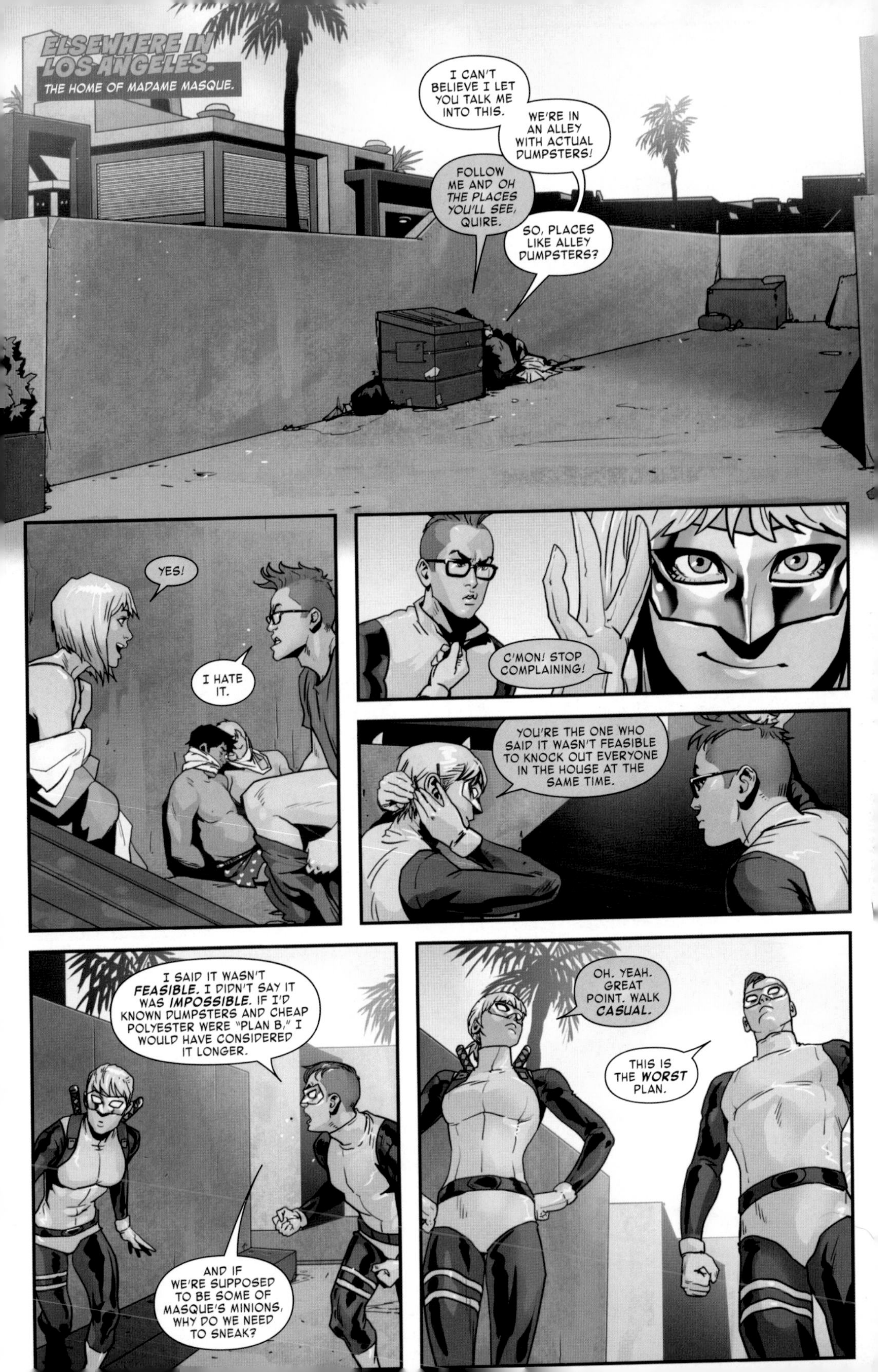
ELSEWHERE IN LOS ANGELES.
THE HOME OF MADAME MASQUE.
I CAN'T BELIEVE I LET YOU TALK ME INTO THIS.
WE'RE IN AN ALLEY WITH ACTUAL DUMPSTERS!
FOLLOW ME AND OH THE PLACES YOU'LL SEE, QUIRE.
SO, PLACES LIKE ALLEY DUMPSTERS?
YES!
I HATE IT.
C'MON! STOP COMPLAINING!
YOU'RE THE ONE WHO SAID IT WASN'T FEASIBLE TO KNOCK OUT EVERYONE IN THE HOUSE AT THE SAME TIME.
I SAID IT WASN'T FEASIBLE. I DIDN'T SAY IT WAS IMPOSSIBLE. IF I'D KNOWN DUMPSTERS AND CHEAP POLYESTER WERE "PLAN B," I WOULD HAVE CONSIDERED IT LONGER.
AND IF WE'RE SUPPOSED TO BE SOME OF MASQUE'S MINIONS, WHY DO WE NEED TO SNEAK?
OH. YEAH. GREAT POINT. WALK CASUAL.
THIS IS THE WORST PLAN.

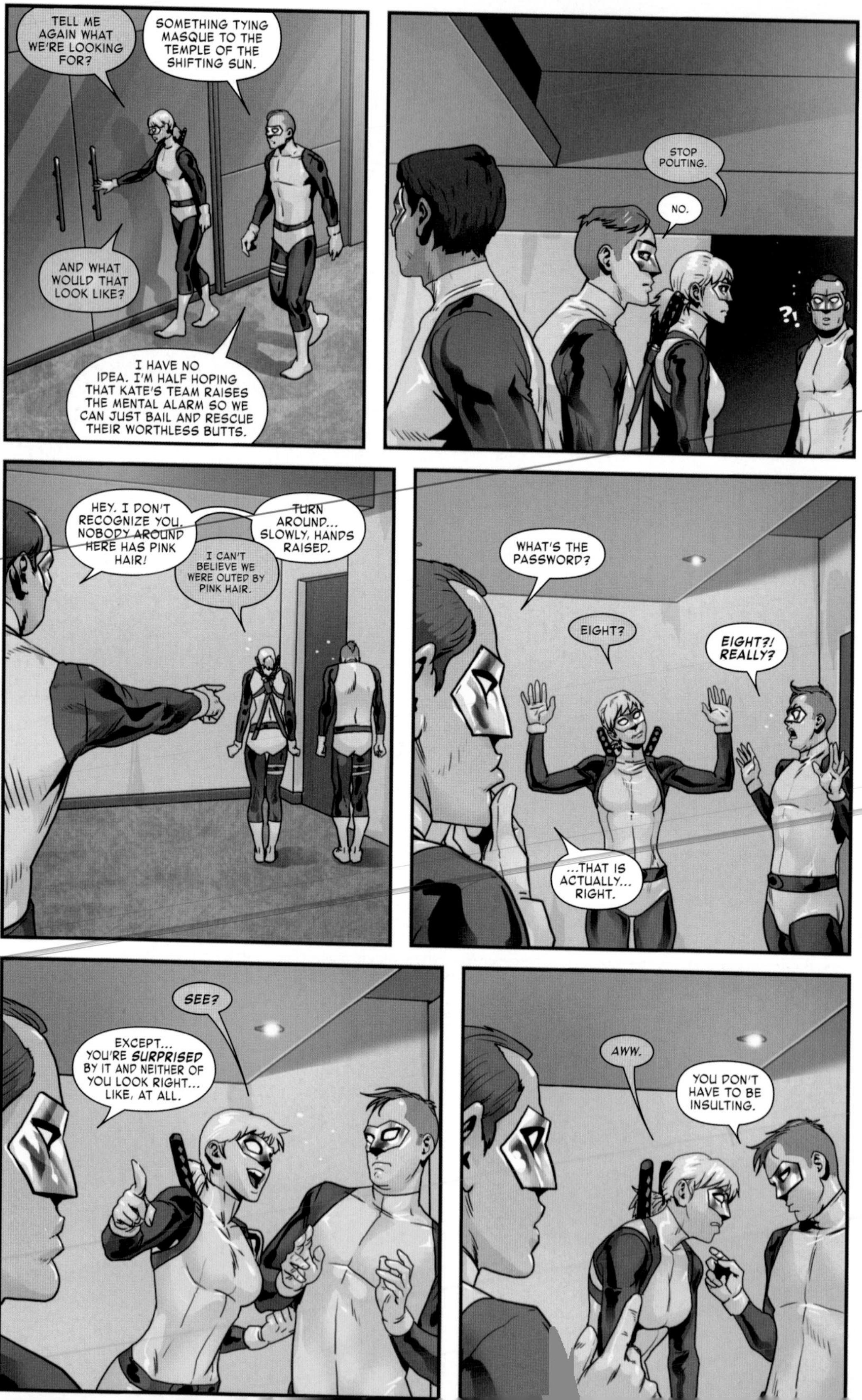
TELL ME AGAIN WHAT WE'RE LOOKING FOR?
SOMETHING TYING MASQUE TO THE TEMPLE OF THE SHIFTING SUN.
AND WHAT WOULD THAT LOOK LIKE?
I HAVE NO IDEA. I'M HALF HOPING THAT KATE'S TEAM RAISES THE MENTAL ALARM SO WE CAN JUST BAIL AND RESCUE THEIR WORTHLESS BUTTS.
STOP POUTING.
NO.
?!
HEY. I DON'T RECOGNIZE YOU. NOBODY AROUND HERE HAS PINK HAIR!
TURN AROUND... SLOWLY, HANDS RAISED.
I CAN'T BELIEVE WE WERE OUTED BY PINK HAIR.
WHAT'S THE PASSWORD?
EIGHT?
EIGHT?! REALLY?
...THAT IS ACTUALLY... RIGHT.
SEE?
EXCEPT... YOU'RE SURPRISED BY IT AND NEITHER OF YOU LOOK RIGHT... LIKE, AT ALL.
AWW.
YOU DON'T HAVE TO BE INSULTING.

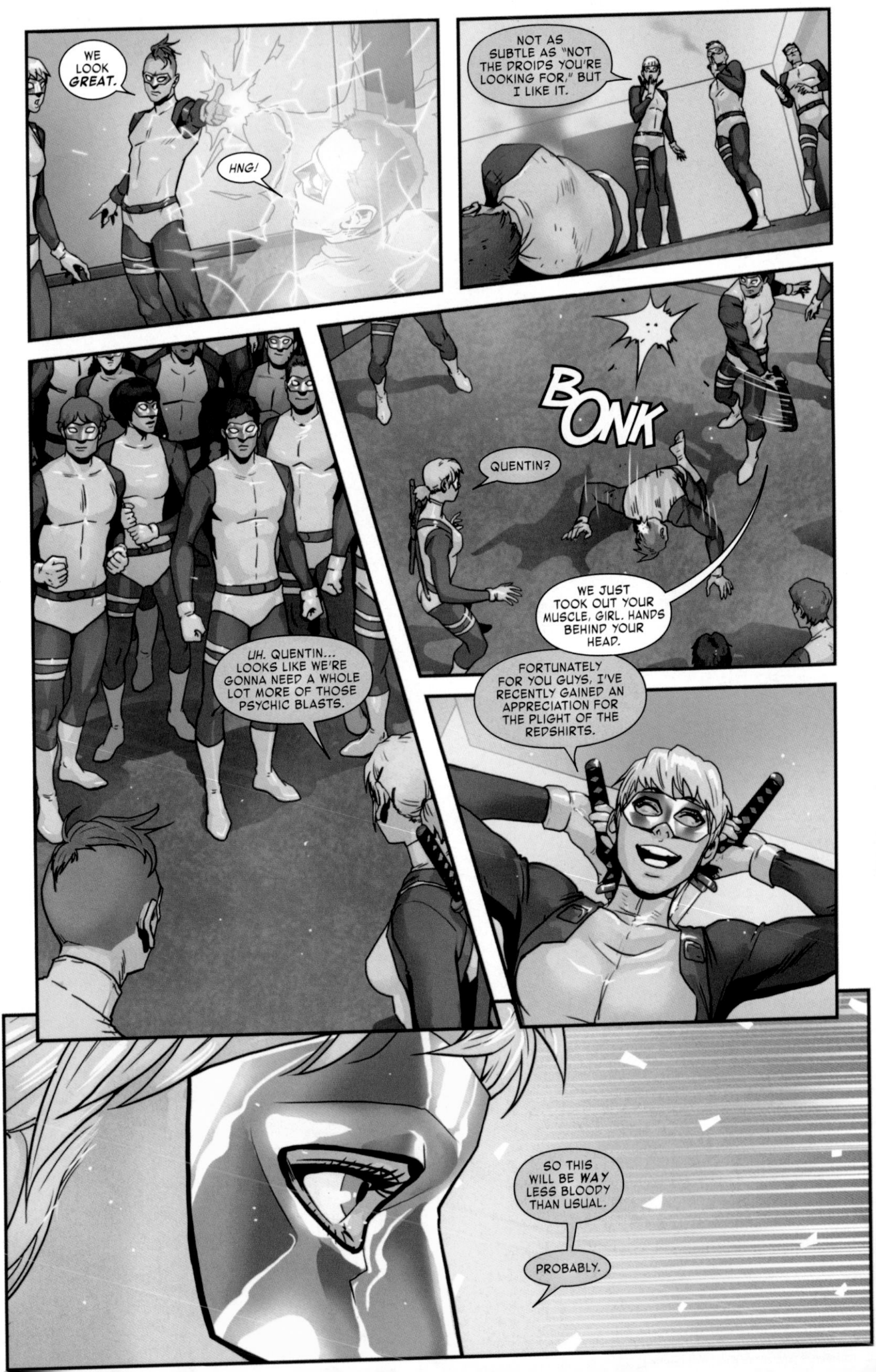
WE LOOK GREAT.
HNG!
NOT AS SUBTLE AS "NOT THE DROIDS YOU'RE LOOKING FOR," BUT I LIKE IT.
UH. QUENTIN... LOOKS LIKE WE'RE GONNA NEED A WHOLE LOT MORE OF THOSE PSYCHIC BLASTS.
BONK
QUENTIN?
WE JUST TOOK OUT YOUR MUSCLE, GIRL. HANDS BEHIND YOUR HEAD.
FORTUNATELY FOR YOU GUYS, I'VE RECENTLY GAINED AN APPRECIATION FOR THE PLIGHT OF THE REDSHIRTS.
SO THIS WILL BE WAY LESS BLOODY THAN USUAL.
PROBABLY.

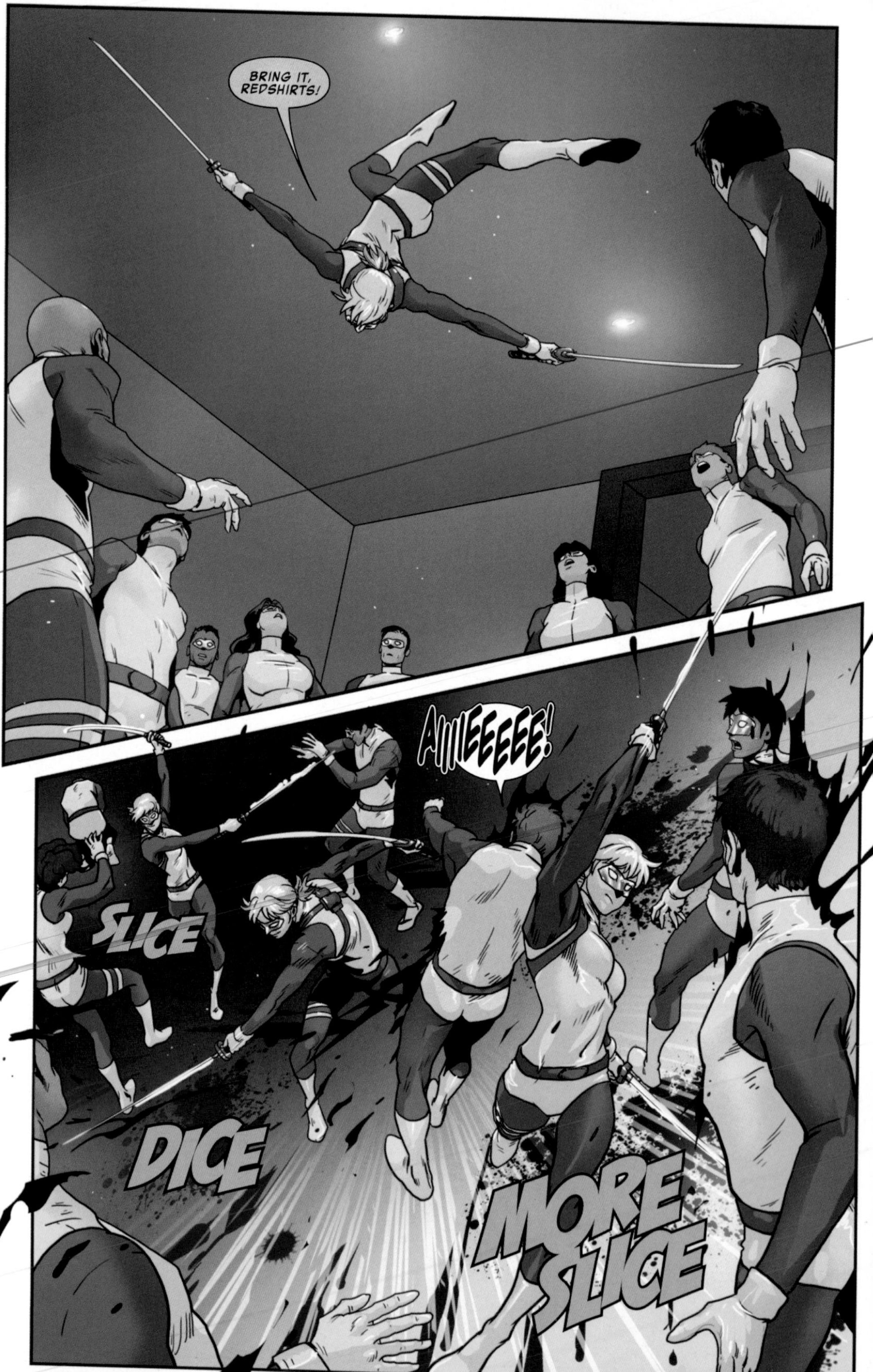
BRING IT, REDSHIRTS!
AIIIEEEEE!
SLICE
DICE
MORE SLICE

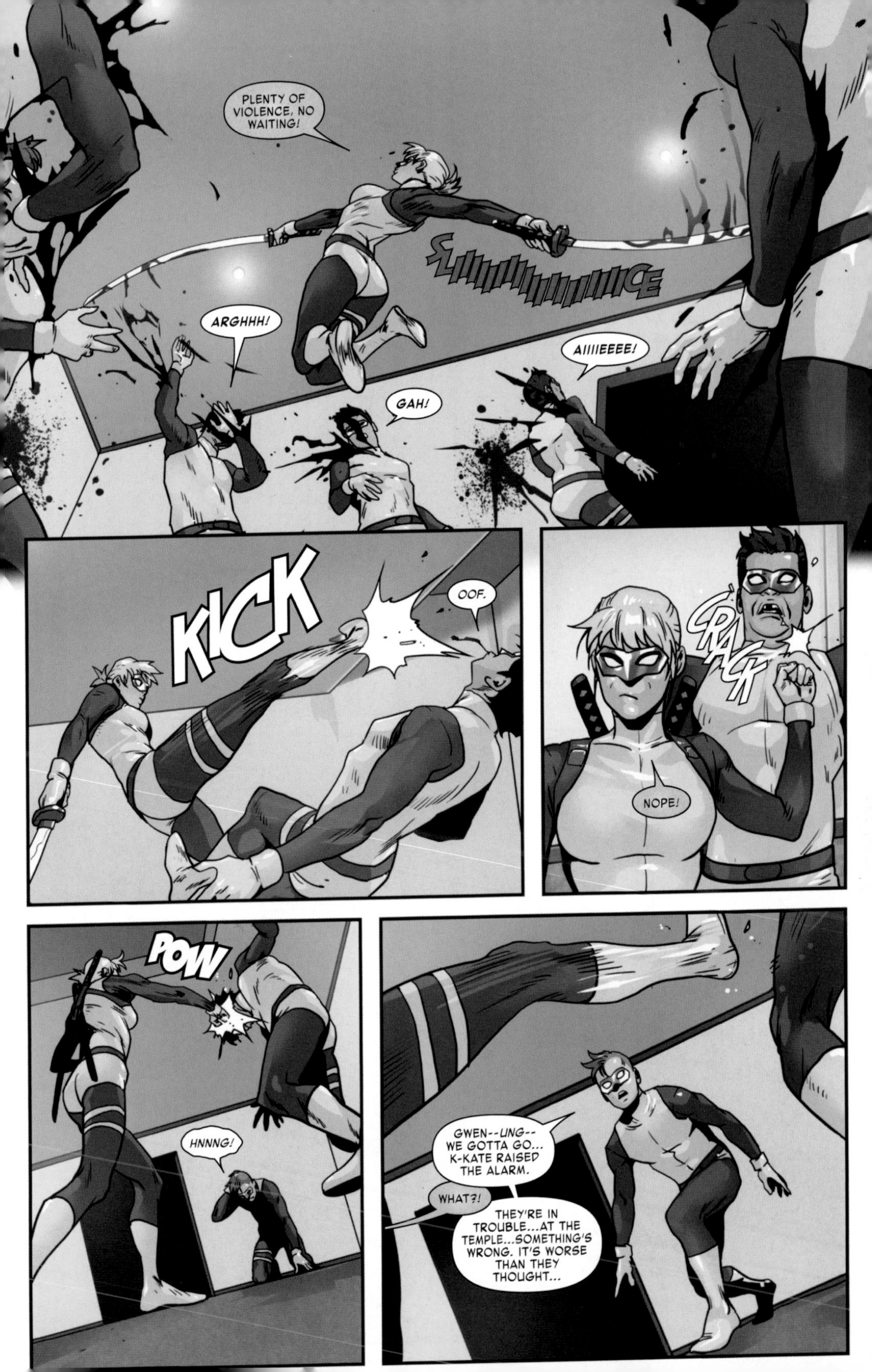
PLENTY OF VIOLENCE, NO WAITING!
SLIIIIIIIIIIIIICE
ARGHHH!
GAH!
AIIIIEEEE!
KICK
OOF.
CRACK
NOPE!
POW
HNNNG!
GWEN--UNG-- WE GOTTA GO... K-KATE RAISED THE ALARM.
WHAT?!
THEY'RE IN TROUBLE...AT THE TEMPLE...SOMETHING'S WRONG. IT'S WORSE THAN THEY THOUGHT...

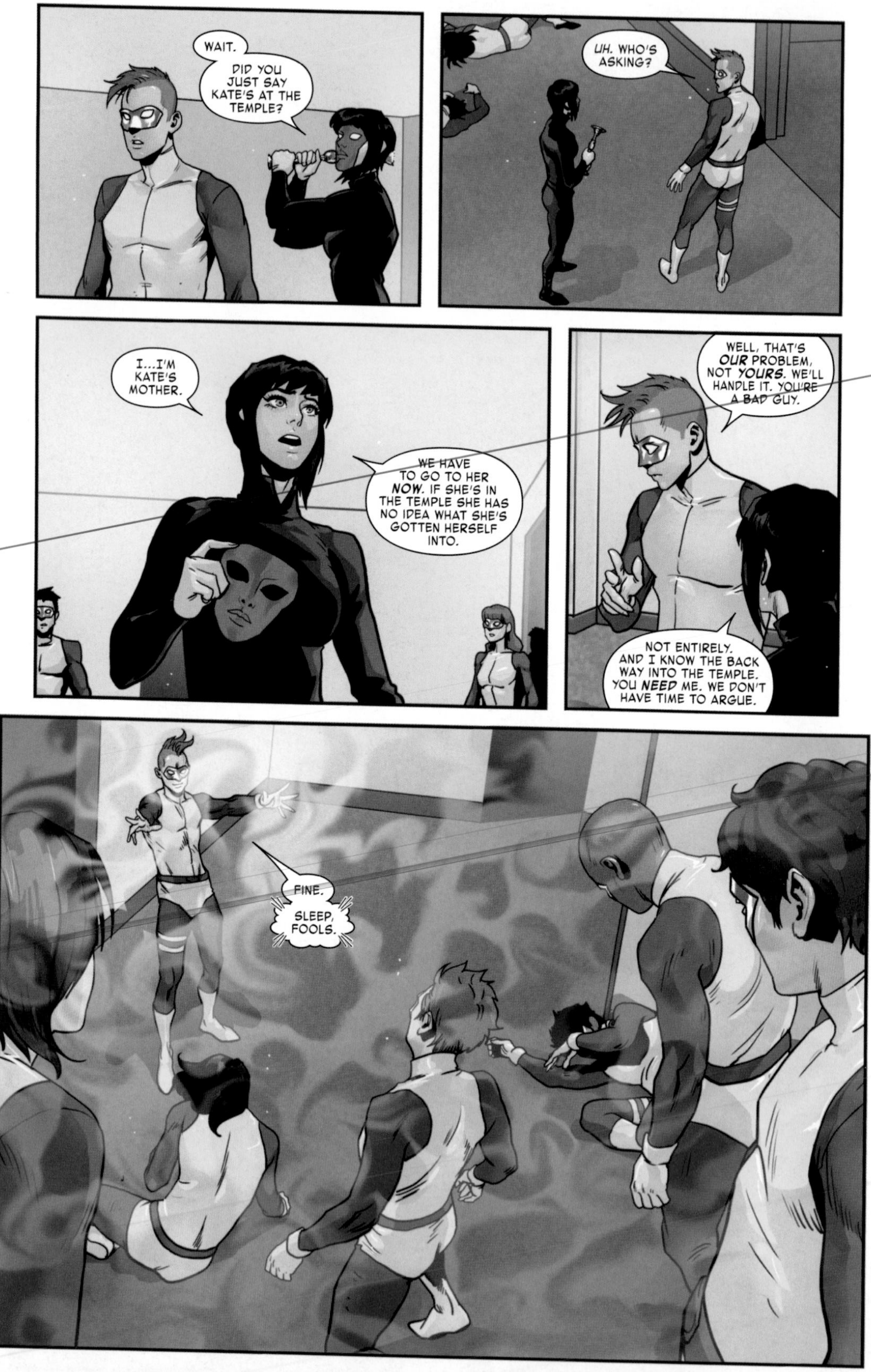
WAIT.
DID YOU JUST SAY KATE'S AT THE TEMPLE?
UH. WHO'S ASKING?
I...I'M KATE'S MOTHER.
WE HAVE TO GO TO HER NOW. IF SHE'S IN THE TEMPLE SHE HAS NO IDEA WHAT SHE'S GOTTEN HERSELF INTO.
WELL, THAT'S OUR PROBLEM, NOT YOURS. WE'LL HANDLE IT. YOU'RE A BAD GUY.
NOT ENTIRELY. AND I KNOW THE BACK WAY INTO THE TEMPLE. YOU NEED ME. WE DON'T HAVE TIME TO ARGUE.
FINE.
SLEEP, FOOLS.

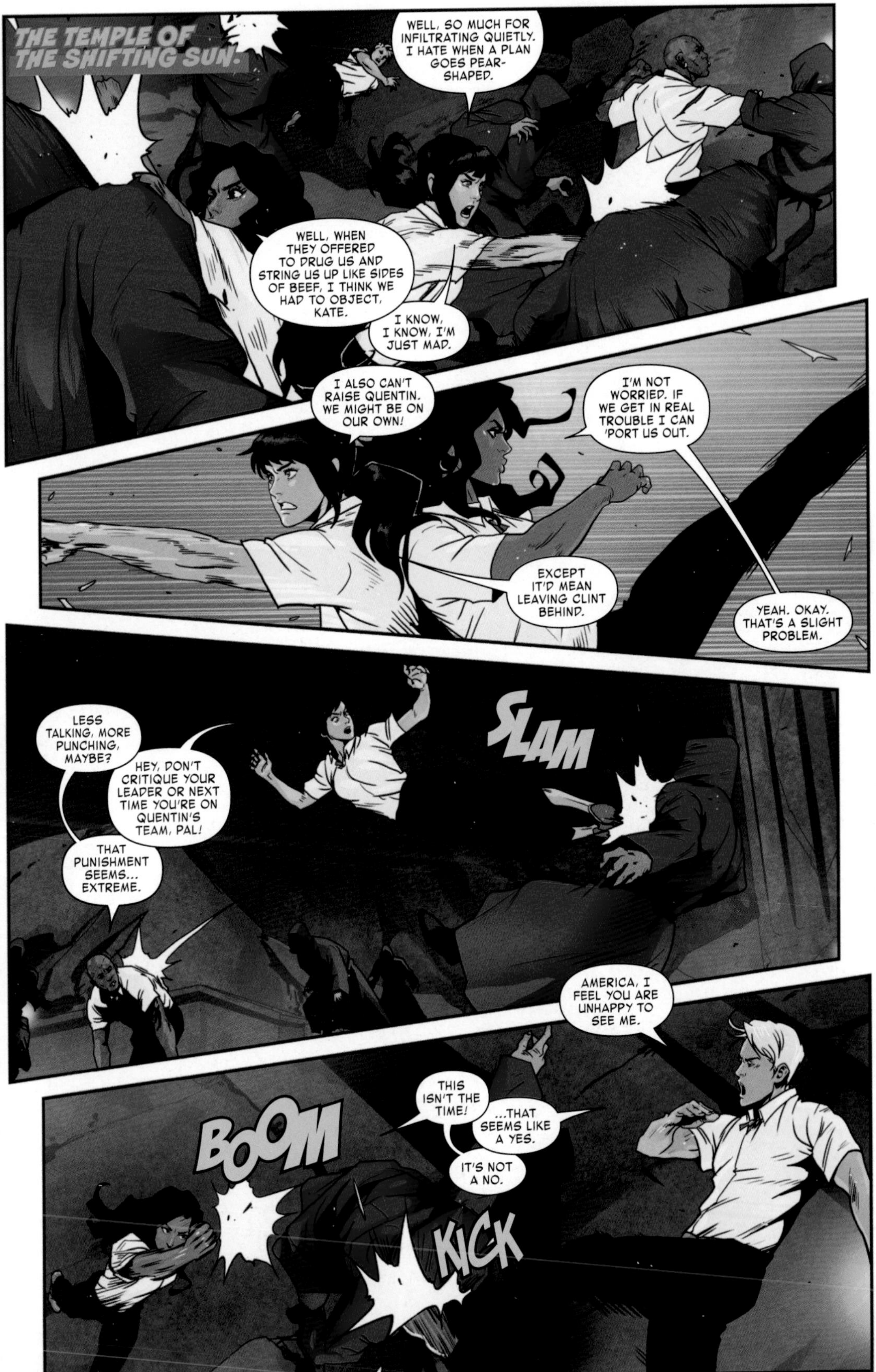
THE TEMPLE OF THE SHIFTING SUN.
WELL, SO MUCH FOR INFILTRATING QUIETLY. I HATE WHEN A PLAN GOES PEAR-SHAPED.
WELL, WHEN THEY OFFERED TO DRUG US AND STRING US UP LIKE SIDES OF BEEF, I THINK WE HAD TO OBJECT, KATE.
I KNOW, I KNOW, I'M JUST MAD.
I ALSO CAN'T RAISE QUENTIN. WE MIGHT BE ON OUR OWN!
I'M NOT WORRIED. IF WE GET IN REAL TROUBLE I CAN 'PORT US OUT.
EXCEPT IT'D MEAN LEAVING CLINT BEHIND.
YEAH. OKAY. THAT'S A SLIGHT PROBLEM.
LESS TALKING, MORE PUNCHING, MAYBE?
HEY, DON'T CRITIQUE YOUR LEADER OR NEXT TIME YOU'RE ON QUENTIN'S TEAM, PAL!
THAT PUNISHMENT SEEMS... EXTREME.
SLAM
AMERICA, I FEEL YOU ARE UNHAPPY TO SEE ME.
BOOM
THIS ISN'T THE TIME!
...THAT SEEMS LIKE A YES.
IT'S NOT A NO.
KICK

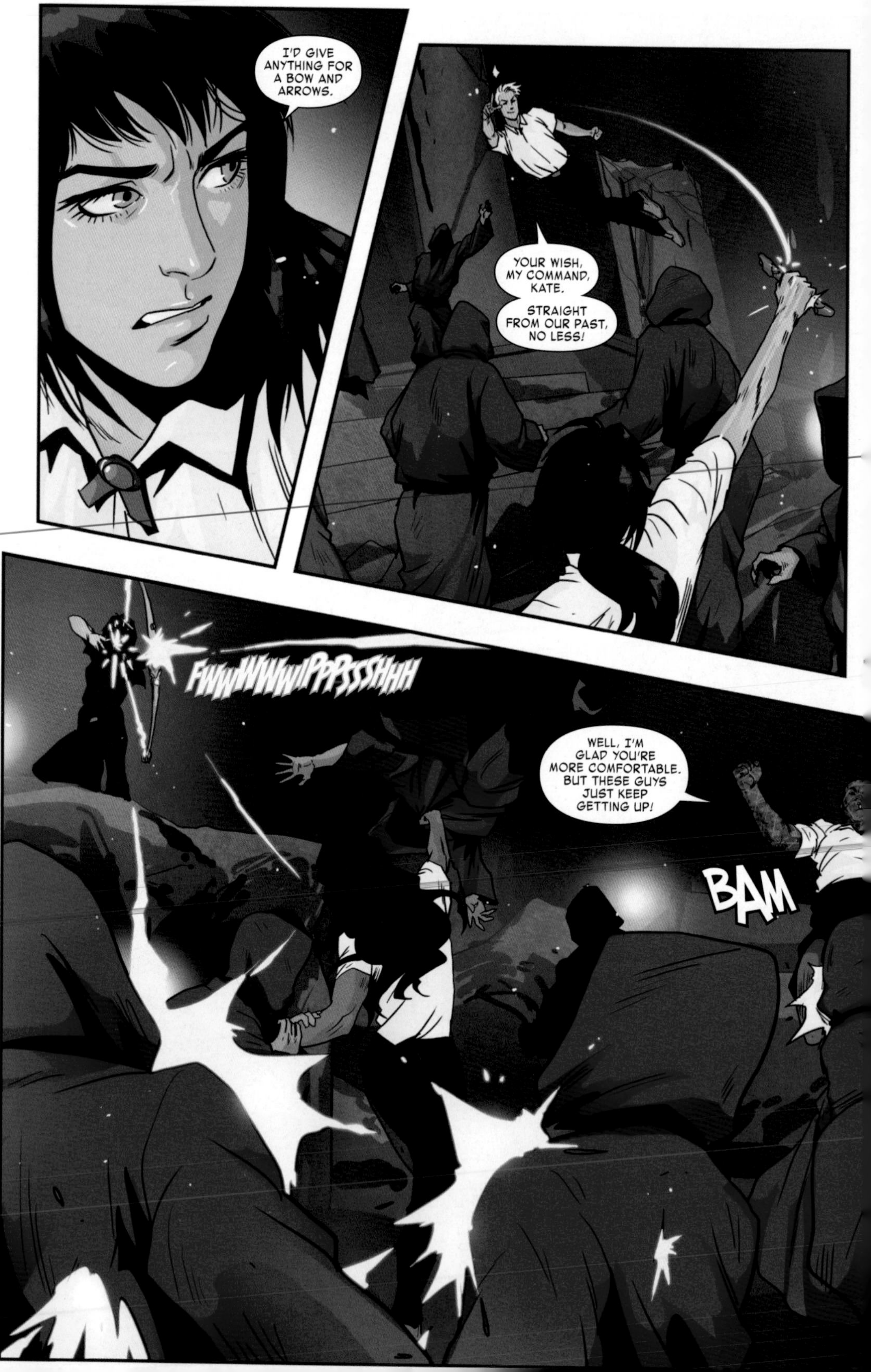
I'D GIVE ANYTHING FOR A BOW AND ARROWS.
YOUR WISH, MY COMMAND, KATE.
STRAIGHT FROM OUR PAST, NO LESS!
FWWWWWWIPPPSSSHHH
WELL, I'M GLAD YOU'RE MORE COMFORTABLE. BUT THESE GUYS JUST KEEP GETTING UP!
BAM

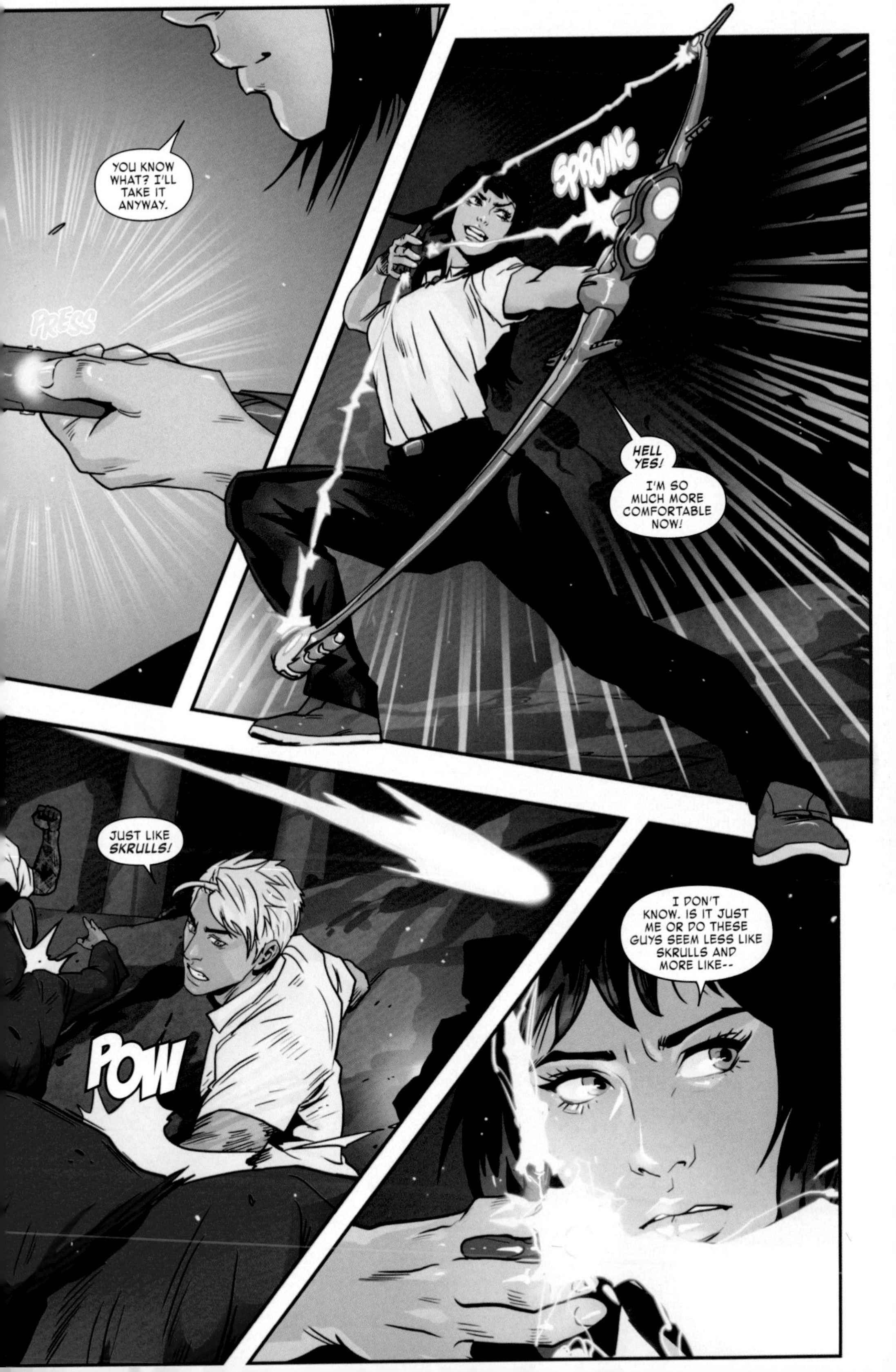
YOU KNOW WHAT? I'LL TAKE IT ANYWAY.
PRESS
SPROING
HELL YES!
I'M SO MUCH MORE COMFORTABLE NOW!
JUST LIKE SKRULLS!
POW
I DON'T KNOW. IS IT JUST ME OR DO THESE GUYS SEEM LESS LIKE SKRULLS AND MORE LIKE--

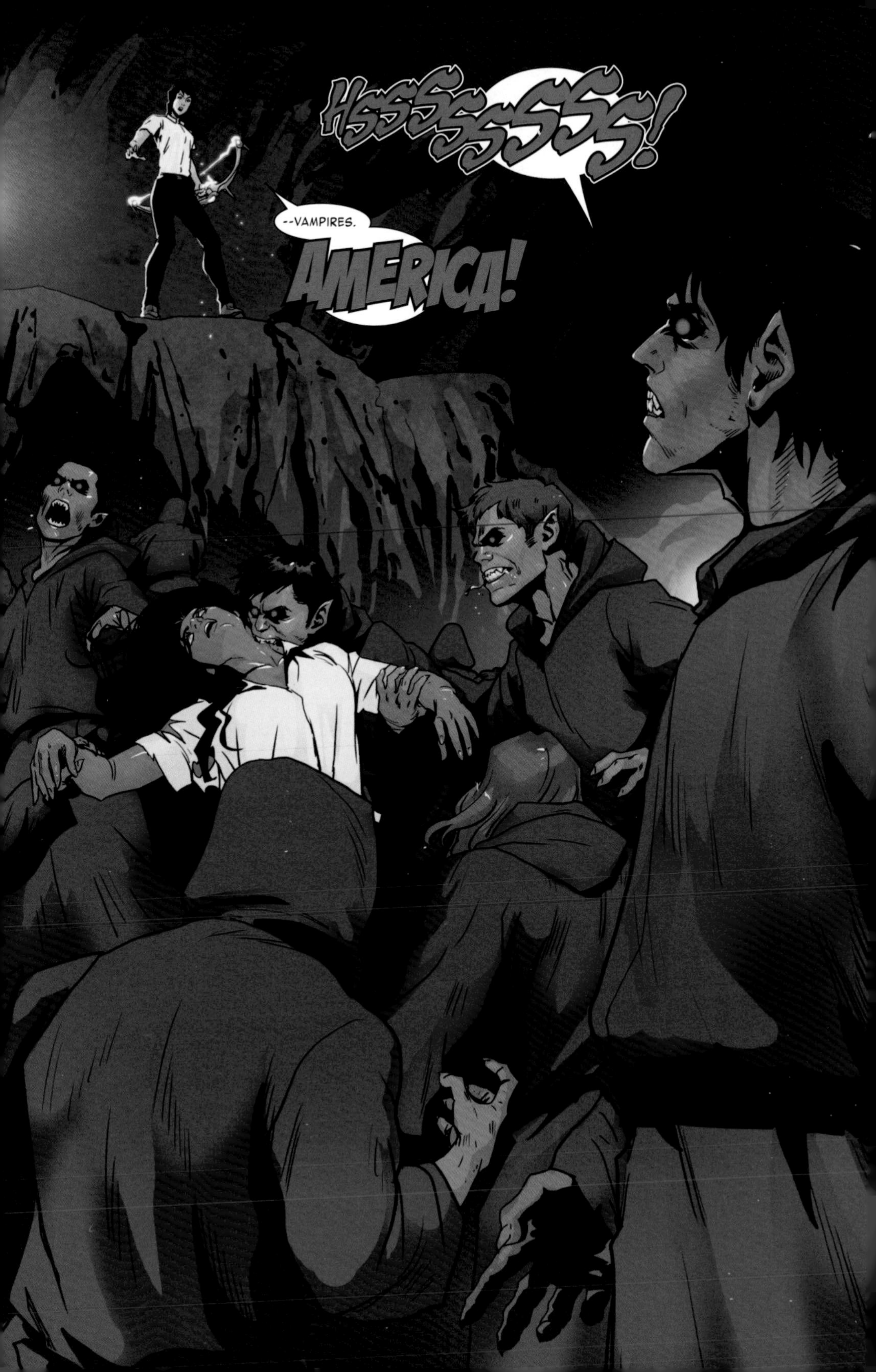
HSSSSSSSS!
--VAMPIRES.
AMERICA!

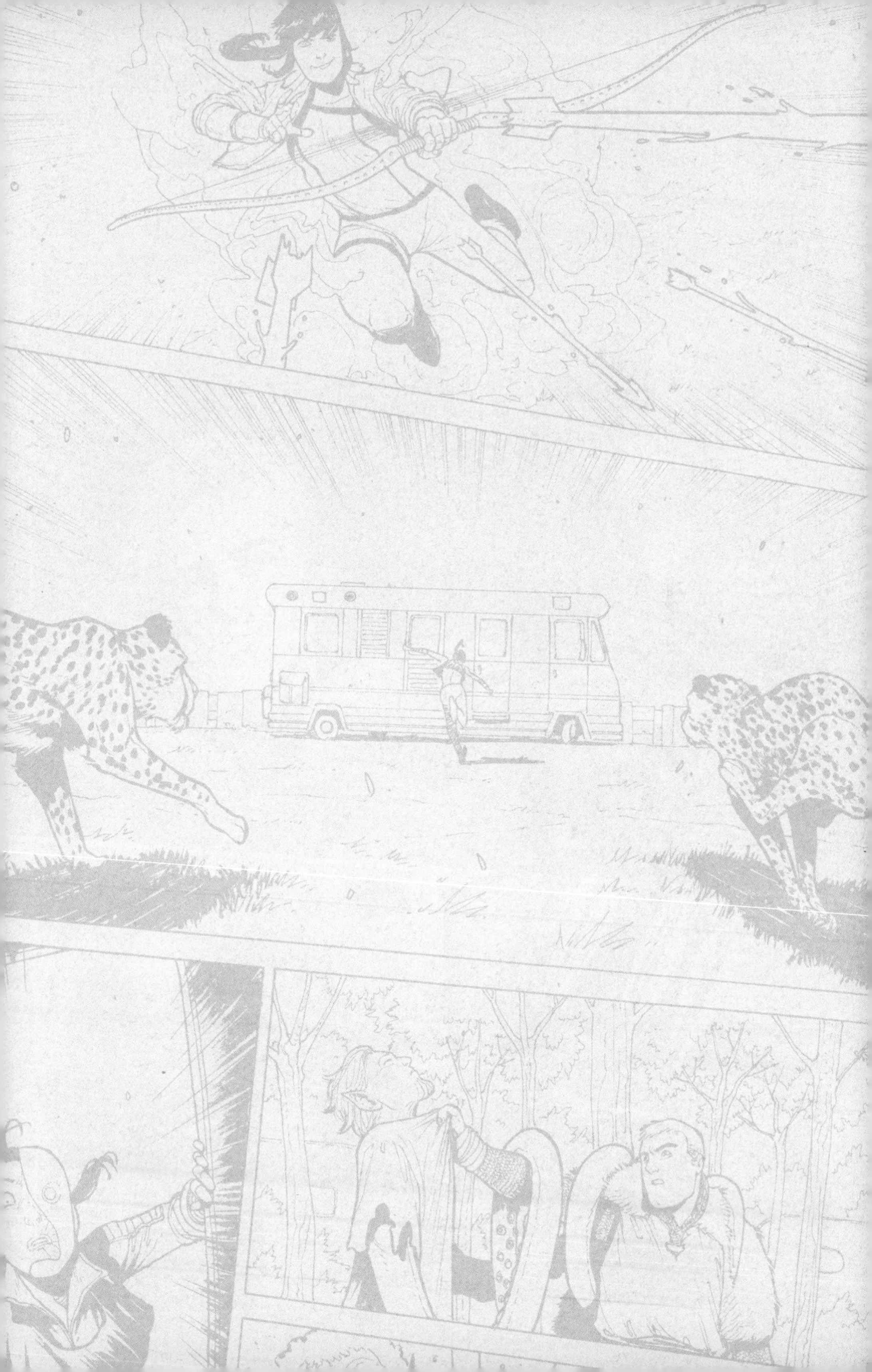

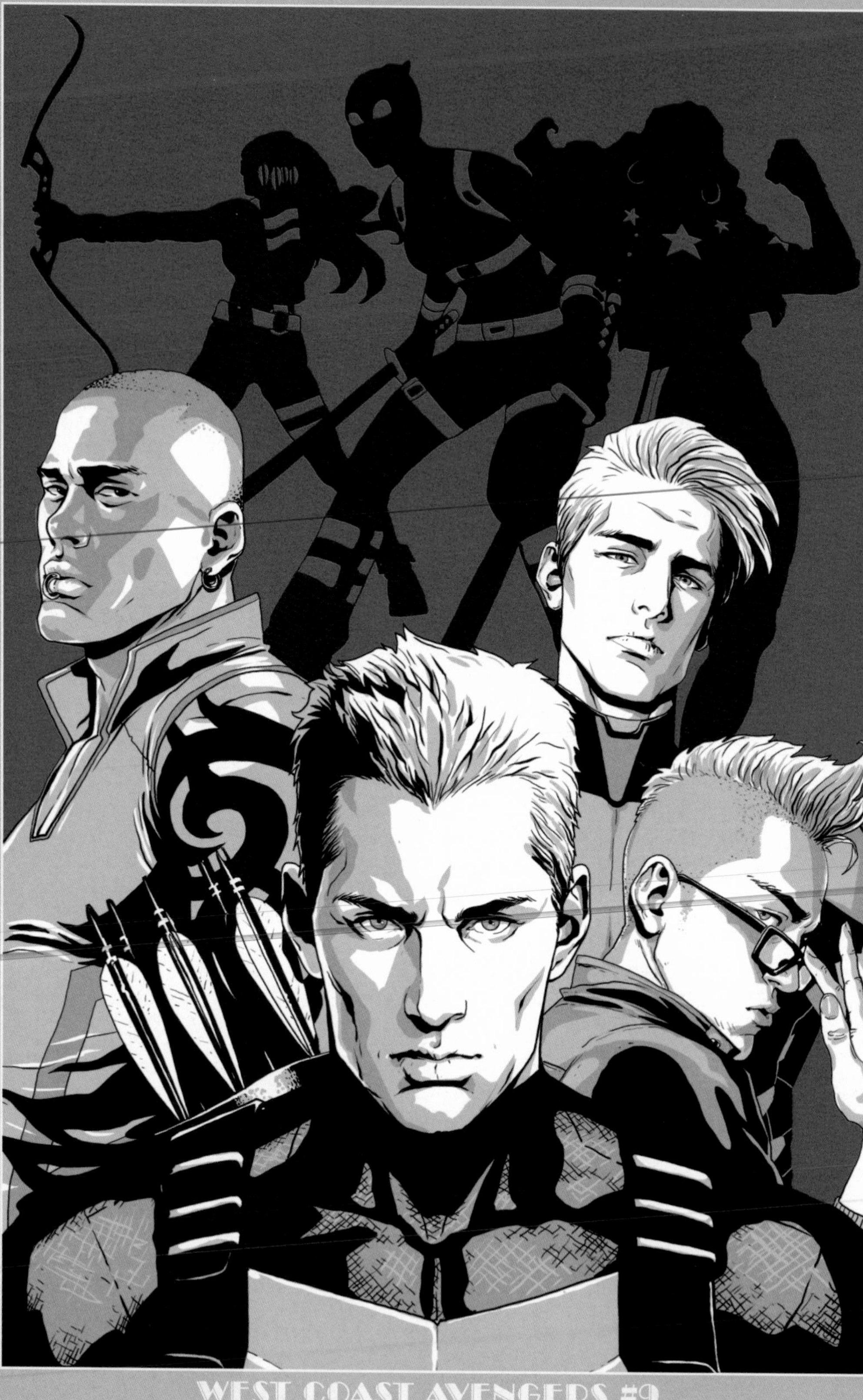

WEST COAST AVENGERS #9

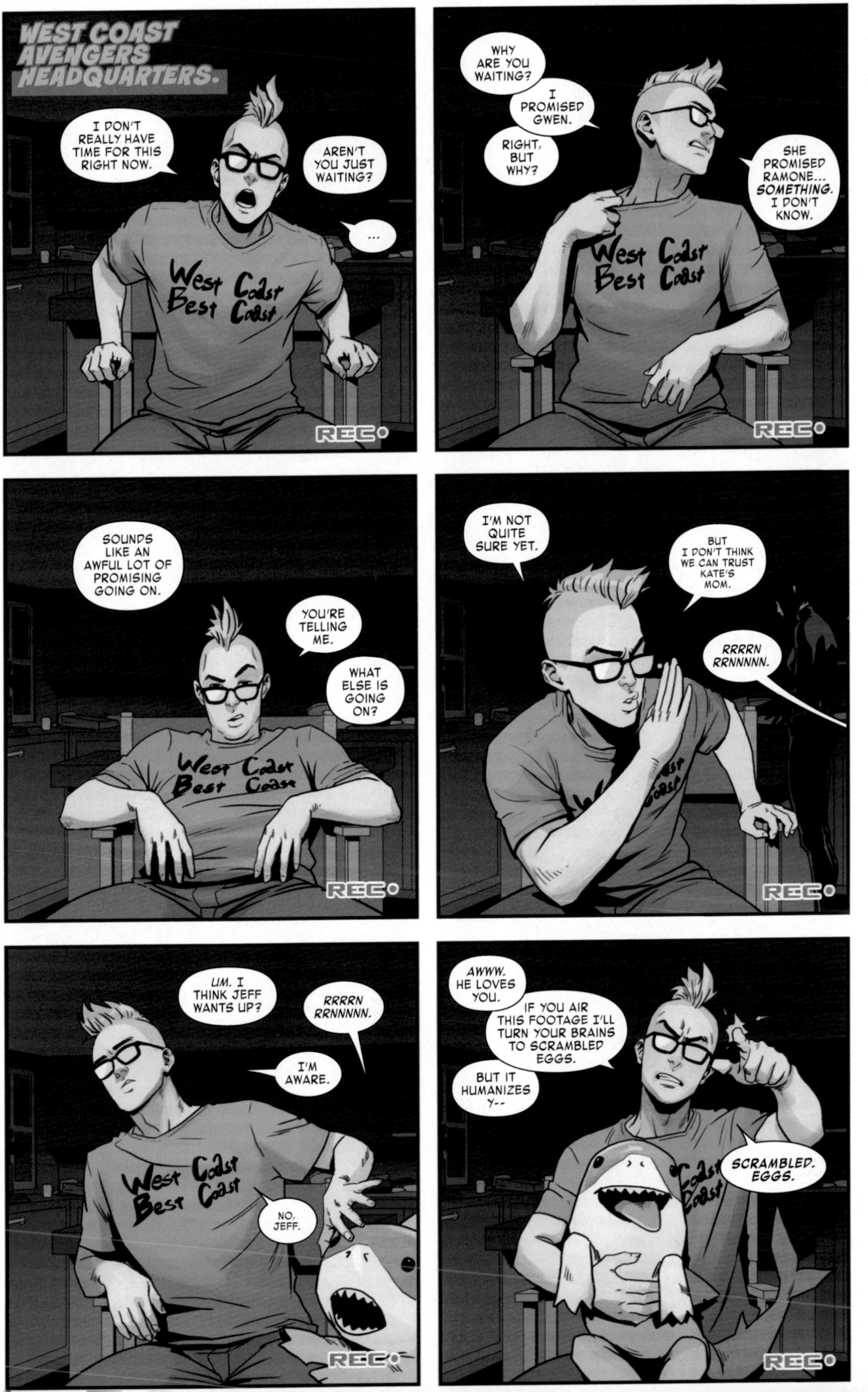
WEST COAST AVENGERS HEADQUARTERS.
I DON'T REALLY HAVE TIME FOR THIS RIGHT NOW.
AREN'T YOU JUST WAITING?
...
West Coast Best Coast
REC
WHY ARE YOU WAITING?
I PROMISED GWEN.
RIGHT, BUT WHY?
SHE PROMISED RAMONE... SOMETHING. I DON'T KNOW.
West Coast Best Coast
REC
SOUNDS LIKE AN AWFUL LOT OF PROMISING GOING ON.
YOU'RE TELLING ME.
WHAT ELSE IS GOING ON?
West Coast Best Coast
REC
I'M NOT QUITE SURE YET.
BUT I DON'T THINK WE CAN TRUST KATE'S MOM.
RRRRN RRNNNNN.
REC
UM. I THINK JEFF WANTS UP?
RRRRN RRNNNNN.
I'M AWARE.
West Coast Best Coast
NO, JEFF.
REC
AWWW. HE LOVES YOU.
IF YOU AIR THIS FOOTAGE I'LL TURN YOUR BRAINS TO SCRAMBLED EGGS.
BUT IT HUMANIZES Y--
SCRAMBLED. EGGS.
REC

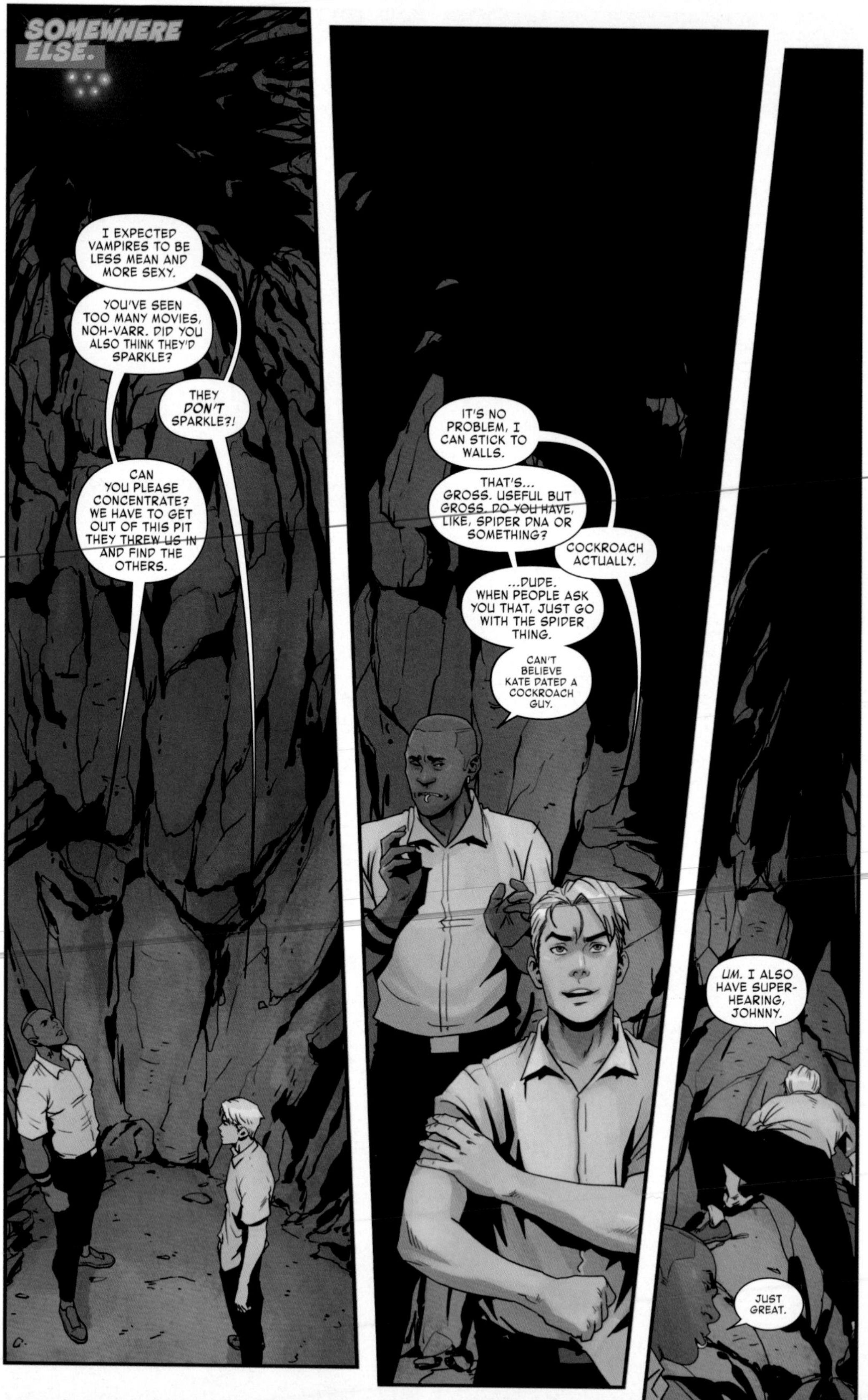
SOMEWHERE ELSE.
I EXPECTED VAMPIRES TO BE LESS MEAN AND MORE SEXY.
YOU'VE SEEN TOO MANY MOVIES, NOH-VARR. DID YOU ALSO THINK THEY'D SPARKLE?
THEY DON'T SPARKLE?!
CAN YOU PLEASE CONCENTRATE? WE HAVE TO GET OUT OF THIS PIT THEY THREW US IN AND FIND THE OTHERS.
IT'S NO PROBLEM, I CAN STICK TO WALLS.
THAT'S... GROSS. USEFUL BUT GROSS. DO YOU HAVE, LIKE, SPIDER DNA OR SOMETHING?
COCKROACH ACTUALLY.
...DUDE. WHEN PEOPLE ASK YOU THAT, JUST GO WITH THE SPIDER THING.
CAN'T BELIEVE KATE DATED A COCKROACH GUY.
UM. I ALSO HAVE SUPER-HEARING, JOHNNY.
JUST GREAT.

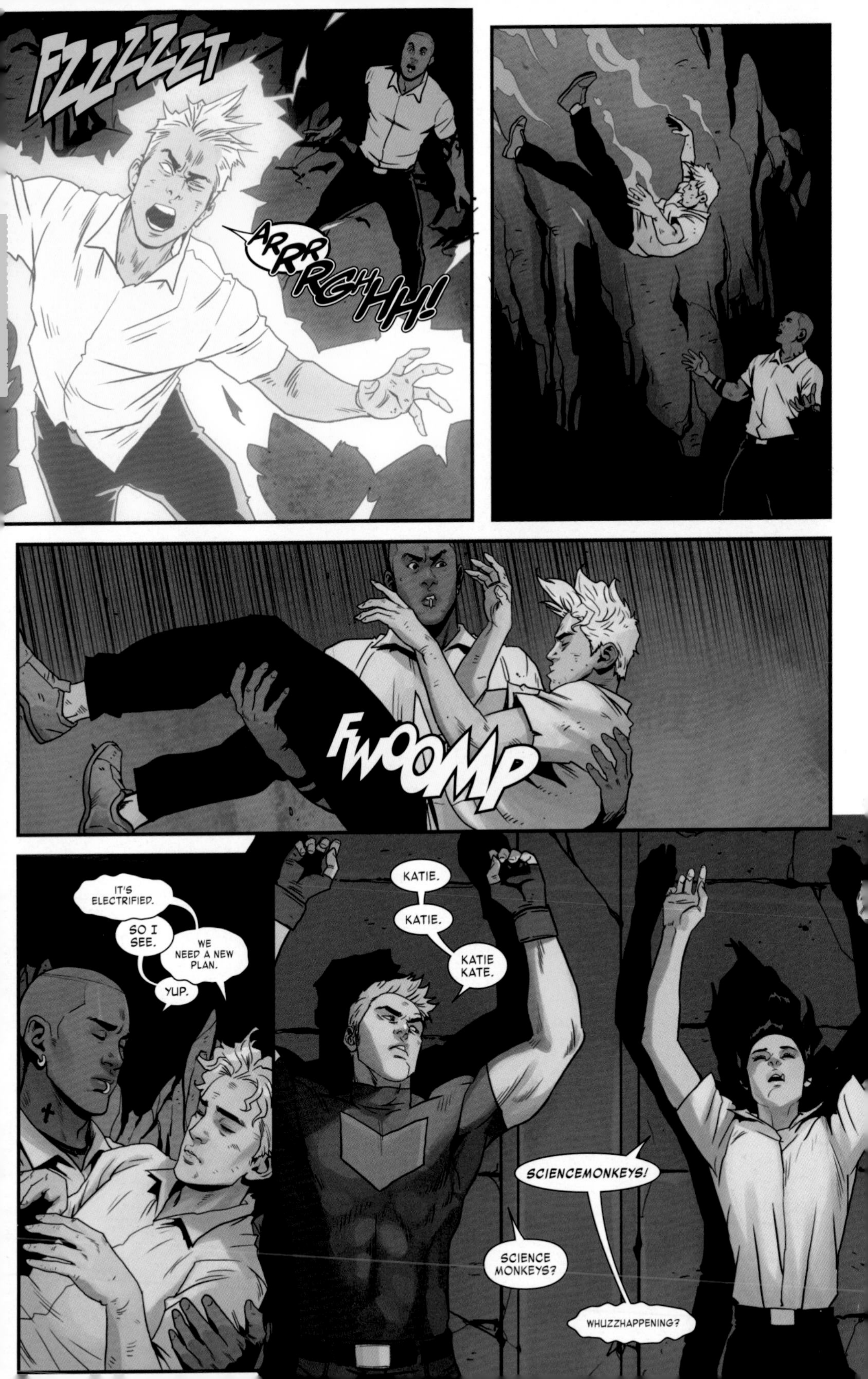
FZZZZZT
ARRRRGHHH!
FWOOMP
IT'S ELECTRIFIED.
SO I SEE.
WE NEED A NEW PLAN.
YUP.
KATIE.
KATIE.
KATIE KATE.
SCIENCEMONKEYS!
SCIENCE MONKEYS?
WHUZZHAPPENING?

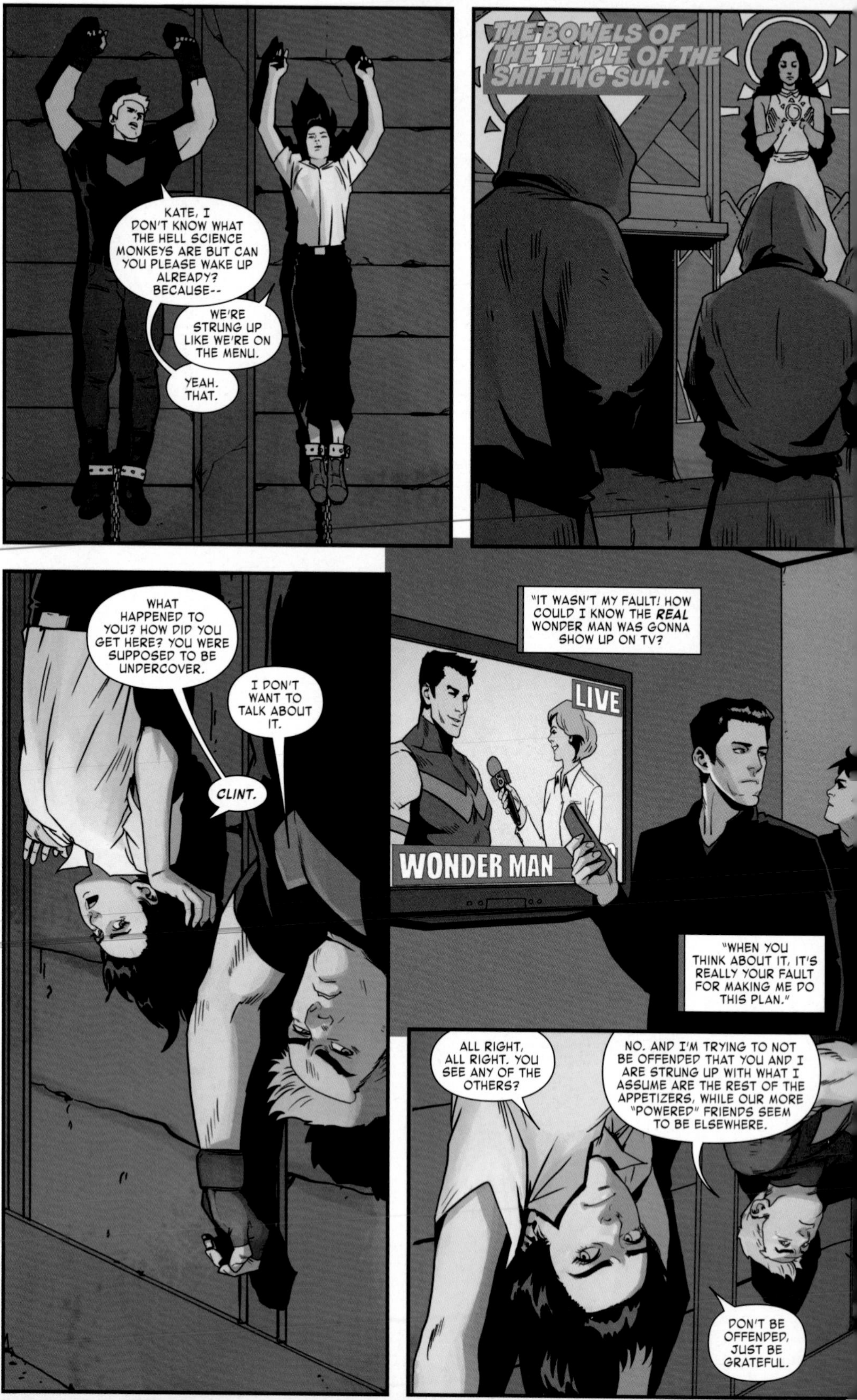
KATE, I DON'T KNOW WHAT THE HELL SCIENCE MONKEYS ARE BUT CAN YOU PLEASE WAKE UP ALREADY? BECAUSE--
WE'RE STRUNG UP LIKE WE'RE ON THE MENU.
YEAH. THAT.
THE BOWELS OF THE TEMPLE OF THE SHIFTING SUN.
WHAT HAPPENED TO YOU? HOW DID YOU GET HERE? YOU WERE SUPPOSED TO BE UNDERCOVER.
I DON'T WANT TO TALK ABOUT IT.
CLINT.
"IT WASN'T MY FAULT! HOW COULD I KNOW THE REAL WONDER MAN WAS GONNA SHOW UP ON TV?
LIVE
WONDER MAN
"WHEN YOU THINK ABOUT IT, IT'S REALLY YOUR FAULT FOR MAKING ME DO THIS PLAN."
ALL RIGHT, ALL RIGHT. YOU SEE ANY OF THE OTHERS?
NO. AND I'M TRYING TO NOT BE OFFENDED THAT YOU AND I ARE STRUNG UP WITH WHAT I ASSUME ARE THE REST OF THE APPETIZERS, WHILE OUR MORE "POWERED" FRIENDS SEEM TO BE ELSEWHERE.
DON'T BE OFFENDED, JUST BE GRATEFUL.

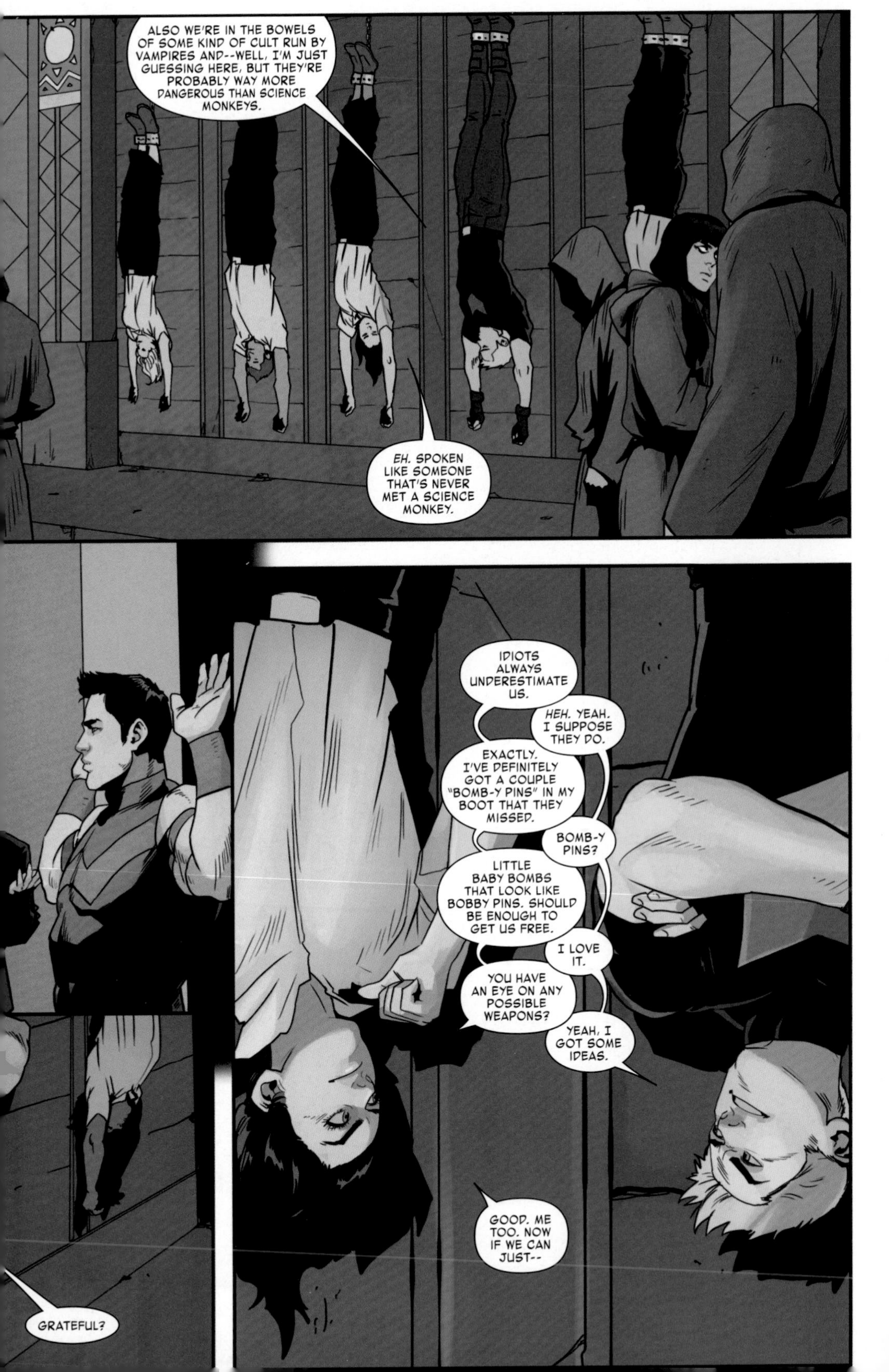
ALSO WE'RE IN THE BOWELS OF SOME KIND OF CULT RUN BY VAMPIRES AND--WELL, I'M JUST GUESSING HERE, BUT THEY'RE PROBABLY WAY MORE DANGEROUS THAN SCIENCE MONKEYS.
EH. SPOKEN LIKE SOMEONE THAT'S NEVER MET A SCIENCE MONKEY.
IDIOTS ALWAYS UNDERESTIMATE US.
HEH. YEAH. I SUPPOSE THEY DO.
EXACTLY. I'VE DEFINITELY GOT A COUPLE "BOMB-Y PINS" IN MY BOOT THAT THEY MISSED.
BOMB-Y PINS?
LITTLE BABY BOMBS THAT LOOK LIKE BOBBY PINS. SHOULD BE ENOUGH TO GET US FREE.
I LOVE IT.
YOU HAVE AN EYE ON ANY POSSIBLE WEAPONS?
YEAH, I GOT SOME IDEAS.
GOOD. ME TOO. NOW IF WE CAN JUST--
GRATEFUL?

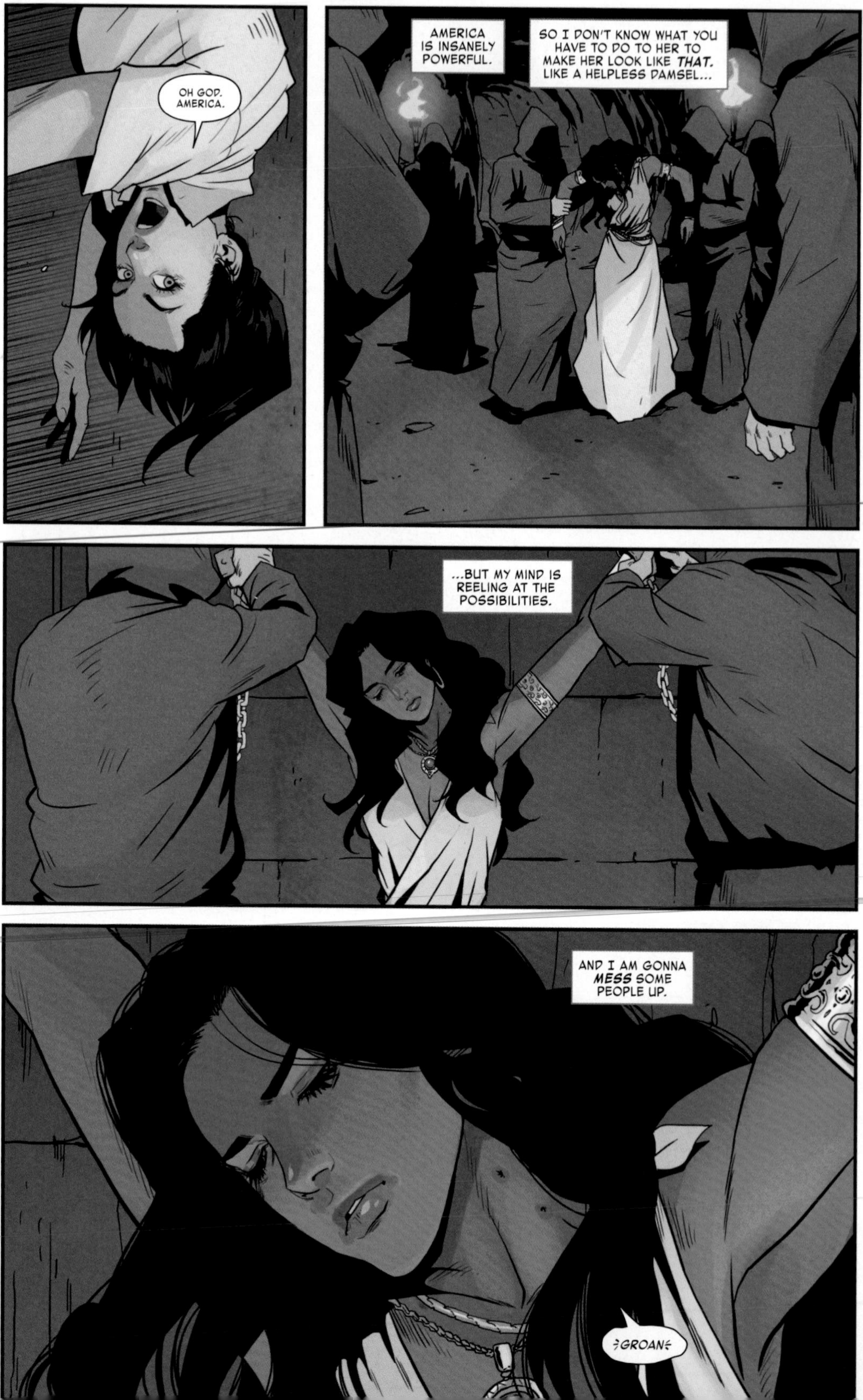
OH GOD. AMERICA.
AMERICA IS INSANELY POWERFUL.
SO I DON'T KNOW WHAT YOU HAVE TO DO TO HER TO MAKE HER LOOK LIKE THAT. LIKE A HELPLESS DAMSEL...
...BUT MY MIND IS REELING AT THE POSSIBILITIES.
AND I AM GONNA MESS SOME PEOPLE UP.
GROAN

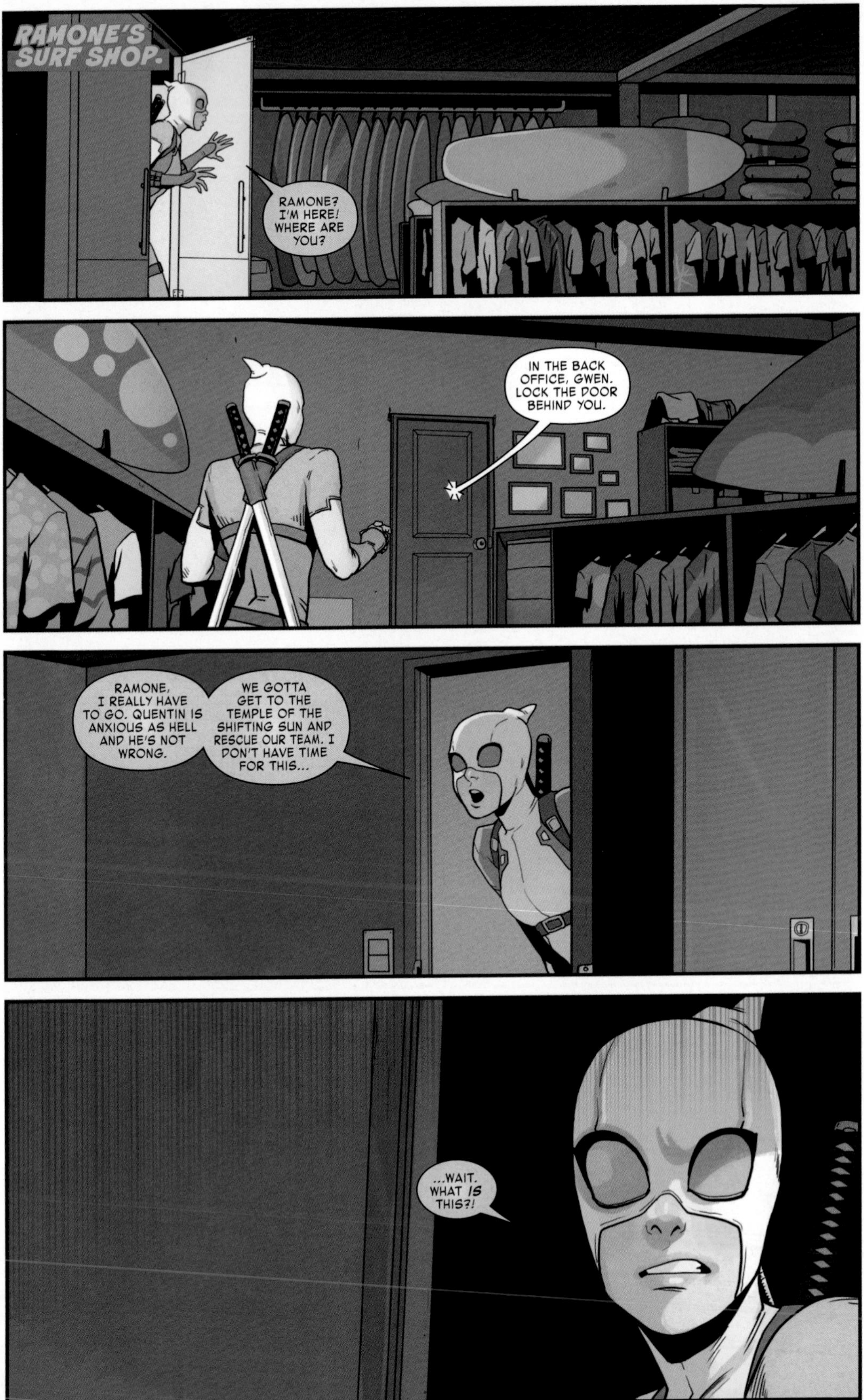
RAMONE'S SURF SHOP.
RAMONE? I'M HERE! WHERE ARE YOU?
IN THE BACK OFFICE, GWEN. LOCK THE DOOR BEHIND YOU.
RAMONE, I REALLY HAVE TO GO. QUENTIN IS ANXIOUS AS HELL AND HE'S NOT WRONG.
WE GOTTA GET TO THE TEMPLE OF THE SHIFTING SUN AND RESCUE OUR TEAM. I DON'T HAVE TIME FOR THIS...
...WAIT. WHAT *IS* THIS?!

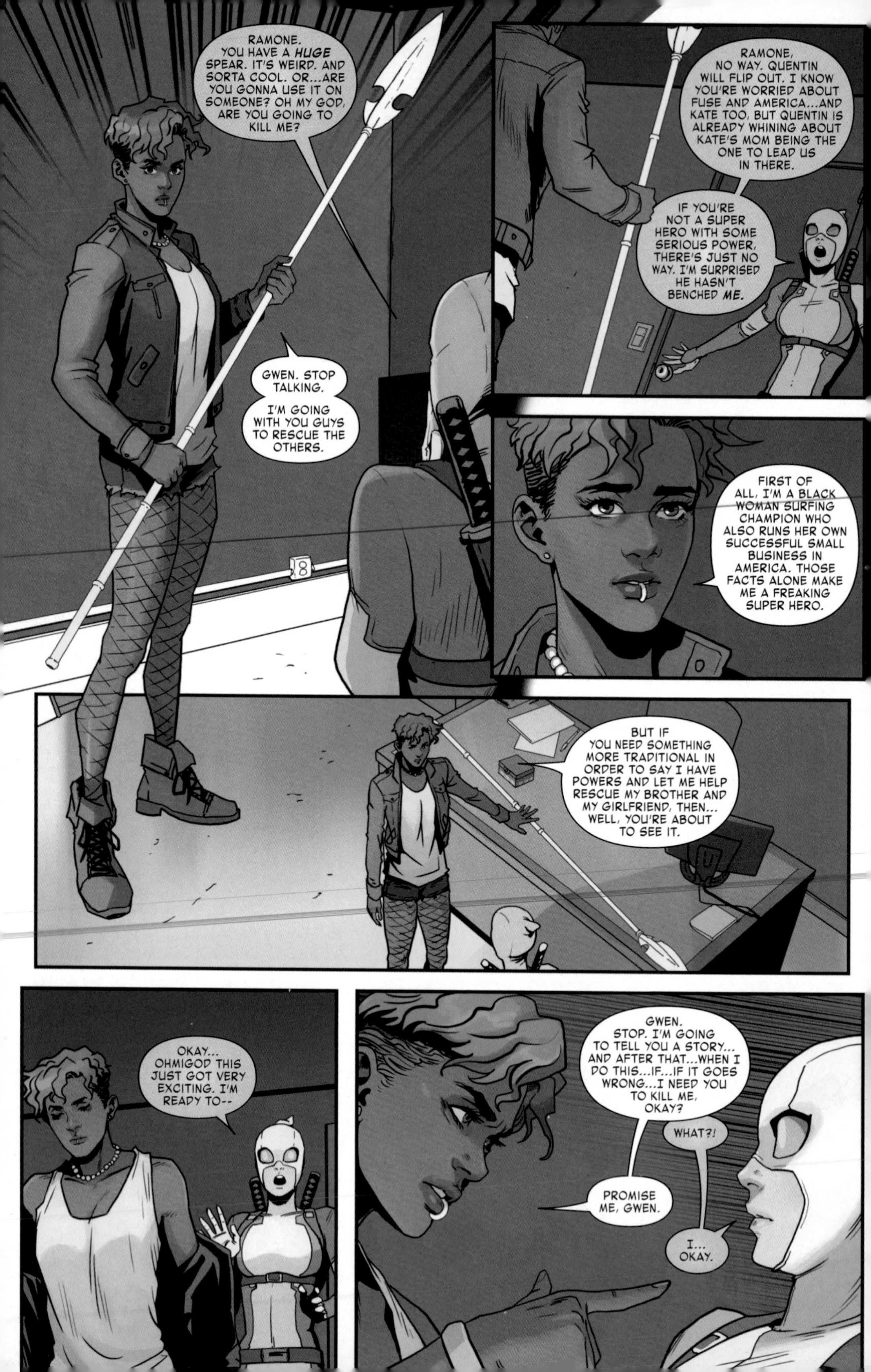
RAMONE. YOU HAVE A ***HUGE*** SPEAR. IT'S WEIRD. AND SORTA COOL. OR...ARE YOU GONNA USE IT ON SOMEONE? OH MY GOD, ARE YOU GOING TO KILL ME?
GWEN. STOP TALKING.
I'M GOING WITH YOU GUYS TO RESCUE THE OTHERS.
RAMONE, NO WAY. QUENTIN WILL FLIP OUT. I KNOW YOU'RE WORRIED ABOUT FUSE AND AMERICA...AND KATE TOO, BUT QUENTIN IS ALREADY WHINING ABOUT KATE'S MOM BEING THE ONE TO LEAD US IN THERE.
IF YOU'RE NOT A SUPER HERO WITH SOME SERIOUS POWER, THERE'S JUST NO WAY. I'M SURPRISED HE HASN'T BENCHED ***ME.***
FIRST OF ALL, I'M A BLACK WOMAN SURFING CHAMPION WHO ALSO RUNS HER OWN SUCCESSFUL SMALL BUSINESS IN AMERICA. THOSE FACTS ALONE MAKE ME A FREAKING SUPER HERO.
BUT IF YOU NEED SOMETHING MORE TRADITIONAL IN ORDER TO SAY I HAVE POWERS AND LET ME HELP RESCUE MY BROTHER AND MY GIRLFRIEND, THEN... WELL, YOU'RE ABOUT TO SEE IT.
OKAY... OHMIGOD THIS JUST GOT VERY EXCITING. I'M READY TO--
GWEN. STOP. I'M GOING TO TELL YOU A STORY... AND AFTER THAT...WHEN I DO THIS...IF...IF IT GOES WRONG...I NEED YOU TO KILL ME, OKAY?
WHAT?!
PROMISE ME, GWEN.
I... OKAY.

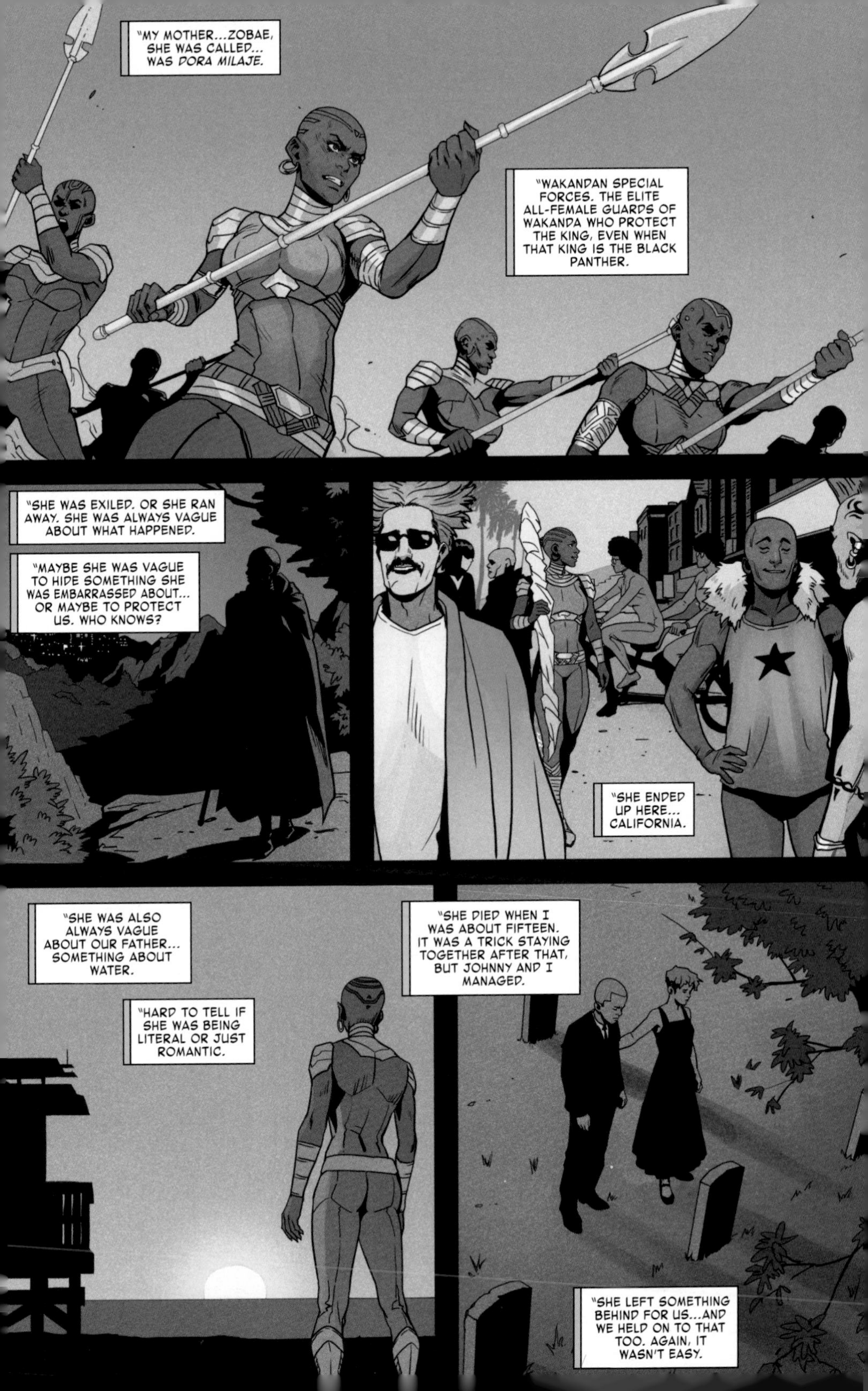
"MY MOTHER...ZOBAE, SHE WAS CALLED... WAS DORA MILAJE.
"WAKANDAN SPECIAL FORCES. THE ELITE ALL-FEMALE GUARDS OF WAKANDA WHO PROTECT THE KING, EVEN WHEN THAT KING IS THE BLACK PANTHER.
"SHE WAS EXILED. OR SHE RAN AWAY. SHE WAS ALWAYS VAGUE ABOUT WHAT HAPPENED.
"MAYBE SHE WAS VAGUE TO HIDE SOMETHING SHE WAS EMBARRASSED ABOUT... OR MAYBE TO PROTECT US. WHO KNOWS?
"SHE ENDED UP HERE... CALIFORNIA.
"SHE WAS ALSO ALWAYS VAGUE ABOUT OUR FATHER... SOMETHING ABOUT WATER.
"HARD TO TELL IF SHE WAS BEING LITERAL OR JUST ROMANTIC.
"SHE DIED WHEN I WAS ABOUT FIFTEEN. IT WAS A TRICK STAYING TOGETHER AFTER THAT, BUT JOHNNY AND I MANAGED.
"SHE LEFT SOMETHING BEHIND FOR US...AND WE HELD ON TO THAT TOO. AGAIN, IT WASN'T EASY.

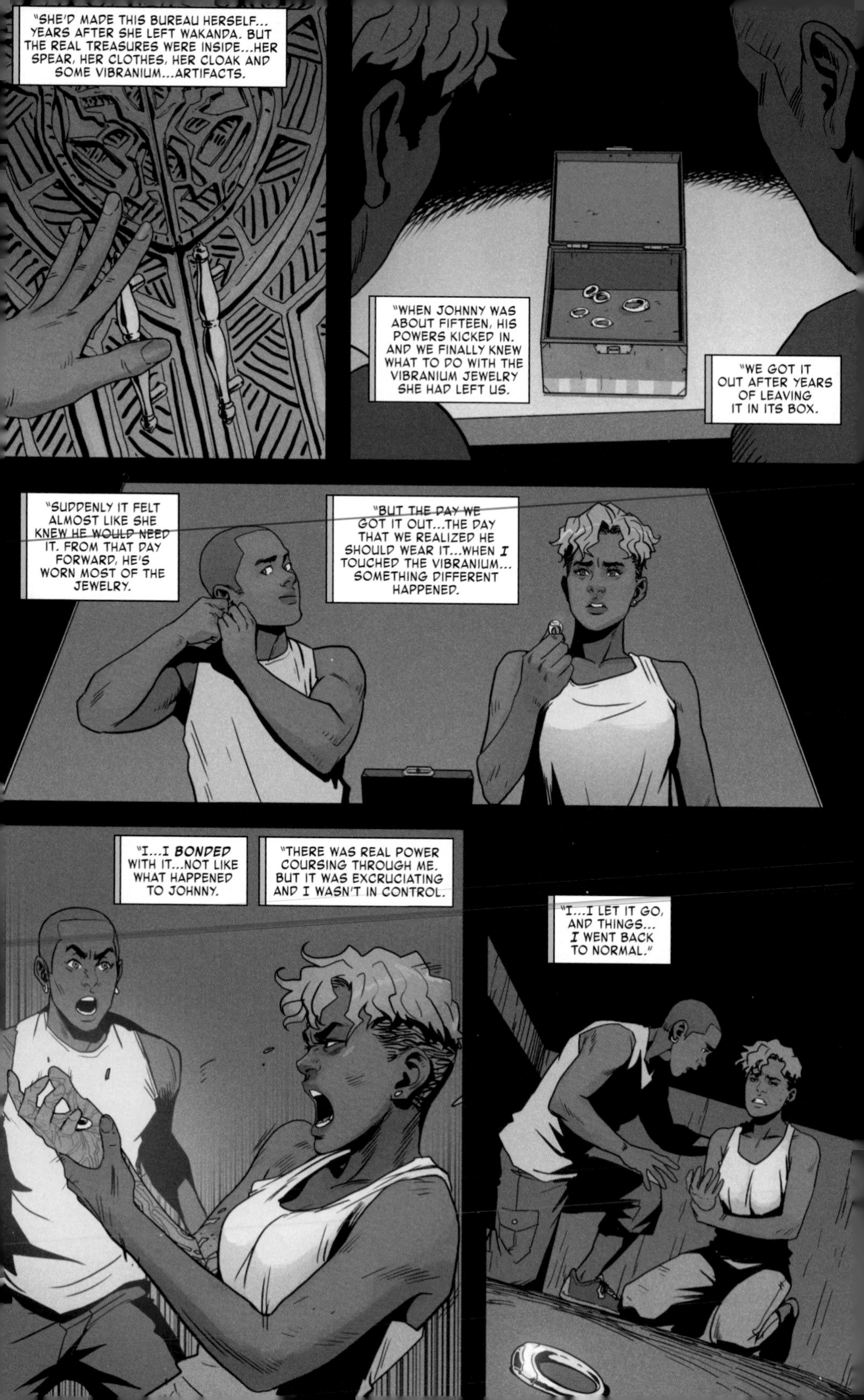
"SHE'D MADE THIS BUREAU HERSELF... YEARS AFTER SHE LEFT WAKANDA. BUT THE REAL TREASURES WERE INSIDE...HER SPEAR, HER CLOTHES, HER CLOAK AND SOME VIBRANIUM...ARTIFACTS.
"WHEN JOHNNY WAS ABOUT FIFTEEN, HIS POWERS KICKED IN. AND WE FINALLY KNEW WHAT TO DO WITH THE VIBRANIUM JEWELRY SHE HAD LEFT US.
"WE GOT IT OUT AFTER YEARS OF LEAVING IT IN ITS BOX.
"SUDDENLY IT FELT ALMOST LIKE SHE KNEW HE WOULD NEED IT. FROM THAT DAY FORWARD, HE'S WORN MOST OF THE JEWELRY.
"BUT THE DAY WE GOT IT OUT...THE DAY THAT WE REALIZED HE SHOULD WEAR IT...WHEN I TOUCHED THE VIBRANIUM... SOMETHING DIFFERENT HAPPENED.
"I...I BONDED WITH IT...NOT LIKE WHAT HAPPENED TO JOHNNY.
"THERE WAS REAL POWER COURSING THROUGH ME. BUT IT WAS EXCRUCIATING AND I WASN'T IN CONTROL.
"I...I LET IT GO, AND THINGS... I WENT BACK TO NORMAL."

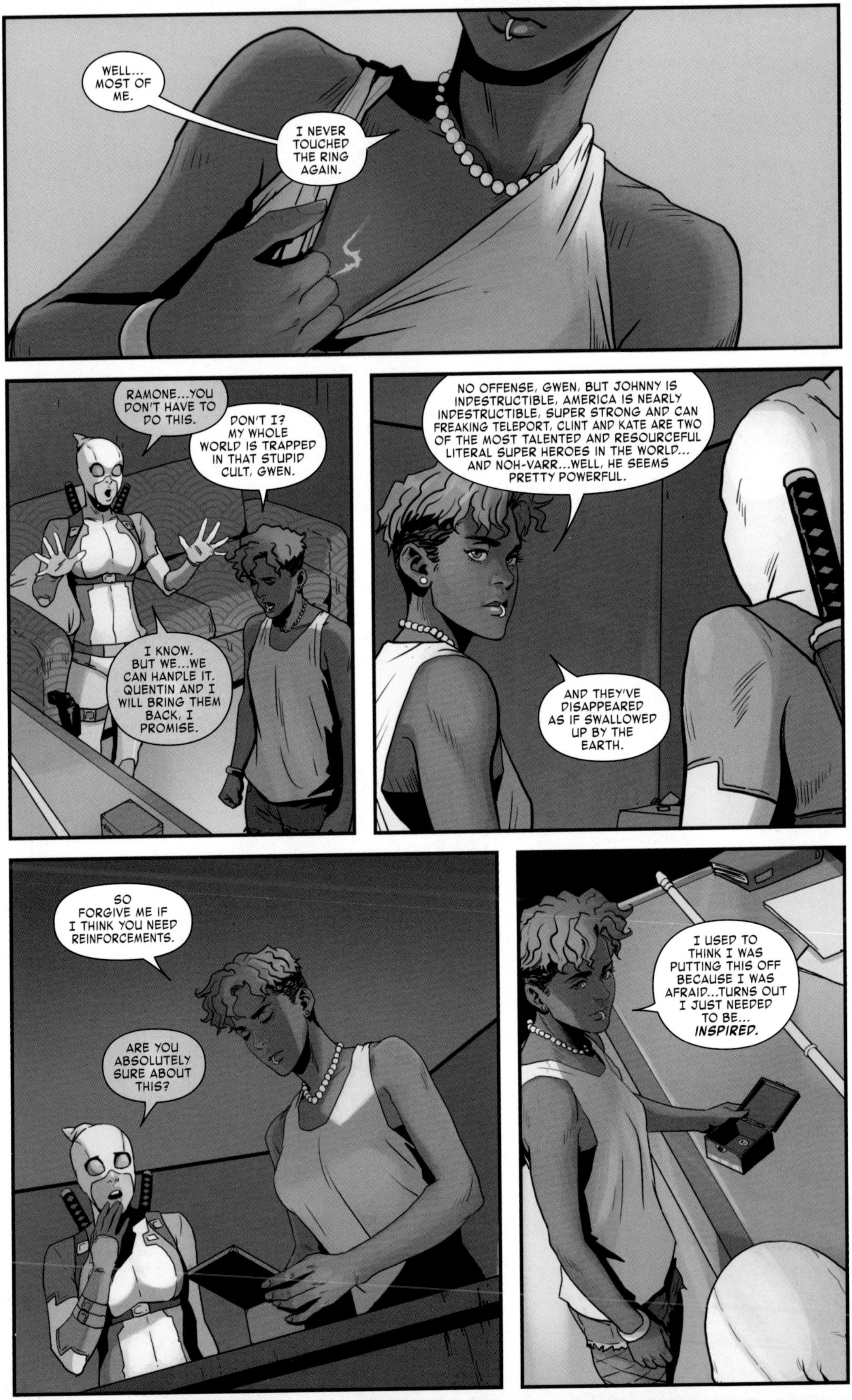
WELL... MOST OF ME.
I NEVER TOUCHED THE RING AGAIN.
RAMONE...YOU DON'T HAVE TO DO THIS.
DON'T I? MY WHOLE WORLD IS TRAPPED IN THAT STUPID CULT, GWEN.
I KNOW. BUT WE...WE CAN HANDLE IT. QUENTIN AND I WILL BRING THEM BACK, I PROMISE.
NO OFFENSE, GWEN, BUT JOHNNY IS INDESTRUCTIBLE, AMERICA IS NEARLY INDESTRUCTIBLE, SUPER STRONG AND CAN FREAKING TELEPORT, CLINT AND KATE ARE TWO OF THE MOST TALENTED AND RESOURCEFUL LITERAL SUPER HEROES IN THE WORLD... AND NOH-VARR...WELL, HE SEEMS PRETTY POWERFUL.
AND THEY'VE DISAPPEARED AS IF SWALLOWED UP BY THE EARTH.
SO FORGIVE ME IF I THINK YOU NEED REINFORCEMENTS.
ARE YOU ABSOLUTELY SURE ABOUT THIS?
I USED TO THINK I WAS PUTTING THIS OFF BECAUSE I WAS AFRAID...TURNS OUT I JUST NEEDED TO BE... INSPIRED.

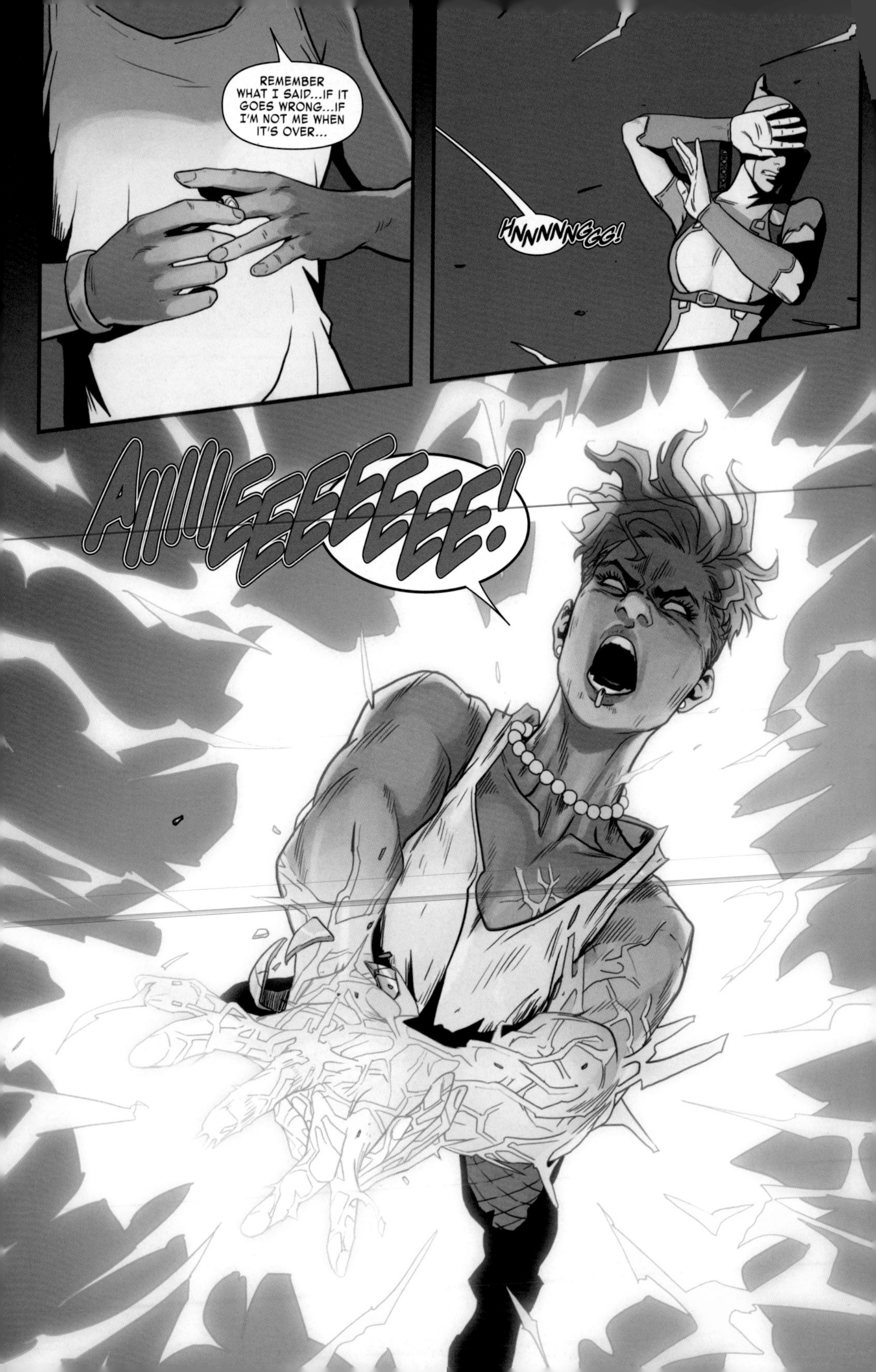
REMEMBER WHAT I SAID...IF IT GOES WRONG...IF I'M NOT ME WHEN IT'S OVER...
HNNNNNGGG!
AIIIIEEEEEEEE!

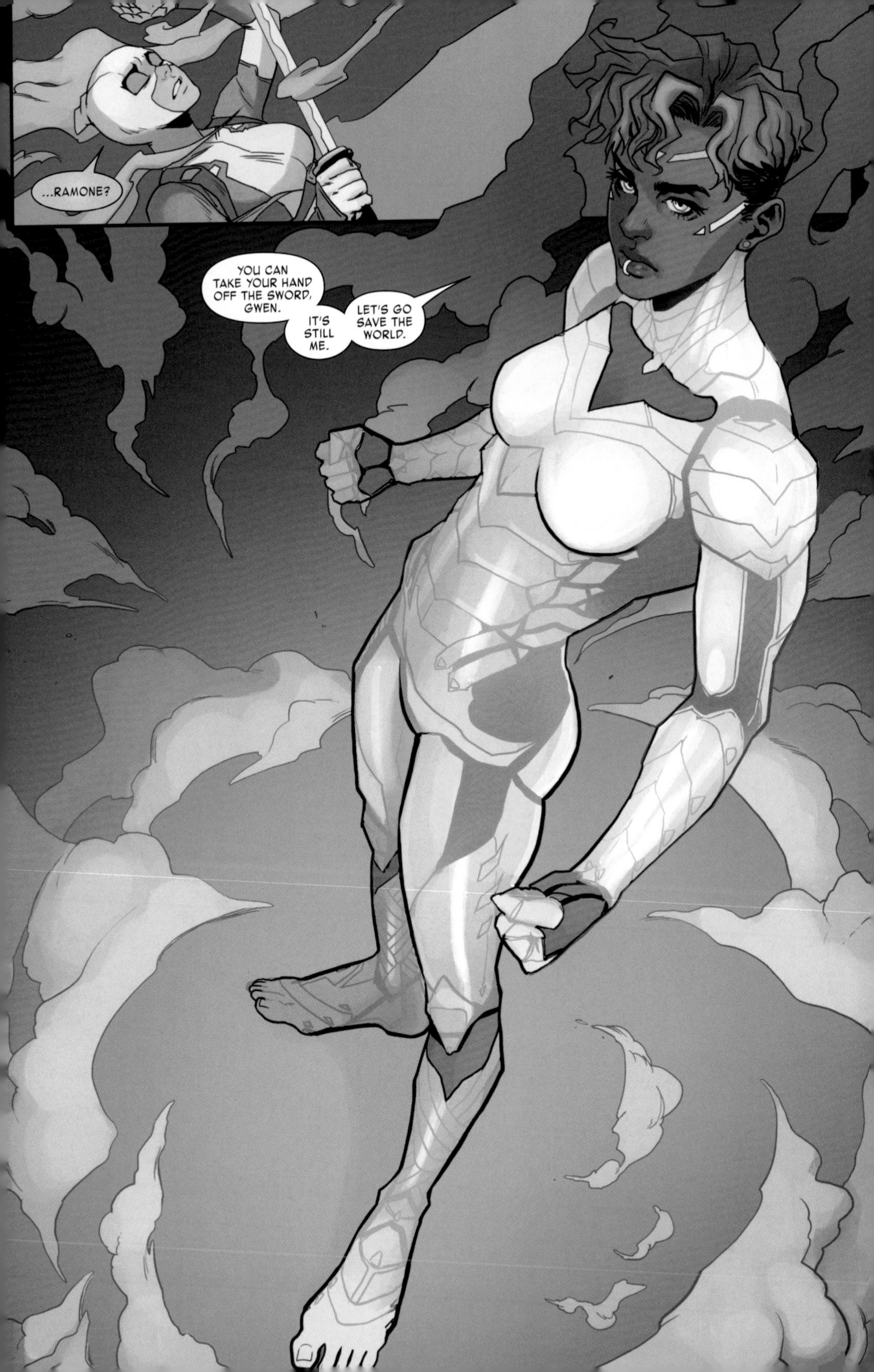
...RAMONE?
YOU CAN TAKE YOUR HAND OFF THE SWORD, GWEN.
IT'S STILL ME.
LET'S GO SAVE THE WORLD.

WHAT... WHAT HAPPENED TO THE RING?

IT MERGED WITH ME.

BUT IF YOU CAN'T TAKE IT OFF...

THIS IS PERMANENT. I KNEW IT WOULD BE.

TIME TO RESCUE MY WHOLE WORLD, GWEN.

...

OKAY, WE'RE HERE. I'M SORRY!

WHAT THE HELL TOOK-- OH. UH. IS THAT YOU, RAMONE?

IT IS.

I'm Ready For The Reboot

WELL, HELL. YES.

THESE ARE THE KIND OF REINFORCEMENTS I'M TALKING ABOUT.

NEARLY UNIRONIC "GO TEAM" THUMBS-UP!

I'm Ready For The Reboot

I'm Ready For

DID YOU... CHANGE YOUR T-SHIRT?

YOU TOOK A VERY LONG TIME.

ALL RIGHT, LET'S GET THIS RESCUE MISSION STARTED!

I'm Ready For The Reboot

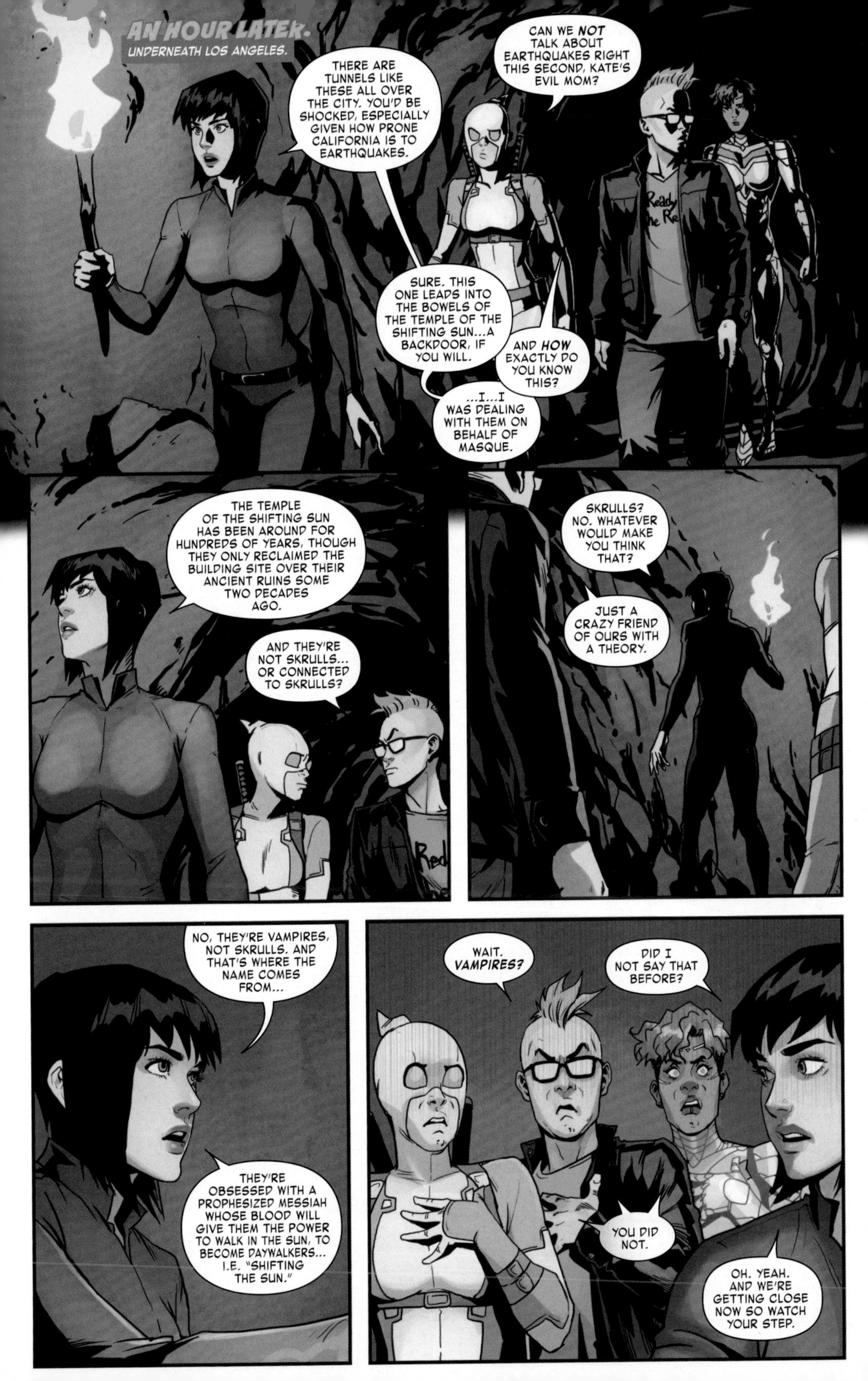
AN HOUR LATER.
UNDERNEATH LOS ANGELES.
THERE ARE TUNNELS LIKE THESE ALL OVER THE CITY. YOU'D BE SHOCKED, ESPECIALLY GIVEN HOW PRONE CALIFORNIA IS TO EARTHQUAKES.
CAN WE NOT TALK ABOUT EARTHQUAKES RIGHT THIS SECOND, KATE'S EVIL MOM?
SURE. THIS ONE LEADS INTO THE BOWELS OF THE TEMPLE OF THE SHIFTING SUN...A BACKDOOR, IF YOU WILL.
AND HOW EXACTLY DO YOU KNOW THIS?
...I...I WAS DEALING WITH THEM ON BEHALF OF MASQUE.
THE TEMPLE OF THE SHIFTING SUN HAS BEEN AROUND FOR HUNDREDS OF YEARS, THOUGH THEY ONLY RECLAIMED THE BUILDING SITE OVER THEIR ANCIENT RUINS SOME TWO DECADES AGO.
AND THEY'RE NOT SKRULLS... OR CONNECTED TO SKRULLS?
SKRULLS? NO. WHATEVER WOULD MAKE YOU THINK THAT?
JUST A CRAZY FRIEND OF OURS WITH A THEORY.
NO, THEY'RE VAMPIRES, NOT SKRULLS. AND THAT'S WHERE THE NAME COMES FROM...
THEY'RE OBSESSED WITH A PROPHESIZED MESSIAH WHOSE BLOOD WILL GIVE THEM THE POWER TO WALK IN THE SUN, TO BECOME DAYWALKERS... I.E. "SHIFTING THE SUN."
WAIT. VAMPIRES?
DID I NOT SAY THAT BEFORE?
YOU DID NOT.
OH. YEAH. AND WE'RE GETTING CLOSE NOW SO WATCH YOUR STEP.

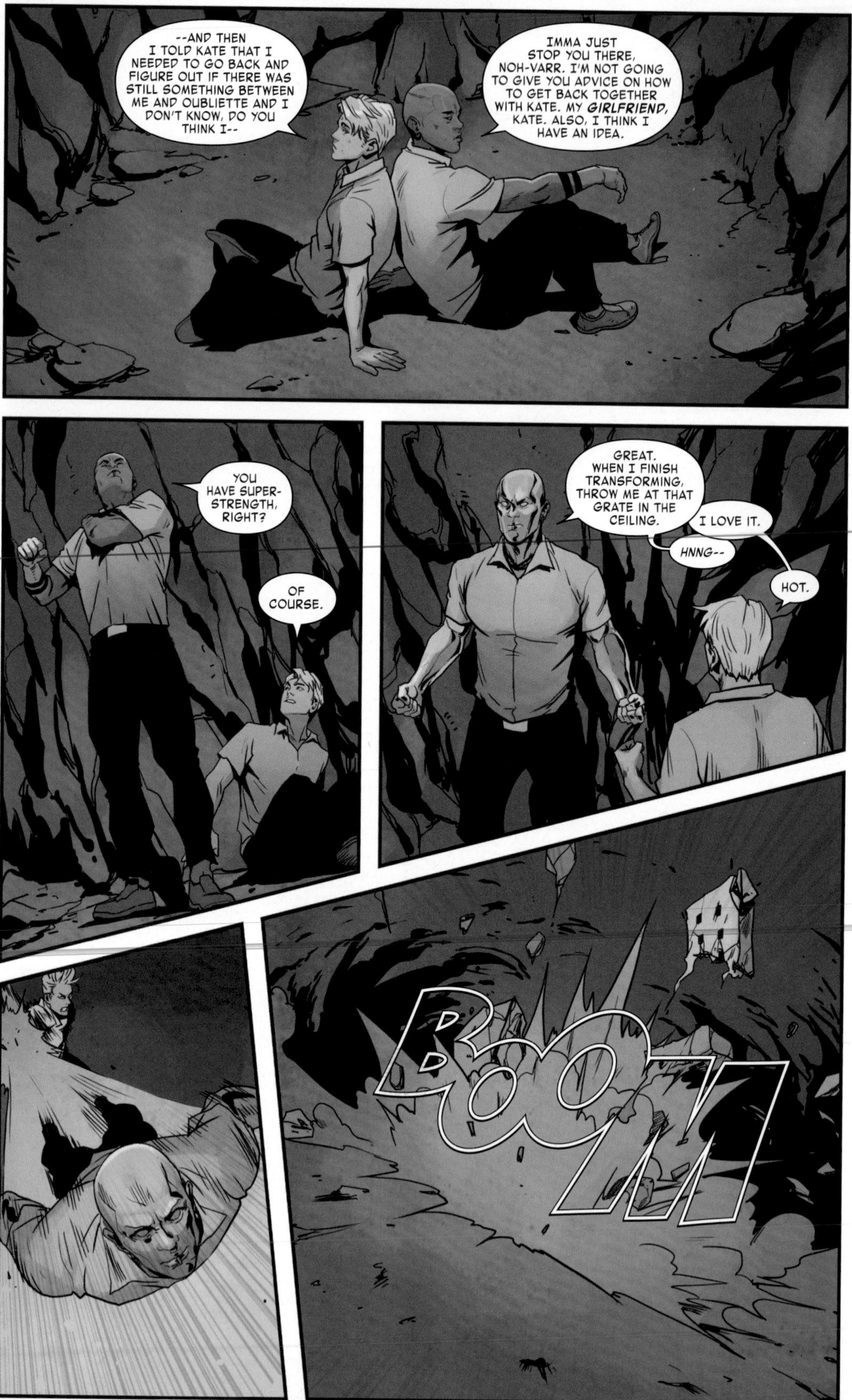
--AND THEN I TOLD KATE THAT I NEEDED TO GO BACK AND FIGURE OUT IF THERE WAS STILL SOMETHING BETWEEN ME AND OUBLIETTE AND I DON'T KNOW, DO YOU THINK I--
IMMA JUST STOP YOU THERE, NOH-VARR. I'M NOT GOING TO GIVE YOU ADVICE ON HOW TO GET BACK TOGETHER WITH KATE. MY GIRLFRIEND, KATE. ALSO, I THINK I HAVE AN IDEA.
YOU HAVE SUPER-STRENGTH, RIGHT?
OF COURSE.
GREAT. WHEN I FINISH TRANSFORMING, THROW ME AT THAT GRATE IN THE CEILING.
HNNG--
I LOVE IT.
HOT.
BOOM

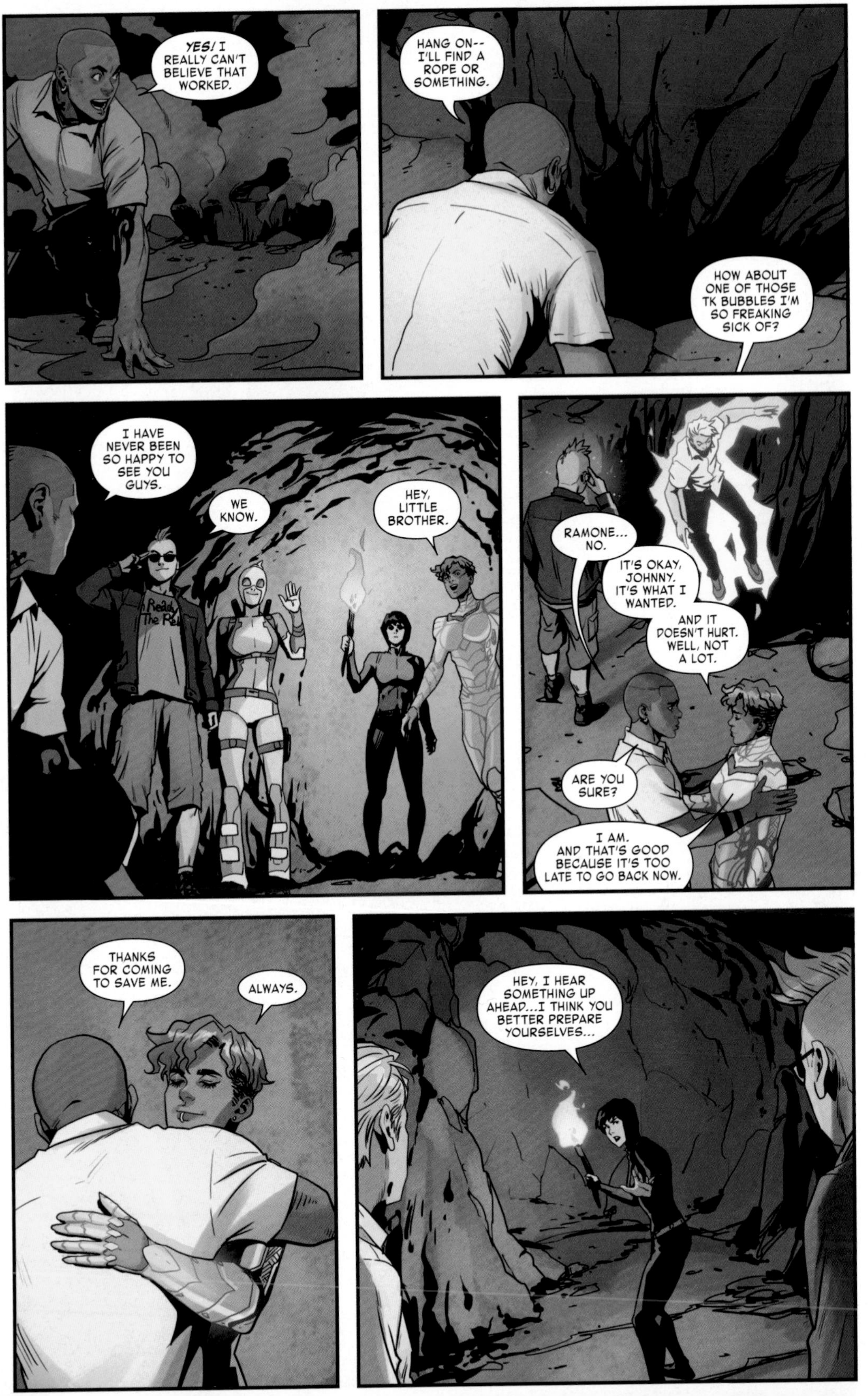
YES! I REALLY CAN'T BELIEVE THAT WORKED.
HANG ON-- I'LL FIND A ROPE OR SOMETHING.
HOW ABOUT ONE OF THOSE TK BUBBLES I'M SO FREAKING SICK OF?
I HAVE NEVER BEEN SO HAPPY TO SEE YOU GUYS.
WE KNOW.
HEY, LITTLE BROTHER.
RAMONE... NO.
IT'S OKAY, JOHNNY. IT'S WHAT I WANTED.
AND IT DOESN'T HURT. WELL, NOT A LOT.
ARE YOU SURE?
I AM. AND THAT'S GOOD BECAUSE IT'S TOO LATE TO GO BACK NOW.
THANKS FOR COMING TO SAVE ME.
ALWAYS.
HEY, I HEAR SOMETHING UP AHEAD...I THINK YOU BETTER PREPARE YOURSELVES...

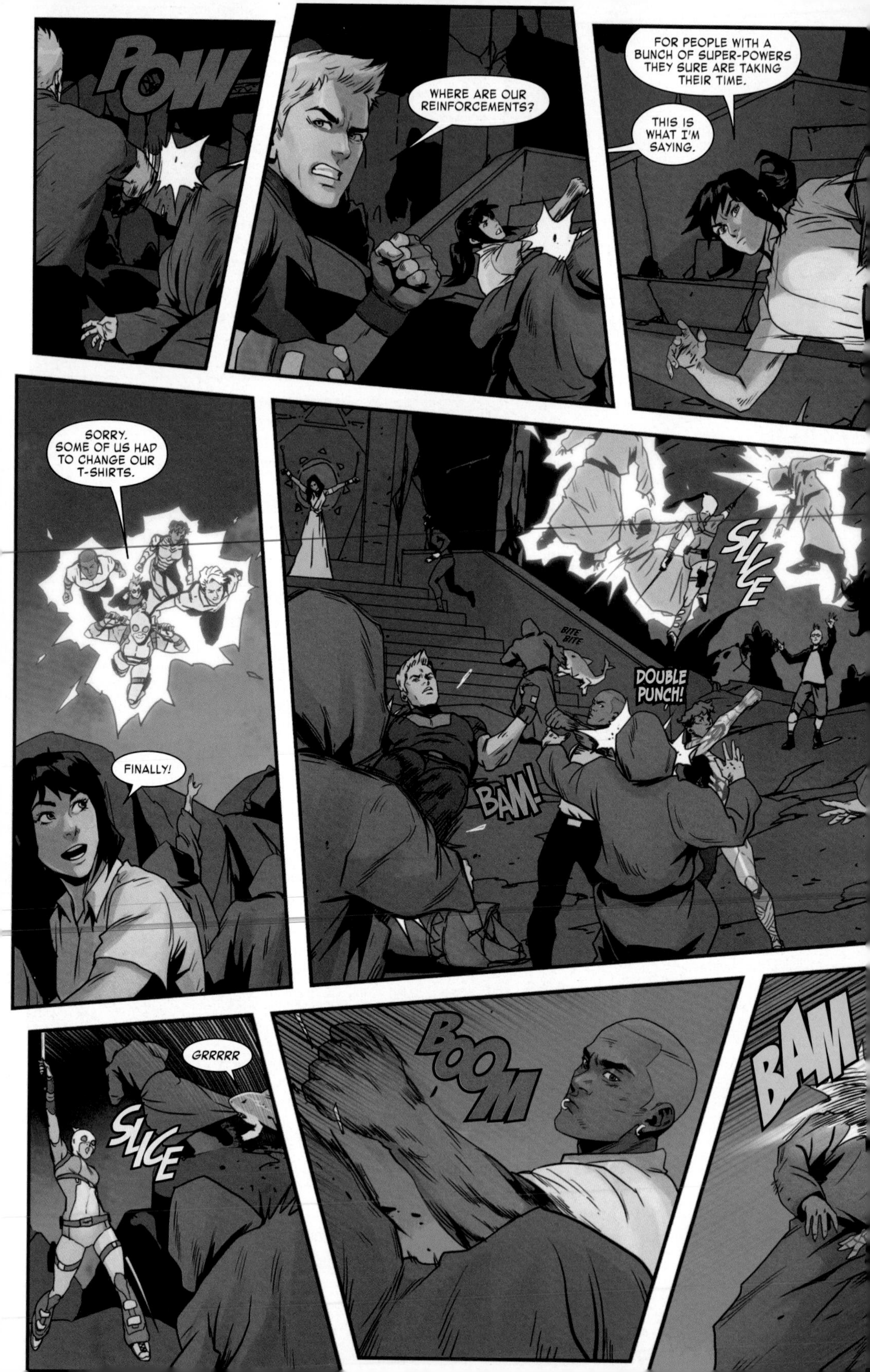
POW
WHERE ARE OUR REINFORCEMENTS?
FOR PEOPLE WITH A BUNCH OF SUPER-POWERS THEY SURE ARE TAKING THEIR TIME.
THIS IS WHAT I'M SAYING.
SORRY. SOME OF US HAD TO CHANGE OUR T-SHIRTS.
FINALLY!
SLICE
BITE BITE
DOUBLE PUNCH!
BAM!
GRRRRR
SLICE
BOOM
BAM

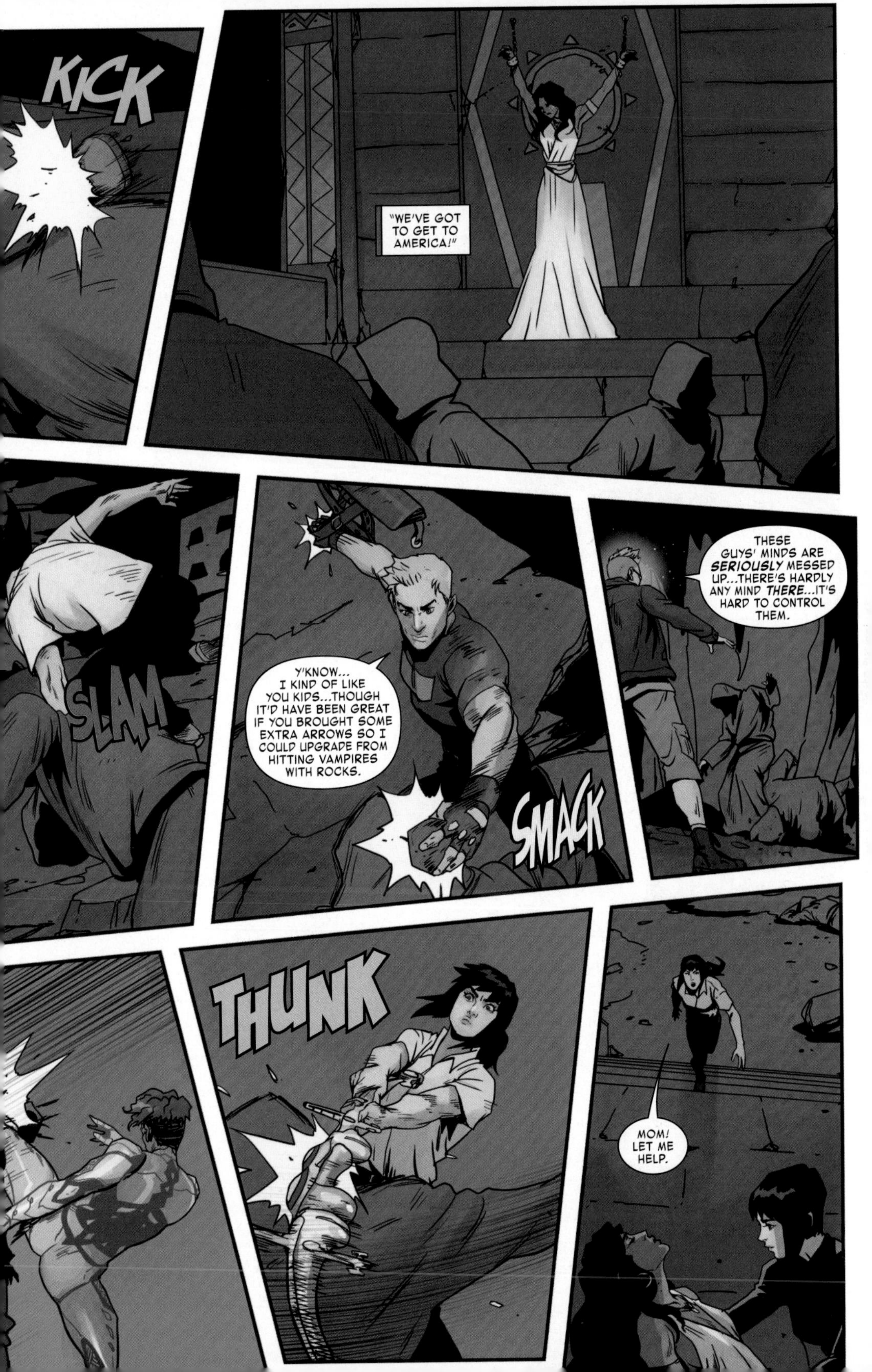
KICK
"WE'VE GOT TO GET TO AMERICA!"
SLAM
Y'KNOW... I KIND OF LIKE YOU KIDS...THOUGH IT'D HAVE BEEN GREAT IF YOU BROUGHT SOME EXTRA ARROWS SO I COULD UPGRADE FROM HITTING VAMPIRES WITH ROCKS.
SMACK
THESE GUYS' MINDS ARE SERIOUSLY MESSED UP...THERE'S HARDLY ANY MIND THERE...IT'S HARD TO CONTROL THEM.
THUNK
MOM! LET ME HELP.

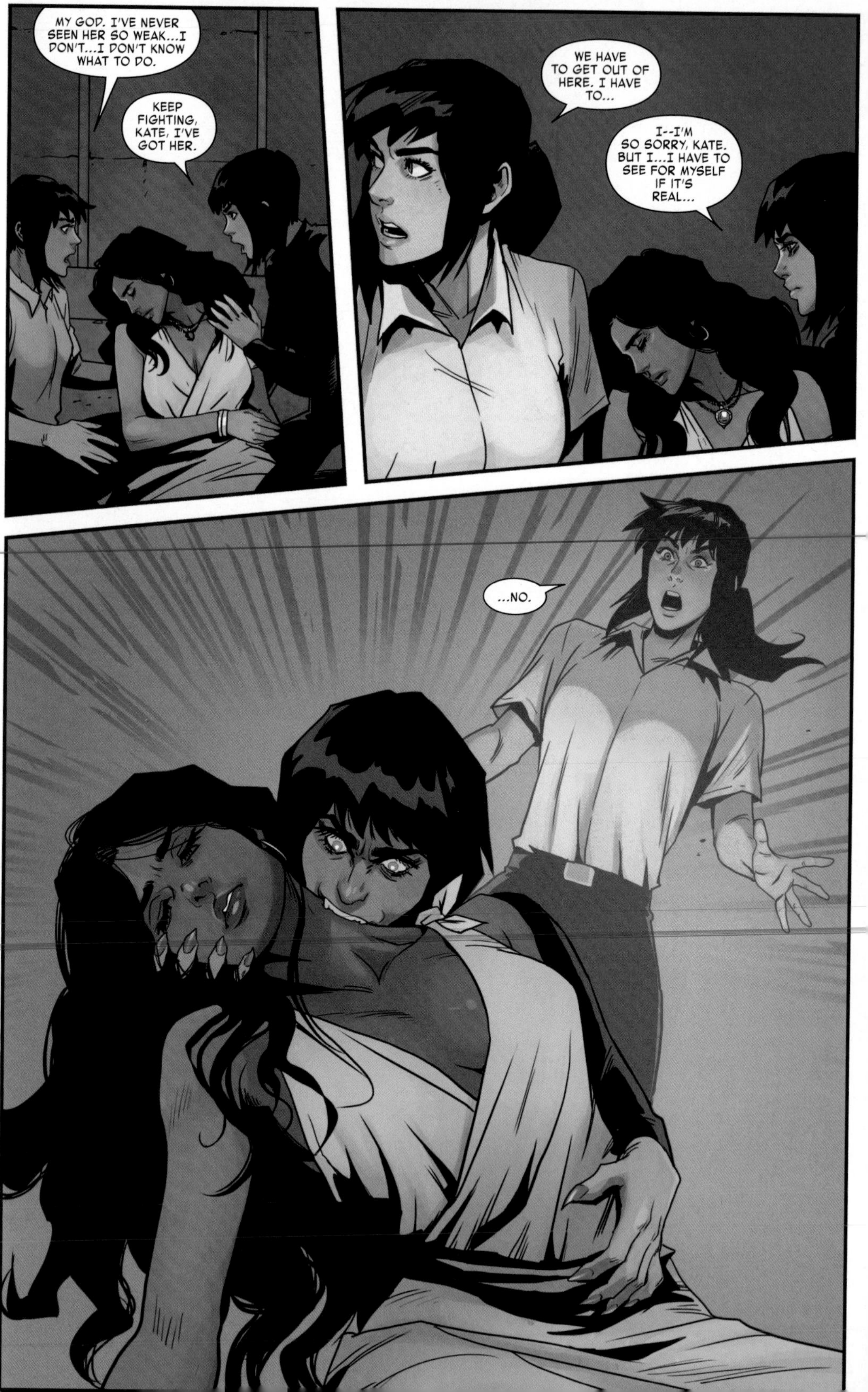
MY GOD. I'VE NEVER SEEN HER SO WEAK...I DON'T...I DON'T KNOW WHAT TO DO.
KEEP FIGHTING, KATE, I'VE GOT HER.
WE HAVE TO GET OUT OF HERE. I HAVE TO...
I--I'M SO SORRY, KATE. BUT I...I HAVE TO SEE FOR MYSELF IF IT'S REAL...
...NO.

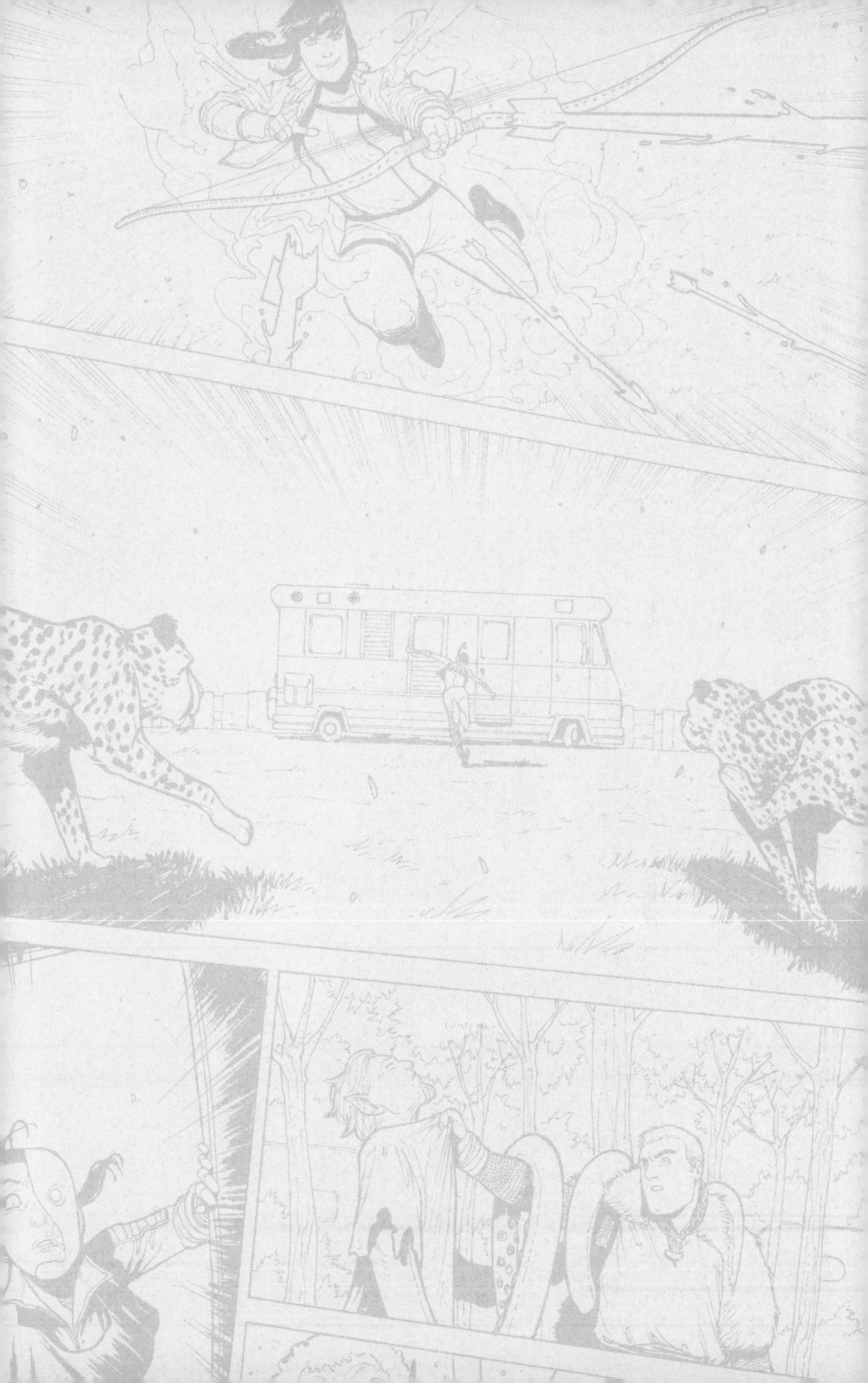

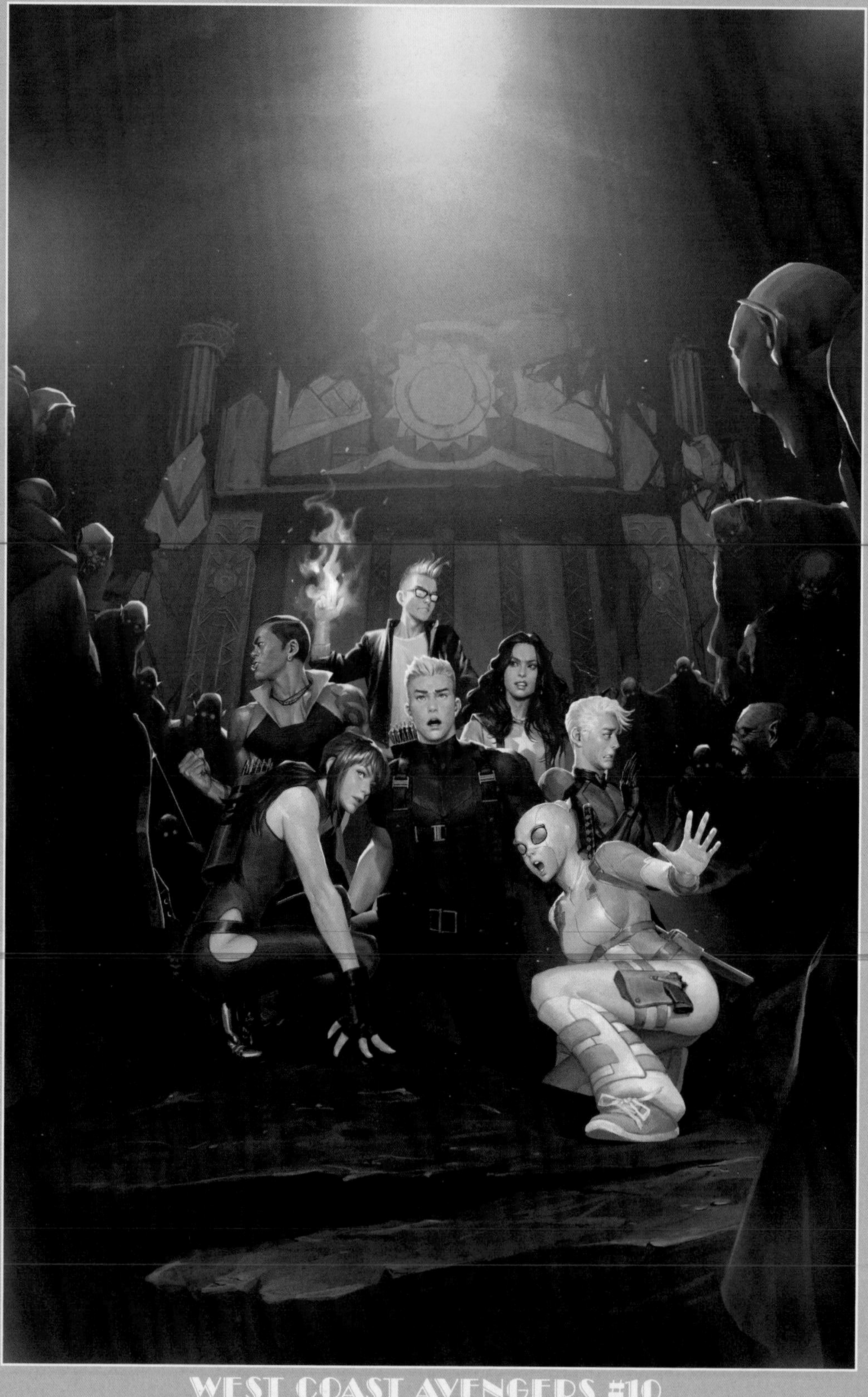

WEST COAST AVENGERS #10

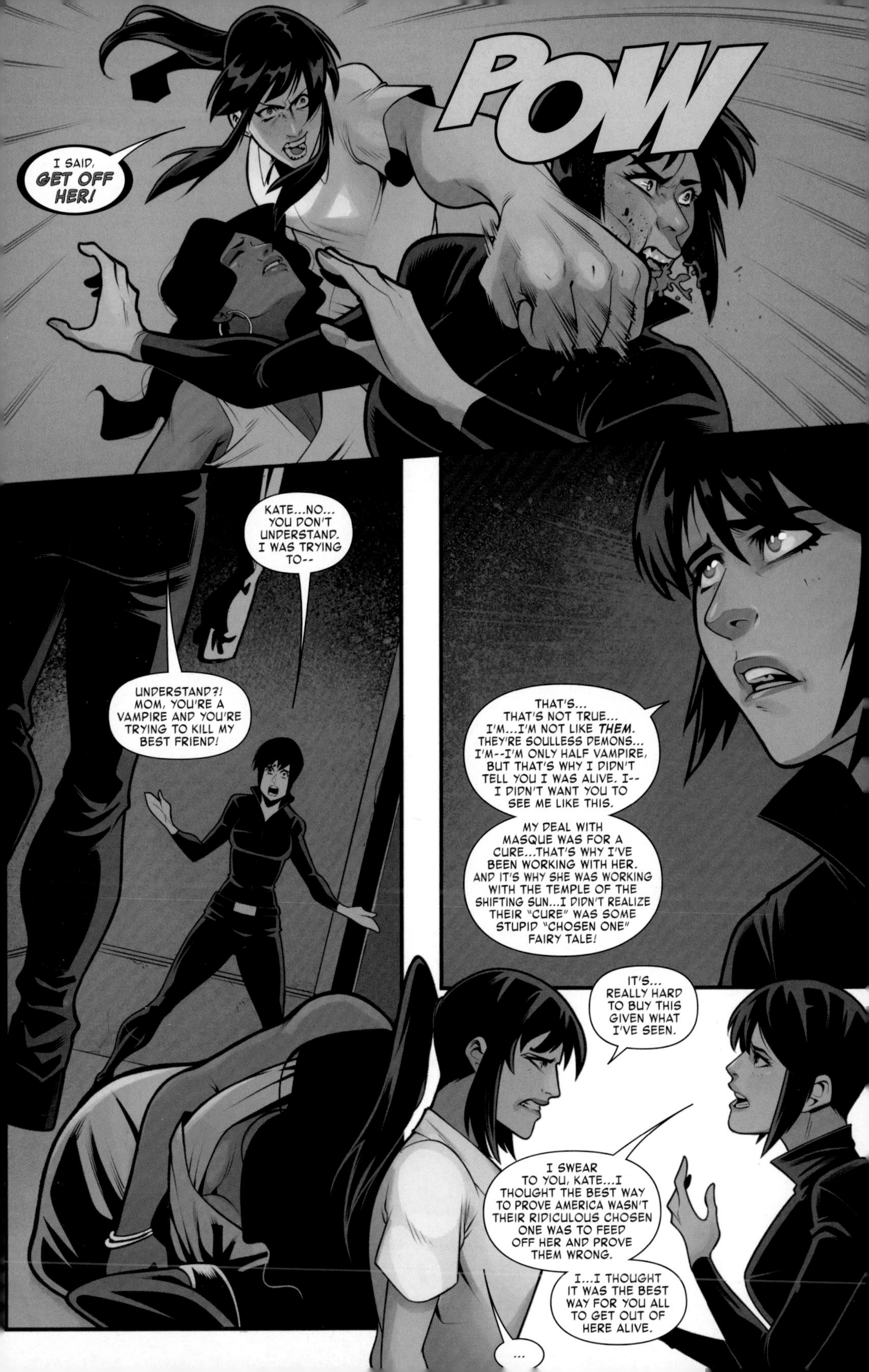
POW
I SAID, GET OFF HER!
KATE...NO... YOU DON'T UNDERSTAND. I WAS TRYING TO--
UNDERSTAND?! MOM, YOU'RE A VAMPIRE AND YOU'RE TRYING TO KILL MY BEST FRIEND!
THAT'S... THAT'S NOT TRUE... I'M...I'M NOT LIKE THEM. THEY'RE SOULLESS DEMONS... I'M--I'M ONLY HALF VAMPIRE, BUT THAT'S WHY I DIDN'T TELL YOU I WAS ALIVE. I-- I DIDN'T WANT YOU TO SEE ME LIKE THIS.
MY DEAL WITH MASQUE WAS FOR A CURE...THAT'S WHY I'VE BEEN WORKING WITH HER. AND IT'S WHY SHE WAS WORKING WITH THE TEMPLE OF THE SHIFTING SUN...I DIDN'T REALIZE THEIR "CURE" WAS SOME STUPID "CHOSEN ONE" FAIRY TALE!
IT'S... REALLY HARD TO BUY THIS GIVEN WHAT I'VE SEEN.
I SWEAR TO YOU, KATE...I THOUGHT THE BEST WAY TO PROVE AMERICA WASN'T THEIR RIDICULOUS CHOSEN ONE WAS TO FEED OFF HER AND PROVE THEM WRONG.
I...I THOUGHT IT WAS THE BEST WAY FOR YOU ALL TO GET OUT OF HERE ALIVE.
...

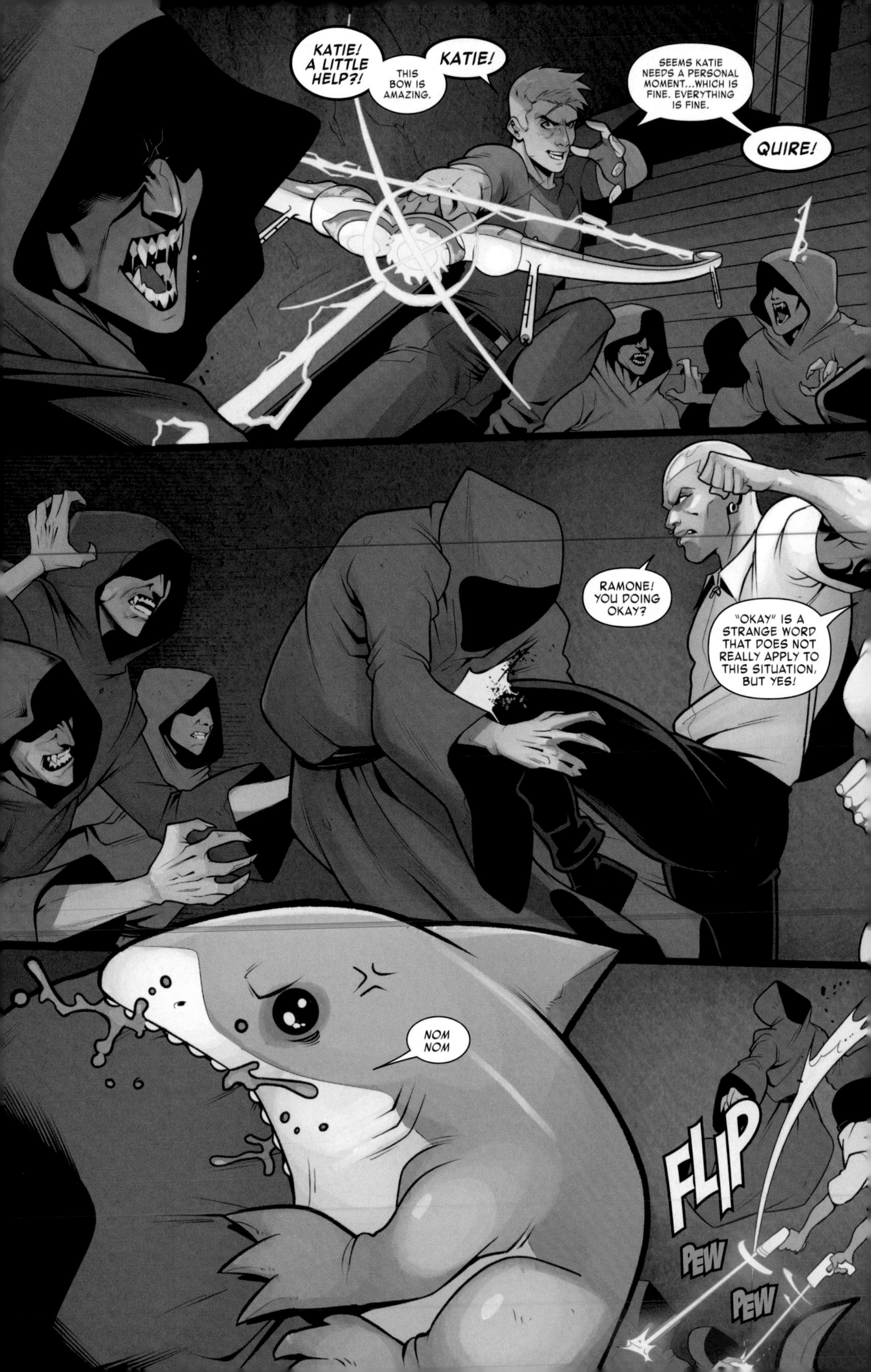
KATIE! A LITTLE HELP?!
THIS BOW IS AMAZING.
KATIE!
SEEMS KATIE NEEDS A PERSONAL MOMENT...WHICH IS FINE. EVERYTHING IS FINE.
QUIRE!
RAMONE! YOU DOING OKAY?
"OKAY" IS A STRANGE WORD THAT DOES NOT REALLY APPLY TO THIS SITUATION, BUT YES!
NOM NOM
FLIP
PEW
PEW

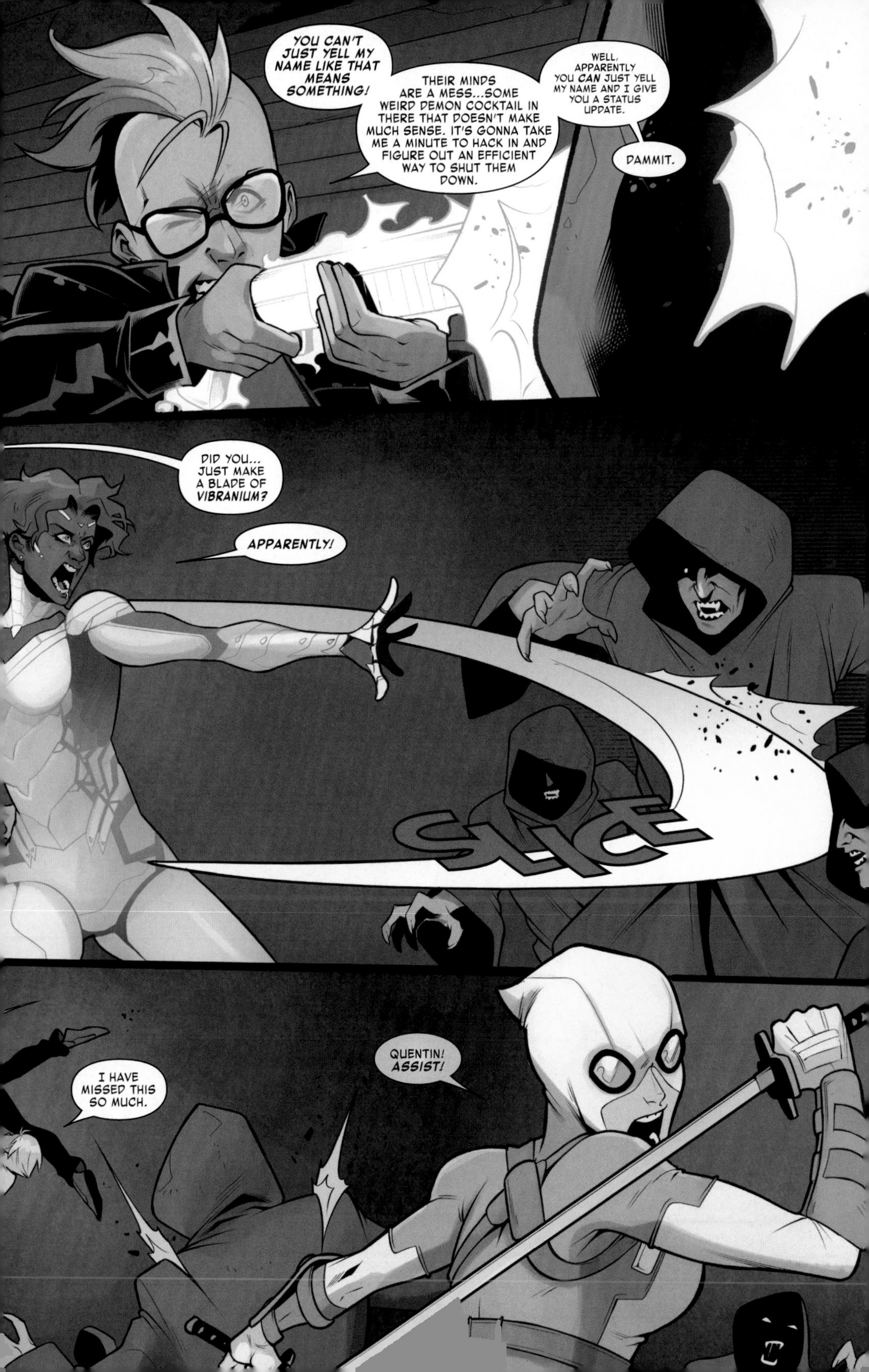

YOU CAN'T JUST YELL MY NAME LIKE THAT MEANS SOMETHING!
THEIR MINDS ARE A MESS...SOME WEIRD DEMON COCKTAIL IN THERE THAT DOESN'T MAKE MUCH SENSE. IT'S GONNA TAKE ME A MINUTE TO HACK IN AND FIGURE OUT AN EFFICIENT WAY TO SHUT THEM DOWN.
WELL, APPARENTLY YOU CAN JUST YELL MY NAME AND I GIVE YOU A STATUS UPDATE.
DAMMIT.
DID YOU... JUST MAKE A BLADE OF VIBRANIUM?
APPARENTLY!
SLICE
QUENTIN! ASSIST!
I HAVE MISSED THIS SO MUCH.

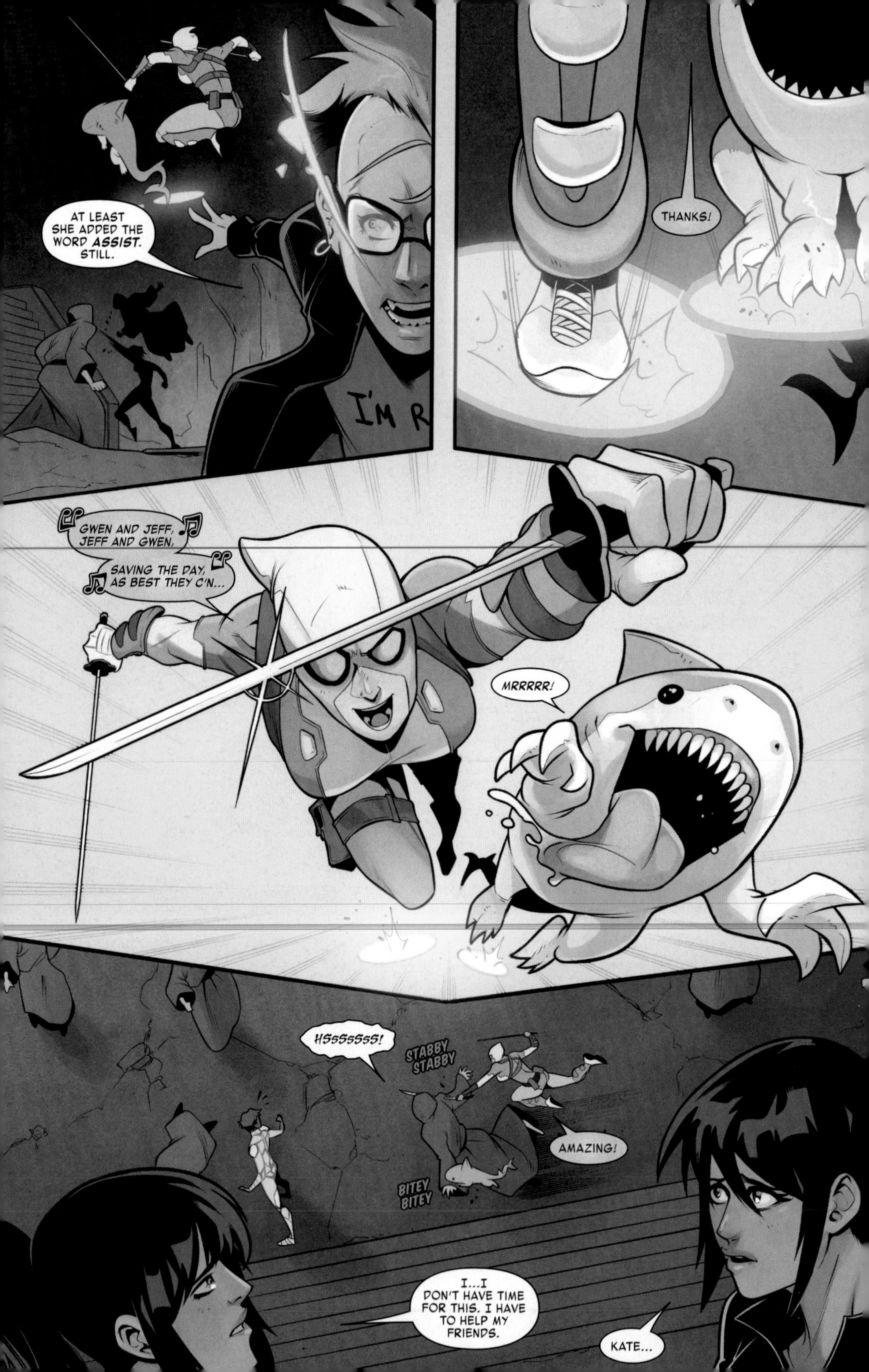
AT LEAST SHE ADDED THE WORD ASSIST. STILL.
I'M R
THANKS!
GWEN AND JEFF, JEFF AND GWEN,
SAVING THE DAY, AS BEST THEY C'N...
MRRRRR!
HSSSSSSS!
STABBY STABBY
AMAZING!
BITEY BITEY
I...I DON'T HAVE TIME FOR THIS. I HAVE TO HELP MY FRIENDS.
KATE...

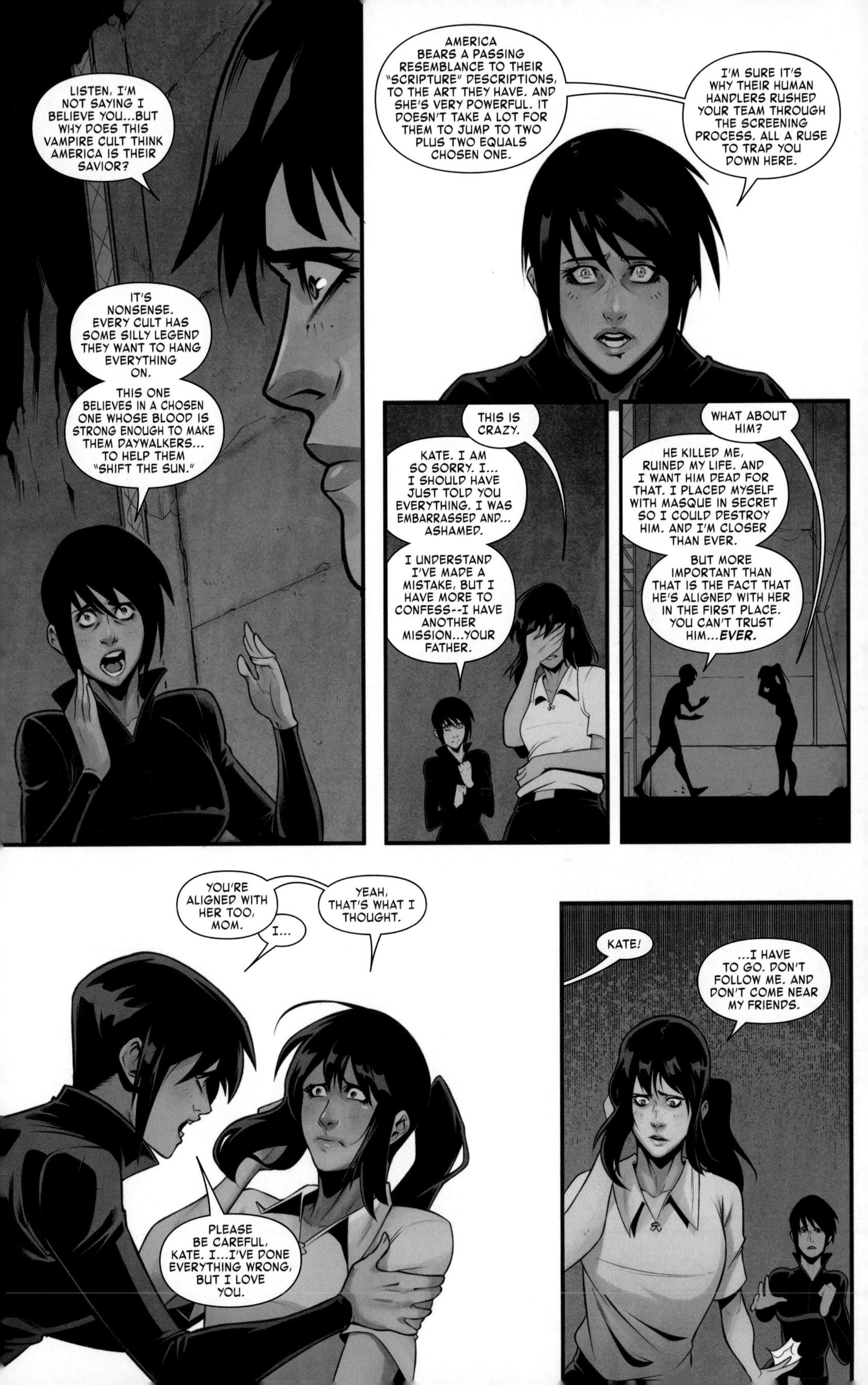

LISTEN, I'M NOT SAYING I BELIEVE YOU...BUT WHY DOES THIS VAMPIRE CULT THINK AMERICA IS THEIR SAVIOR?
IT'S NONSENSE. EVERY CULT HAS SOME SILLY LEGEND THEY WANT TO HANG EVERYTHING ON.
THIS ONE BELIEVES IN A CHOSEN ONE WHOSE BLOOD IS STRONG ENOUGH TO MAKE THEM DAYWALKERS... TO HELP THEM "SHIFT THE SUN."
AMERICA BEARS A PASSING RESEMBLANCE TO THEIR "SCRIPTURE" DESCRIPTIONS, TO THE ART THEY HAVE. AND SHE'S VERY POWERFUL. IT DOESN'T TAKE A LOT FOR THEM TO JUMP TO TWO PLUS TWO EQUALS CHOSEN ONE.
I'M SURE IT'S WHY THEIR HUMAN HANDLERS RUSHED YOUR TEAM THROUGH THE SCREENING PROCESS. ALL A RUSE TO TRAP YOU DOWN HERE.
THIS IS CRAZY.
KATE. I AM SO SORRY. I... I SHOULD HAVE JUST TOLD YOU EVERYTHING. I WAS EMBARRASSED AND... ASHAMED.
I UNDERSTAND I'VE MADE A MISTAKE, BUT I HAVE MORE TO CONFESS--I HAVE ANOTHER MISSION...YOUR FATHER.
WHAT ABOUT HIM?
HE KILLED ME, RUINED MY LIFE. AND I WANT HIM DEAD FOR THAT. I PLACED MYSELF WITH MASQUE IN SECRET SO I COULD DESTROY HIM. AND I'M CLOSER THAN EVER.
BUT MORE IMPORTANT THAN THAT IS THE FACT THAT HE'S ALIGNED WITH HER IN THE FIRST PLACE. YOU CAN'T TRUST HIM...EVER.
YOU'RE ALIGNED WITH HER TOO, MOM.
I...
YEAH, THAT'S WHAT I THOUGHT.
PLEASE BE CAREFUL, KATE. I...I'VE DONE EVERYTHING WRONG, BUT I LOVE YOU.
KATE!
...I HAVE TO GO. DON'T FOLLOW ME. AND DON'T COME NEAR MY FRIENDS.

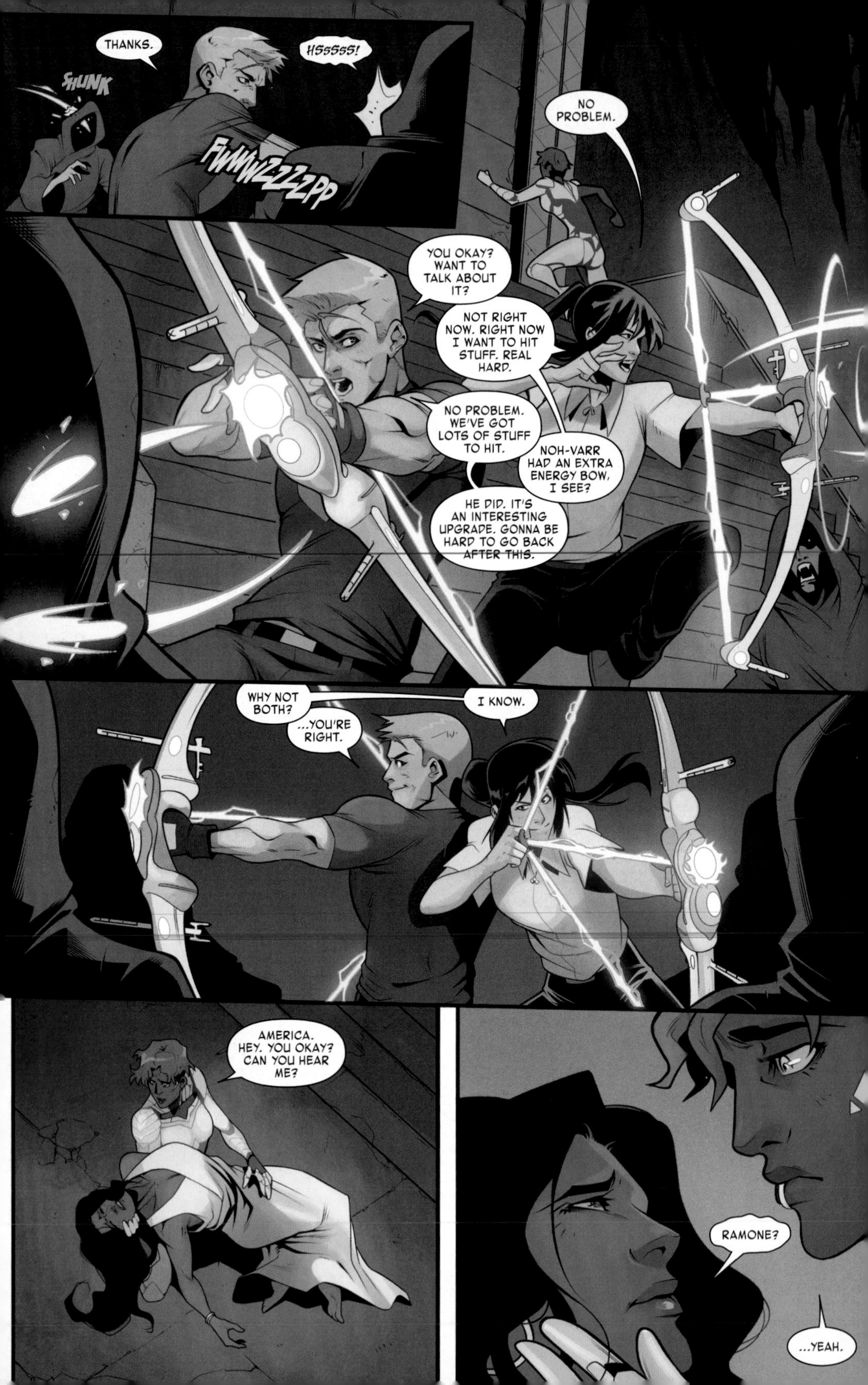
THANKS.
SHUNK
HSSSSS!
FWWWZZZZZPP
NO PROBLEM.
YOU OKAY? WANT TO TALK ABOUT IT?
NOT RIGHT NOW. RIGHT NOW I WANT TO HIT STUFF. REAL HARD.
NO PROBLEM. WE'VE GOT LOTS OF STUFF TO HIT.
NOH-VARR HAD AN EXTRA ENERGY BOW, I SEE?
HE DID. IT'S AN INTERESTING UPGRADE. GONNA BE HARD TO GO BACK AFTER THIS.
WHY NOT BOTH?
I KNOW.
...YOU'RE RIGHT.
AMERICA. HEY. YOU OKAY? CAN YOU HEAR ME?
RAMONE?
...YEAH.

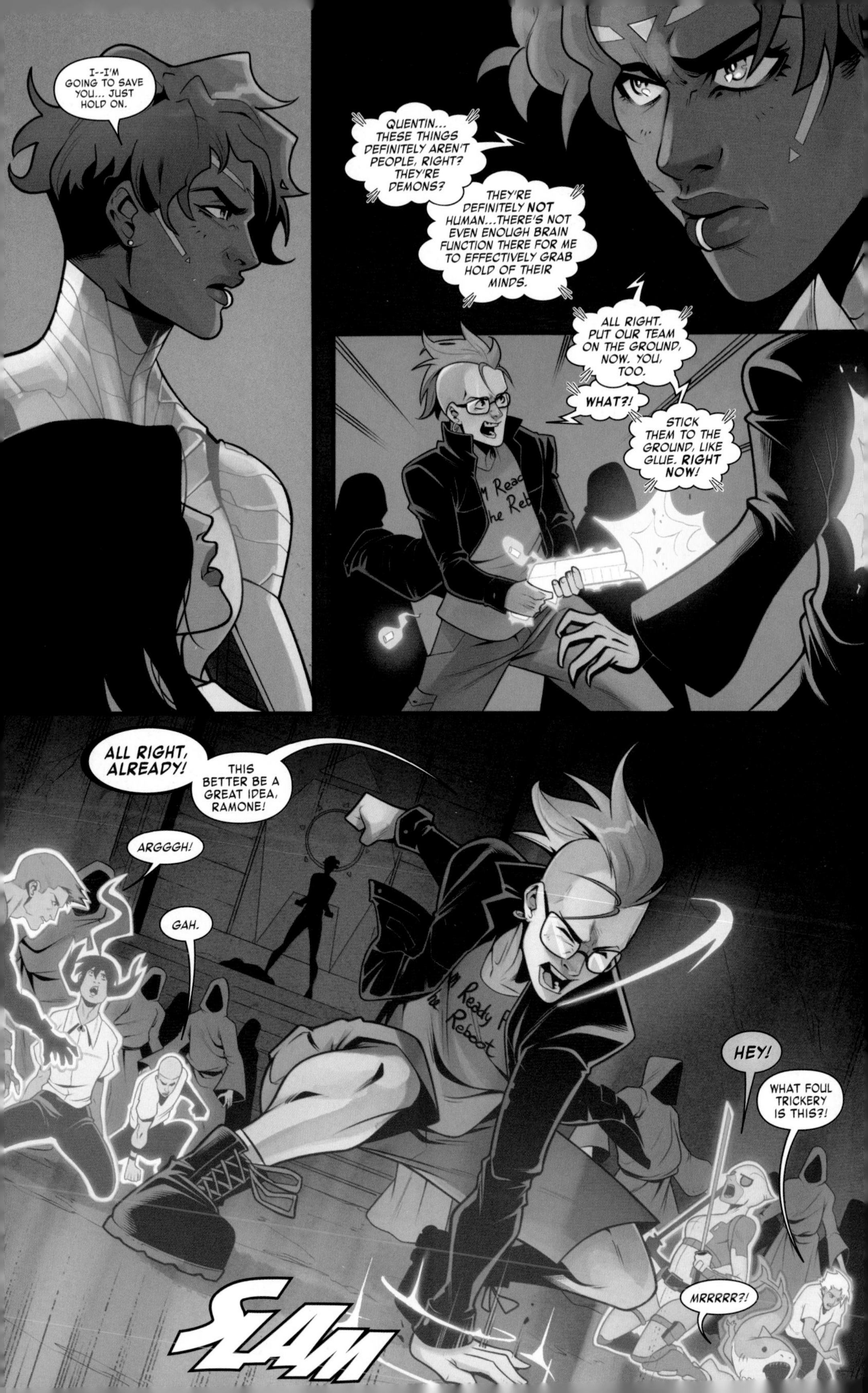
I--I'M GOING TO SAVE YOU... JUST HOLD ON.
QUENTIN... THESE THINGS DEFINITELY AREN'T PEOPLE, RIGHT? THEY'RE DEMONS?
THEY'RE DEFINITELY **NOT** HUMAN...THERE'S NOT EVEN ENOUGH BRAIN FUNCTION THERE FOR ME TO EFFECTIVELY GRAB HOLD OF THEIR MINDS.
ALL RIGHT. PUT OUR TEAM ON THE GROUND, NOW. YOU, TOO.
WHAT?!
STICK THEM TO THE GROUND, LIKE GLUE. **RIGHT NOW!**
ALL RIGHT, ALREADY!
THIS BETTER BE A GREAT IDEA, RAMONE!
ARGGGH!
GAH.
HEY!
WHAT FOUL TRICKERY IS THIS?!
MRRRRR?!
SLAM

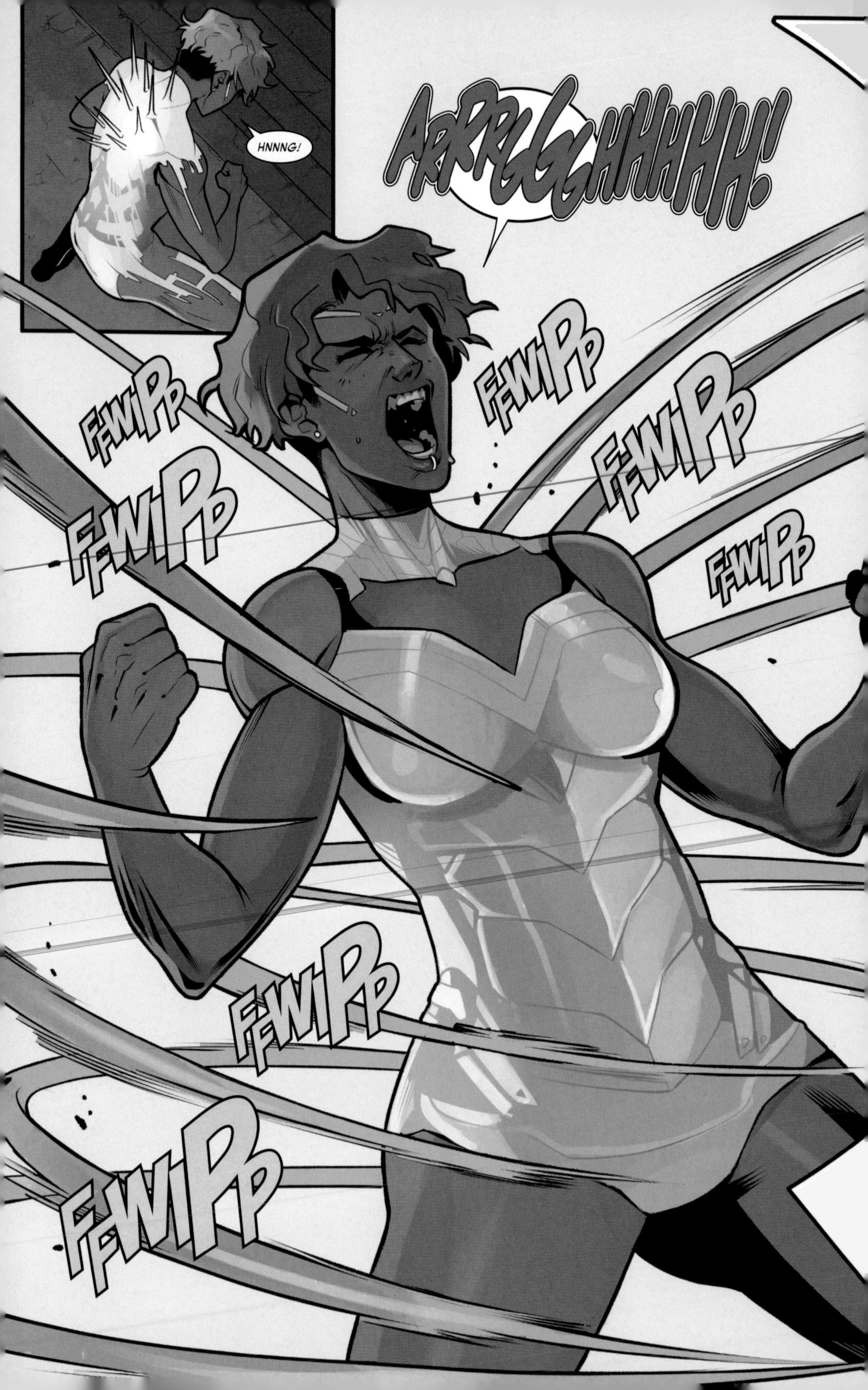
HNNNG!
ARRRGGGHHHHHH!
FFWIPP
FFWIPP
FFWIPP
FFWIPP
FFWIPP
FFWIPP
FFWIPP

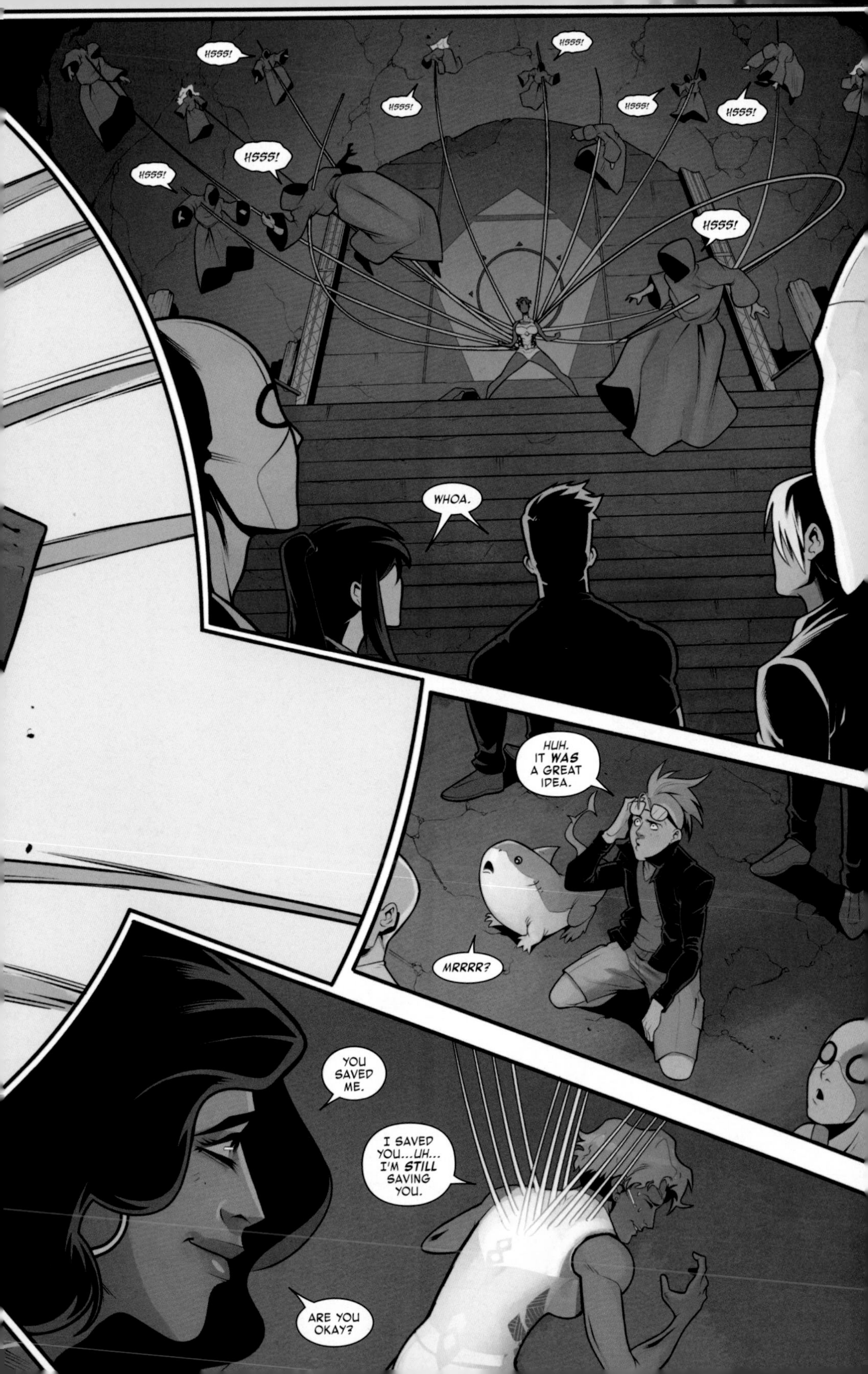
HSSS!
HSSS!
HSSS!
HSSS!
HSSS!
HSSS!
HSSS!
HSSS!
HSSS!
WHOA.
HUH. IT WAS A GREAT IDEA.
MRRRR?
YOU SAVED ME.
I SAVED YOU...UH... I'M STILL SAVING YOU.
ARE YOU OKAY?

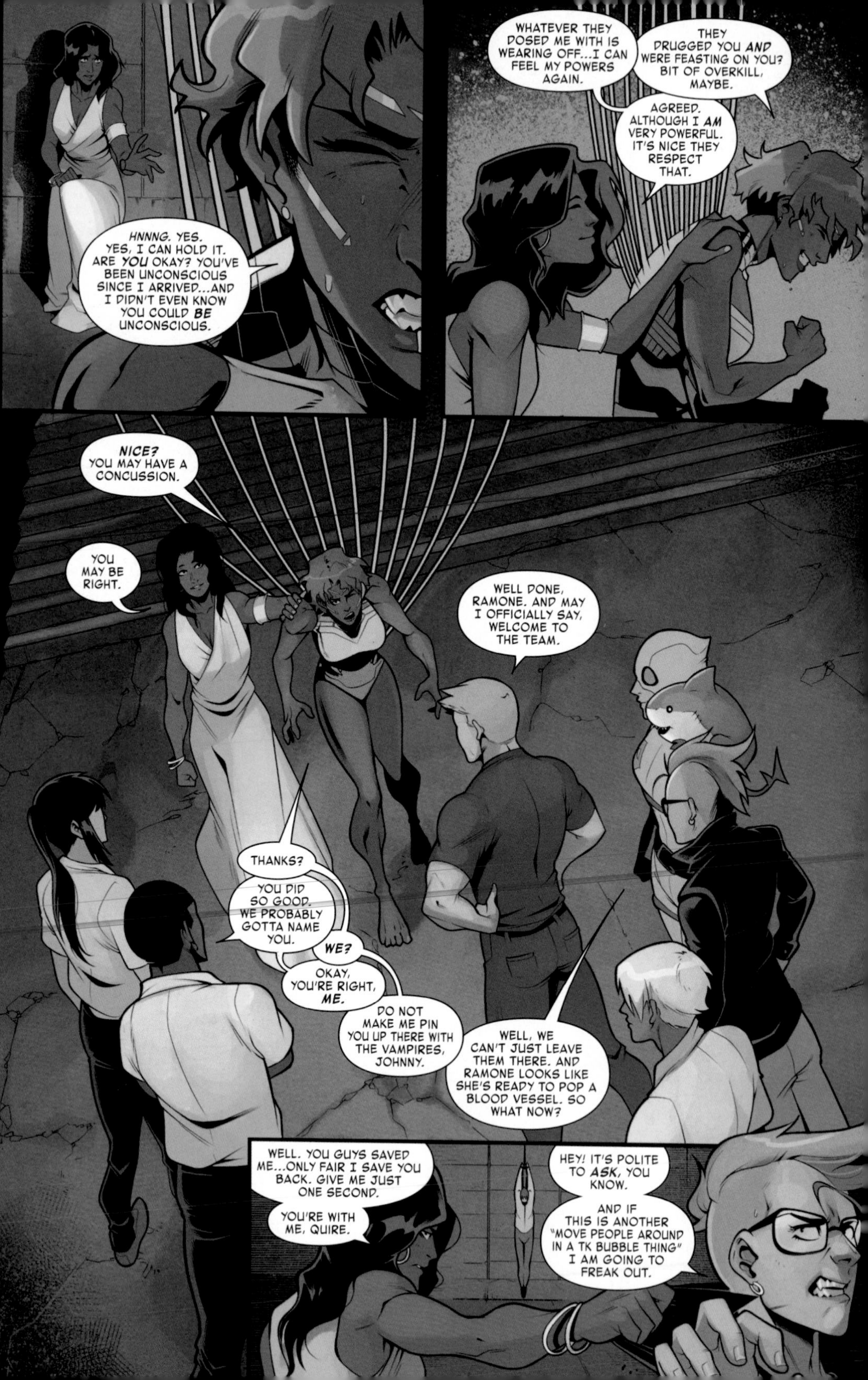

HNNNG. YES. YES, I CAN HOLD IT. ARE YOU OKAY? YOU'VE BEEN UNCONSCIOUS SINCE I ARRIVED...AND I DIDN'T EVEN KNOW YOU COULD BE UNCONSCIOUS.
WHATEVER THEY DOSED ME WITH IS WEARING OFF...I CAN FEEL MY POWERS AGAIN.
THEY DRUGGED YOU AND WERE FEASTING ON YOU? BIT OF OVERKILL, MAYBE.
AGREED. ALTHOUGH I AM VERY POWERFUL. IT'S NICE THEY RESPECT THAT.
NICE? YOU MAY HAVE A CONCUSSION.
YOU MAY BE RIGHT.
WELL DONE, RAMONE. AND MAY I OFFICIALLY SAY, WELCOME TO THE TEAM.
THANKS?
YOU DID SO GOOD. WE PROBABLY GOTTA NAME YOU.
WE?
OKAY, YOU'RE RIGHT, ME.
DO NOT MAKE ME PIN YOU UP THERE WITH THE VAMPIRES, JOHNNY.
WELL, WE CAN'T JUST LEAVE THEM THERE. AND RAMONE LOOKS LIKE SHE'S READY TO POP A BLOOD VESSEL. SO WHAT NOW?
WELL. YOU GUYS SAVED ME...ONLY FAIR I SAVE YOU BACK. GIVE ME JUST ONE SECOND.
YOU'RE WITH ME, QUIRE.
HEY! IT'S POLITE TO ASK, YOU KNOW.
AND IF THIS IS ANOTHER "MOVE PEOPLE AROUND IN A TK BUBBLE THING" I AM GOING TO FREAK OUT.

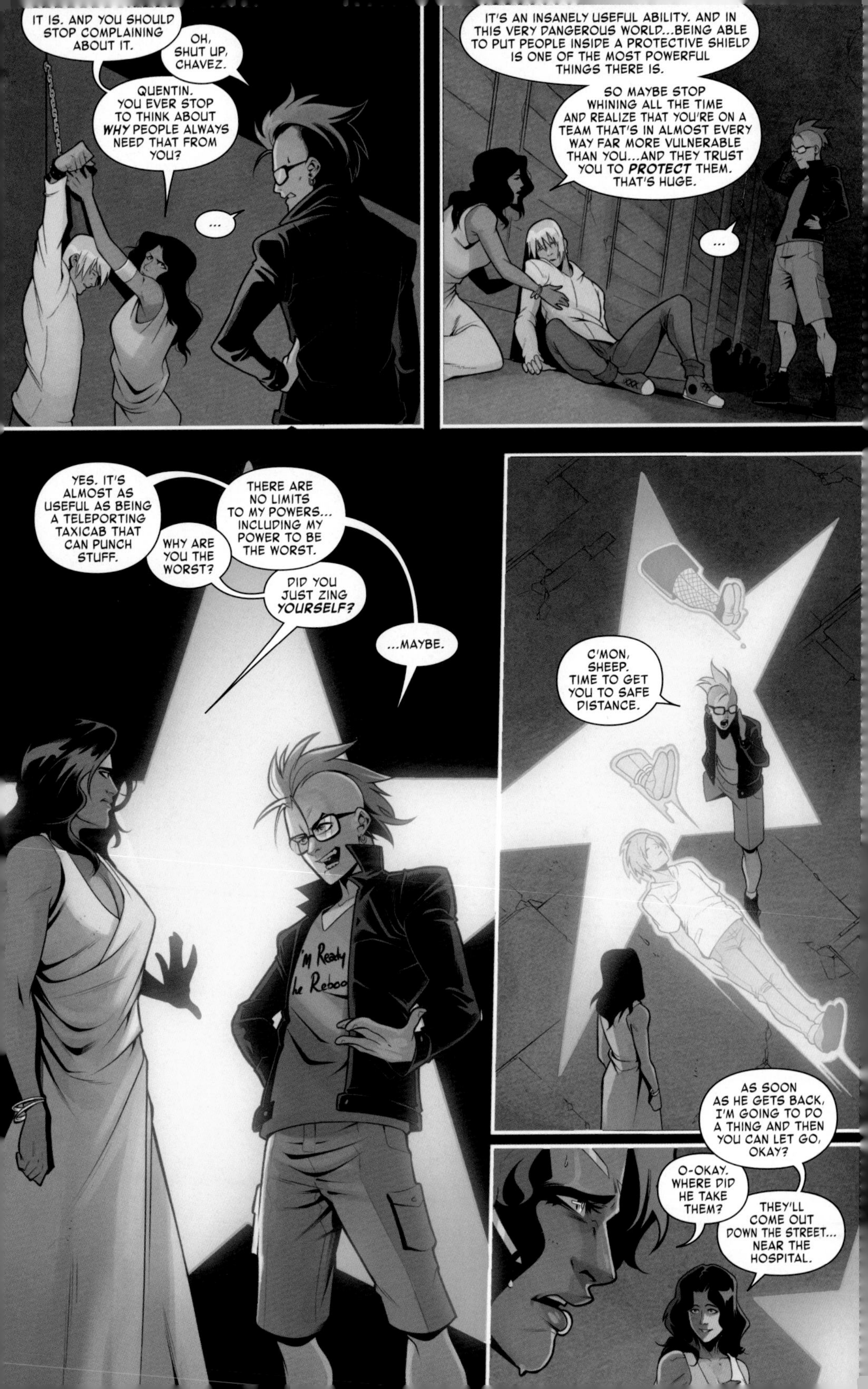
IT IS. AND YOU SHOULD STOP COMPLAINING ABOUT IT.
OH, SHUT UP, CHAVEZ.
QUENTIN. YOU EVER STOP TO THINK ABOUT WHY PEOPLE ALWAYS NEED THAT FROM YOU?
...
IT'S AN INSANELY USEFUL ABILITY. AND IN THIS VERY DANGEROUS WORLD...BEING ABLE TO PUT PEOPLE INSIDE A PROTECTIVE SHIELD IS ONE OF THE MOST POWERFUL THINGS THERE IS.
SO MAYBE STOP WHINING ALL THE TIME AND REALIZE THAT YOU'RE ON A TEAM THAT'S IN ALMOST EVERY WAY FAR MORE VULNERABLE THAN YOU...AND THEY TRUST YOU TO PROTECT THEM. THAT'S HUGE.
...
YES. IT'S ALMOST AS USEFUL AS BEING A TELEPORTING TAXICAB THAT CAN PUNCH STUFF.
THERE ARE NO LIMITS TO MY POWERS... INCLUDING MY POWER TO BE THE WORST.
WHY ARE YOU THE WORST?
DID YOU JUST ZING YOURSELF?
...MAYBE.
C'MON, SHEEP. TIME TO GET YOU TO SAFE DISTANCE.
AS SOON AS HE GETS BACK, I'M GOING TO DO A THING AND THEN YOU CAN LET GO, OKAY?
O-OKAY. WHERE DID HE TAKE THEM?
THEY'LL COME OUT DOWN THE STREET... NEAR THE HOSPITAL.

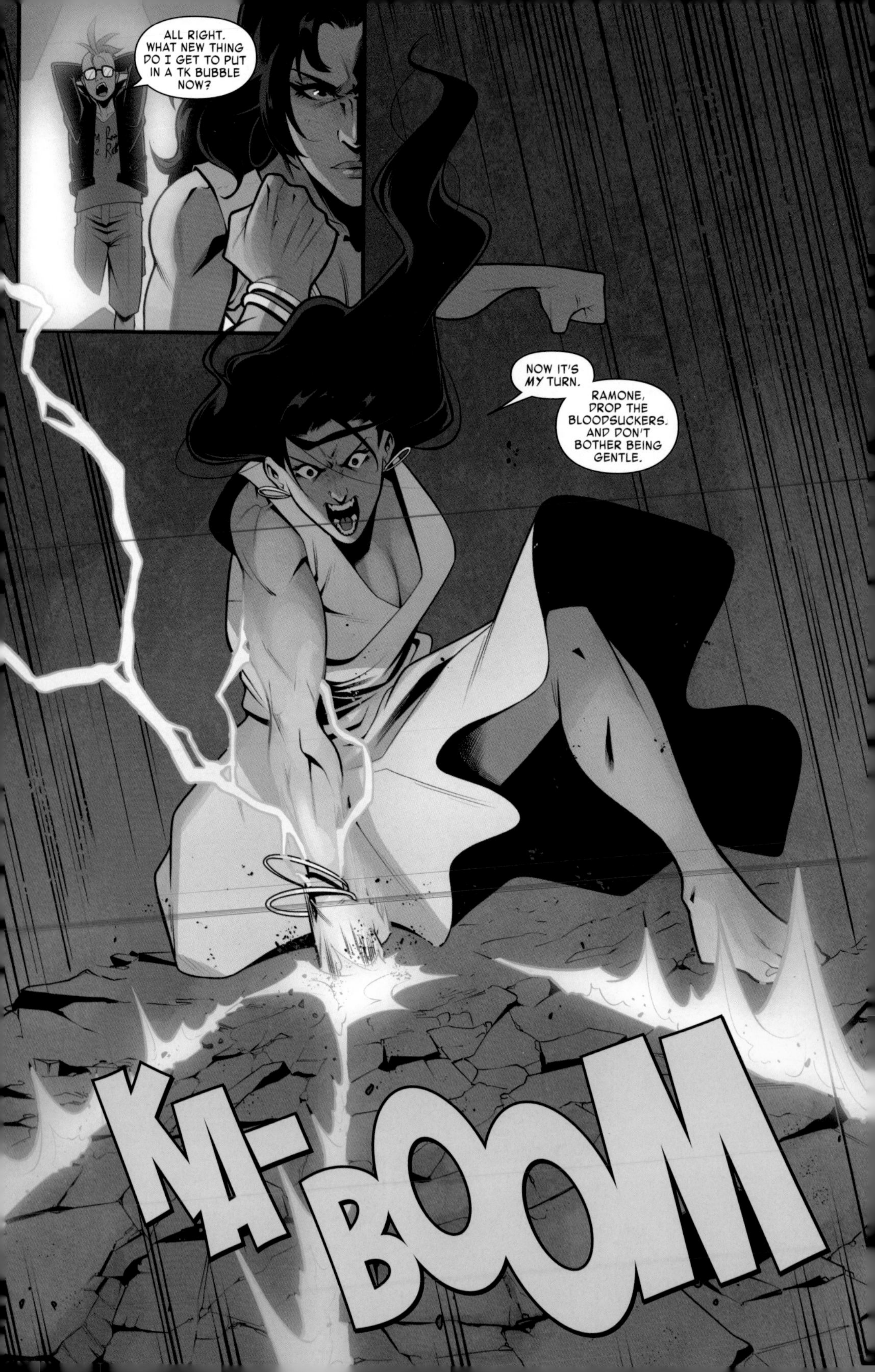
ALL RIGHT. WHAT NEW THING DO I GET TO PUT IN A TK BUBBLE NOW?
NOW IT'S *MY* TURN.
RAMONE, DROP THE BLOODSUCKERS. AND DON'T BOTHER BEING GENTLE.
KA-BOOM

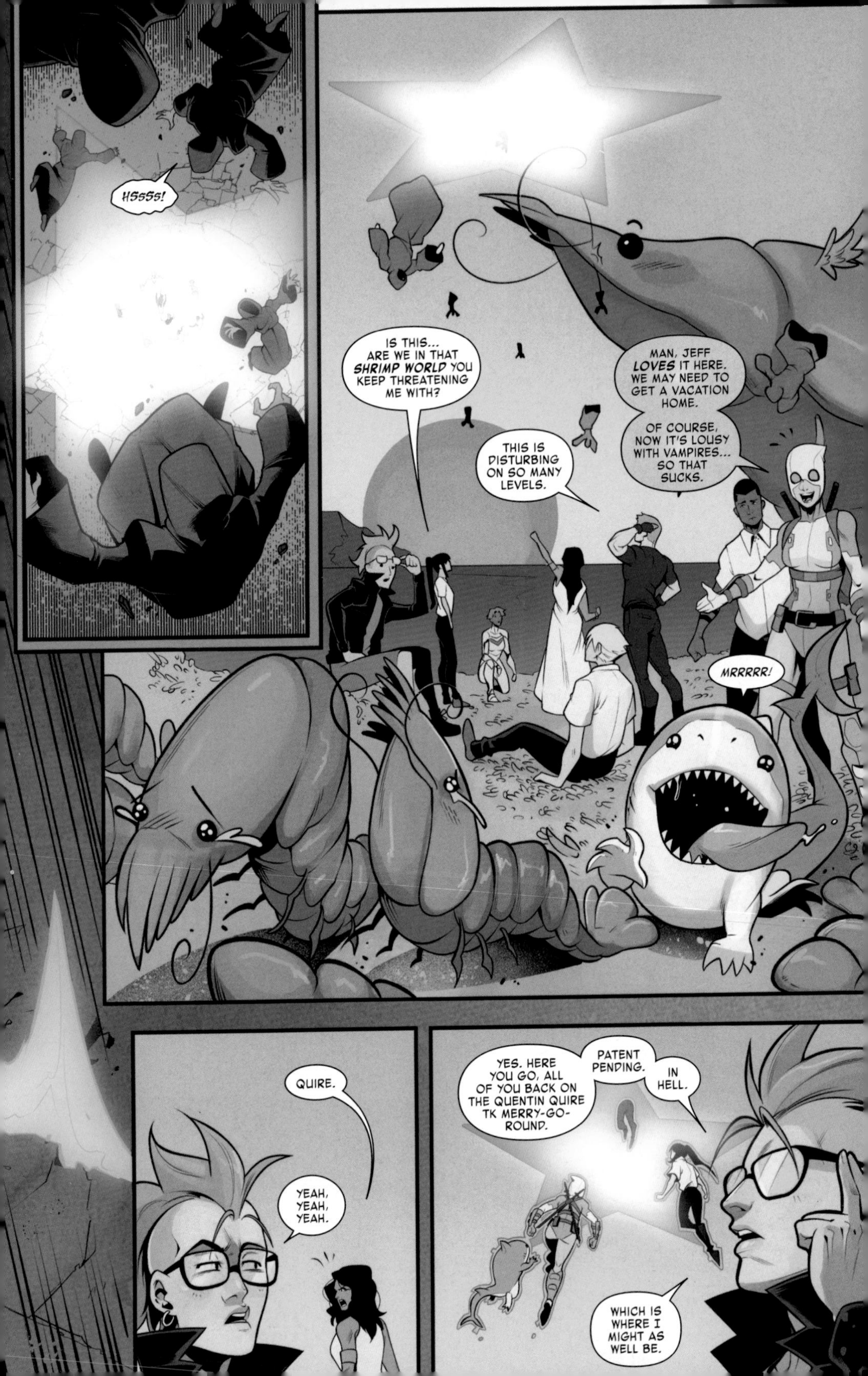
HSsSs!
IS THIS... ARE WE IN THAT SHRIMP WORLD YOU KEEP THREATENING ME WITH?
THIS IS DISTURBING ON SO MANY LEVELS.
MAN, JEFF LOVES IT HERE. WE MAY NEED TO GET A VACATION HOME.
OF COURSE, NOW IT'S LOUSY WITH VAMPIRES... SO THAT SUCKS.
MRRRRR!
QUIRE.
YEAH, YEAH, YEAH.
YES. HERE YOU GO, ALL OF YOU BACK ON THE QUENTIN QUIRE TK MERRY-GO-ROUND.
PATENT PENDING.
IN HELL.
WHICH IS WHERE I MIGHT AS WELL BE.

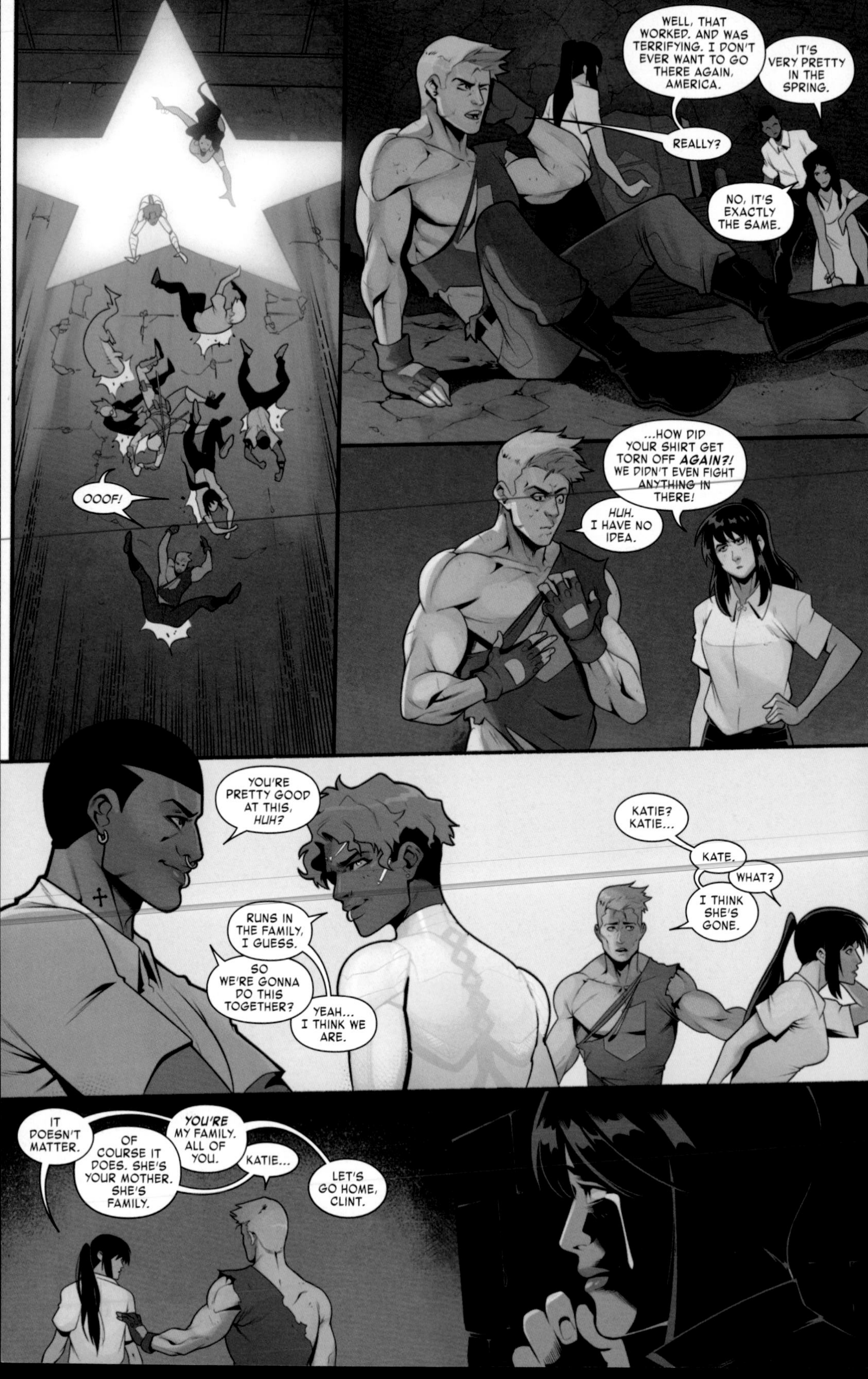
OOOF!
WELL, THAT WORKED. AND WAS TERRIFYING. I DON'T EVER WANT TO GO THERE AGAIN, AMERICA.
REALLY?
IT'S VERY PRETTY IN THE SPRING.
NO, IT'S EXACTLY THE SAME.
...HOW DID YOUR SHIRT GET TORN OFF AGAIN?! WE DIDN'T EVEN FIGHT ANYTHING IN THERE!
HUH. I HAVE NO IDEA.
YOU'RE PRETTY GOOD AT THIS, HUH?
RUNS IN THE FAMILY, I GUESS.
SO WE'RE GONNA DO THIS TOGETHER?
YEAH... I THINK WE ARE.
KATIE? KATIE...
KATE.
WHAT?
I THINK SHE'S GONE.
IT DOESN'T MATTER.
OF COURSE IT DOES. SHE'S YOUR MOTHER. SHE'S FAMILY.
YOU'RE MY FAMILY. ALL OF YOU.
KATIE...
LET'S GO HOME, CLINT.

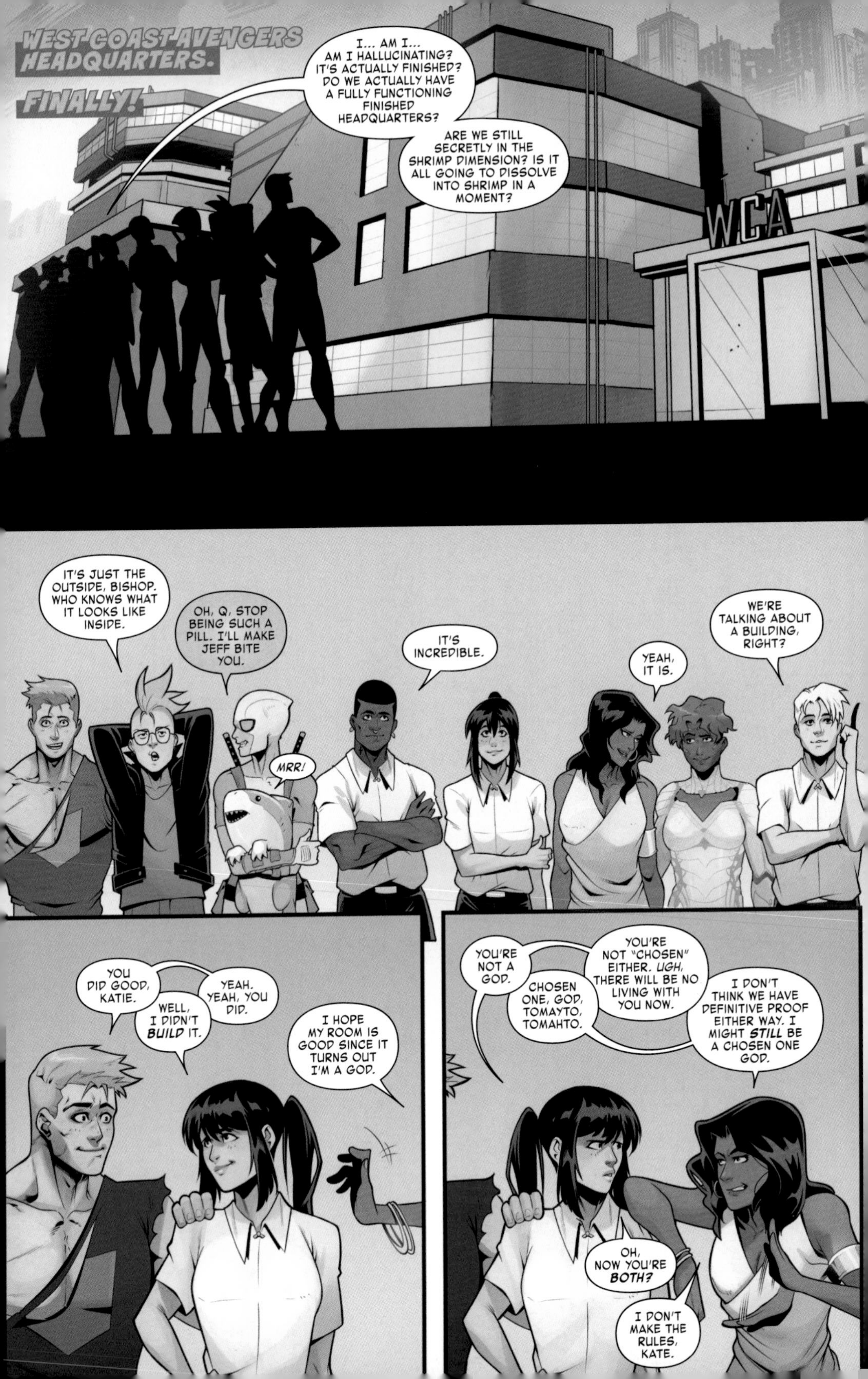
WEST COAST AVENGERS HEADQUARTERS.
FINALLY!
I... AM I... AM I HALLUCINATING? IT'S ACTUALLY FINISHED? DO WE ACTUALLY HAVE A FULLY FUNCTIONING FINISHED HEADQUARTERS?
ARE WE STILL SECRETLY IN THE SHRIMP DIMENSION? IS IT ALL GOING TO DISSOLVE INTO SHRIMP IN A MOMENT?
WCA
IT'S JUST THE OUTSIDE, BISHOP. WHO KNOWS WHAT IT LOOKS LIKE INSIDE.
OH, Q, STOP BEING SUCH A PILL. I'LL MAKE JEFF BITE YOU.
MRR!
IT'S INCREDIBLE.
YEAH, IT IS.
WE'RE TALKING ABOUT A BUILDING, RIGHT?
YOU DID GOOD, KATIE.
WELL, I DIDN'T BUILD IT.
YEAH. YEAH, YOU DID.
I HOPE MY ROOM IS GOOD SINCE IT TURNS OUT I'M A GOD.
YOU'RE NOT A GOD.
CHOSEN ONE, GOD, TOMAYTO, TOMAHTO.
YOU'RE NOT "CHOSEN" EITHER. UGH, THERE WILL BE NO LIVING WITH YOU NOW.
I DON'T THINK WE HAVE DEFINITIVE PROOF EITHER WAY. I MIGHT STILL BE A CHOSEN ONE GOD.
OH, NOW YOU'RE BOTH?
I DON'T MAKE THE RULES, KATE.

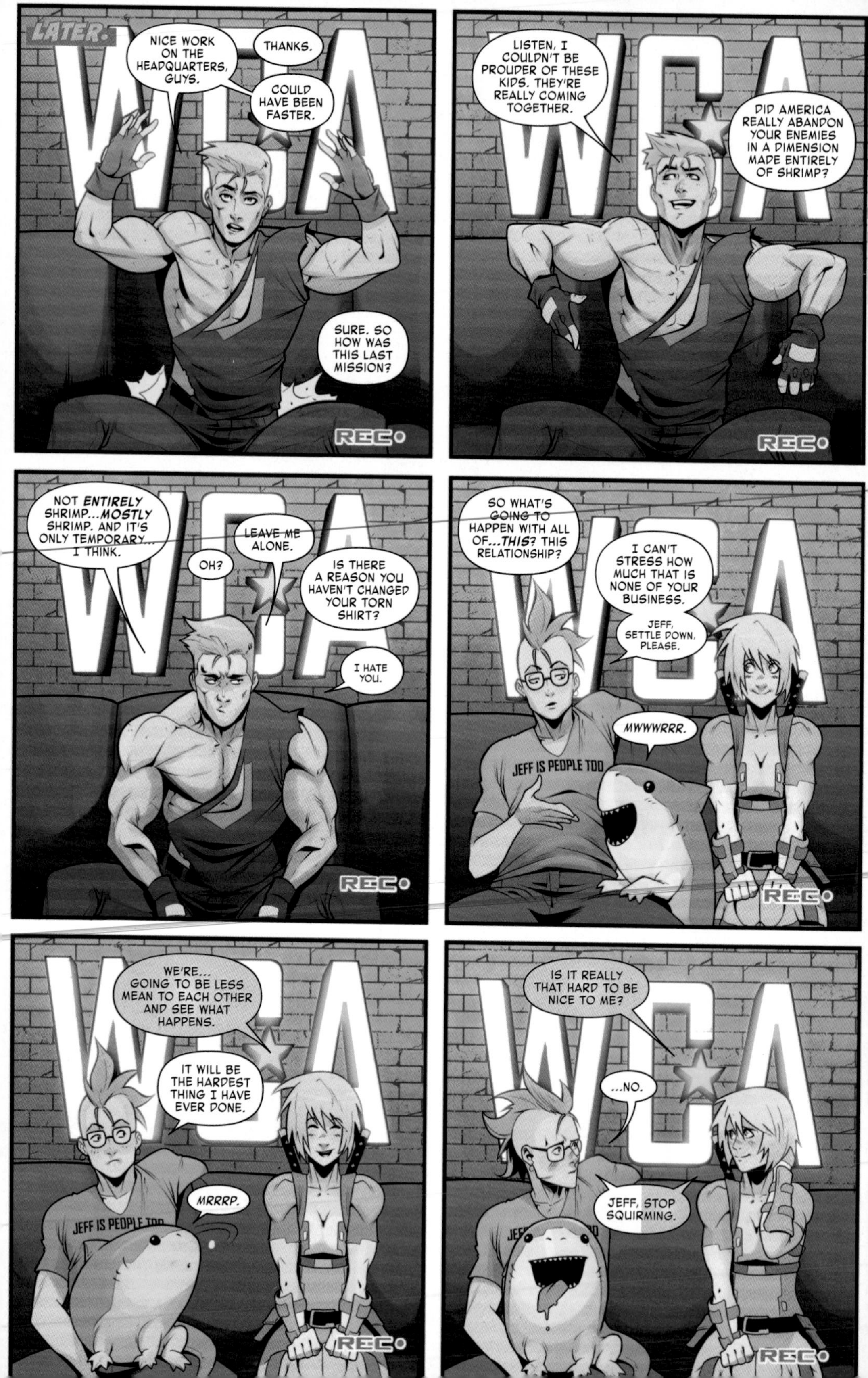
LATER.
NICE WORK ON THE HEADQUARTERS, GUYS.
THANKS.
COULD HAVE BEEN FASTER.
SURE. SO HOW WAS THIS LAST MISSION?
REC
LISTEN, I COULDN'T BE PROUDER OF THESE KIDS. THEY'RE REALLY COMING TOGETHER.
DID AMERICA REALLY ABANDON YOUR ENEMIES IN A DIMENSION MADE ENTIRELY OF SHRIMP?
REC
NOT ENTIRELY SHRIMP...MOSTLY SHRIMP. AND IT'S ONLY TEMPORARY... I THINK.
OH?
LEAVE ME ALONE.
IS THERE A REASON YOU HAVEN'T CHANGED YOUR TORN SHIRT?
I HATE YOU.
REC
SO WHAT'S GOING TO HAPPEN WITH ALL OF...THIS? THIS RELATIONSHIP?
I CAN'T STRESS HOW MUCH THAT IS NONE OF YOUR BUSINESS.
JEFF, SETTLE DOWN, PLEASE.
MWWWRRR.
JEFF IS PEOPLE TOO
REC
WE'RE... GOING TO BE LESS MEAN TO EACH OTHER AND SEE WHAT HAPPENS.
IT WILL BE THE HARDEST THING I HAVE EVER DONE.
MRRRP.
REC
IS IT REALLY THAT HARD TO BE NICE TO ME?
...NO.
JEFF, STOP SQUIRMING.
REC

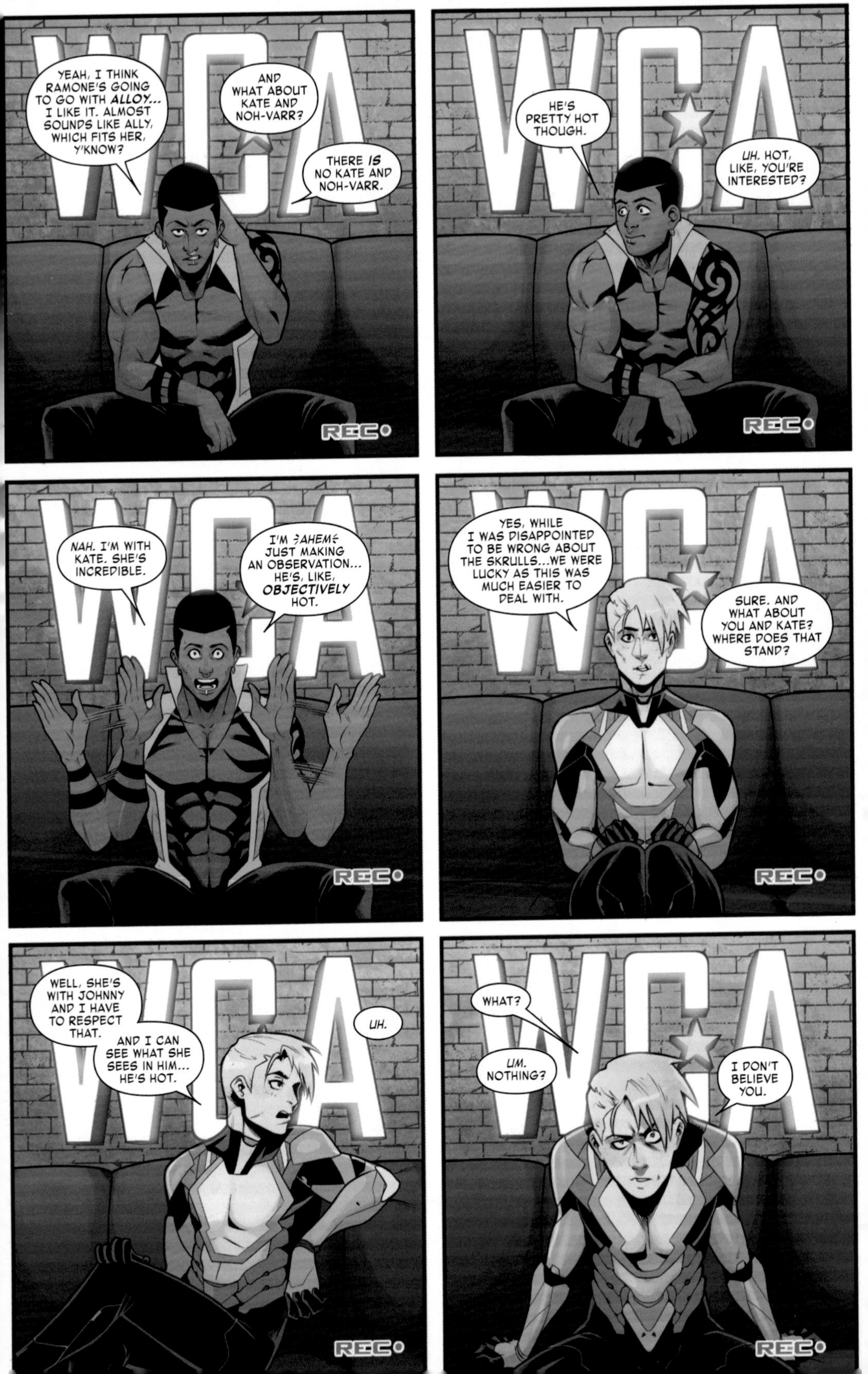
YEAH, I THINK RAMONE'S GOING TO GO WITH ALLOY... I LIKE IT. ALMOST SOUNDS LIKE ALLY, WHICH FITS HER, Y'KNOW?
AND WHAT ABOUT KATE AND NOH-VARR?
THERE IS NO KATE AND NOH-VARR.
REC
HE'S PRETTY HOT THOUGH.
UH. HOT, LIKE, YOU'RE INTERESTED?
REC
NAH. I'M WITH KATE. SHE'S INCREDIBLE.
I'M AHEM JUST MAKING AN OBSERVATION... HE'S, LIKE, OBJECTIVELY HOT.
REC
YES, WHILE I WAS DISAPPOINTED TO BE WRONG ABOUT THE SKRULLS...WE WERE LUCKY AS THIS WAS MUCH EASIER TO DEAL WITH.
SURE. AND WHAT ABOUT YOU AND KATE? WHERE DOES THAT STAND?
REC
WELL, SHE'S WITH JOHNNY AND I HAVE TO RESPECT THAT.
AND I CAN SEE WHAT SHE SEES IN HIM... HE'S HOT.
UH.
REC
WHAT?
UM. NOTHING?
I DON'T BELIEVE YOU.
REC

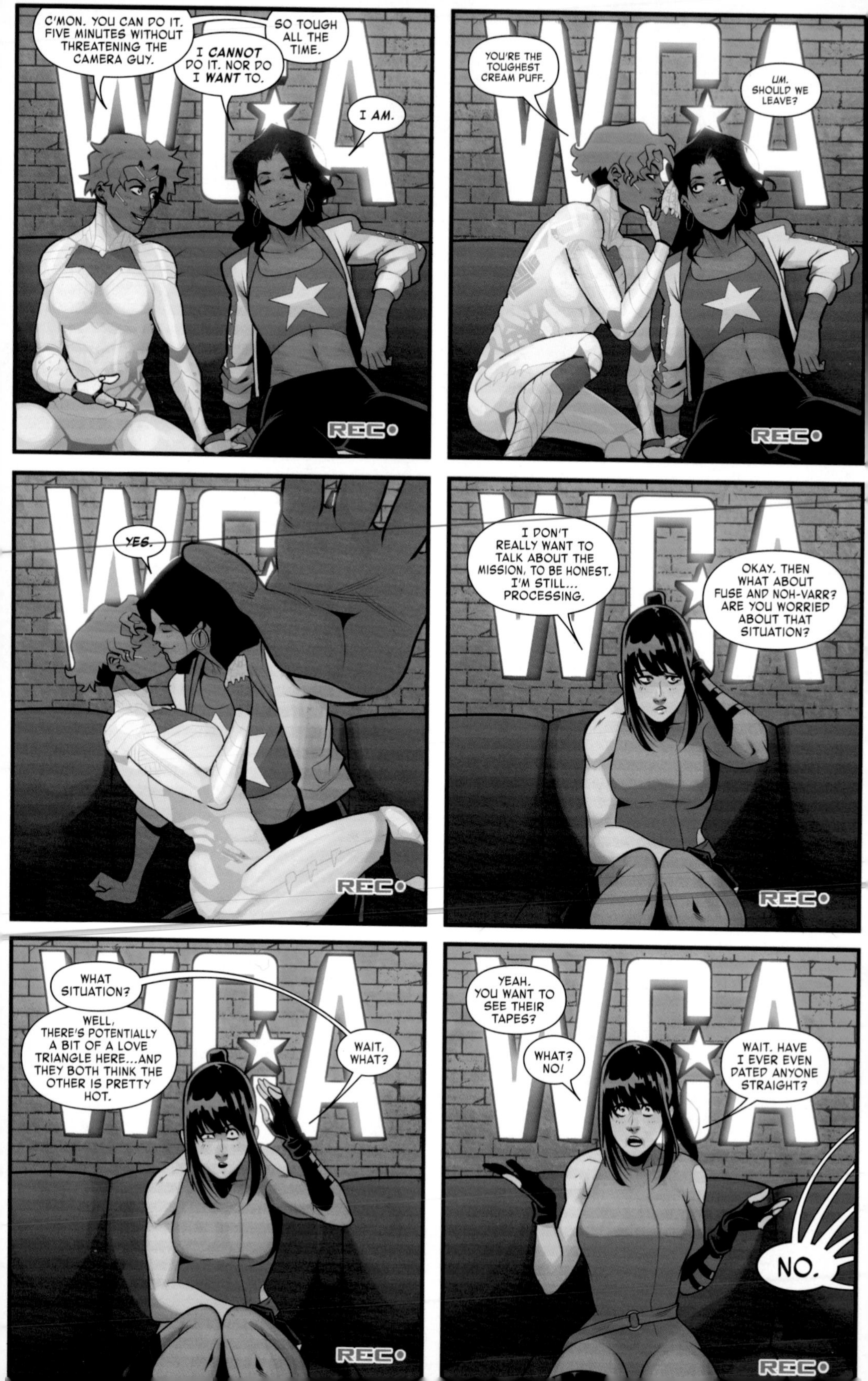
C'MON. YOU CAN DO IT. FIVE MINUTES WITHOUT THREATENING THE CAMERA GUY.
SO TOUGH ALL THE TIME.
I CANNOT DO IT. NOR DO I WANT TO.
I AM.
REC
YOU'RE THE TOUGHEST CREAM PUFF.
UM. SHOULD WE LEAVE?
REC
YES.
REC
I DON'T REALLY WANT TO TALK ABOUT THE MISSION, TO BE HONEST. I'M STILL... PROCESSING.
OKAY. THEN WHAT ABOUT FUSE AND NOH-VARR? ARE YOU WORRIED ABOUT THAT SITUATION?
REC
WHAT SITUATION?
WELL, THERE'S POTENTIALLY A BIT OF A LOVE TRIANGLE HERE...AND THEY BOTH THINK THE OTHER IS PRETTY HOT.
WAIT, WHAT?
REC
YEAH. YOU WANT TO SEE THEIR TAPES?
WHAT? NO!
WAIT. HAVE I EVER EVEN DATED ANYONE STRAIGHT?
NO.
REC

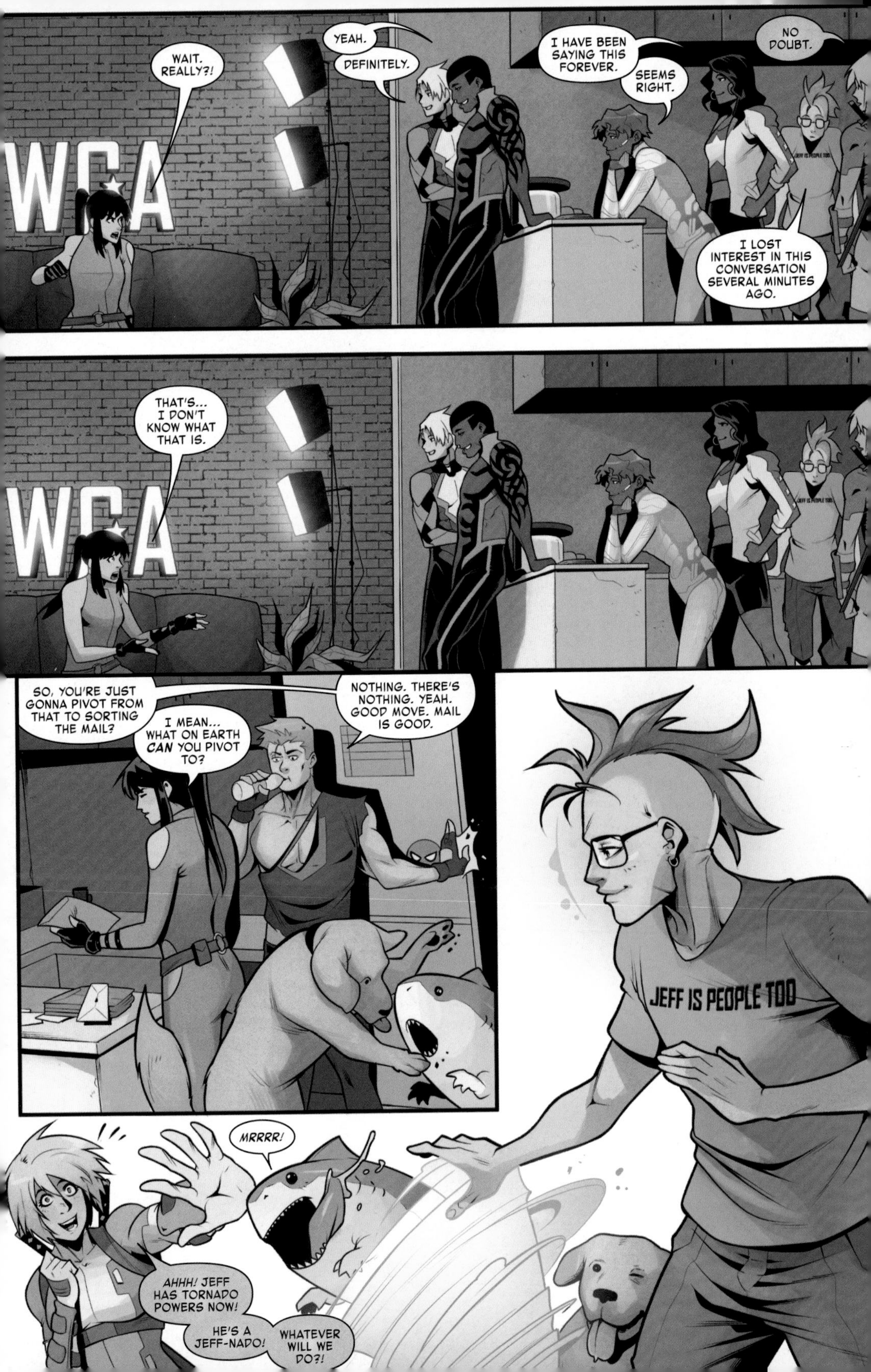

WCA
WAIT. REALLY?!
YEAH.
DEFINITELY.
I HAVE BEEN SAYING THIS FOREVER.
SEEMS RIGHT.
NO DOUBT.
JEFF IS PEOPLE TOO
I LOST INTEREST IN THIS CONVERSATION SEVERAL MINUTES AGO.
WCA
THAT'S... I DON'T KNOW WHAT THAT IS.
JEFF IS PEOPLE TOO
SO, YOU'RE JUST GONNA PIVOT FROM THAT TO SORTING THE MAIL?
NOTHING. THERE'S NOTHING. YEAH. GOOD MOVE. MAIL IS GOOD.
I MEAN... WHAT ON EARTH **CAN** YOU PIVOT TO?
JEFF IS PEOPLE TOO
MRRRR!
AHHH! JEFF HAS TORNADO POWERS NOW!
HE'S A JEFF-NADO!
WHATEVER WILL WE DO?!

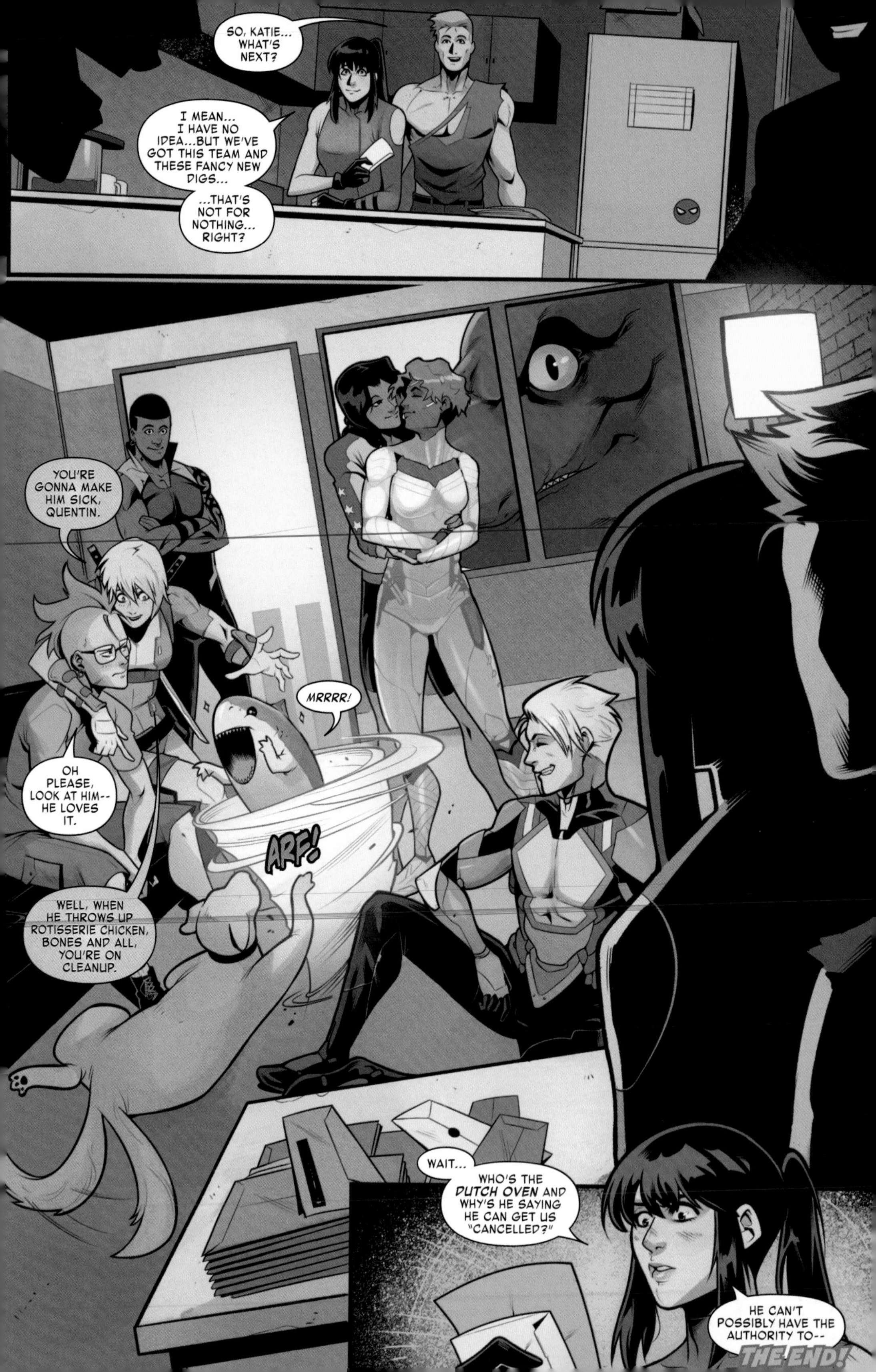
SO, KATIE... WHAT'S NEXT?
I MEAN... I HAVE NO IDEA...BUT WE'VE GOT THIS TEAM AND THESE FANCY NEW DIGS...
...THAT'S NOT FOR NOTHING... RIGHT?
YOU'RE GONNA MAKE HIM SICK, QUENTIN.
MRRRR!
OH PLEASE, LOOK AT HIM-- HE LOVES IT.
ARF!
WELL, WHEN HE THROWS UP ROTISSERIE CHICKEN, BONES AND ALL, YOU'RE ON CLEANUP.
WAIT...
WHO'S THE DUTCH OVEN AND WHY'S HE SAYING HE CAN GET US "CANCELLED?"
HE CAN'T POSSIBLY HAVE THE AUTHORITY TO--
THE END!

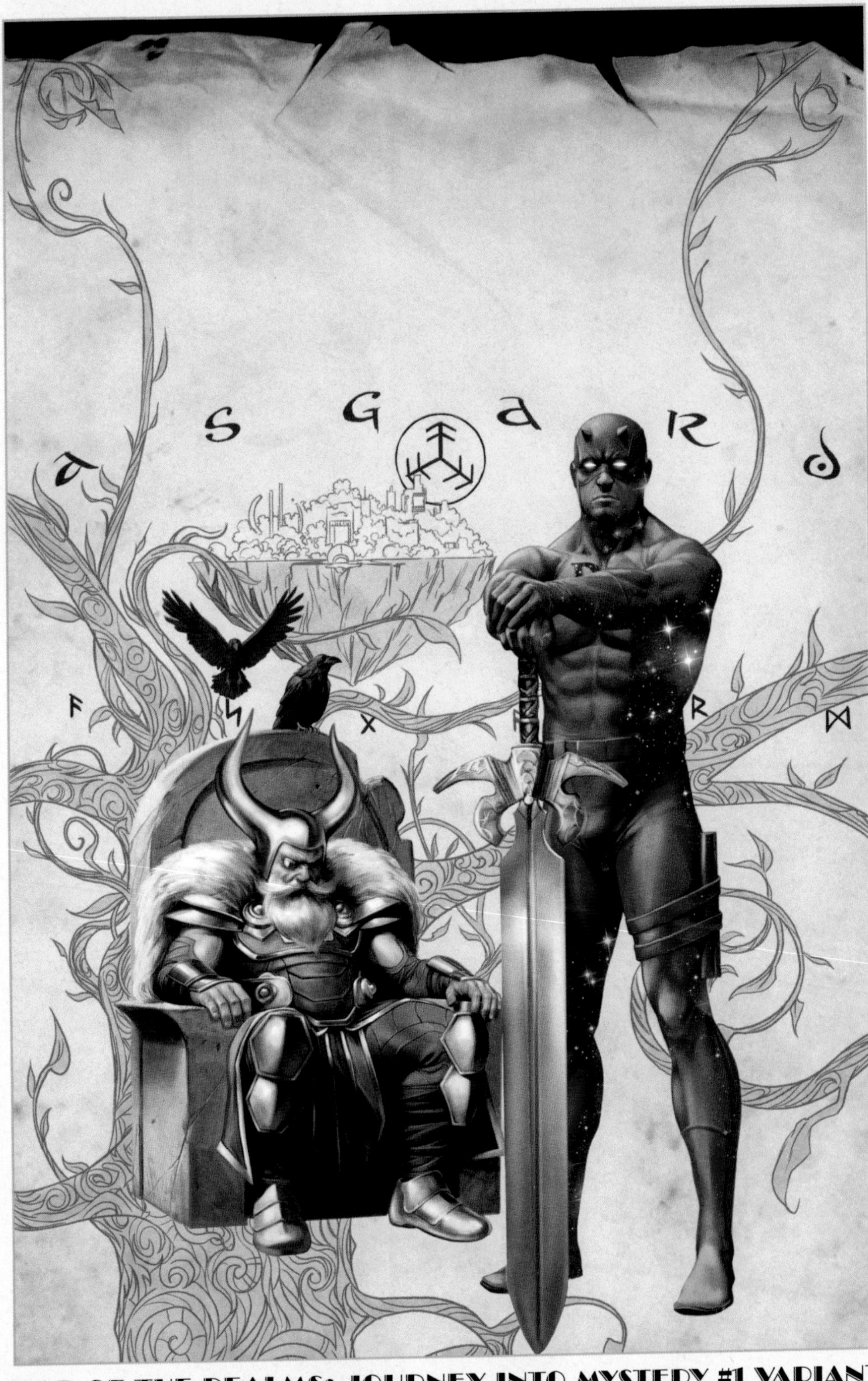
ASGARD

WAR OF THE REALMS: JOURNEY INTO MYSTERY #1 VARIANT
BY GUISEPPE CAMUNCOLI & ELIA BONETTI

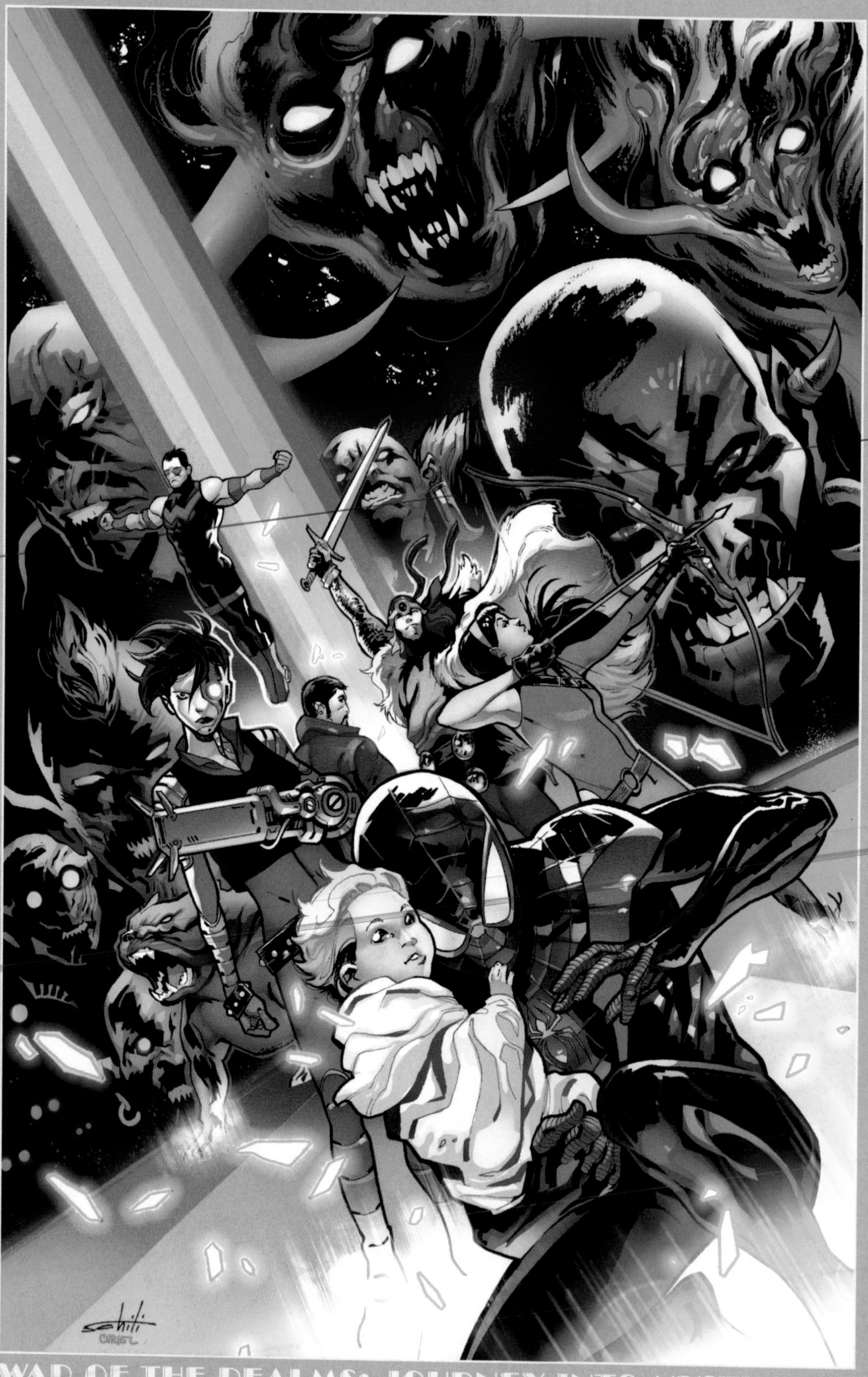

WAR OF THE REALMS: JOURNEY INTO MYSTERY #1

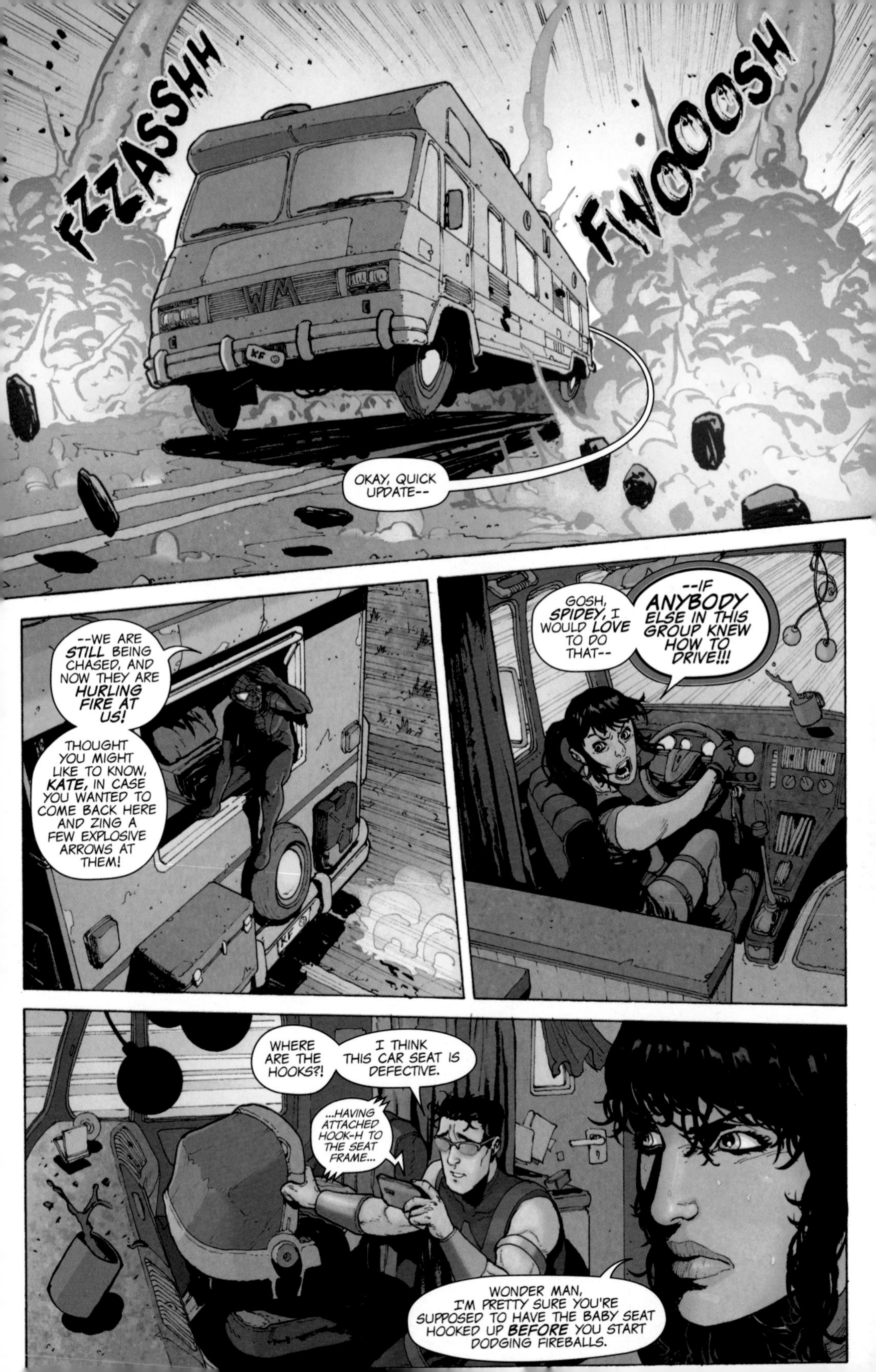
FZZASSHH
FWOOOSH
OKAY, QUICK UPDATE--
--WE ARE STILL BEING CHASED, AND NOW THEY ARE HURLING FIRE AT US!
THOUGHT YOU MIGHT LIKE TO KNOW, KATE, IN CASE YOU WANTED TO COME BACK HERE AND ZING A FEW EXPLOSIVE ARROWS AT THEM!
GOSH, SPIDEY, I WOULD LOVE TO DO THAT--
--IF ANYBODY ELSE IN THIS GROUP KNEW HOW TO DRIVE!!!
WHERE ARE THE HOOKS?!
I THINK THIS CAR SEAT IS DEFECTIVE.
...HAVING ATTACHED HOOK-H TO THE SEAT FRAME...
WONDER MAN, I'M PRETTY SURE YOU'RE SUPPOSED TO HAVE THE BABY SEAT HOOKED UP BEFORE YOU START DODGING FIREBALLS.

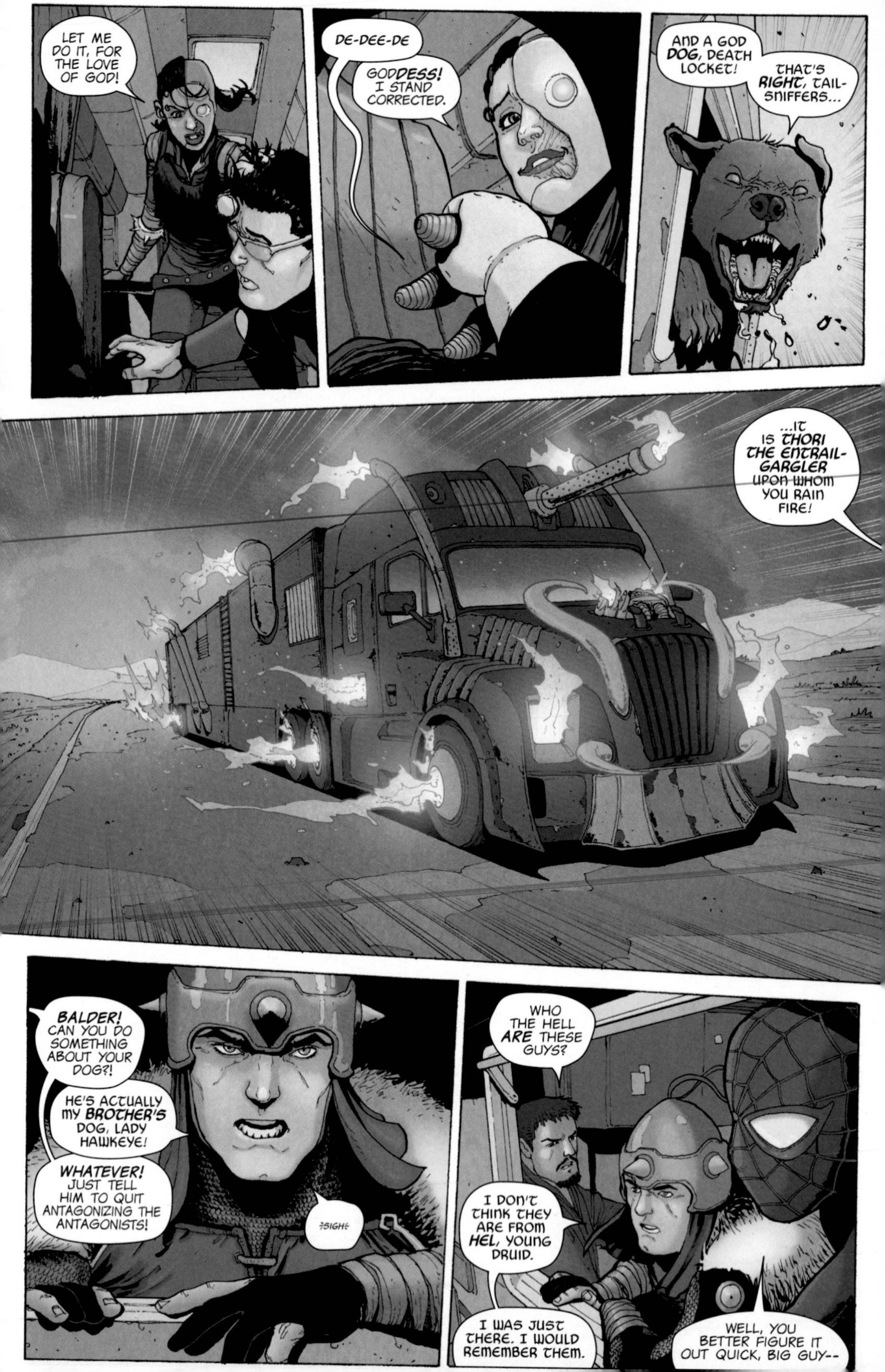
LET ME DO IT, FOR THE LOVE OF GOD!
DE-DEE-DE
GODDESS! I STAND CORRECTED.
AND A GOD DOG, DEATH LOCKET!
THAT'S RIGHT, TAIL-SNIFFERS...
...IT IS THORI THE ENTRAIL-GARGLER UPON WHOM YOU RAIN FIRE!
BALDER! CAN YOU DO SOMETHING ABOUT YOUR DOG?!
HE'S ACTUALLY MY BROTHER'S DOG, LADY HAWKEYE!
WHATEVER! JUST TELL HIM TO QUIT ANTAGONIZING THE ANTAGONISTS!
SIGH
WHO THE HELL ARE THESE GUYS?
I DON'T THINK THEY ARE FROM HEL, YOUNG DRUID.
I WAS JUST THERE. I WOULD REMEMBER THEM.
WELL, YOU BETTER FIGURE IT OUT QUICK, BIG GUY--

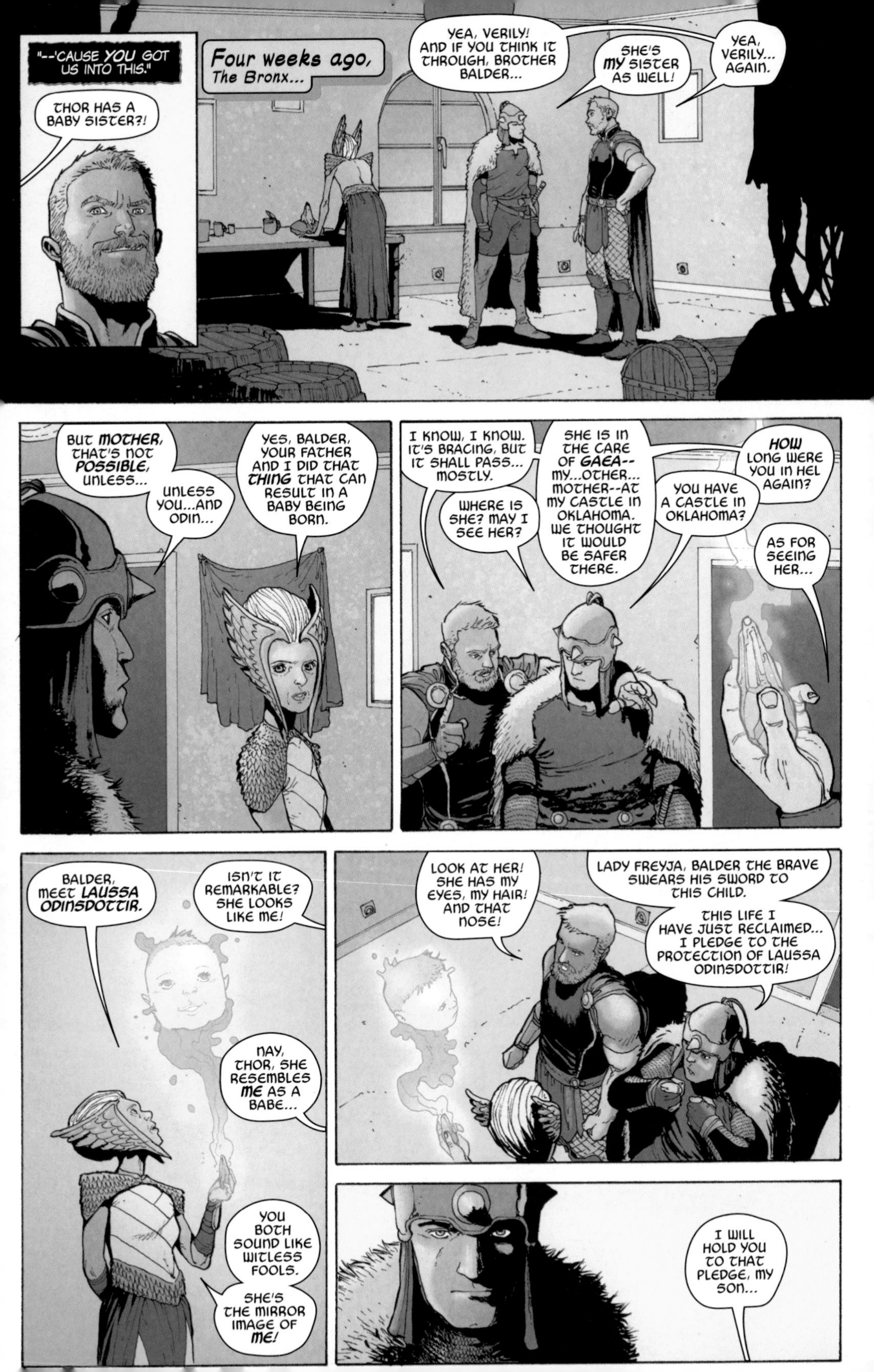
"--'CAUSE YOU GOT US INTO THIS."
THOR HAS A BABY SISTER?!
Four weeks ago, The Bronx...
YEA, VERILY! AND IF YOU THINK IT THROUGH, BROTHER BALDER...
SHE'S MY SISTER AS WELL!
YEA, VERILY... AGAIN.
BUT MOTHER, THAT'S NOT POSSIBLE, UNLESS...
UNLESS YOU...AND ODIN...
YES, BALDER, YOUR FATHER AND I DID THAT THING THAT CAN RESULT IN A BABY BEING BORN.
I KNOW, I KNOW. IT'S BRACING, BUT IT SHALL PASS... MOSTLY.
WHERE IS SHE? MAY I SEE HER?
SHE IS IN THE CARE OF GAEA-- MY...OTHER... MOTHER--AT MY CASTLE IN OKLAHOMA. WE THOUGHT IT WOULD BE SAFER THERE.
YOU HAVE A CASTLE IN OKLAHOMA?
HOW LONG WERE YOU IN HEL AGAIN?
AS FOR SEEING HER...
BALDER, MEET LAUSSA ODINSDOTTIR.
ISN'T IT REMARKABLE? SHE LOOKS LIKE ME!
NAY, THOR, SHE RESEMBLES ME AS A BABE...
YOU BOTH SOUND LIKE WITLESS FOOLS.
SHE'S THE MIRROR IMAGE OF ME!
LOOK AT HER! SHE HAS MY EYES, MY HAIR! AND THAT NOSE!
LADY FREYJA, BALDER THE BRAVE SWEARS HIS SWORD TO THIS CHILD.
THIS LIFE I HAVE JUST RECLAIMED... I PLEDGE TO THE PROTECTION OF LAUSSA ODINSDOTTIR!
I WILL HOLD YOU TO THAT PLEDGE, MY SON...

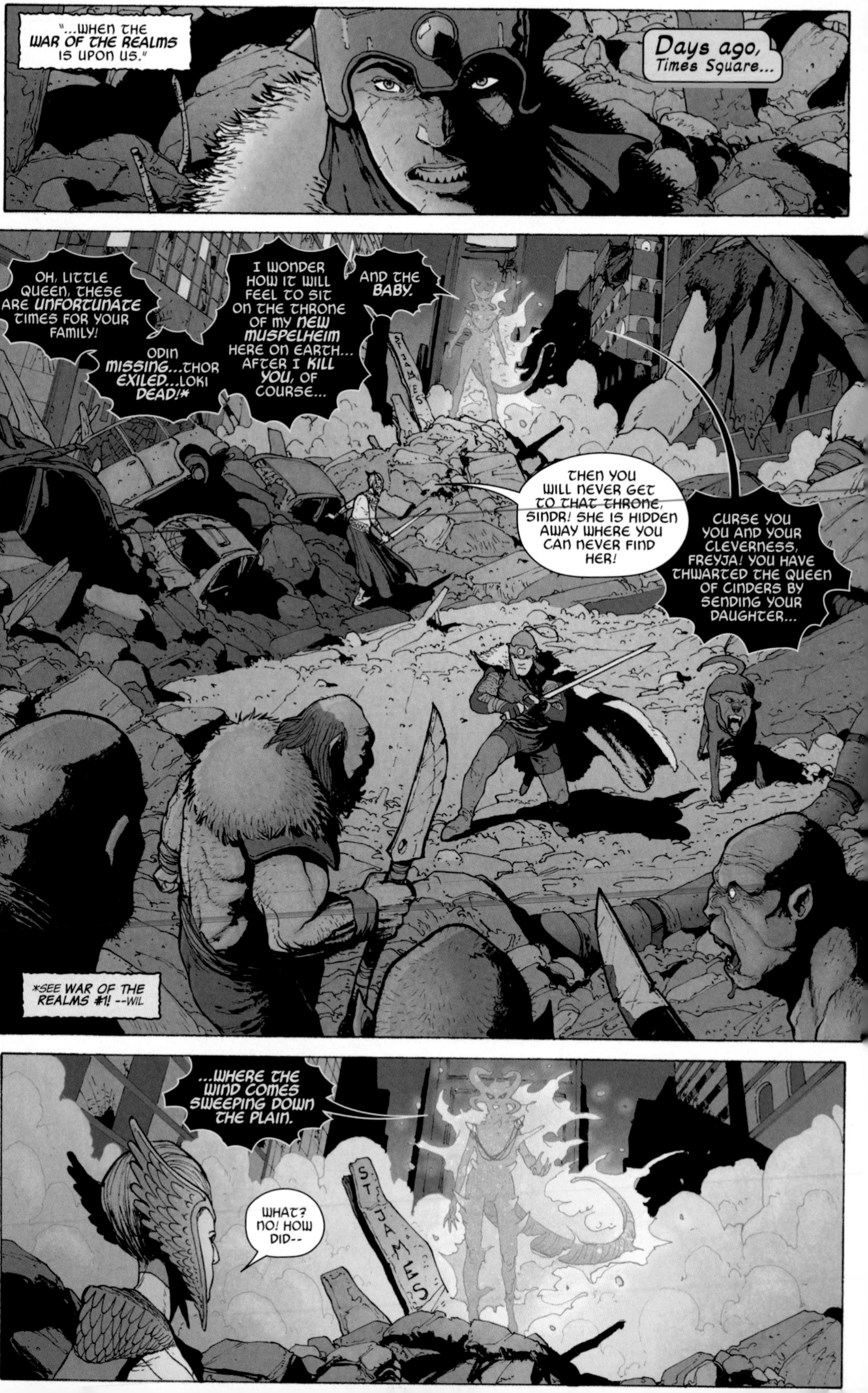
"...WHEN THE WAR OF THE REALMS IS UPON US."
Days ago, Times Square...
OH, LITTLE QUEEN, THESE ARE UNFORTUNATE TIMES FOR YOUR FAMILY!
ODIN MISSING...THOR EXILED...LOKI DEAD!*
I WONDER HOW IT WILL FEEL TO SIT ON THE THRONE OF MY NEW MUSPELHEIM HERE ON EARTH... AFTER I KILL YOU, OF COURSE...
AND THE BABY.
ST JAMES
THEN YOU WILL NEVER GET TO THAT THRONE, SINDR! SHE IS HIDDEN AWAY WHERE YOU CAN NEVER FIND HER!
CURSE YOU YOU AND YOUR CLEVERNESS, FREYJA! YOU HAVE THWARTED THE QUEEN OF CINDERS BY SENDING YOUR DAUGHTER...
*SEE WAR OF THE REALMS #1! --WIL
...WHERE THE WIND COMES SWEEPING DOWN THE PLAIN.
WHAT? NO! HOW DID--
ST JAMES

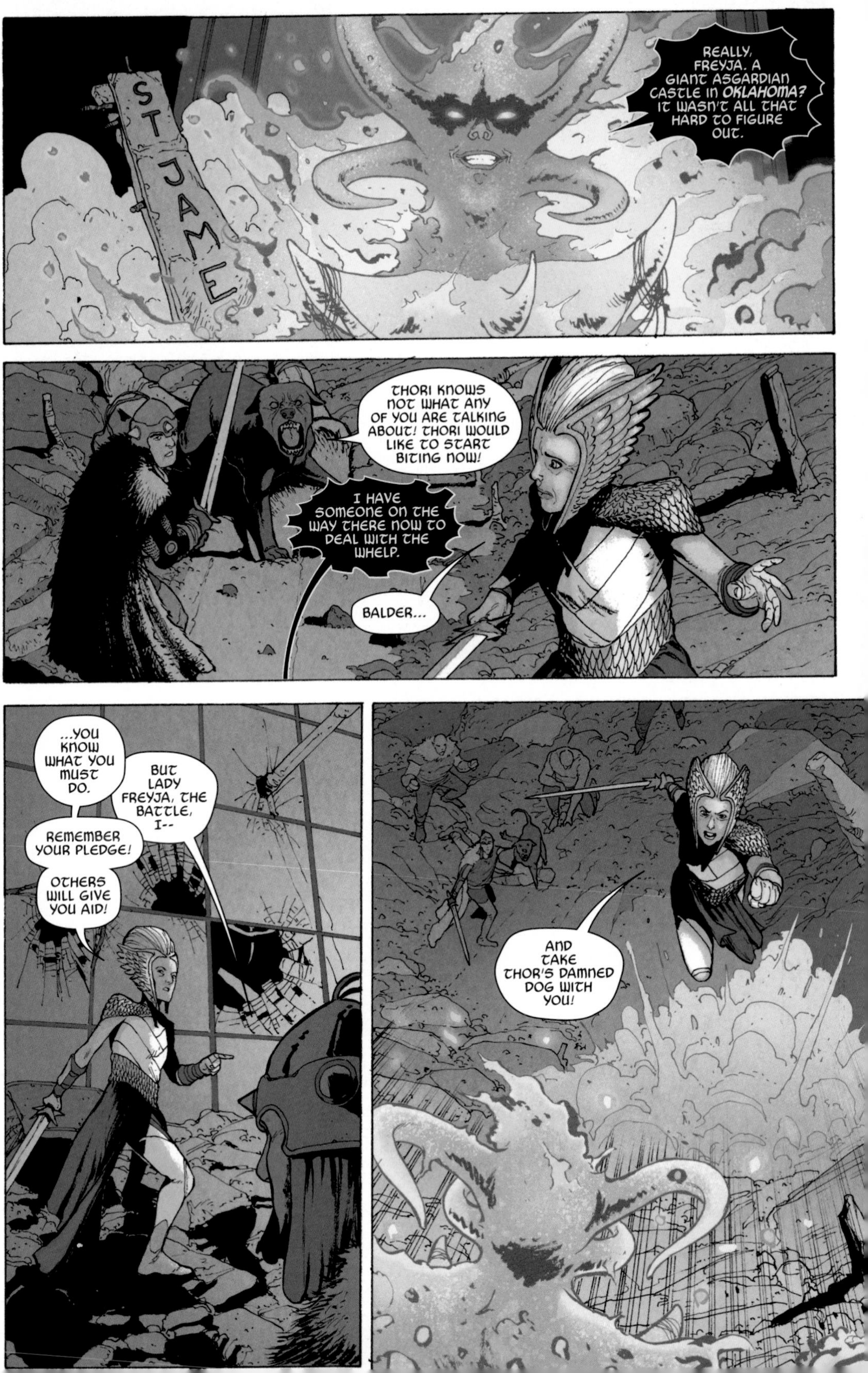

ST JAME
REALLY, FREYJA. A GIANT ASGARDIAN CASTLE IN OKLAHOMA? IT WASN'T ALL THAT HARD TO FIGURE OUT.
THORI KNOWS NOT WHAT ANY OF YOU ARE TALKING ABOUT! THORI WOULD LIKE TO START BITING NOW!
I HAVE SOMEONE ON THE WAY THERE NOW TO DEAL WITH THE WHELP.
BALDER...
...YOU KNOW WHAT YOU MUST DO.
BUT LADY FREYJA, THE BATTLE, I--
REMEMBER YOUR PLEDGE!
OTHERS WILL GIVE YOU AID!
AND TAKE THOR'S DAMNED DOG WITH YOU!

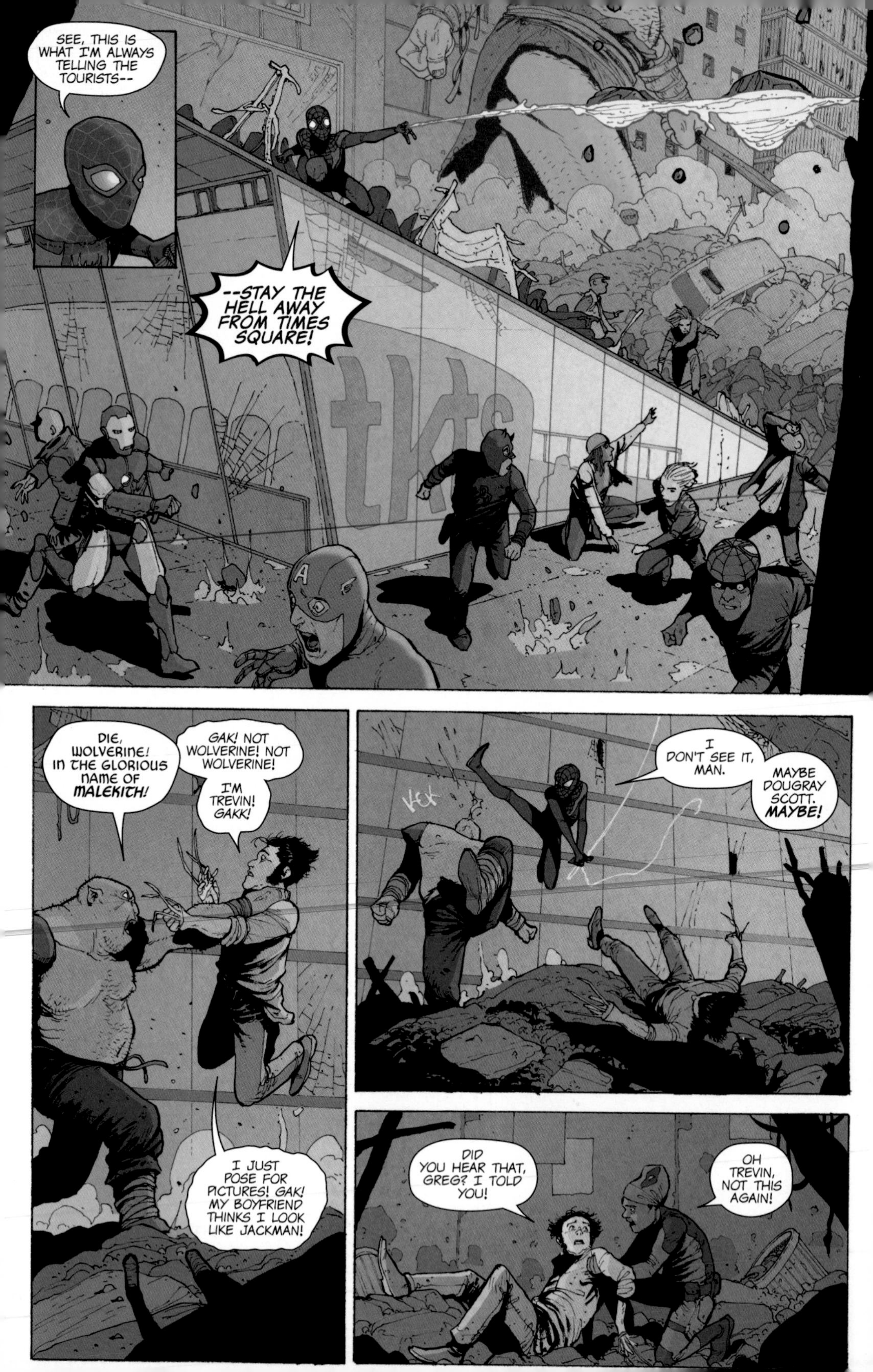
SEE, THIS IS WHAT I'M ALWAYS TELLING THE TOURISTS--
--STAY THE HELL AWAY FROM TIMES SQUARE!
tkts
DIE, WOLVERINE! IN THE GLORIOUS NAME OF MALEKITH!
GAK! NOT WOLVERINE! NOT WOLVERINE!
I'M TREVIN! GAKK!
I JUST POSE FOR PICTURES! GAK! MY BOYFRIEND THINKS I LOOK LIKE JACKMAN!
I DON'T SEE IT, MAN.
MAYBE DOUGRAY SCOTT. MAYBE!
DID YOU HEAR THAT, GREG? I TOLD YOU!
OH TREVIN, NOT THIS AGAIN!

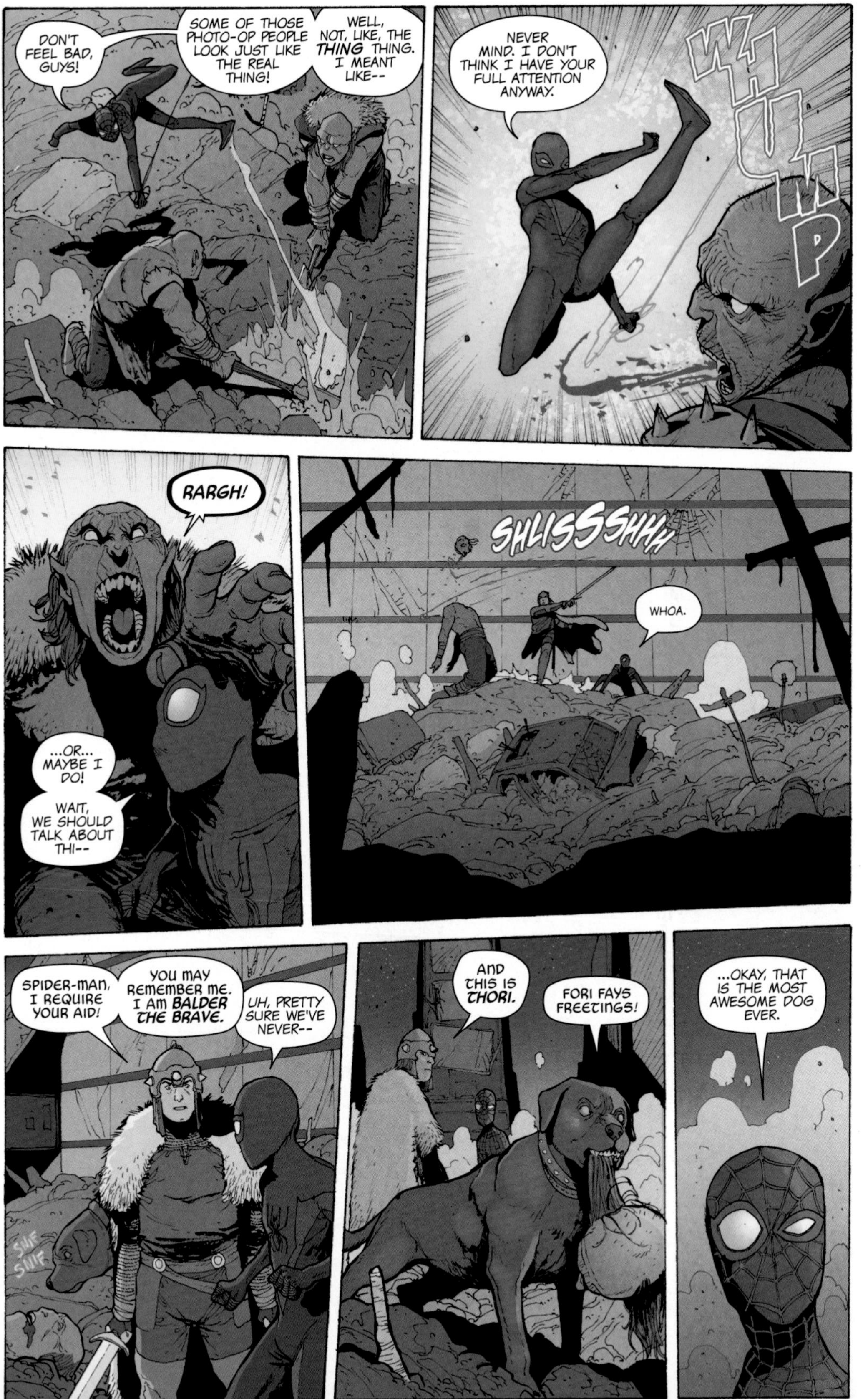
DON'T FEEL BAD, GUYS!
SOME OF THOSE PHOTO-OP PEOPLE LOOK JUST LIKE THE REAL THING!
WELL, NOT, LIKE, THE THING THING. I MEANT LIKE--
NEVER MIND. I DON'T THINK I HAVE YOUR FULL ATTENTION ANYWAY.
WHUMP
RARGH!
...OR... MAYBE I DO!
WAIT, WE SHOULD TALK ABOUT THI--
SHLISSSHHH
WHOA.
SPIDER-MAN, I REQUIRE YOUR AID!
YOU MAY REMEMBER ME. I AM BALDER THE BRAVE.
UH, PRETTY SURE WE'VE NEVER--
SNIF SNIF
AND THIS IS THORI.
FORI FAYS FREETINGS!
...OKAY, THAT IS THE MOST AWESOME DOG EVER.

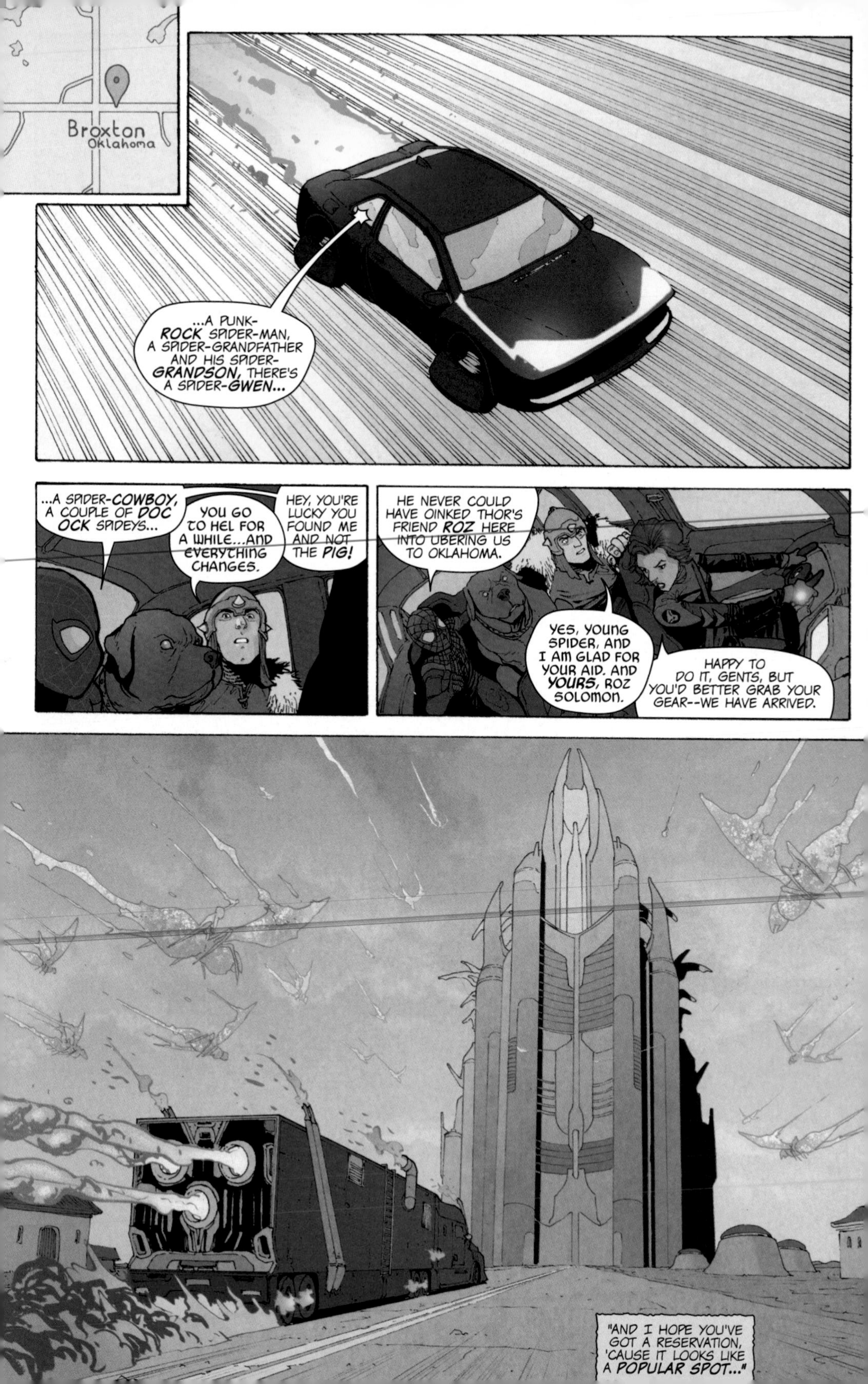
Broxton
Oklahoma
...A PUNK-ROCK SPIDER-MAN, A SPIDER-GRANDFATHER AND HIS SPIDER-GRANDSON, THERE'S A SPIDER-GWEN...
...A SPIDER-COWBOY, A COUPLE OF DOC OCK SPIDEYS...
YOU GO TO HEL FOR A WHILE...AND EVERYTHING CHANGES.
HEY, YOU'RE LUCKY YOU FOUND ME AND NOT THE PIG!
HE NEVER COULD HAVE OINKED THOR'S FRIEND ROZ HERE INTO UBERING US TO OKLAHOMA.
YES, YOUNG SPIDER, AND I AM GLAD FOR YOUR AID. AND YOURS, ROZ SOLOMON.
HAPPY TO DO IT, GENTS, BUT YOU'D BETTER GRAB YOUR GEAR--WE HAVE ARRIVED.
"AND I HOPE YOU'VE GOT A RESERVATION, 'CAUSE IT LOOKS LIKE A POPULAR SPOT..."

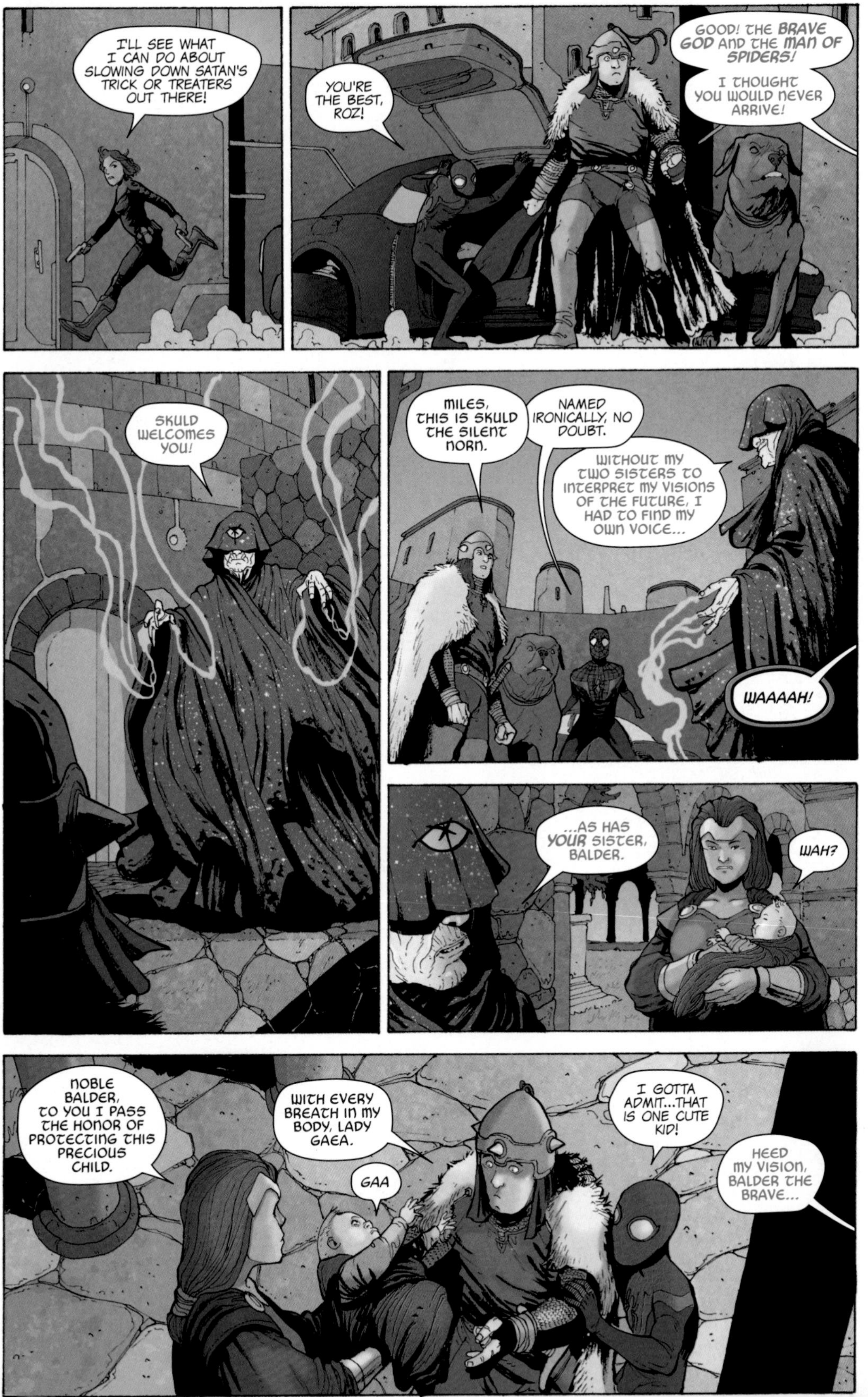
I'LL SEE WHAT I CAN DO ABOUT SLOWING DOWN SATAN'S TRICK OR TREATERS OUT THERE!
YOU'RE THE BEST, ROZ!
GOOD! THE BRAVE GOD AND THE MAN OF SPIDERS!
I THOUGHT YOU WOULD NEVER ARRIVE!
SKULD WELCOMES YOU!
MILES, THIS IS SKULD THE SILENT NORN.
NAMED IRONICALLY, NO DOUBT.
WITHOUT MY TWO SISTERS TO INTERPRET MY VISIONS OF THE FUTURE, I HAD TO FIND MY OWN VOICE...
WAAAAH!
...AS HAS YOUR SISTER, BALDER.
WAH?
NOBLE BALDER, TO YOU I PASS THE HONOR OF PROTECTING THIS PRECIOUS CHILD.
WITH EVERY BREATH IN MY BODY, LADY GAEA.
GAA
I GOTTA ADMIT...THAT IS ONE CUTE KID!
HEED MY VISION, BALDER THE BRAVE...

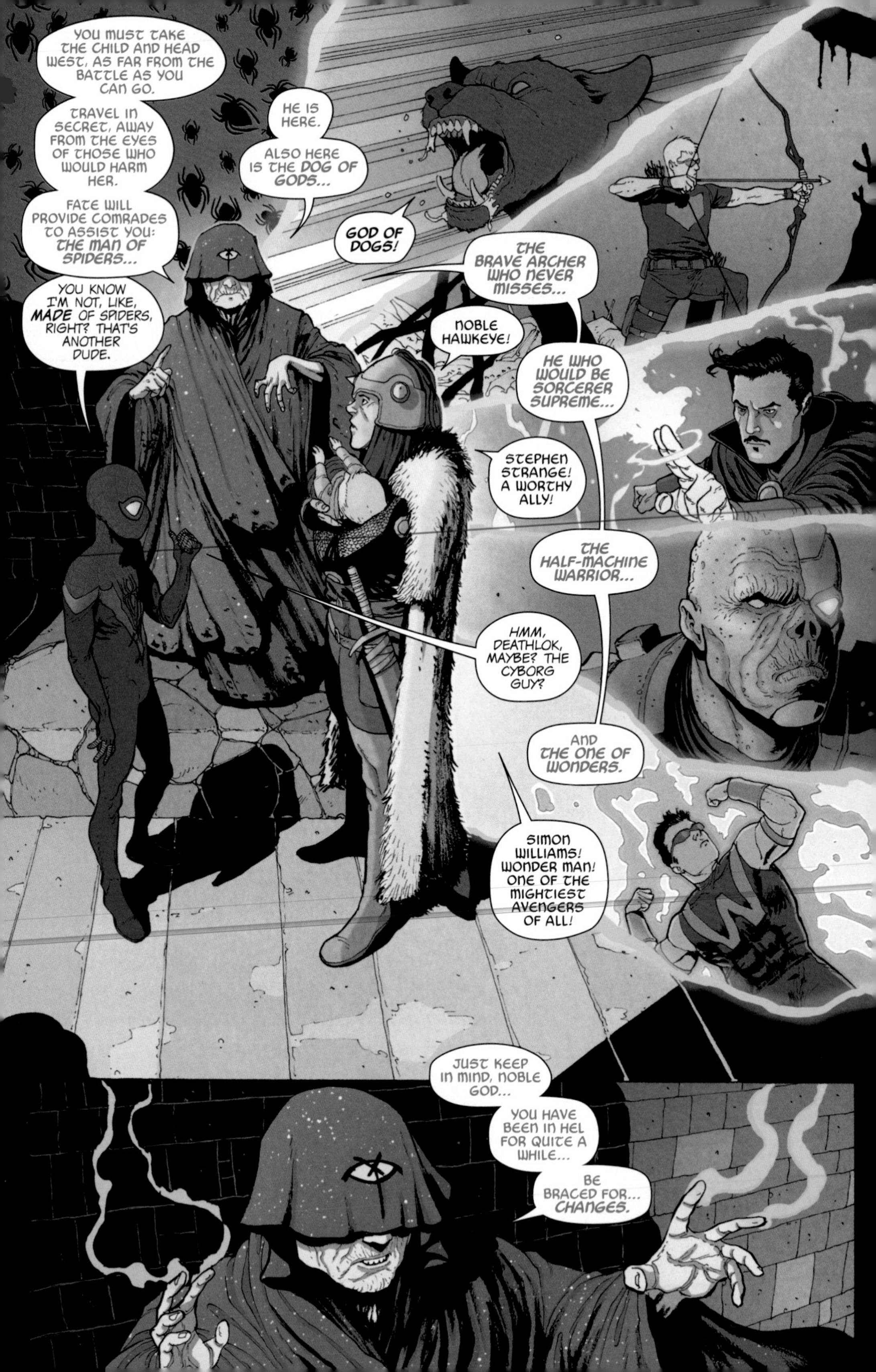

YOU MUST TAKE THE CHILD AND HEAD WEST, AS FAR FROM THE BATTLE AS YOU CAN GO.
TRAVEL IN SECRET, AWAY FROM THE EYES OF THOSE WHO WOULD HARM HER.
FATE WILL PROVIDE COMRADES TO ASSIST YOU: THE MAN OF SPIDERS...
YOU KNOW I'M NOT, LIKE, MADE OF SPIDERS, RIGHT? THAT'S ANOTHER DUDE.
HE IS HERE.
ALSO HERE IS THE DOG OF GODS...
GOD OF DOGS!
THE BRAVE ARCHER WHO NEVER MISSES...
NOBLE HAWKEYE!
HE WHO WOULD BE SORCERER SUPREME...
STEPHEN STRANGE! A WORTHY ALLY!
THE HALF-MACHINE WARRIOR...
HMM, DEATHLOK, MAYBE? THE CYBORG GUY?
AND THE ONE OF WONDERS.
SIMON WILLIAMS! WONDER MAN! ONE OF THE MIGHTIEST AVENGERS OF ALL!
JUST KEEP IN MIND, NOBLE GOD...
YOU HAVE BEEN IN HEL FOR QUITE A WHILE...
BE BRACED FOR... CHANGES.

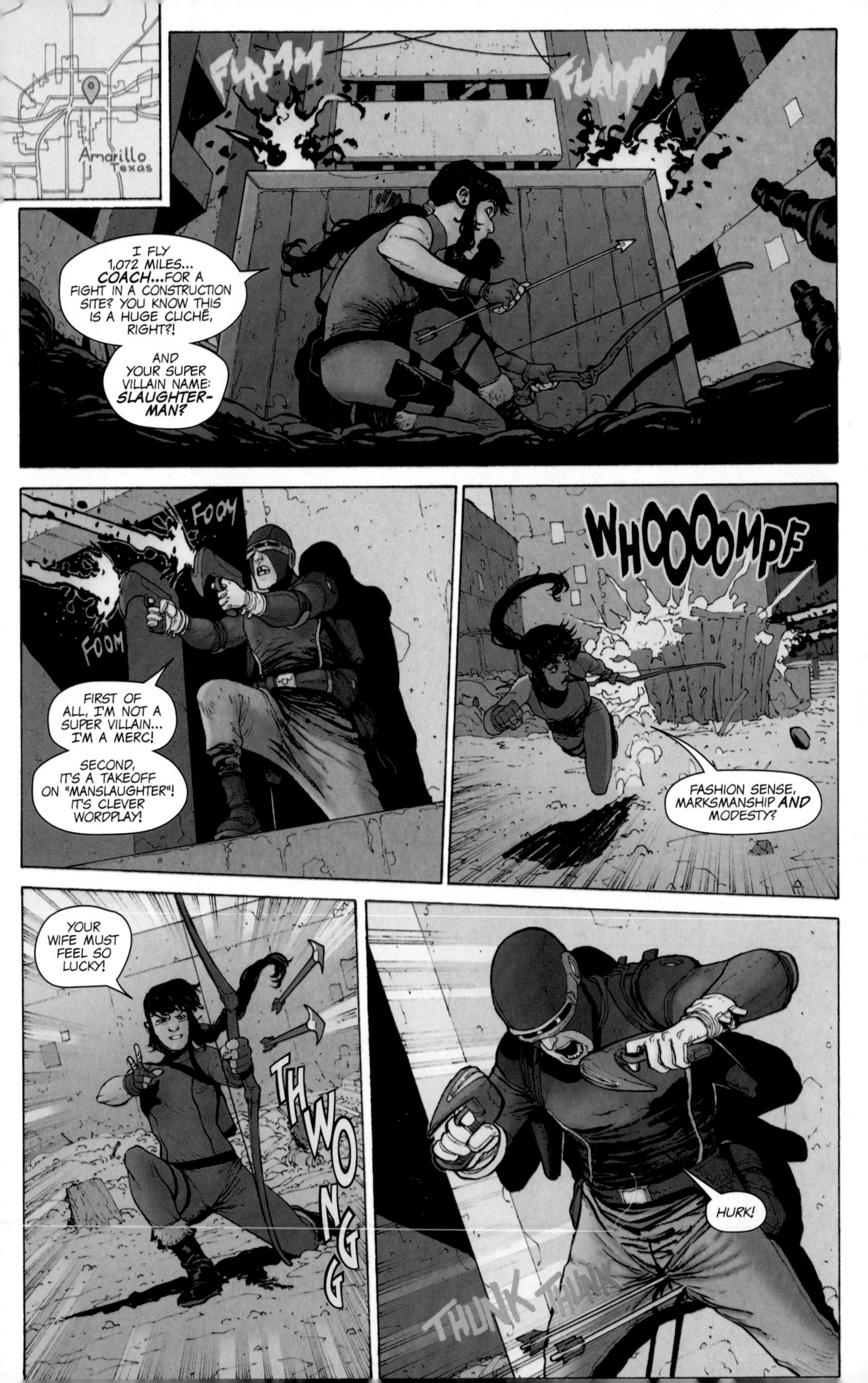
Amarillo Texas
FLAMM
FLAMM
I FLY 1,072 MILES... COACH...FOR A FIGHT IN A CONSTRUCTION SITE? YOU KNOW THIS IS A HUGE CLICHÉ, RIGHT?!
AND YOUR SUPER VILLAIN NAME: SLAUGHTER-MAN?
FOOM
FOOM
FIRST OF ALL, I'M NOT A SUPER VILLAIN... I'M A MERC!
SECOND, IT'S A TAKEOFF ON "MANSLAUGHTER"! IT'S CLEVER WORDPLAY!
WHOOOOOMPF
FASHION SENSE, MARKSMANSHIP AND MODESTY?
YOUR WIFE MUST FEEL SO LUCKY!
THWONGG
HURK!
THUNK THUNK

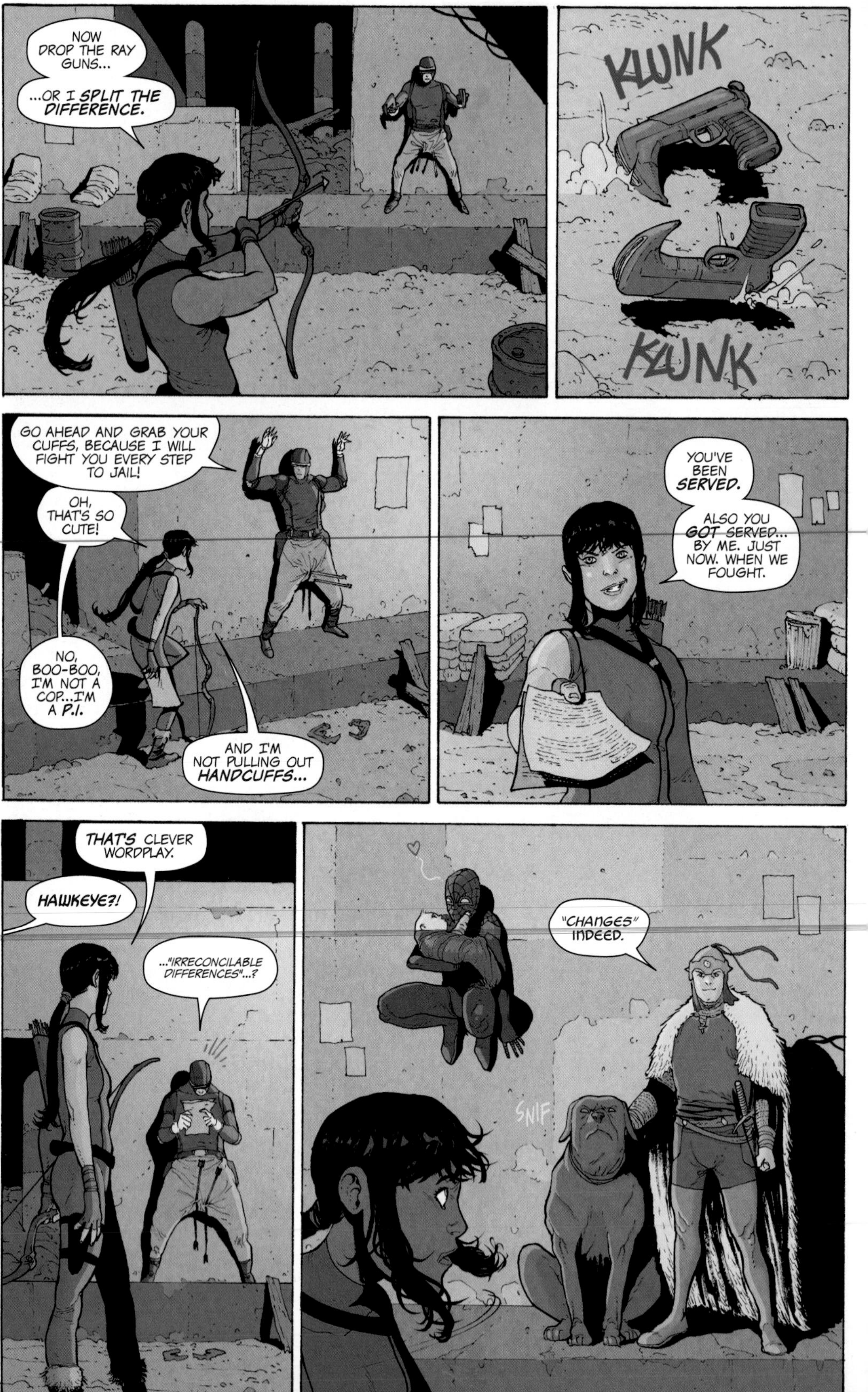
NOW DROP THE RAY GUNS...
...OR I SPLIT THE DIFFERENCE.
KLUNK
KLUNK
GO AHEAD AND GRAB YOUR CUFFS, BECAUSE I WILL FIGHT YOU EVERY STEP TO JAIL!
OH, THAT'S SO CUTE!
NO, BOO-BOO, I'M NOT A COP...I'M A P.I.
AND I'M NOT PULLING OUT HANDCUFFS...
YOU'VE BEEN SERVED.
ALSO YOU GOT SERVED... BY ME. JUST NOW. WHEN WE FOUGHT.
THAT'S CLEVER WORDPLAY.
HAWKEYE?!
..."IRRECONCILABLE DIFFERENCES"...?
"CHANGES" INDEED.
SNIF

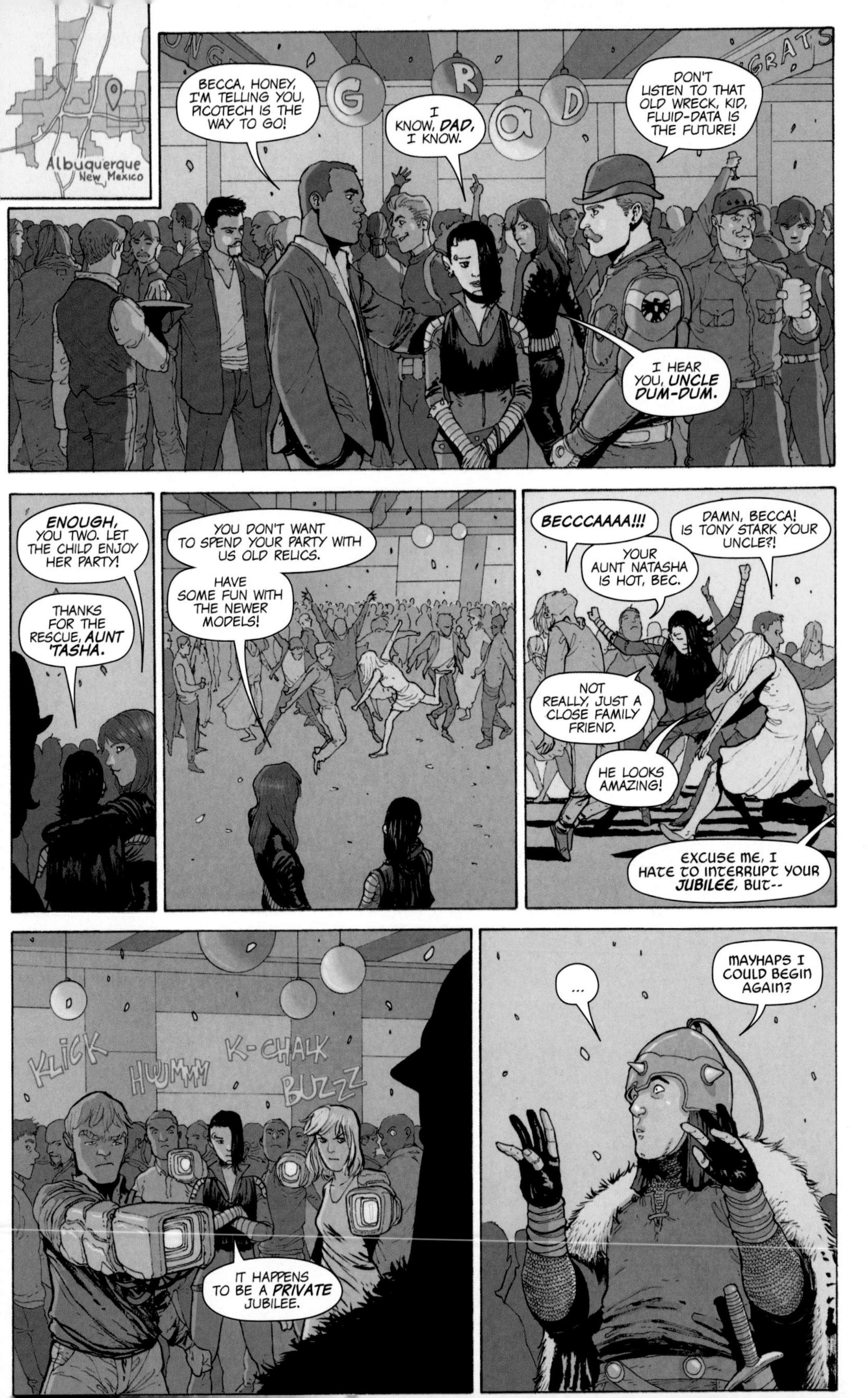
Albuquerque
New Mexico
CONGRATS
G R a D
BECCA, HONEY, I'M TELLING YOU, PICOTECH IS THE WAY TO GO!
I KNOW, DAD, I KNOW.
DON'T LISTEN TO THAT OLD WRECK, KID, FLUID-DATA IS THE FUTURE!
I HEAR YOU, UNCLE DUM-DUM.
ENOUGH, YOU TWO. LET THE CHILD ENJOY HER PARTY!
THANKS FOR THE RESCUE, AUNT 'TASHA.
YOU DON'T WANT TO SPEND YOUR PARTY WITH US OLD RELICS.
HAVE SOME FUN WITH THE NEWER MODELS!
BECCCAAAA!!!
YOUR AUNT NATASHA IS HOT, BEC.
DAMN, BECCA! IS TONY STARK YOUR UNCLE?!
NOT REALLY, JUST A CLOSE FAMILY FRIEND.
HE LOOKS AMAZING!
EXCUSE ME, I HATE TO INTERRUPT YOUR JUBILEE, BUT--
KLICK
HWMMM
K-CHALK
BUZZZ
IT HAPPENS TO BE A PRIVATE JUBILEE.
...
MAYHAPS I COULD BEGIN AGAIN?

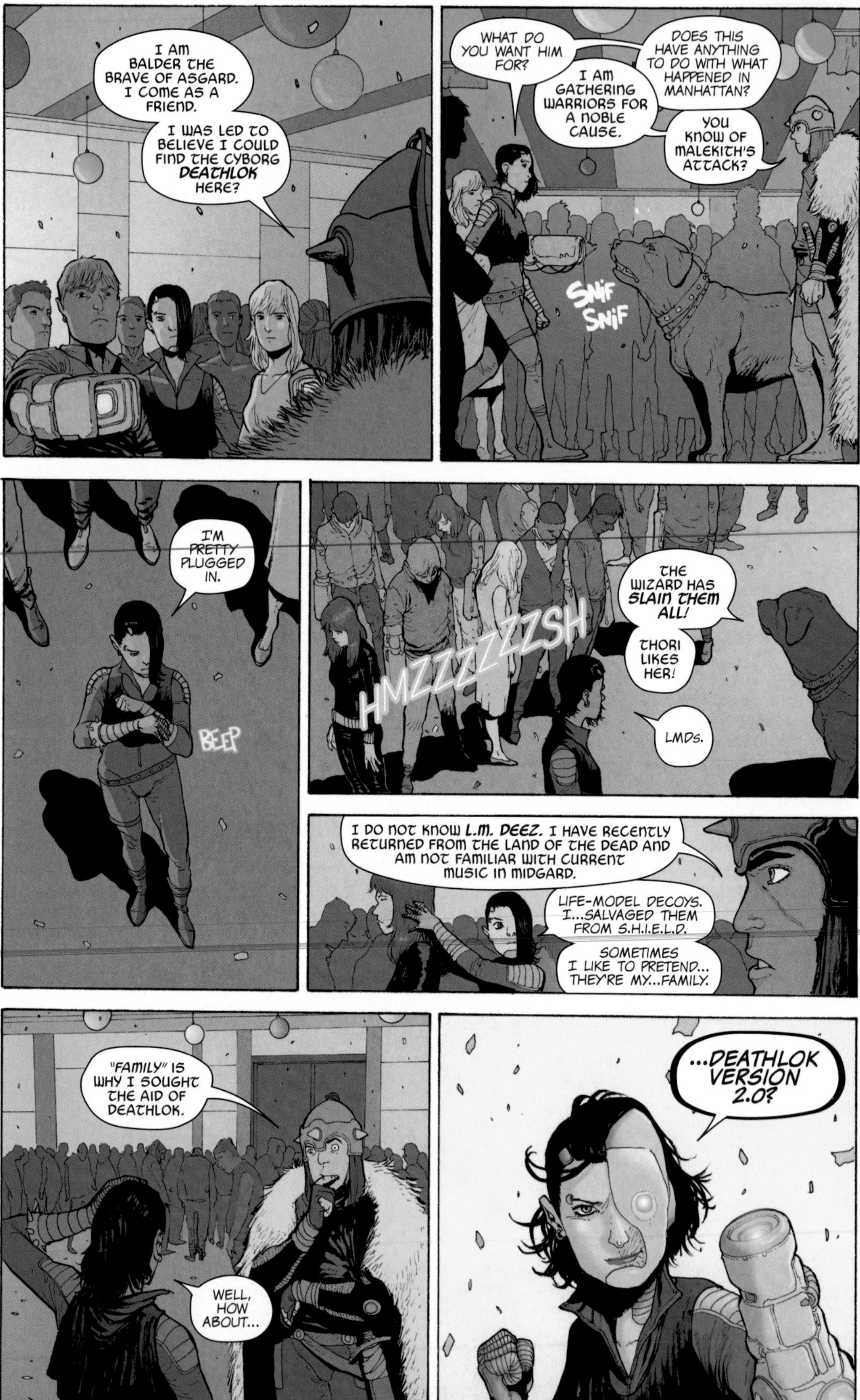

I AM BALDER THE BRAVE OF ASGARD. I COME AS A FRIEND.
I WAS LED TO BELIEVE I COULD FIND THE CYBORG DEATHLOK HERE?
WHAT DO YOU WANT HIM FOR?
I AM GATHERING WARRIORS FOR A NOBLE CAUSE.
DOES THIS HAVE ANYTHING TO DO WITH WHAT HAPPENED IN MANHATTAN?
YOU KNOW OF MALEKITH'S ATTACK?
SNIF SNIF
I'M PRETTY PLUGGED IN.
BEEP
HMZZZZZZZSH
THE WIZARD HAS SLAIN THEM ALL!
THORI LIKES HER!
LMDs.
I DO NOT KNOW L.M. DEEZ. I HAVE RECENTLY RETURNED FROM THE LAND OF THE DEAD AND AM NOT FAMILIAR WITH CURRENT MUSIC IN MIDGARD.
LIFE-MODEL DECOYS. I...SALVAGED THEM FROM S.H.I.E.L.D.
SOMETIMES I LIKE TO PRETEND... THEY'RE MY...FAMILY.
"FAMILY" IS WHY I SOUGHT THE AID OF DEATHLOK.
WELL, HOW ABOUT...
...DEATHLOK VERSION 2.0?

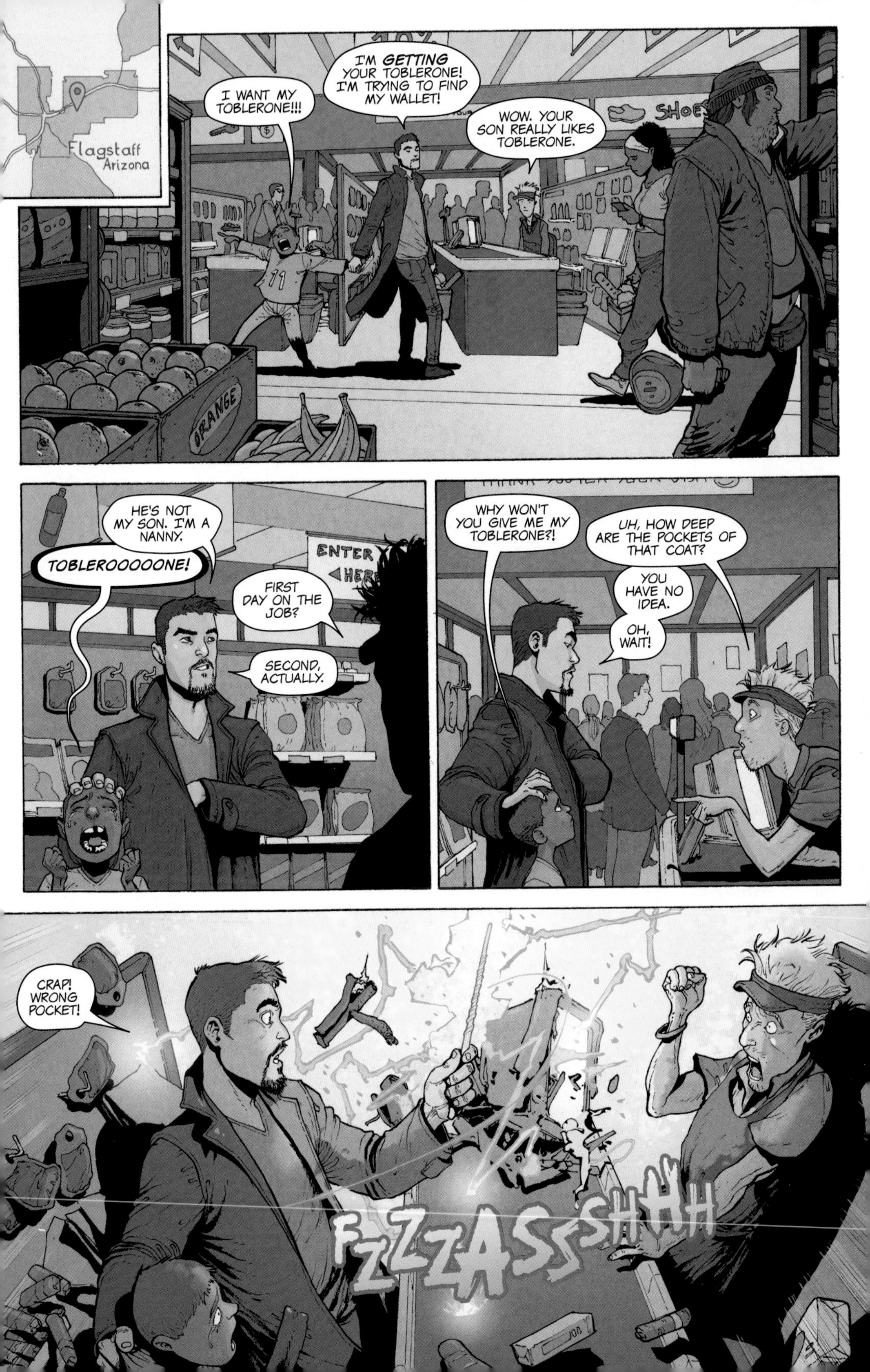
Flagstaff
Arizona
I WANT MY TOBLERONE!!!
I'M GETTING YOUR TOBLERONE! I'M TRYING TO FIND MY WALLET!
WOW. YOUR SON REALLY LIKES TOBLERONE.
SHOES
ORANGE
HE'S NOT MY SON. I'M A NANNY.
TOBLEROOOOONE!
ENTER HERE
FIRST DAY ON THE JOB?
SECOND, ACTUALLY.
WHY WON'T YOU GIVE ME MY TOBLERONE?!
UH, HOW DEEP ARE THE POCKETS OF THAT COAT?
YOU HAVE NO IDEA.
OH, WAIT!
CRAP! WRONG POCKET!
FZZZASSHHH

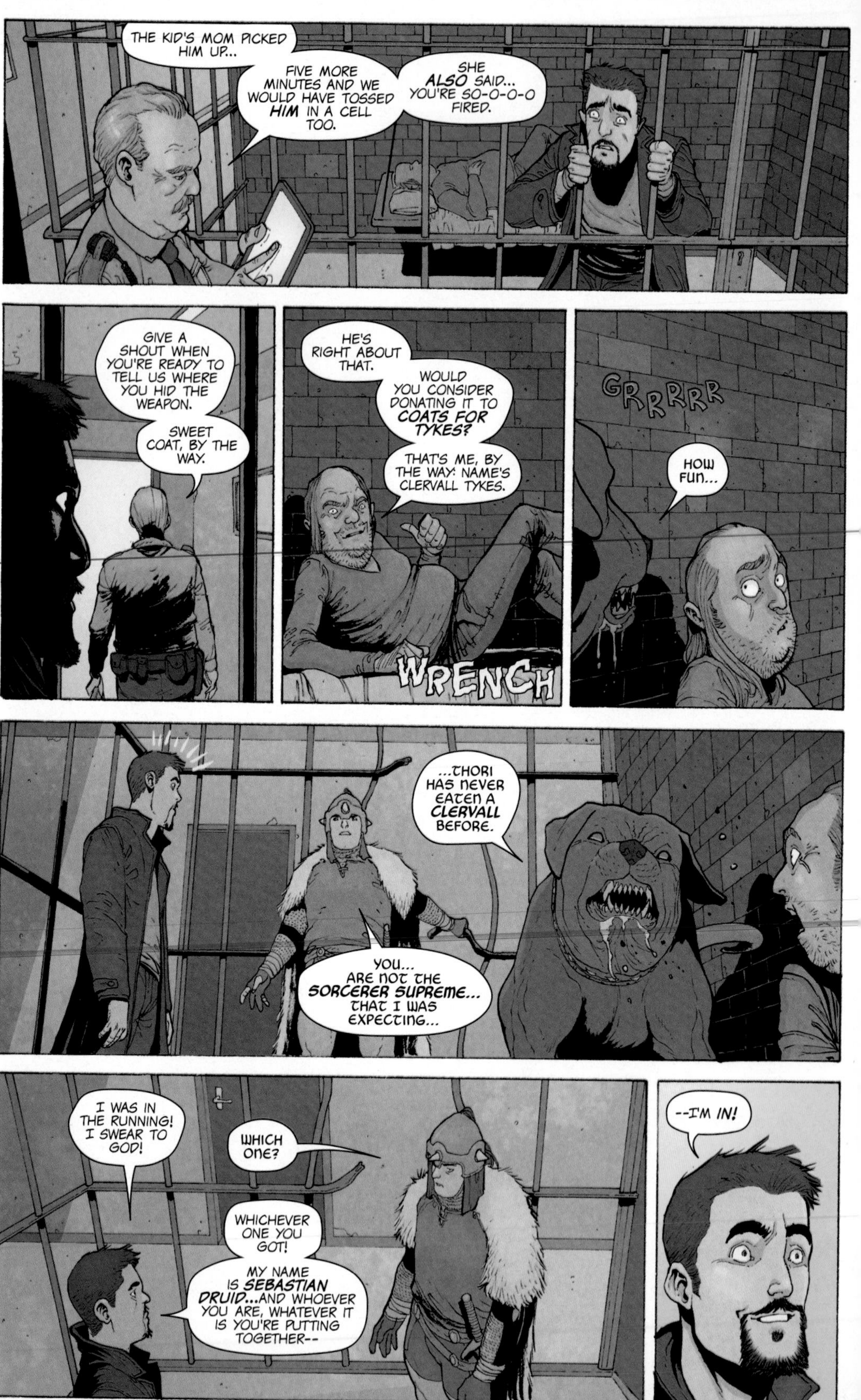
THE KID'S MOM PICKED HIM UP...
FIVE MORE MINUTES AND WE WOULD HAVE TOSSED HIM IN A CELL TOO.
SHE ALSO SAID... YOU'RE SO-O-O-O FIRED.
GIVE A SHOUT WHEN YOU'RE READY TO TELL US WHERE YOU HID THE WEAPON.
SWEET COAT, BY THE WAY.
HE'S RIGHT ABOUT THAT.
WOULD YOU CONSIDER DONATING IT TO COATS FOR TYKES?
THAT'S ME, BY THE WAY: NAME'S CLERVALL TYKES.
WRENCH
GRRRRR
HOW FUN...
...THORI HAS NEVER EATEN A CLERVALL BEFORE.
YOU... ARE NOT THE SORCERER SUPREME... THAT I WAS EXPECTING...
I WAS IN THE RUNNING! I SWEAR TO GOD!
WHICH ONE?
WHICHEVER ONE YOU GOT!
MY NAME IS SEBASTIAN DRUID...AND WHOEVER YOU ARE, WHATEVER IT IS YOU'RE PUTTING TOGETHER--
--I'M IN!

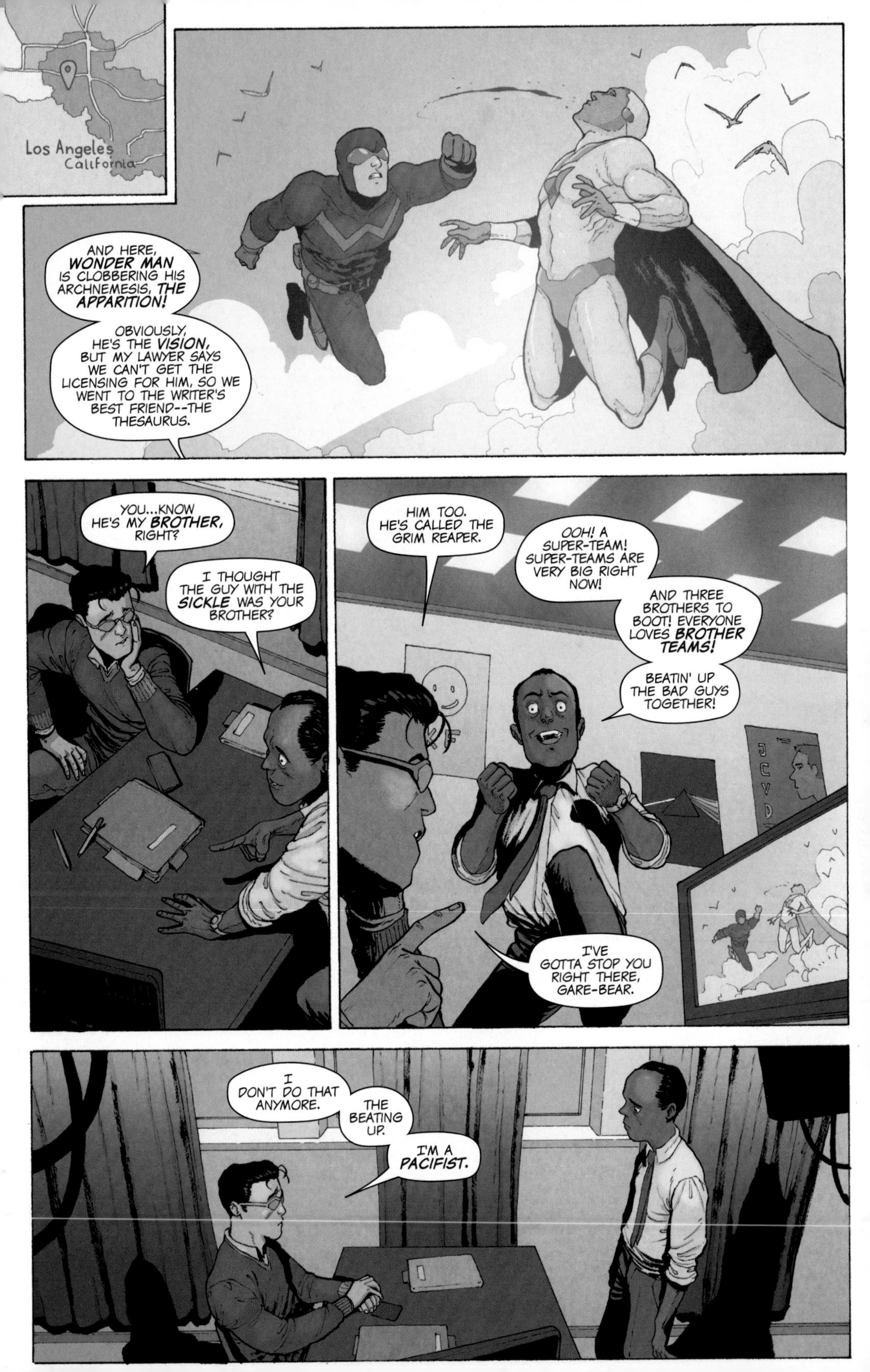
Los Angeles
California
AND HERE, WONDER MAN IS CLOBBERING HIS ARCHNEMESIS, THE APPARITION!
OBVIOUSLY, HE'S THE VISION, BUT MY LAWYER SAYS WE CAN'T GET THE LICENSING FOR HIM, SO WE WENT TO THE WRITER'S BEST FRIEND--THE THESAURUS.
YOU...KNOW HE'S MY BROTHER, RIGHT?
I THOUGHT THE GUY WITH THE SICKLE WAS YOUR BROTHER?
HIM TOO. HE'S CALLED THE GRIM REAPER.
OOH! A SUPER-TEAM! SUPER-TEAMS ARE VERY BIG RIGHT NOW!
AND THREE BROTHERS TO BOOT! EVERYONE LOVES BROTHER TEAMS!
BEATIN' UP THE BAD GUYS TOGETHER!
I'VE GOTTA STOP YOU RIGHT THERE, GARE-BEAR.
I DON'T DO THAT ANYMORE.
THE BEATING UP.
I'M A PACIFIST.

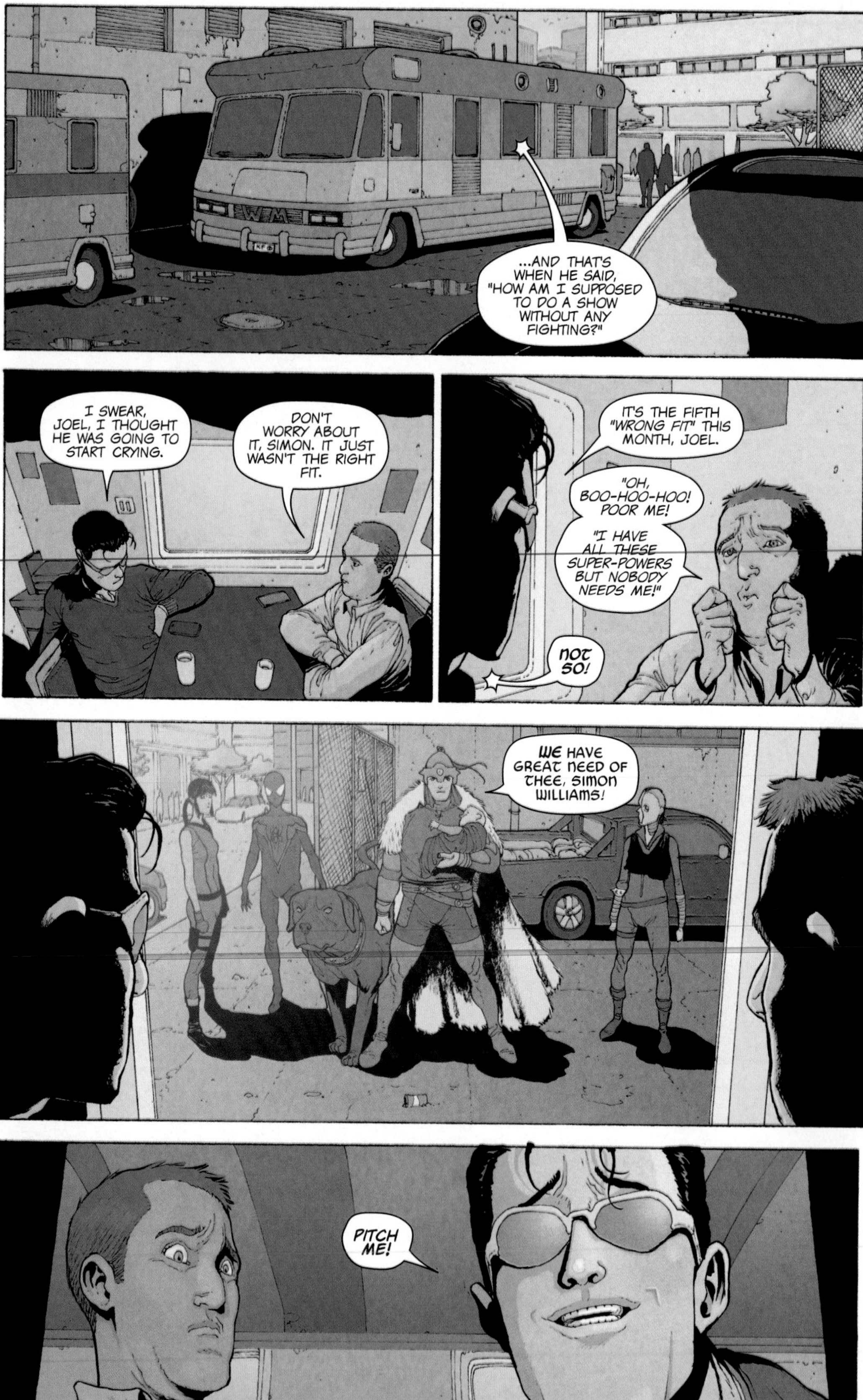
...AND THAT'S WHEN HE SAID, "HOW AM I SUPPOSED TO DO A SHOW WITHOUT ANY FIGHTING?"
I SWEAR, JOEL, I THOUGHT HE WAS GOING TO START CRYING.
DON'T WORRY ABOUT IT, SIMON. IT JUST WASN'T THE RIGHT FIT.
IT'S THE FIFTH "WRONG FIT" THIS MONTH, JOEL.
"OH, BOO-HOO-HOO! POOR ME!
"I HAVE ALL THESE SUPER-POWERS BUT NOBODY NEEDS ME!"
NOT SO!
WE HAVE GREAT NEED OF THEE, SIMON WILLIAMS!
PITCH ME!

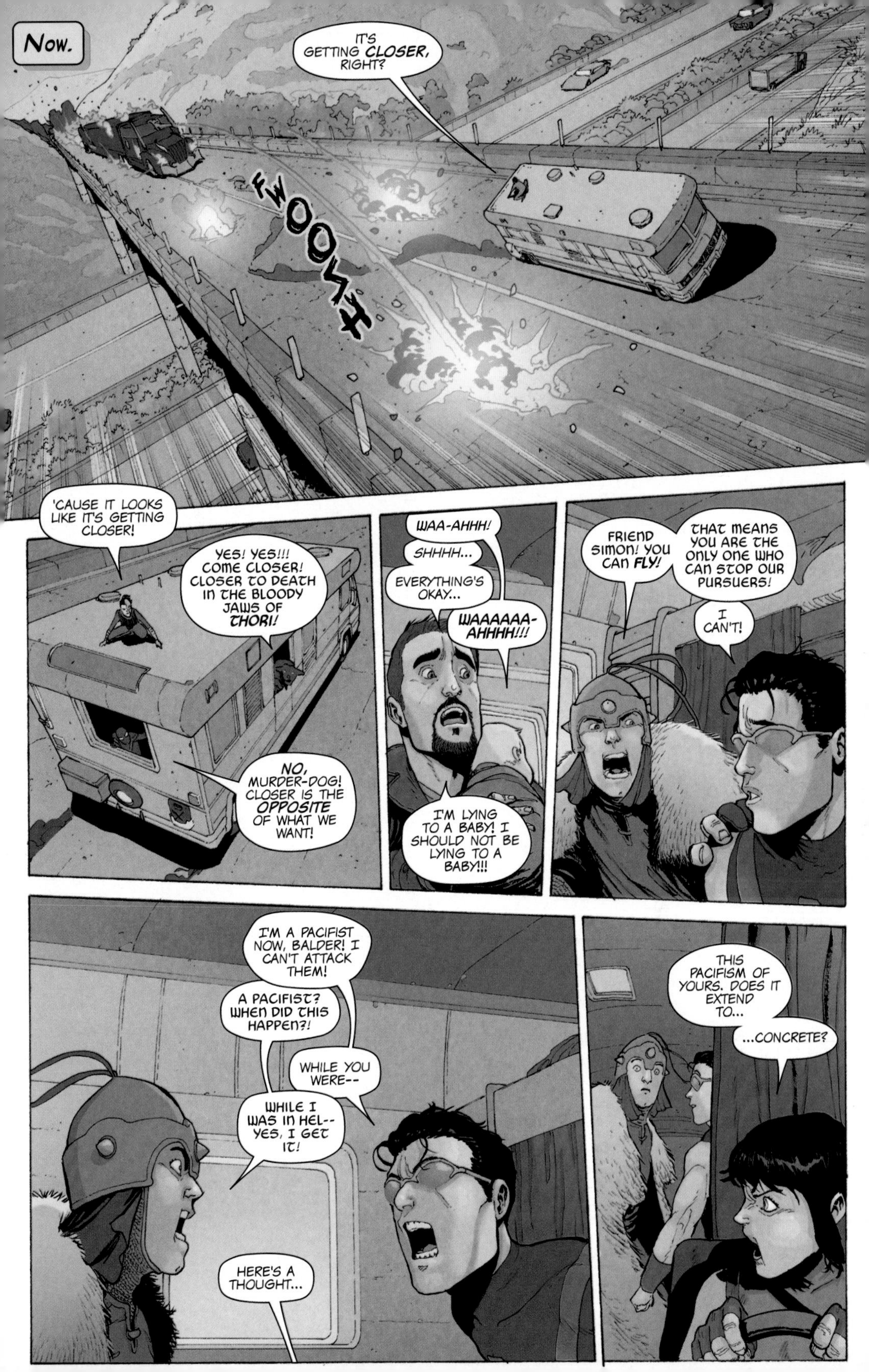
Now.
IT'S GETTING CLOSER, RIGHT?
FWOOSH
'CAUSE IT LOOKS LIKE IT'S GETTING CLOSER!
YES! YES!!! COME CLOSER! CLOSER TO DEATH IN THE BLOODY JAWS OF THORI!
NO, MURDER-DOG! CLOSER IS THE OPPOSITE OF WHAT WE WANT!
WAA-AHHH!
SHHHH...
EVERYTHING'S OKAY...
WAAAAAA-AHHHH!!!
I'M LYING TO A BABY! I SHOULD NOT BE LYING TO A BABY!!!
FRIEND SIMON! YOU CAN FLY!
THAT MEANS YOU ARE THE ONLY ONE WHO CAN STOP OUR PURSUERS!
I CAN'T!
I'M A PACIFIST NOW, BALDER! I CAN'T ATTACK THEM!
A PACIFIST? WHEN DID THIS HAPPEN?!
WHILE YOU WERE--
WHILE I WAS IN HEL-- YES, I GET IT!
HERE'S A THOUGHT...
THIS PACIFISM OF YOURS. DOES IT EXTEND TO...
...CONCRETE?

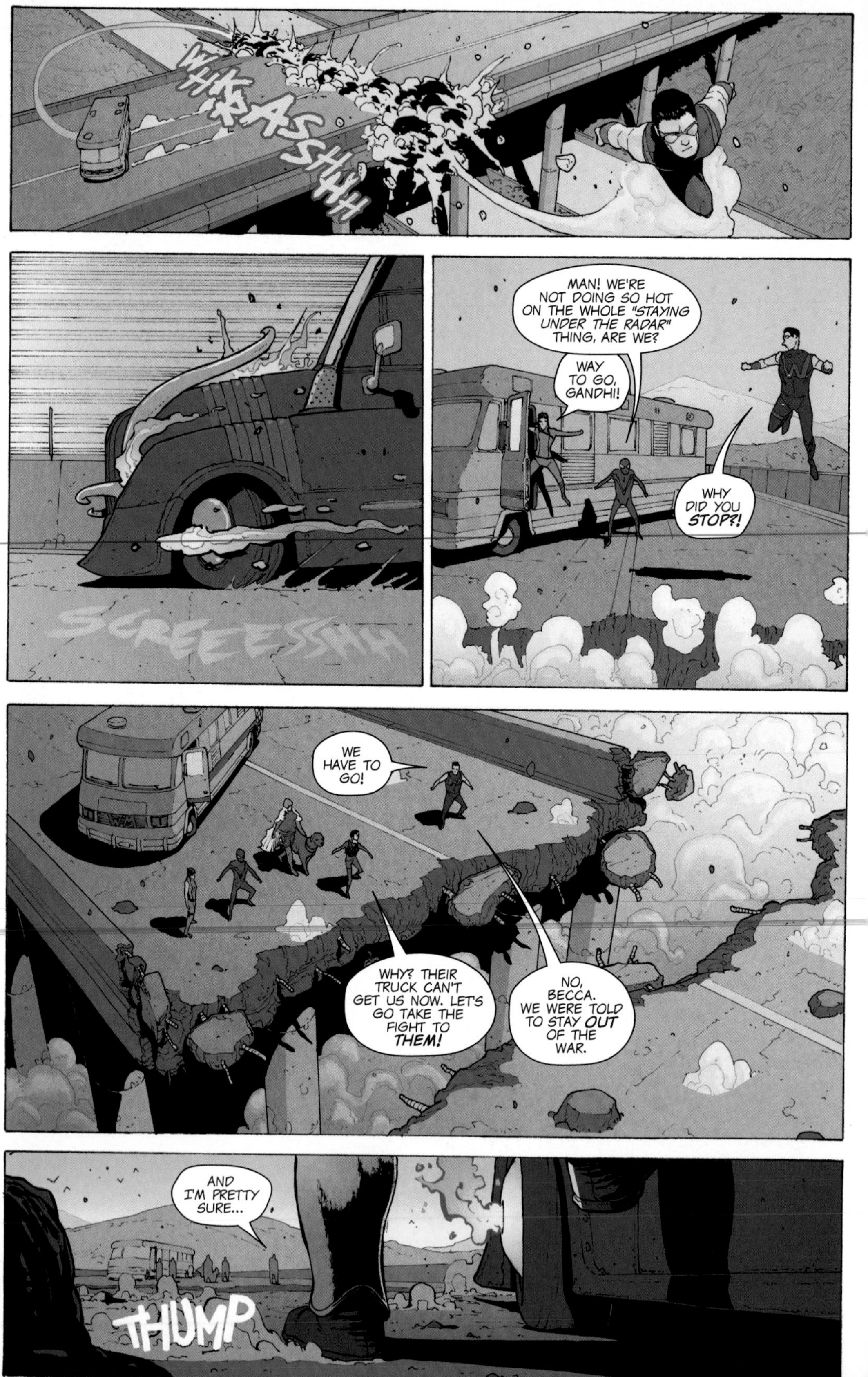
WHKRASHHH
SCREEESSHH
MAN! WE'RE NOT DOING SO HOT ON THE WHOLE "STAYING UNDER THE RADAR" THING, ARE WE?
WAY TO GO, GANDHI!
WHY DID YOU STOP?!
WE HAVE TO GO!
WHY? THEIR TRUCK CAN'T GET US NOW. LET'S GO TAKE THE FIGHT TO THEM!
NO, BECCA. WE WERE TOLD TO STAY OUT OF THE WAR.
AND I'M PRETTY SURE...
THUMP

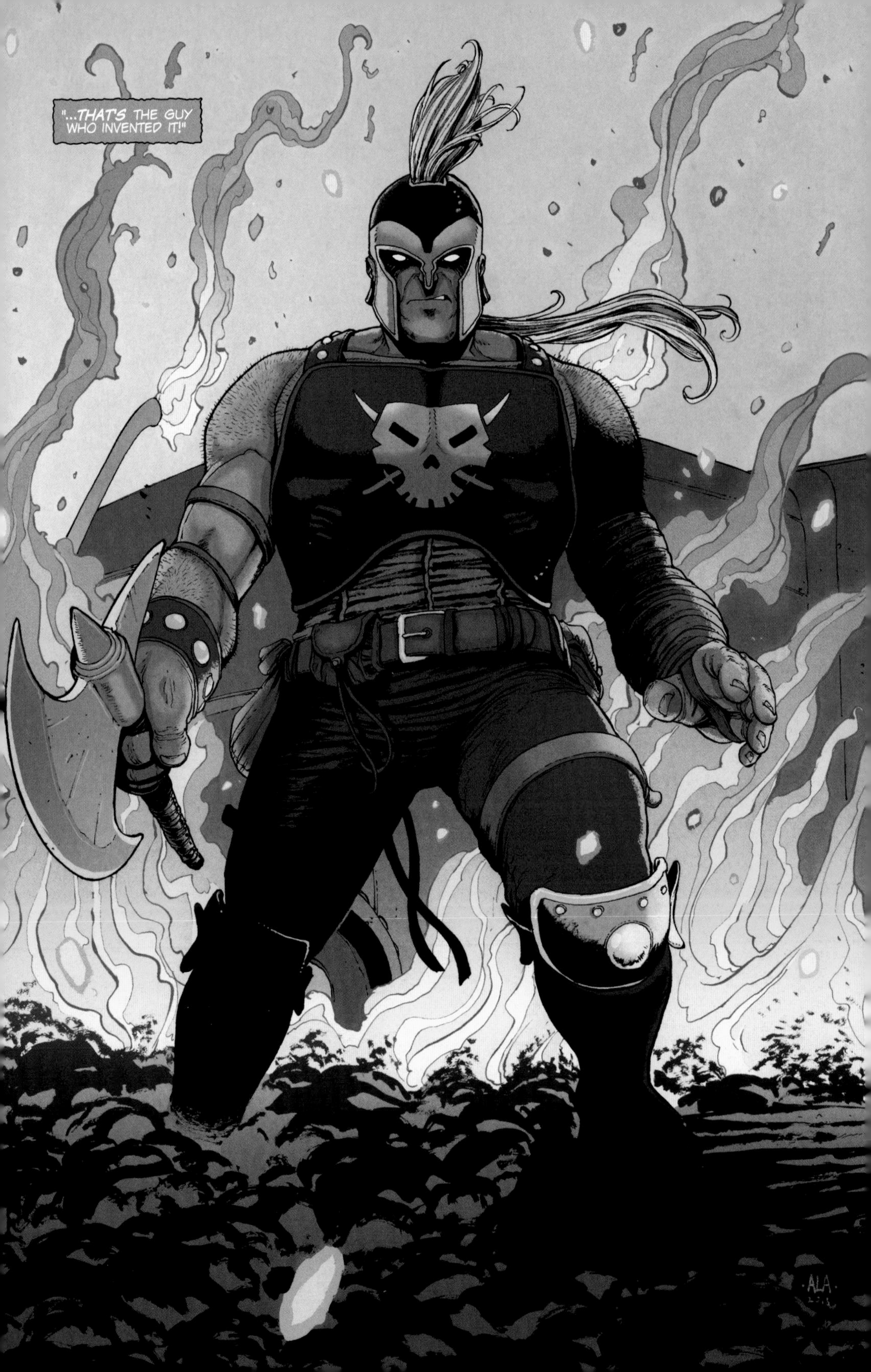
"...THAT'S THE GUY WHO INVENTED IT!"
ALA

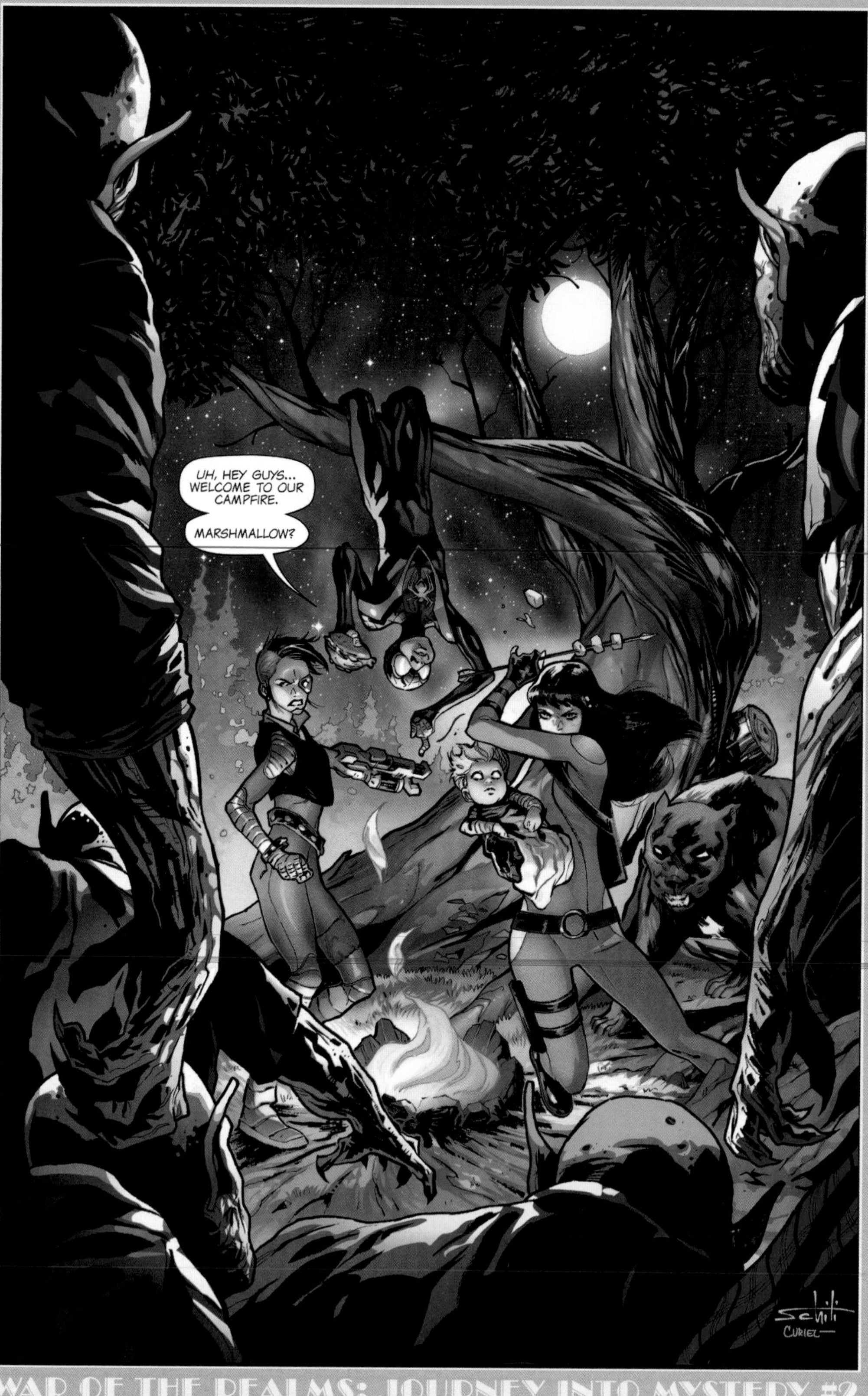
UH, HEY GUYS... WELCOME TO OUR CAMPFIRE.
MARSHMALLOW?
SCHITI
CURIEL

WAR OF THE REALMS: JOURNEY INTO MYSTERY #2

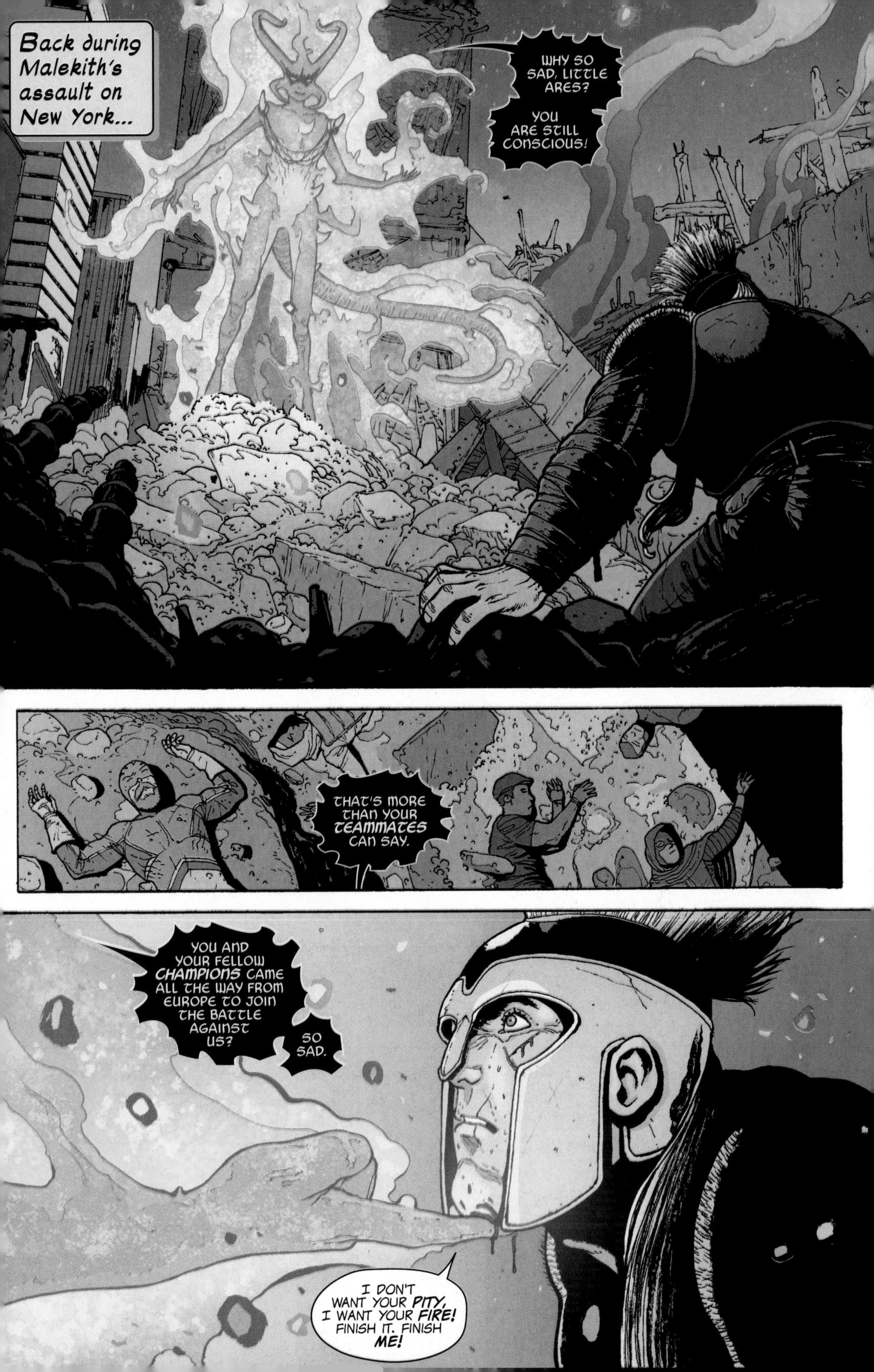
Back during Malekith's assault on New York...
WHY SO SAD, LITTLE ARES?
YOU ARE STILL CONSCIOUS!
THAT'S MORE THAN YOUR TEAMMATES CAN SAY.
YOU AND YOUR FELLOW CHAMPIONS CAME ALL THE WAY FROM EUROPE TO JOIN THE BATTLE AGAINST US?
SO SAD.
I DON'T WANT YOUR PITY, I WANT YOUR FIRE! FINISH IT. FINISH ME!

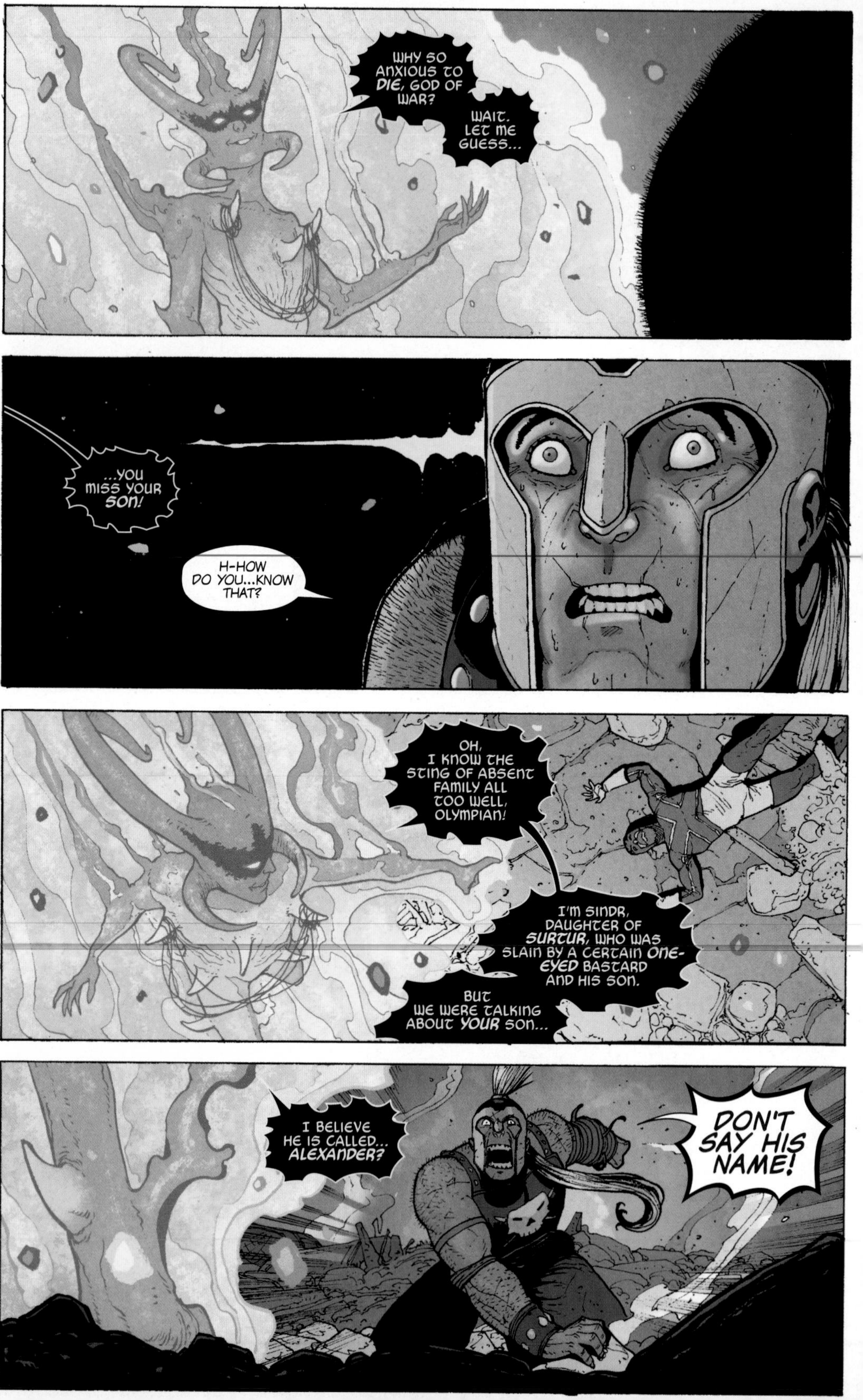
WHY SO ANXIOUS TO DIE, GOD OF WAR?
WAIT. LET ME GUESS...
...YOU MISS YOUR SON!
H-HOW DO YOU...KNOW THAT?
OH, I KNOW THE STING OF ABSENT FAMILY ALL TOO WELL, OLYMPIAN!
I'M SINDR, DAUGHTER OF SURTUR, WHO WAS SLAIN BY A CERTAIN ONE-EYED BASTARD AND HIS SON.
BUT WE WERE TALKING ABOUT YOUR SON...
I BELIEVE HE IS CALLED... ALEXANDER?
DON'T SAY HIS NAME!

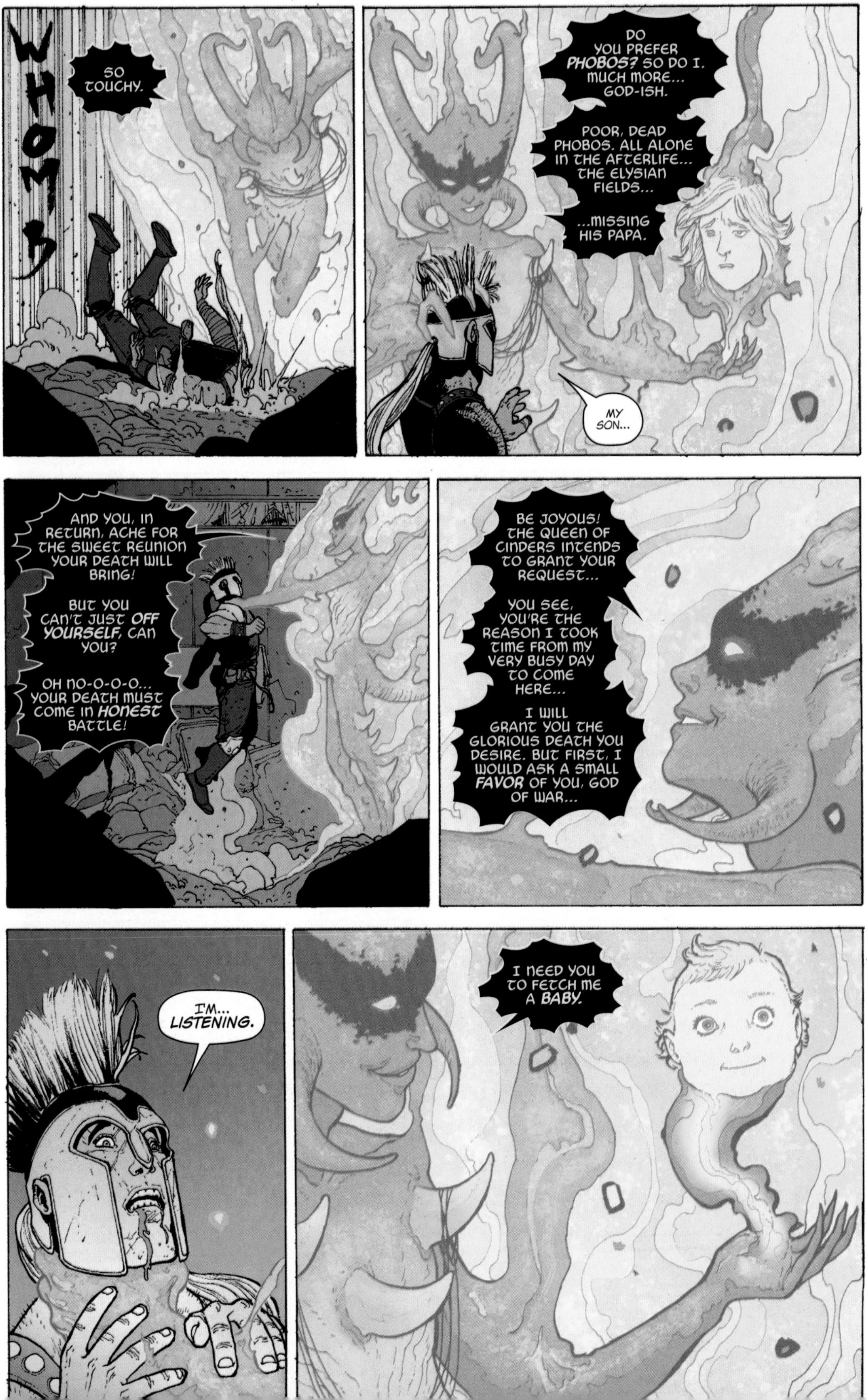

WHOMB
SO TOUCHY.
DO YOU PREFER PHOBOS? SO DO I. MUCH MORE... GOD-ISH.
POOR, DEAD PHOBOS. ALL ALONE IN THE AFTERLIFE... THE ELYSIAN FIELDS...
...MISSING HIS PAPA.
MY SON...
AND YOU, IN RETURN, ACHE FOR THE SWEET REUNION YOUR DEATH WILL BRING!
BUT YOU CAN'T JUST OFF YOURSELF, CAN YOU?
OH NO-O-O-O... YOUR DEATH MUST COME IN HONEST BATTLE!
BE JOYOUS! THE QUEEN OF CINDERS INTENDS TO GRANT YOUR REQUEST...
YOU SEE, YOU'RE THE REASON I TOOK TIME FROM MY VERY BUSY DAY TO COME HERE...
I WILL GRANT YOU THE GLORIOUS DEATH YOU DESIRE. BUT FIRST, I WOULD ASK A SMALL FAVOR OF YOU, GOD OF WAR...
I'M... LISTENING.
I NEED YOU TO FETCH ME A BABY.

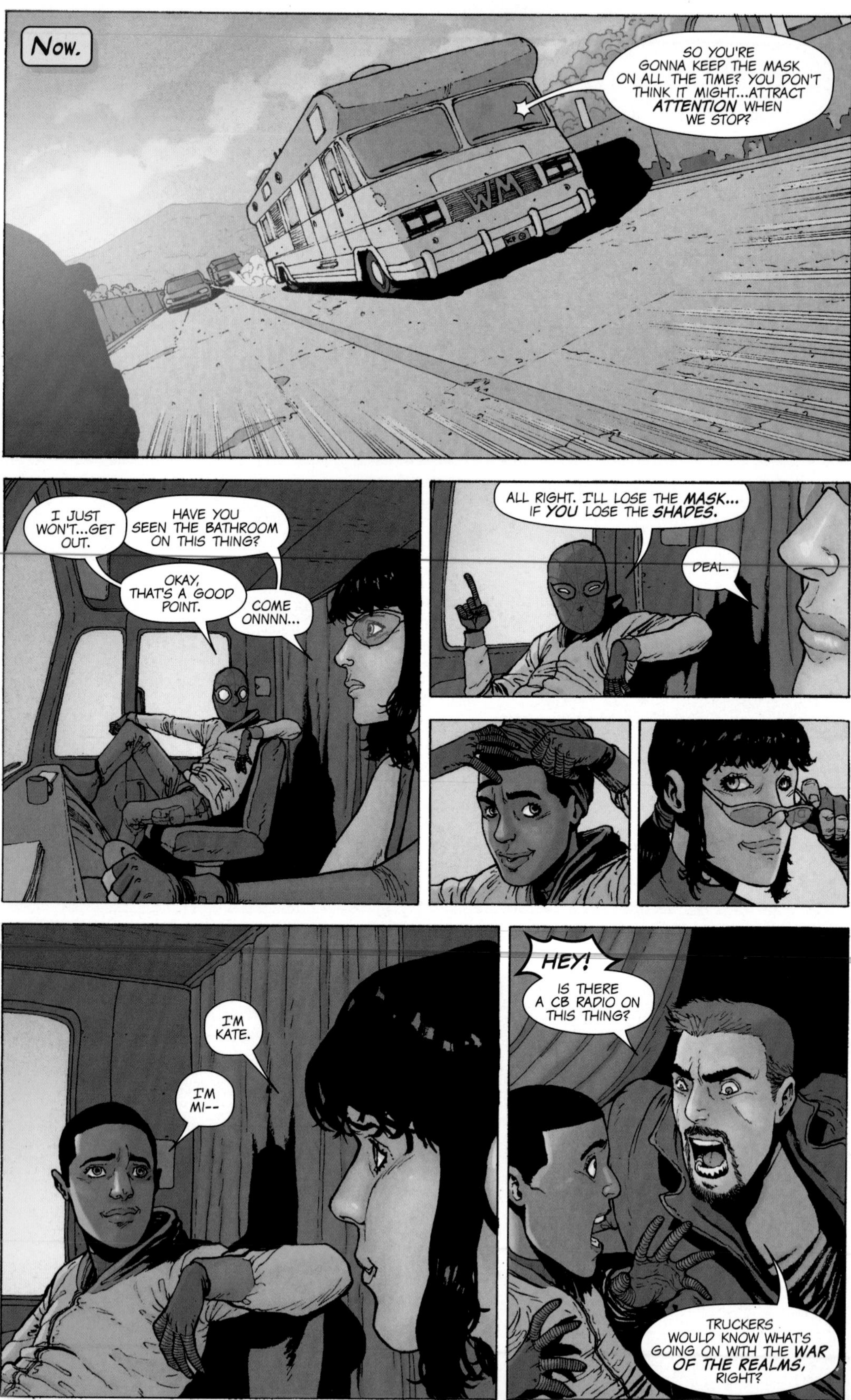

Now.
SO YOU'RE GONNA KEEP THE MASK ON ALL THE TIME? YOU DON'T THINK IT MIGHT...ATTRACT ATTENTION WHEN WE STOP?
I JUST WON'T...GET OUT.
HAVE YOU SEEN THE BATHROOM ON THIS THING?
OKAY, THAT'S A GOOD POINT.
COME ONNNN...
ALL RIGHT. I'LL LOSE THE MASK... IF YOU LOSE THE SHADES.
DEAL.
I'M KATE.
I'M MI--
HEY!
IS THERE A CB RADIO ON THIS THING?
TRUCKERS WOULD KNOW WHAT'S GOING ON WITH THE WAR OF THE REALMS, RIGHT?

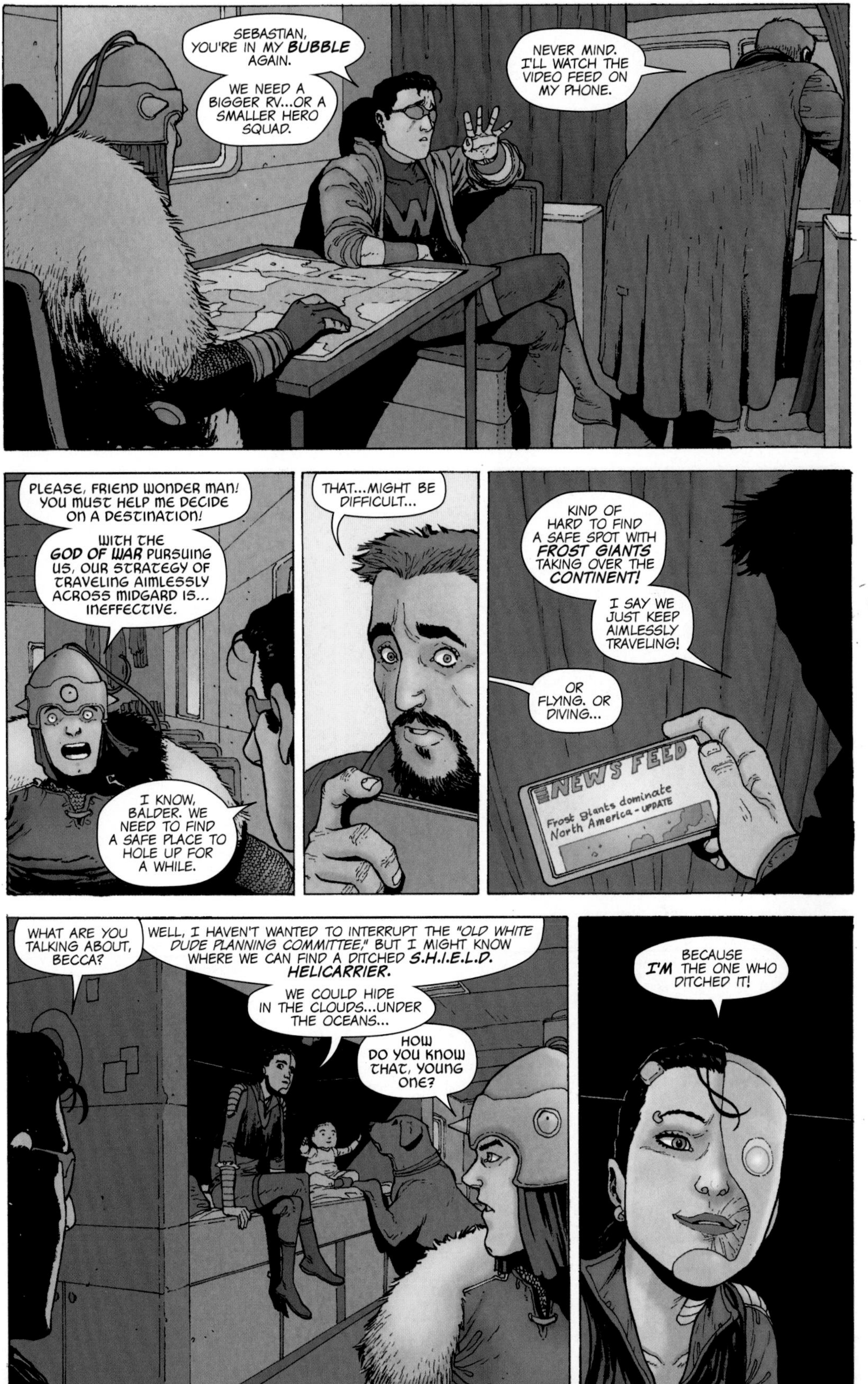
SEBASTIAN, YOU'RE IN MY BUBBLE AGAIN.
WE NEED A BIGGER RV...OR A SMALLER HERO SQUAD.
NEVER MIND. I'LL WATCH THE VIDEO FEED ON MY PHONE.
PLEASE, FRIEND WONDER MAN! YOU MUST HELP ME DECIDE ON A DESTINATION!
WITH THE GOD OF WAR PURSUING US, OUR STRATEGY OF TRAVELING AIMLESSLY ACROSS MIDGARD IS... INEFFECTIVE.
I KNOW, BALDER. WE NEED TO FIND A SAFE PLACE TO HOLE UP FOR A WHILE.
THAT...MIGHT BE DIFFICULT...
KIND OF HARD TO FIND A SAFE SPOT WITH FROST GIANTS TAKING OVER THE CONTINENT!
I SAY WE JUST KEEP AIMLESSLY TRAVELING!
OR FLYING. OR DIVING...
NEWS FEED
Frost Giants dominate North America - UPDATE
WHAT ARE YOU TALKING ABOUT, BECCA?
WELL, I HAVEN'T WANTED TO INTERRUPT THE "OLD WHITE DUDE PLANNING COMMITTEE," BUT I MIGHT KNOW WHERE WE CAN FIND A DITCHED S.H.I.E.L.D. HELICARRIER.
WE COULD HIDE IN THE CLOUDS...UNDER THE OCEANS...
HOW DO YOU KNOW THAT, YOUNG ONE?
BECAUSE I'M THE ONE WHO DITCHED IT!

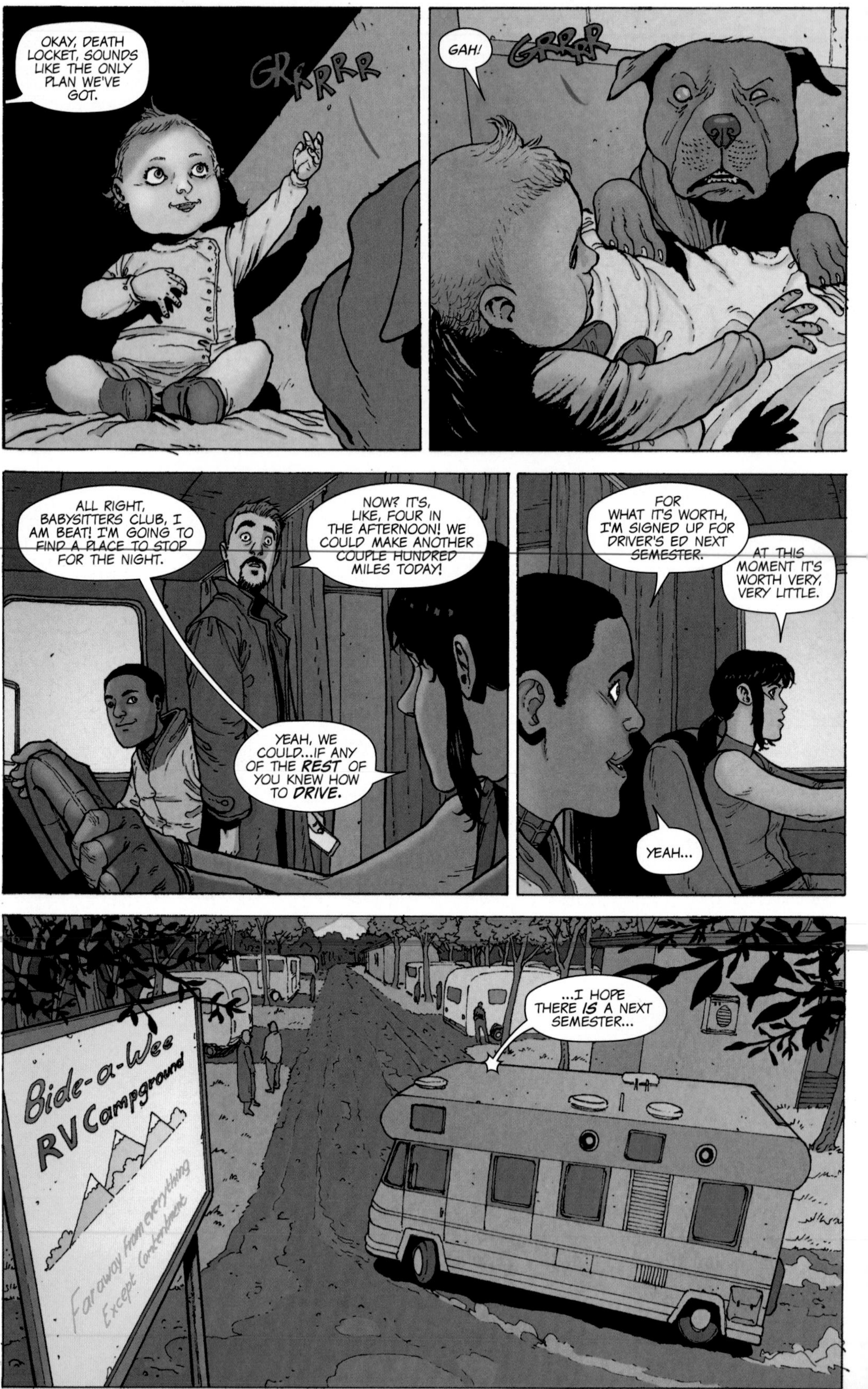
OKAY, DEATH LOCKET, SOUNDS LIKE THE ONLY PLAN WE'VE GOT.
GRRRRR
GAH!
GRRRR
ALL RIGHT, BABYSITTERS CLUB, I AM BEAT! I'M GOING TO FIND A PLACE TO STOP FOR THE NIGHT.
NOW? IT'S, LIKE, FOUR IN THE AFTERNOON! WE COULD MAKE ANOTHER COUPLE HUNDRED MILES TODAY!
YEAH, WE COULD...IF ANY OF THE *REST* OF YOU KNEW HOW TO *DRIVE.*
FOR WHAT IT'S WORTH, *I'M* SIGNED UP FOR DRIVER'S ED NEXT SEMESTER.
AT THIS MOMENT IT'S WORTH VERY, VERY LITTLE.
YEAH...
...I HOPE THERE *IS* A NEXT SEMESTER...
Bide-a-Wee
RV Campground
Faraway from everything
Except Contentment

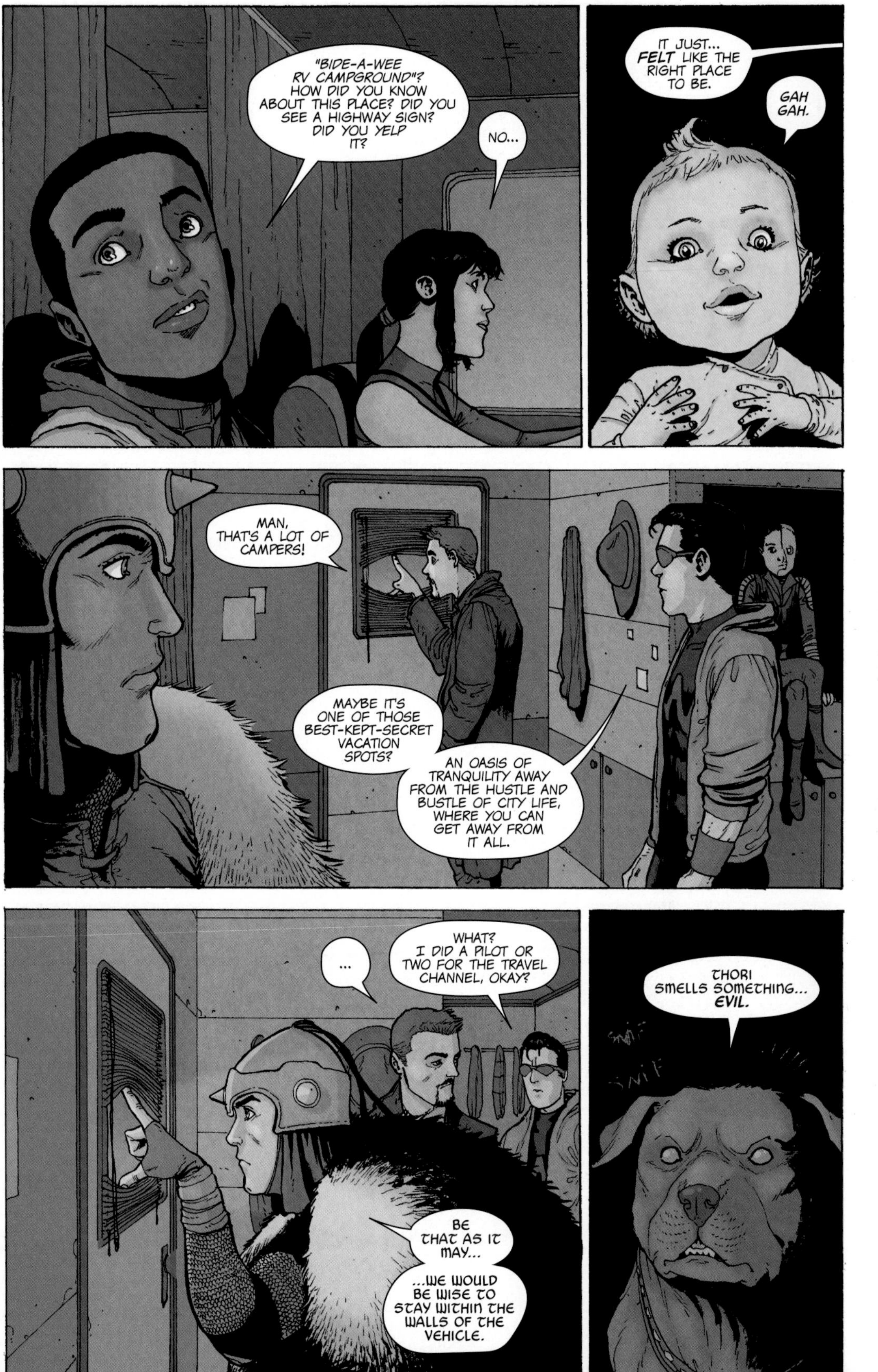
"BIDE-A-WEE RV CAMPGROUND"? HOW DID YOU KNOW ABOUT THIS PLACE? DID YOU SEE A HIGHWAY SIGN? DID YOU YELP IT?
NO...
IT JUST... FELT LIKE THE RIGHT PLACE TO BE.
GAH GAH.
MAN, THAT'S A LOT OF CAMPERS!
MAYBE IT'S ONE OF THOSE BEST-KEPT-SECRET VACATION SPOTS?
AN OASIS OF TRANQUILITY AWAY FROM THE HUSTLE AND BUSTLE OF CITY LIFE, WHERE YOU CAN GET AWAY FROM IT ALL.
...
WHAT? I DID A PILOT OR TWO FOR THE TRAVEL CHANNEL, OKAY?
BE THAT AS IT MAY...
...WE WOULD BE WISE TO STAY WITHIN THE WALLS OF THE VEHICLE.
THORI SMELLS SOMETHING... EVIL.

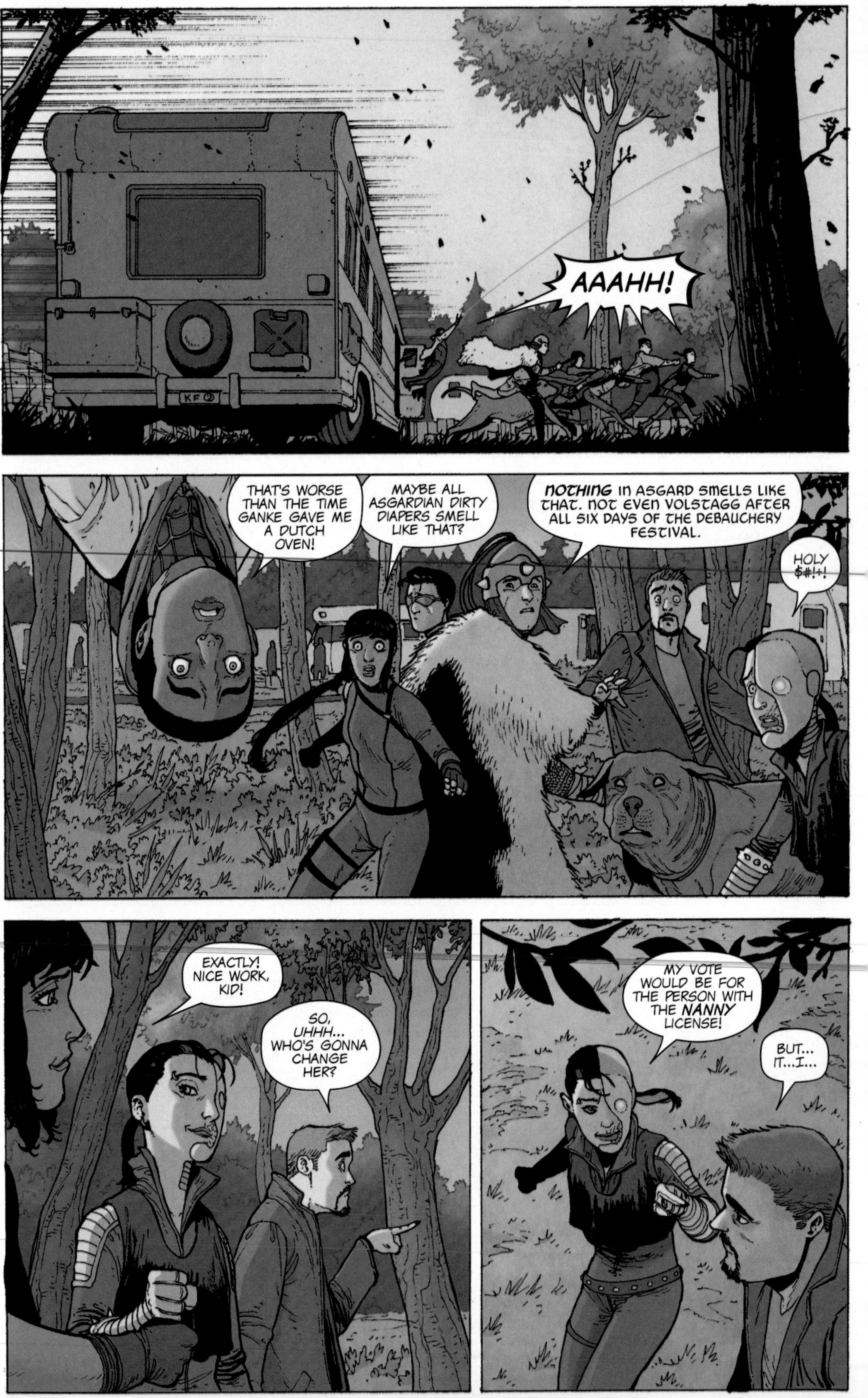
AAAHH!
THAT'S WORSE THAN THE TIME GANKE GAVE ME A DUTCH OVEN!
MAYBE ALL ASGARDIAN DIRTY DIAPERS SMELL LIKE THAT?
NOTHING IN ASGARD SMELLS LIKE THAT. NOT EVEN VOLSTAGG AFTER ALL SIX DAYS OF THE DEBAUCHERY FESTIVAL.
HOLY $#!+!
EXACTLY! NICE WORK, KID!
SO, UHHH... WHO'S GONNA CHANGE HER?
MY VOTE WOULD BE FOR THE PERSON WITH THE NANNY LICENSE!
BUT... IT...I...

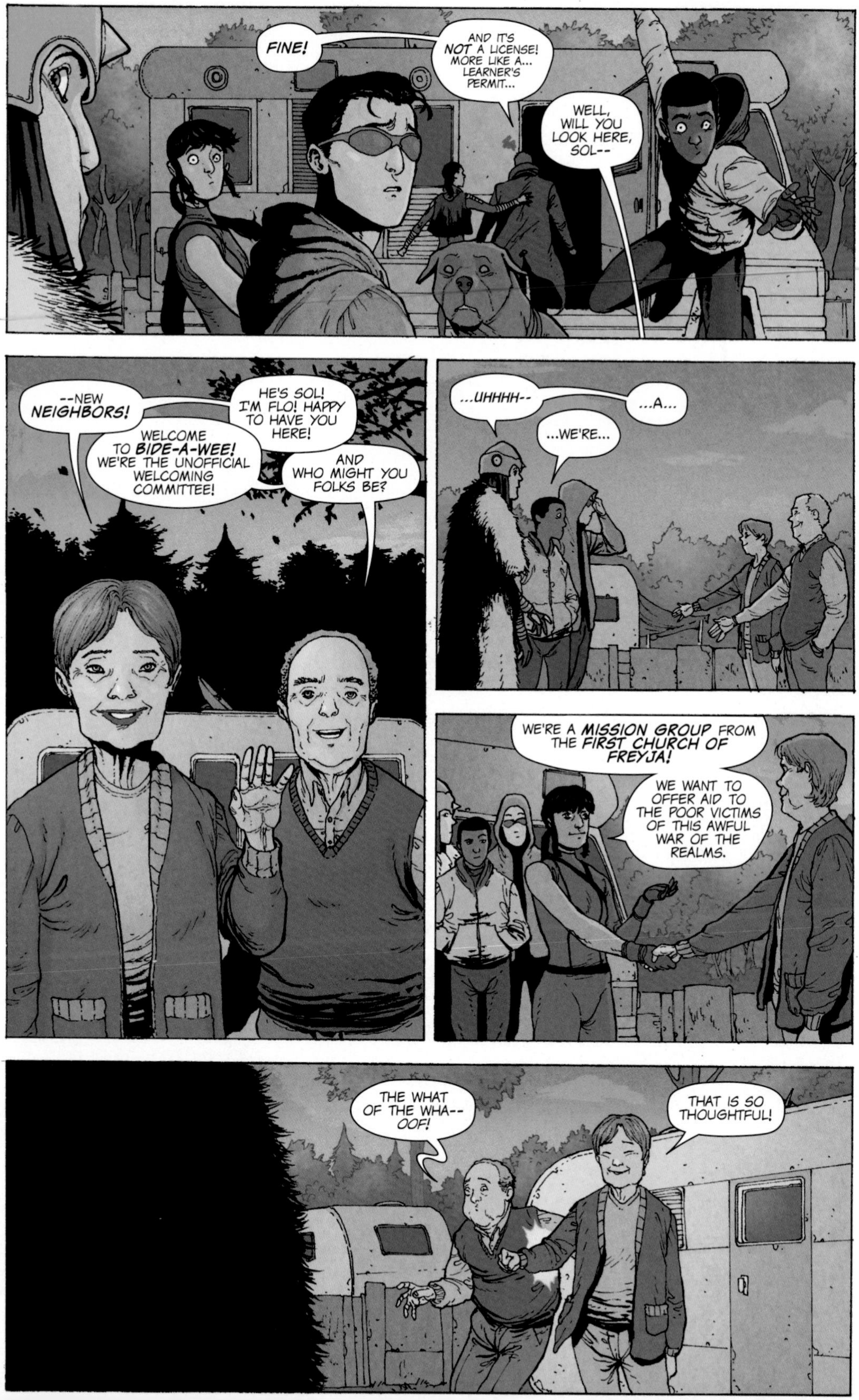
FINE!
AND IT'S NOT A LICENSE! MORE LIKE A... LEARNER'S PERMIT...
WELL, WILL YOU LOOK HERE, SOL--
--NEW NEIGHBORS!
HE'S SOL! I'M FLO! HAPPY TO HAVE YOU HERE!
WELCOME TO BIDE-A-WEE! WE'RE THE UNOFFICIAL WELCOMING COMMITTEE!
AND WHO MIGHT YOU FOLKS BE?
...UHHHH--
...A...
...WE'RE...
WE'RE A MISSION GROUP FROM THE FIRST CHURCH OF FREYJA!
WE WANT TO OFFER AID TO THE POOR VICTIMS OF THIS AWFUL WAR OF THE REALMS.
THE WHAT OF THE WHA-- OOF!
THAT IS SO THOUGHTFUL!

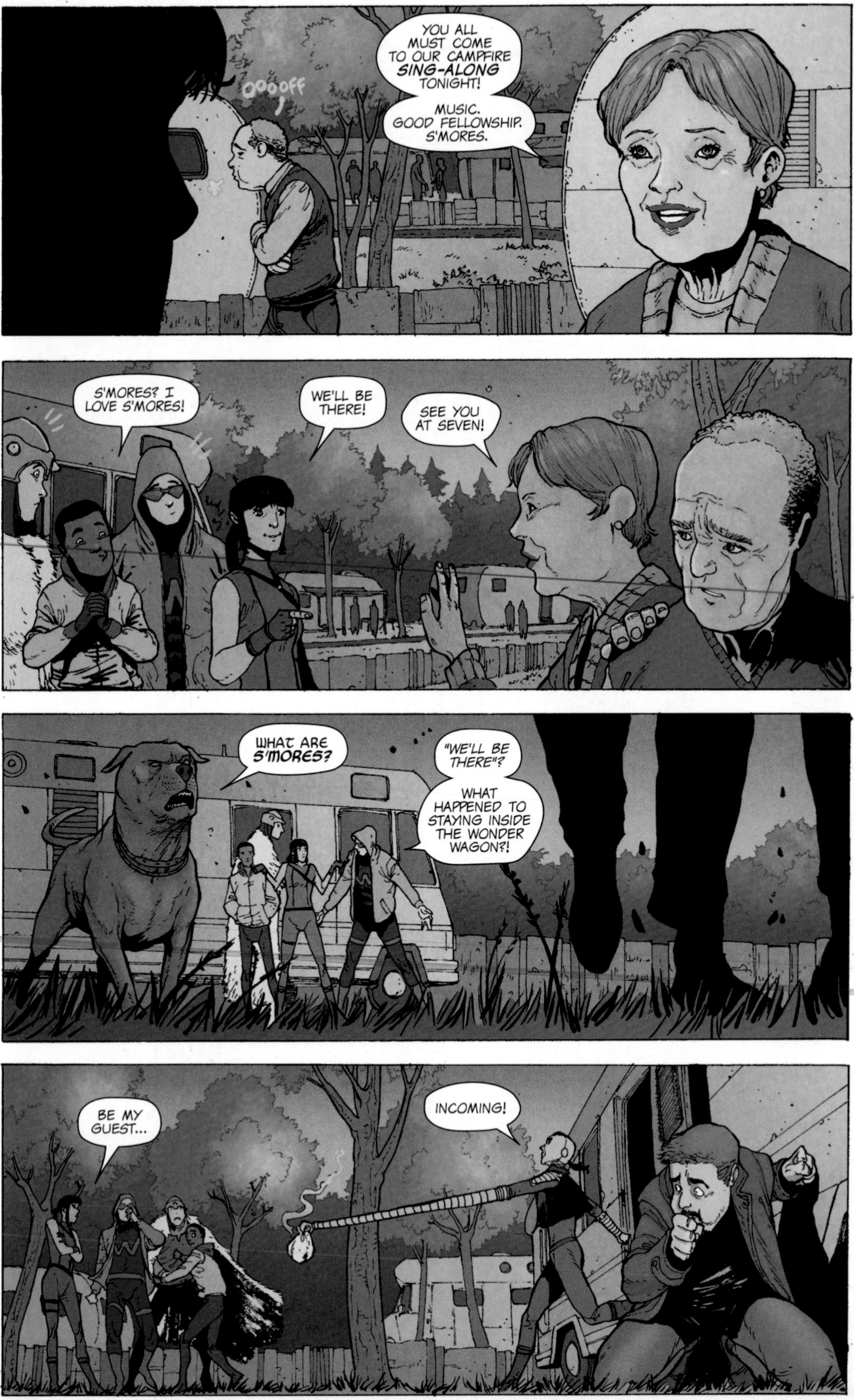
YOU ALL MUST COME TO OUR CAMPFIRE SING-ALONG TONIGHT!
OOOOFF
MUSIC. GOOD FELLOWSHIP. S'MORES.
S'MORES? I LOVE S'MORES!
WE'LL BE THERE!
SEE YOU AT SEVEN!
WHAT ARE S'MORES?
"WE'LL BE THERE"?
WHAT HAPPENED TO STAYING INSIDE THE WONDER WAGON?!
BE MY GUEST...
INCOMING!

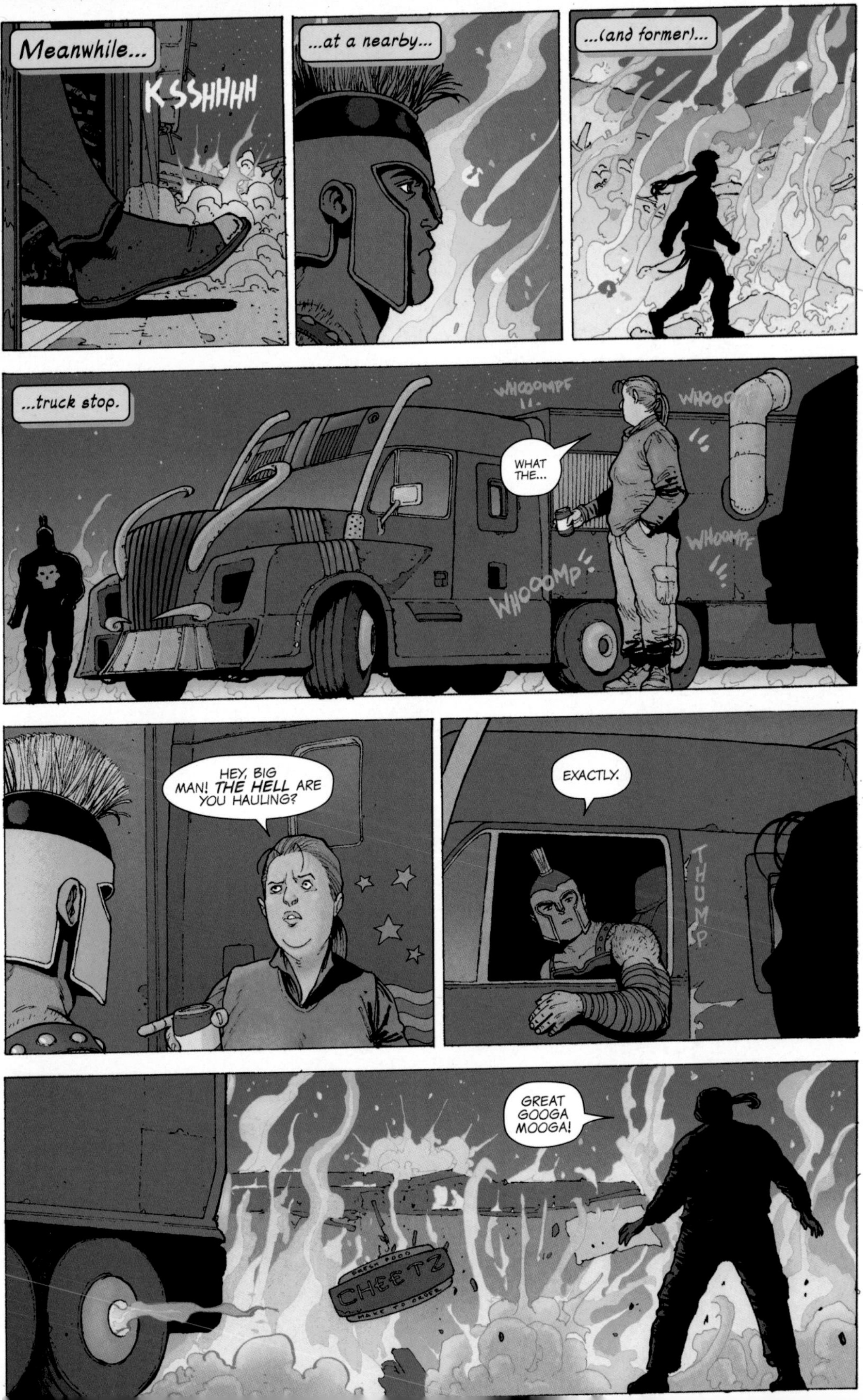
Meanwhile...
KSSHHHH
...at a nearby...
...(and former)...
...truck stop.
WHOOMPF
WHOOO
WHAT THE...
WHOOMPF
WHOOOMP
HEY, BIG MAN! THE HELL ARE YOU HAULING?
EXACTLY.
THUMP
GREAT GOOGA MOOGA!
CHEETZ

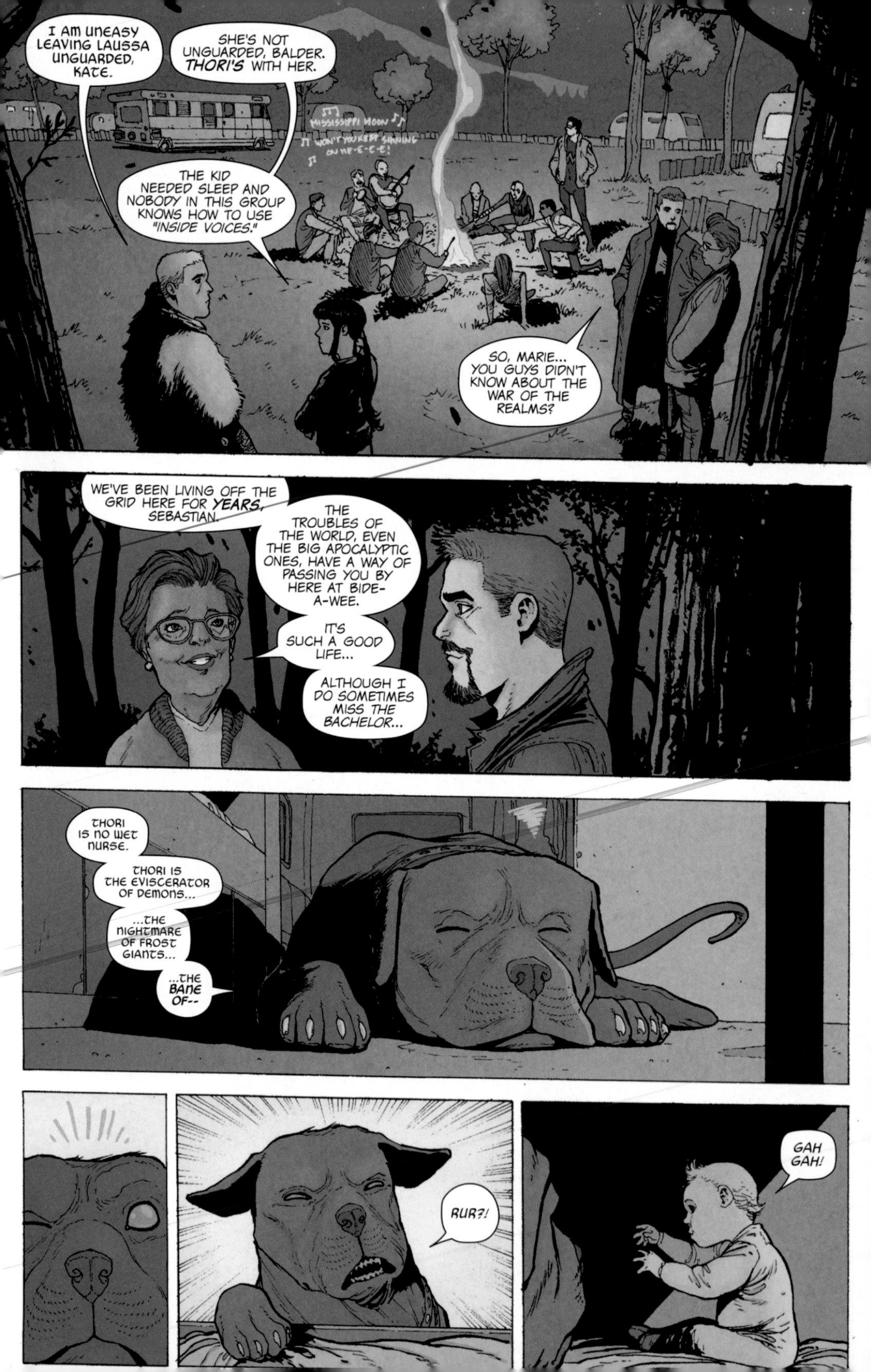
I AM UNEASY LEAVING LAUSSA UNGUARDED, KATE.
SHE'S NOT UNGUARDED, BALDER. THORI'S WITH HER.
MISSISSIPPI MOON
WON'T YOU KEEP SHINING ON ME-E-E-E!
THE KID NEEDED SLEEP AND NOBODY IN THIS GROUP KNOWS HOW TO USE "INSIDE VOICES."
SO, MARIE... YOU GUYS DIDN'T KNOW ABOUT THE WAR OF THE REALMS?
WE'VE BEEN LIVING OFF THE GRID HERE FOR YEARS, SEBASTIAN.
THE TROUBLES OF THE WORLD, EVEN THE BIG APOCALYPTIC ONES, HAVE A WAY OF PASSING YOU BY HERE AT BIDE-A-WEE.
IT'S SUCH A GOOD LIFE...
ALTHOUGH I DO SOMETIMES MISS THE BACHELOR...
THORI IS NO WET NURSE.
THORI IS THE EVISCERATOR OF DEMONS...
...THE NIGHTMARE OF FROST GIANTS...
...THE BANE OF--
RUR?!
GAH GAH!

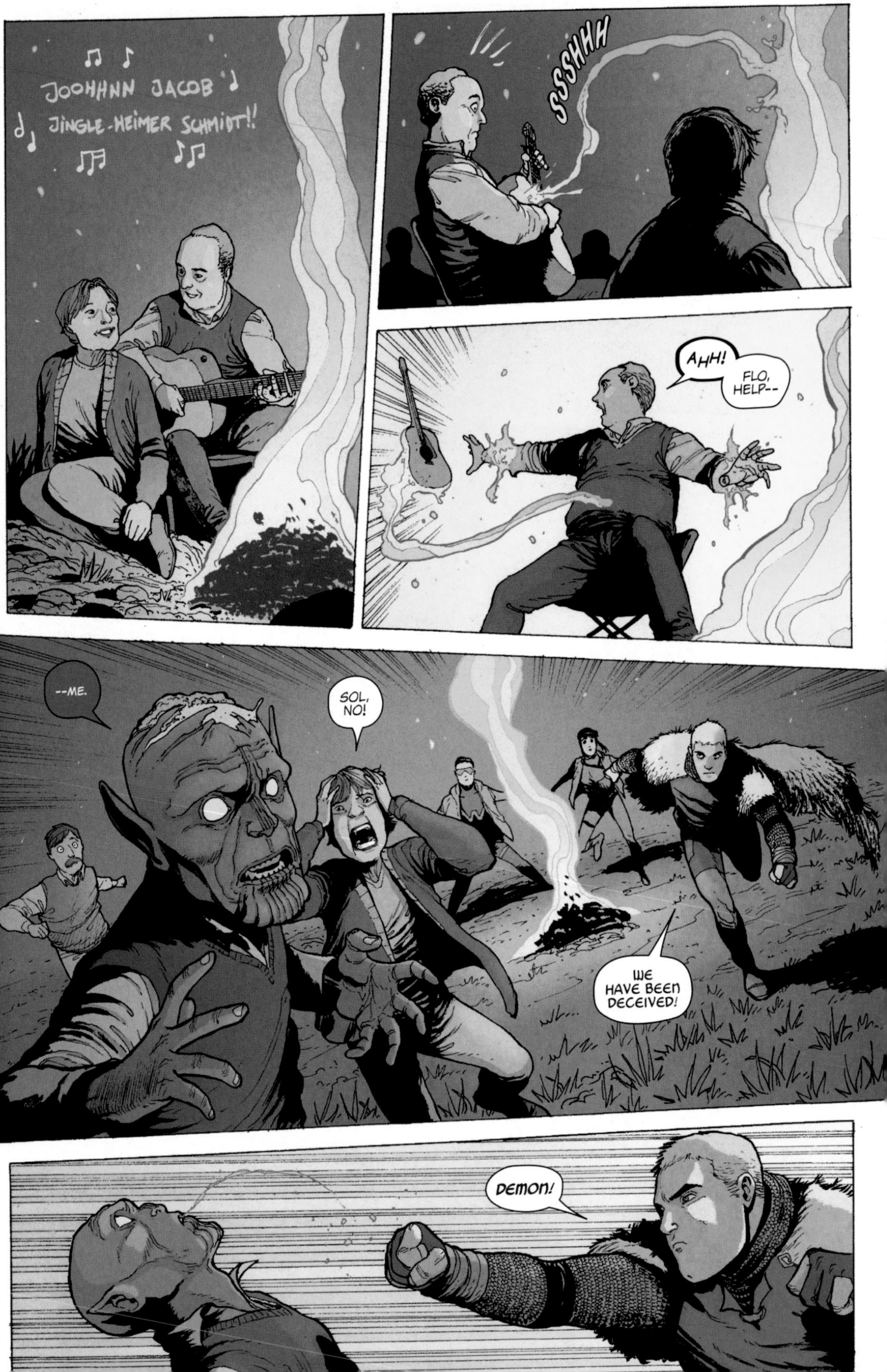
JOOHHNN JACOB
JINGLE-HEIMER SCHMIDT!!
SSSHHH
AHH!
FLO, HELP--
--ME.
SOL, NO!
WE HAVE BEEN DECEIVED!
DEMON!

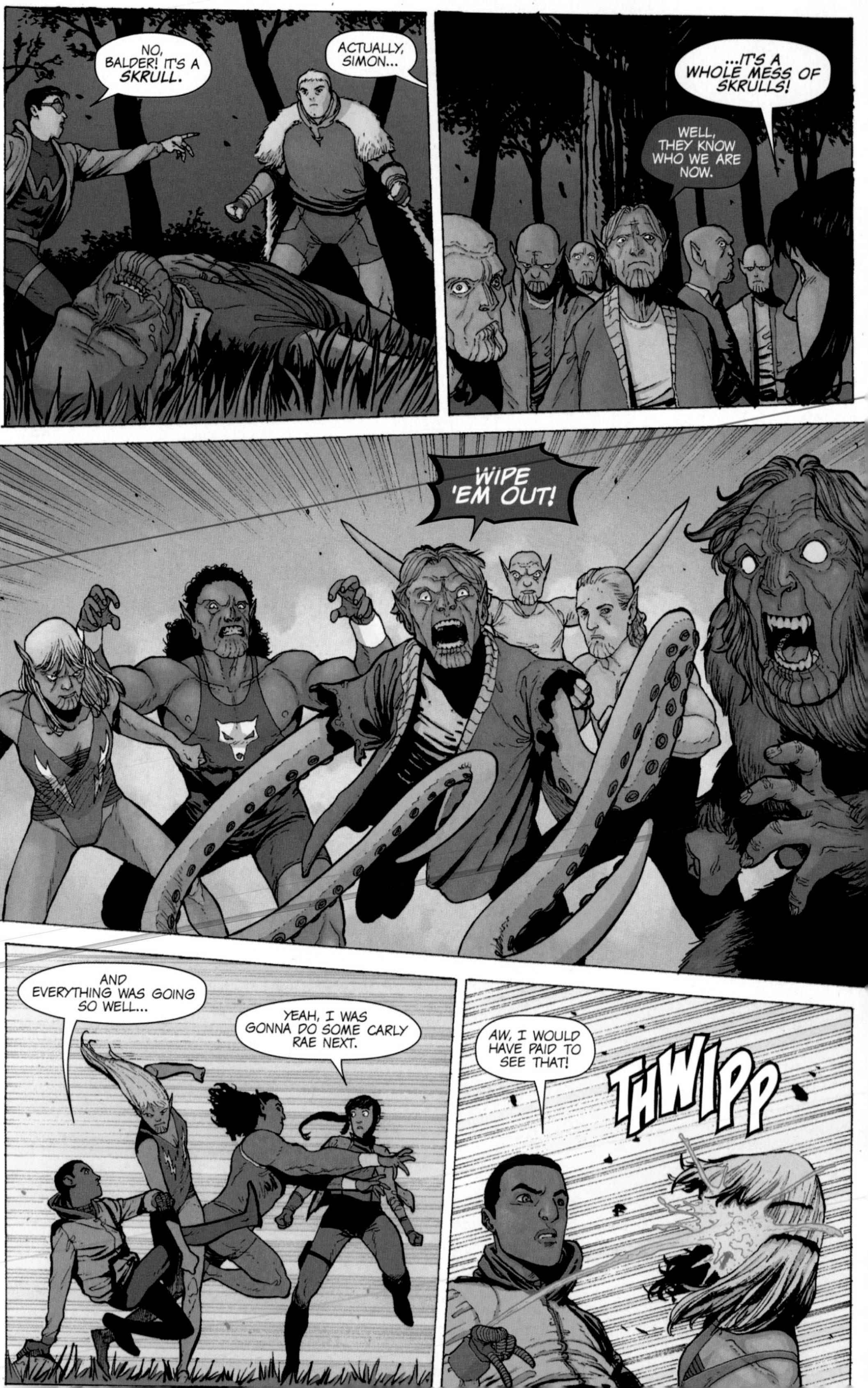
NO, BALDER! IT'S A SKRULL.
ACTUALLY, SIMON...
...IT'S A WHOLE MESS OF SKRULLS!
WELL, THEY KNOW WHO WE ARE NOW.
WIPE 'EM OUT!
AND EVERYTHING WAS GOING SO WELL...
YEAH, I WAS GONNA DO SOME CARLY RAE NEXT.
AW, I WOULD HAVE PAID TO SEE THAT!
THWIPP

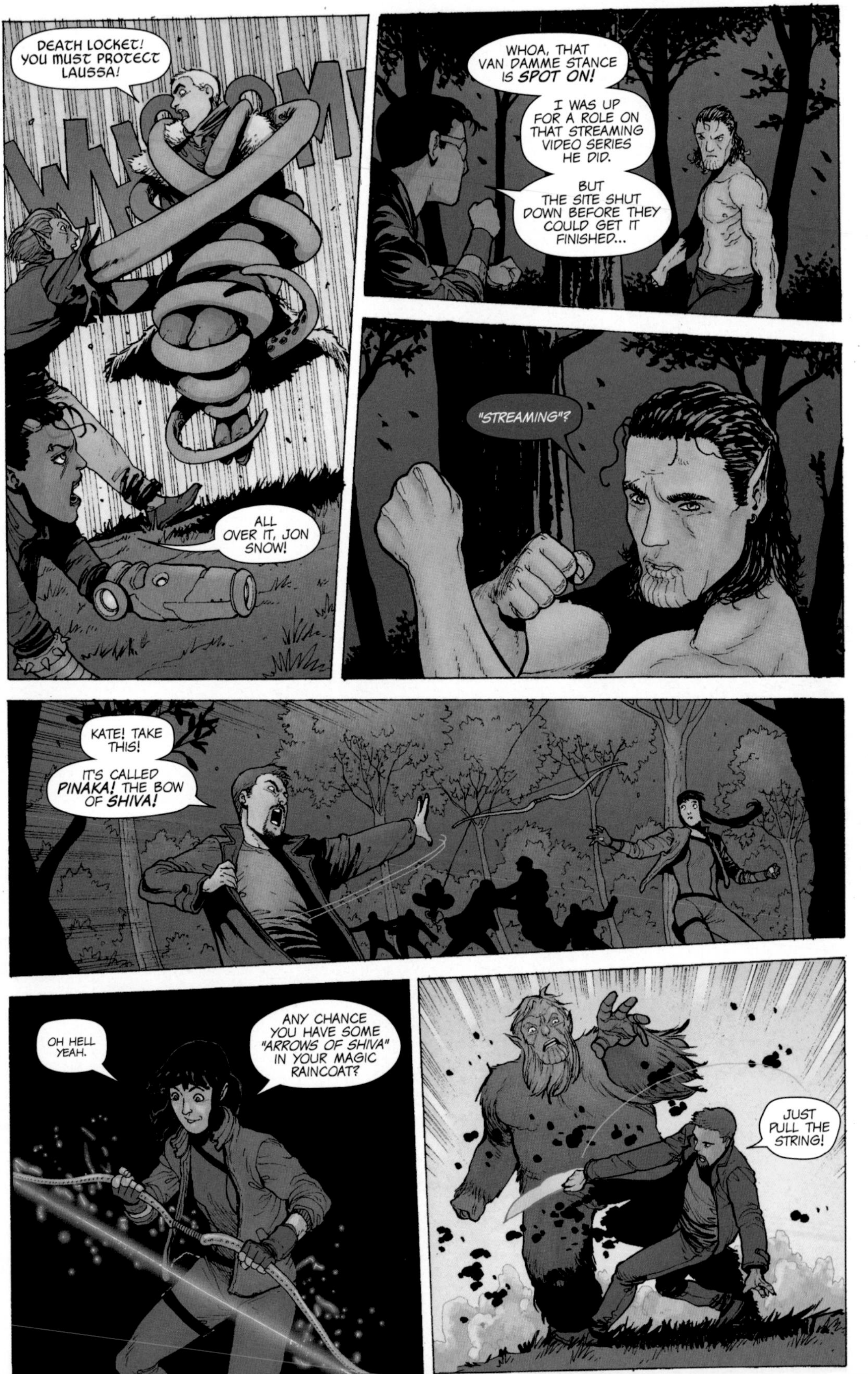
DEATH LOCKET! YOU MUST PROTECT LAUSSA!
WHOOM
ALL OVER IT, JON SNOW!
WHOA, THAT VAN DAMME STANCE IS SPOT ON!
I WAS UP FOR A ROLE ON THAT STREAMING VIDEO SERIES HE DID.
BUT THE SITE SHUT DOWN BEFORE THEY COULD GET IT FINISHED...
"STREAMING"?
KATE! TAKE THIS!
IT'S CALLED PINAKA! THE BOW OF SHIVA!
OH HELL YEAH.
ANY CHANCE YOU HAVE SOME "ARROWS OF SHIVA" IN YOUR MAGIC RAINCOAT?
JUST PULL THE STRING!

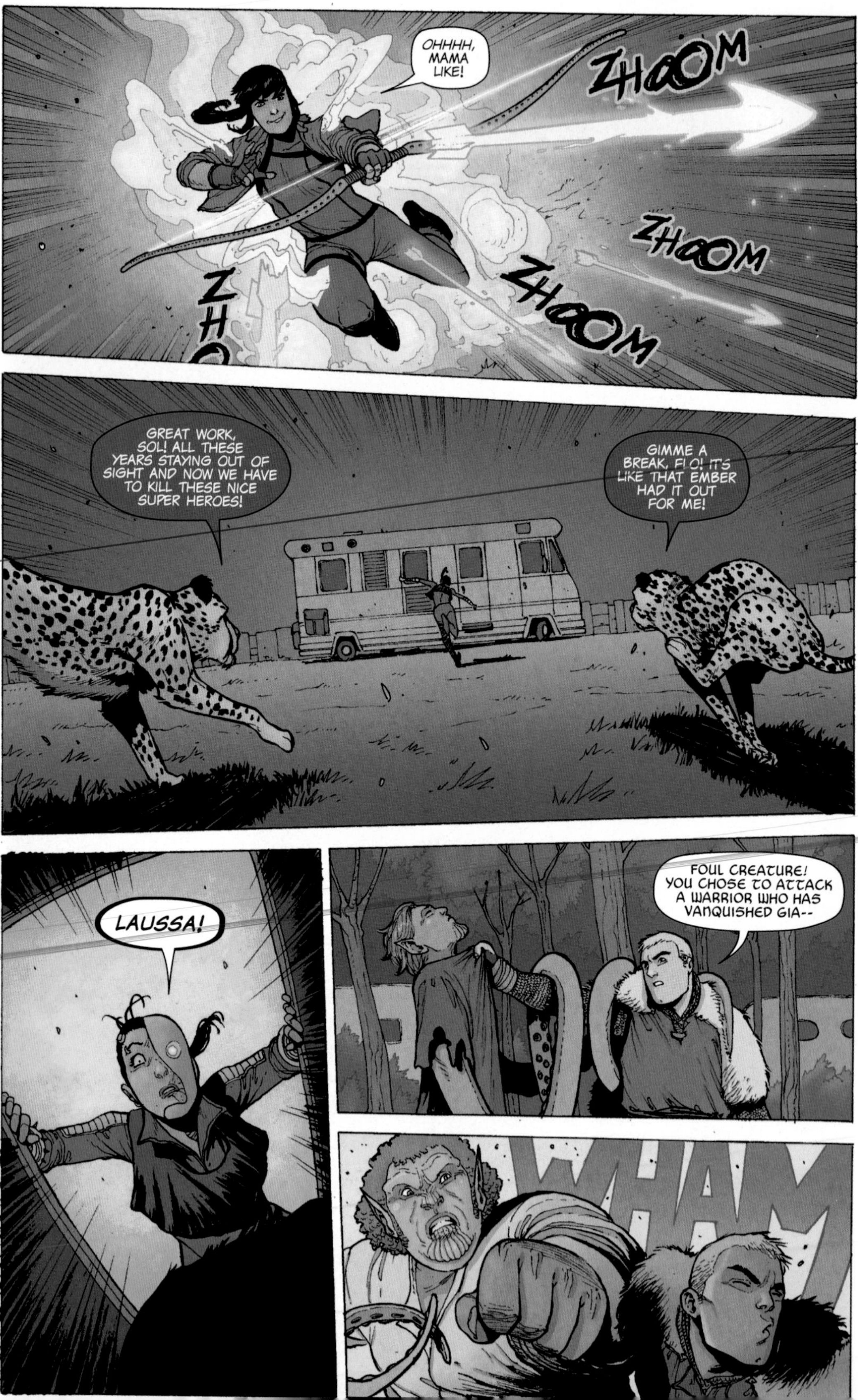
OHHHH, MAMA LIKE!
ZHOOM
ZHOOM
ZHOOM
ZHO
GREAT WORK, SOL! ALL THESE YEARS STAYING OUT OF SIGHT AND NOW WE HAVE TO KILL THESE NICE SUPER HEROES!
GIMME A BREAK, FLO! ITS LIKE THAT EMBER HAD IT OUT FOR ME!
LAUSSA!
FOUL CREATURE! YOU CHOSE TO ATTACK A WARRIOR WHO HAS VANQUISHED GIA--
WHAM

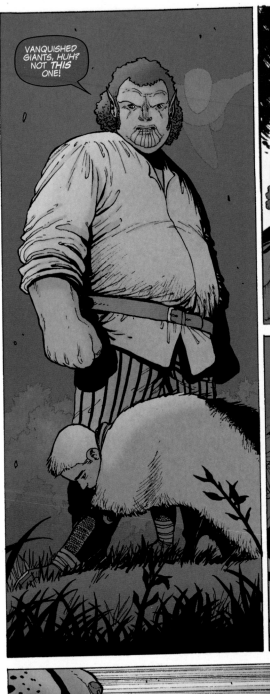

VANQUISHED GIANTS, HUH? NOT *THIS* ONE!

WHAT'S WITH ALL THE '90s JUNK? YOU PEOPLE REALLY *HAVE* BEEN OFF THE GRID!

AGH!

FIRST OFF, THE PRINCESS BRIDE CAME OUT IN 1987.

AND *SECOND,* IT'S A TIMELESS CLASSIC THAT SHAPED-- *not NOW,* DRUID--

--THE SKRULLS HAVE SET UPON LAUSSA!

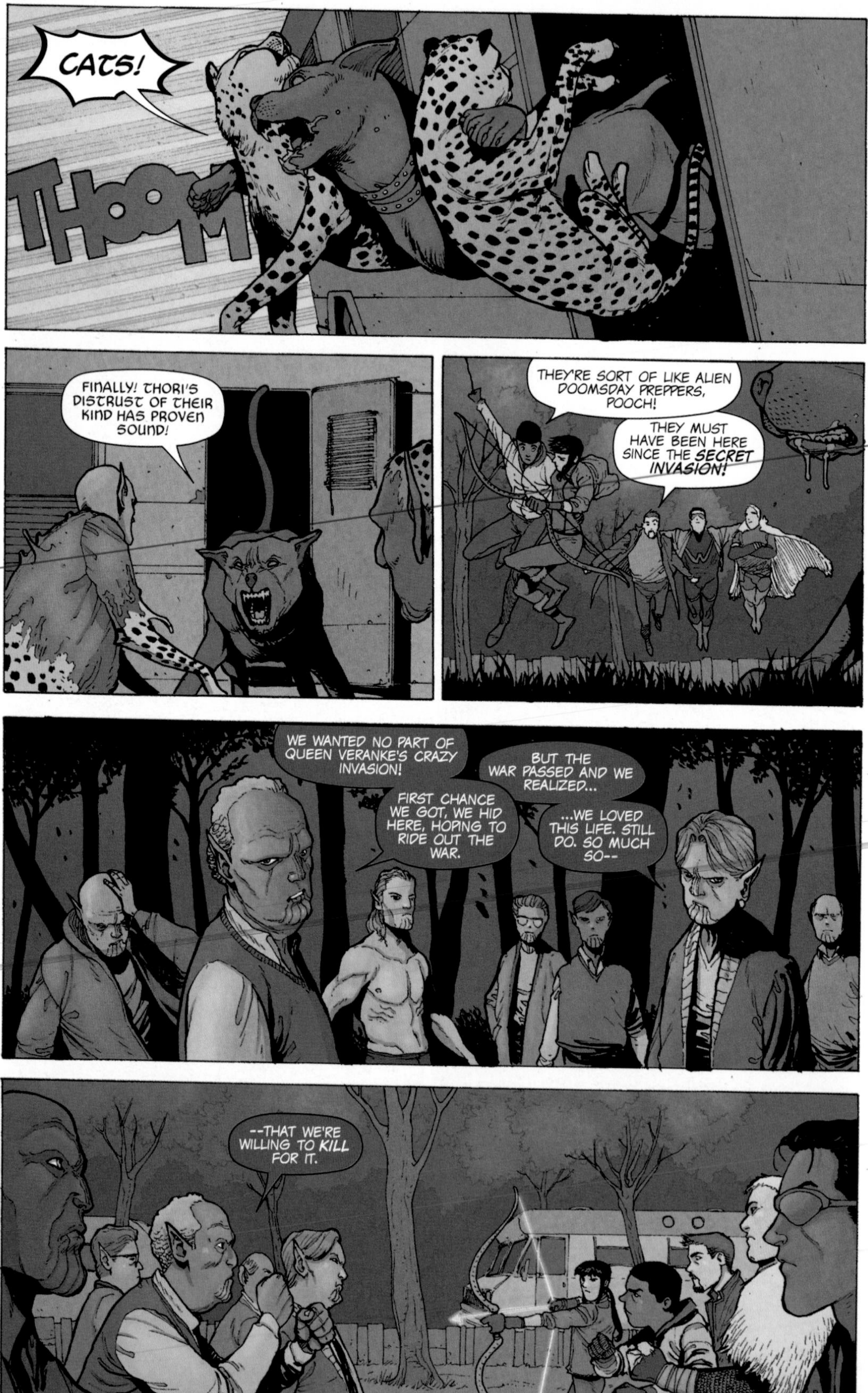
CATS!
THOOM
FINALLY! THORI'S DISTRUST OF THEIR KIND HAS PROVEN SOUND!
THEY'RE SORT OF LIKE ALIEN DOOMSDAY PREPPERS, POOCH!
THEY MUST HAVE BEEN HERE SINCE THE SECRET INVASION!
WE WANTED NO PART OF QUEEN VERANKE'S CRAZY INVASION!
FIRST CHANCE WE GOT, WE HID HERE, HOPING TO RIDE OUT THE WAR.
BUT THE WAR PASSED AND WE REALIZED...
...WE LOVED THIS LIFE. STILL DO. SO MUCH SO--
--THAT WE'RE WILLING TO KILL FOR IT.

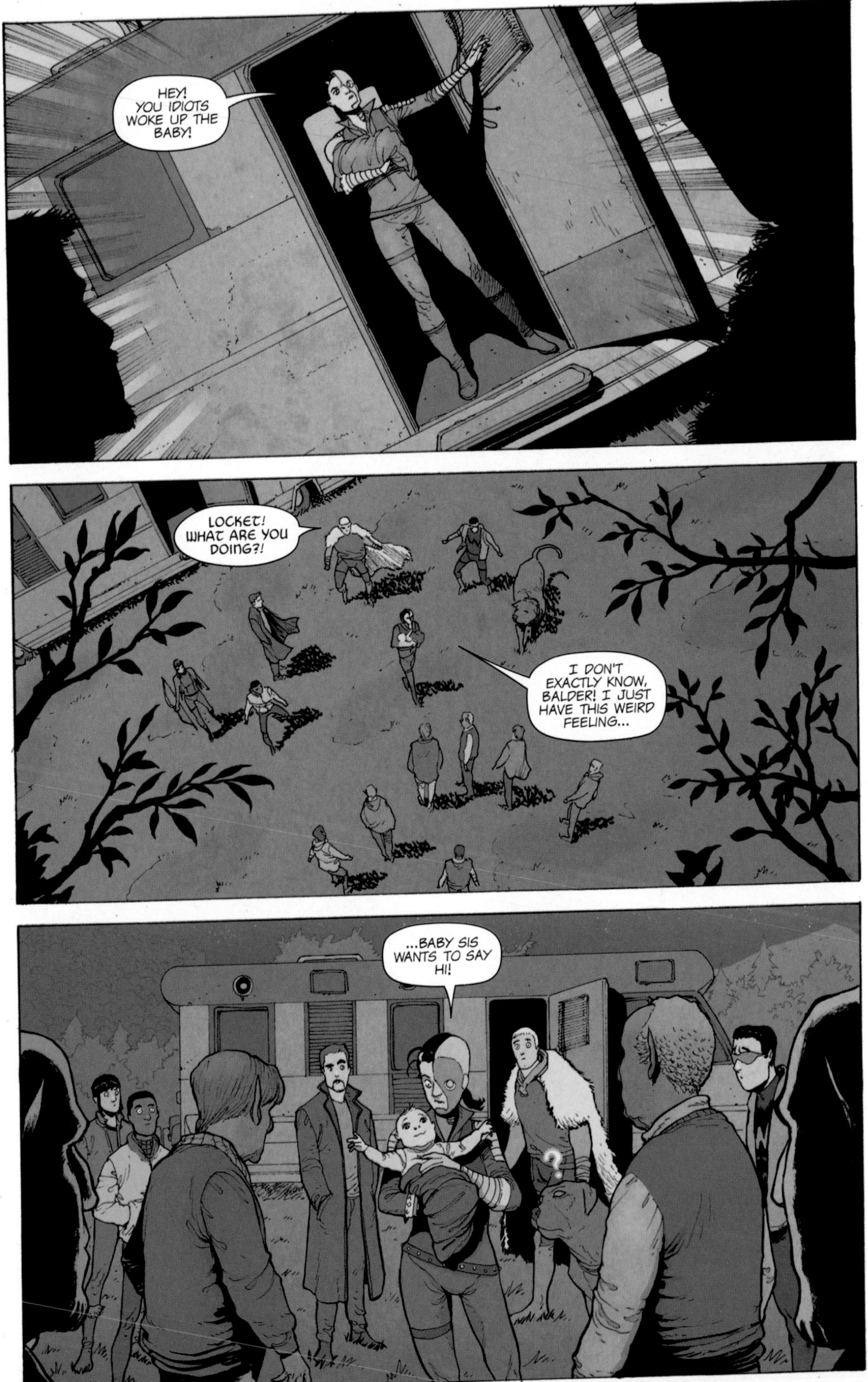
HEY! YOU IDIOTS WOKE UP THE BABY!
LOCKET! WHAT ARE YOU DOING?!
I DON'T EXACTLY KNOW, BALDER! I JUST HAVE THIS WEIRD FEELING...
...BABY SIS WANTS TO SAY HI!
?

OH MY GAWD! LOOK AT HER!

AWMMMWW!

WHO'S A PRETTY GIRL? WHO'S A PRETTY GIRL?

GOO-GOO-GOO! GOO-GOO-GOO!

WHAT A DOLL!

SHE'S PERFECT!

WHAT... THE... HELL?!

IT'S LIKE THEY'VE MORPHED INTO MY GRANDPARENTS.

WEIRD, THEY STILL LOOK LIKE SKRULLS TO ME.

SO DO GRAN-GRAN AND PEEPS.

BALDER, HAVE YOU EVER SEEN ANYTHING LIKE THIS?

NO, FRIEND DRUID. I HAVE NOT.

THORI IS NOT HAPPY...

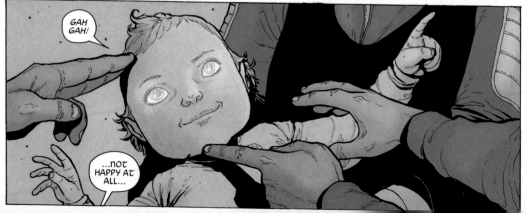

GAH GAH!

...NOT HAPPY AT ALL...

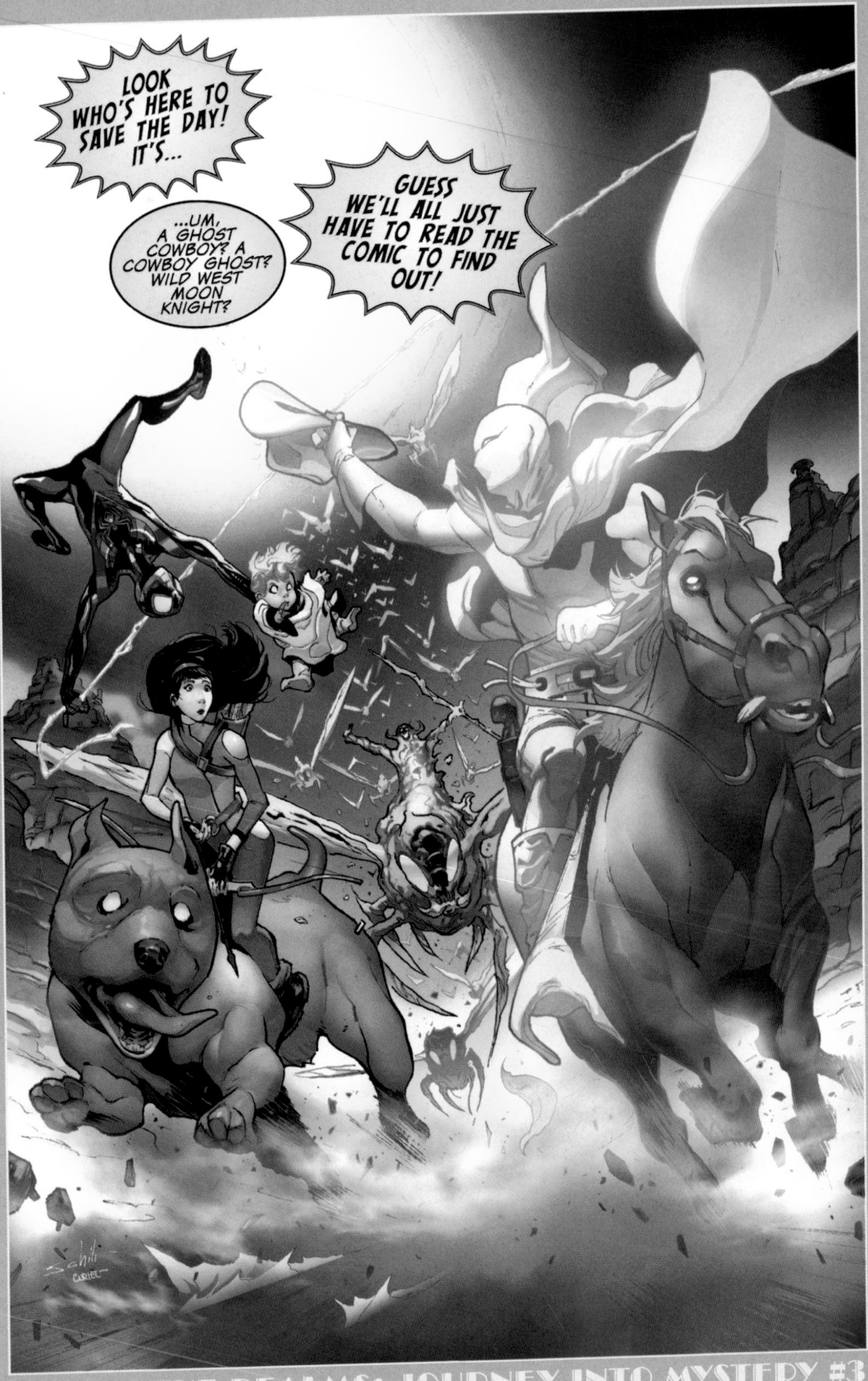
LOOK WHO'S HERE TO SAVE THE DAY! IT'S...
...UM, A GHOST COWBOY? A COWBOY GHOST? WILD WEST MOON KNIGHT?
GUESS WE'LL ALL JUST HAVE TO READ THE COMIC TO FIND OUT!

WAR OF THE REALMS: JOURNEY INTO MYSTERY #3

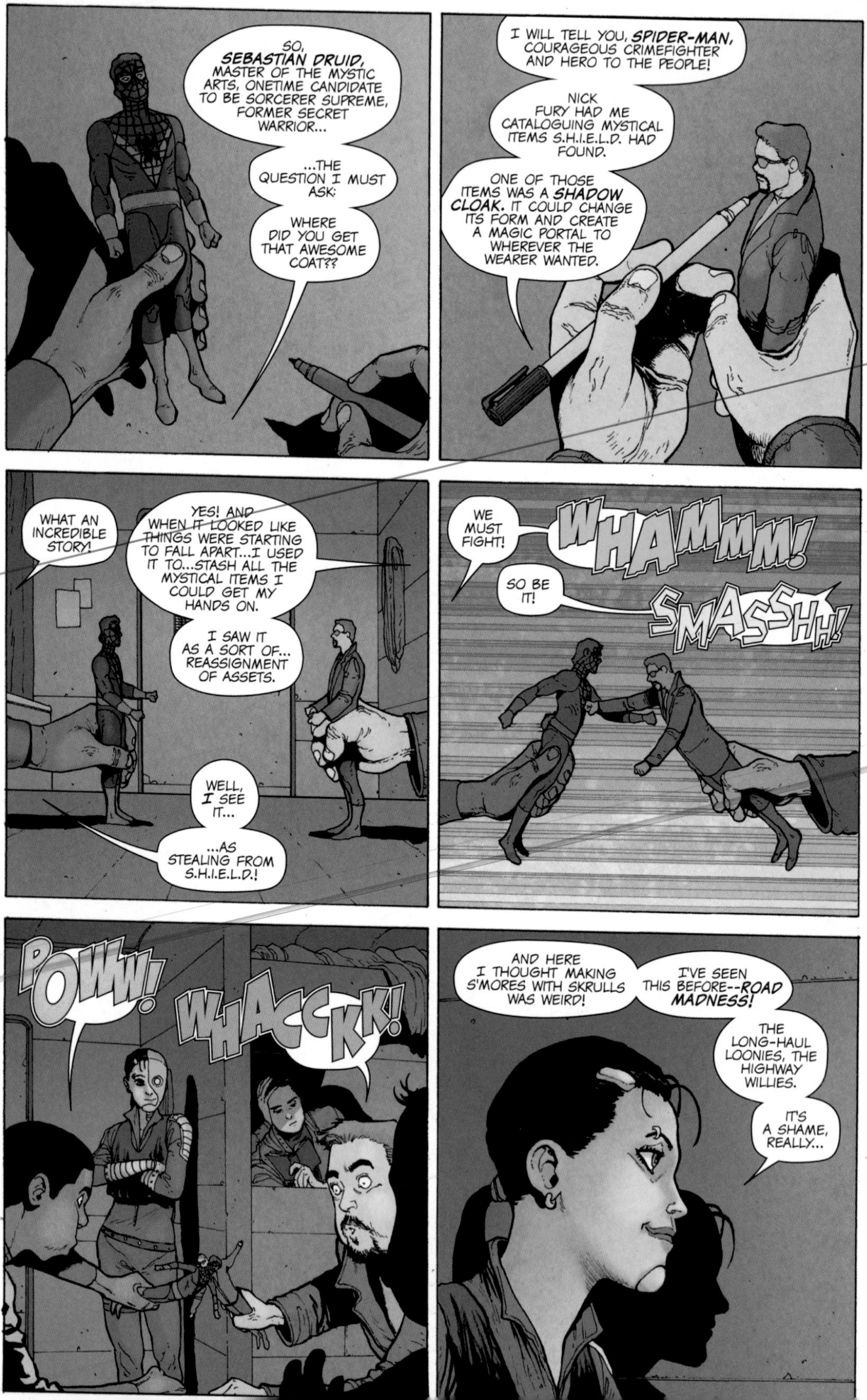
SO, SEBASTIAN DRUID, MASTER OF THE MYSTIC ARTS, ONETIME CANDIDATE TO BE SORCERER SUPREME, FORMER SECRET WARRIOR...
...THE QUESTION I MUST ASK:
WHERE DID YOU GET THAT AWESOME COAT??
I WILL TELL YOU, SPIDER-MAN, COURAGEOUS CRIMEFIGHTER AND HERO TO THE PEOPLE!
NICK FURY HAD ME CATALOGUING MYSTICAL ITEMS S.H.I.E.L.D. HAD FOUND.
ONE OF THOSE ITEMS WAS A SHADOW CLOAK. IT COULD CHANGE ITS FORM AND CREATE A MAGIC PORTAL TO WHEREVER THE WEARER WANTED.
WHAT AN INCREDIBLE STORY!
YES! AND WHEN IT LOOKED LIKE THINGS WERE STARTING TO FALL APART...I USED IT TO...STASH ALL THE MYSTICAL ITEMS I COULD GET MY HANDS ON.
I SAW IT AS A SORT OF... REASSIGNMENT OF ASSETS.
WELL, I SEE IT...
...AS STEALING FROM S.H.I.E.L.D.!
WE MUST FIGHT!
WHAMMMM!
SO BE IT!
SMASSHH!
POWW!
WHACCKK!
AND HERE I THOUGHT MAKING S'MORES WITH SKRULLS WAS WEIRD!
I'VE SEEN THIS BEFORE--ROAD MADNESS!
THE LONG-HAUL LOONIES, THE HIGHWAY WILLIES.
IT'S A SHAME, REALLY...

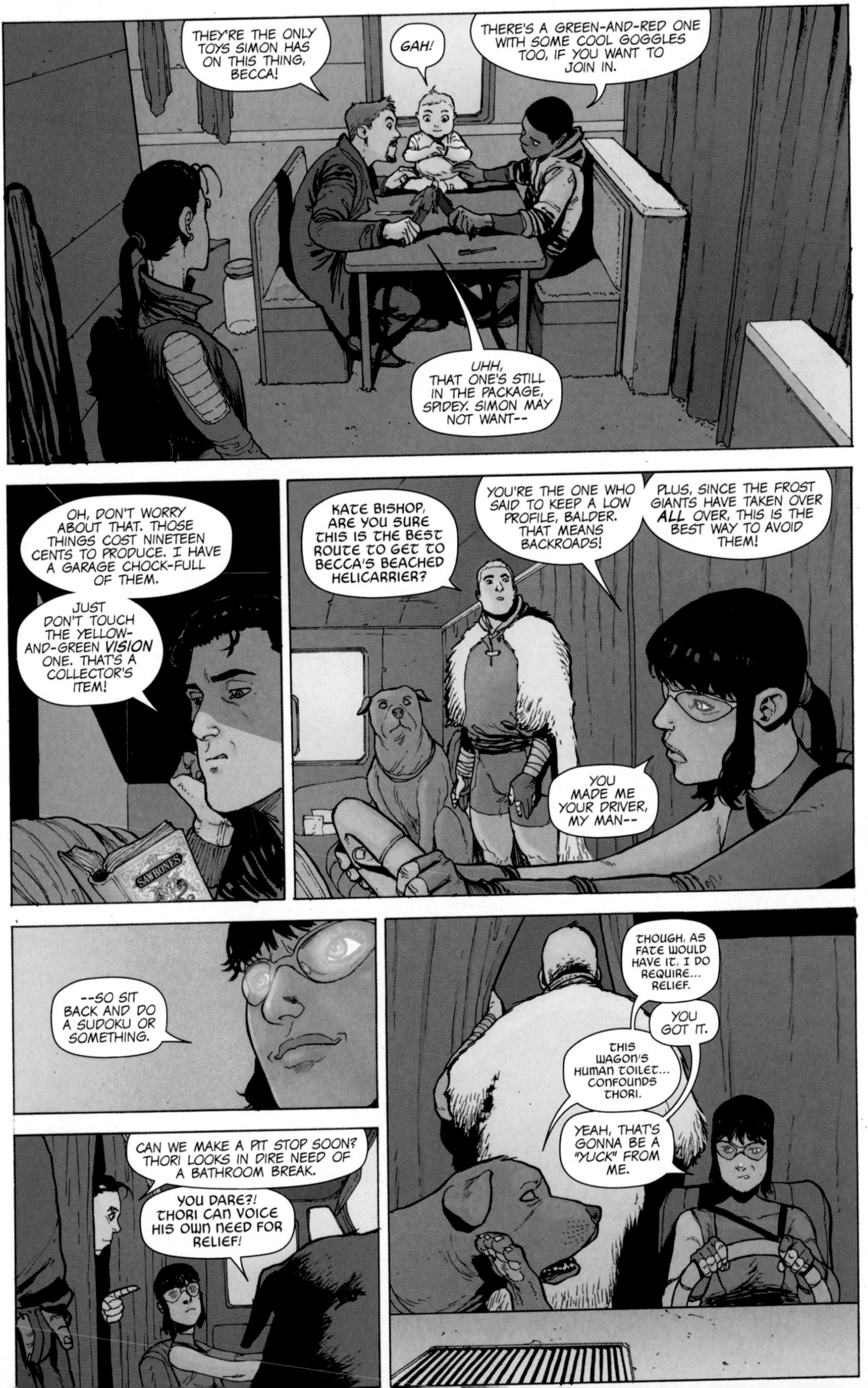
THEY'RE THE ONLY TOYS SIMON HAS ON THIS THING, BECCA!
GAH!
THERE'S A GREEN-AND-RED ONE WITH SOME COOL GOGGLES TOO, IF YOU WANT TO JOIN IN.
UHH, THAT ONE'S STILL IN THE PACKAGE, SPIDEY. SIMON MAY NOT WANT--
OH, DON'T WORRY ABOUT THAT. THOSE THINGS COST NINETEEN CENTS TO PRODUCE. I HAVE A GARAGE CHOCK-FULL OF THEM.
JUST DON'T TOUCH THE YELLOW-AND-GREEN VISION ONE. THAT'S A COLLECTOR'S ITEM!
SAWBONES
KATE BISHOP, ARE YOU SURE THIS IS THE BEST ROUTE TO GET TO BECCA'S BEACHED HELICARRIER?
YOU'RE THE ONE WHO SAID TO KEEP A LOW PROFILE, BALDER. THAT MEANS BACKROADS!
PLUS, SINCE THE FROST GIANTS HAVE TAKEN OVER ALL OVER, THIS IS THE BEST WAY TO AVOID THEM!
YOU MADE ME YOUR DRIVER, MY MAN--
--SO SIT BACK AND DO A SUDOKU OR SOMETHING.
CAN WE MAKE A PIT STOP SOON? THORI LOOKS IN DIRE NEED OF A BATHROOM BREAK.
YOU DARE?! THORI CAN VOICE HIS OWN NEED FOR RELIEF!
THOUGH, AS FATE WOULD HAVE IT, I DO REQUIRE... RELIEF.
YOU GOT IT.
THIS WAGON'S HUMAN TOILET... CONFOUNDS THORI.
YEAH, THAT'S GONNA BE A "YUCK" FROM ME.

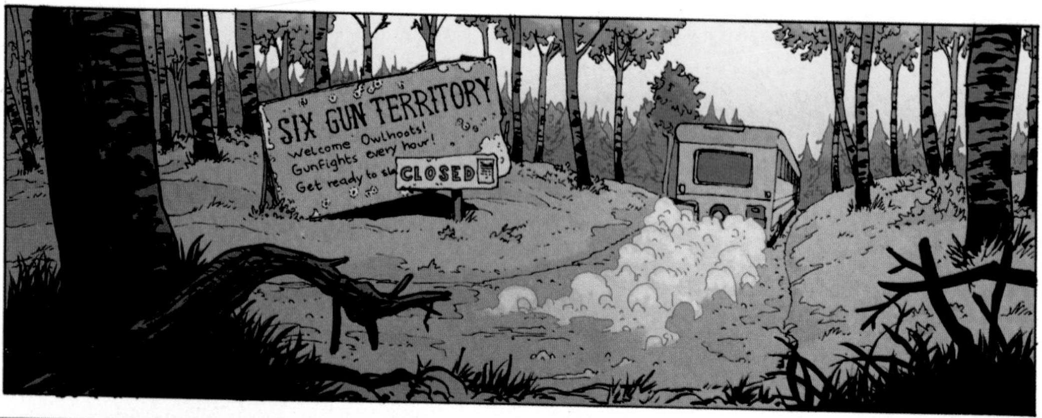
SIX GUN TERRITORY
Welcome Owlhoots!
Gunfights every hour!
Get ready to sl
CLOSED

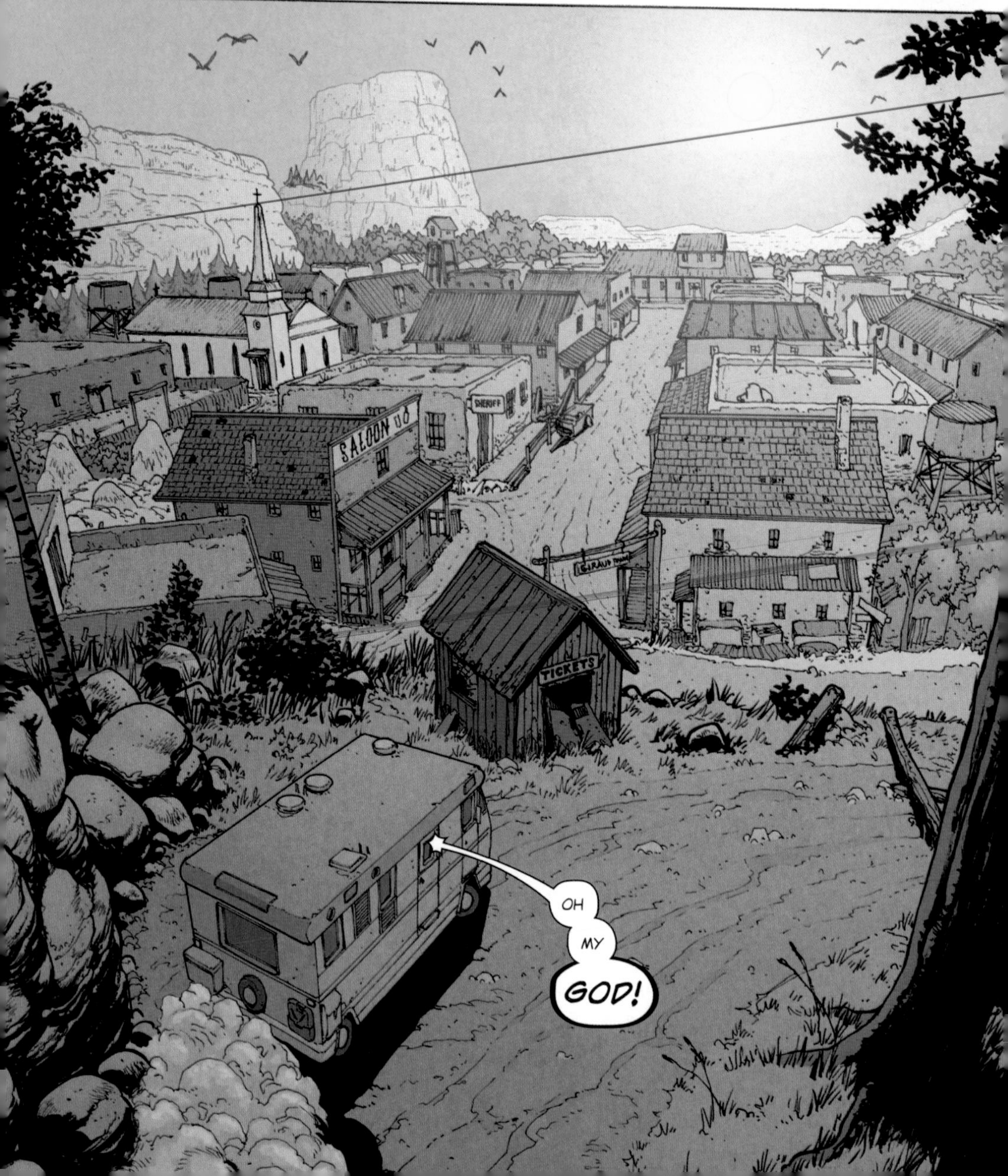
SALOON
SHERIFF
TICKETS
OH MY GOD!

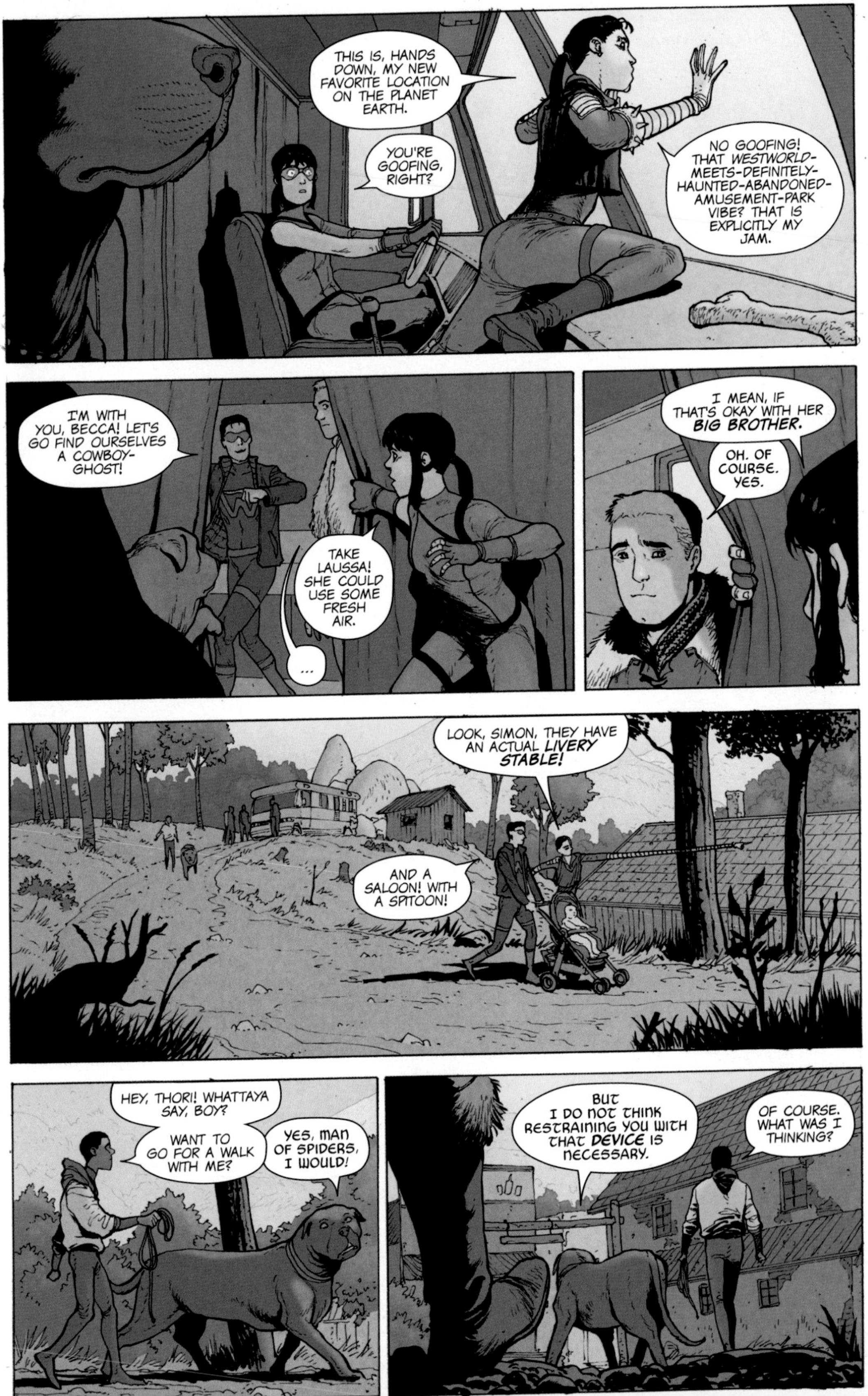

THIS IS, HANDS DOWN, MY NEW FAVORITE LOCATION ON THE PLANET EARTH.
YOU'RE GOOFING, RIGHT?
NO GOOFING! THAT WESTWORLD-MEETS-DEFINITELY-HAUNTED-ABANDONED-AMUSEMENT-PARK VIBE? THAT IS EXPLICITLY MY JAM.
I'M WITH YOU, BECCA! LET'S GO FIND OURSELVES A COWBOY-GHOST!
TAKE LAUSSA! SHE COULD USE SOME FRESH AIR.
...
I MEAN, IF THAT'S OKAY WITH HER BIG BROTHER.
OH. OF COURSE. YES.
LOOK, SIMON, THEY HAVE AN ACTUAL LIVERY STABLE!
AND A SALOON! WITH A SPITOON!
HEY, THORI! WHATTAYA SAY, BOY?
WANT TO GO FOR A WALK WITH ME?
YES, MAN OF SPIDERS, I WOULD!
BUT I DO NOT THINK RESTRAINING YOU WITH THAT DEVICE IS NECESSARY.
OF COURSE. WHAT WAS I THINKING?

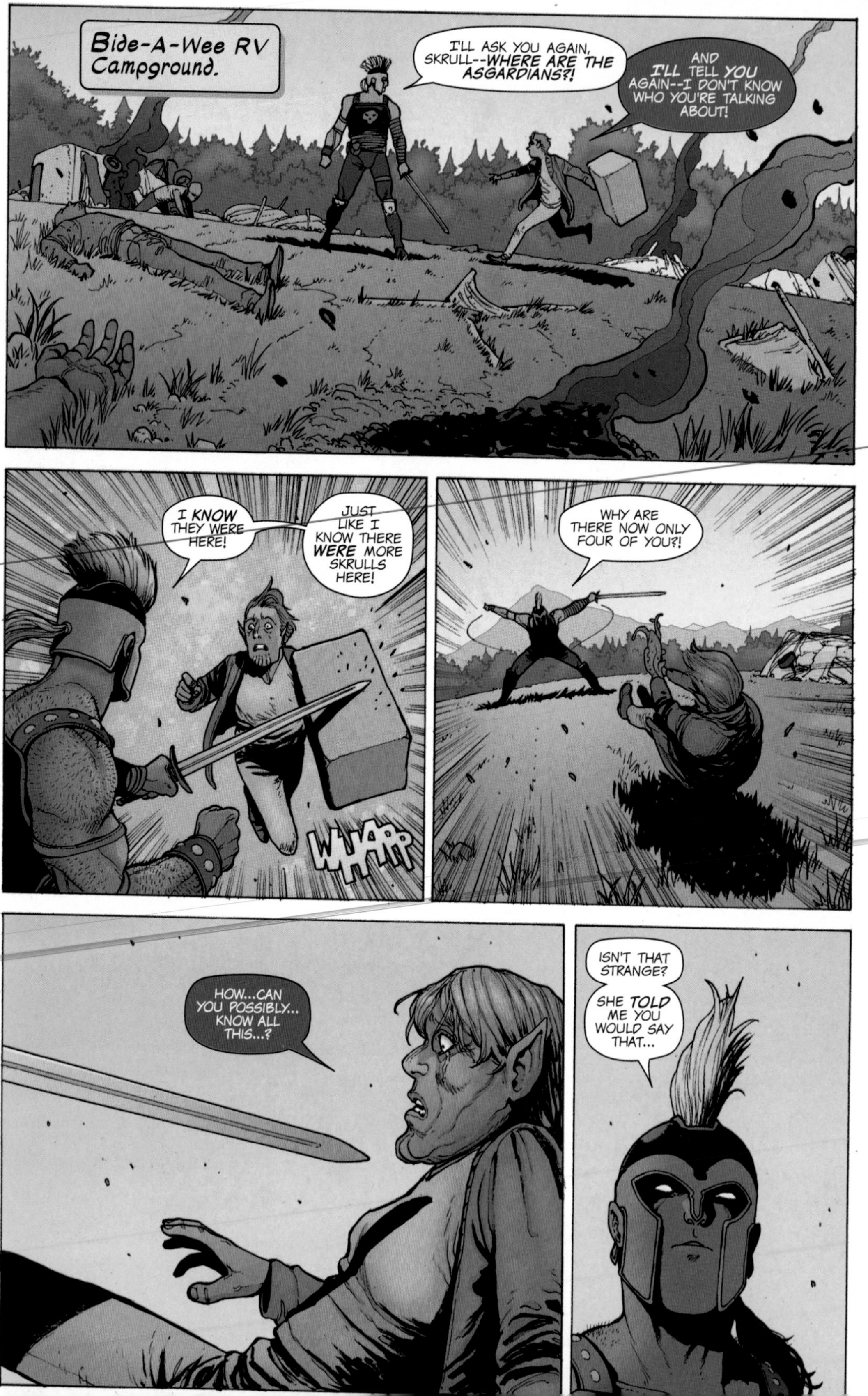

Bide-A-Wee RV Campground.
I'LL ASK YOU AGAIN, SKRULL--WHERE ARE THE ASGARDIANS?!
AND I'LL TELL YOU AGAIN--I DON'T KNOW WHO YOU'RE TALKING ABOUT!
I KNOW THEY WERE HERE!
JUST LIKE I KNOW THERE WERE MORE SKRULLS HERE!
WHAPP
WHY ARE THERE NOW ONLY FOUR OF YOU?!
HOW...CAN YOU POSSIBLY... KNOW ALL THIS...?
ISN'T THAT STRANGE?
SHE TOLD ME YOU WOULD SAY THAT...

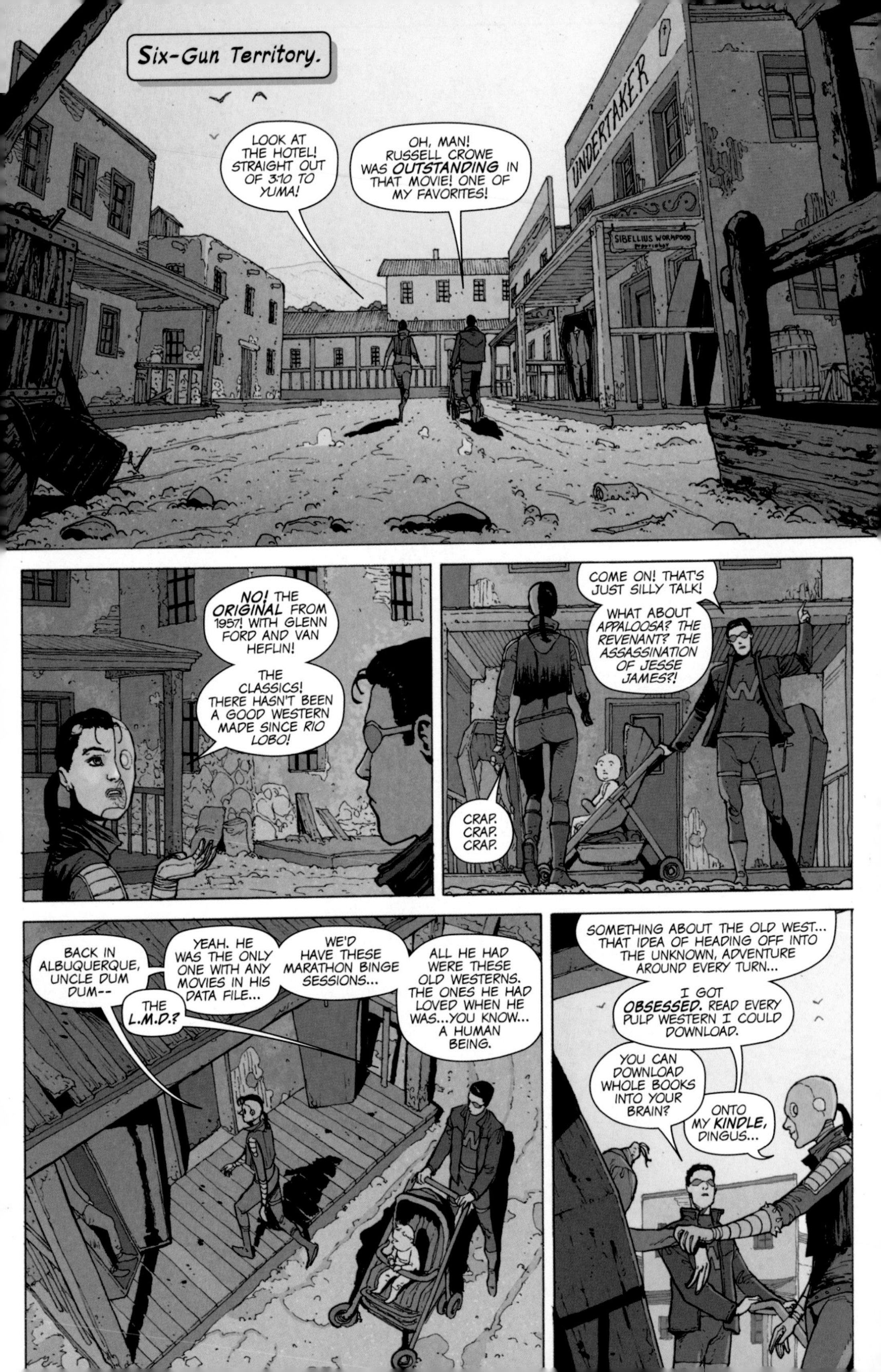
Six-Gun Territory.
LOOK AT THE HOTEL! STRAIGHT OUT OF 3:10 TO YUMA!
OH, MAN! RUSSELL CROWE WAS OUTSTANDING IN THAT MOVIE! ONE OF MY FAVORITES!
UNDERTAKER
SIBELLIUS WORMFOOD
NO! THE ORIGINAL FROM 1957! WITH GLENN FORD AND VAN HEFLIN!
THE CLASSICS! THERE HASN'T BEEN A GOOD WESTERN MADE SINCE RIO LOBO!
COME ON! THAT'S JUST SILLY TALK!
WHAT ABOUT APPALOOSA? THE REVENANT? THE ASSASSINATION OF JESSE JAMES?!
CRAP. CRAP. CRAP.
BACK IN ALBUQUERQUE, UNCLE DUM DUM--
THE L.M.D.?
YEAH. HE WAS THE ONLY ONE WITH ANY MOVIES IN HIS DATA FILE...
WE'D HAVE THESE MARATHON BINGE SESSIONS...
ALL HE HAD WERE THESE OLD WESTERNS. THE ONES HE HAD LOVED WHEN HE WAS...YOU KNOW... A HUMAN BEING.
SOMETHING ABOUT THE OLD WEST... THAT IDEA OF HEADING OFF INTO THE UNKNOWN, ADVENTURE AROUND EVERY TURN...
I GOT OBSESSED. READ EVERY PULP WESTERN I COULD DOWNLOAD.
YOU CAN DOWNLOAD WHOLE BOOKS INTO YOUR BRAIN?
ONTO MY KINDLE, DINGUS...

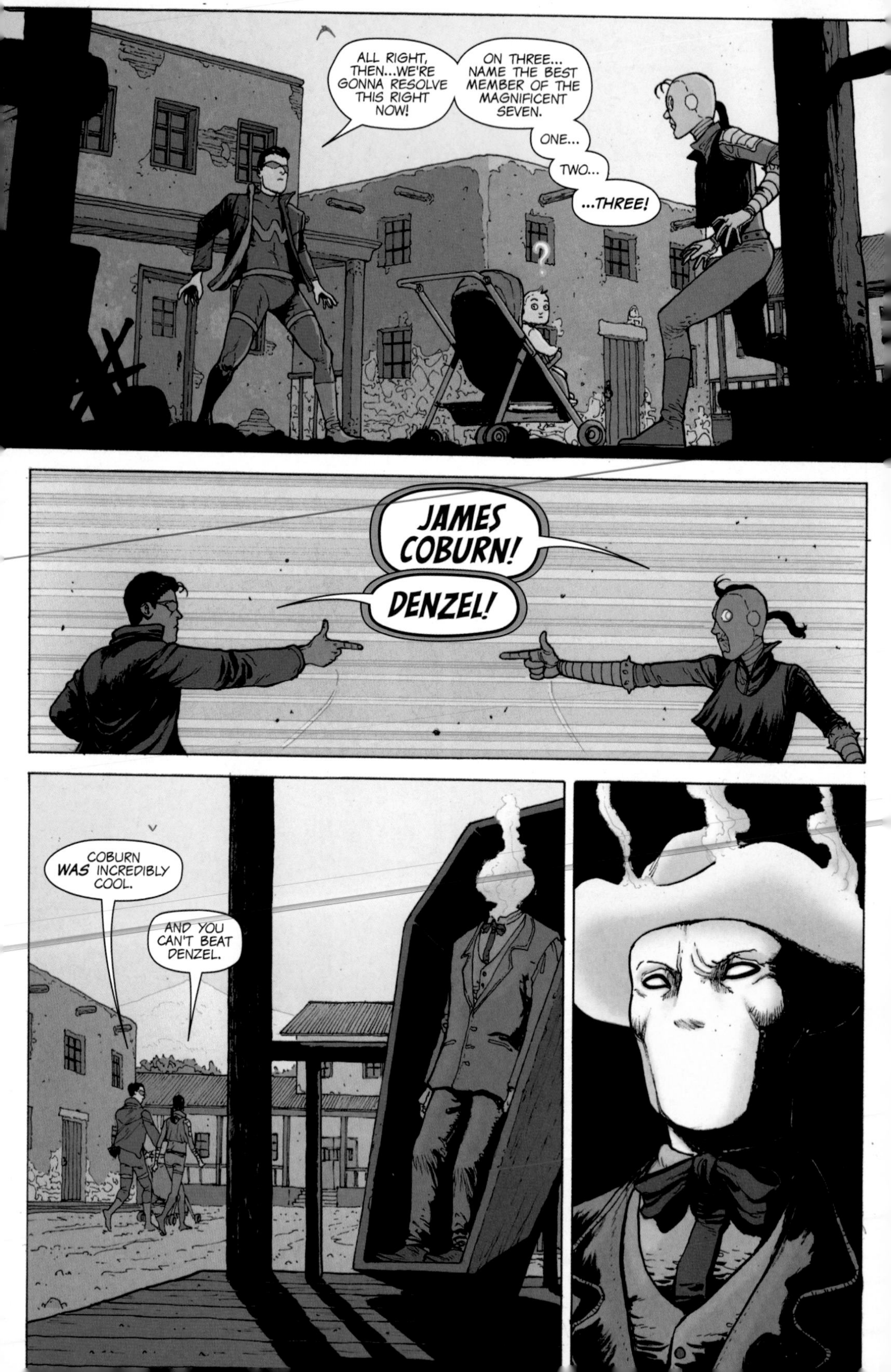
ALL RIGHT, THEN...WE'RE GONNA RESOLVE THIS RIGHT NOW!
ON THREE... NAME THE BEST MEMBER OF THE MAGNIFICENT SEVEN.
ONE...
TWO...
...THREE!
JAMES COBURN!
DENZEL!
COBURN WAS INCREDIBLY COOL.
AND YOU CAN'T BEAT DENZEL.

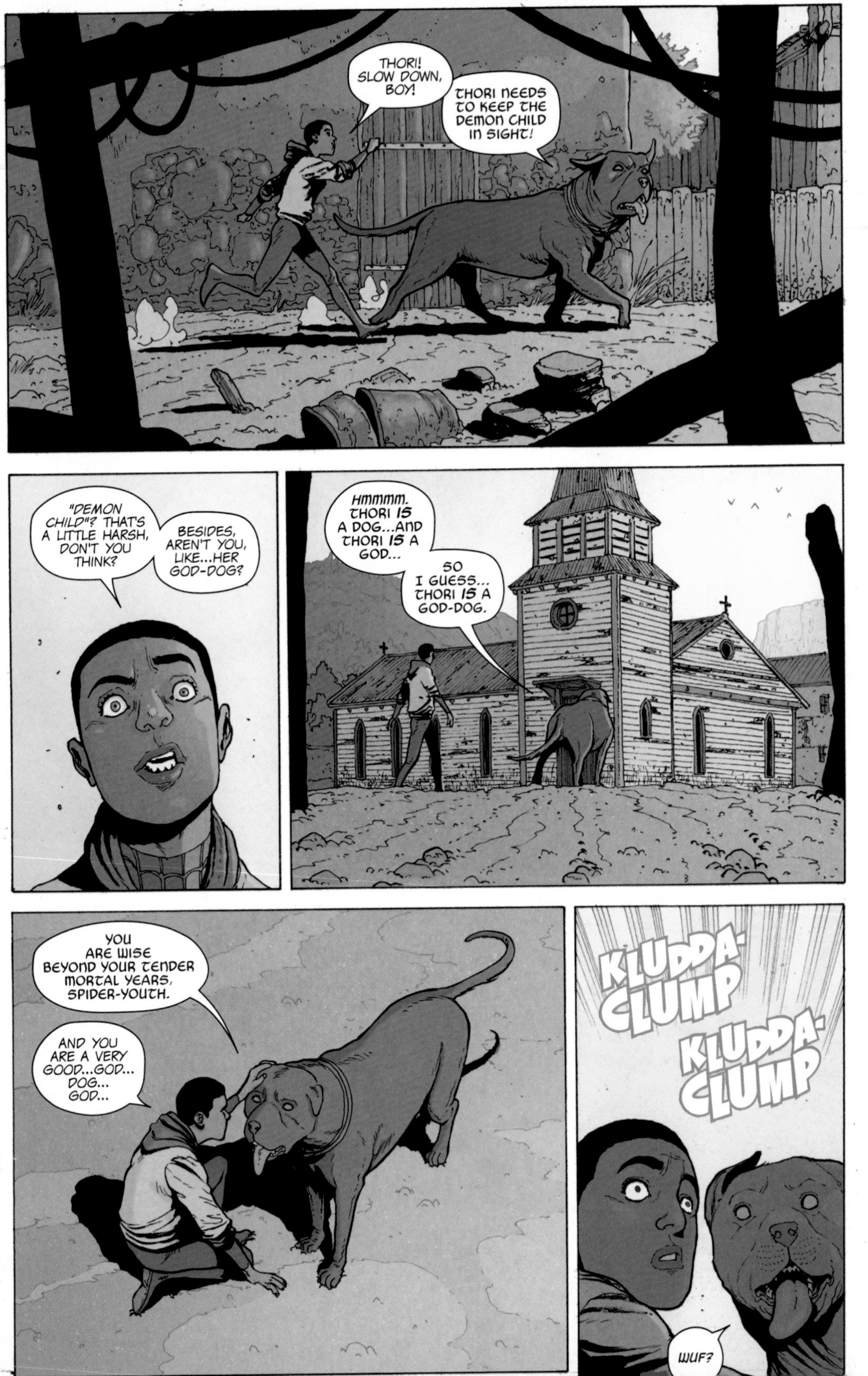
THORI! SLOW DOWN, BOY!
THORI NEEDS TO KEEP THE DEMON CHILD IN SIGHT!
"DEMON CHILD"? THAT'S A LITTLE HARSH, DON'T YOU THINK?
BESIDES, AREN'T YOU, LIKE...HER GOD-DOG?
HMMMM. THORI IS A DOG...AND THORI IS A GOD...
SO I GUESS... THORI IS A GOD-DOG.
YOU ARE WISE BEYOND YOUR TENDER MORTAL YEARS, SPIDER-YOUTH.
AND YOU ARE A VERY GOOD...GOD... DOG... GOD...
KLUDDA-CLUMP
KLUDDA-CLUMP
WUF?

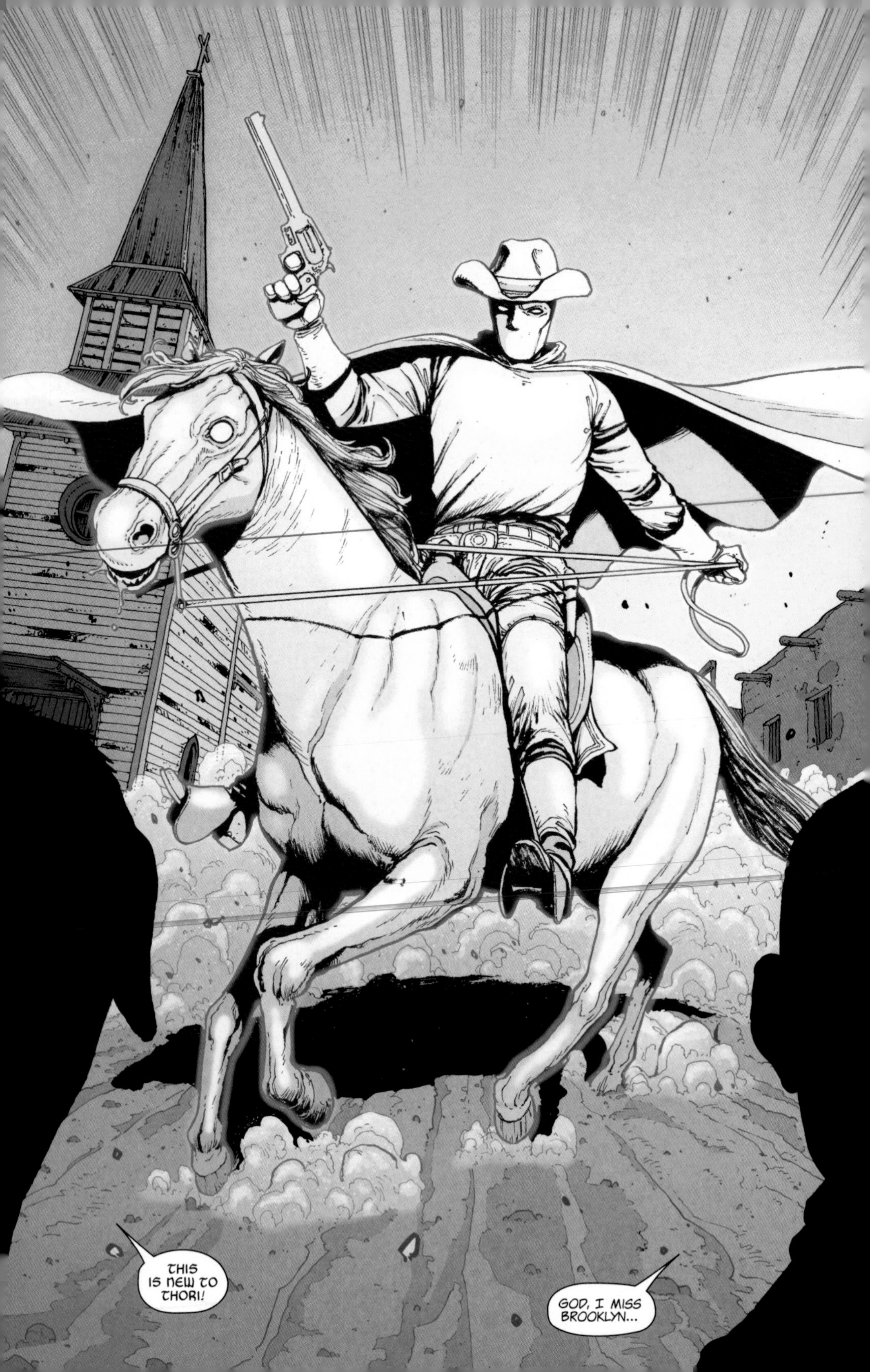
THIS IS NEW TO THORI!
GOD, I MISS BROOKLYN...

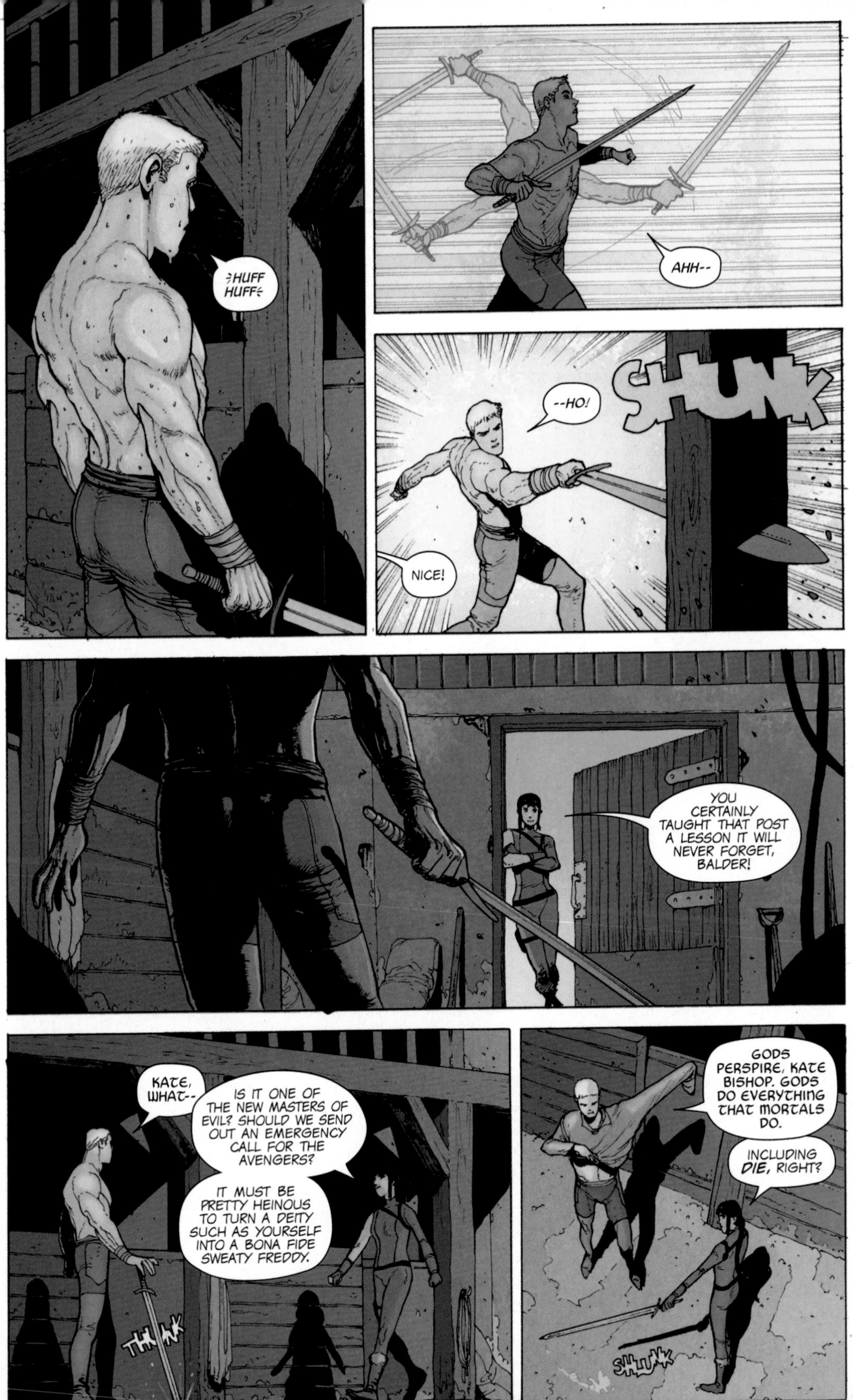
HUFF HUFF
AHH--
--HO!
SHUNK
NICE!
YOU CERTAINLY TAUGHT THAT POST A LESSON IT WILL NEVER FORGET, BALDER!
KATE, WHAT--
IS IT ONE OF THE NEW MASTERS OF EVIL? SHOULD WE SEND OUT AN EMERGENCY CALL FOR THE AVENGERS?
IT MUST BE PRETTY HEINOUS TO TURN A DEITY SUCH AS YOURSELF INTO A BONA FIDE SWEATY FREDDY.
THWNK
GODS PERSPIRE, KATE BISHOP. GODS DO EVERYTHING THAT MORTALS DO.
INCLUDING DIE, RIGHT?
SHUNK

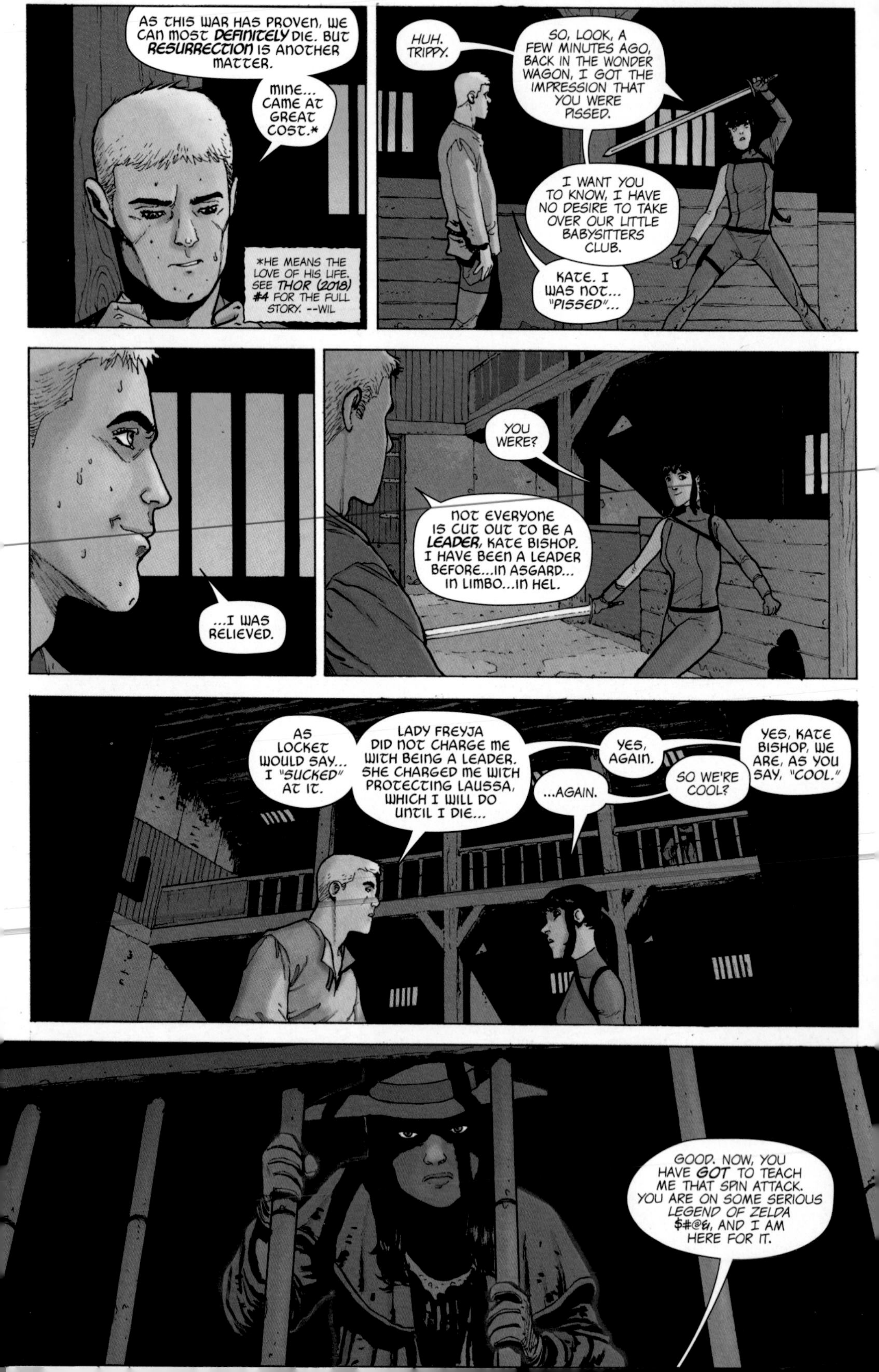
AS THIS WAR HAS PROVEN, WE CAN MOST DEFINITELY DIE. BUT RESURRECTION IS ANOTHER MATTER.
MINE... CAME AT GREAT COST.*
*HE MEANS THE LOVE OF HIS LIFE. SEE THOR (2018) #4 FOR THE FULL STORY. --WIL
HUH. TRIPPY.
SO, LOOK, A FEW MINUTES AGO, BACK IN THE WONDER WAGON, I GOT THE IMPRESSION THAT YOU WERE PISSED.
I WANT YOU TO KNOW, I HAVE NO DESIRE TO TAKE OVER OUR LITTLE BABYSITTERS CLUB.
KATE. I WAS NOT... "PISSED"...
...I WAS RELIEVED.
YOU WERE?
NOT EVERYONE IS CUT OUT TO BE A LEADER, KATE BISHOP. I HAVE BEEN A LEADER BEFORE...IN ASGARD... IN LIMBO...IN HEL.
AS LOCKET WOULD SAY... I "SUCKED" AT IT.
LADY FREYJA DID NOT CHARGE ME WITH BEING A LEADER. SHE CHARGED ME WITH PROTECTING LAUSSA, WHICH I WILL DO UNTIL I DIE...
...AGAIN.
YES, AGAIN.
SO WE'RE COOL?
YES, KATE BISHOP, WE ARE, AS YOU SAY, "COOL."
GOOD. NOW, YOU HAVE GOT TO TEACH ME THAT SPIN ATTACK. YOU ARE ON SOME SERIOUS LEGEND OF ZELDA $#@&, AND I AM HERE FOR IT.

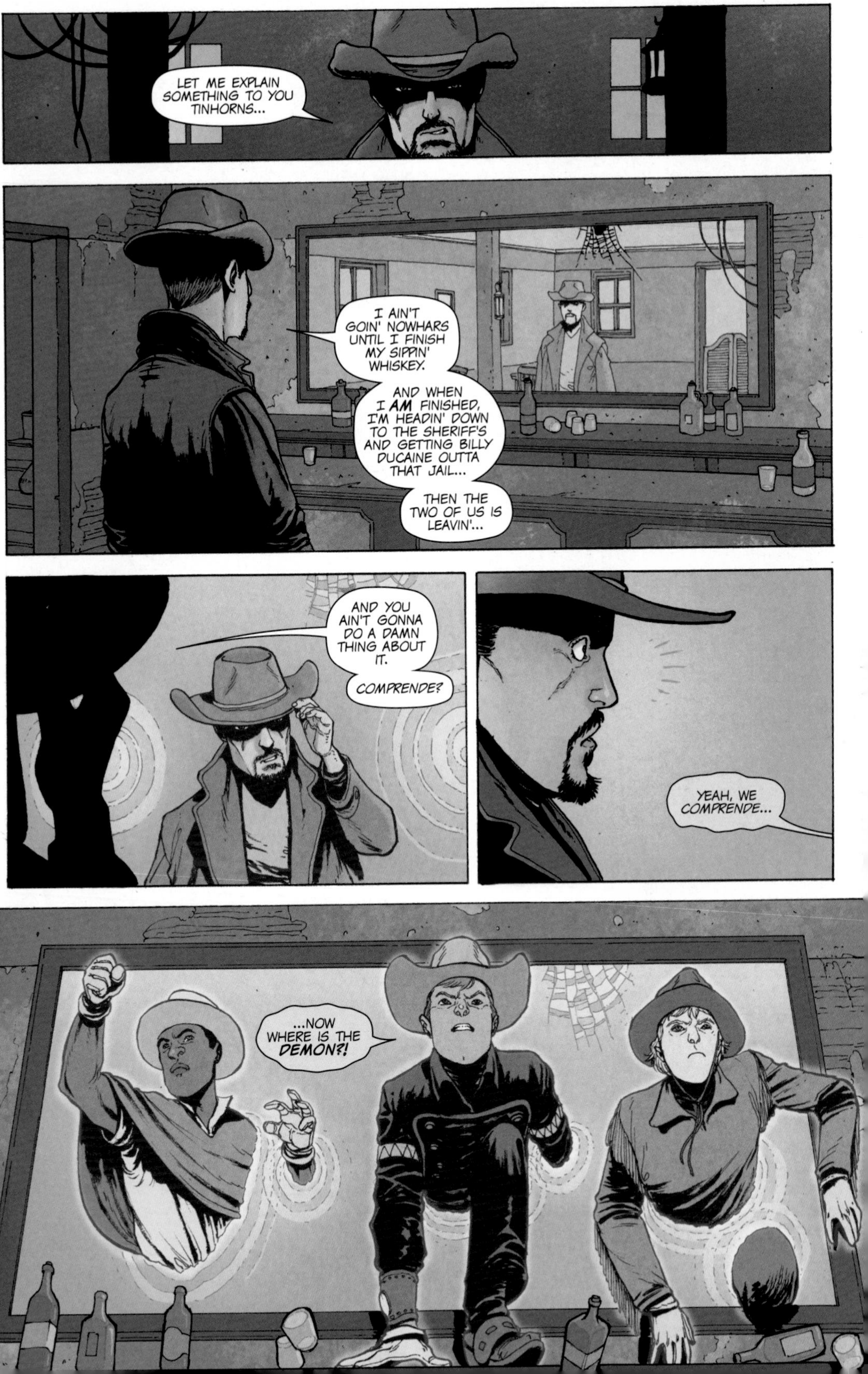
LET ME EXPLAIN SOMETHING TO YOU TINHORNS...
I AIN'T GOIN' NOWHARS UNTIL I FINISH MY SIPPIN' WHISKEY.
AND WHEN I **AM** FINISHED, I'M HEADIN' DOWN TO THE SHERIFF'S AND GETTING BILLY DUCAINE OUTTA THAT JAIL...
THEN THE TWO OF US IS LEAVIN'...
AND YOU AIN'T GONNA DO A DAMN THING ABOUT IT.
COMPRENDE?
YEAH, WE *COMPRENDE*...
...NOW WHERE IS THE ***DEMON?!***

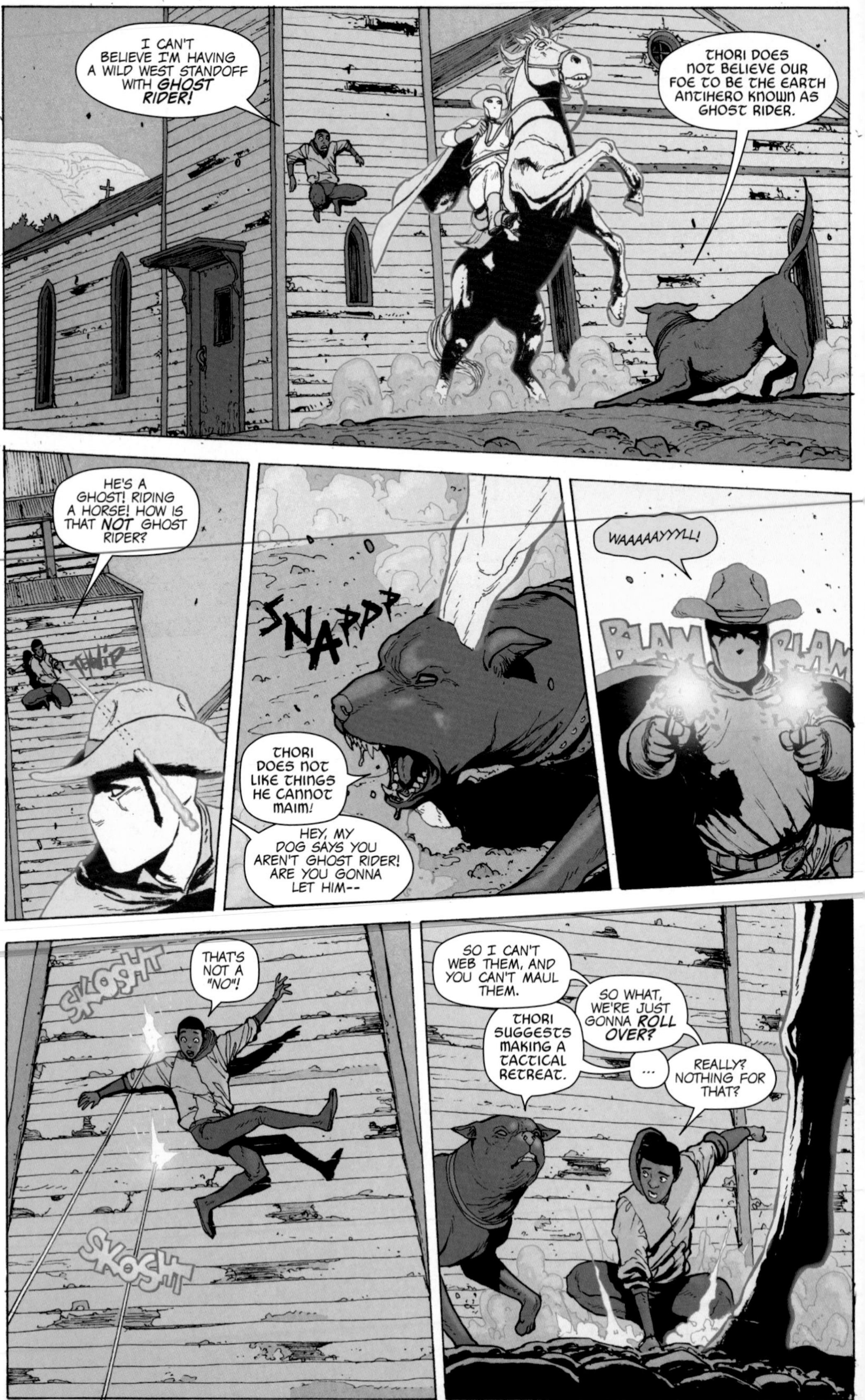
I CAN'T BELIEVE I'M HAVING A WILD WEST STANDOFF WITH GHOST RIDER!
THORI DOES NOT BELIEVE OUR FOE TO BE THE EARTH ANTIHERO KNOWN AS GHOST RIDER.
HE'S A GHOST! RIDING A HORSE! HOW IS THAT NOT GHOST RIDER?
THWIP
SNAPPP
THORI DOES NOT LIKE THINGS HE CANNOT MAIM!
HEY, MY DOG SAYS YOU AREN'T GHOST RIDER! ARE YOU GONNA LET HIM--
WAAAAAYYYLL!
BLAM BLAM
SKOSH
THAT'S NOT A "NO"!
SKOSH
SO I CAN'T WEB THEM, AND YOU CAN'T MAUL THEM.
SO WHAT, WE'RE JUST GONNA ROLL OVER?
THORI SUGGESTS MAKING A TACTICAL RETREAT.
...
REALLY? NOTHING FOR THAT?

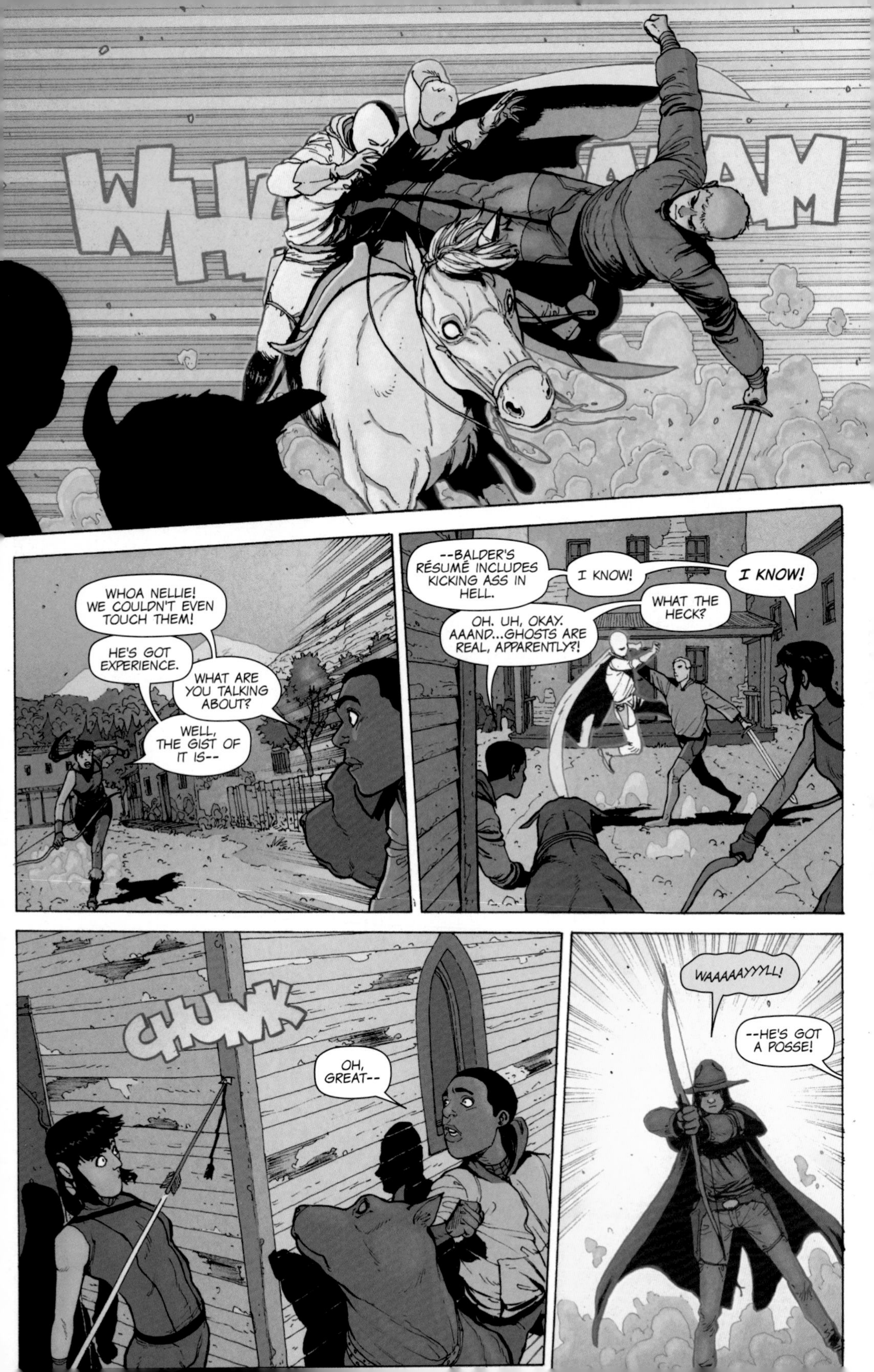

WHAAAM
WHOA NELLIE! WE COULDN'T EVEN TOUCH THEM!
HE'S GOT EXPERIENCE.
WHAT ARE YOU TALKING ABOUT?
WELL, THE GIST OF IT IS--
--BALDER'S RÉSUMÉ INCLUDES KICKING ASS IN HELL.
I KNOW!
I KNOW!
OH. UH, OKAY. AAAND...GHOSTS ARE REAL, APPARENTLY?!
WHAT THE HECK?
CHUNK
OH, GREAT--
WAAAAAYYYLL!
--HE'S GOT A POSSE!

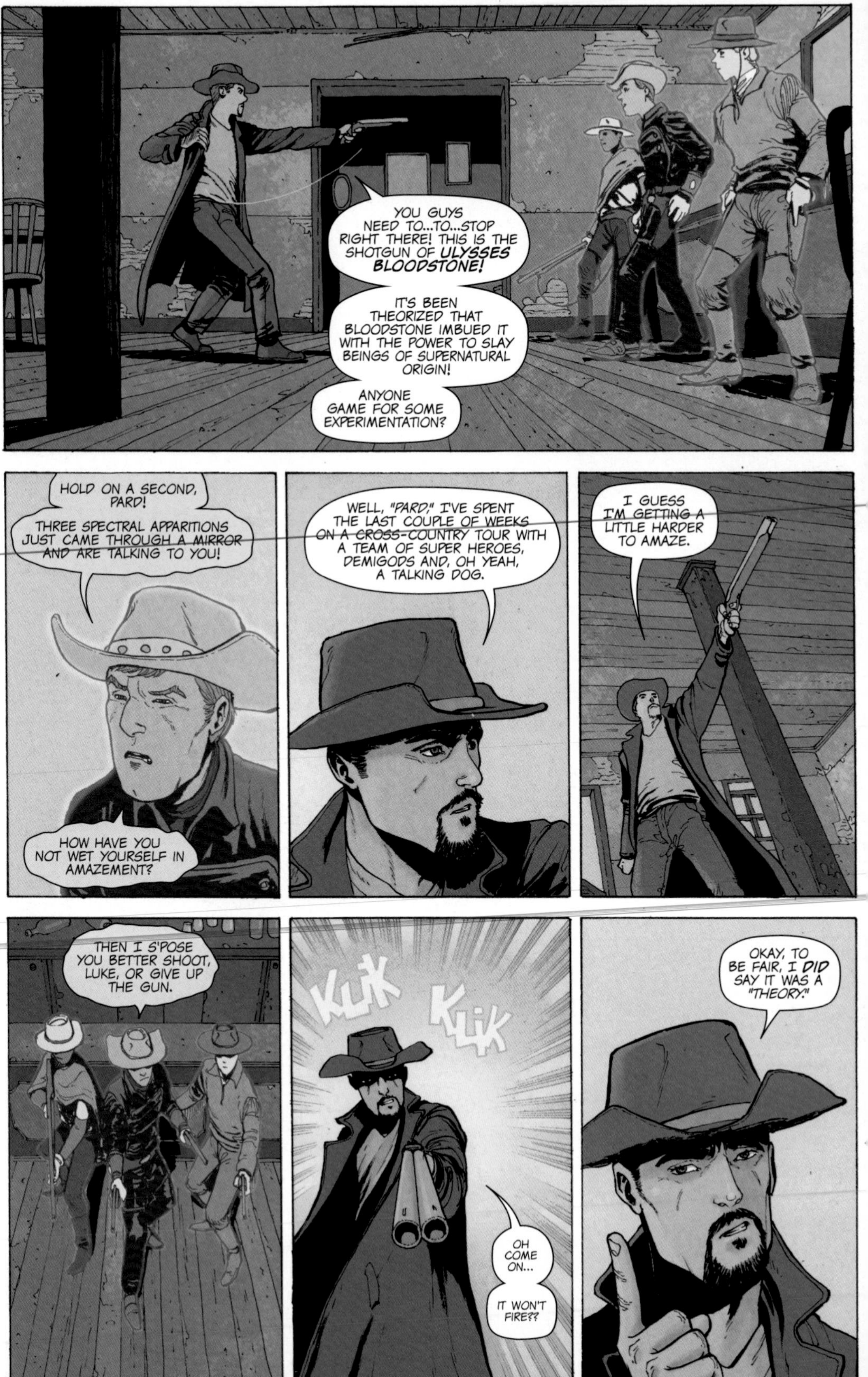
YOU GUYS NEED TO...TO...STOP RIGHT THERE! THIS IS THE SHOTGUN OF ULYSSES BLOODSTONE!
IT'S BEEN THEORIZED THAT BLOODSTONE IMBUED IT WITH THE POWER TO SLAY BEINGS OF SUPERNATURAL ORIGIN!
ANYONE GAME FOR SOME EXPERIMENTATION?
HOLD ON A SECOND, PARD!
THREE SPECTRAL APPARITIONS JUST CAME THROUGH A MIRROR AND ARE TALKING TO YOU!
HOW HAVE YOU NOT WET YOURSELF IN AMAZEMENT?
WELL, "PARD," I'VE SPENT THE LAST COUPLE OF WEEKS ON A CROSS-COUNTRY TOUR WITH A TEAM OF SUPER HEROES, DEMIGODS AND, OH YEAH, A TALKING DOG.
I GUESS I'M GETTING A LITTLE HARDER TO AMAZE.
THEN I S'POSE YOU BETTER SHOOT, LUKE, OR GIVE UP THE GUN.
KLIK
KLIK
OH COME ON...
IT WON'T FIRE??
OKAY, TO BE FAIR, I DID SAY IT WAS A "THEORY."

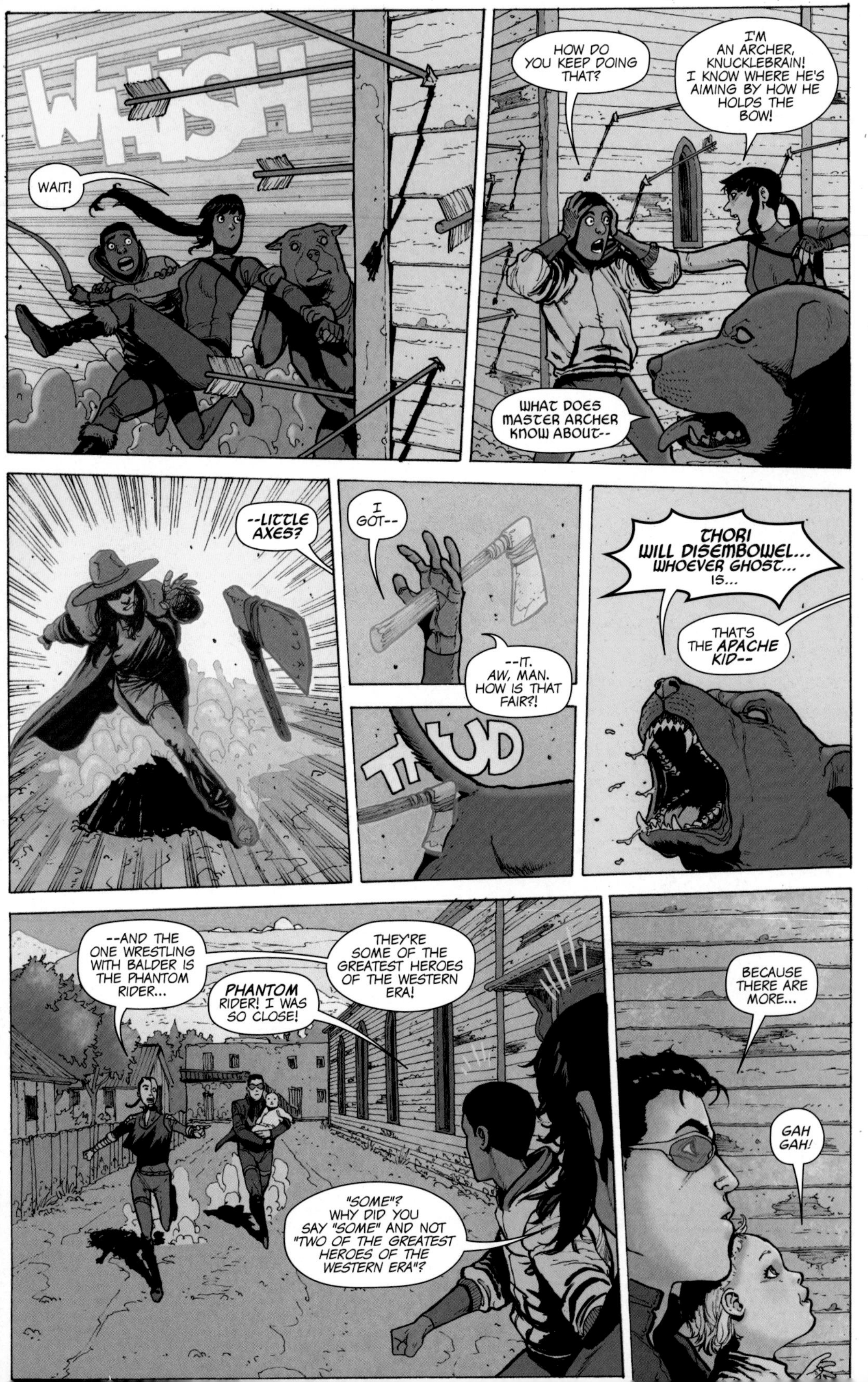
WHISH
WAIT!
HOW DO YOU KEEP DOING THAT?
I'M AN ARCHER, KNUCKLEBRAIN! I KNOW WHERE HE'S AIMING BY HOW HE HOLDS THE BOW!
WHAT DOES MASTER ARCHER KNOW ABOUT--
--LITTLE AXES?
I GOT--
--IT. AW, MAN. HOW IS THAT FAIR?!
THUD
THORI WILL DISEMBOWEL... WHOEVER GHOST... IS...
THAT'S THE APACHE KID--
--AND THE ONE WRESTLING WITH BALDER IS THE PHANTOM RIDER...
THEY'RE SOME OF THE GREATEST HEROES OF THE WESTERN ERA!
PHANTOM RIDER! I WAS SO CLOSE!
"SOME"? WHY DID YOU SAY "SOME" AND NOT "TWO OF THE GREATEST HEROES OF THE WESTERN ERA"?
BECAUSE THERE ARE MORE...
GAH GAH!

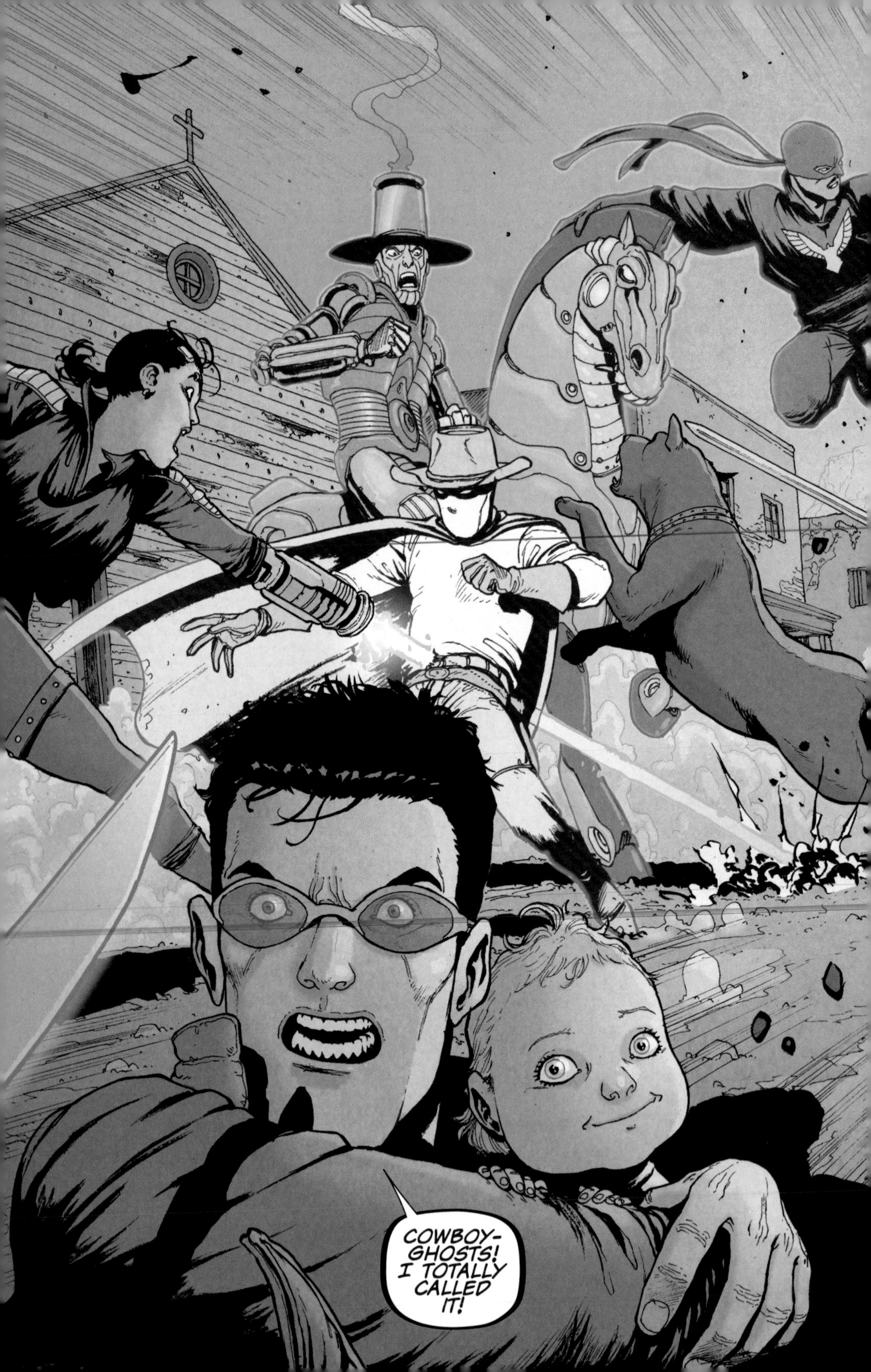
COWBOY-GHOSTS! I TOTALLY CALLED IT!

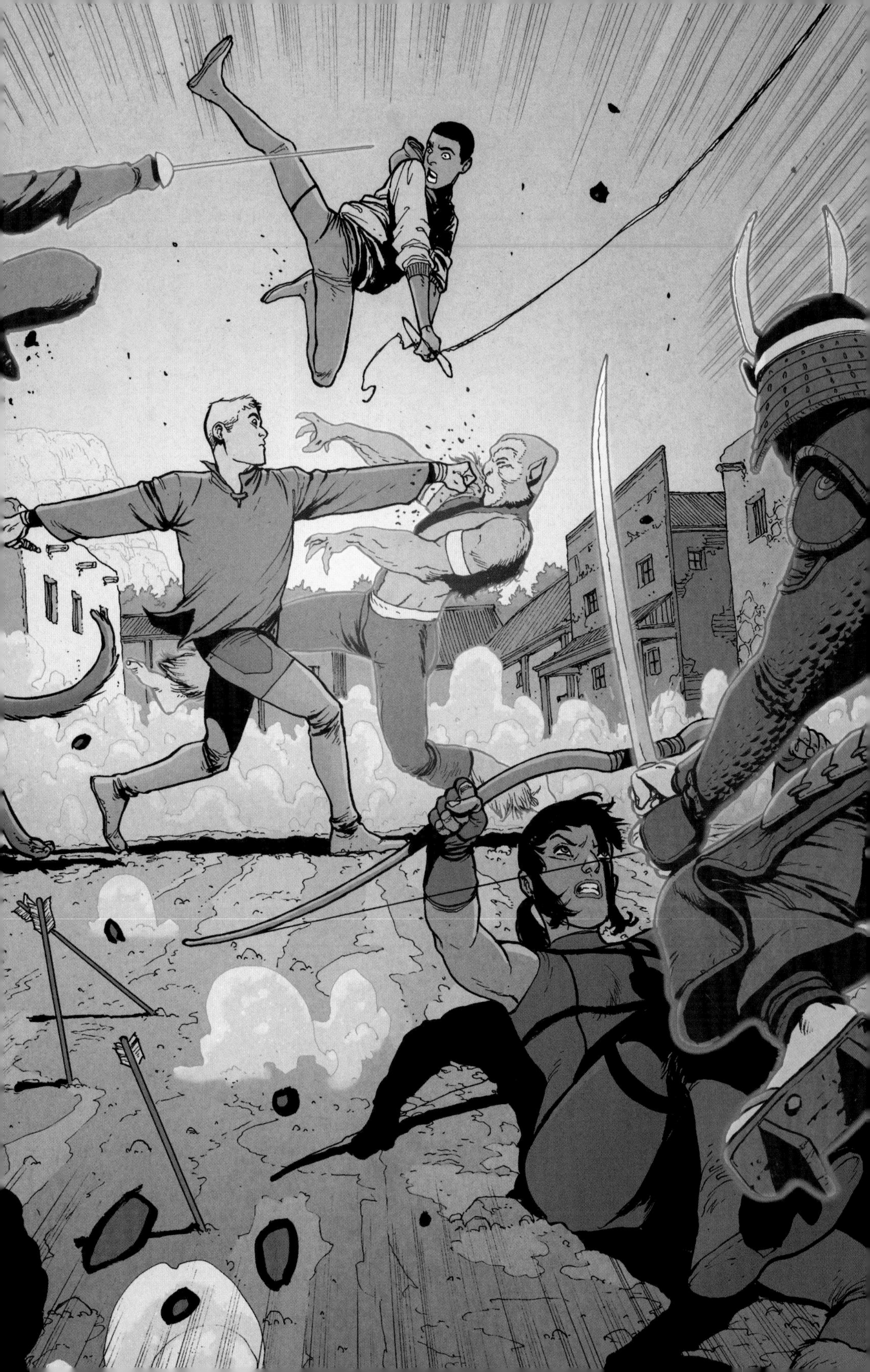

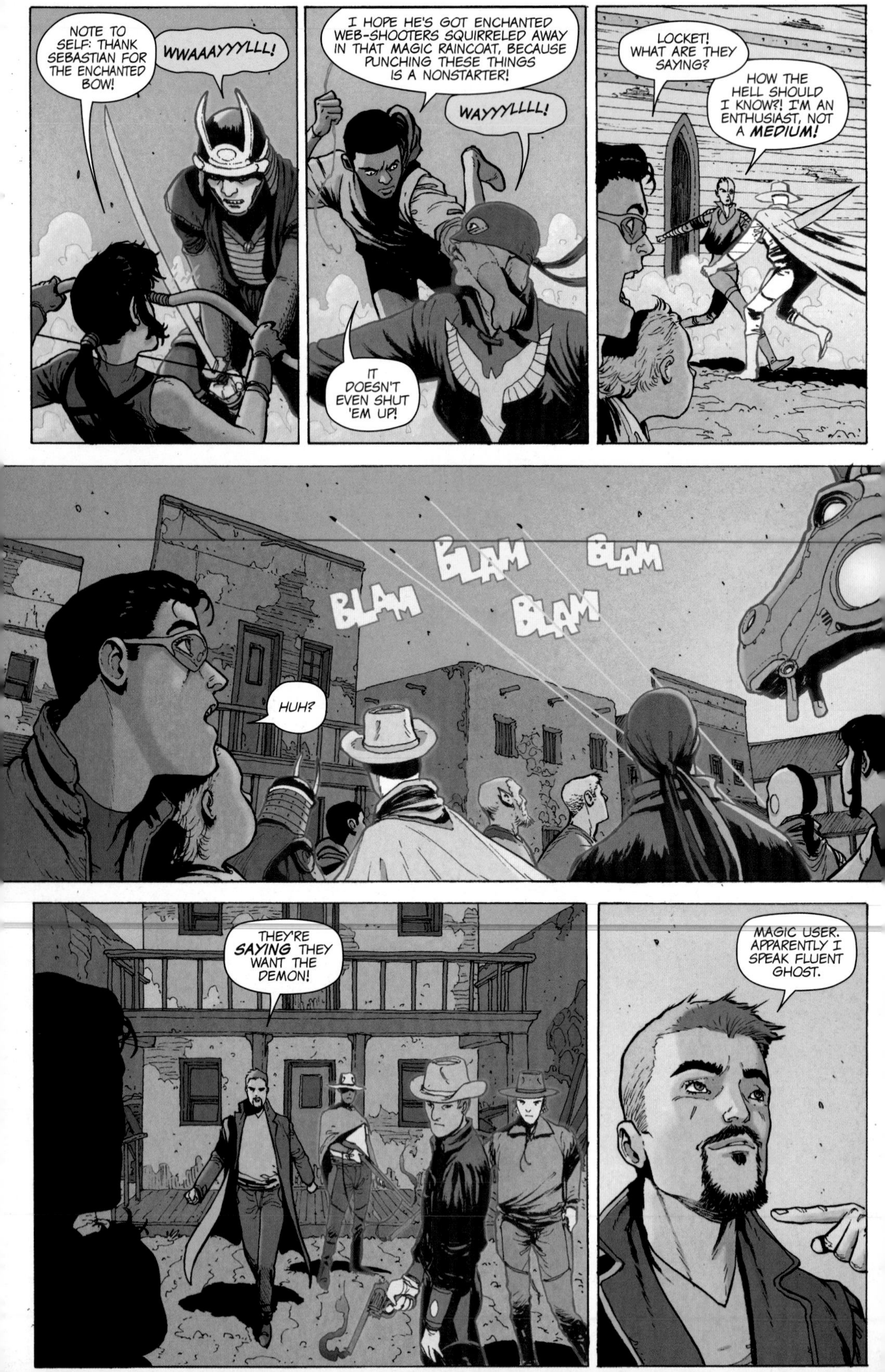
NOTE TO SELF: THANK SEBASTIAN FOR THE ENCHANTED BOW!
WWAAAAYYYLLL!
I HOPE HE'S GOT ENCHANTED WEB-SHOOTERS SQUIRRELED AWAY IN THAT MAGIC RAINCOAT, BECAUSE PUNCHING THESE THINGS IS A NONSTARTER!
WAYYYLLLL!
IT DOESN'T EVEN SHUT 'EM UP!
LOCKET! WHAT ARE THEY SAYING?
HOW THE HELL SHOULD I KNOW?! I'M AN ENTHUSIAST, NOT A MEDIUM!
BLAM
BLAM
BLAM
BLAM
HUH?
THEY'RE SAYING THEY WANT THE DEMON!
MAGIC USER. APPARENTLY I SPEAK FLUENT GHOST.

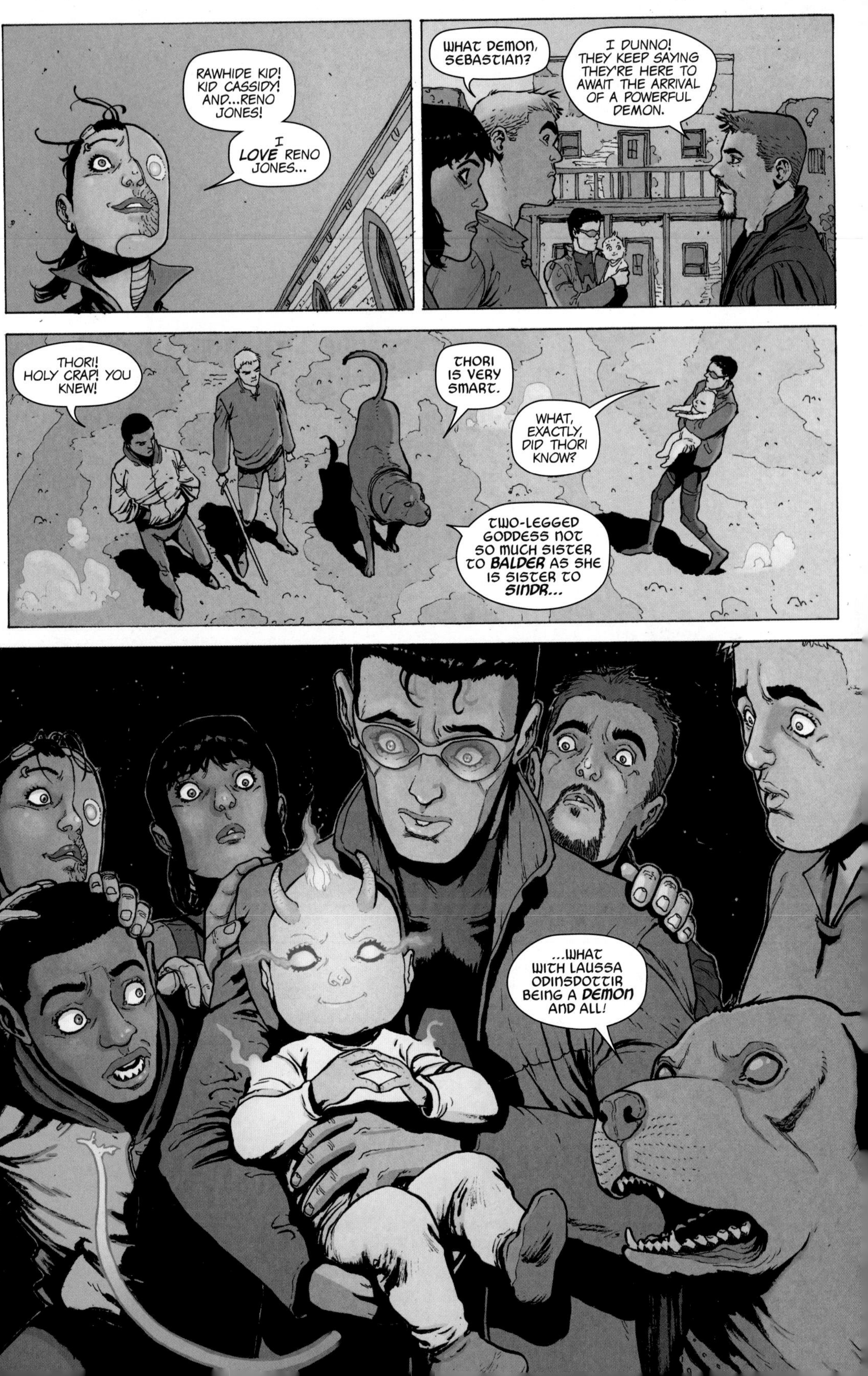
RAWHIDE KID! KID CASSIDY! AND...RENO JONES!
I LOVE RENO JONES...
WHAT DEMON, SEBASTIAN?
I DUNNO! THEY KEEP SAYING THEY'RE HERE TO AWAIT THE ARRIVAL OF A POWERFUL DEMON.
THORI! HOLY CRAP! YOU KNEW!
THORI IS VERY SMART.
WHAT, EXACTLY, DID THORI KNOW?
TWO-LEGGED GODDESS NOT SO MUCH SISTER TO BALDER AS SHE IS SISTER TO SINDR...
...WHAT WITH LAUSSA ODINSDOTTIR BEING A DEMON AND ALL!

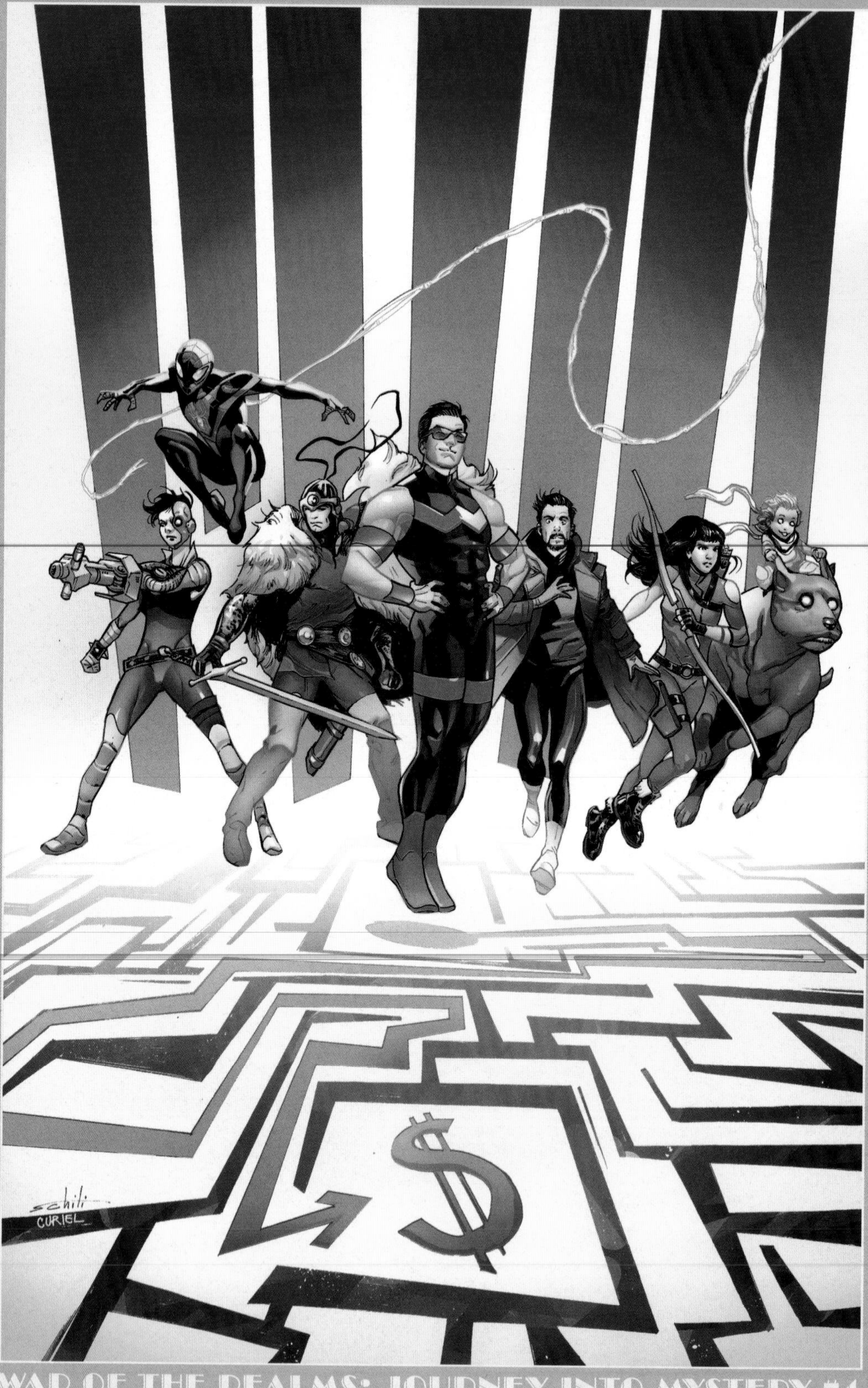
schiti
CURIEL

WAR OF THE REALMS: JOURNEY INTO MYSTERY #4

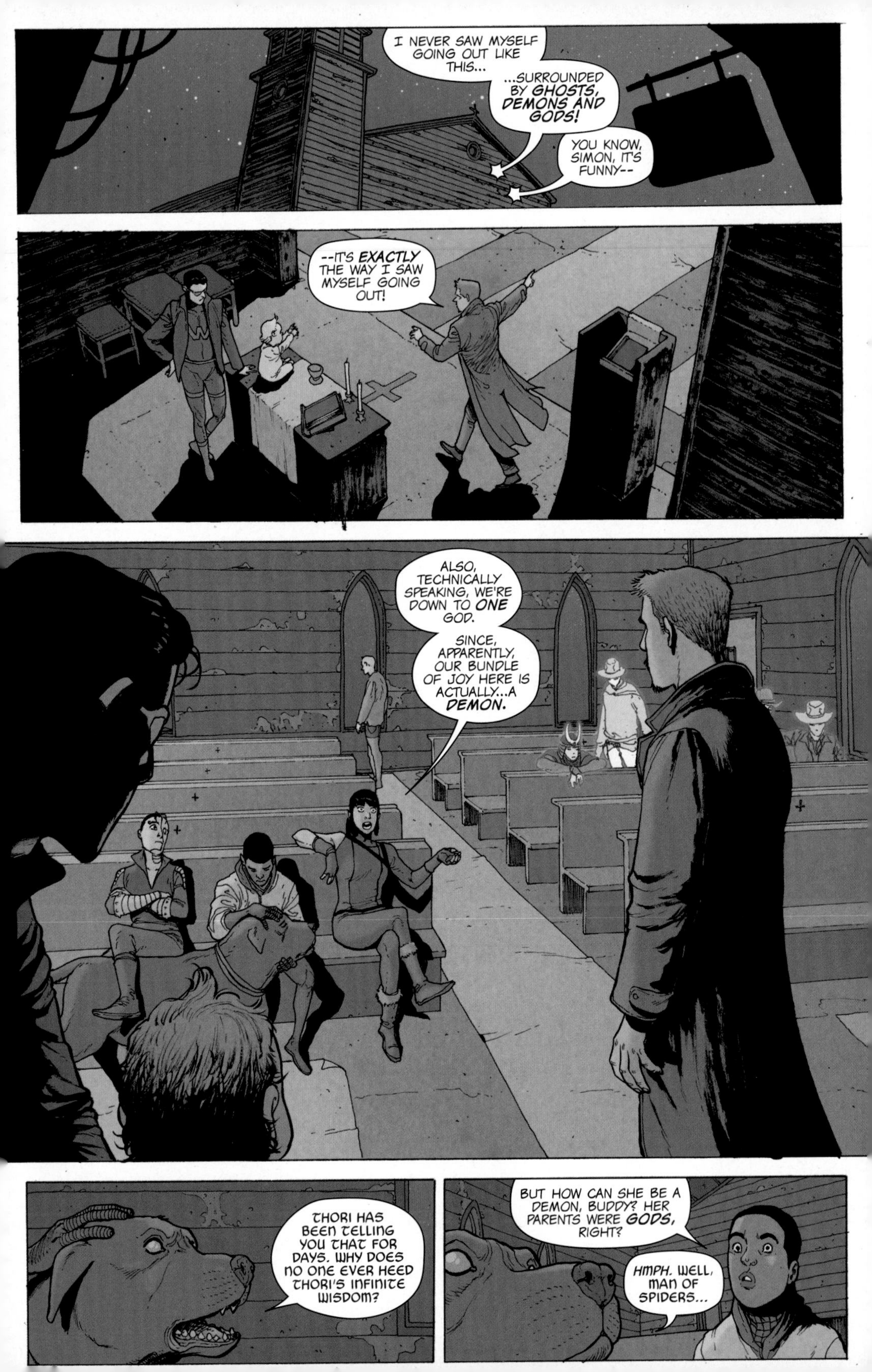
I NEVER SAW MYSELF GOING OUT LIKE THIS...
...SURROUNDED BY GHOSTS, DEMONS AND GODS!
YOU KNOW, SIMON, IT'S FUNNY--
--IT'S EXACTLY THE WAY I SAW MYSELF GOING OUT!
ALSO, TECHNICALLY SPEAKING, WE'RE DOWN TO ONE GOD.
SINCE, APPARENTLY, OUR BUNDLE OF JOY HERE IS ACTUALLY...A DEMON.
THORI HAS BEEN TELLING YOU THAT FOR DAYS. WHY DOES NO ONE EVER HEED THORI'S INFINITE WISDOM?
BUT HOW CAN SHE BE A DEMON, BUDDY? HER PARENTS WERE GODS, RIGHT?
HMPH. WELL, MAN OF SPIDERS...

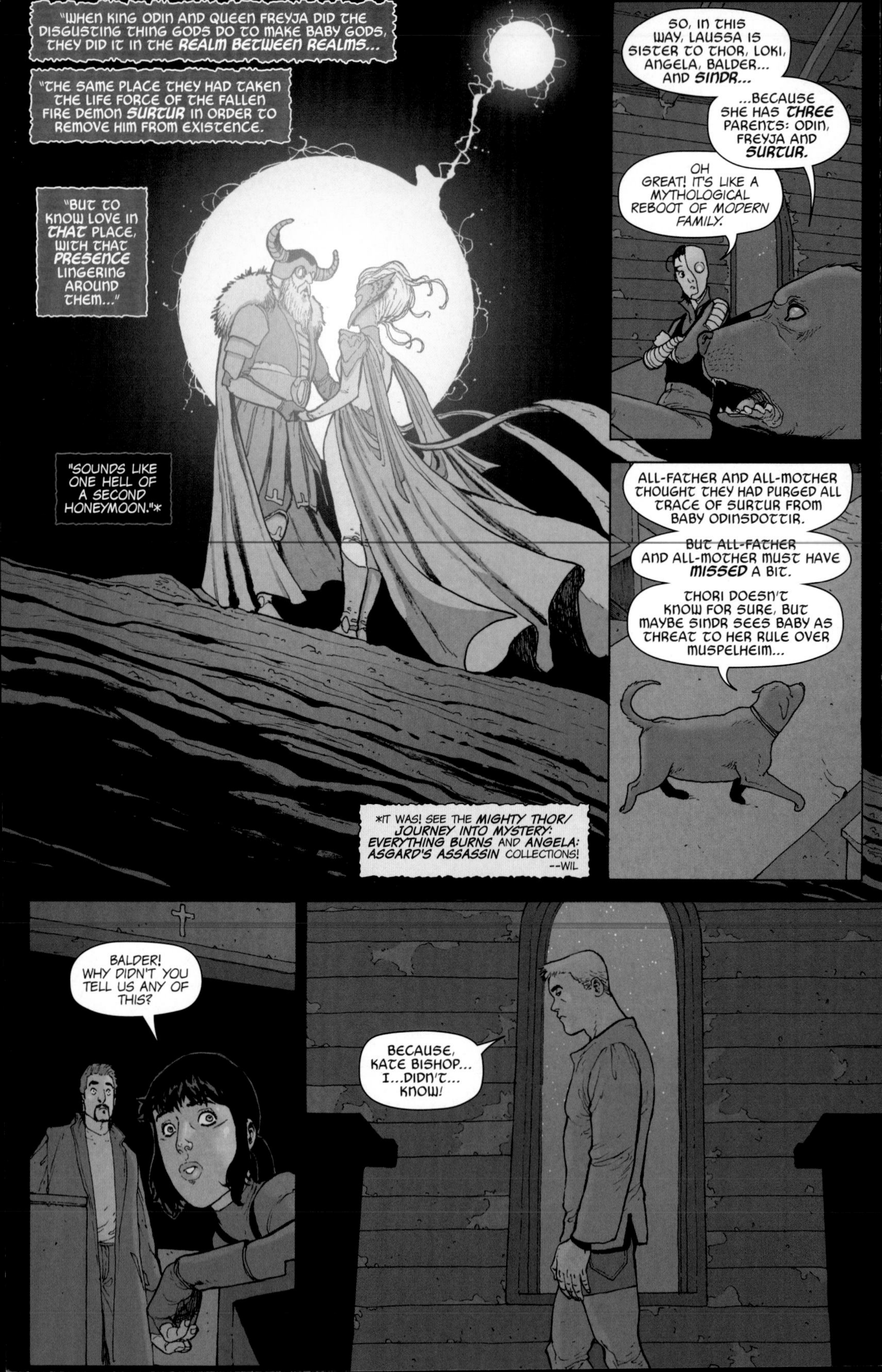

"WHEN KING ODIN AND QUEEN FREYJA DID THE DISGUSTING THING GODS DO TO MAKE BABY GODS, THEY DID IT IN THE REALM BETWEEN REALMS...
"THE SAME PLACE THEY HAD TAKEN THE LIFE FORCE OF THE FALLEN FIRE DEMON SURTUR IN ORDER TO REMOVE HIM FROM EXISTENCE.
"BUT TO KNOW LOVE IN THAT PLACE, WITH THAT PRESENCE LINGERING AROUND THEM..."
"SOUNDS LIKE ONE HELL OF A SECOND HONEYMOON."*
*IT WAS! SEE THE MIGHTY THOR/ JOURNEY INTO MYSTERY: EVERYTHING BURNS AND ANGELA: ASGARD'S ASSASSIN COLLECTIONS! --WIL
SO, IN THIS WAY, LAUSSA IS SISTER TO THOR, LOKI, ANGELA, BALDER... AND SINDR...
...BECAUSE SHE HAS THREE PARENTS: ODIN, FREYJA AND SURTUR.
OH GREAT! IT'S LIKE A MYTHOLOGICAL REBOOT OF MODERN FAMILY.
ALL-FATHER AND ALL-MOTHER THOUGHT THEY HAD PURGED ALL TRACE OF SURTUR FROM BABY ODINSDOTTIR.
BUT ALL-FATHER AND ALL-MOTHER MUST HAVE MISSED A BIT.
THORI DOESN'T KNOW FOR SURE, BUT MAYBE SINDR SEES BABY AS THREAT TO HER RULE OVER MUSPELHEIM...
BALDER! WHY DIDN'T YOU TELL US ANY OF THIS?
BECAUSE, KATE BISHOP... I...DIDN'T... KNOW!

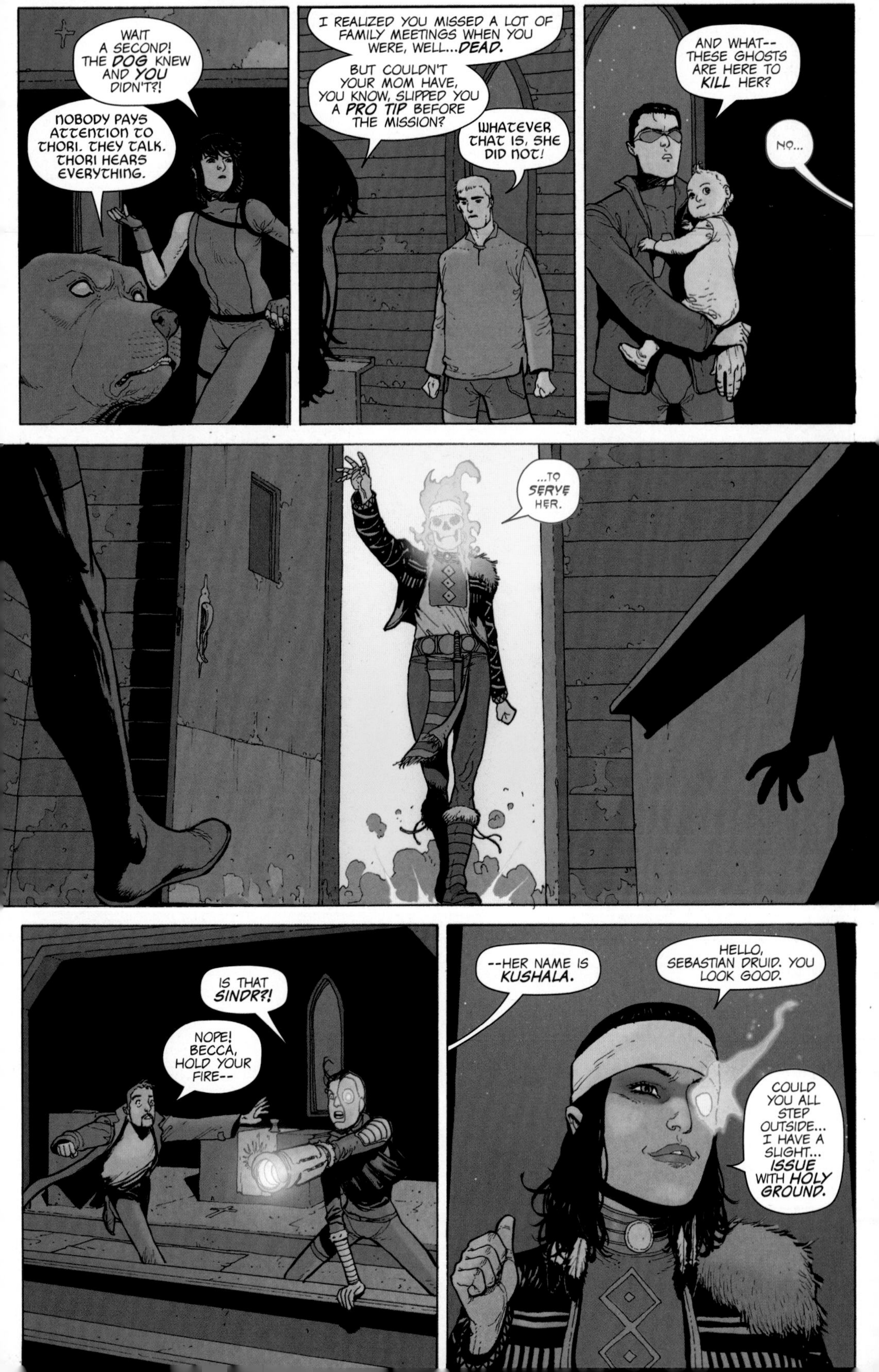
WAIT A SECOND! THE DOG KNEW AND YOU DIDN'T?!
NOBODY PAYS ATTENTION TO THORI. THEY TALK. THORI HEARS EVERYTHING.
I REALIZED YOU MISSED A LOT OF FAMILY MEETINGS WHEN YOU WERE, WELL...DEAD.
BUT COULDN'T YOUR MOM HAVE, YOU KNOW, SLIPPED YOU A PRO TIP BEFORE THE MISSION?
WHATEVER THAT IS, SHE DID NOT!
AND WHAT-- THESE GHOSTS ARE HERE TO KILL HER?
NO...
...TO SERVE HER.
IS THAT SINDR?!
NOPE! BECCA, HOLD YOUR FIRE--
--HER NAME IS KUSHALA.
HELLO, SEBASTIAN DRUID. YOU LOOK GOOD.
COULD YOU ALL STEP OUTSIDE... I HAVE A SLIGHT... ISSUE WITH HOLY GROUND.

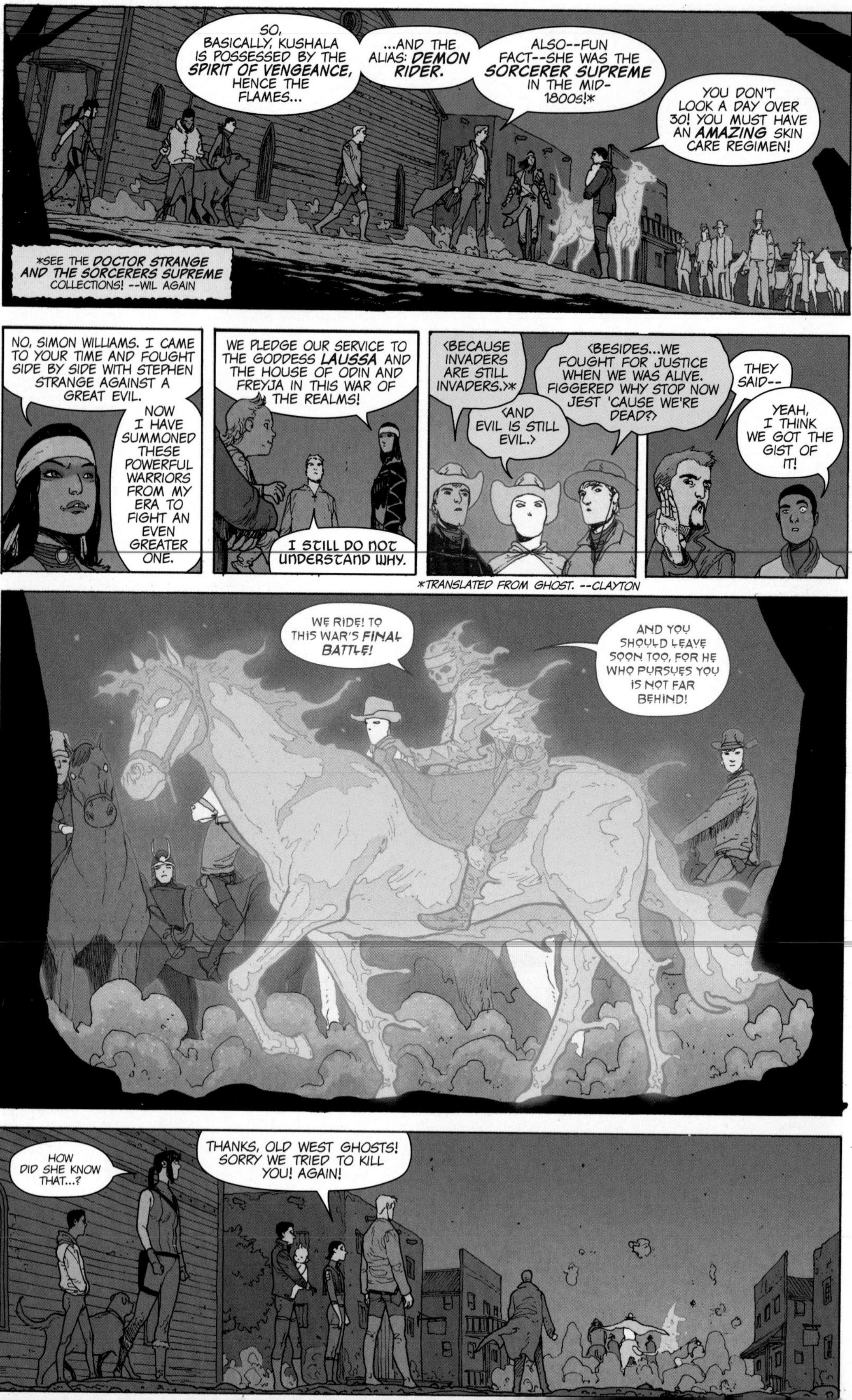

SO, BASICALLY, KUSHALA IS POSSESSED BY THE SPIRIT OF VENGEANCE, HENCE THE FLAMES...
...AND THE ALIAS: DEMON RIDER.
ALSO--FUN FACT--SHE WAS THE SORCERER SUPREME IN THE MID-1800s!*
YOU DON'T LOOK A DAY OVER 30! YOU MUST HAVE AN AMAZING SKIN CARE REGIMEN!
*SEE THE DOCTOR STRANGE AND THE SORCERERS SUPREME COLLECTIONS! --WIL AGAIN
NO, SIMON WILLIAMS. I CAME TO YOUR TIME AND FOUGHT SIDE BY SIDE WITH STEPHEN STRANGE AGAINST A GREAT EVIL.
NOW I HAVE SUMMONED THESE POWERFUL WARRIORS FROM MY ERA TO FIGHT AN EVEN GREATER ONE.
WE PLEDGE OUR SERVICE TO THE GODDESS LAUSSA AND THE HOUSE OF ODIN AND FREYJA IN THIS WAR OF THE REALMS!
I STILL DO NOT UNDERSTAND WHY.
<BECAUSE INVADERS ARE STILL INVADERS.>*
<AND EVIL IS STILL EVIL.>
<BESIDES...WE FOUGHT FOR JUSTICE WHEN WE WAS ALIVE. FIGGERED WHY STOP NOW JEST 'CAUSE WE'RE DEAD?>
THEY SAID--
YEAH, I THINK WE GOT THE GIST OF IT!
*TRANSLATED FROM GHOST. --CLAYTON
WE RIDE! TO THIS WAR'S FINAL BATTLE!
AND YOU SHOULD LEAVE SOON TOO, FOR HE WHO PURSUES YOU IS NOT FAR BEHIND!
HOW DID SHE KNOW THAT...?
THANKS, OLD WEST GHOSTS! SORRY WE TRIED TO KILL YOU! AGAIN!

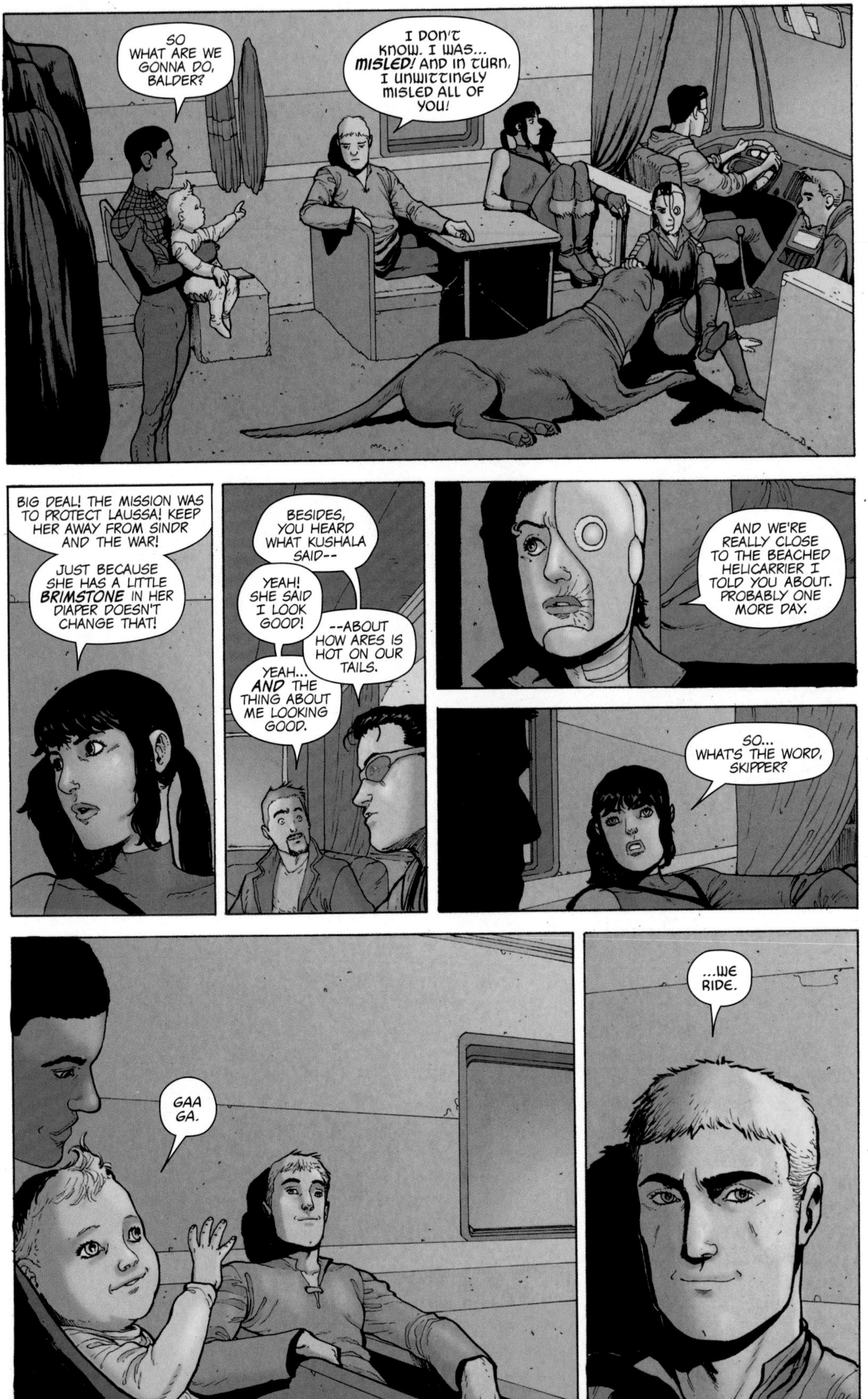
SO WHAT ARE WE GONNA DO, BALDER?
I DON'T KNOW. I WAS... MISLED! AND IN TURN, I UNWITTINGLY MISLED ALL OF YOU!
BIG DEAL! THE MISSION WAS TO PROTECT LAUSSA! KEEP HER AWAY FROM SINDR AND THE WAR!
JUST BECAUSE SHE HAS A LITTLE BRIMSTONE IN HER DIAPER DOESN'T CHANGE THAT!
BESIDES, YOU HEARD WHAT KUSHALA SAID--
YEAH! SHE SAID I LOOK GOOD!
--ABOUT HOW ARES IS HOT ON OUR TAILS.
YEAH... AND THE THING ABOUT ME LOOKING GOOD.
AND WE'RE REALLY CLOSE TO THE BEACHED HELICARRIER I TOLD YOU ABOUT. PROBABLY ONE MORE DAY.
SO... WHAT'S THE WORD, SKIPPER?
GAA GA.
...WE RIDE.

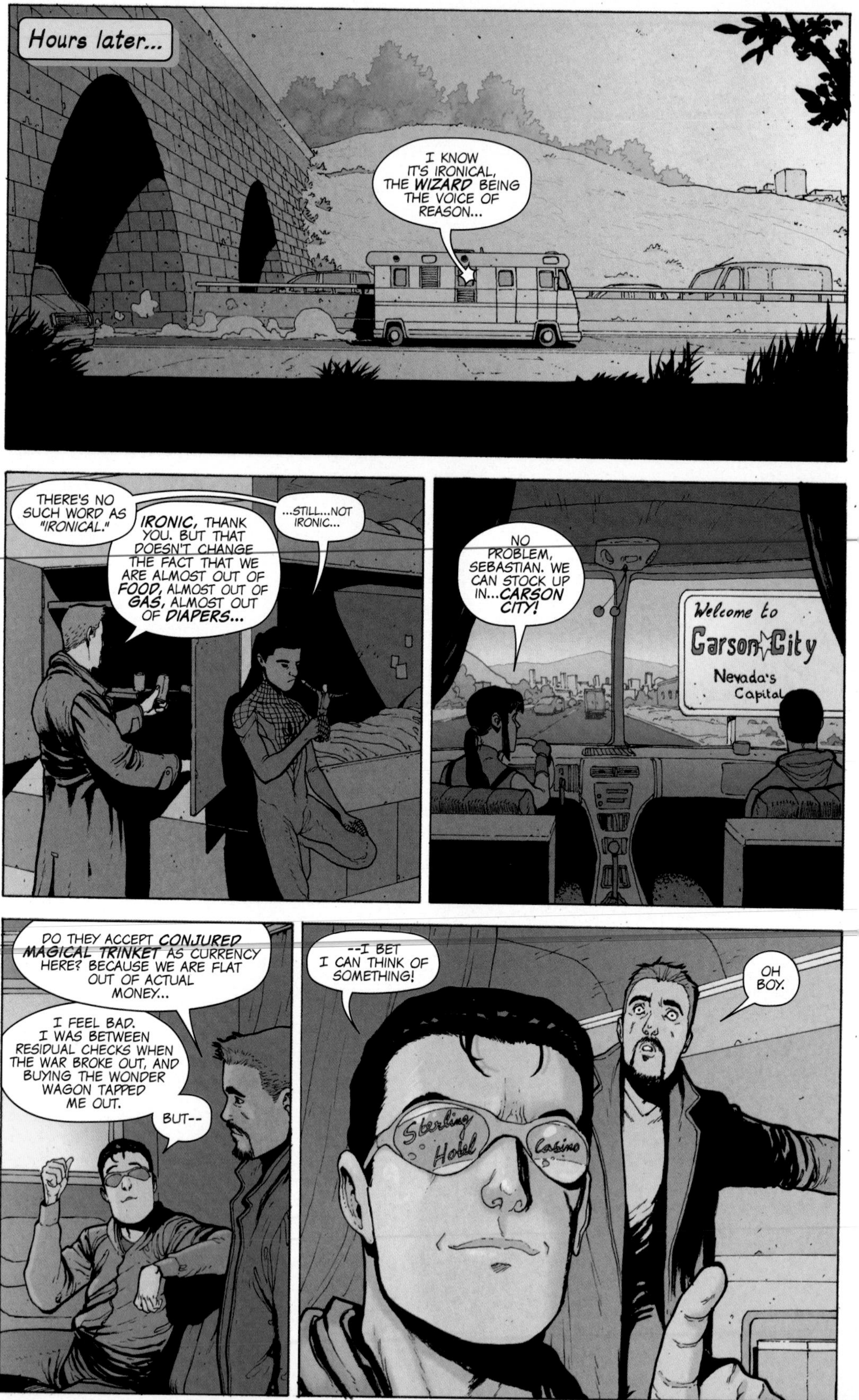
Hours later...
I KNOW IT'S IRONICAL, THE WIZARD BEING THE VOICE OF REASON...
THERE'S NO SUCH WORD AS "IRONICAL."
IRONIC, THANK YOU. BUT THAT DOESN'T CHANGE THE FACT THAT WE ARE ALMOST OUT OF FOOD, ALMOST OUT OF GAS, ALMOST OUT OF DIAPERS...
...STILL...NOT IRONIC...
NO PROBLEM, SEBASTIAN. WE CAN STOCK UP IN...CARSON CITY!
Welcome to
Carson City
Nevada's Capital
DO THEY ACCEPT CONJURED MAGICAL TRINKET AS CURRENCY HERE? BECAUSE WE ARE FLAT OUT OF ACTUAL MONEY...
I FEEL BAD. I WAS BETWEEN RESIDUAL CHECKS WHEN THE WAR BROKE OUT, AND BUYING THE WONDER WAGON TAPPED ME OUT.
BUT--
--I BET I CAN THINK OF SOMETHING!
OH BOY.
Sterling Hotel Casino

SO THE "SOMETHING" YOU THOUGHT OF WAS...THROW ON DISGUISES AND **WIN A BUNCH OF MONEY?**

YES! I'M GONNA HIT THE CRAPS TABLE. I HAVE A NEVER-FAIL SYSTEM!

SAID EVERY SOON-TO-BE-BROKE GAMBLER...

NO, LISTEN, I GOT THIS! I WAS IN THE TOP 30 FOR JAMES BOND!

WHICH MOVIE?

UM. THE VIDEO GAME. GOLDENEYE... *RELOADED.*

-SIGH- HERE. JUST PLAY **SMART,** OKAY? WE DON'T HAVE MUCH TO BET!

WAIT A SEC! THIS IS BAD! LOOK AT... EVERYBODY!

THIS PLACE IS LOUSY WITH **SUPER VILLAINS!**

The Sterling Hotel & Casino SHC
proudly welcomes you to:
HENCHFEST

IT'S **LOUSY** ALL RIGHT, BUT...NOT EXACTLY WITH **SUPER** VILLAINS...

The Sterling Hotel & Casino SHC
proudly welcomes you to:
HENCHFEST
"*While the villains are away, the henches do play.*"

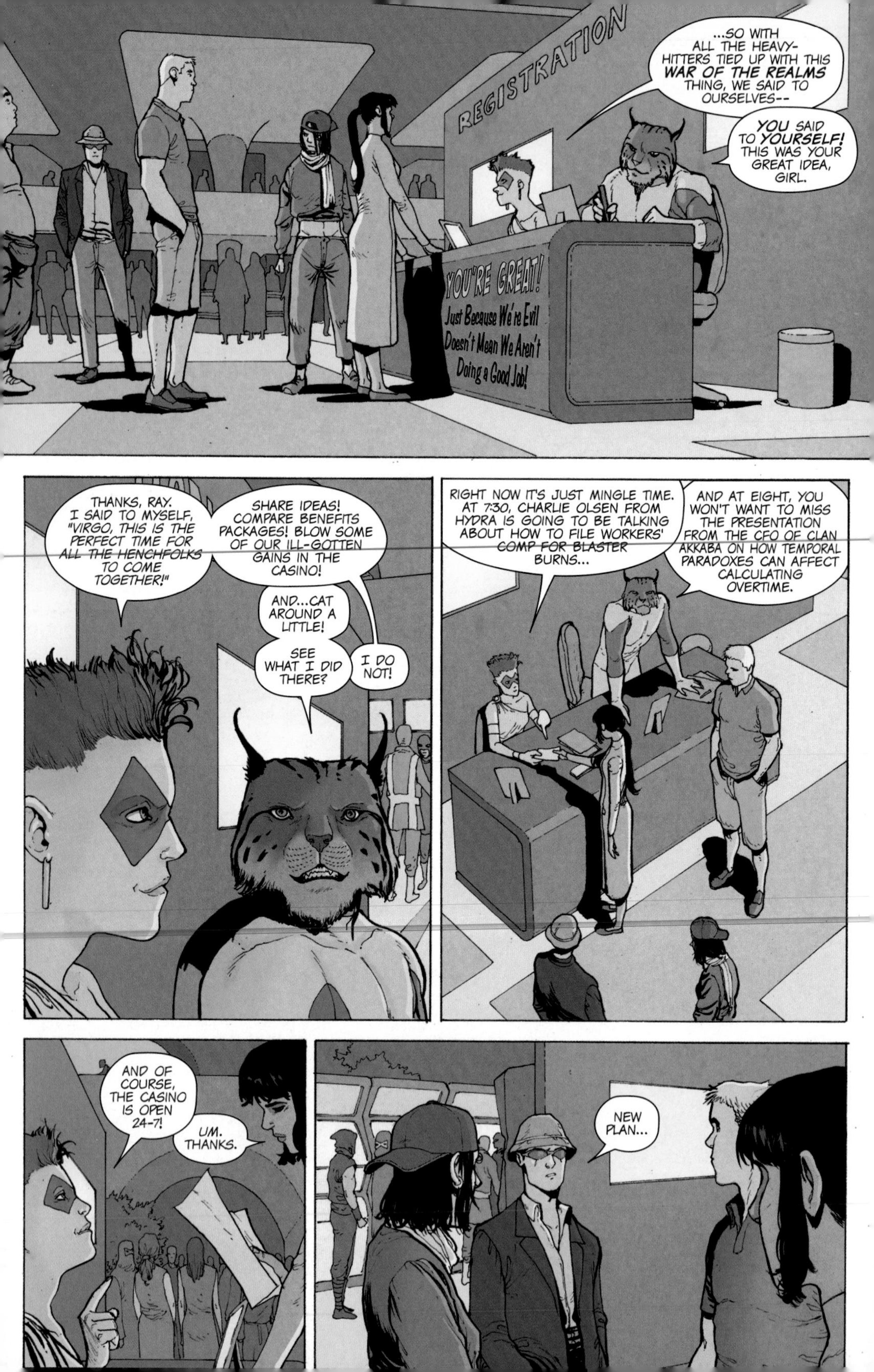
REGISTRATION
...SO WITH ALL THE HEAVY-HITTERS TIED UP WITH THIS WAR OF THE REALMS THING, WE SAID TO OURSELVES--
YOU SAID TO YOURSELF! THIS WAS YOUR GREAT IDEA, GIRL.
YOU'RE GREAT! Just Because We're Evil Doesn't Mean We Aren't Doing a Good Job!
THANKS, RAY. I SAID TO MYSELF, "VIRGO, THIS IS THE PERFECT TIME FOR ALL THE HENCHFOLKS TO COME TOGETHER!"
SHARE IDEAS! COMPARE BENEFITS PACKAGES! BLOW SOME OF OUR ILL-GOTTEN GAINS IN THE CASINO!
AND...CAT AROUND A LITTLE!
SEE WHAT I DID THERE?
I DO NOT!
RIGHT NOW IT'S JUST MINGLE TIME. AT 7:30, CHARLIE OLSEN FROM HYDRA IS GOING TO BE TALKING ABOUT HOW TO FILE WORKERS' COMP FOR BLASTER BURNS...
AND AT EIGHT, YOU WON'T WANT TO MISS THE PRESENTATION FROM THE CFO OF CLAN AKKABA ON HOW TEMPORAL PARADOXES CAN AFFECT CALCULATING OVERTIME.
AND OF COURSE, THE CASINO IS OPEN 24-7!
UM. THANKS.
NEW PLAN...

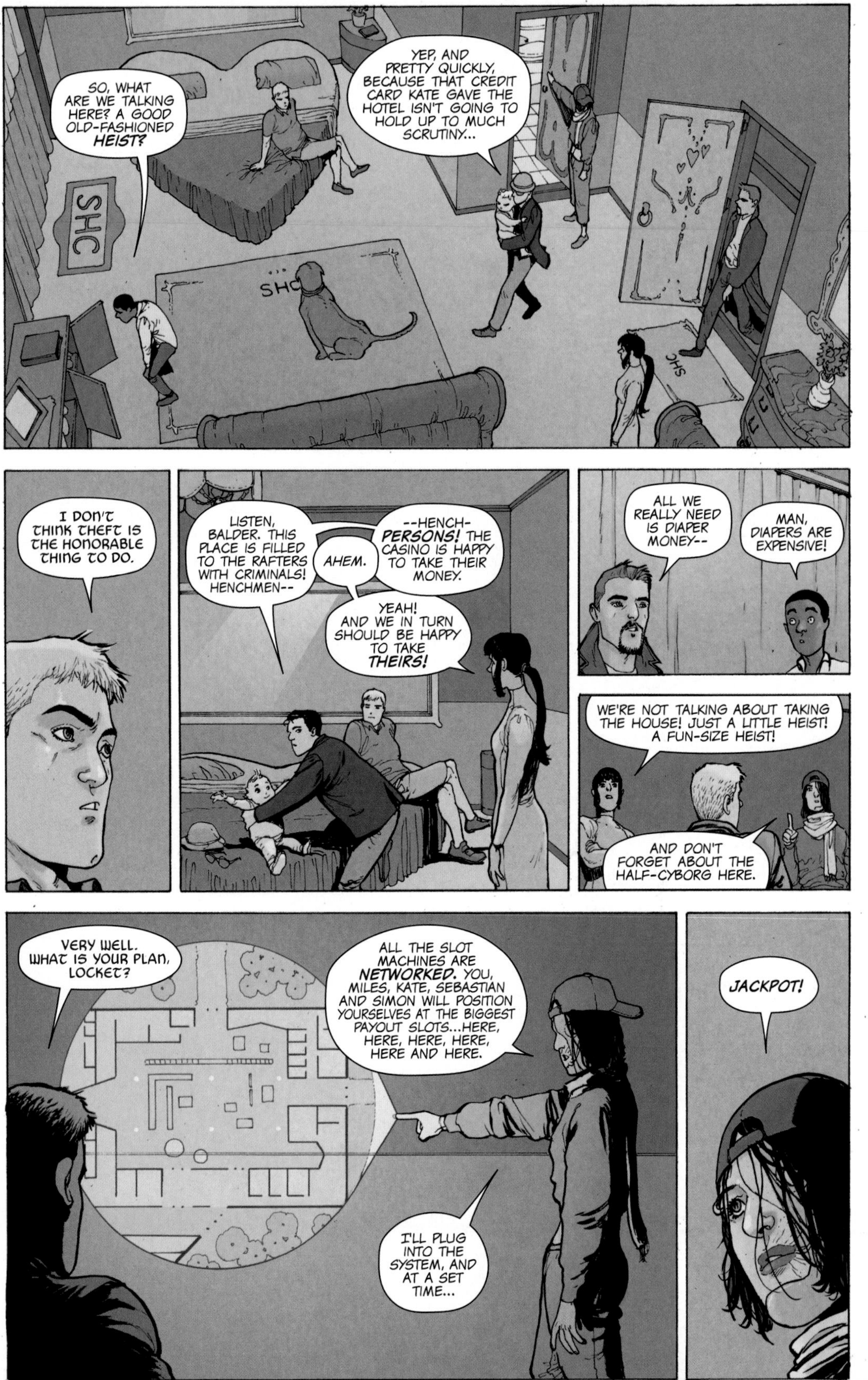
SO, WHAT ARE WE TALKING HERE? A GOOD OLD-FASHIONED HEIST?
YEP, AND PRETTY QUICKLY, BECAUSE THAT CREDIT CARD KATE GAVE THE HOTEL ISN'T GOING TO HOLD UP TO MUCH SCRUTINY...
SHC
SHC
SHC
I DON'T THINK THEFT IS THE HONORABLE THING TO DO.
LISTEN, BALDER. THIS PLACE IS FILLED TO THE RAFTERS WITH CRIMINALS! HENCHMEN--
AHEM.
--HENCH-PERSONS! THE CASINO IS HAPPY TO TAKE THEIR MONEY.
YEAH! AND WE IN TURN SHOULD BE HAPPY TO TAKE THEIRS!
ALL WE REALLY NEED IS DIAPER MONEY--
MAN, DIAPERS ARE EXPENSIVE!
WE'RE NOT TALKING ABOUT TAKING THE HOUSE! JUST A LITTLE HEIST! A FUN-SIZE HEIST!
AND DON'T FORGET ABOUT THE HALF-CYBORG HERE.
VERY WELL. WHAT IS YOUR PLAN, LOCKET?
ALL THE SLOT MACHINES ARE NETWORKED. YOU, MILES, KATE, SEBASTIAN AND SIMON WILL POSITION YOURSELVES AT THE BIGGEST PAYOUT SLOTS...HERE, HERE, HERE, HERE, HERE AND HERE.
I'LL PLUG INTO THE SYSTEM, AND AT A SET TIME...
JACKPOT!

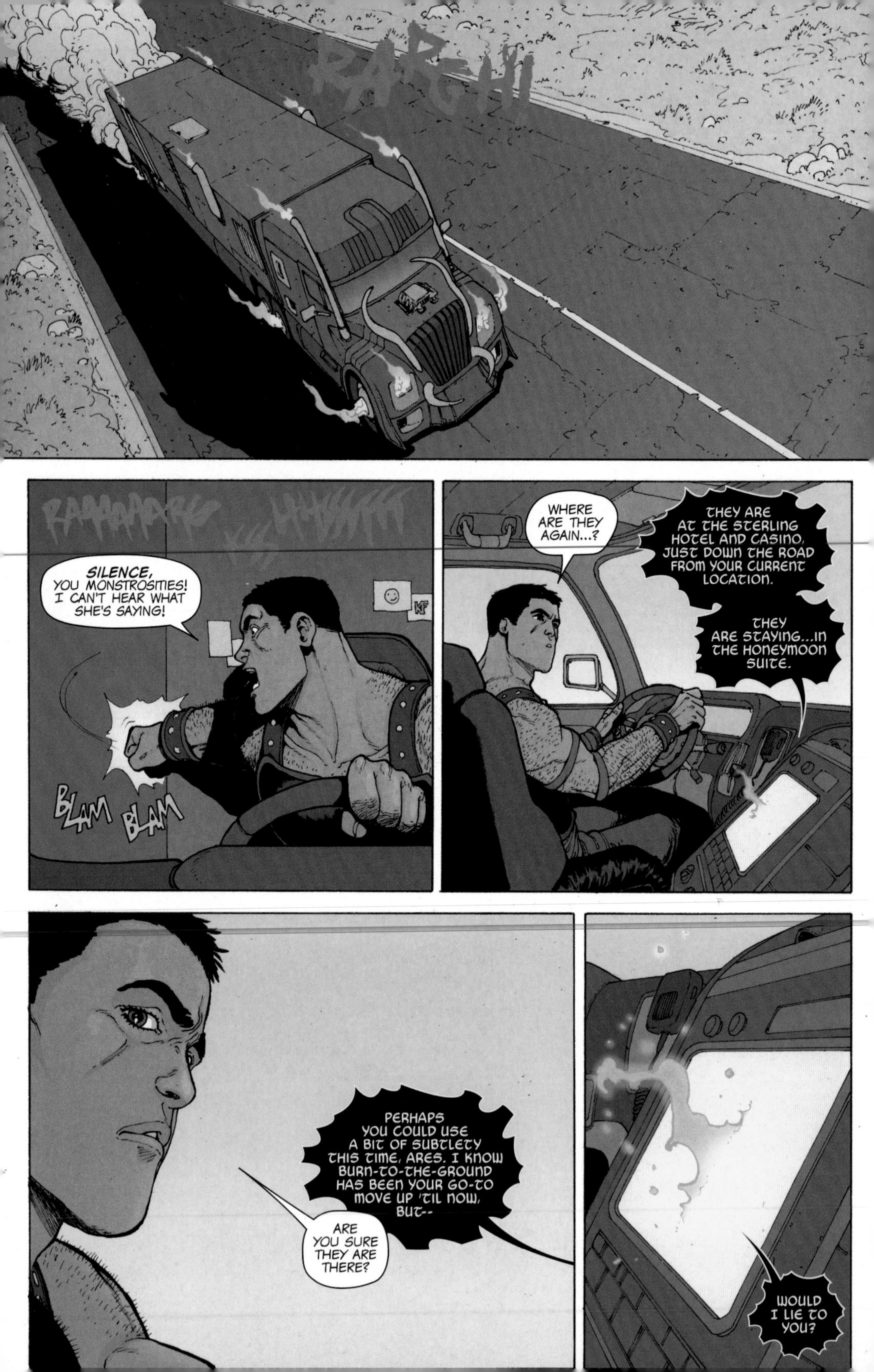
RARGH!
SILENCE, YOU MONSTROSITIES! I CAN'T HEAR WHAT SHE'S SAYING!
BLAM BLAM
WHERE ARE THEY AGAIN...?
THEY ARE AT THE STERLING HOTEL AND CASINO, JUST DOWN THE ROAD FROM YOUR CURRENT LOCATION.
THEY ARE STAYING...IN THE HONEYMOON SUITE.
PERHAPS YOU COULD USE A BIT OF SUBTLETY THIS TIME, ARES. I KNOW BURN-TO-THE-GROUND HAS BEEN YOUR GO-TO MOVE UP 'TIL NOW, BUT--
ARE YOU SURE THEY ARE THERE?
WOULD I LIE TO YOU?

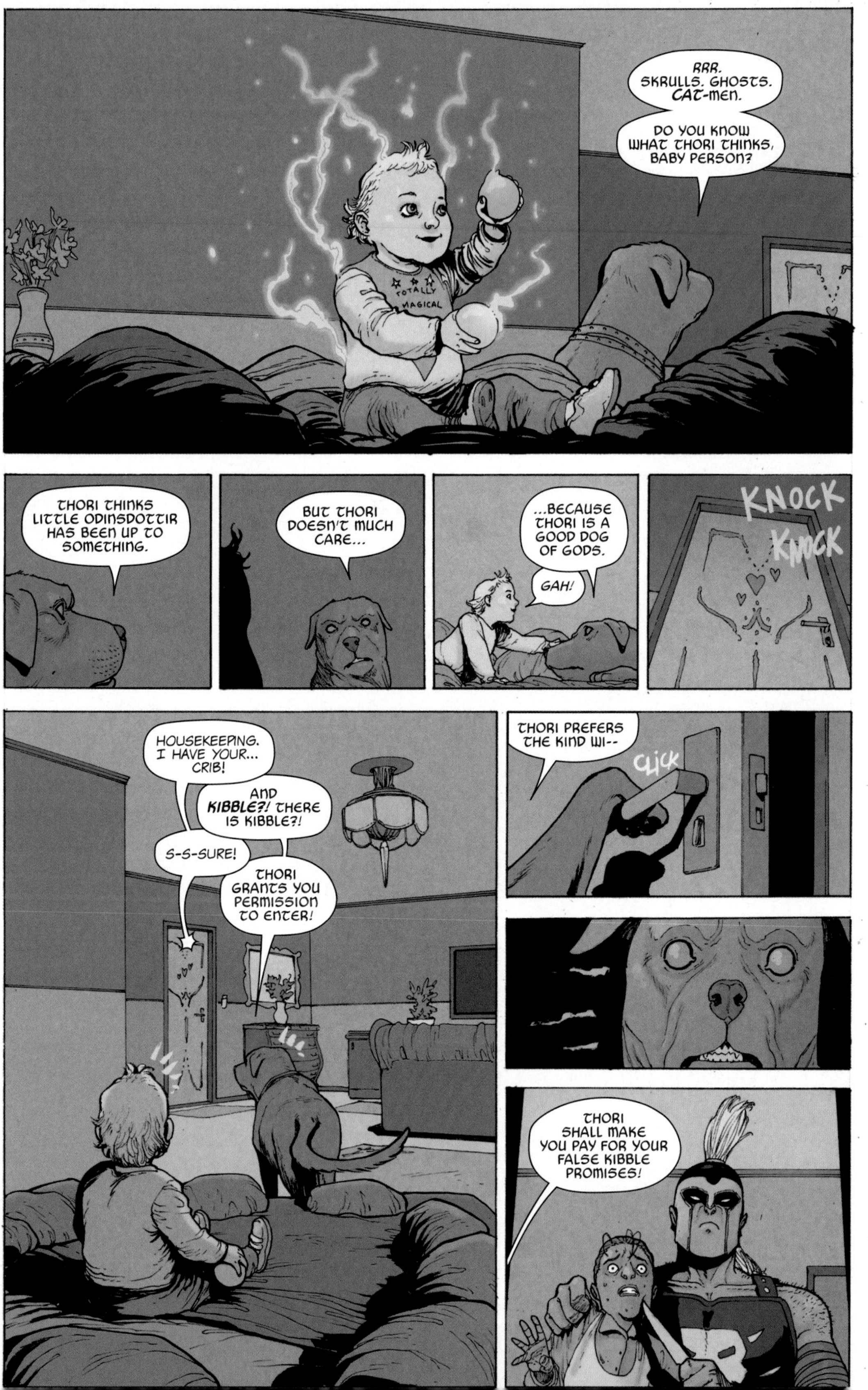

RRR. SKRULLS. GHOSTS. CAT-MEN.
DO YOU KNOW WHAT THORI THINKS, BABY PERSON?
TOTALLY MAGICAL
THORI THINKS LITTLE ODINSDOTTIR HAS BEEN UP TO SOMETHING.
BUT THORI DOESN'T MUCH CARE...
...BECAUSE THORI IS A GOOD DOG OF GODS.
GAH!
KNOCK
KNOCK
HOUSEKEEPING. I HAVE YOUR... CRIB!
AND KIBBLE?! THERE IS KIBBLE?!
S-S-SURE!
THORI GRANTS YOU PERMISSION TO ENTER!
THORI PREFERS THE KIND WI--
CLICK
THORI SHALL MAKE YOU PAY FOR YOUR FALSE KIBBLE PROMISES!

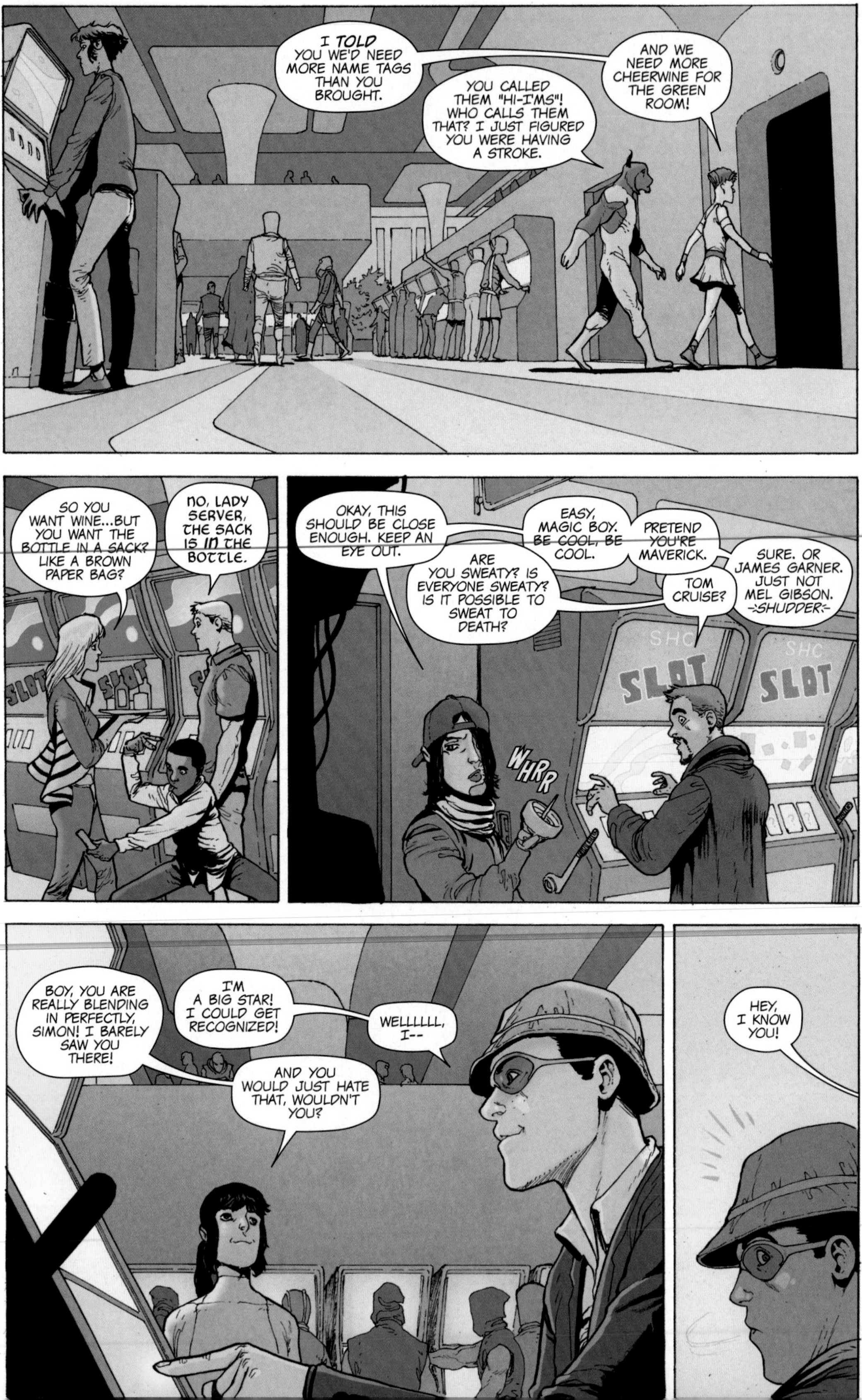
I TOLD YOU WE'D NEED MORE NAME TAGS THAN YOU BROUGHT.
YOU CALLED THEM "HI-I'MS"! WHO CALLS THEM THAT? I JUST FIGURED YOU WERE HAVING A STROKE.
AND WE NEED MORE CHEERWINE FOR THE GREEN ROOM!
SO YOU WANT WINE...BUT YOU WANT THE BOTTLE IN A SACK? LIKE A BROWN PAPER BAG?
NO, LADY SERVER, THE SACK IS IN THE BOTTLE.
OKAY, THIS SHOULD BE CLOSE ENOUGH. KEEP AN EYE OUT.
EASY, MAGIC BOY. BE COOL, BE COOL.
ARE YOU SWEATY? IS EVERYONE SWEATY? IS IT POSSIBLE TO SWEAT TO DEATH?
PRETEND YOU'RE MAVERICK.
TOM CRUISE?
SURE. OR JAMES GARNER. JUST NOT MEL GIBSON. -SHUDDER-
SHC
SLOT
SHC
SLOT
WHRR
BOY, YOU ARE REALLY BLENDING IN PERFECTLY, SIMON! I BARELY SAW YOU THERE!
I'M A BIG STAR! I COULD GET RECOGNIZED!
WELLLLLL, I--
AND YOU WOULD JUST HATE THAT, WOULDN'T YOU?
HEY, I KNOW YOU!

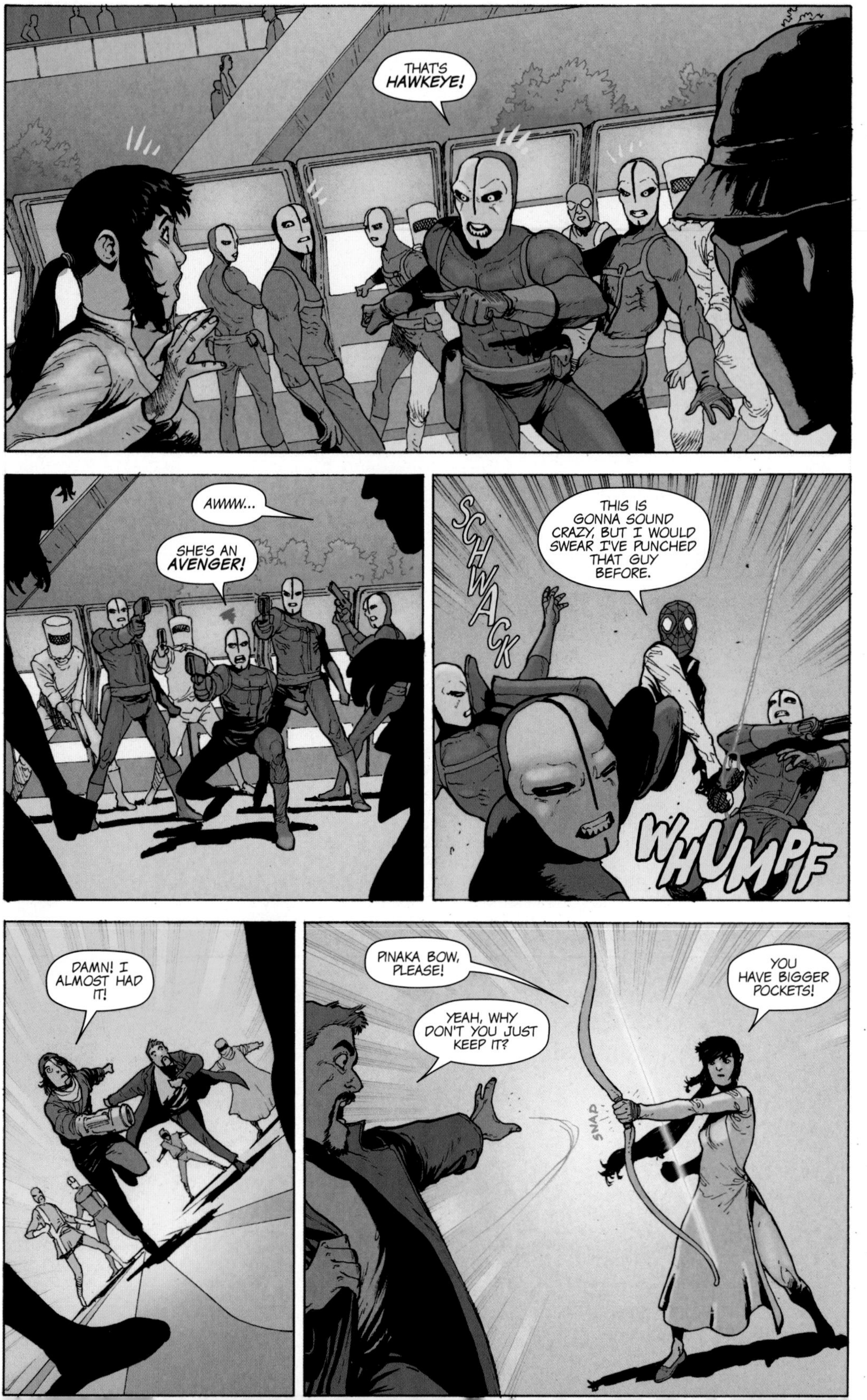
THAT'S HAWKEYE!
AWWW...
SHE'S AN AVENGER!
SCHWACK
THIS IS GONNA SOUND CRAZY, BUT I WOULD SWEAR I'VE PUNCHED THAT GUY BEFORE.
WHUMPF
DAMN! I ALMOST HAD IT!
PINAKA BOW, PLEASE!
YEAH, WHY DON'T YOU JUST KEEP IT?
YOU HAVE BIGGER POCKETS!
SNAP

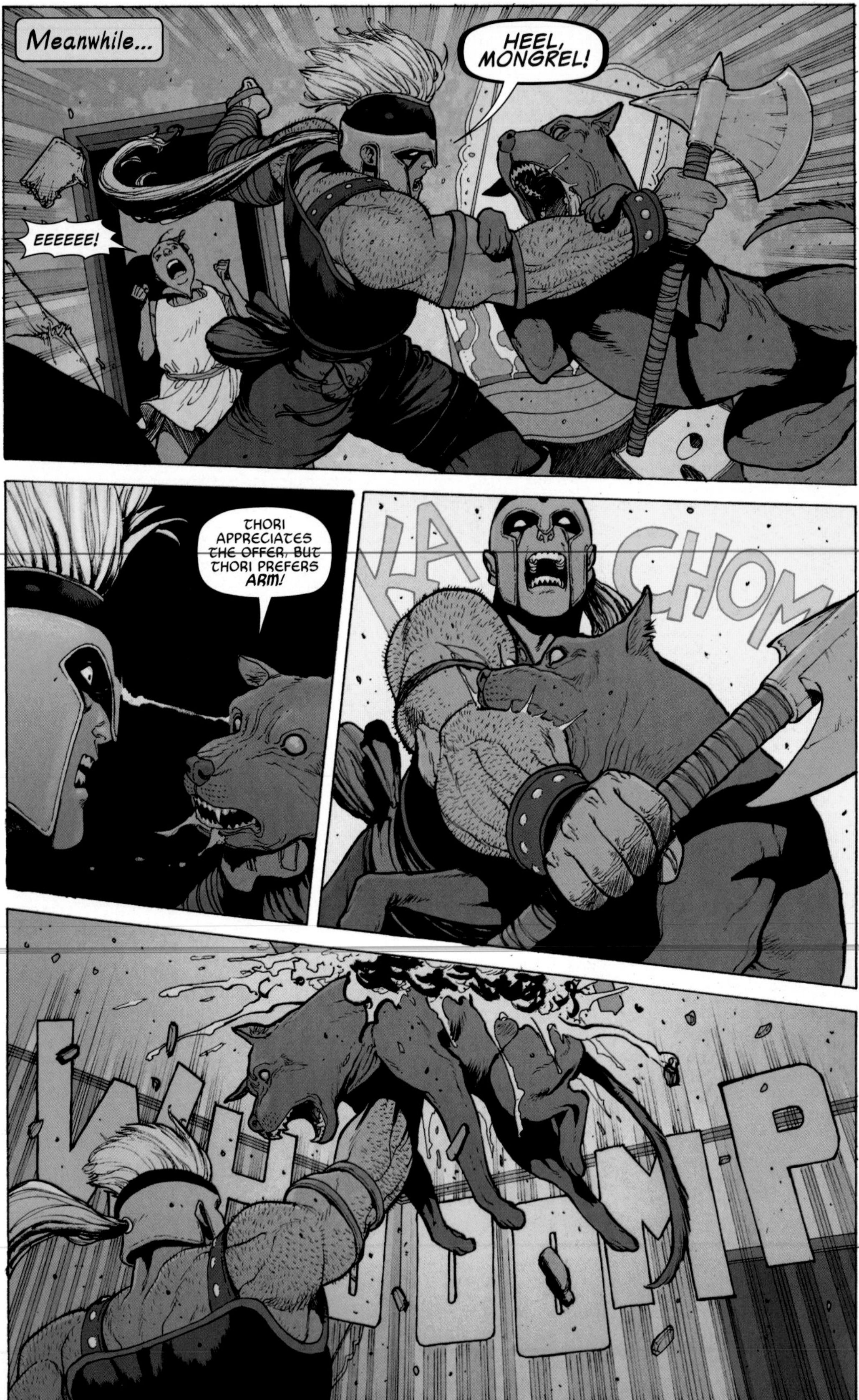
Meanwhile...
HEEL, MONGREL!
EEEEEE!
THORI APPRECIATES THE OFFER, BUT THORI PREFERS ARM!
KA-CHOM
WHUDOMP

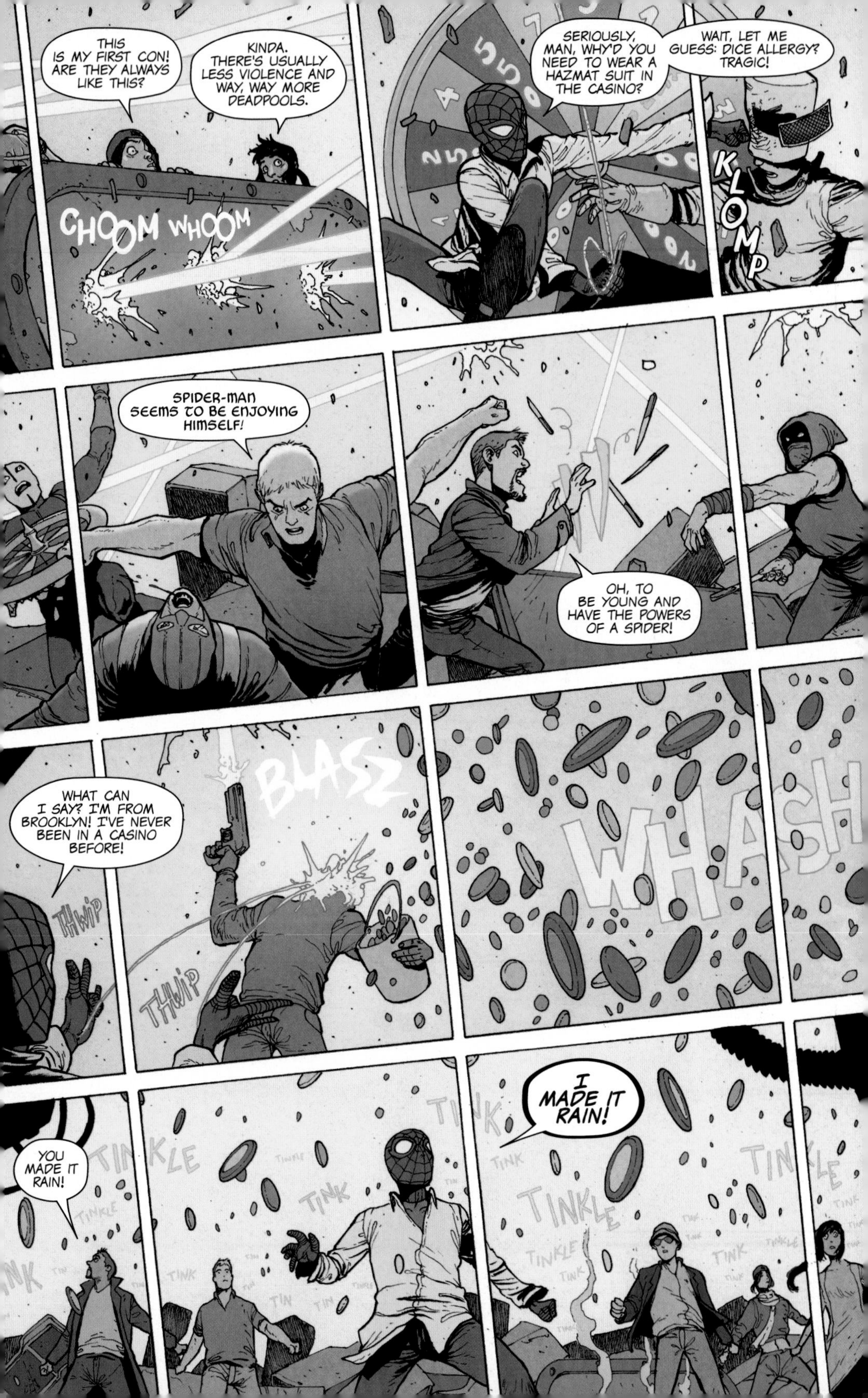

THIS IS MY FIRST CON! ARE THEY ALWAYS LIKE THIS?
KINDA. THERE'S USUALLY LESS VIOLENCE AND WAY, WAY MORE DEADPOOLS.
CHOOM WHOOM
SERIOUSLY, MAN, WHY'D YOU NEED TO WEAR A HAZMAT SUIT IN THE CASINO?
WAIT, LET ME GUESS: DICE ALLERGY? TRAGIC!
KLOMP
SPIDER-MAN SEEMS TO BE ENJOYING HIMSELF!
OH, TO BE YOUNG AND HAVE THE POWERS OF A SPIDER!
WHAT CAN I SAY? I'M FROM BROOKLYN! I'VE NEVER BEEN IN A CASINO BEFORE!
THWIP
THWIP
BLASZ
WHASH
YOU MADE IT RAIN!
I MADE IT RAIN!
TINKLE
TINK
TINKLE
TINK
TINKLE
TINKLE

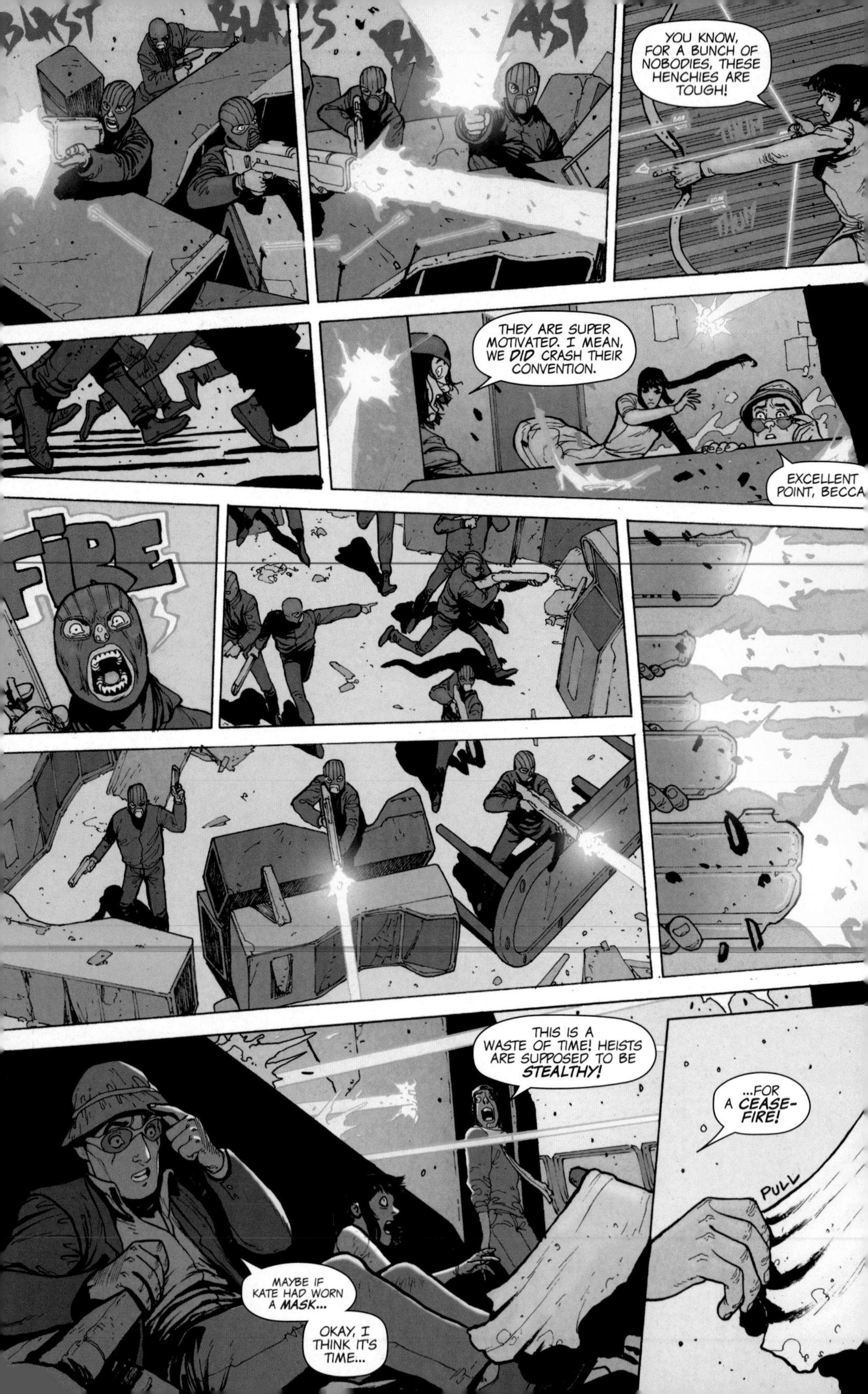
BLAST
BLAST
BLAST
YOU KNOW, FOR A BUNCH OF NOBODIES, THESE HENCHIES ARE TOUGH!
THUM
THUM
THEY ARE SUPER MOTIVATED. I MEAN, WE DID CRASH THEIR CONVENTION.
EXCELLENT POINT, BECCA
FIRE
THIS IS A WASTE OF TIME! HEISTS ARE SUPPOSED TO BE STEALTHY!
MAYBE IF KATE HAD WORN A MASK...
OKAY, I THINK IT'S TIME...
...FOR A CEASE-FIRE!
PULL

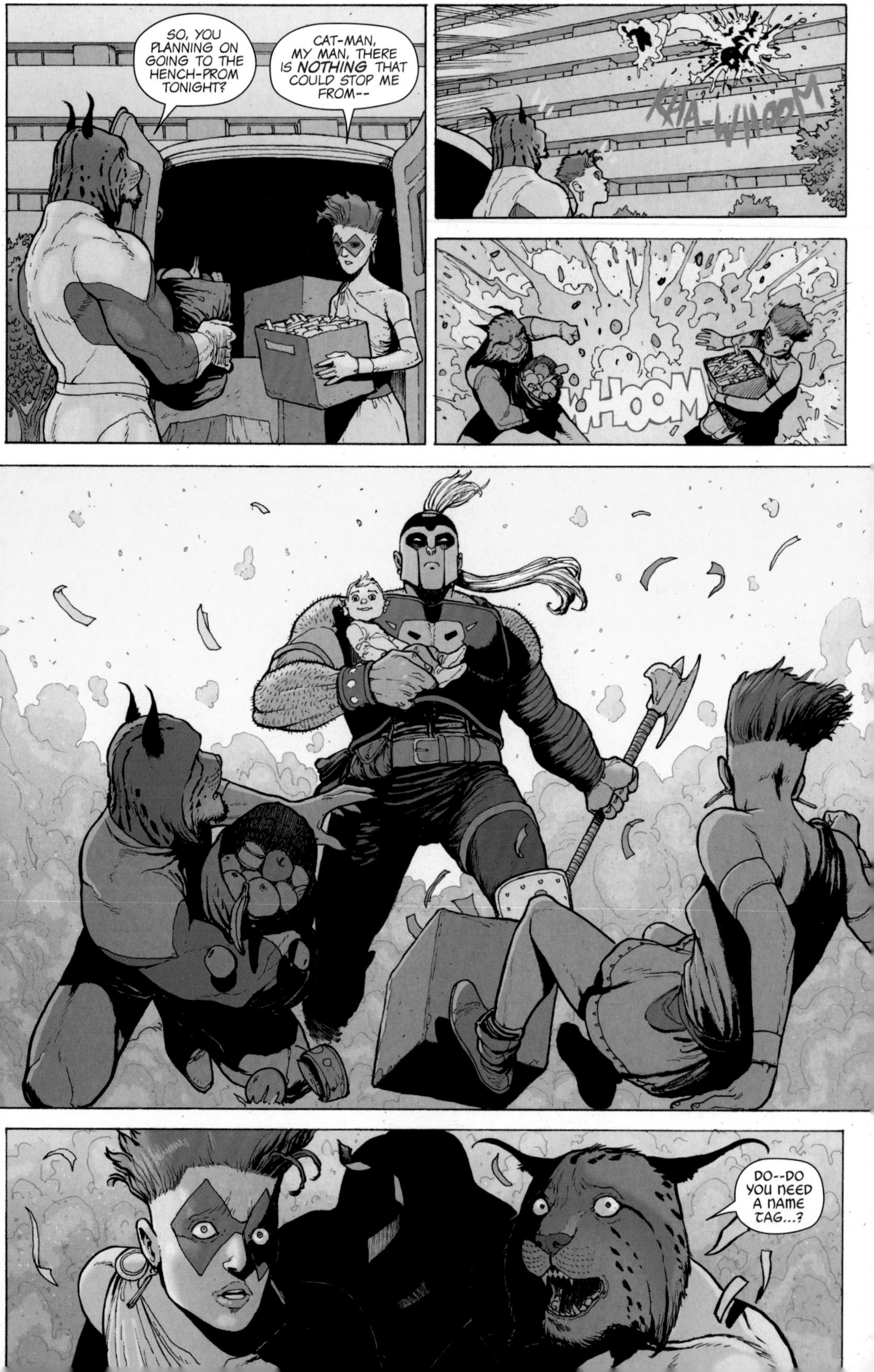
SO, YOU PLANNING ON GOING TO THE HENCH-PROM TONIGHT?
CAT-MAN, MY MAN, THERE IS NOTHING THAT COULD STOP ME FROM--
KHA-WHOOM
WHOOM
DO--DO YOU NEED A NAME TAG...?

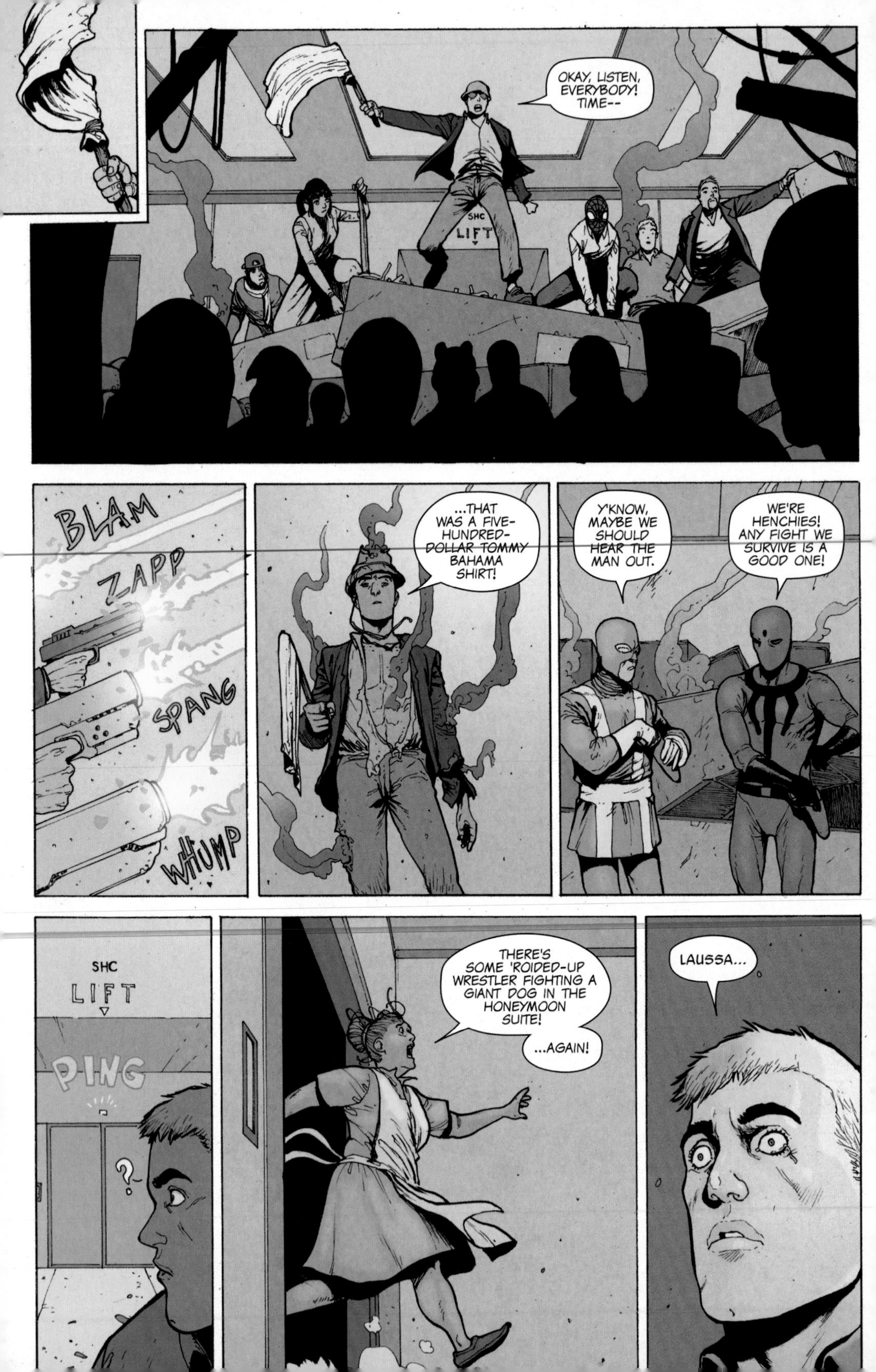
OKAY, LISTEN, EVERYBODY! TIME--
SHC LIFT
BLAM
ZAPP
SPANG
WHUMP
...THAT WAS A FIVE-HUNDRED-DOLLAR TOMMY BAHAMA SHIRT!
Y'KNOW, MAYBE WE SHOULD HEAR THE MAN OUT.
WE'RE HENCHIES! ANY FIGHT WE SURVIVE IS A GOOD ONE!
SHC LIFT
PING
?
THERE'S SOME 'ROIDED-UP WRESTLER FIGHTING A GIANT DOG IN THE HONEYMOON SUITE!
...AGAIN!
LAUSSA...

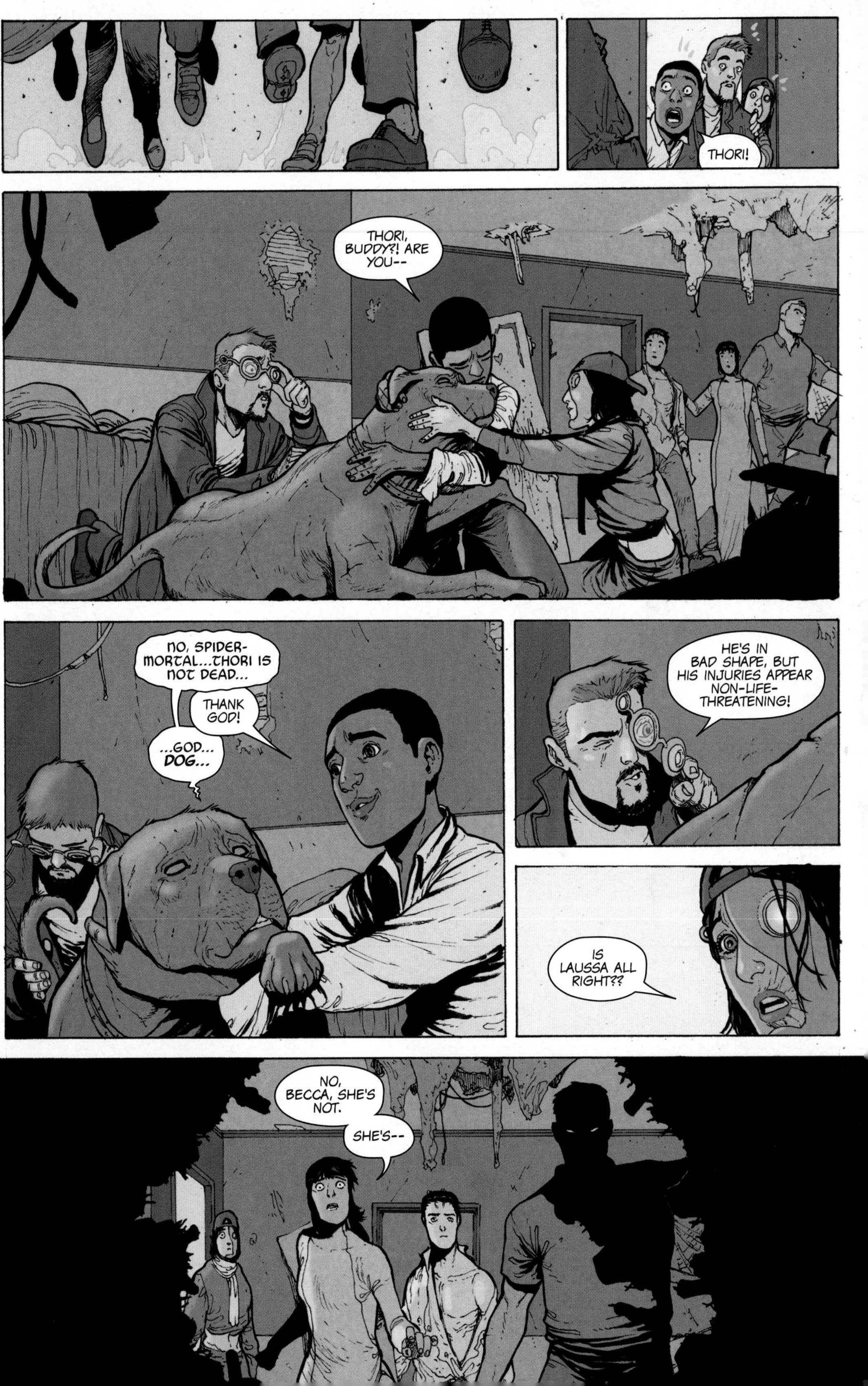
THORI!
THORI, BUDDY?! ARE YOU--
NO, SPIDER-MORTAL...THORI IS NOT DEAD...
THANK GOD!
...GOD... DOG...
HE'S IN BAD SHAPE, BUT HIS INJURIES APPEAR NON-LIFE-THREATENING!
IS LAUSSA ALL RIGHT??
NO, BECCA, SHE'S NOT.
SHE'S--

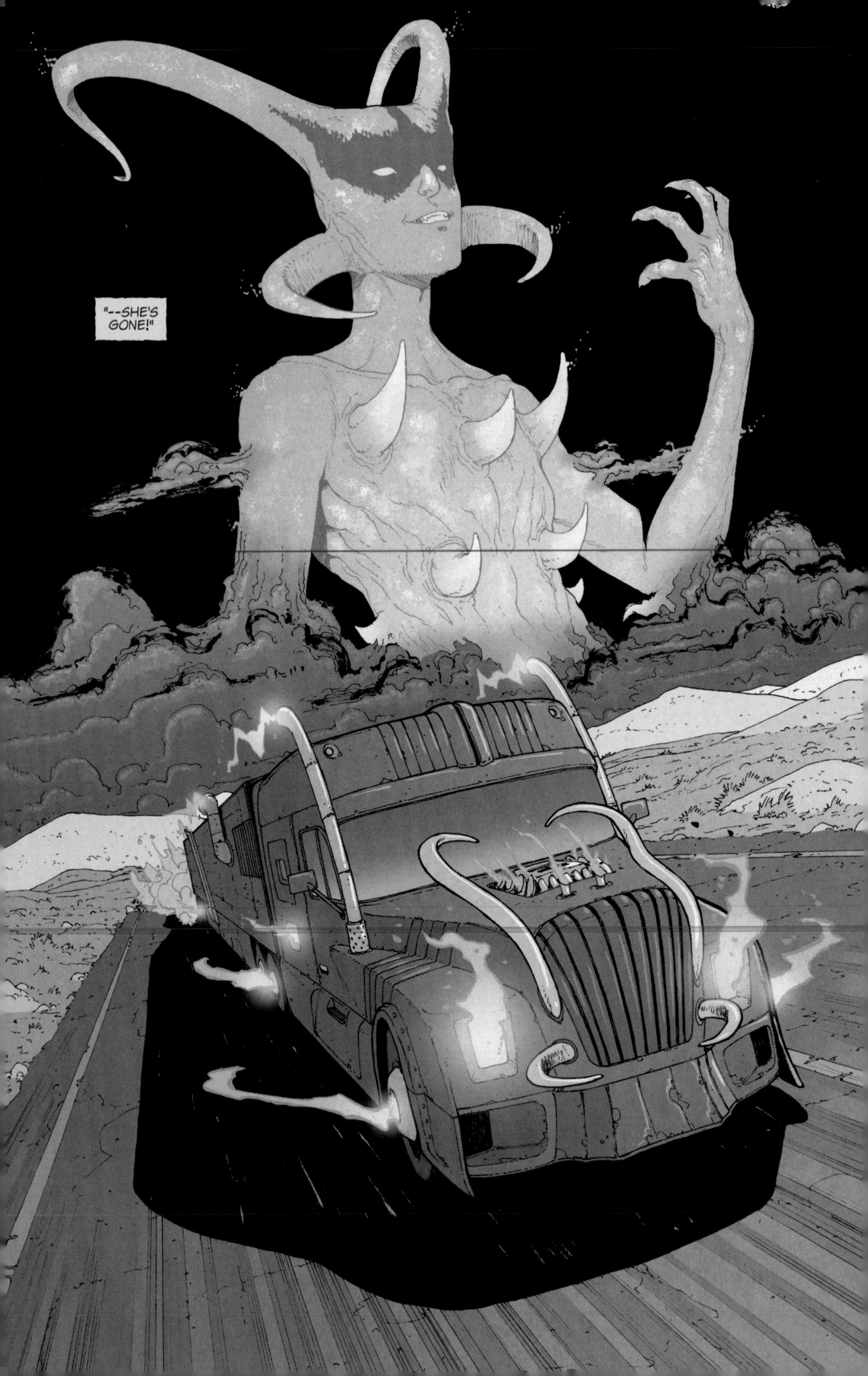
"--SHE'S GONE!"

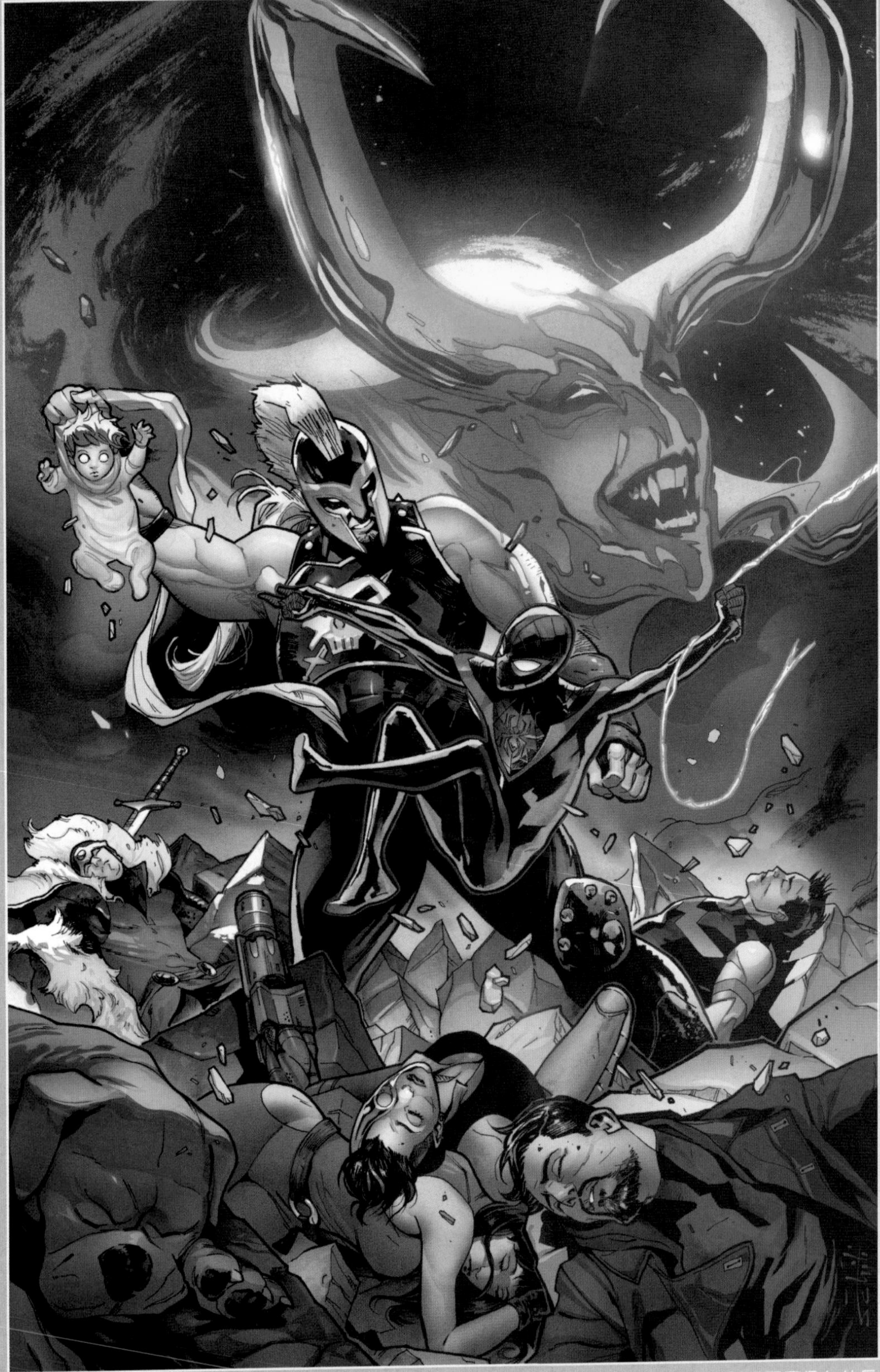

WAR OF THE REALMS: JOURNEY INTO MYSTERY #5

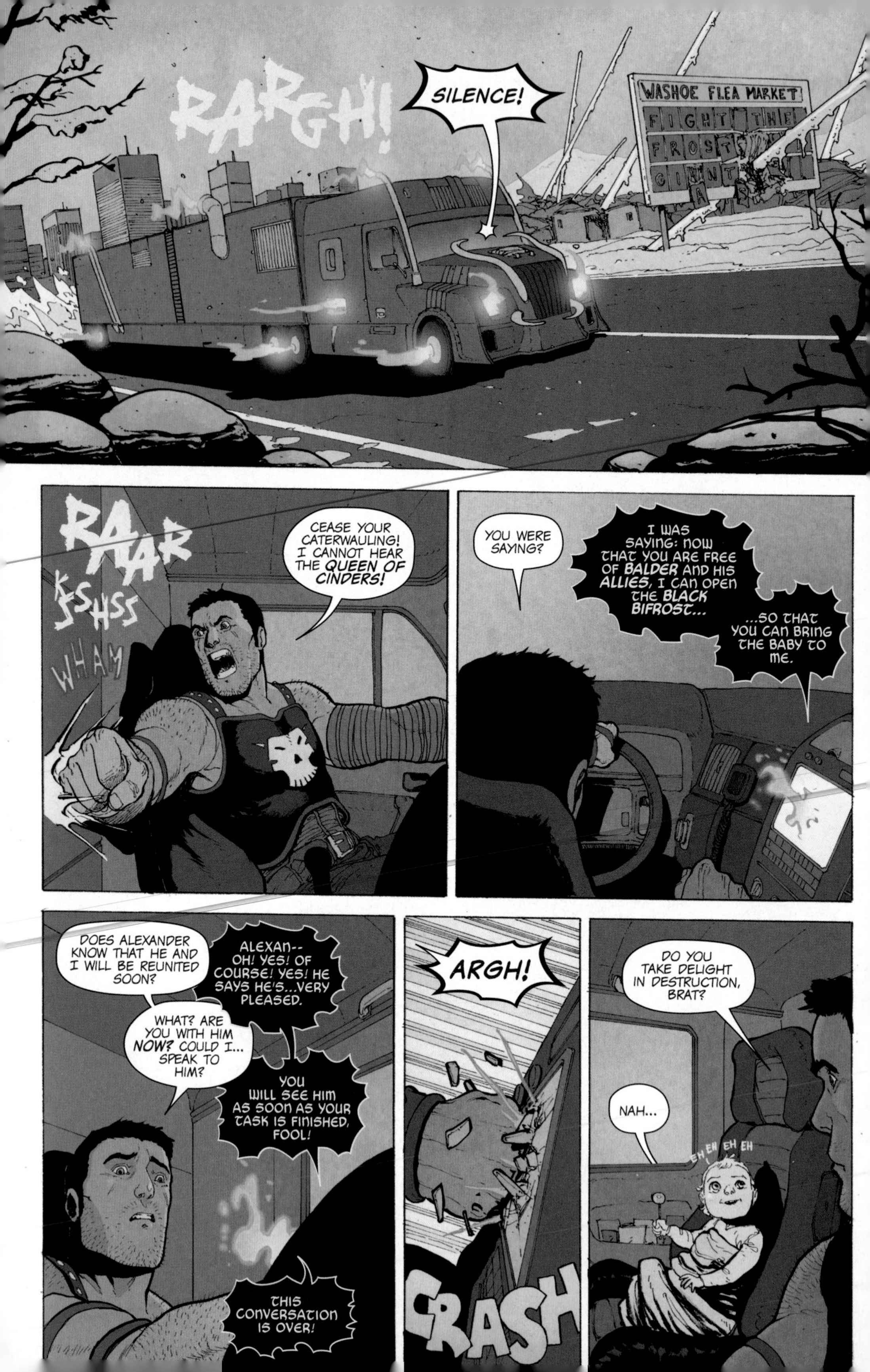
RARGH!
SILENCE!
WASHOE FLEA MARKET
FIGHT THE FROST GIANT
RAAR
KSHSS
WHAM
CEASE YOUR CATERWAULING! I CANNOT HEAR THE QUEEN OF CINDERS!
YOU WERE SAYING?
I WAS SAYING: NOW THAT YOU ARE FREE OF BALDER AND HIS ALLIES, I CAN OPEN THE BLACK BIFROST...
...SO THAT YOU CAN BRING THE BABY TO ME.
DOES ALEXANDER KNOW THAT HE AND I WILL BE REUNITED SOON?
ALEXAN-- OH! YES! OF COURSE! YES! HE SAYS HE'S...VERY PLEASED.
WHAT? ARE YOU WITH HIM NOW? COULD I... SPEAK TO HIM?
YOU WILL SEE HIM AS SOON AS YOUR TASK IS FINISHED, FOOL!
THIS CONVERSATION IS OVER!
ARGH!
CRASH
DO YOU TAKE DELIGHT IN DESTRUCTION, BRAT?
NAH...
EH EH EH EH

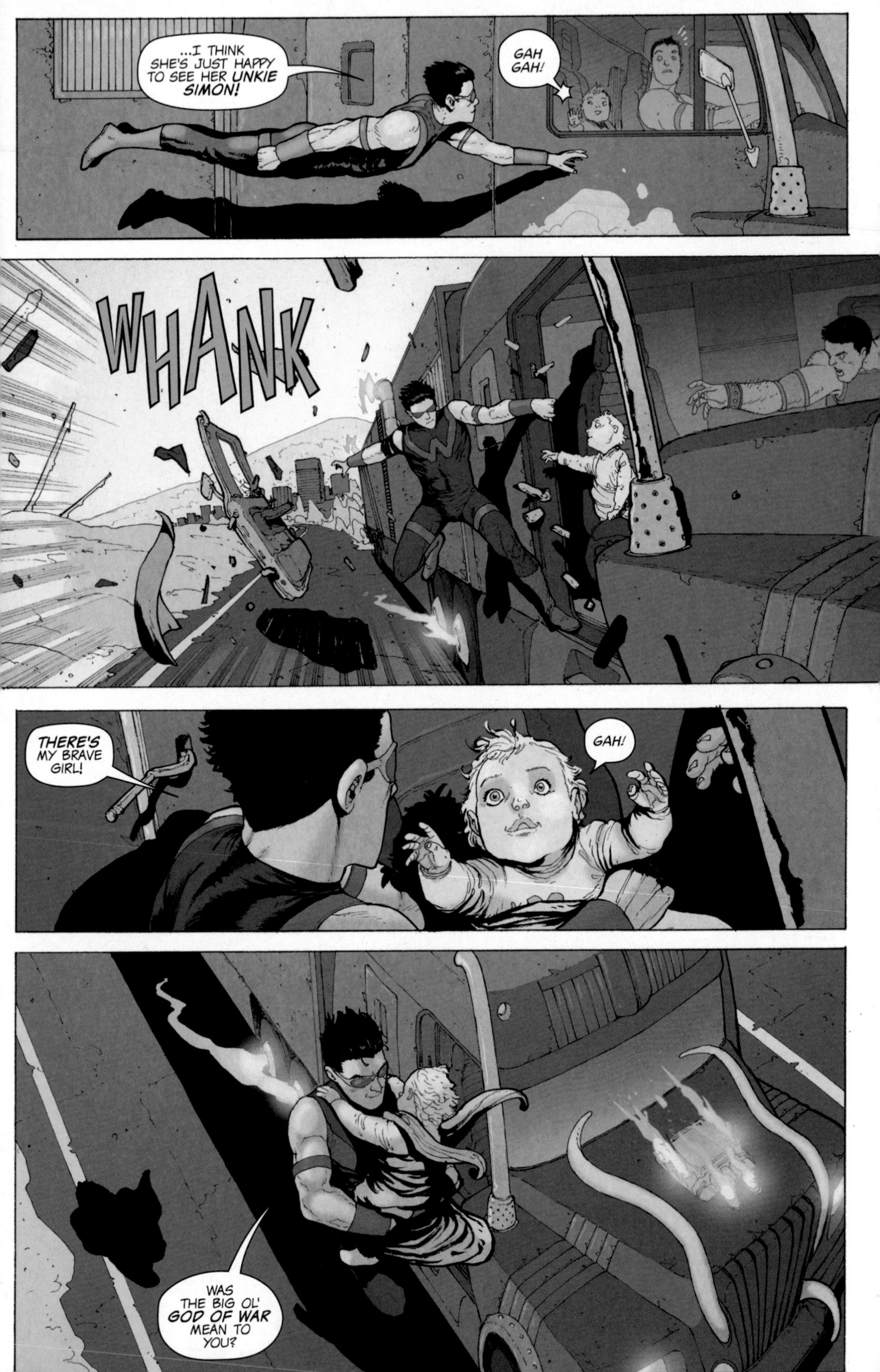
...I THINK SHE'S JUST HAPPY TO SEE HER UNKIE SIMON!
GAH GAH!
WHANK
THERE'S MY BRAVE GIRL!
GAH!
WAS THE BIG OL' GOD OF WAR MEAN TO YOU?

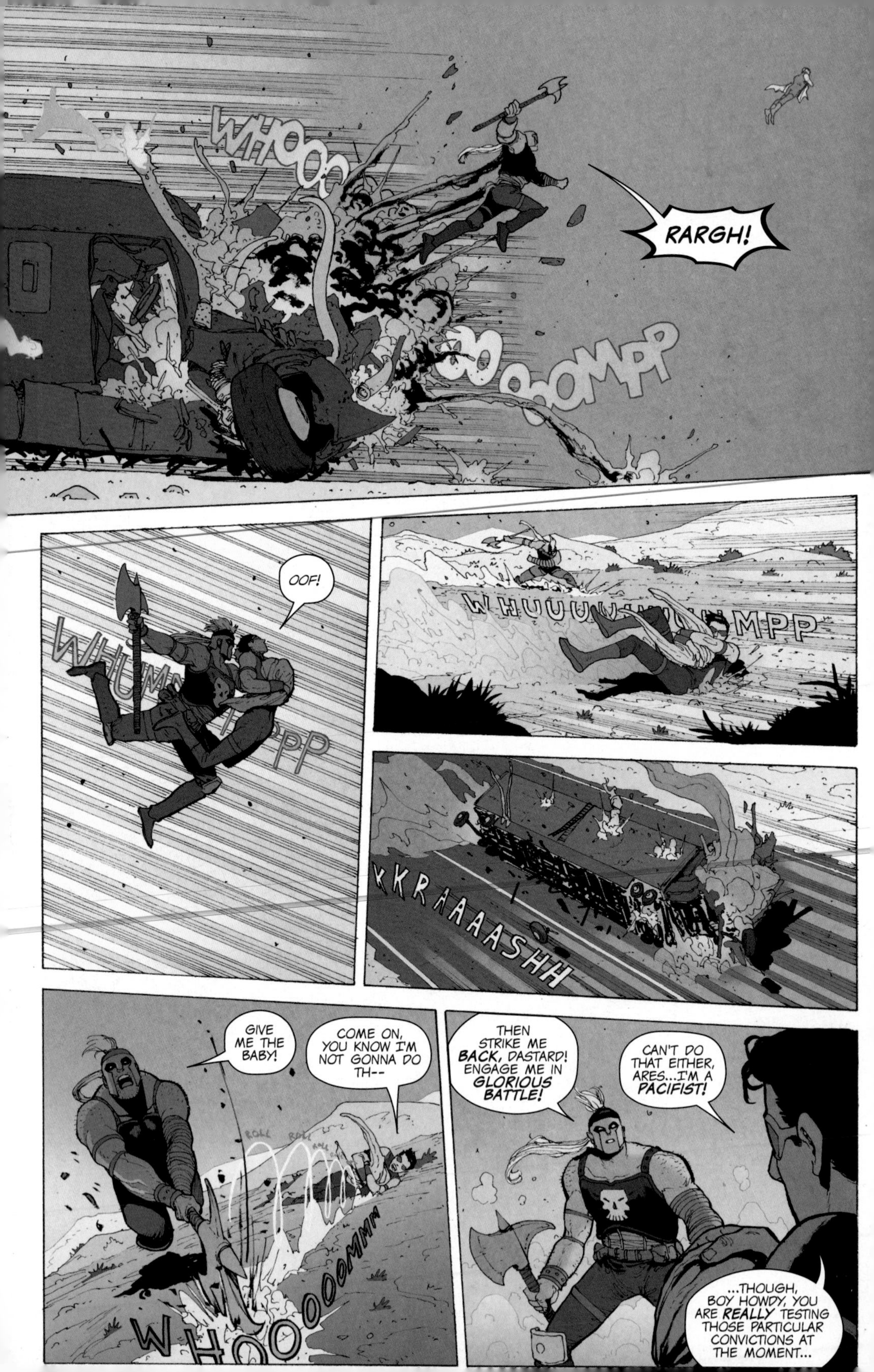
WHOOO
OOOOMPP
RARGH!
WHUMMPP
OOF!
WHUUUUMPP
KKRAAAAASHH
GIVE ME THE BABY!
COME ON, YOU KNOW I'M NOT GONNA DO TH--
ROLL ROLL ROLL
WHOOOOOMM
THEN STRIKE ME BACK, DASTARD! ENGAGE ME IN GLORIOUS BATTLE!
CAN'T DO THAT EITHER, ARES...I'M A PACIFIST!
...THOUGH, BOY HOWDY, YOU ARE REALLY TESTING THOSE PARTICULAR CONVICTIONS AT THE MOMENT...

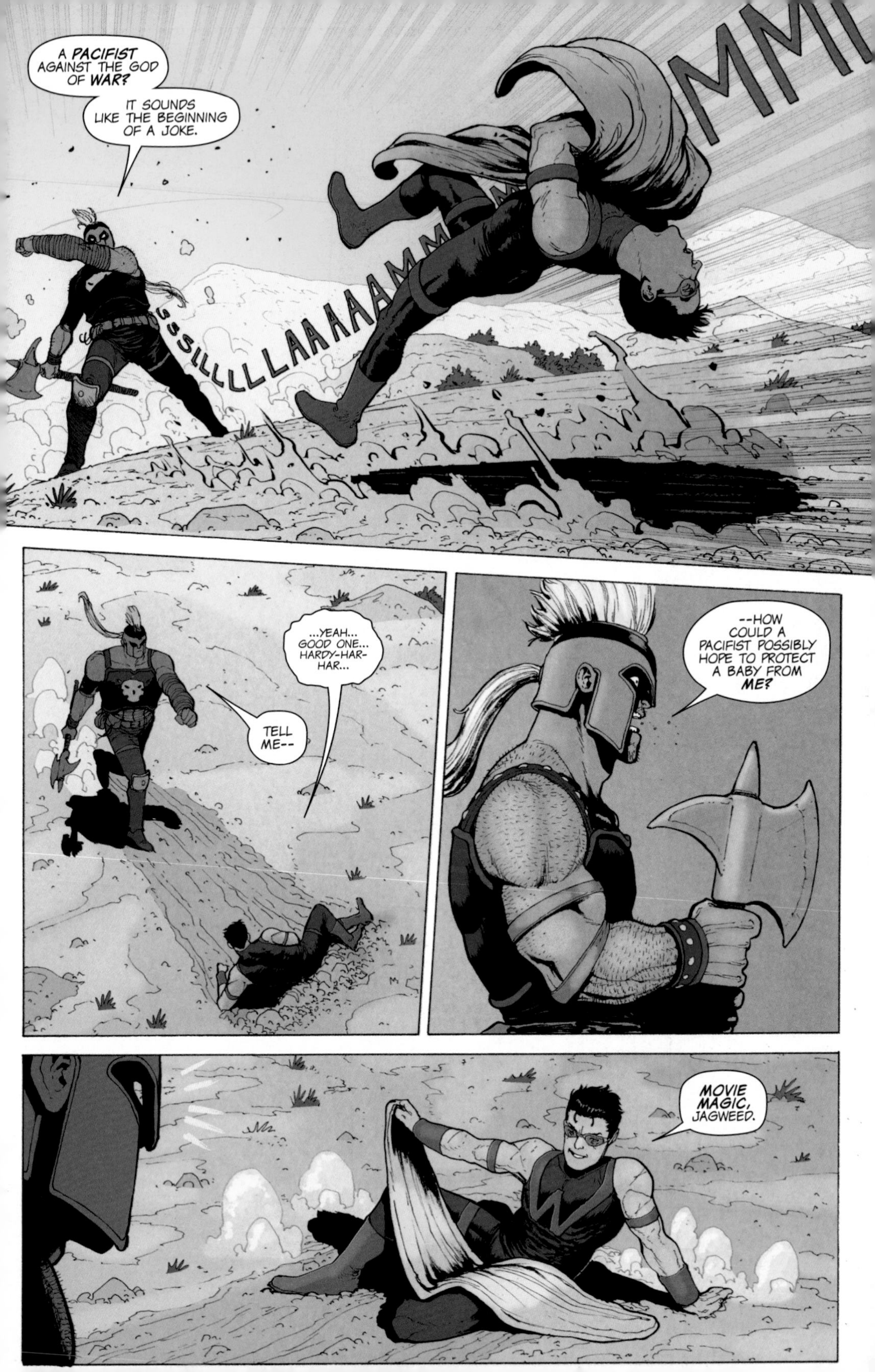
A PACIFIST AGAINST THE GOD OF WAR?
IT SOUNDS LIKE THE BEGINNING OF A JOKE.
SSSLLLLLLAAAAAAAMMMMMMMM
...YEAH... GOOD ONE... HARDY-HAR-HAR...
TELL ME--
--HOW COULD A PACIFIST POSSIBLY HOPE TO PROTECT A BABY FROM ME?
MOVIE MAGIC, JAGWEED.

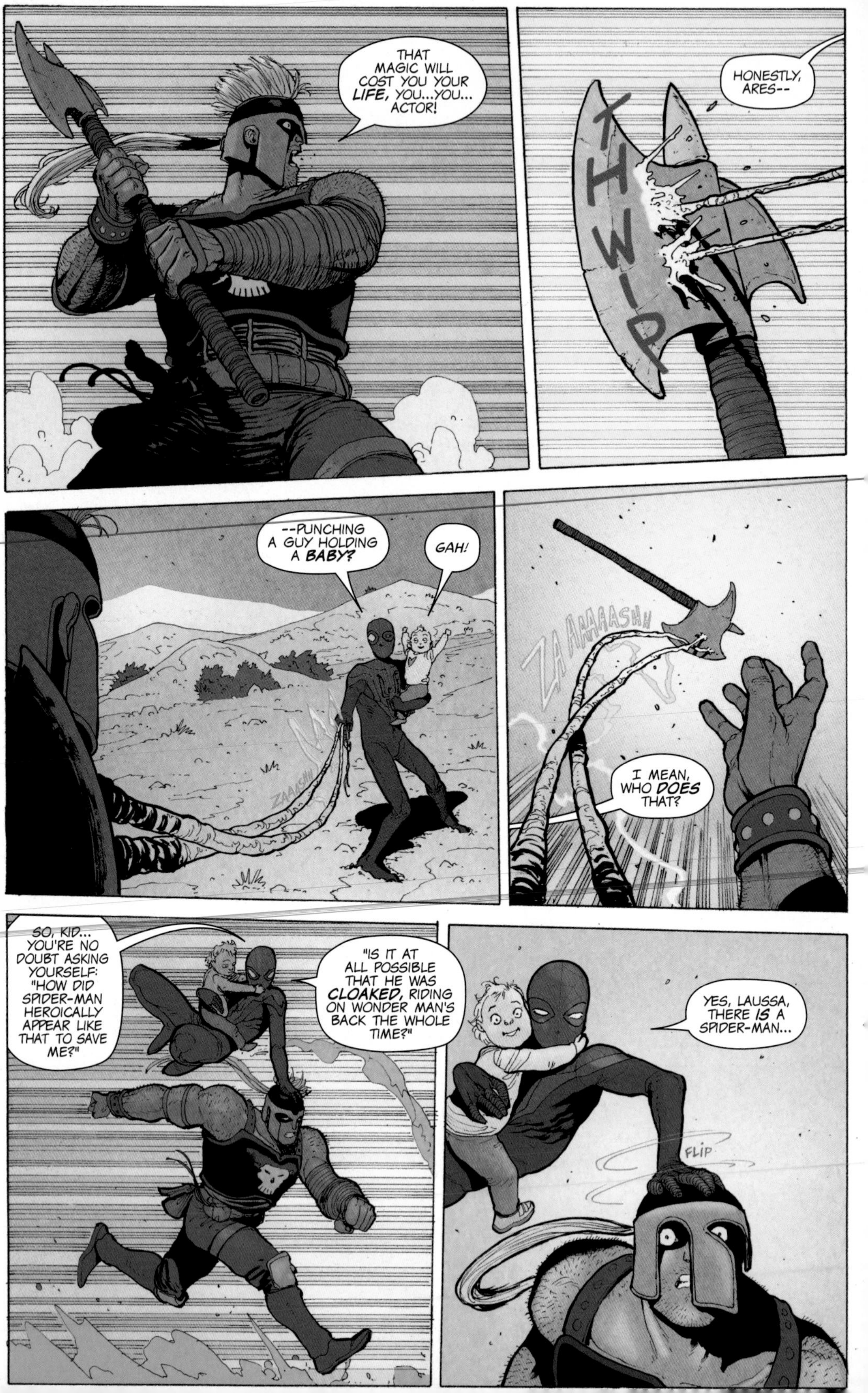

THAT MAGIC WILL COST YOU YOUR LIFE, YOU...YOU... ACTOR!
HONESTLY, ARES--
THWIP
--PUNCHING A GUY HOLDING A BABY?
GAH!
ZAAASHH
ZAAAAAASHH
I MEAN, WHO DOES THAT?
SO, KID... YOU'RE NO DOUBT ASKING YOURSELF: "HOW DID SPIDER-MAN HEROICALLY APPEAR LIKE THAT TO SAVE ME?"
"IS IT AT ALL POSSIBLE THAT HE WAS CLOAKED, RIDING ON WONDER MAN'S BACK THE WHOLE TIME?"
YES, LAUSSA, THERE IS A SPIDER-MAN...
FLIP

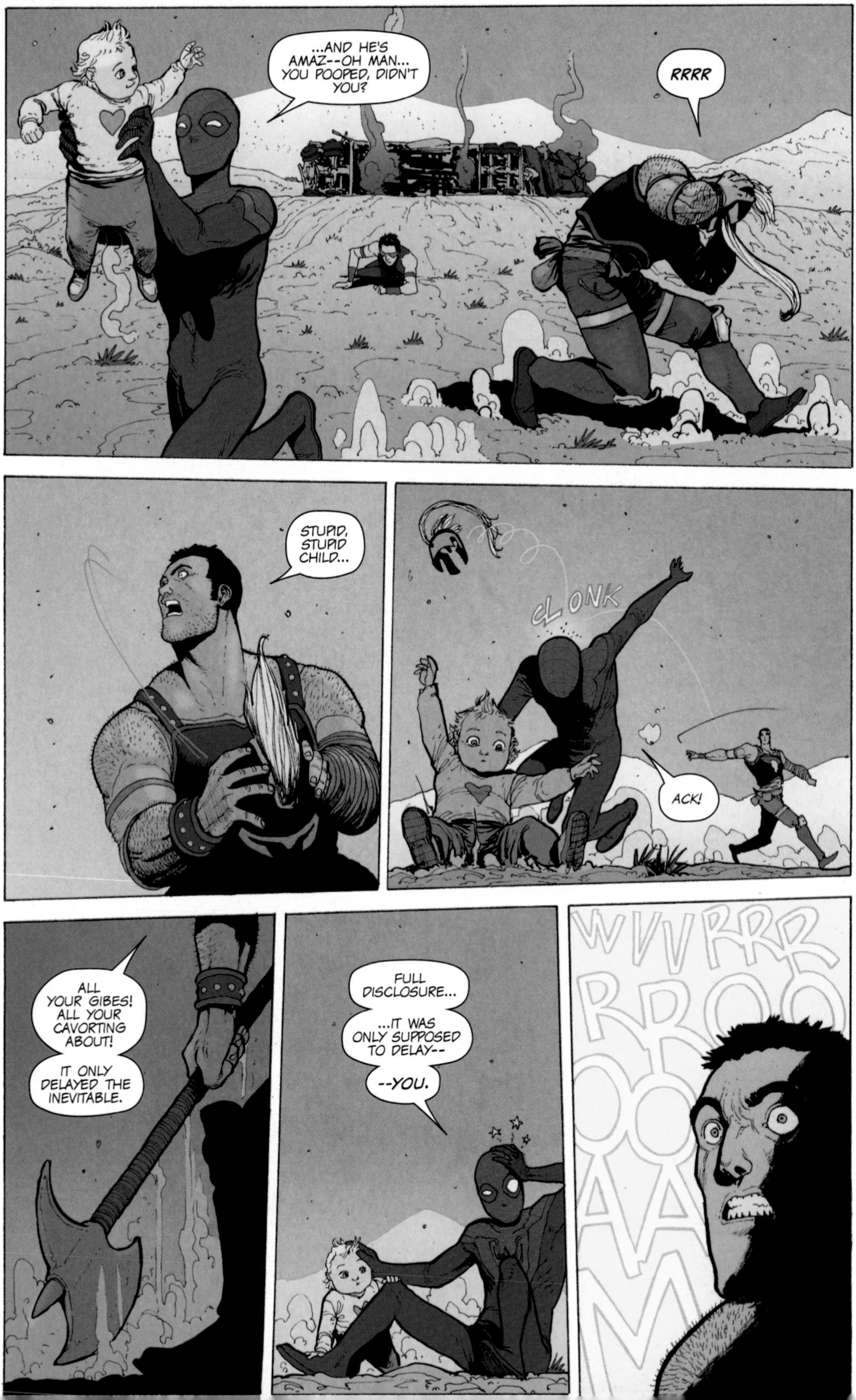
...AND HE'S AMAZ--OH MAN... YOU POOPED, DIDN'T YOU?
RRRR
STUPID, STUPID CHILD...
CLONK
ACK!
ALL YOUR GIBES! ALL YOUR CAVORTING ABOUT!
IT ONLY DELAYED THE INEVITABLE.
FULL DISCLOSURE...
...IT WAS ONLY SUPPOSED TO DELAY--
--YOU.
WVVRRR RROOOOAAMM

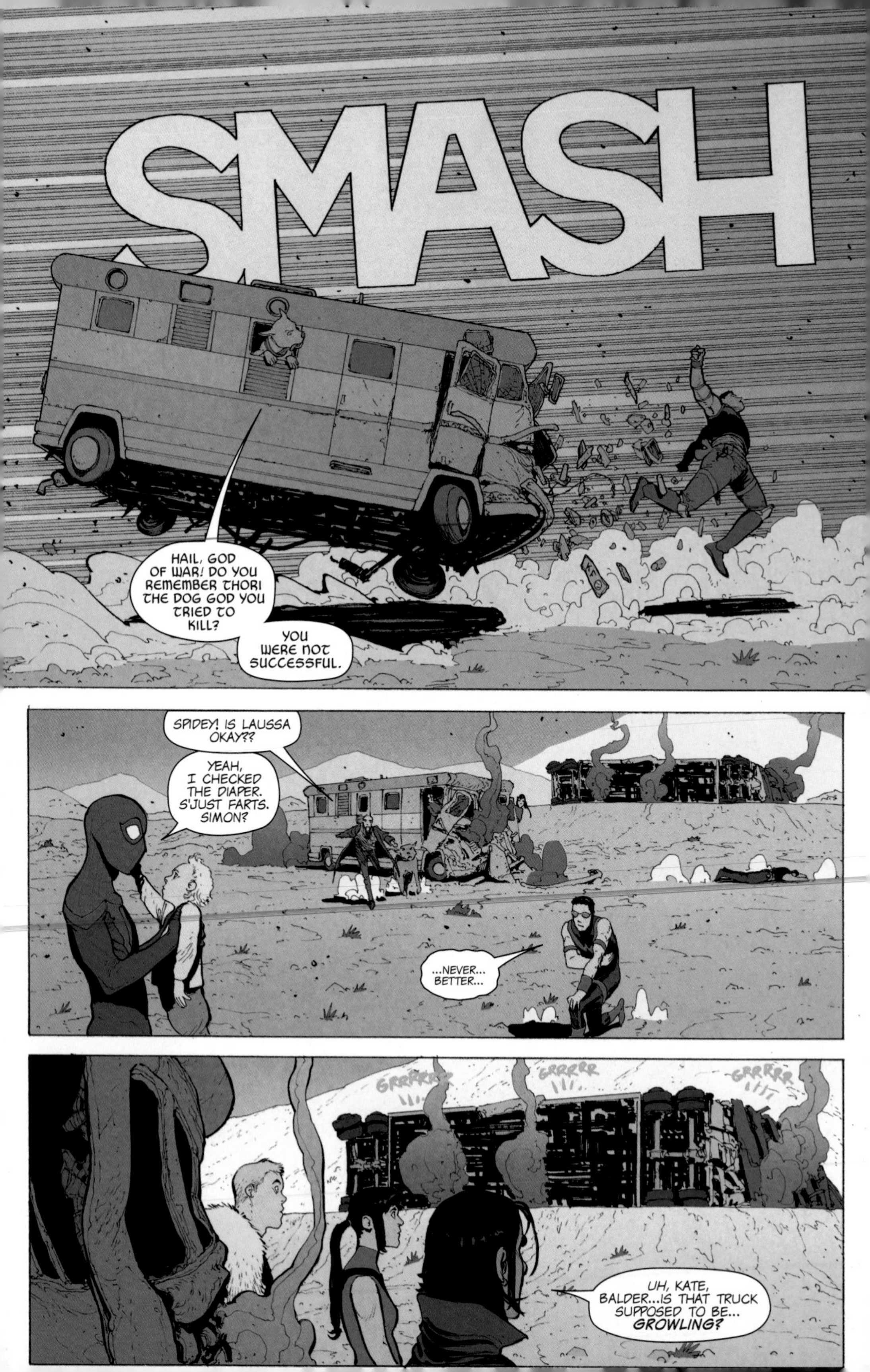
SMASH
HAIL, GOD OF WAR! DO YOU REMEMBER THORI THE DOG GOD YOU TRIED TO KILL?
YOU WERE NOT SUCCESSFUL.
SPIDEY! IS LAUSSA OKAY??
YEAH, I CHECKED THE DIAPER. S'JUST FARTS. SIMON?
...NEVER... BETTER...
GRRRRRR
GRRRRR
GRRRRR
UH, KATE, BALDER...IS THAT TRUCK SUPPOSED TO BE... GROWLING?

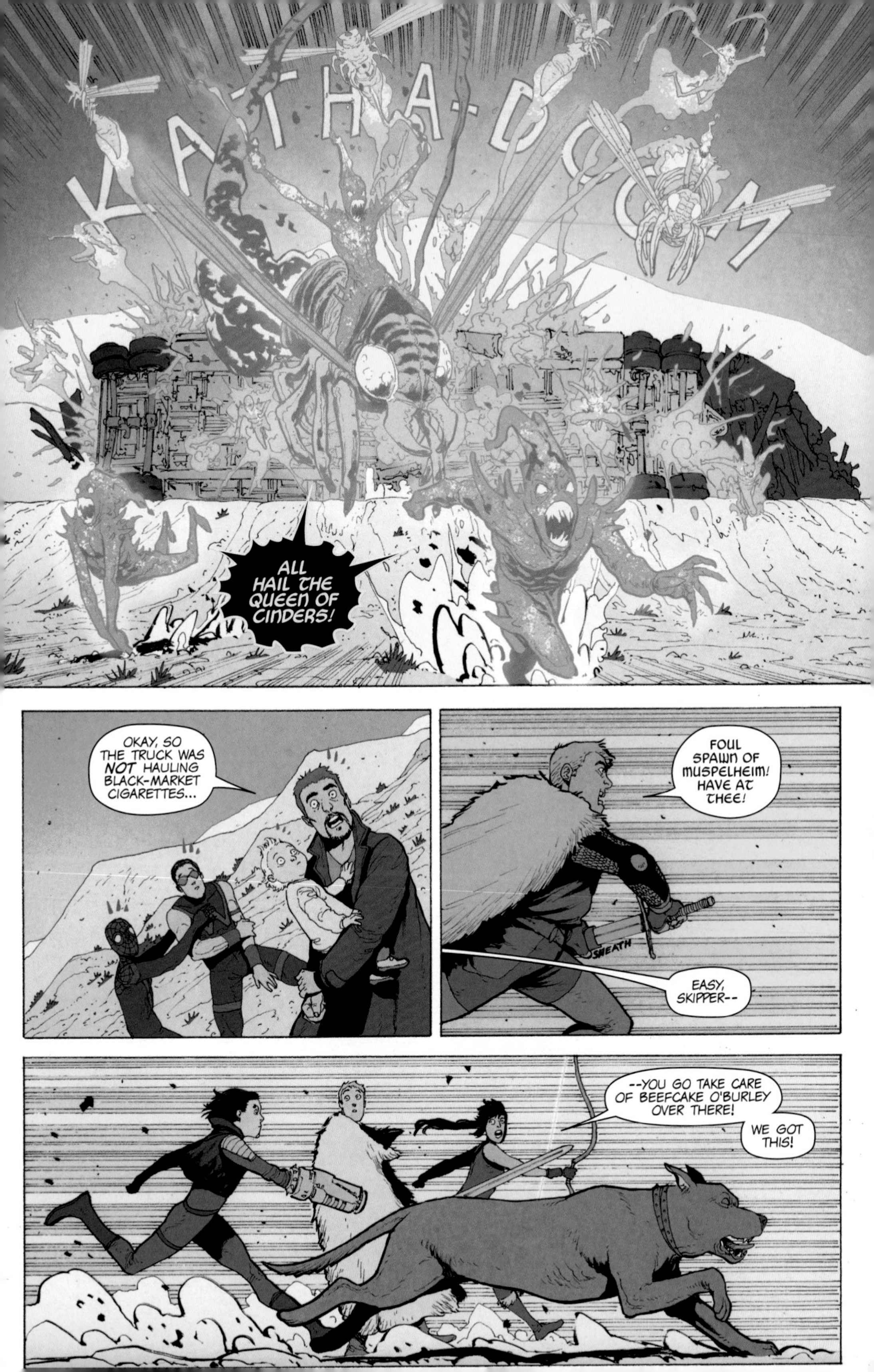
KATHA-DOOM
ALL HAIL THE QUEEN OF CINDERS!
OKAY, SO THE TRUCK WAS NOT HAULING BLACK-MARKET CIGARETTES...
FOUL SPAWN OF MUSPELHEIM! HAVE AT THEE!
SHEATH
EASY, SKIPPER--
--YOU GO TAKE CARE OF BEEFCAKE O'BURLEY OVER THERE!
WE GOT THIS!

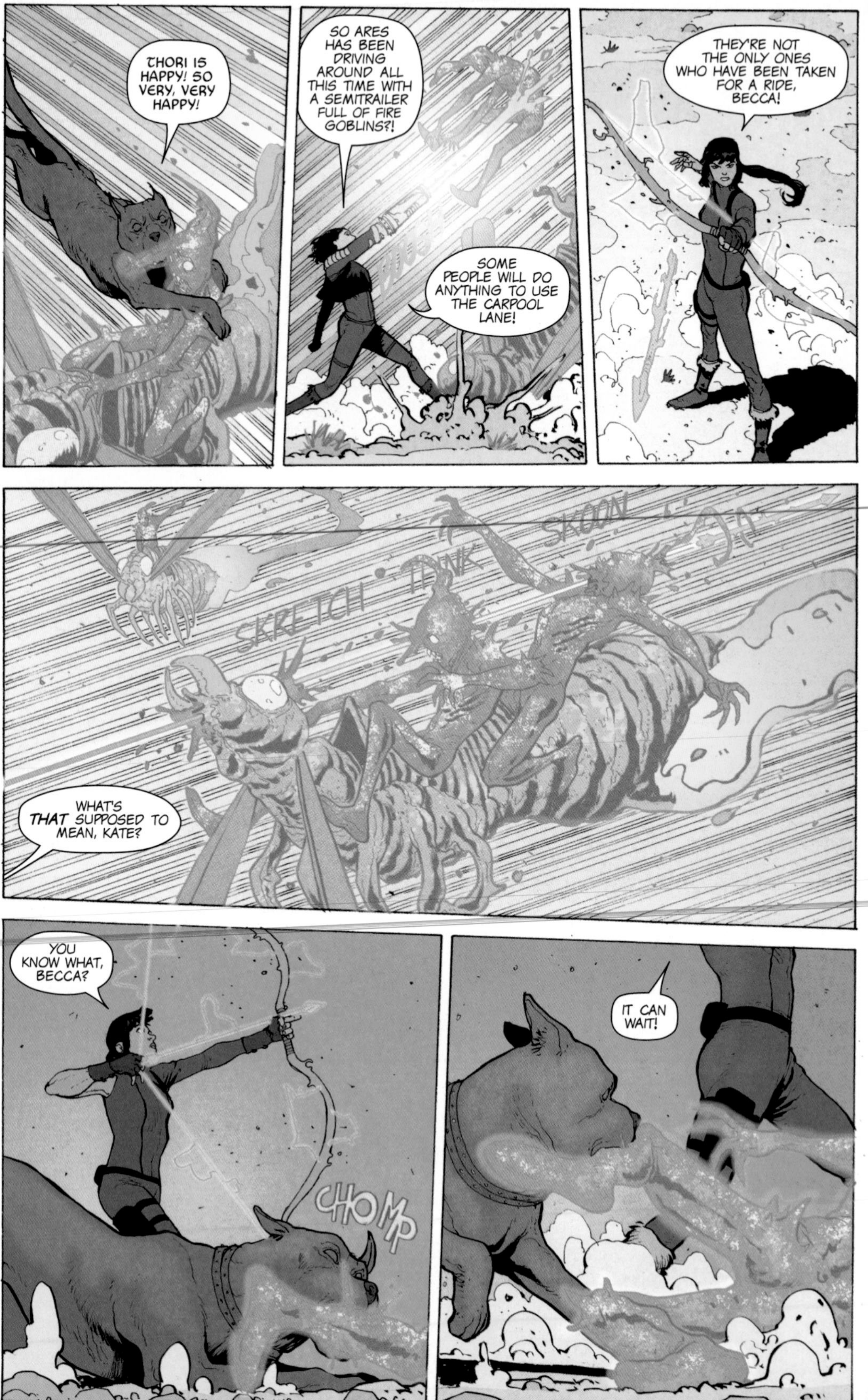
THORI IS HAPPY! SO VERY, VERY HAPPY!
SO ARES HAS BEEN DRIVING AROUND ALL THIS TIME WITH A SEMITRAILER FULL OF FIRE GOBLINS?!
SOME PEOPLE WILL DO ANYTHING TO USE THE CARPOOL LANE!
THEY'RE NOT THE ONLY ONES WHO HAVE BEEN TAKEN FOR A RIDE, BECCA!
SKRETCH
TINK
SKOON
WHAT'S *THAT* SUPPOSED TO MEAN, KATE?
YOU KNOW WHAT, BECCA?
CHOMP
IT CAN WAIT!

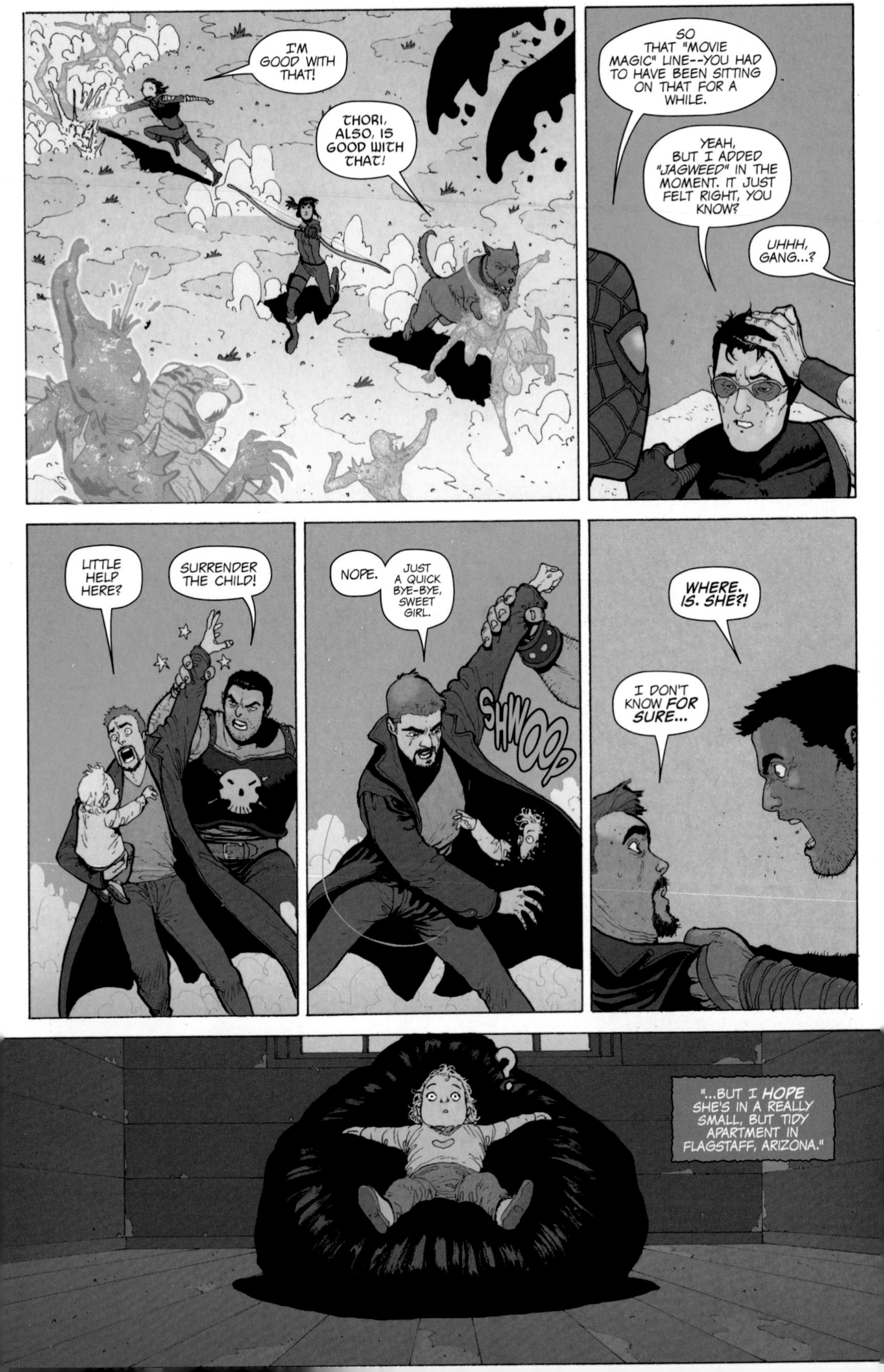
I'M GOOD WITH THAT!
THORI, ALSO, IS GOOD WITH THAT!
SO THAT "MOVIE MAGIC" LINE--YOU HAD TO HAVE BEEN SITTING ON THAT FOR A WHILE.
YEAH, BUT I ADDED "JAGWEED" IN THE MOMENT. IT JUST FELT RIGHT, YOU KNOW?
UHHH, GANG...?
LITTLE HELP HERE?
SURRENDER THE CHILD!
NOPE.
JUST A QUICK BYE-BYE, SWEET GIRL.
SHWOOP
WHERE. IS. SHE?!
I DON'T KNOW FOR SURE...
"...BUT I HOPE SHE'S IN A REALLY SMALL, BUT TIDY APARTMENT IN FLAGSTAFF, ARIZONA."

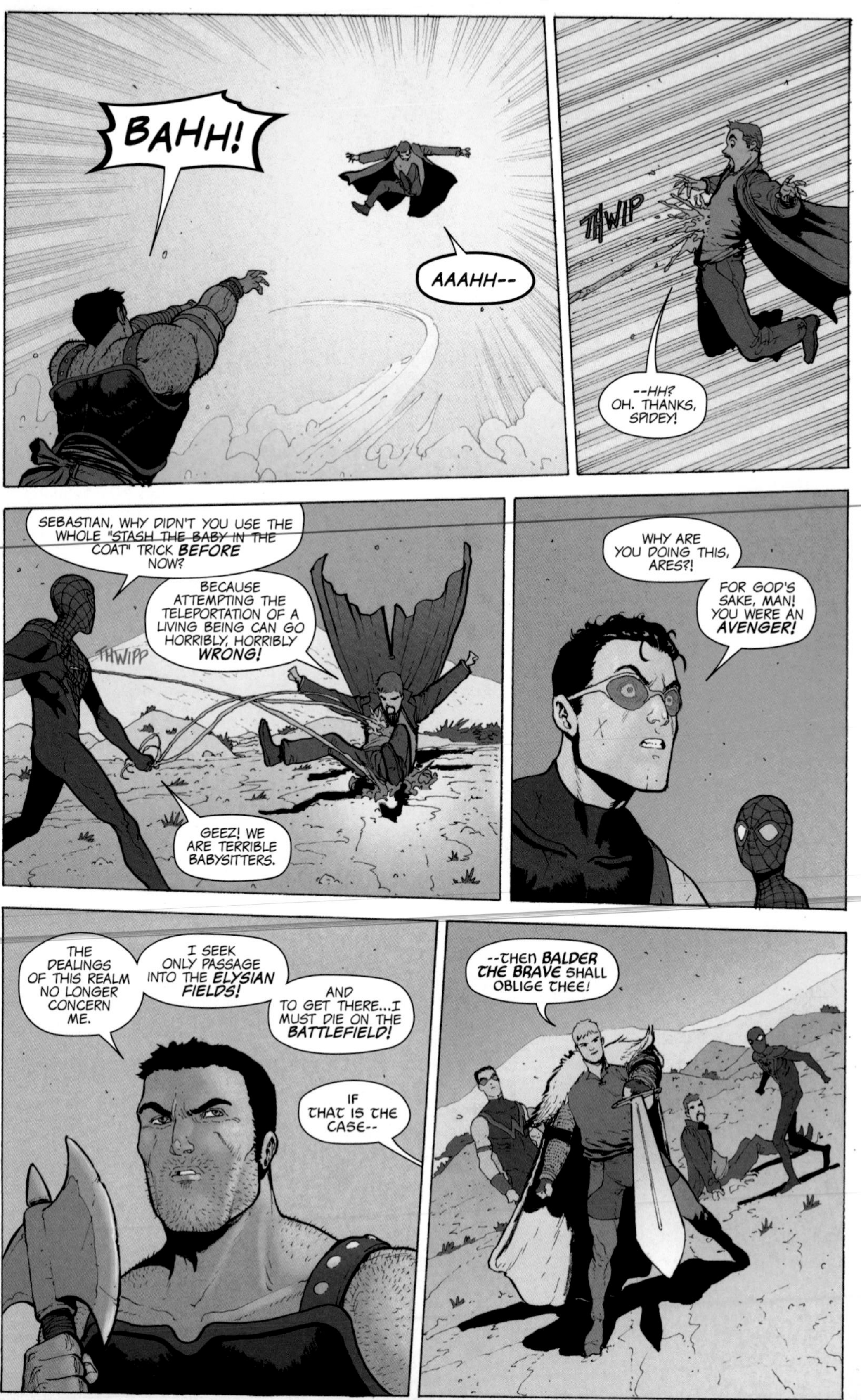
BAHH!
AAAHH--
THWIP
--HH? OH. THANKS, SPIDEY!
SEBASTIAN, WHY DIDN'T YOU USE THE WHOLE "STASH THE BABY IN THE COAT" TRICK BEFORE NOW?
BECAUSE ATTEMPTING THE TELEPORTATION OF A LIVING BEING CAN GO HORRIBLY, HORRIBLY WRONG!
THWIPP
GEEZ! WE ARE TERRIBLE BABYSITTERS.
WHY ARE YOU DOING THIS, ARES?!
FOR GOD'S SAKE, MAN! YOU WERE AN AVENGER!
THE DEALINGS OF THIS REALM NO LONGER CONCERN ME.
I SEEK ONLY PASSAGE INTO THE ELYSIAN FIELDS!
AND TO GET THERE...I MUST DIE ON THE BATTLEFIELD!
IF THAT IS THE CASE--
--THEN BALDER THE BRAVE SHALL OBLIGE THEE!

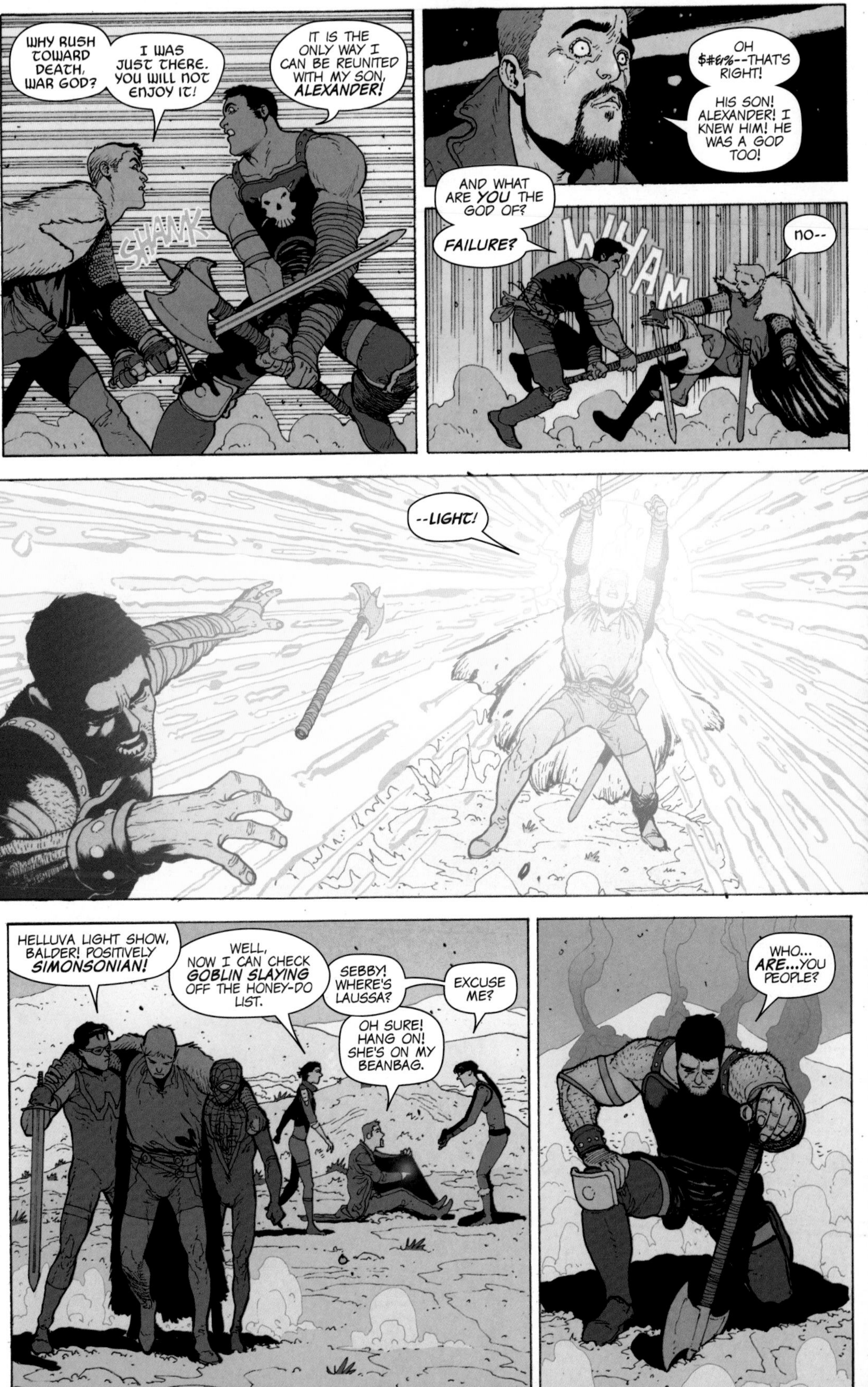
WHY RUSH TOWARD DEATH, WAR GOD?
I WAS JUST THERE. YOU WILL NOT ENJOY IT!
IT IS THE ONLY WAY I CAN BE REUNITED WITH MY SON, ALEXANDER!
SHANK
OH $#&%--THAT'S RIGHT!
HIS SON! ALEXANDER! I KNEW HIM! HE WAS A GOD TOO!
AND WHAT ARE YOU THE GOD OF?
FAILURE?
WHAM
no--
--LIGHT!
HELLUVA LIGHT SHOW, BALDER! POSITIVELY SIMONSONIAN!
WELL, NOW I CAN CHECK GOBLIN SLAYING OFF THE HONEY-DO LIST.
SEBBY! WHERE'S LAUSSA?
EXCUSE ME?
OH SURE! HANG ON! SHE'S ON MY BEANBAG.
WHO... ARE...YOU PEOPLE?

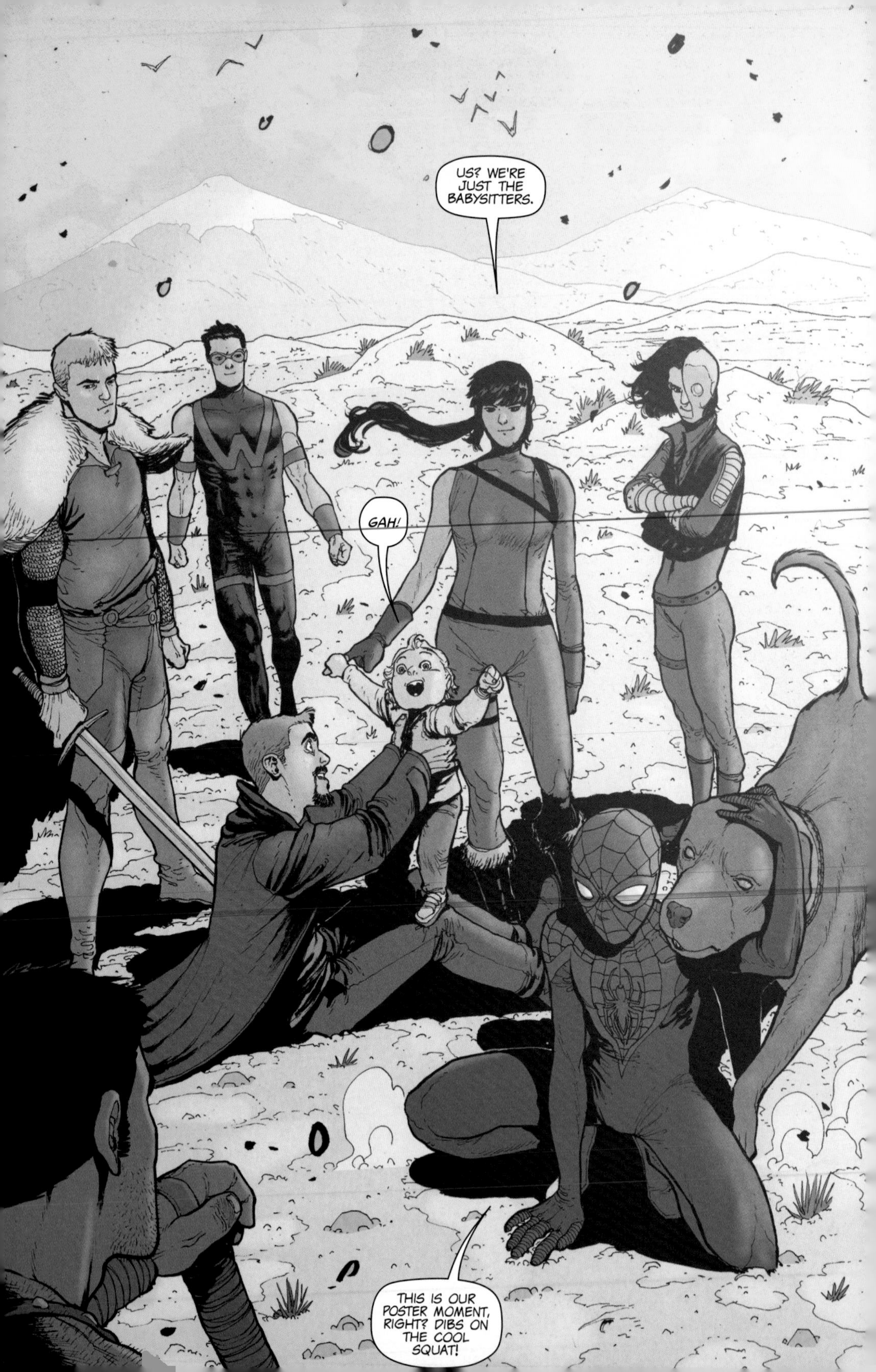
US? WE'RE JUST THE BABYSITTERS.
GAH!
THIS IS OUR POSTER MOMENT, RIGHT? DIBS ON THE COOL SQUAT!

IT MATTERS... NOT...

I WAS GUIDED BY **DIVINE PROVIDENCE** TO THIS PLACE, AT THIS MOMENT, AND PROMISED BY THE QUEEN OF CINDERS--

ACTUALLY...

...THAT WAS ME!

MORE DEMONS! THORI IS SO VERY TIRED OF DEMONS.

DEMON **RIDER**, THORI. WE MET THIS ONE, REMEMBER?

HELLO AGAIN, SEBASTIAN DRUID.

HI-HO, KUSHALA.

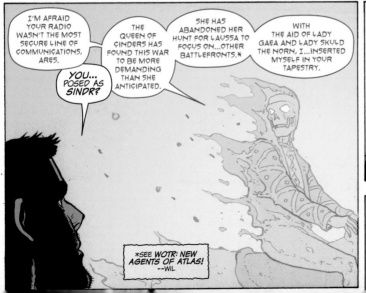

I'M AFRAID YOUR RADIO WASN'T THE MOST SECURE LINE OF COMMUNICATIONS, ARES.

YOU... POSED AS SINDR?

THE QUEEN OF CINDERS HAS FOUND THIS WAR TO BE MORE DEMANDING THAN SHE ANTICIPATED.

SHE HAS ABANDONED HER HUNT FOR LAUSSA TO FOCUS ON...OTHER BATTLEFRONTS.*

WITH THE AID OF LADY GAEA AND LADY SKULD THE NORN, I...INSERTED MYSELF IN YOUR TAPESTRY.

*SEE WOTR: NEW AGENTS OF ATLAS! --WIL

BUT WHY?

BECAUSE SHE ASKED ME TO.

SINDR?

NO...

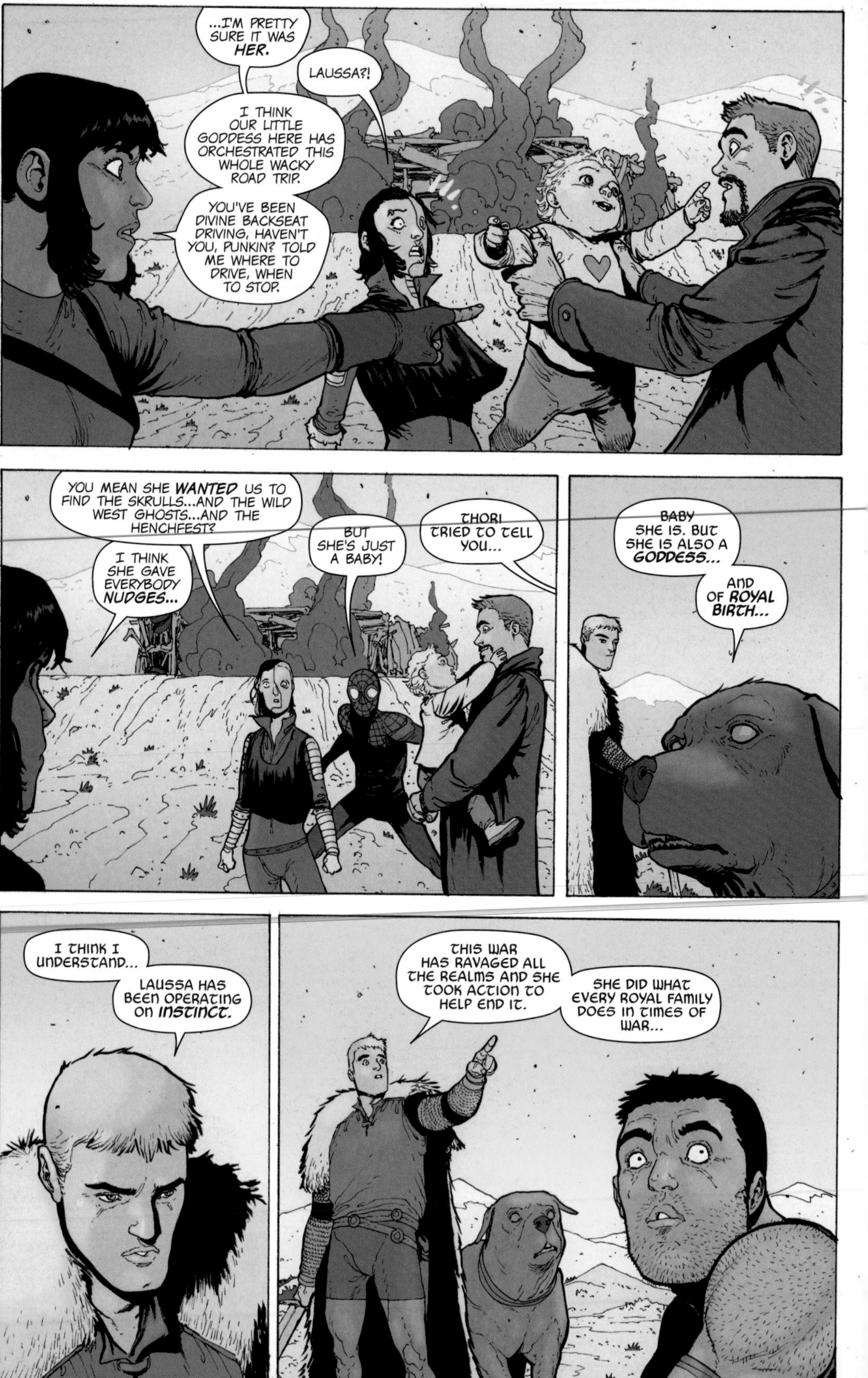
...I'M PRETTY SURE IT WAS HER.
LAUSSA?!
I THINK OUR LITTLE GODDESS HERE HAS ORCHESTRATED THIS WHOLE WACKY ROAD TRIP.
YOU'VE BEEN DIVINE BACKSEAT DRIVING, HAVEN'T YOU, PUNKIN? TOLD ME WHERE TO DRIVE, WHEN TO STOP.
YOU MEAN SHE WANTED US TO FIND THE SKRULLS...AND THE WILD WEST GHOSTS...AND THE HENCHFEST?
I THINK SHE GAVE EVERYBODY NUDGES...
BUT SHE'S JUST A BABY!
THOR! TRIED TO TELL YOU...
BABY SHE IS. BUT SHE IS ALSO A GODDESS...
AND OF ROYAL BIRTH...
I THINK I UNDERSTAND...
LAUSSA HAS BEEN OPERATING ON INSTINCT.
THIS WAR HAS RAVAGED ALL THE REALMS AND SHE TOOK ACTION TO HELP END IT.
SHE DID WHAT EVERY ROYAL FAMILY DOES IN TIMES OF WAR...

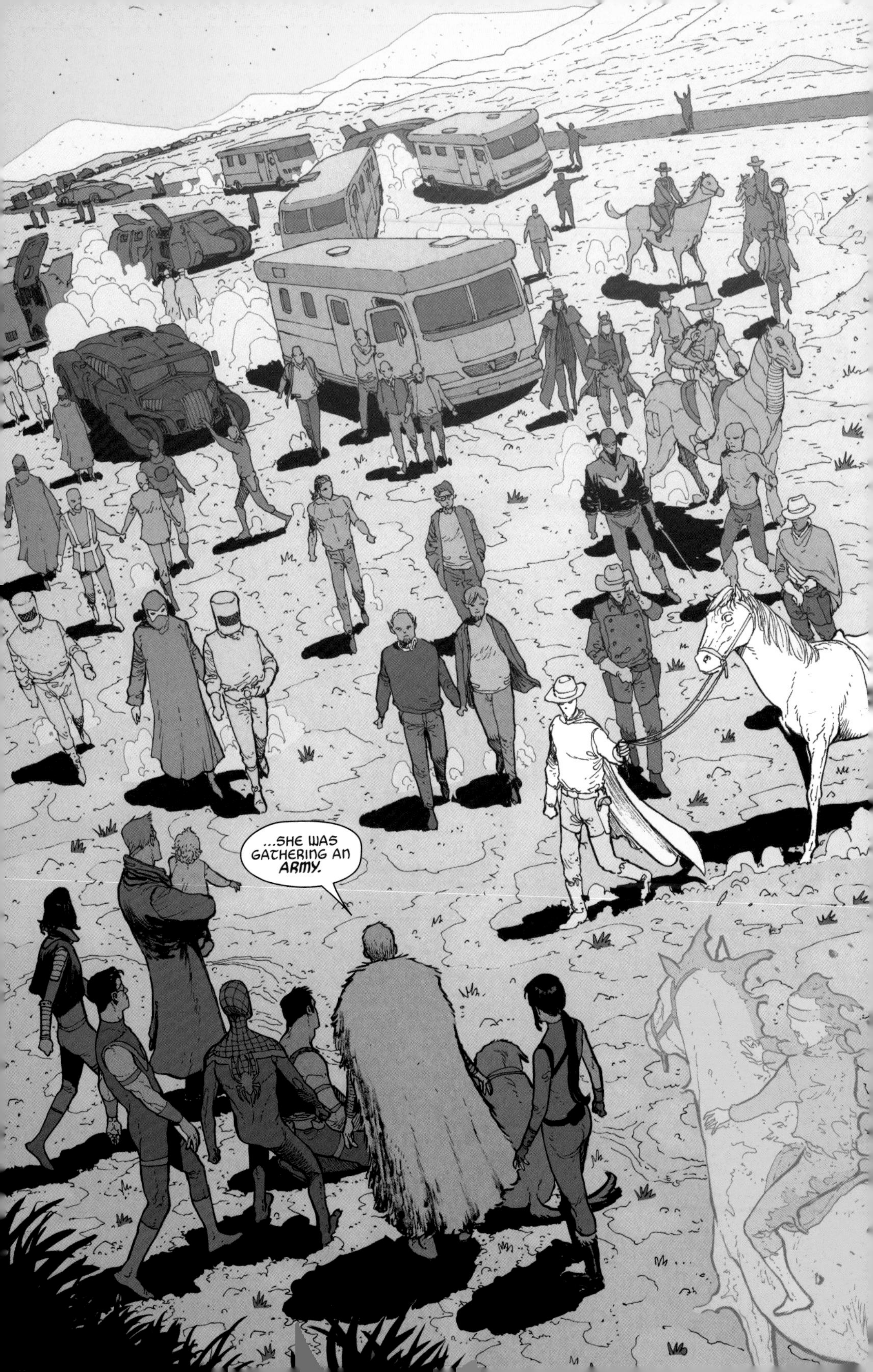
...SHE WAS GATHERING AN ARMY.

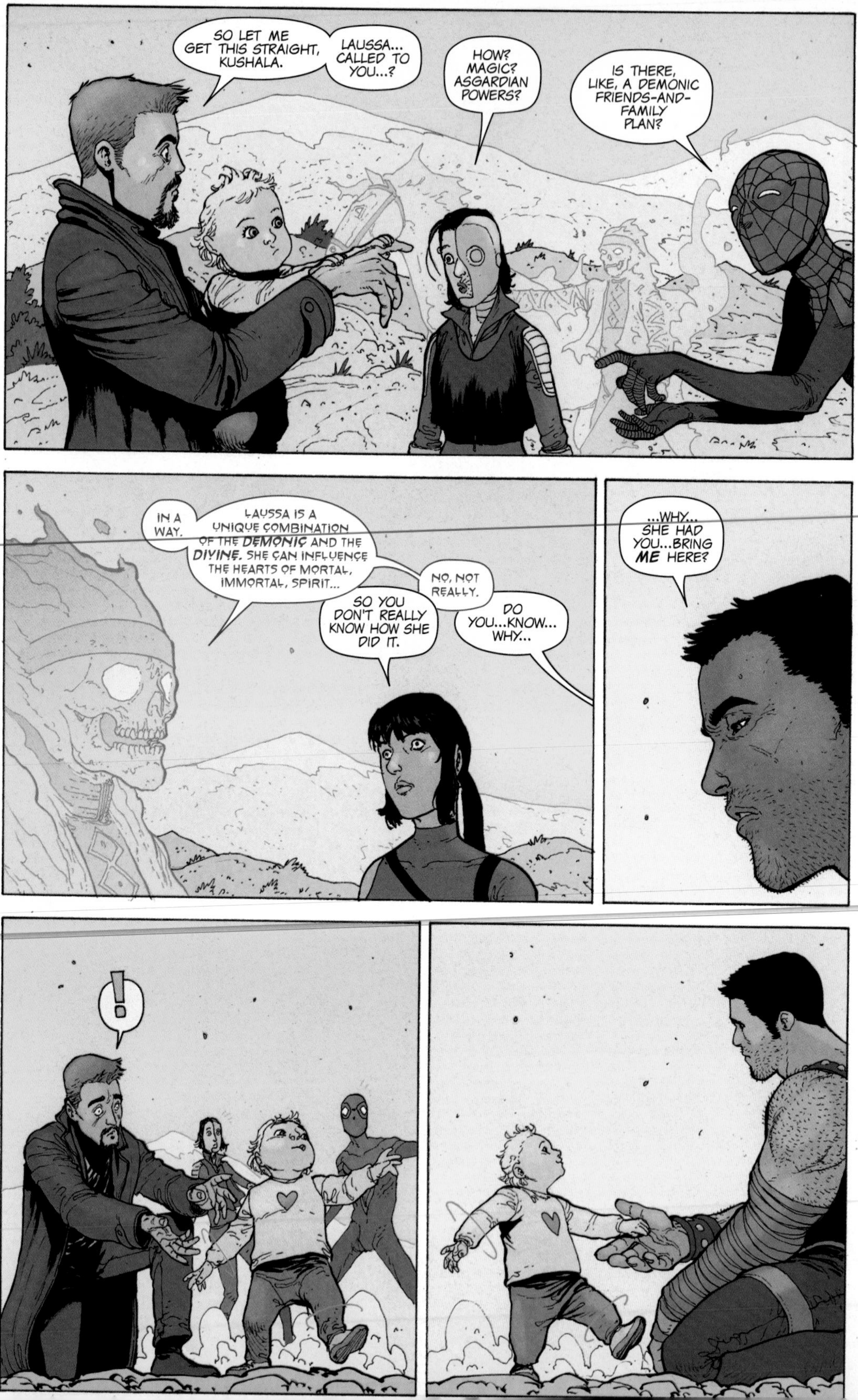
SO LET ME GET THIS STRAIGHT, KUSHALA.
LAUSSA... CALLED TO YOU...?
HOW? MAGIC? ASGARDIAN POWERS?
IS THERE, LIKE, A DEMONIC FRIENDS-AND-FAMILY PLAN?
IN A WAY.
LAUSSA IS A UNIQUE COMBINATION OF THE DEMONIC AND THE DIVINE. SHE CAN INFLUENCE THE HEARTS OF MORTAL, IMMORTAL, SPIRIT...
NO, NOT REALLY.
SO YOU DON'T REALLY KNOW HOW SHE DID IT.
DO YOU...KNOW... WHY...
...WHY... SHE HAD YOU...BRING ME HERE?
!

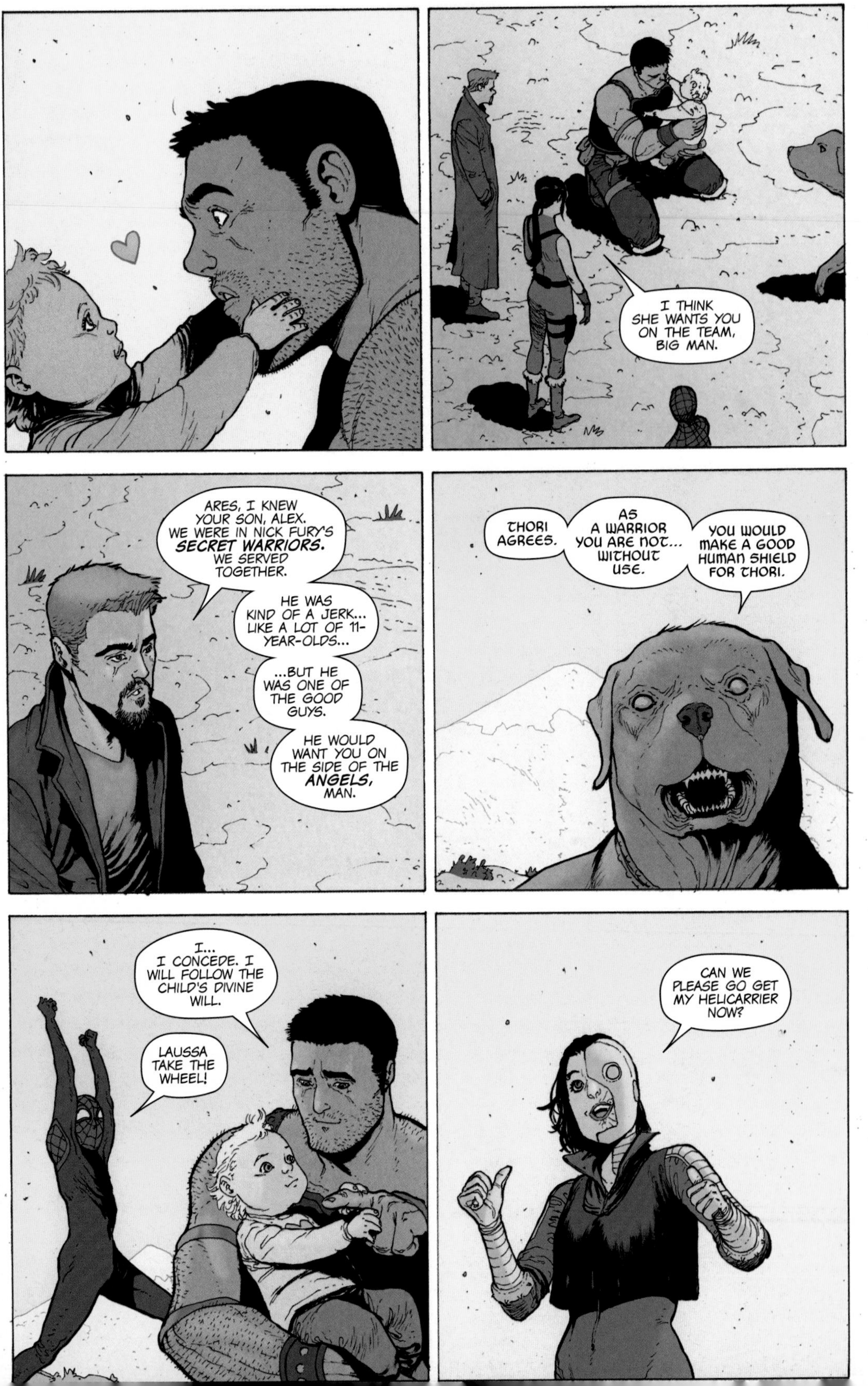
I THINK SHE WANTS YOU ON THE TEAM, BIG MAN.
ARES, I KNEW YOUR SON, ALEX. WE WERE IN NICK FURY'S SECRET WARRIORS. WE SERVED TOGETHER.
HE WAS KIND OF A JERK... LIKE A LOT OF 11-YEAR-OLDS...
...BUT HE WAS ONE OF THE GOOD GUYS.
HE WOULD WANT YOU ON THE SIDE OF THE ANGELS, MAN.
THORI AGREES.
AS A WARRIOR YOU ARE NOT... WITHOUT USE.
YOU WOULD MAKE A GOOD HUMAN SHIELD FOR THORI.
I... I CONCEDE. I WILL FOLLOW THE CHILD'S DIVINE WILL.
LAUSSA TAKE THE WHEEL!
CAN WE PLEASE GO GET MY HELICARRIER NOW?

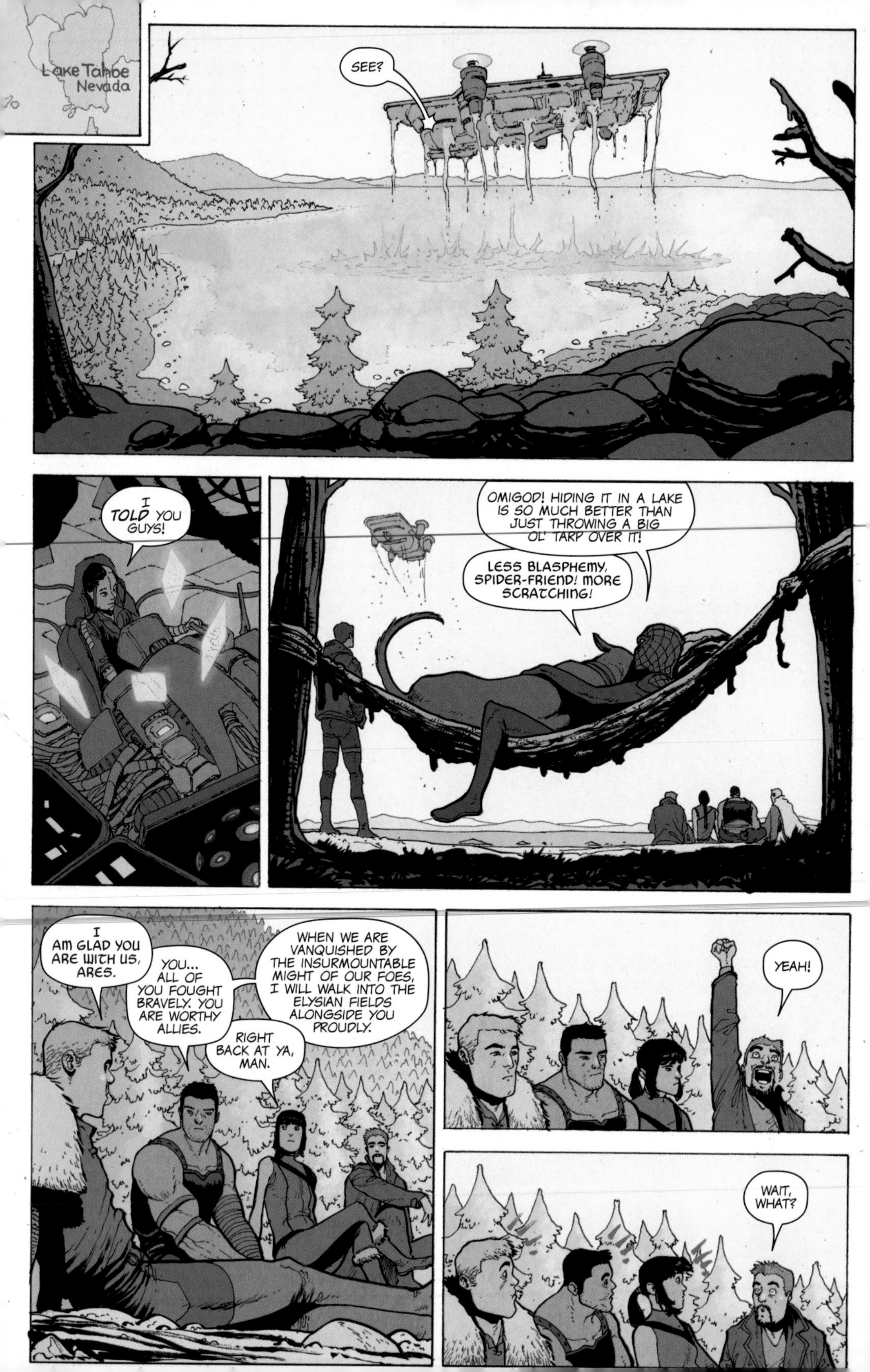
Lake Tahoe
Nevada
SEE?
I TOLD YOU GUYS!
OMIGOD! HIDING IT IN A LAKE IS SO MUCH BETTER THAN JUST THROWING A BIG OL' TARP OVER IT!
LESS BLASPHEMY, SPIDER-FRIEND! MORE SCRATCHING!
I AM GLAD YOU ARE WITH US, ARES.
YOU... ALL OF YOU FOUGHT BRAVELY. YOU ARE WORTHY ALLIES.
WHEN WE ARE VANQUISHED BY THE INSURMOUNTABLE MIGHT OF OUR FOES, I WILL WALK INTO THE ELYSIAN FIELDS ALONGSIDE YOU PROUDLY.
RIGHT BACK AT YA, MAN.
YEAH!
WAIT, WHAT?

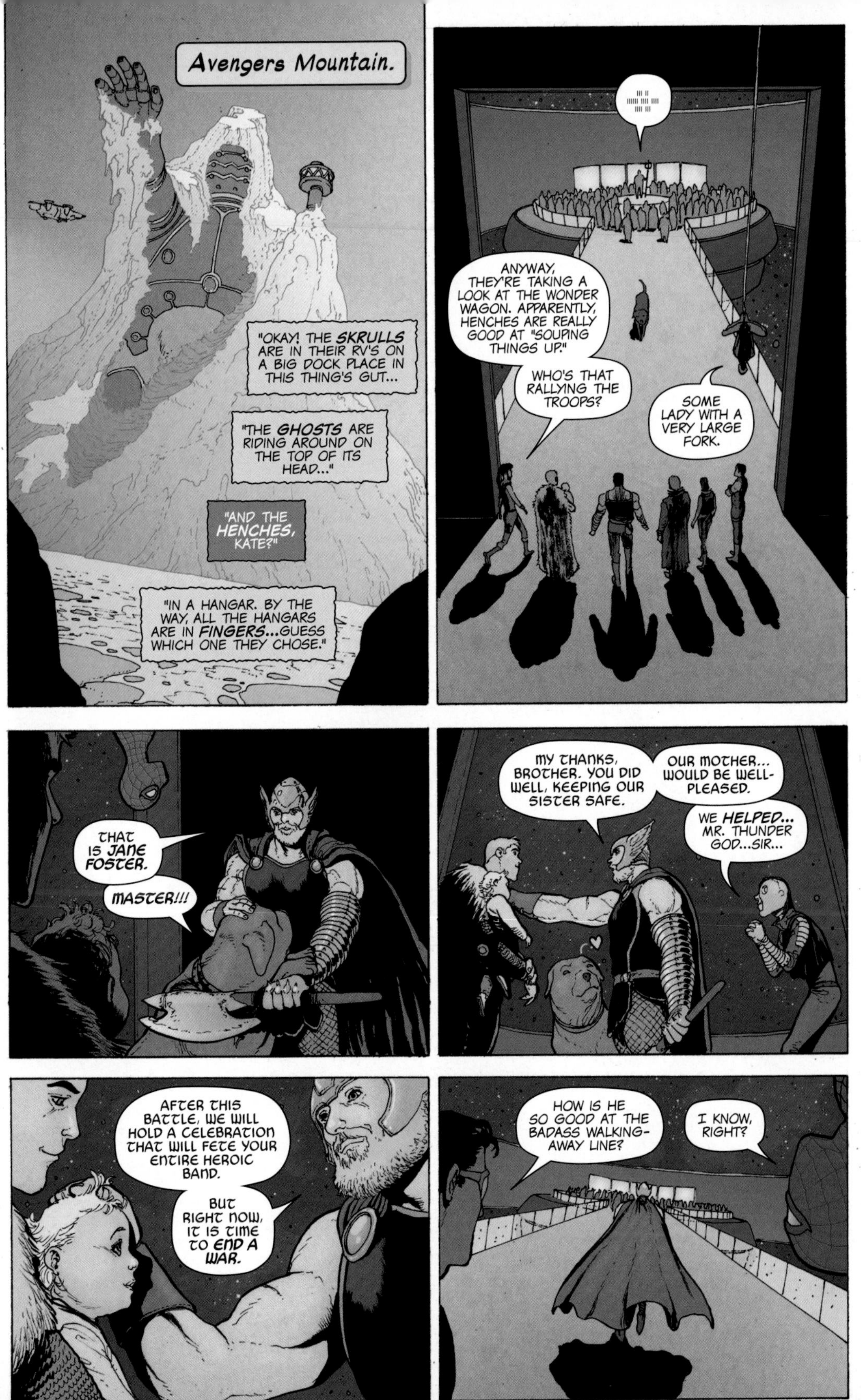
Avengers Mountain.
"OKAY! THE SKRULLS ARE IN THEIR RV'S ON A BIG DOCK PLACE IN THIS THING'S GUT...
"THE GHOSTS ARE RIDING AROUND ON THE TOP OF ITS HEAD..."
"AND THE HENCHES, KATE?"
"IN A HANGAR. BY THE WAY, ALL THE HANGARS ARE IN FINGERS...GUESS WHICH ONE THEY CHOSE."
ANYWAY, THEY'RE TAKING A LOOK AT THE WONDER WAGON. APPARENTLY, HENCHES ARE REALLY GOOD AT "SOUPING THINGS UP."
WHO'S THAT RALLYING THE TROOPS?
SOME LADY WITH A VERY LARGE FORK.
THAT IS JANE FOSTER.
MASTER!!!
MY THANKS, BROTHER. YOU DID WELL, KEEPING OUR SISTER SAFE.
OUR MOTHER... WOULD BE WELL-PLEASED.
WE HELPED... MR. THUNDER GOD...SIR...
AFTER THIS BATTLE, WE WILL HOLD A CELEBRATION THAT WILL FETE YOUR ENTIRE HEROIC BAND.
BUT RIGHT NOW, IT IS TIME TO END A WAR.
HOW IS HE SO GOOD AT THE BADASS WALKING-AWAY LINE?
I KNOW, RIGHT?

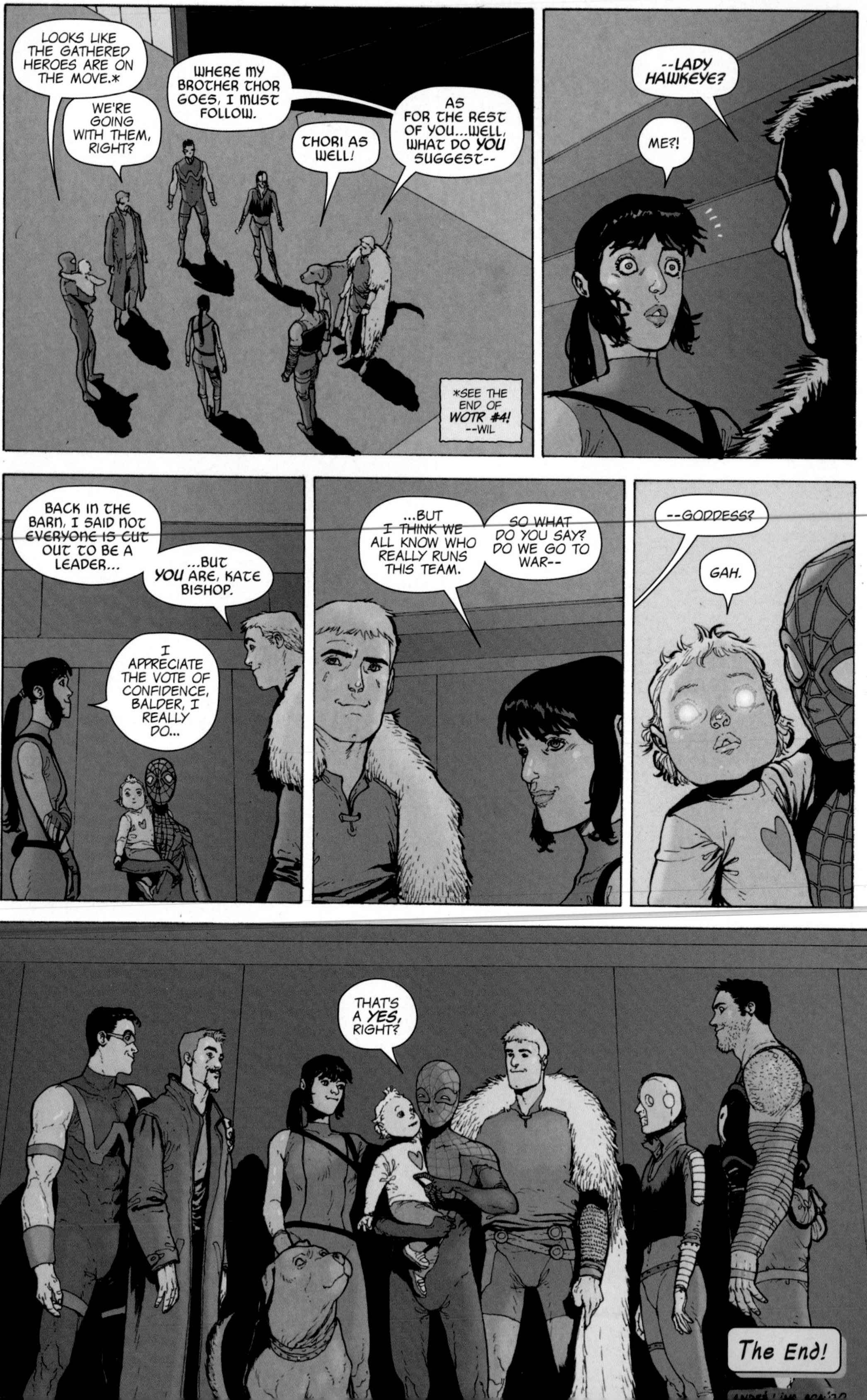
LOOKS LIKE THE GATHERED HEROES ARE ON THE MOVE.*
WE'RE GOING WITH THEM, RIGHT?
WHERE MY BROTHER THOR GOES, I MUST FOLLOW.
THORI AS WELL!
AS FOR THE REST OF YOU...WELL, WHAT DO YOU SUGGEST--
*SEE THE END OF WOTR #4! --WIL
--LADY HAWKEYE?
ME?!
BACK IN THE BARN, I SAID NOT EVERYONE IS CUT OUT TO BE A LEADER...
...BUT YOU ARE, KATE BISHOP.
I APPRECIATE THE VOTE OF CONFIDENCE, BALDER, I REALLY DO...
...BUT I THINK WE ALL KNOW WHO REALLY RUNS THIS TEAM.
SO WHAT DO YOU SAY? DO WE GO TO WAR--
--GODDESS?
GAH.
THAT'S A YES, RIGHT?
The End!

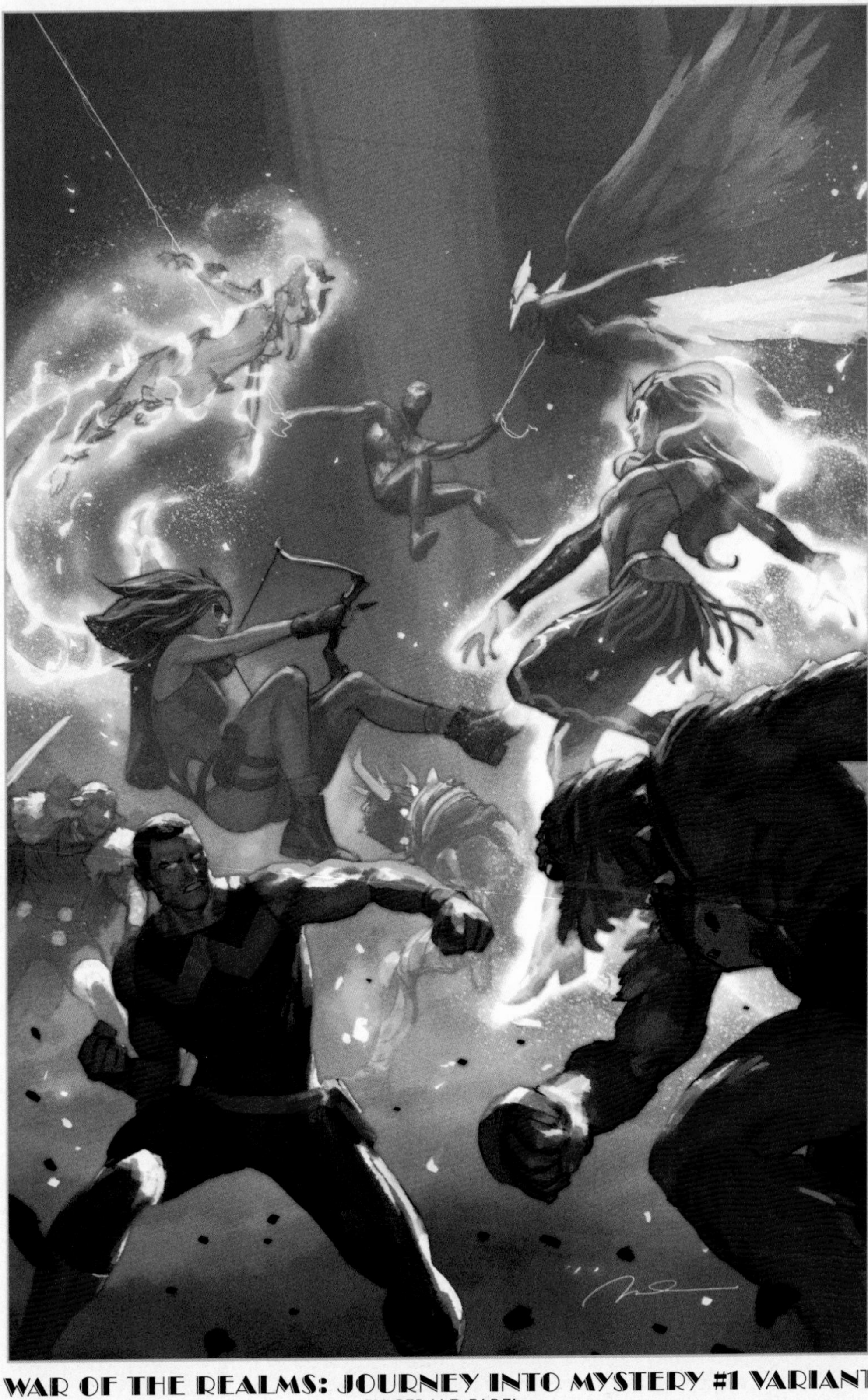

WAR OF THE REALMS: JOURNEY INTO MYSTERY #1 VARIANT
BY GERALD PAREL

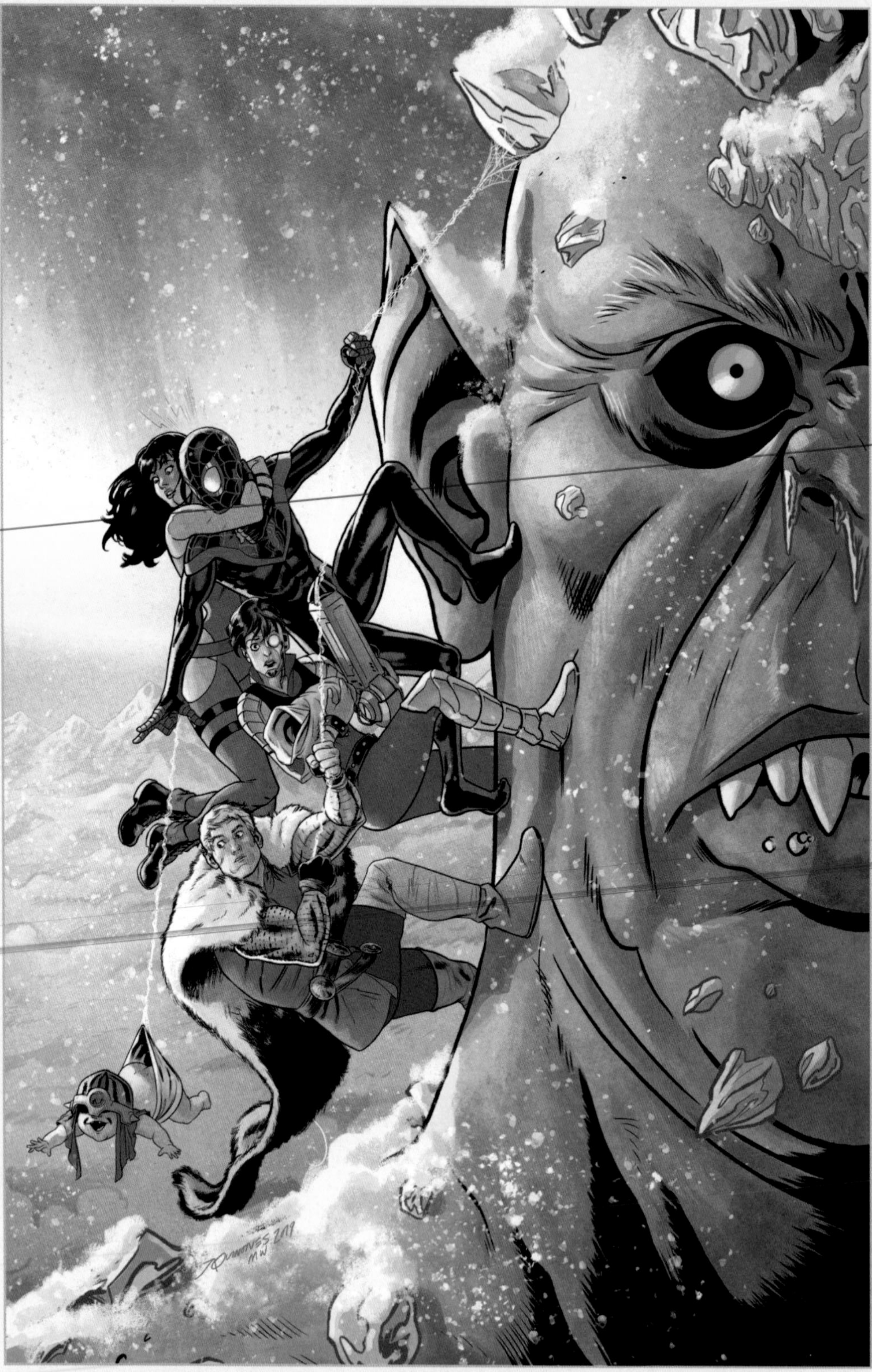

WAR OF THE REALMS: JOURNEY INTO MYSTERY #1 VARIANT
BY JOE QUINONES & MATTHEW WILSON